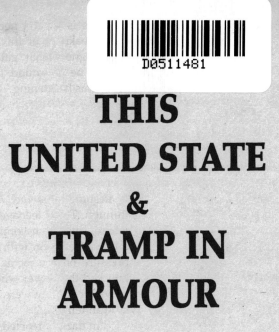

THIS
UNITED STATE
&
TRAMP IN
ARMOUR

Colin Forbes writes a novel every year. For the past twenty-five years, he has earned his living solely as a full-time writer.

He visits all the locations which will appear in a new novel. Forbes says, 'It is essential for me to see for myself where the book will take place. Only in this way can I conjure up the unique atmosphere of the chosen locales.'

He has explored most of Western Europe, the East and West coasts of America, and has made excursions to Africa and Asia. Each new book appears on all major bestseller lists. He is translated into thirty languages.

Surveys have shown his readership is divided equally between women and men.

COLIN FORBES
THIS
UNITED STATE
&
TRAMP IN
ARMOUR

PAN BOOKS

This United State first published 1999
by Macmillan and first published by Pan Books 1999
Tramp in Armour first published 1969
by William Collins Sons & Co. and first published by Pan Books 1971

This omnibus edition published 2002 by Pan Books
an imprint of Pan Macmillan Ltd
Pan Macmillan, 20 New Wharf Road, London N1 9RR
Basingstoke and Oxford
Associated companies throughout the world
www.panmacmillan.com

ISBN 0 330 41820 3

1 3 5 7 9 8 6 4 2

A CIP catalogue record for this book is available from
the British Library.

Typeset by Set Systems Ltd, Saffron Walden, Essex
Printed and bound in Great Britain by
Mackays of Chatham plc, Chatham, Kent

THIS UNITED STATE

Author's Note

For
JANET

Prologue

Paula Grey's nightmare began at exactly 10 p.m. on a cold February night in Albemarle Street, the heart of Mayfair, London.

She walked out of Brown's Hotel, left hand clutching the collar of her coat, shoulder bag slung over her right arm. A taxi pulled in to the kerb, the door was flung open, a man dived out. Cord Dillon, Deputy Director of the CIA. The last person in the world she'd expected to see. He stopped abruptly, close to her.

'Paula, get away from me. You'll get killed.'

'Cord, what the devil—'

'That white Cadillac coming up the street. Full of men trying to shoot me—'

'Come this way. My town. Don't argue!'

She grabbed the right arm of the large American, guided him swiftly up the street, away from the approaching car. The rear window on their side lowered as she hustled Dillon. She had a glimpse of a bald man holding a handgun.

A taxi cut in front of the Cadillac, delaying it. They were already beyond the façade of Brown's Hotel. She hauled Dillon into the partial shelter of a setback, in front of a large plate-glass window. *Crack!* She had heard no sound of a shot fired. Glancing behind them she saw the bullet hole in the window. A huge triangular section of plate glass toppled. Inwards, away from them.

'Keep moving,' she ordered. 'A truck has swerved in front of the Cadillac.'

'You'd better leave me—'

'Shut up! Keep moving,' she repeated. 'I didn't hear a shot.'

'They use silencers on their weapons.'

Arriving at a T-junction, she urged him across the road, turned right along Grafton Street. This was crazy – trying to murder someone in Mayfair. At that time of night Albemarle Street was usually a haven of peace. Just a few parked cars. No one on foot – not in this cold. All the buildings without lights – except for the hotel. Out of sight of Albemarle Street she heard a vehicle coming up behind them. A taxi with its lights on. She flagged it down.

'Victoria Station,' she told the driver.

'Hop in, then.'

They were already inside, the door closed. The taxi drove off. Paula glanced through the rear window. The Cadillac had turned the corner. The driver had seen them board the taxi. Paula extracted a ten-pound note from her wallet. Leaning forward, she passed it through a gap in the glass partition separating them from the driver.

'This is your tip. There's a white Cadillac behind us. Please lose it well before we reach Victoria. My husband's behind the wheel.'

'Righty-ho, lady. Will do.'

The cockney cabbie tucked the banknote inside a pocket, closed the partition, pressed his foot down. Paula lost track of the devious route the cabbie took, racing down side streets, turning at speed round corners. When she looked back there was no sign of the Cadillac. She heaved a sigh of relief.

'Why Victoria Station?' Dillon asked.

'Don't want to lead them to Park Crescent.'

'They know about Tweed's HQ . . .'

2

'Leave it to me.'

'Have you got a gun?' he whispered.

'Yes.'

Her right hand was inside the special compartment of her shoulder bag, holding the butt of her Browning .32. She glanced at Dillon. His craggy, clean-shaven face was so familiar. She noticed a touch of grey in his hair, his haggard drawn look.

'Better let me have the gun,' he suggested.

'No. Leave it to me. You're short of sleep, aren't you?'

'I came straight off a flight from Montreal at Heathrow. Didn't sleep a wink during the whole flight. Never stopped checking the other passengers.'

'Why from Montreal?'

'I guessed they'd be watching flights from Washington to London. So I flew to Montreal first.'

'Who is after you?'

'A small army. Let's keep that for Tweed . . .'

Arriving at Victoria Station, she paid the driver, led Dillon inside the cavernous terminus. Very few people about. An old man in shabby clothes sat on a seat, drinking from a bottle of beer. She scanned the concourse, then led the American back the way they had come.

'What are we doing now?' he asked.

'I wanted that cab we took to go away. I saw a passenger get inside while we were walking in. There's another taxi. We'll take that to Park Crescent.'

Dillon wore a camelhair coat, carried a large executive case. In his late forties, he had a pugnacious jaw, a strong nose and a determined mouth. In many ways he was a typical American – tall, wide-shouldered, the build of a quarterback. He lapsed into silence during the drive. Paula sensed he was near the end of his tether and kept quiet. She checked the rear window several times. No Cadillac.

3

She was paying the driver generously as he turned into Park Crescent. They left the cab and she pushed open the heavy door with a plate alongside it on the wall. General & Cumbria Assurance. George, the guard, was standing behind his desk as they entered the hall.

'Tweed's in, I hope?' she queried.

'Yes. He has Bob Newman with him.'

'Ask Monica to tell Tweed we're on our way up. This is Cord Dillon.'

'I remember Mr Dillon.'

'And I remember you, sharpie,' the American growled.

'The strain's telling on you,' Paula rebuked him as they mounted the staircase.

When she opened the door on the first floor Tweed was seated in his swivel chair behind his desk, hands clasped behind the back of his neck. Of medium height, clean-shaven, of a certain age, he wore horn-rimmed glasses. The Deputy Director of the SIS was a man you could pass in the street without noticing, something which had proved invaluable in his work. He stood up to shake hands, his penetrating eyes studying his visitor as he ushered him to a chair facing the desk.

'You look washed out, Cord.'

'You could say that. Tell you about it when I get my heard screwed on again.'

'You've met Monica.'

Dillon twisted round to look at the small middle-aged woman who kept her grey hair tied up in a bun. Tweed's close assistant for many years, she sat behind her desk which supported several telephones, a fax, a word processor.

'Guess I should remember you, Monica, by now. Can't understand why you go on working for this monster.'

'Coffee?' Monica suggested, standing up. 'How do you like it these days?'

'Black as sin.' Dillon grunted. 'And there's plenty of that comin' into town here from the States.'

'What kind of sin is that?' queried Bob Newman.

The world-famous foreign correspondent, in his forties, had fair hair, a wry smile on his strong face. Also clean-shaven, five feet ten tall, he was well built and women found him engaging – an advantage he exploited only spasmodically. Fully vetted, he had worked with Tweed in a number of dangerous situations.

'Hi, Bob. Been a long time.' Dillon paused. 'The sin is a wolf pack of professional thugs infiltrating this country by devious routes. Top guns.'

'Give me a devious route.'

'The one they like is fly to Paris from Washington. Then come in here by Eurostar by rail.'

'Why that route?'

'I guess they figure there's less of a check arriving by train. They dress as Brits – the contemporary businessman's uniform. A suit as black as night, a flash tie. They really worked this one out. Suits in different sizes bought here, flown to the States. They carry American diplomatic passports.'

'Here's your coffee,' said Monica, who had returned with a tray.

'Thanks. This I really need.'

'While you're drinking it maybe I could tell Tweed and Bob how we came to meet this evening,' Paula suggested.

She did, after Dillon had nodded his agreement. Paula had a gift for describing complex events tersely. Tweed watched her as she sat behind her desk, hands clasped in her lap. She was very calm, matter-of-fact.

'It was a million-to-one chance that I came out of

Brown's when I did,' she concluded. 'I'd met my informant, then waited ten minutes to give the informant time
to get clear without risk of our being seen together.'

'I think, Cord, we'd better get you out of London,'
suggested Tweed. 'Right away. Bob, could you drive
Cord down to the Bunker in Kent? You left your luggage
downstairs, I presume, Cord?'

'Left it on the carousel at Heathrow. Decided I'd
better get a cab out to Brown's fast. I remembered you
use the hotel a lot. I was going to phone you from there.
Didn't want to risk leading the people after me here. To
hell with my case back at the airport.'

'Any personal identification on the case – or inside
it?' Tweed persisted.

'No. The label only gives the flight number and
destination. Not a thing inside.'

'Then we'd better get moving down to Kent,' Newman said, standing up. 'We'll go in my Merc.'

'Not so fast. Wait.' Tweed took a pair of powerful
night glasses out of a drawer, went towards the large
window masked by drawn curtains. 'Monica, switch out
the lights, please.'

With the room in darkness he opened a gap in the
curtains, focused the glasses. His action had created an
air of tension. No one moved but Paula was close enough
to peer over his shoulder. The large office overlooking
Regent's Park in the distance was full of an ominous
silence.

'Did you get the registration number of that Cadillac?'
Tweed asked.

'Of course.'

She recited it from memory. Tweed called over Newman, handed him the glasses. Then he quietly walked
back and sat behind his desk before he spoke.

'The same Cadillac is parked on the main road at the

right-hand entrance to Park Crescent. Four men inside. Obviously watching this building.

'I'll go out and move them. They're illegally parked,' Newman announced after checking through the glasses.

'You can't,' Tweed informed him. 'Paula, have you checked the car too?'

'Yes, it's the same one.'

She handed the glasses back to Tweed, having first carefully closed the curtains. Monica put on the lights again. Everyone stared at each other and Dillon then spoke.

'We're trapped.'

'I'm going out to move the bastards,' Newman insisted.

'You can't,' Tweed repeated. 'That Cadillac has diplomatic plates.'

'And the rats inside will all have diplomatic passports,' Dillon told them. 'Before I left Washington I heard the staff at the Grosvenor Square Embassy had been increased by two hundred. All with diplomatic passports.'

'You still want Cord taken to the Bunker?' Newman demanded.

'Yes. As soon as possible.'

'Then we'll leave now. We'll alter your appearance.' Standing up, Newman studied the American. 'We're about the same build – you can wear my trench coat. That camelhair is a giveaway.'

'And Marler's beret is in the cupboard,' chimed in Paula as she fetched it. 'The fit may be a bit tight but it will do the trick.'

'And,' Tweed suggested, 'walk more slowly, Cord. Not your usual stride. Take shorter steps. Body language identifies anyone.'

'I'll put your executive case inside a canvas holder,' Monica decided.

'And I'll carry it,' said Newman.

'Harry,' instructed Tweed over his phone. 'A small immediate problem. We're smuggling someone out of the building into Newman's car. A white Cadillac with gunmen is parked on the main road. I don't think they'll risk opening fire on our visitor – although they did just that in Albemarle Street.'

'I'll wait outside with a smoke bomb.'

'Only use it if you have to. They're on their way down.'

'They'll shoot me if they can,' Dillon said over his shoulder at the doorway. 'And I have things to tell you . . .'

'Tell Bob on your way to the Bunker. He'll relay what you say to me. If necessary, I can call you down there on a safe phone. Go!'

The beret was a tight fit but it concealed the American's hair. The trench coat Newman had given him fitted better. The camelhair coat was left on a chair. The horn-rimmed glasses, provided by Paula, perched comfortably on his broken nose. George, the guard, waited by the door after taking a brief call from Tweed.

'Where's Harry Butler?' Newman asked, the executive case tucked under his arm inside its canvas covering.

'Went outside,' George reported. 'Said he was going for a quick stroll . . .'

Butler, a burly man, armed with a Walther 9mm automatic pistol inside his hip holster, had his right hand holding the smoke bomb concealed under his windcheater. He was halfway to where the Cadillac was parked when Newman emerged, unlocked his Merc, ushered Dillon into the front passenger seat. Unfortunately, the exhausted American forgot to disguise his normal way of walking.

As Newman started the engine Butler was in two minds about hurling the smoke bomb at the Cadillac.

Remembering Tweed's explicit order he resisted the temptation until trouble started. Newman drove at speed out of the Crescent, turned along the main road in the opposite direction to where the enemy was parked. As he did so the driver of the Cadillac, who had kept the engine running, purred after him.

'They're coming,' said Dillon, twisted round in his seat.

'Let them,' Newman replied. 'Plenty of time to lose them on the way south . . .'

'This sounds to be getting more dangerous,' Paula said to Tweed when the two men had left.

'It's certainly getting interesting,' Tweed responded, seated casually in his chair, hands again clasped behind his head.

'Interesting? Two hundred men sent to the American Embassy. A brazen attempt to murder the Deputy Director of the CIA in the middle of London in an American car carrying diplomatic plates. Another horde of thugs flying to Paris, then coming in here via Eurostar. And you call it interesting?'

'I need more data to work out what is happening. Cord Dillon may provide that when he talks to Newman.'

'Why did you take all that trouble creating the Bunker down in Kent? It's almost like a stand-by headquarters.'

'That's exactly what it is. In case we have to move out of here quickly.'

'This is getting scary. You only got back from Washington three days ago. But you didn't seem surprised when Dillon turned up.'

'I heard a rumour from a source that Cord was on his way out – that he was being replaced by a man called Ed Osborne. A very tough ruthless gentleman.'

'I meant to ask you,' Paula went on, 'where is Marler?'

'He's in Paris, meeting some of his informants. He'll be back any day now.'

'And you'll go all cryptic on me if I ask you what Marler is trying to find out.'

'Incidentally,' Tweed mused, 'I found Washington in a state of feverish activity. No one knew why – or they wouldn't tell me. Like a volcano about to explode.'

'You didn't answer my question about Marler.'

'Marler?' Tweed suppressed a yawn. 'He's attempting to discover who assassinated our Prime Minister in Manchester last week.'

1

'This traffic is as bad as I've seen in LA,' Dillon commented. 'And the Cadillac has picked us up again – it's three cars behind us.'

Newman was driving his Merc among an armada of speeding cars in the dark moonless night. He chose his moment carefully for the manoeuvre when a huge truck masked the Cadillac, then turned in to the left-hand lane. They climbed a hill via a slip road and the traffic had disappeared.

'We were on the M20 motorway driving south,' Newman explained. 'So much traffic at this late hour was due to the accident which held us up further back. Now the poor devils back on the motorway are ramming their feet down to get home hours late.' He checked his rear-view mirror again. 'We've lost the Cadillac.'

'So where are we headed for?'

'Canterbury, eventually. Which is where we don't want to go. So at the next roundabout we'll turn back and rejoin the M20. I want to turn off it at Junction Eight. Are you too tired to talk?'

'Guess not. Strange things are happening in Washington. A heavy delegation is heading for Britain – some have arrived.'

'Give me some names.'

'Sharon Mandeville, for one. Taking up some position at the Grosvenor Square Embassy.'

'She's made the papers a lot. A girl friend of the President?'

'Never. She's too smart to risk upsetting the President's wife. She carries a lot of clout. Then Jefferson Morgenstern himself is coming over,' Dillon said.

'The Secretary of State. Very big gun. Went to the States from Europe as a young man. They say he would have been the President one day if he'd been born an American. Clever as Kissinger and similar background. Here's the roundabout – we can turn back, rejoin the motorway . . .'

Scores of headlights glared like marauding tigers. Side by side, almost touching, a torrent of cars roared south at dangerous speeds. Risks were taken. Everyone seemed to sacrifice safety in their urge to get home, knowing they were very late.

'Never seen anything like this,' Dillon commented, glancing back. 'Like an enemy attack.'

'Were you looking for the enemy?'

'No. I guess you lost him for good.'

'Don't be too sure . . .'

They reached Junction Eight, left the motorway for a country lane. The sudden quiet and solitude in the night was startling. Dillon sagged with relief. Newman turned off the lane down another empty hedge-lined country road, switched his beams full on as they approached a series of bends.

'Anyone else important coming in from Washington?' Newman asked.

'Yes. Ed Osborne, the roughneck who has got my job. A tough guy. Dangerous. You never know what he's thinking.'

'Any ideas why they tried to gun you down in Albermarle Street?'

'I knew too much. I'd ferreted around checking on

12

people. A huge operation is planned but I couldn't get the hang of it.'

Newman sensed that his companion was making an effort to think. The American was close to a state of total exhaustion. They had driven some distance along the lonely country lane without meeting another car when the headlights illuminated a road sign. PARHAM.

'This is an old village,' Newman commented. 'There's another one of the same name in Suffolk, I think. And a good three miles north of us is a very good hotel, Chilston Park. Tweed has stayed there—' He broke off as they swung round a bend, dipped his headlights, slowed down. 'Well, well – look what's ahead of us. The white Cadillac.'

'Have you got a gun I could have?' Dillon growled, jerking himself into his normal alertness.

'I'm carrying my usual Smith & Wesson .38 – and you can't have it. We don't want to start a shooting war out here.'

'Those guys in the Cadillac will see us.'

'I don't think so. I've experienced this before. One car tails another, loses it. From then on the occupants are looking in front of them. They rarely look back. Might be interesting to see where they're headed for.'

Parham was a working village. Even at this late hour lights were on in pubs and restaurants. The Cadillac drove slowly along a narrow street lined on both sides with white clapboard houses. Newman was familiar with the place laid out in a series of chessboard-like squares, one leading into another, an old village typical of the area. A cutting icy wind had been blowing in the countryside but the village was sheltered by the layout of its buildings.

'Looks like they've arrived somewhere,' Dillon commented.

'Let's find out where . . .'

Everyone was indoors. There was not a soul on the deserted narrow streets, lit at intervals by ancient lanterns. They followed the Cadillac into one small square and then it turned into another even smaller square. Newman parked his Merc by the kerb.

'That's a dead end. Let's follow on foot.'

'Bloody cold night,' Dillon observed, standing on the cobbled pavement.

'You'll feel it – you're very tired. Now where have they gone?'

Leading the way, he peered round a corner into the smaller square. The Cadillac had stopped at one side in front of tall gates which gave no view of what lay beyond them. On either side the property was further concealed by old twelve-foot-high brick walls. A hand protruded from the driver's window. Both huge gates slowly moved inwards automatically.

'That's weird,' Newman whispered as Dillon stared over his left shoulder. 'They're electronically controlled and the driver has the gadget which opens them.'

They watched as the Cadillac drove slowly forward up a curving drive. At the end they had a glimpse of a large grim-looking mansion built of stone with turrets at the corners. All the windows were masked by closed shutters and there was no sign that the place was inhabited – until the front door opened and light streamed on to the drive. Then the gates closed and the mansion was gone.

'Let's take a closer look,' Newman suggested.

They crept into the square and on the three other sides were more high brick walls almost hiding the large houses behind them. Newman handed Dillon a pair of gloves, told him to put them on. The American was shivering with cold and fatigue. Newman had a torch in his left hand as they reached the outside of the mansion where the Cadillac had disappeared. The gates were constructed of tall iron rails and attached to them on the inside were sheets of metal, obstructing any view. On the right-hand brick pillar was a metal plate which gave the name when Newman switched on his torch. *Irongates*.

'Let's get back to the car,' Newman whispered.

Once inside the Merc they savoured the warmth of the heaters. Newman had left the engine running in case they had to make a quick getaway. He drove back into the large square, took another exit and suddenly Parham vanished and they were out in lonely countryside, moving along another deserted country lane.

'Irongates,' Newman said half to himself. 'I know who lives there. Sir Guy Strangeways. Spent over twenty years in the States building up a property empire. Never met him.'

'I have,' Dillon told him. 'A mogul. Had the right contacts with certain senators in Washington. Money changes hands and he always got permission to buy an old building to erect a high rise after demolition. He was over there a long time but stayed very British.'

'Never went native?'

'I guess that's what you think we Yanks are – just a bunch of natives.'

'I always respect other people's opinion of themselves,' Newman joked back.

Dillon must have woken up to be capable of a wisecrack. Probably the brief excursion into the cold night air, Newman decided. They drove on through the night, each smoking a cigarette. Dillon looked to his left. The moon had risen, illuminating a range of low hills which fanned away into the distance.

'Thought this part of the world was flat,' he remarked.

'It is. Wait till we get beyond Ashford. A very ordinary town but difficult to drive through if you don't know it. Have to get into the right lane – otherwise you're going miles out of your way.'

Newman had turned onto a wide highway which stretched south as far as the eye could see. No traffic now. Hardly a village. They passed through a deserted Ashford and continued along a highway. Dillon saw what Newman had meant. The world was flat as a billiard table. On both sides fields stretched away to nowhere. Newman slowed down as they approached a signpost. Ivychurch. He turned left off the highway, drove slowly along a twisting narrow lane. Ivychurch was an isolated church, a handful of cottages, then nothing.

'What is the Bunker?' Dillon asked.

'You'll see when we get there.'

'Where are we now?'

'A place where you'll be safe,' Newman said.

'Tells me everything.'

'Gunmen in Cadillacs will never track us here.'

'You don't know those boys.'

'Maybe I do,' Newman retorted. 'Let's stop for a minute. We could get out for a moment.'

Putting on Newman's gloves again, Dillon stepped out of the car. The wind had dropped, the night air was still. There was a heavy silence which seemed to press down on him. Bare hedges, networks of bleak twigs, lined the narrow road. Beyond them flat fields sprawled away for ever. Here and there was dotted the silhouette of a leafless tree, its extremities like skeletal hands clawing upwards towards the sky. No sign of any kind of habitation or life anywhere.

'Too damned quiet for my liking,' Dillon commented. 'Reminds me of certain parts of the Midwest back home. Where the hell are we?'

'We're inside Romney Marsh,' said Newman who

had joined him. 'This side of that hedge is a wide gulley, a drainage ditch – they're all over the place.'

'Think I'd like to get back in the car. Where to next?'

'Deeper inside the marsh . . .'

Dillon lost track of the number of lonely forks and crossroads they came across. Newman seemed to know the way even with his headlights dimmed. They met no traffic, passed through two tiny villages with no lights in the huddled cottages. Dillon thought this was the most desolate area he'd ever encountered. Would they ever reach the mysterious Bunker?

'Will I be out here long?' he eventually asked without enthusiasm.

'You'll be safe. That's the object of the exercise.'

'Anyone to talk to?'

'Yes. We're close now.'

Ahead of them, just off the road, a strange shape loomed in the night. A large round windmill, its four huge sails motionless. Dillon stared at this first sign of civilization.

'What's that thing?'

'A windmill. The only one on Romney Marsh, so far as I know. It's five storeys high and they say the view from the top is awesome.'

'There was a light in the top window. It's gone out. Any idea who lives there?'

'A hermit, I gather. No one ever sees him. We're close to the Bunker – and not so far from the sea. At times a mist, even a fog, comes rolling in. The atmosphere is pretty ghostly when that happens.'

'Goddam ghostly now . . .'

Newman had slowed to a crawl. They turned yet another curving bend and what appeared to be an old farm gate closed off a track leading through a gap in the hedge. Stopping as the car faced the gate, Newman

17

flashed his lights in an irregular series. The gate slowly swung inwards, Newman drove through on to the track, the gate closed behind them.

'While I remember,' Dillon remarked, 'Washington has also sent a team of top communication experts to the Embassy. No idea why.'

'Useful to know.'

A large old tumbledown farmhouse stood at the end of the track. Laid out on three sides it enclosed a cobbled yard Newman drove onto. They got out of the Merc as an old wooden door opened and a small plump woman in her fifties was framed in the light behind her. She wore a flowered print dress with an apron over it. Dillon's idea of a typical Brit's farmer's wife.

She had red apple cheeks and a warm smile. Her grey hair was tied back in a bun, reminding the American of Monica's hairstyle. She ushered her guests inside and Newman patted her affectionately on the rump.

'Meet your hostess, Cord. This is Mrs Carson. She runs the Bunker and we take orders from her. This is Cord Dillon – just arrived from the States,' he introduced. 'No sleep for days and hungry as a hunter, I'm sure.'

'That door has a solid steel plate on the inside,' observed Dillon as Mrs Carson closed and attended to three sophisticated locks.

'Behind the closed shutters of every window is armour-plated glass,' Newman told him.

'Place looks like a series of shacks and turns out to be a fortress. Who protects it if we come under attack?'

'I do,' said Mrs Carson. 'Not that anyone will find us.'

Dillon stared at her in disbelief. His expression became more pronounced as she slipped her hand inside a large canvas shopping bag perched on a shelf and took out a Heckler & Koch MP5 9mm sub-machine-gun.

Effortlessly she inserted a magazine, then, still smiling, looked at Newman.

'Is he trustworthy?'

'Totally. And he may be staying here for a while. He's on the run from gunmen.'

'You'd better have this, then,' she said, handing the weapon to Dillon. 'You do know how to use it?' she asked.

'Cord is very familiar with it,' Newman assured her.

'I have another one ready hanging in a cupboard,' she assured her guest. 'And down in the cellars we have an armoury. Handguns, machine-guns, smoke bombs, grenades. I'll show you, then you can have supper. Tweed phoned me, said he thought you'd need a good hot home-cooked meal . . .'

They were standing in a large kitchen-breakfast room with a wooden table laid for three people to eat. The atmosphere was warm, cosy and Dillon detected a slight humming sound.

'You've even got air-conditioning, for Pete's sake.'

'We have,' Newman told him. 'Powered by our own generator. We have a spare as back-up in case of a breakdown.'

'Are you a drinking man?' Mrs Carson enquired. 'I haven't Bourbon but I could supply a double Scotch. You look as though you could do with it.'

'I sure could. Thank you.'

'Nothing for me,' Newman chimed in. 'I may have to drive back tonight. I'll know when I've phoned Tweed.'

Their hostess had walked quickly to check what was happening on her Aga cooker, lifting lids of several pans, stirring one gently. She then opened a cupboard, brought out a bottle of very expensive whisky, poured a generous double Scotch, handed it to her guest.

'Get that inside you. Supper's not quite ready. I'll show you your sleeping quarters underground.'

19

'This is what I need.' Dillon took a large swallow. 'The weakness of this place is that a mob of gunmen could ignore that gate, scramble through the hedge. They'd be all round this farmhouse before you knew what was happening.'

'No, they couldn't,' Mrs Carson said sharply. 'Look at this.' She opened a large white metal panel on the wall. Behind it was a series of small porthole windows, each with a number above it. 'There's an electric tripwire all round all the hedges. If there are intruders a buzzer goes off. I only have to check this and whichever number is flashing tells me which sectors they're coming in through. Three teenage boys did try to break in. I knew where, saw them coming through my binoculars, went out to meet them with my miniature water cannon. The pressure on the jet is very powerful. It is so strong I knocked them over when I aimed it at them. And it was in winter so they were soaked in icy water. They ran for it, I can tell you.'

'I'm dazed,' reacted Dillon.

'Must be the drink,' Mrs Carson suggested, pulling his leg. 'Now follow me . . .'

Crossing to the opposite panelled wall, she pressed a button. A section of the panel slid back, revealing a doorway. Telling Dillon to mind the steps, she switched on a light and led the way down a flight of concrete steps with a handrail on either side.

The underground complex was vast, one cellar leading to another. The floors, walls and tunnel-like ceiling were painted white. There was nothing primitive about the complex. Opening one door, she ushered her visitor into a comfortably furnished bedroom with a modern bathroom leading off it. Dillon could hardly believe it as she escorted him to more rooms. Taking out two keys she unlocked a steel door and a light came on inside automatically.

'The armoury.'

Dillon stared in amazement as he wandered slowly round, looking at the racks holding a vast majority of guns amd grenades. Below each rack holding weapons was another rack stacked with the correct ammunition. As he turned round Mrs Carson was checking her watch.

'Must have taken you ages to excavate all this,' he said.

'No, it didn't,' Newman explained. 'This place has a history of being used by smugglers in the old days. The cellars were here so they just had to be modernized. Marler supervised the development.'

'Difficult to keep it secret. Workers talk.'

'Not the workers who created this. Marler recruited them in Eastern Europe. Brought them in secretly aboard small launches by night. They never knew where they were. Marler could talk to them in their own lingo. A lot were miners – used to working underground. They never left the place until it was done. Then they were transported secretly back to where they'd come from – with a load of dollars, their favourite currency. For the sophisticated technical work we used boffins from Park Crescent and the training mansion down in Surrey.'

'You two will be gabbling all night and the meal is ready,' Mrs Carson said severely.

'What do they think about the assassination of our Prime Minister in the States?' Newman asked as they followed her upstairs.

'The rumour they spread was it was the work of a splinter group of the IRA.'

'Who might "they" be?'

'Top-flight spin doctors. Incidentally, a team of them have also arrived at the Embassy. Experts in TV, radio and the Internet. Why, I don't know. Something very big is being planned.' Dillon drank the rest of his Scotch.

'When I said top-flight I meant it – recruited from private industry.'

'What do these spin doctors do in America?' Newman asked as they entered the kitchen-breakfast room.

'Brainwash people. Which is why the President is still in the White House.'

'Stop chattering, you two,' Mrs Carson ordered. 'Supper is ready. I hope you like roast beef and Yorkshire pudding, Mr Dillon?'

'Lead me to it. And call me Cord.'

'I must call Tweed from the office here,' Newman told her. 'I may not have time to eat anything. Back in a minute.'

Opening another door, he went into a small room after switching on the light. Closing the door, he sat in a swivel chair behind a desk. Its surface contained a phone, the machine Mrs Carson typed her reports on, but no fax. Security was very tight at the Bunker. When Monica answered he asked for Tweed.

'I'm on the line . . .' Tweed's voice.

'Be careful. I'm not sure this is any longer a safe phone.' Newman was recalling Dillon's reference to a team of communication experts arriving at Grosvenor Square. 'I've arrived here with the parcel.'

'Any important data?'

'Yes, but I don't think I should give you it on the phone. I propose to drive straight back. I can give it to you in the morning.'

'I'd like it tonight. I'll wait for you.'

'I'm on my way . . .'

Going back into the other room, he found Dillon ravenously devouring Mrs Carson's meal. She had refilled his whisky glass and was eating a small portion herself. The aroma made Newman suddenly feel hungry. Mrs Carson was an excellent cook, besides being a crack shot with a variety of weapons.

'Sorry,' he said, 'but I have to drive straight back to London. Cord, I have a full outfit of clothes down here, including pyjamas and shaving kit. You'll find everything you need.'

'Thank you, friend, for bringing me here.' Dillon had stood up, left hand holding his napkin, shaking Newman's with the other. 'How long will I be in the Bunker?'

'Until it's safe to come out. There are fifteen acres round the farmhouse. Mrs Carson will show you outside. She'll give you some old farmer's clothes in case anyone sees you. They'll think you're a yokel.'

'Better practise my yokel accent.'

Mrs Carson was putting the plates of food in a warming drawer. She produced her keys, ready to let Newman out.

'One more thing, Cord, before I go. All the things you have seen recently, what has happened to you. Any idea what it's all about?'

'The whole grim business is a mystery.'

Mrs Carson dimmed the lights before unlocking the main door. Newman hugged her, went out into the breathtaking cold air to his car. He drove slowly back up the track and Mrs Carson timed the opening of the gate perfectly.

Leaving the farmhouse behind, he turned his lights on full beam. As he navigated the maze of lanes half his mind was on driving the car, half on what Dillon had told him. Why did he have a sense of imminent doom?

When Newman walked into Tweed's office in the middle
of the night there was a tense atmosphere. Paula and
Monica sat silently behind their desks. Tweed was leaning forward in his chair chatting to a man in his thirties
who Newman detested. Basil Windermere.

Leaning against a wall, smoking a king-size, stood
Marler, a key member of Tweed's team, reputed to be
the best marksman in the whole of Western Europe.
Shorter than Newman – he was five feet seven tall –
Marler was slim and, as usual, smartly dressed. Wearing
a grey suit with a Prince of Wales check, his trouser
creases were knife-edged, his white shirt fresh from the
dry-cleaner, his blue silk tie decorated with a subtle chain
link design. His dark hair was neatly trimmed and his
clean-shaven face had an expression suggesting he was
miles away in thought.

'I think you know Basil,' Tweed said.

'We've met,' Newman replied without enthusiasm.

'Good to see you, old chap.' Windermere extended a
hand which Newman ignored. 'What a bunch of night
birds we are,' he went on in the soft voice which made
many women fall over backwards. 'I'm here to put
Tweed on to a good thing. Heard on the grapevine
Sharon Mandeville is up for insurance to the tune of
thirty million dollars.'

'Thought she was in America,' Newman lied.

'My dear chap, you're the world's greatest foreign
correspondent. Thought you kept up to date. The delectable Sharon is in town here. Some big job with the
American Embassy. Thought of Tweed at once. His

insurance company handles protective cover against eminent souls being kidnapped.'

Which confirmed to Newman that Windermere had no idea the General & Cumbria Assurance plate on the door at the entrance was a cover for the secret HQ of the SIS. He simply nodded. Windermere turned back to Tweed.

'I'm a bit short of the readies.' He flicked index finger and thumb. 'Some of the folding stuff for the tip would most certainly not come amiss.'

'Who is proposing to pay this enormous premium?' Tweed asked.

'Presumably her latest billionaire boy friend back in the US of A.'

'Presumably? The boy friend has a name?'

'Sorry, I haven't got that far.'

'Maybe this anonymous boy friend hasn't got that far either. He could just hope to.'

'Mind if I smoke?'

Windermere extracted a gold cigarette case from his pocket and selected a Turkish cigarette with a flourish. On the outside was engraved a royal-looking crown. Undoubtedly a fake, Newman decided. Just like the owner.

Windermere was known to live off rich women. Once a male model, he was six feet tall, and took care to keep his weight down at a health club. This was one place where he encountered female prospects. He was wearing a white linen suit, which was ridiculous for the time of the year. He hardly ever stopped smiling, which Newman described as a smirk. He had a head of thick hair and too-perfect features.

'How did you come by this information?' Tweed probed.

'Met her at a party, didn't I? She's something else

25

again – a real knock-out. Intelligent with it. Told me during the course of our long conversation. Think she rather liked me. I took the liberty of mentioning your organization.'

'Who mentioned my name?'

'She did, as a matter of fact. Hope you don't mind.'

'Don't do it again,' Tweed said. 'I don't tout for any of my business.'

'Any chance of a small advance for the tip?'

'None at all. Too vague.'

'A couple of hundred pounds would make me happy.'

'Try your luck with the lottery.'

'Suppose I'd better love you and leave you.' Windermere stood up. The hostile reception has at last penetrated his thick skull, Newman said to himself. 'I had a coat.'

Monica was already taking down his white coat from a hook. She simply handed it to him without making any effort to help him on with it. Windermere stood very still, glancing round the spartan office. Newman could see why he would be attractive to a certain type of woman.

'Don't think I know you,' Windermere remarked, addressing Marler.

'You don't.'

'And what a charming lady,' Windermere went on, gazing at Paula.

She had her head down, studying some papers. She appeared not to have heard him.

'Newman will accompany you to the door,' Tweed told him.

'Let's keep in touch, you beautiful people . . .'

Newman had the door open. As he closed it and followed their visitor down the stairs Windermere began talking over his shoulder.

'I say, Bob, maybe we could have a drink together one evening.'

'Maybe.'

'I frequent Bentleys in Swallow Street. You'd find me there about eight in the evening. In their sumptuous bar downstairs.'

'George,' Newman called out, 'our visitor is leaving if you'd unlock the door . . .'

Windermere paused just outside the exit to button up his coat. Newman stayed inside after glancing outside across the Crescent. As George was closing the door Newman ran back upstairs into Tweed's office. He looked annoyed.

'Why on earth did you let that gigolo get inside here?' he asked.

'To see if he'd provide me with any information. He did,' Tweed replied.

'You mean about someone insuring Sharon Mandeville for thirty million dollars?'

'No. That was nonsense. His excuse for coming here to check up on my staff, to identify as many as he could. Marler caught on and so did Paula. So who could be anxious to penetrate our organization?'

'Sharon Mandeville,' Newman suggested.

'Not necessarily. Windermere babbles on but is a stranger to the truth. He may not have even met the delectable Sharon, as he described her.'

'Well,' Newman retorted as he sat down, 'you might be interested to know that everyone who leaves this building is being photographed. This time a Lincoln Continental is parked out on the main road. I caught a glimpse of a man aiming a camera at Windermere as he was leaving.'

'Get a picture of you?' Tweed enquired.

'No, I kept well back.'

'I don't understand it,' protested Paula. 'First a Cadillac,

27

now a Lincoln Continental. If it is an American gang you'd think they'd use British cars. Why American?'

'To intimidate us,' Tweed told her. 'I expect their campaign to get a lot worse, even more aggressive. But enough of that. Bob, you arrived back just in time. Marler has discovered who assassinated the Prime Minister.'

'Up to a point,' Marler drawled in his upper-crust accent. 'I'm just back from Paris,' he explained to Newman. 'While over in Gay Paree, as the Yanks used to call it, I met three of my informants in various seedy parts of the city. The first two couldn't give me the time of day.'

'They didn't know?' Newman queried.

'The question scared them stiff. Then I met the Ear in another low-down bar.'

'The Ear?' asked Paula, puzzled.

'That's his nickname in the French underworld. He has guts. He plays both sides. For money, of course. By both sides I'm referring to the police and the underworld. And what I have just said is utterly confidential.'

'He's playing a dangerous game,' Newman commented.

'With great skill,' Marler told him. 'He's helped the Prefect of Paris to put some very lethal saboteurs – especially from Algeria – behind bars. Bit of a patriot, the Ear.'

'And was he also scared stiff when you put the question to him?' Newman suggested.

'Not a bit of it. He just doubled his normal fee, which I was happy to pay. This assassin is pretty damned good. He killed that French Minister a few weeks ago, the one who made a powerful speech attacking the Americans, accusing them of trying to take over the world. A month before that he took out Heinz Keller, the German politician who is anti-American and might have one day become Chancellor of Germany.'

'Sounds as though the assassin is American,' Paula speculated.

'That's one thing he isn't,' Marler corrected her. 'It makes sense when you come to think of it. If he was ever caught Washington would take worldwide flak. Our friends across the Atlantic appear to have become more sophisticated. Diabolical might be the word.'

'Do we get a name?' Newman prodded impatiently.

'Why not?' Marler said offhandedly. 'He's called the Phantom.'

'He sounds very sinister,' Paula commented.

'Sinister,' Marler agreed, 'highly skilled and professional. He assassinated the heavily guarded Prime Minister. Afterwards Special Branch never found the rifle he used. Imagine smuggling that away with a horde of security men checking everyone they could find. And the devil's firing point was the rooftop of a warehouse used for storing books. A repeat of Dallas all those years ago.'

'Has the Ear any clue as to his nationality?' pressed Newman.

'He's European, could even be an Englishman. The Ear stressed that was a rumour. He didn't know whether it was true.'

'So his identity is completely unknown?' Newman asked.

'Completely. Rumoured he has a number of girl friends. Again the Ear emphasized that also was no more than a rumour.'

'So we have no name.'

'None at all. As yet. The Ear is going on digging. Speaks good English. He'll contact me here if he finds out more. Monica, he'll give the name of Maurice and leave a message. Maybe just an address and a time and day.'

'Any other clue?'

'Only one, which could be misleading. The Ear says it's known he's paid in dollars. That could be a smoke-screen. Could be some other nation is his paymaster.'

'You've done well,' said Tweed. 'Now I think we should all hear what Bob has to tell us.' He looked at Marler. 'He has just returned from escorting Cord Dillon to the Bunker. Come to think of it, maybe Paula had better put you in the picture first. She had a bit of an adventure late yesterday evening.'

'A bit of an adventure,' Paula repeated ironically. 'That's one way of describing it. Here goes . . .'

Newman and Marler watched her as she gave a terse account of her experience with Cord Dillon. She started with her leaving the hotel in Albermarle Street. Yet again Newman thought that Paula was a very attractive woman. In her thirties, slim with a very good pair of legs, her black hair had a glossy sheen, falling just short of her collar. She had a face with strong bone structure and a determined chin. Her voice was soft but he could hear clearly every word she said. Smartly dressed in a two-piece navy blue suit she was a woman men in the street turned to look at. Above all else she was enor-mously capable and had great stamina.

'That's it,' she ended. 'And that's enough, I'd say.'

'Tough cookie,' said Marler, squeezing her shoulder.

'If you say so.'

'Now it's Bob's turn to bring us up to date,' Tweed suggested.

He made occasional notes as Newman outlined everything that had happened when he'd escorted Dillon to the Bunker. Monica was recording the entire story, as she had with Paula.

'That's it,' Newman concluded, 'to quote Paula.'

'It's a lot,' Tweed said. 'Some of it very disturbing. Now we have quite an array of players in this grim game. Monica, in the morning I'd like you to start building profiles on these people. Jefferson Morgenstern, esteemed Secretary of State, whom I know. Ed Osborne, the new Deputy Director of the CIA. Both now in London. Sir Guy Strangeways, who lives at the mansion called Irongates at Parham. And . . .' He paused. 'Sharon Mandeville. Her whole history, which could be interesting.' He stared at the ceiling. 'Add Basil Windermere to that list if you would, please.'

'I'll start tonight,' Monica announced. 'New York is five hours behind us and some of my contacts work late. Then San Francisco – they're eight hours behind us so I'll catch my contacts there. Don't look at me like that. I'm fresh as a daisy.'

The phone rang. Monica picked it up, frowned, put her hand over the mouthpiece, looked at Marler.

'It's for you. Maurice on the line . . .'

'Marler speaking. Where are you?'

'On a public phone at Heathrow. Need to see you urgently.'

'Hang on a moment.'

Marler put his own hand over the mouthpiece. He spoke to Tweed, spoke quickly.

'The Ear has turned up at Heathrow. Needs to speak to me. Can he come here? He thinks I work for an insurance outfit.'

'Yes. Tell him to take a cab. You can see him in the waiting room.'

The moment Marler ended the brief call, giving the Ear the address, Tweed reacted. He gestured towards the curtained windows.

'We have to shift that Lincoln Continental fast. If it's still there they'll photograph the Ear.'

'I'll handle that,' Newman said, standing up. 'There's

31

going to be an accident. I'll take the four-wheel drive. Could you get the police here yesterday?'

'I'll call my old sparring partner, Roy Buchanan at the Yard. I've already reported the attack in Albemarle Street. He's not best pleased with the Americans.'

Newman snatched a scarf and his trench coat off a hook. As he hurried downstairs he was wrapping the scarf round the lower part of his face, covering his nose. He pulled up the military-style lapels, darted out of the front door and round a corner to where the vehicle with a ram was parked.

He drove a roundabout route which brought him back on to the main road. A plane was flying very low overhead as he saw the Lincoln parked at the edge of the Crescent. He pressed his foot down, slammed into the back of the American car, smashing up its rear badly. He then reversed, dragged metal off the damaged car.

'Made of tin,' he said under his breath.

Turning off his engine, he got out as a tough-looking passenger jumped out of the back of the Lincoln. He had a boxer's nose and the face of a moron. His head was bald. He swaggered up to Newman, now standing in the road as a car pulled up alongside him. Chief Inspector Roy Buchanan was at the wheel with Sergeant Warden, a heavily built man, beside him.

'Buddy, I'm going to put all your teeth down your throat,' the thug said with a rough American accent.

'You could try it,' Newman replied.

'Here it comes then. Kiss your mouth goodbye.'

Newman timed it carefully. As a huge bunched fist slammed towards his mouth he jerked his head sideways, took the punch on the side of his jaw. The fist slid off him. Newman made no attempt to retaliate as Buchanan appeared with Sergeant Warden on his heels.

'This car was illegally parked,' Newman told him. 'A

plane flew very low and distracted me. You don't expect a car parked here at any time.'

'And I saw you assault this man,' Buchanan said grimly.

'Who the friggin' hell are you?' the thug snarled.

'Chief Inspector Buchanan of the CID . . .'

'I've got a diplomatic passport, so frig off.'

The thug raised one finger almost in Buchanan's face. Then he swore foully.

'I wish you hadn't done that. Diplomatic passport? And the moon is blue.'

'Look at the licence plates, buddy,' the thug ranted on. 'It has diplomatic plates.'

In the distance Newman heard police sirens coming closer. Buchanan folded his arms and studied the thug. Then three police cars with uniformed officers aboard appeared and pulled up, forming a laager round the Lincoln. Buchanan was a tall lanky man in his forties, wearing a dark suit, an ironic smile on his lean intelligent face. Villains found something disturbing about his casual manner.

'I think I recognize you,' he said, addressing the thug. 'A bank raid in the City a month ago. No money taken – just security documents about a number of prominent British citizens. One of the raiders was caught on video. Looked just like you. I'd appreciate you giving me your name.'

'See for yourself,' snapped the American. 'Hank Waltz.' He shoved a diplomatic passport at Buchanan.

'Sometimes known as Diamond Waltz,' Newman remarked. 'Look at all the flashy rings on his stubby fingers. Fakes, I imagine.'

'Fakes?' Waltz clenched his fist. 'You want another one?'

'Cool it, chum.'

33

One of the uniformed police who had spilled out of the cars stood very close to the American. While Buchanan was examining the passport the driver of the Lincoln stepped out and came up to them.

Tall, with the appearance of a quarterback, his manner was very different from Waltz's. Wearing a Savile Row suit, he was smiling, conciliatory, his American accent soft.

'Good evening. I'm sorry if we've caused any problems. And Hank has a short fuse. He's fond of the Lincoln – normally he drives the car.'

'I do?'

'Hank, now the Chief Inspector has given you back your passport I suggest you get back to your seat. Every time you open that mouth of yours you shove your big foot in it.'

'Could I have your name?' Buchanan asked stiffly.

'Sure. Why not? I'm Chuck Venacki. Attaché at the Embassy.'

'What are your duties, sir?' Buchanan demanded.

'Public relations.'

'Diamond Waltz isn't going to help you much in that direction.'

'Hank Waltz. He's a bodyguard. The new American Ambassador has received threatening warnings. You'd like to see my passport?'

'I don't think that will be necessary.'

As Buchanan replied there was a heavy rumbling noise behind them. Newman glanced back to see a large vehicle transporter pulling in behind them. Men in working clothes got out, started walking round the Lincoln.

'May I ask what is happening?' Venacki enquired smoothly.

'You may. That Lincoln is blocking the road. The transporter will take it on board and move it. I'll get you a taxi.'

34

'Taxi coming,' said Newman, flagging it down.

'Good.' Buchanan stared coldly at Venacki. 'That will take you wherever you were going.'

'And the Lincoln?'

'Will be dumped outside your Embassy. Alternatively it could be taken to a maintenance garage to see if repair is possible.'

'No, thank you,' Venacki said hastily. 'Grosvenor Square will do nicely.'

'Then I suggest all four of you are on your way in the cab. I may add that if he hadn't had a diplomatic passport Diamond Waltz would have been arrested on a criminal charge. An incident here a month ago.'

'Thank you for your help, Chief Inspector.'

'I suggest you leave at once. Meter's ticking up on the cab.'

Buchanan had offered to drive Tweed home. He was talking as the Lincoln was swiftly manoeuvred aboard the transporter. Newman had earlier used gloves to wrench off the wreckage he had hauled off the Lincoln. The four-wheel drive was in perfect driving condition.

'I saw the light was still on in his office,' Buchanan said as they mounted the stairs together. 'Time he went home.'

'I suppose you're right,' Tweed agreed when Buchanan made his offer. 'Monica is staying on, checking the names I gave her. And Roy can tell me what happened outside – plus I have a few things to tell him.'

'What about Paula?' Newman asked as they went back down the stairs with Buchanan.

'She's staying on too . . .'

This had been Marler's suggestion.

'The Ear will be more comfortable if I have Paula with me in the waiting room,' he explained to Tweed.

35

'He relaxes more in women's company – that is, the few he can trust.'

'He may not trust me,' Paula pointed out.

'He will. His ability to weigh up people is remarkable. He has an uncanny knowledge of human nature. But only if you feel up to it.'

'I can't wait to meet the Ear,' she replied.

3

When Newman had left the building with Tweed and Buchanan, Marler set the stage for the arrival of the Ear. He raided the drinks cupboard of Howard, the Director. Holding three glasses and a bottle of white wine he took them downstairs and laid them on the bare wooden table in the waiting room. He then upset George.

'I'll guard the front door. You go upstairs and make yourself at home in one of the offices. Not Tweed's.'

'I'm supposed to be the guard,' the red-faced ex-army sergeant protested.

'I know. We have someone coming who won't want to be recognized.'

'Have it your own way.'

'I'm going to . . .'

With Paula seated at one of the three chairs round the table, Marler waited behind George's desk, listening for the sound of a taxi pulling up. Instead, after half an hour someone rang the bell. Peering through the spy-hole in the heavy front door Marler stared in surprise, then opened it. He ushered the Ear into the waiting room, closed the door.

'This is Paula. I hope you don't mind her being with us.'

Paula looked at their visitor. She hadn't expected such a small man. No more than five feet tall, he had shuffled in and now he gazed at her through thick pebble glasses, perched on the bridge of a hooked nose. He took off the glasses, glanced at Marler before reverting his gaze to Paula.

'Disguise,' he explained. 'Nice name, Paula,' he went on, still staring at her in a way she did not find offensive.

Without the glasses he became a different person. His nose seemed even more hooked, his thin mouth was firm, his jaw pointed. Penetrating blue eyes surveyed her. His cheekbones were prominent and his thick dark eyebrows curled upwards. He reminded her of a Dickensian character.

'I shall be very happy for the lady to be present,' he decided. 'I like your clothes,' he told Paula. 'Smart but not a mantrap.'

'He does speak his mind,' Marler said quickly.

'I think he has a wonderful sense of humour.' Paula laughed. 'His description of me is perfect.'

'And very practical shoes. For moving silently or running.'

He doesn't miss a thing, thought Paula, who had her legs crossed, exposing the rubber sole of one shoe. The explanation he had given was precisely the reason she wore them. Marler pulled out a chair for their visitor to sit down. He extended a hand to Paula. His grip was firm.

'I am Kurt Schwarz.'

'I don't think Kurt will mind my telling you his base is in Switzerland. In Basle.'

Marler sat down in a chair facing them. The Ear put down on the floor an old trilby hat he had been carrying. He wore a shabby windcheater with patches on the sleeves and a pair of denims which had seen better days.

37

Below the sharp nose his Adam's apple was also promi-nent, heightening the Dickensian impression. He picked up the bottle of wine, glanced at it, put the bottle down.

'Not bad, could be better,' he told Marler.

'You don't have to drink it.'

'That would be impolite. And I wish to toast the health of this charming lady.'

'Flattery will get you somewhere. How did you find those old clothes? You look like a tramp.'

'I saw a junk shop still open on the way from the airport. I told the cab driver to drop me there. They had a selection of second-hand clothes. There was a public lavatory nearby. I went into it after leaving the shop and changed in a cubicle.'

'Kurt,' commented Paula, 'your English is very good.'

'I once spent two years in Hammersmith. Is it still there?'

'Unfortunately, yes.'

'Well, Hammersmith is like Hampstead compared to half of Paris. Tourists don't see the slums I know so well.' He watched Marler struggling with a gadget to extract the cork from the wine bottle. 'I could get that cork out now with my teeth. Maybe yours are false.'

'That's enough of that.'

Marler poured the wine. The Ear raised his glass. 'To Paula, a long and happy life.'

'Thank you,' she said as they clinked glasses.

'What did you do with the clothes you came across in?' Marler asked.

'Put them inside the canvas hold-all by the side of my chair.' He reached down, pulled out a black beret, fitted it on to his thick grey hair. He still reminded Paula of a Dickensian character. Even his voice fitted – it was hoarse but warm. 'Now, shall we be serious?'

'That's why you're here,' Marler replied.

'The Americans have transmitted electronically one

hundred million dollars to an account at the Zürcher Kredit Bank on Bankverein.'

'That's in Basle?'

'Yes.'

'You're sure of your information?'

'Of course. I shouldn't let you know but I have a teller in that bank who is a contact. For a fee.'

'That's staggering,' said Paula.

'They also have some kind of base in the area. Not in the city.' He turned to Paula. 'You probably know the city is unique. Three countries meet there. Switzerland, Germany and France. You can slip across the border easily. They have a unit somewhere, but not in the city,' he repeated. 'So my next mission is to locate their base.' He sipped more wine. 'I will inform you when I discover it. This wine is not bad.'

'Which means he'd like more,' said Marler, refilling his glass. 'And you'd better be careful. There are some pretty nasty types floating about.'

'There always are.'

'You were very late phoning me from Heathrow,' Marler remarked casually. 'The last flight from Paris had arrived ages before.'

'I was tailed. I had to lose him before I came here. I headed for the multi-storey car park. As you know, it has many levels. Eventually I hid behind a car and he lost me. But I was cautious – I waited a long time before I left the place. Then I called you.'

'How did the tail spot you?'

'He happened to be on my flight. I made a bad mistake. I had been talking to the stewardess in French. Then she dropped a tray and I said, "Don't worry. I'll help you to pick them up." In English. I think the tail heard me. That's what always gets you in the end. Random chance.'

'Any more dope on the Phantom?'

'I was coming to that. The rumours that he's English are now stronger. But they are still rumours. No name. And he's very cautious.'

'I'll say he is,' agreed Marler. 'He assassinated the Prime Minister over here. The security people only think they found his firing point on the rooftop of a warehouse. If they did, he left behind no spent cartridge, nothing.'

'The same as when he killed the German, Heinz Keller – and the French Minister. Bear in mind he could be a Frenchman, a German – or an Uzbek.'

'How are we going to get you away from here? It's late.'

'That is easy,' Kurt explained. 'There are many areas not far from here with cheap hotels. You get a room for the night – providing you pay in advance.'

'You've been here – I mean in London – recently, haven't you?' Paula suggested intuitively.

'Clever lady.' Kurt smiled, his lips twisting in a crooked way, but the smile was very human. 'Yes, I have. On several occasions.'

'You didn't tell me that in Paris,' Marler said sharply.

'Why should I? When I am not certain what I have found out? I only pass on information when what I say is positive. I take your fees. To do otherwise would be dishonest. I will tell you that something very strange and dangerous is happening here. England is facing the greatest enemy since it fought Hitler.'

'What we'll do,' Paula said decisively, 'is the three of us will drive to my flat in the Fulham Road. It won't take me long to prepare a meal, and I'm hungry. I think you are, Kurt.'

'And I'm starving,' Marler lied. 'Afterwards I can drive Kurt to my place for the night. I have a spare bedroom. It's not far from Paula's flat.'

'Don't argue,' Paula said severely as Kurt opened his mouth.

'I surrender.' Kurt threw up both hands. 'I am grateful . . .'

He travelled alongside Paula in her Ford while Marler followed in his station wagon. On the way Paula found Kurt's phrase repeating itself time and again in her mind. '. . . *something very strange and dangerous is happening here. England is facing the greatest enemy since it fought Hitler.*'

4

'Sharon Mandeville,' Monica announced. 'Let's start with the profile I've built up on her – so far as it goes . . .'

It was the morning of the same day that Paula had provided a meal for her two guests. Newman sat in an armchair, his long legs casually crossed. Paula, hiding a yawn, was behind her desk, and Tweed was leaning forward in his swivel chair.

'Sharon is forty-two years old, looks younger,' Monica began. 'I obtained a recent photo of her from the editor of a fashion magazine, a friend of mine. Here it is.'

Newman took it from her. Sitting down again, he studied the glossy print. Then he whistled before passing it to Tweed.

'She's a blonde stunner.'

'She's enigmatic,' commented Tweed. 'I met her at a party in Washington. Not the most recent visit. When I was there three weeks ago.' He passed it to Paula. 'What do you think?'

'Hard to say,' she said eventually. 'A photo can mislead.'

'If I could proceed,' Monica said impatiently. 'Sharon was born in Washington, DC. So she's an American citizen. Her mother was English, her father an American industrialist with money. Sharon was partly educated in

England, partly in the US. When Sharon was fifteen the three of them moved here. Apparently her father thought he could make more money in Britain. Result? He lost everything on the stock market and they all returned to the States. Soon after they got back the parents were both killed in a car crash. Sharon was eighteen. A year later she married a Texan oil millionaire. There was a prenuptial agreement. Twenty months later she divorced him and was a rich woman.'

'Because of the prenuptial arrangement?' Tweed suggested.

'Exactly,' Monica confirmed. 'There's a pattern. To cut it short, she remarried three times, always to millionaires or, in one case, to a billionaire. Always there was a prenuptial agreement with a generous settlement for her. Now she may be the richest woman in America.'

'Gold-digger,' said Newman.

'Not necessarily,' Tweed objected. 'Didn't strike me like that when I met her. You have to remember it's a jungle in the US. Rich men treat their wives like trophies, but they can be mean and unreliable. Maybe Sharon spotted that – hence the prenuptial agreements.'

'If I may go on,' snapped Monica. 'So now she's single with four husbands behind her. After the fourth fiasco – if you can call it that – she bought an apartment in luxurious Chevvy Chase and mixed with high society in Washington. She became a friend of the President's wife and was given various jobs.'

'I'd say Newman was right. Gold-digger,' said Marler. He had come into the office a few minutes earlier, nodded and now had taken up his usual stance, leaning against a wall. 'And very attractive,' he concluded, handing back the print.

'You can't always tell from the photo what someone is like,' Paula protested.

'Jefferson Morgenstern, Secretary of State,' Monica

continued, 'is difficult. I'll get there but I concentrated on Sharon. Morgenstern, as I'm sure you know, originated in Europe. Not sure where yet. His real name is Gerhard Morgenstern. He's now at the American Embassy here, like Sharon.'

'You've done very well,' said Tweed.

'Haven't finished yet. Sir Guy Strangeways, who lives now at Irongates in the village of Parham, made his pile as a property developer in the States. An ex-Guards officer, I gather he's still very British. He was in America for twenty years and for some time he lived in Washington. Travels a lot all over the world. There are mysterious gaps in his whereabouts at certain periods. More later.'

'When did he come back here?' Tweed asked. 'He was still in Washington when I was there three weeks ago.'

'Came back two weeks ago. A sudden departure.'

'That's interesting,' Tweed remarked.

'Now, Ed Osborne,' Monica went on. 'The most mysterious of the lot. He also had an English mother and an American father. He was born in New York, in Hoboken. Not the most salubrious part of that place. His father was an unsuccessful locksmith. His childhood was poverty-stricken. Then, Heaven knows how, he's at Harvard. Afterwards there are huge gaps in his life. No knowledge as to whether he was somewhere in the States or somewhere abroad. Then he joins the CIA and rockets up. I'm still digging.'

'Keep on digging,' Tweed suggested.

'Finally, Basil Windermere. Chucked out of Tonbridge when he was discovered with an under-age girl. I've only just started to build up his file. That's it for now.'

'So, Tweed,' Marler enquired, 'what's your reaction?'

'Menace.'

'How do you make that out?' Paula asked.

'Sixth sense.'

'Now you're going cryptic again.'

As soon as she had spoken it struck her that Kurt Schwarz and Tweed had one thing in common. They never revealed their thinking until they were sure. She guessed why this was. Tweed was careful not to point his team in any direction until he was sure he had worked out what was happening. This made his team think for themselves, come to their own conclusions.

'I simply don't have enough to go on,' said Tweed, answering Paula's comment. 'Incidentally, you'll find several key people here have disappeared. In the night I sent them down to the Bunker. A skeleton team, if you like.'

'You said that casually,' Newman told him. 'When you talk like that it usually means there's a major emergency.'

'There is.'

'I've had an idea,' Newman remarked. 'Basil Windermere came up with the suggestion that I meet him in a bar during the evening. I wasn't encouraging, but I think I'll have a chat with him. Might help Monica to build up her file on him.'

'Good idea,' agreed Tweed.

'If that's all, think I'll mosey off,' said Marler.

'Another good idea. I know you're all short of sleep. So go home and catch up on some rest.'

'Half a mo,' Marler replied. 'Your camp bed is pushed against that wall behind Paula's desk.'

'I noticed that too,' Paula agreed. 'Decided not to ask any questions.'

'Well, I've just asked one,' Marler insisted. 'Tweed, Bob told me you went home soon after midnight.'

'I did.'

'So why is your camp bed out of the cupboard?'

'My fault,' Monica piped up. 'I managed to get the

44

linen to the laundry, then you all came storming in before I could put the bed away.'

'I'll confess,' Tweed said with mock humility. 'I came back from my flat by cab in the middle of the night. I wanted to supervise those members of the team who were going down to the Bunker. They'd been warned in advance.'

'So we wouldn't know,' Marler accused.

'So I didn't have a lot of questions asked in the middle of the move. Then I slept here instead of another trip back to my flat. Off you go, all of you.'

The phone rang before anyone had time to leave the room. Monica answered it, frowned before she looked across at Tweed.

'George says there is an Ed Osborne downstairs. The gentleman wants to see you.'

'Wheel him up, then. The rest of you stay for a while.'

'How the hell did he find out this address?' demanded Newman.

'Maybe Cord had no time to erase certain confidential information from the computer in Langley, Virginia.'

A restless, guarded atmosphere had spread through the office. Only Tweed seemed unaffected, undisturbed. He looked up as George opened the door and a six-foot aggressive American burst inside. It was as though a hurricane had entered. The new arrival was big in every way, radiating dynamic energy. His thick hair was grey-white, his expression dominant, and ice-cold blue eyes swept round the room. Above them were shaggy white brows, below them a straight wide nose and below that a broad thick-lipped mouth. His gaze homed on Paula.

'Hi, baby, you're lookin' good. You and I could make music.'

'I don't think so, Mr Osborne,' she replied coldly.

'You must be Tweed.' He swung round, extended a large hand, looked surprised as he gripped Tweed's hand and squeezed it with the force of a powershovel. Tweed's grip was equally strong.

'You'd better sit down,' he invited his visitor. 'I do prefer people to phone me for an appointment.'

'Waste of time. I just crash the barrier.'

Osborne lowered his bulk into an armchair. Newman had already resumed his seat in his own chair close to the American's. The American lifted his legs, planted his feet encased in very large shoes on the edge of Tweed's desk. Newman leaned forward, grasped both feet by the crossed ankles, dropped them on the floor.

'We don't do that sort of thing over here,' he explained. 'We like good manners.'

'Get you nowhere. World's movin' on. Move with it or get left behind.'

'Britain has been around for quite a time. Your lot has been on the planet only two hundred years.'

'You're Bob Newman, the foreign correspondent. Hoped we'd get on together. Any time you want to interview me, I'm available. Might give you something to write about. They've set up an outfit at the Embassy called the Executive Action Department. Don't know what it does – if anything. You might enquire about it – just for laughs. EAD, they call it. I'm the new Deputy Director of the CIA. They handed me the job on a plate when Cord Dillon went. Don't forget. EAD.'

'You Americans love initials,' Newman commented.

'Saves time. We like to move fast. I'm at the Embassy.'

'Maybe, Mr Osborne, you could enlighten us as to why you have come here?' Tweed suggested.

'Sure. Why not? And who's the thin streak of a guy holding up the wall?'

'He just called in for a cup of coffee,' said Newman.

'That I could do with myself.'

46

Monica rose slowly from her chair. Tweed had nodded his agreement. Osborne swung round in his chair, stared at her.

'Black, honey. Don't ruin it with milk or sugar.'

Her lips pursed, Monica left the room. I hope she doesn't put poison in it, Marler thought. Although it might not be a bad idea.

'Why am I here?' Osborne rumbled on in his deep, aggressive voice. 'We have this special relationship with you Brits. We think it ought to be strengthened. A lot more close cooperation. A lot more exchange of information about what's really goin' on in the world. The way I see it we're natural partners. We have to sit on the same bench. Be buddies.'

'Why?' asked Tweed.

'We have the same problems. A lot of dangerous characters have been flooding in to your country . . .'

'We have noticed,' Newman informed him.

'Mafia men from Eastern Europe. Saboteurs from fanatic Muslim outfits. Same in the States. Sneaking in over the Canadian and Mexican borders. Take the bomb at the World Trade Center in New York. We need tough controls before both our countries go down in chaos.'

Osborne took a gulp of the coffee Monica had put down on the desk close to him. His face screwed up and he choked briefly.

'This is like tar.'

'It's the strong coffee you asked for,' Monica said and sat down behind her computer.

'Fell a friggin' ox.'

'Watch the language,' Tweed said. 'Ladies present.'

'And they probably use worse language than I do.'

'I doubt that's possible,' Newman interjected.

'Screw yourself.'

'If you can't control your language I suggest you get up and go,' Newman snapped.

47

'Mr Osborne—' Tweed began.

'Ed.'

'If there are issues we should discuss I suggest we set up a proper meeting in advance.'

'At the Embassy,' Osborne growled. 'When?'

'When an opportunity comes up I will get in touch. Thank you for calling in to see me.'

'Guess it's time to leave you folks.' Osborne, wearing a loose windcheater, the zip half open, exposing a wild sweater of many colours, and corduroy slacks, stood up. He was calm, stared all round, looking longest at Marler. 'I'll know you when we meet again.'

'I'll know you,' Marler responded offhandedly.

'At least we've got to know each other,' Osborne said, looking at Tweed. 'We'll get to know each other much better, I'm sure.'

'Thank you again for calling in,' Tweed replied.

'I can let myself out.' Osborne paused as he opened the door, his gaze again sweeping the room. 'Have a nice day.'

'My God, what a bloody boor,' Paula exclaimed.

'American,' Marler drawled. 'All brawn, no brain.'

'I'd say,' Tweed disagreed, 'that he's highly dangerous and it would be a great mistake to underestimate him.'

'In that case,' Newman said after a pause, 'maybe he's the man in charge of all the thugs flooding into London. He could handle that job.'

'You may be right. That strange organization they've set up. EAD. Executive Action Department. I don't too much like the sound of it.'

'As long as the first word doesn't mean Execution,' Paula ruminated.

'I'm really going to check that man out,' Monica announced venomously.

'Do that,' Tweed urged her. 'Try to fill in some of those large gaps in his life. Now, I think all of you really should go home and get some rest. I'll stay here awhile. I have a lot to think about.'

'Could I stay on for a few minutes?' Paula requested. 'I want to ask you about something.'

'Of course you may . . .'

As they left the office Marler followed Newman downstairs and walked alongside him to his Merc. They were both wearing sheepskins and the wind was bitter, the temperature way down. Along the main road beyond the Crescent people hurried, shoulders hunched, heads down. Girls walked with their arms folded to give extra protection.

'You mentioned when you phoned me this morning before leaving your flat that you'd decided to take Basil Windermere up on his invitation to meet you at Bentleys this evening,' Marler said.

'That's right. At eight o'clock. Downstairs bar. Why?'

'I'd rather like to be there. Not with you,' Marler added as Newman frowned.

'Windermere will recognize you.'

'No, he won't. You may not either. You don't mind?'

'Why this interest in Windermere?' Newman questioned.

'For one thing I happen to know he's made a number of extended trips to the Continent recently. And prior to that he was seen in Paris frequently.'

'Join the party, then,' Newman said reluctantly. 'But you'd better not be seen.'

'I'll be the Invisible Man.'

*

49

'You wanted to ask me questions,' Tweed said to Paula. 'Fire away.'

'This Bunker down on Romney Marsh – which, of course, I've seen. It must have taken months to build. What triggered off the idea? You've made three trips to Washington, which is unusual for you. One several months ago, two more recently.'

'First, the Bunker was completed in thirty days.'

'I can't believe it.'

'Marler kept his imported workers going hard at it. The main reason it was put together so quickly was the maze of cellars which already existed under that old farmhouse. I heard about it from a historian. I'm sure it was once used by smugglers ages ago. One distant tunnel comes up underneath an abandoned old bell tower not far from the sea.'

'I didn't see that.'

'Because I didn't show it to you. The door at the end of the tunnel is concealed. You'll see it the next time I take you down there. Satisfied?'

'No. You're evading the second part of my question. I also asked what triggered off the idea. Your trips to Washington?'

'You've forgotten.' Tweed smiled. 'I've also made trips to Paris recently.'

'There he goes again,' Paula said to Monica. 'As cryptic as Marler's friend,' she commented, switching her gaze to Tweed.

'What happened to him? When I called you after getting back to my flat last night you said the three of you were having a marvellous time – that your guest had a great sense of humour.'

'He has. He said he was flying back this morning. Now, time for me to go.'

'She's probably off to her health club,' Monica informed Tweed.

'Health club?'

'I haven't bothered to mention it,' said Paula as she put on her coat. 'For the past six months I've attended this health club.'

'Aerobics and all that.' Monica snorted. 'She's on a health kick. Fit as the proverbial fiddle and strong as a horse.'

'I approve,' said Tweed. Paula was just leaving when he called out to her. 'Did Marler's friend say where he was flying to?'

'Paris.'

Tweed remained behind his desk when Paula had gone. Monica was using her computer to record certain aspects of a profile she was working on. None of it was on the network. Tweed had warned her earlier to work in this way. He was writing groups of names on a large pad, then circling groups and drawing lines from one to another, trying to work out whether they linked up. The phone rang.

'American Embassy on the line,' Monica called out.

'Not that pest, Osborne?'

'No. Sharon Mandeville. Said she'd met you at a party once in Washington.'

'Tweed speaking.'

'This is Sharon Mandeville. I don't know whether you'll remember me. We had a long chat at a Washington cocktail party.'

The voice was soft, tentative, appealing. Tweed detected a note of hesitancy.

'Remember you well, Ms Mandeville. What can I do for you?'

'I need to talk to you privately. Would it be too much to ask you to come over to the Embassy to see me?'

'Of course not. When do you suggest?'

'It's probably inconvenient for you, but I was wondering whether you could come over this morning – at your convenience?'

'I could come now.'

'I'll be waiting for you. Just ask for me at reception. Till then . . .'

'I'm off to the American Embassy to meet her,' he told Monica as he put on his overcoat.

'Don't fall for her.'

'Hardly likely. And it fits in nicely with my driving down to Parham this afternoon. I want to have a long talk with Sir Guy Strangeways. See if I can find out what *he* is up to.'

5

Tweed asked his cab driver to drop him just outside Grosvenor Square. March had come in like a lion and a biting wind was battering at him. Above the elegant square an armada of low dark clouds scudded across the sky, threatening a cloudburst.

Tweed paused at a corner, gazing at the huge white modern building facing the central garden. It reared up, solid as a steel wall with windows. A monument to the immense world power it represented. Tweed grunted, mounted the deserted flight of wide steps, pushed his way through a new revolving door. A short walk took him to the reception desk. Behind it an attractive brunette watched him coming warily.

'Ms Mandeville is expecting me. Tweed is the name.'

'You have identification, sir?'

She spoke in a broad American accent. Her voice was nasal, harsh. Tweed took out his wallet, extracted a card which showed him as Chief Investigator, General & Cumbria Assurance. She studied it as though it might be forged, which it was.

'I'll let you know when she can see you. Take a seat over there.'

'I'll stay here. I have an appointment now.'

The receptionist made a moue of displeasure. She expected people to do what she said. After speaking on the phone she gestured towards the lift. No attempt to escort him.

'Take the elevator. Floor One. Room Twenty-one. To your left as you get out.'

'Thank you.'

He glanced at an obvious guard in plain clothes. A weapon bulged under his left armpit. Eyes like stones stared at Tweed, who gave him a little wave on his way to the lift. Cosy atmosphere these days at the American Embassy – almost as though they were expecting an attack.

Tweed strolled over to the lift, pressed the button for Floor One. The door opened silently. He stepped inside. The door closed silently, the lift began to ascend. He was struck by the silence of the building. Like a stage setting prepared for his arrival.

The door slid open, again making no sound. He stepped out into a wide corridor, his rubber-soled shoes as soundless as the lift door, then stopped. To his left, further along the corridor, he saw the back of Jefferson Morgenstern, Secretary of State, America's Foreign Minister. Tweed recognized the small man because he had met him at a party in Washington. Morgenstern was carrying a thick black file.

He was accompanied by two tall men, one on either side of the most powerful man in the American administration. Expecting that at any moment one of the three men would see him, Tweed remained perfectly still. They didn't see him. They appeared too intent on where they were going.

Pausing before a closed door on the right, one of the aides took out a key, unlocked the door and Morgenstern hurried inside. Since they hadn't closed the door Tweed guessed they would be coming out again when they had finished whatever task they were engaged on. He began to walk along the corridor.

Slowing down as he reached the open door, Tweed glanced into the room. A safe like a bank vault set into one wall was open. Morgenstern bent down, slipped the file inside. Tweed walked on. He had already observed the odd numbers were on his left side. He had also noticed the number of the room Morgenstern had entered. Number 16. In addition he had seen the metal plate on the half-open door engraved with one word: SECURITY.

He quickened his pace. Arriving at Room 21 he raised his hand to knock. Before his knuckles could reach the surface the door opened in his face. The woman he had come to see ushered him inside, closed her door. Tweed was under cover before anyone emerged from Security.

It was as though he had met Sharon Mandeville the day before. Her manner was restrained but easy. Tweed reflected that she looked more like a mature thirty-five than her real age, forty-two. She escorted him to two leather-covered swivel chairs by the side of her massive desk. Behind the desk was another chair but as soon as he was seated she occupied the chair next to him.

'Thank you for coming to see me so quickly,' she said in her soft voice. No trace of an American accent. 'I'm sure you would like some coffee. It's a bitter day.'

'That would be very acceptable.'

'Black, if I remember rightly. No sugar. No milk.'

'You have a remarkable memory.'

'And you're wearing the same suit you wore in Washington. I like a man to look smart.'

'Again, your memory.'

'A woman notices small things . . .'

As she conversed she was pouring two cups of coffee from a silver pot perched on a silver tray on a side table. Tweed studied her. She had beautiful blonde hair, very thick, arranged in waves and falling so it just touched her shoulders. As in Washington, it was her large greenish eyes which held him. She had a strong chin without spoiling the striking appearance of her pale face. Her forehead was high. Her mouth was wide but the lips were not full.

Five foot six tall, she was slim and was wearing a pale green dress which went well with her intense eyes. It was high at the neck. She crossed her elegant legs, sipped at her coffee, put the cup down and turned to face her visitor.

'What are you doing over here, if I may ask?' said Tweed.

'It's rather confidential. No, don't worry. I will tell you. The first time we met I decided you could be trusted.'

She paused. Her hypnotic eyes held his. She was a very unusual woman, Tweed was thinking. It was not just a matter of beauty, her graceful movements. Any time she walked into a room full of people all the men would stop talking while they gazed at her. She had *impact*.

'I'm not even sure what my job here is,' she went on. 'I don't know why, but I get on well with the President's wife. She's given me various assignments in the past. I do know that over here I'm supposed to keep an eye on a man called Ed Osborne, the new Deputy Director of the CIA. He's a rough diamond and my main task is to smooth the path for him. Don't let him upset the Brits, is what I was told by the President's wife. I hate that word Brit. Typically American. Osborne will probably try to get in touch with you,' she warned.

'Why would he do that?' Tweed asked innocently.

'He told me you were a friend of his predecessor, Cord Dillon.'

'That's true. What has happened to Dillon?'

'I suppose he's retired. I asked Ed that question myself and all he said was, "He's gone fishin'" – which told me a lot.' She paused, took a cigarette from a silver box. Tweed produced a lighter, lit her cigarette.

'Thank you,' she said.

The typical American woman would have said, 'I can do that for myself,' Tweed thought.

'I'm not offering you one because you don't smoke,' she went on.

'You could produce a file on me,' Tweed joked.

She frowned, then half-smiled. 'I told you I remember trivial things.' She used her other hand to push back a wave of hair.

Tweed knew she was a natural blonde. In Washington she had produced two colour photos of herself from her evening bag. One of herself at twelve and the other when she was eighteen. In both photos her thick blonde hair had jumped out at him. She had apologized for showing them to him.

'I don't carry these about with me,' she had explained. 'I want to give them to a man here who is good at framing photos. To remind me I'm getting old.'

'Hardly.'

'Thank you.'

'Why did you ask me over here?' Tweed now asked. 'Is there something I can help you with?'

'Yes, there might be.' Her eyes still gazed at him.

'Dillon apparently told the President's wife you were a key figure over here, that you know a lot of people. Washington is trying to strengthen the bonds between the two countries. I was hoping you'd introduce me to people who matter from time to time.'

Tweed's expression was neutral. He took his time finishing off his coffee, then refused more. He stared round the room. On a side desk was a pile of folders, some with a red tab attached. The furniture was expensive. The windows looked out on to a side street.

'They should give you an office overlooking the square,' he suggested.

'I prefer it back here – on my own. Osborne has an office the size of a tennis court looking out on the square. How is the insurance business? I suppose you are rich?'

'Not really. I certainly couldn't compete with you. Four husbands must have been a roller-coaster ride.'

'Something like that,' she said after a long pause. 'When I first went – was taken – to the States, I realized my English accent was a passport to successful men. When you're young you're easily flattered. I suppose I did exploit my accent. Does that sound awful?'

'No.'

'Money isn't everything.'

'How is it you still speak perfect English, after all that time spent over there?'

'I came back over here frequently. I have a small mansion in Dorset. Sometimes I think I'd like to live here for good. I find America raw. You glanced at your watch.'

'I've enjoyed our conversation. I hope you'll excuse me – I have an important appointment this afternoon.'

'Of course.'

A light had been flashing on her phone for several minutes. It had been reflected in a mirror close to the door. Tweed collected his coat from the hanger she had put it on while Sharon sat behind her desk. Picking up her phone she listened, then answered.

'Yes. Yes. Yes. Now don't bother me again.'

She got up and walked slowly towards him. Again it occurred to Tweed that she was an incredibly elegant woman. She shook hands with him.

'When you have the time perhaps we could meet again for lunch or dinner to chat some more.'

'It will be my pleasure . . .'

He walked into the corridor, she closed the door and he felt very alone.

There was something about the atmosphere of the building which Tweed found disturbing. No sign of anyone. No sound. He'd have expected the Embassy to be a hive of activity. He had paused, was about to turn to his right when the door across the corridor opened.

A tall American with a smooth face and a blank expression stood facing him. Tweed had the impression of a man conscious of his position in the pecking order. When the American spoke he wondered how he had known Tweed would be in the corridor. Sharon Mandeville had finished speaking before she opened the door, which had not made a hint of noise.

'Tweed?' the American enquired.

'Yes. Who are you?'

'Chuck Venacki.'

The penny dropped. Tweed recalled Chief Inspector Buchanan's story of the encounter when Newman had rammed the Lincoln Continental on the edge of Park Crescent. This physically impressive man had said he was an attaché at the Embassy.

'Main elevator you came up in is out of order,' Venacki said tersely. 'Turn left, end of corridor turn left

58

again. Take the elevator there. There's a door to the side street.'

'Thank you.'

Venacki didn't hear his reaction. He had closed the door in Tweed's face. A certain lack of warmth, Tweed said to himself. As though Venacki resented his presence. And there had been an air of hostility. Tweed turned right, heading for the elevator which had brought him up.

There was a notice hanging from the elevator's closed door. *Out of order*. He pressed a button. Nothing happened. Next to the elevator was a wide staircase which, presumably, led to the exit floor below. He was just descending the first step when he looked back along the corridor. Chuck Venacki was outside his office, watching him. He disappeared instantly, as though he had dashed back into his quarters. Tweed frowned.

He descended the several short flights of stairs slowly, listening. Still not a sound. Peculiar. The atmosphere now seemed menacing. He reached the bottom and the spacious hall was empty – except for the receptionist behind her desk. Her phone rang. She answered it, slammed down the receiver, got up, vanished through a door behind her. Tweed walked quickly to the door. When he tried to open it the door wouldn't move.

He turned round, headed for the revolving door leading out to the square. Close to it was a small desk with a phone. He was about to pass the desk when the phone buzzed faintly. Carefully, Tweed lifted the receiver. A man's voice he didn't recognize was speaking.

'The operation's under way. Double-check with Charlie . . .'

What operation? And who the heck was Charlie? Tweed moved swiftly, pressed a hand on the revolving door. It remained stationary. He couldn't get out the way he had come in. He was trapped. Calmly he surveyed the reception hall. There was no one he could contact. No doubt about it – he was imprisoned inside the building.

He peered out beyond the immobile revolving door. A stretch limo had pulled in behind a blue Chrysler parked at the kerb. Without waiting for his uniformed chauffeur to alight, a passenger jumped out of the rear seat, slammed the door shut, ran up the steps. On his arrival Tweed had noticed two video cameras aimed down the flight of steps. He recognized – from pictures in the papers – the lean energetic man running up the steps. The recently appointed American Ambassador.

Taking no notice of the man inside, the Ambassador pushed at the doors and they began revolving. Tweed walked out as the Ambassador walked in. The keen cold air hit him after the warmth of the air-conditioned building. Tweed paused at the top of the steps, scanning the street. Then he ran one hand over the top of his head, smoothing down his hair.

He had almost reached the bottom step when three tough-looking men emerged from the Chrysler. One opened the rear door. Another addressed him in a harsh American accent.

'Mr Tweed?'

'Yes . . .'

'We'll drive you back to where you're going. Get in.'

'No, thank you . . .'

'I said get in, Buddy.'

Something hard and circular was rammed into his back. Two men took him by the arms, began to hustle him inside the rear of the car. On the far rear seat a small bald man was playing with a Colt automatic pistol, grinning unpleasantly at Tweed.

Tweed became aware of a commotion, a scuffle

60

behind him. He was released from the hand grips. Newman hit one thug over the head with the barrel of his gun. Marler hit another of them with the stiffened side of his hand, the blow connecting with the side of his neck. Harry Butler pointed a wide-barrelled gun, aimed inside the car, pulled the trigger. The interior was sprayed with Mace gas. The bald man and the driver behind the wheel collapsed, choking, unable to see. Newman heaved one unconscious thug into the rear of the car, Marler bundled the second unconscious bundle inside. Butler, who had earlier broken the jaw of the third assailant, shoved him in, fired one more blast of Mace gas, slammed the door shut.

'Let's go,' Newman said to Tweed. 'Merc's parked over there.'

'I know. I saw it.'

'What brought you here?' Tweed asked as Butler drove the Merc back to Park Crescent.

'Monica,' Newman replied, for once seated beside Tweed in the rear. 'When she told us you'd gone to the Embassy we decided you might need back-up. Too many not-nice people floating around our city these days.'

'Well, thank you all. I don't know what they had in mind for me if they'd pulled off the kidnap. Maybe interrogation, maybe murder . . .'

He then explained concisely his experiences inside the Embassy. When he'd finished he looked out of the window where a drizzle of rain was smearing London.

'One key is to find out who Charlie is. I think he may be the real leader behind their Executive Action Department.'

6

At four in the afternoon Tweed was driving his Ford
Sierra along a narrow twisting lane approaching Parham.
By his side Paula sat keeping quiet. She sensed Tweed
was thinking as he drove.

It was almost dark and his headlights shone through
the gloom. Overhead dark clouds massed as though
preparing for a cloudburst. She noticed he kept glancing
in his rear-view mirror. He slowed down at an isolated
spot where he could see the lane ahead for some distance, pulled over onto the grass verge, put one hand out
of the window he had lowered, gestured for a car behind
to stop.

'We have company.'

'Hostile?'

She reached into her shoulder bag and gripped the
.32 Browning. When she looked back as Tweed climbed
out she saw Newman's Merc pull in behind them. She
got out to join Tweed. In the rear seat behind Newman
sat Harry Butler and his partner, Pete Nield.

'Just what is the meaning of this?' Tweed demanded.

'Simple,' replied Newman, still seated behind the
wheel. 'We think you need protection.'

'I thought I emphasized before I left Park Crescent
that I was coming down here by myself.'

'You've got Paula with you.'

'Paula met Sir Guy Strangeways awhile ago at a
dinner in London. They got on well. I think he'll be more
relaxed with Paula present. He won't be if he sees you
three. He's a bit of a martinet.'

'May I remind you,' Newman told him, 'that when I
was bringing Cord Dillon this way we saw the Cadillac

with four American thugs drive inside Irongates? Those gentlemen may still be there. Have you forgotten your experience at the Embassy?'

'I have not. Strangeways is English. Now that you're here find a place open in Parham. Go in and have afternoon tea.'

'I don't think you can get afternoon tea in this country these days,' Nield remarked amiably.

Harry Butler and Pete Nield worked well as a team. There was a great contrast between the two men. Butler was short, burly, with broad shoulders, his dark hair roughly brushed, a man who used words as though he regarded them as money. Pete Nield was slim, had fairish hair and a thin moustache. Unlike Butler, wearing a shabby windcheater and a pair of well-worn slacks, Nield took trouble with his appearance. He was clad in a smart grey suit, a pair of shoes from Aquascutum, a raincoat from the same shop. He was never backward in voicing his thoughts.

'You'll find a tea shop in Parham,' Tweed told him. 'Just keep away from Irongates. This will be a quiet visit.'

'Famous last words,' Paula said under her breath.

Returning with her to his car, Tweed drove on. In his rear-view mirror he noted the Merc was still stationary. Paula was furious.

'That's no way to talk to them after what happened this morning. They rescued you from God knows what.'

'And I thanked them when we got back to Park Crescent. Here is the beginning of Parham.'

He guided the car along the old village street, turned into the first, larger square, then into the smaller square with no other exit. There was no sign of life outside the large mansion and the gates were closed. Tweed stopped the car.

'There's a speakphone in the right-hand pillar. Would you mind letting our host know we've arrived?'

'Of course not,' she snapped.

She got out, still steaming. Tweed was taking risks in a situation which had already proved potentially lethal. It was not only the incident at the American Embassy she had in mind. She was recalling the brutal attempt to murder Cord Dillon in the middle of London. Pressing a button by the side of the speakphone, she waited. A buzz. Then a commanding voice she recognized. Strangeways.

'Who the hell is it?'

'Paula Grey. I have Mr Tweed with me. We understood you—'

'Enter.'

'The gates are closed.'

'Use your eyes.'

She caught sight of movement. The large gates were opening inwards. She ran to the car, jumped into her seat. Tweed immediately drove forward at a slow pace. Behind them the gates closed, making no sound.

'Hinges must be well oiled,' Tweed remarked.

Their tyres crunched on the gravel surface. High banks of rhododendron bushes masked any view on both sides. Paula was experiencing a feeling of claustrophobia – shut away from the outside world like the approach to a monastery where the monks had an evil reputation. At the end of the gently curving drive crouched the house, an ancient mansion, three storeys high and dormer windows in the mansard roof, round like ports for cannons. The style of the mansion was Gothic, grim, its dark stone bleak. Gargoyles leered down at them below the turrets flanking each end of the house.

'Strangeways himself answered me,' Paula recalled. 'He sounded strange – no pun intended. Like a bear with a sore head. When I sat next to him at that dinner he was charming. Amiable and jokey.'

'Interesting.'

She realized Tweed was only half-listening to her. He was peering up at the right-hand turret. He parked the car at the foot of a wide flight of old stone steps leading up to a balustraded terrace. As he locked the car Tweed again looked up at the turret.

'What a ghastly place to live,' Paula whispered.

'You have to remember Strangeways spent twenty years in the army as a young man before he went into business. Prior to that he was at a public school. That sort of background does not make you aware of your surroundings. You take no interest in taste or comfort.'

A heavy front door opened as they reached it. Framed in the doorway was Strangeways. Five foot ten tall, well built, his fleshy face was red, his nose like a hawk's, the eyes dark and forbidding, his mouth tight-lipped above an aggressive jaw. Grey-haired, he sported a trim moustache, stood ramrod erect and was wearing a blue business suit.

'You're late,' he rapped out.

'We're on time. Your watch must be wrong,' Tweed said mildly.

'I pride myself on punctuality,' Strangeways barked. 'An old army habit.'

'My watch is an Accurist. Greenwich mean time. Better buy one for yourself,' Tweed rapped back. 'Are we going to stand out here all afternoon in the cold?'

'Of course not. Please do come in.' Their host's manner had mellowed. As he closed the door he lowered his voice. 'My apologies to you both, but my wretched son turned up out of the blue. I'll introduce you, then tell him to push off . . .'

They followed Strangeways across a large stark hall with woodblock flooring. The only furniture was a large ugly oak chest stood against one wall. No pictures. Strangeways opened a door into a large room, again without a carpet or rugs. Close to the left-hand wall was a plain desk supporting an outsize globe and behind it a map of the world. A heavy oak table occupied the middle of the room and the chairs which surrounded it were hard-backed and looked uncomfortable to Paula. The interior of the house reminded her of a prison.

'This is my son, Rupert,' their host said without enthusiasm.

Sprawled on a couch was a man of about thirty. He wore riding kit with jodhpurs thrust inside gleaming knee-length boots. His right hand held a riding crop which he was tapping against his thigh. His boots were resting on the end of the couch.

'Get those damned boots off the furniture,' Strangeways growled. 'This is a friend of mine with his assistant, Paula.'

Rupert took his time about planting his boots on the floor. He stood up, five feet eight inches tall, a slim man, his jet-black hair neatly trimmed. He had his father's hawkish nose, his dark eyes alert, and a foxy chin, and he surveyed Paula insolently. She bridled inwardly as he slowly took in her legs, higher up her body and then her face.

'Rather like the look of you, Paula. You're not bad.'

'I'm supposed to take that as a compliment?'

'I take my time.'

Tweed had been studying Rupert, who ignored him. Strangeways guided Tweed to a seat at the table. Standing behind him he stood erect, looking embarrassed. He coughed, glanced at Paula.

'I don't quite know how to phrase this. The last thing I want to do is to appear impolite.'

'But you'd prefer it if the two of you could talk alone,' Paula suggested with a smile.

'My dear, there's a library on your left as you go back into the hall. If you're interested in books it's quite an unusual collection I've built up over the years.'

'I'd be happy to wait there.'

'Not so fast.' He went over to the wall, pressed an old-fashioned bell. 'The housekeeper, Mrs Belloc, can provide you with tea and cakes. Indian, Darjeeling, Earl Grey? And I'd better warn you Mrs Belloc is an odd character. Goes around with a black shawl over her head. A hard worker but it's difficult keeping local servants. They don't like her. Ah, here she is.'

Paula had a shock. When the door opened a short powerfully built woman walked slowly in. The black shawl was worn so it concealed most of her features, exposing only gimlet eyes and a nose like a parrot's. A black dress reached almost to her ankles. There was something sinister about her.

'You wanted me, sir?' she asked, addressing her employer.

Strangeways gave her instructions to serve Paula tea in the library. Mrs Belloc was staring at Tweed while she listened. Then she withdrew without a word.

Rupert opened the door again, bowed in an exaggerated way. He was smiling sardonically. Without a backward glance at the two men in the room, he closed the door and caught up with Paula.

'You don't want to waste your time in the library. Let's go riding. I can give you a gentle nag.'

'I want to see the library. And Mrs Belloc is bringing me tea.'

'Never read a book in my life,' he replied jauntily, following her as she opened the door on her left.

'Might do you good if you did read a few.'

'I seem to get by without them.'

She was already inside a large room, the walls lined with bookcases. A wheeled ladder was attached to one wall so the high shelves could be reached easily. Nondescript coffee tables were scattered round the room near large leather couches which looked as though they'd been there for generations. The room was chilly. She pulled out a book on Alexander the Great and perched at the end of a couch. Rupert joined her.

'You'll end up with that old horror, Mrs Belloc, for company. I'm much more fun.'

'I'm sure you are.'

'Please yourself, then,' he said acidly. 'Bury your nose in a crummy book. You don't know what you're missing. We could shoot a few birds instead of riding.'

'That idea doesn't appeal to me.'

'Playing hard to get.' He stood up. 'Have it your own way.'

It was a relief to Paula when he left the room, closing the door behind him. Something caught her eye. She looked at a side window, jumped up, ran into the mullioned bay. Outside was Harry Butler, one finger to his lips. Behind him a trim lawn stretched away to a hedge and beyond it was a field. Wrestling with the old security catch, she pushed open a casement window.

'What on earth are you doing out there?'

'Prowling. And keeping an eye on Tweed. Newman's orders. Got over the side wall with a telescopic ladder he carries in the boot of his car.'

'Get out of sight! Quick! The housekeeper is bringing me tea . . .'

'I'll have a cuppa,' said Butler and was gone.

She was struggling to close the window, had just managed it, when she heard a sound. She hadn't heard the door open but now she heard the sound she had heard when Mrs Belloc entered the other room earlier. The rustle of the stiff black material she wore as a dress. Paula froze.

'Wouldn't have anything to do with him if I were you,' a harsh voice advised.

For a tense moment she thought the housekeeper was

referring to Butler. Then, in the field beyond the hedge, she saw Rupert riding a large stallion. He reined in his mount suddenly. It bucked, reared into the air. Rupert stayed in the saddle, waved his whip at her as his steed's forelegs dropped to the ground.

'Showing off, as usual,' Mrs Belloc complained.

Paula turned round and the squat hooded woman was laying on a table a sparkling silver tray containing the tea. The tray looked genuine and Paula guessed it was an heirloom. It was difficult to imagine Strangeways bothering to purchase the tray.

'Milk and sugar in your tea?'

'Just milk, please. This is very kind of you. And the cakes look scrumptious.'

Mrs Belloc showed no inclination to leave as Paula sat down.

She had closed the door when she came into the library and now she stood close to Paula as she perched on the couch and sampled the tea. Her large, ugly hands were clasped across her middle, her penetrating eyes fixed on Paula.

'This tea is perfect,' said Paula. 'Thank you.'

'Rupert goes to the Continent a lot. Takes one of his fancy ladies with him. He's had a harem of floozies. No, that's not quite right. They're a snooty type, well educated, with not a hint of a brain.'

'Really?'

'He likes the casinos over there. Gambles heavily. Must cost him a packet.'

'I expect he can afford it.'

'Don't know he can. When his mother died she left him some kind of regular allowance. Wouldn't have thought it ran to the sort of life he lives.'

'I see.'

Paula ate one of the cakes. She was being careful not

to say much. She didn't like gossip. Above all she didn't want to say anything which might be repeated to Rupert's father.

'He likes shooting. Pheasants. Boasts about it. He's always saying one bullet, one bird. I'd better leave you now. I'm going up to the turret.'

'What's up there?'

'Gives me a good view of what Rupert is up to. You mind my words. Give Rupert a clear berth.'

On this note she ambled slowly to the door, left the library, closing the door behind her. Paula selected another cake. As she consumed it her mind whirled with thoughts. She was also wondering how Tweed was getting on with his host.

'How about a double Scotch?' Strangeways had suggested as soon as they were alone.

'No, thank you. I'm driving.'

He watched Strangeways walk briskly to a cabinet against a wall. Taking out a glass and a bottle of expensive whisky, his host poured a generous drink. As the bottle touched the rim of the glass it rattled. He drank half the contents, returned to the table, sat facing Tweed.

'That's better. I needed it.'

'You're worried about something?'

'Tweed, you know I've spent a long time in the States. By now I know America. I know a lot of the top people. I know the way they're thinking. Incidentally, I'm having dinner with Jefferson Morgenstern in town this evening.'

'Is he worried?'

'I think so. Look at it from their point of view. Globally. They feel encircled. Across the Pacific they have China facing them. That's a distance, but not in these days of inter-continental ballistic missiles. They think the Russians are going to ally themselves with the Chinese.

That's looking west from where they sit. Now take Europe and the Middle East. Iran, to mention only one Muslim state, is building a nuclear arsenal. If it combined with Turkey – which could soon become a Muslim state again – they might over-run Europe. Turkey, as you know, is close to having a population of a hundred and fifty million. Bigger than any nation in Western Europe.'

'Iran is a long way from America,' Tweed pointed out, glancing at the wall map of the world facing him.

'London is roughly half the distance Beijing is from San Francisco – and they're worried about Beijing.'

'Why mention London?'

'It's much closer to the East Coast of America.'

'Why is that relevant?'

'If an enormous Muslim power took over Britain, America would be an isolated fortress, menaced on both coasts.'

'Why do they think that would happen?' Tweed enquired.

'Because they think this European Union idea is a shambles. Umpteen nations, speaking different languages, with different histories, many secretly hating each other. They quote the old Austro-Hungarian Empire – also a goulash of nationalities – which collapsed at the end of the First World War. More recently, they point to Yugoslavia. Again a mix of races with their own languages, religions. Tito dies and the whole house of cards comes tumbling down.

'So?'

'They foresee a scenario whereby an overwhelming Muslim force could conquer Western Europe. Supposing a federated Europe was attacked. Imagine the indecision in Brussels. They'd still be working out what to do when the Muslims crossed the Rhine. There'd be a large element arguing that any life would be better than death.'

'So what do the Americans propose to do about it?'

'They have a plan. I do know that. Morgenstern, remember, was born in Europe. Was in Europe until he was a young man and went to the States.'

'It's his plan?'

'I don't know. But he carries tremendous influence in Washington.'

'What is the plan?' Tweed asked point blank.

'I don't know. They never forget I'm English.' Strangeways finished off his drink. 'So they don't confide in me.'

'But you seem to know a lot.'

'I simply know how they're thinking. What about you? Have you a clue as to what is going on?'

'Nothing, really,' Tweed replied evasively.

'I do know they think very highly of you, Tweed,' Strangeways said casually.

Strangeways was looking at the wall as he said this. His right hand was playing with his empty glass. For a moment Tweed detected a hint of shiftiness in his host, something he had never seen before.

'Why me?' he asked.

'They respect your global outlook. Your achievements in the past. Above all, you're not a politician. Morgenstern once described you as having the brain of a statesman.'

'Nice of him. Do you agree with what is happening?'

'Damn it, I can't make up my mind. The world is changing day by day. There's no precedent for the present grim situation.'

'Why did you ask me down here, Guy? If I may call you that?'

'Of course you may. I felt a strong need for a sounding board. To get your reaction. I'm going to have another drink.'

'I hope you don't mind – ' Tweed checked his watch – 'but I'll have to be going soon.'

He looked round the chilly uncomfortable room. Yes, it all came from a boarding-school upbringing. There was an atmosphere in the room he didn't like, a restlessness which he felt sure originated in his host. He also felt alarmed and couldn't put his finger on the reason for this sensation.

'Sorry, Tweed,' Strangeways said, returning with his refilled glass. 'I've been pouring out my anxieties to you. Not like me.'

'Why do you think the Prime Minister was assassinated?' Tweed asked suddenly.

Strangeways was sitting down. He froze. The liquid in his glass shook. Then he stood up, his expression grim.

'That was a nasty business.' He drank more whisky. 'But I'm detaining you.'

He accompanied Tweed into the forbidding hall, went over and opened the library door. Paula was immersed in her book. She looked up and smiled.

'I've really enjoyed the peace and quiet in here.'

'Rupert hasn't been bothering you, has he?'

'Heavens, no.'

She spoke over her shoulder as she carefully replaced the volume where she had found it. Strangeways watched her action with approval.

'You know something,' he told her, 'you're the first visitor who hasn't taken out a book and then left it on one of the couches. Tweed is leaving now . . .'

The three of them were walking across the hall when the front door was hurled open. Rupert entered, slapping his crop against his thigh. He stared hard at Tweed.

'Don't know you.'

'No, you don't,' Tweed replied abruptly.

'But I must say goodbye to the alluring Paula.'

'Go straight upstairs to your room,' Strangeways snapped.

'Your wish is my command.'

73

Rupert began running up a wide curving staircase to the left of the doorway Tweed and his father had just left. As he ran he twirled his riding crop in a way which reminded Paula of an American girl leading a parade before a sports match, manipulating her symbolic stick. He's athletic, she thought. Then Rupert threw the crop into the air, caught it with one hand as it fell behind his back. And quick reflexes, she said to herself.

'I'll give you a buzz,' he called down to Paula. 'We'll have dinner in London.'

She didn't reply, Strangeways tightened his mouth and then his son was gone. The doorway where Rupert had entered was still open. Paula thanked their host as they left and Tweed turned on the terrace.

'Enjoy your dinner with Morgenstern,' he said.

Strangeways said nothing, merely nodded before closing the door. At the bottom of the steps Tweed paused with Paula, glanced up at the right-hand turret before getting behind the wheel of his car.

'Someone is watching us.'

'I know. Mrs Belloc, seeing us off the premises. I'm glad we are going. Something creepy about that place.'

7

Tweed had a shock when he arrived back at Park Crescent. He had found the Merc parked outside a tea shop in Parham. Newman had emerged immediately with Butler and Nield. Paula was secretly relieved to see Butler. During the drive back Tweed had told her he would explain what had happened with Strangeways when they got back. This made Paula resolve to say nothing about her encounter with Rupert for the moment.

It was dry and bitterly cold when Tweed parked his

car and they entered the SIS building. George, who let them in, pointed to the waiting room.

'You'll never guess who is waiting to see you.'

'Then I won't try.'

Newman and Nield were heading up the stairs to Tweed's office when George called out to them, 'Marler has arrived. You'll find him up there.'

Butler paused. He made no attempt to follow the two men up to the first floor. He spoke tersely before heading for the door to the basement. 'I have to visit the boffins. They're cooking up a new gadget for Marler.'

'Well, George, what is it?' Tweed asked when he was alone with Paula.

'And you'll never guess what he said to me. Chief Inspector Roy Buchanan has been waiting for almost an hour. He told me that if anyone at the Metropolitan Police asked if he was here I was to say I hadn't see him.'

'He used the phrase Metropolitan Police?' Tweed checked in a puzzled tone.

'His very words.'

'Sorry to keep you waiting so long, Roy,' Tweed apologized as he entered the waiting room with Paula. 'You didn't phone to let me know you were coming.'

'Deliberately. My office may be bugged.'

Paula was gazing at their visitor. Normally Buchanan's manner was sardonic, deceptively offhand. Now he looked like a man under pressure, his expression grim. She recalled the bizarre change in Strangeways' appearance, how the jokey amiability had been replaced by tension. He had struck her at Irongates as being taut as a guitar string under unbearable strain. What on earth was happening to these men?

'Roy,' said Tweed briskly, 'in my office there are Newman, Nield and Marler. And, of course, Monica. Would you sooner they didn't hear what you have to say?'

'I'd sooner they did. At least *they* are trustworthy . . .'

When they were all settled in his office Monica suggested some coffee. Buchanan accepted the offer gratefully. Paula sensed that Monica had noticed the change in the Chief Inspector. Their guest normally lounged in his armchair. Now he was sitting bolt upright.

'Fire away, Roy,' Tweed invited.

'Something terrible is happening to this country,' Buchanan began. 'Like a monster octopus extending its tentacles round every key position. I've been told to lay off the Americans,' he said savagely.

'In what way?' Tweed enquired.

'For starters, no investigation of the outrage in Albemarle Street. No witnesses . . .'

'Oh, yes, there are!' Paula exploded. 'I'm a witness – that is, if Tweed agrees. But I can't reveal the identity of the man they tried to kill.'

'I know it was Cord Dillon, ex-Deputy Director of the CIA,' the Chief Inspector replied. 'Tweed called me at home from his flat. I gather he's in hiding and there are no other witnesses.'

'The street was empty,' Paula went on vehemently. 'It was a freezing night. And it happened just after ten o'clock. No one was about – which isn't surprising.'

'Then,' Buchanan went on, 'I've been told to destroy my report on the Lincoln Continental incident, when Newman rammed it outside here. Again, lay off the Americans.'

'Who told you this?' Tweed asked.

'The Commissioner himself. Had me in his office this morning. Just the two of us. He was apologetic, defensive. The trouble is there's a strong rumour he's going to be replaced. And he's the best man in the country to hold down the job.'

'He was adamant?' Tweed suggested.

'Not entirely. He was escorting me to the door and then said, "You must use your own judgement, Roy."'

The phone rang. Monica had just returned and served

Buchanan with coffee. She picked up the phone, listened, looked across at Tweed.

'Sorry to interrupt. Butler's on the line from the basement. Said it was urgent.'

'What is it, Harry?' Tweed asked on his own phone.

'Thought I'd better own up. While you were at Irongates I used a telescopic ladder to scale the side wall. Wanted to check you were OK. Then explored round the back, found a big garage. Padlocked shut but there was a gap in the old doors. Shone my torch inside and there was the Chrysler they tried to shove you into outside the American Embassy.'

'You're certain?'

'Same number plate.'

'You did well. I need that information.'

Putting down the phone, Tweed told Buchanan there was something he ought to know. He then described the attempt to kidnap him and Butler's Chrysler report. Buchanan's expression changed. He relaxed in his chair.

'Now I've got something I can get my teeth into. Kidnapping – or the attempt – is a major crime. And, if you agree, Tweed, I've got witnesses. Newman and Butler would do.'

'I agree,' Tweed said promptly.

'You can keep the SIS out of this?' enquired Marler, standing against a wall.

'Newman would make the perfect witness,' Buchanan pointed out. 'He's the best-known foreign correspondent on Earth. Butler works for the General & Cumbria Insurance outfit. Tweed is its chief investigator. His speciality is supposed to be the insurance of prominent men against being kidnapped. A clever counsel could link the whole thing up – someone Tweed has insured is in danger of being kidnapped.'

'Any idea why the Prime Minister was assassinated?' Tweed asked out of the blue.

'None at all.'

'I think I have. Normally we know who would have taken his place. But the Cabinet and the MPs rebelled. They chose someone else. An apparently neutral figure. Whoever paid for the assassination banked on their own man getting the job.'

'That's shrewd,' Buchanan commented. 'Incidentally, Interpol contacted me about the possible identity of the assassin.'

'Who did they come up with?' interjected Marler.

'I know why you've asked. If anybody eventually locates the bastard you will. Interpol told me it could be the Phantom. They're sure he killed that German, Keller, and the French Minister. They then told me – emphasizing it was no more than a rumour – that the Phantom could be an Englishman.'

'So what about the Chrysler?' Tweed prodded. 'You've been told to lay off the Americans.'

'Blow that. I'm getting a search warrant for Irongates so we can open up that garage. If I get the sack, then I do. I'll send a team down there. Think I'd better get moving.'

'Watch your back,' warned Tweed.

'I've been doing that for years – some of the people I've had to deal with.' Buchanan stood up, grabbed the overcoat Monica had put on a hanger in a corner near the door. 'And thanks, Monica, for the coffee. You make the best in London.'

With one hand on the door handle, he turned to look quickly at everyone. He pulled a wry face.

'Don't do anything I would. Otherwise you'll get yourselves into a proper pickle . . .'

'He's his old self,' said Paula when Buchanan had gone. 'Must be the coffee.'

'We gave him something he can get hold of,' Tweed asserted.

'Oh, I had an early morning phone call before I left my flat,' Newman announced.

'Give,' rapped out Paula. 'You look pleased with yourself.'

'Sharon Mandeville wants me to have dinner with her tomorrow evening. How she got hold of my ex-directory number I have no idea. She suggested Santorini's, the new place down by the river.'

'And you're going to oblige the lady?'

'Thought I might get some information out of her.'

'Of course. That ravishing photo of her we showed you had nothing to do with it.'

'I just wonder,' Tweed mused, 'whether she's had it up to here with America. Maybe she's decided to settle down over here. Hence her buying a house in Dorset. In which case she'll be keen to build up a circle of friends.'

'I've just found out about that,' Monica intervened. 'She's actually bought a small manor in Dorset.'

'Which backs up my theory about her,' Tweed remarked.

'I'd better get moving,' Newman said, standing up. 'I want to go home and freshen up. I'll need my wits about me. I'm meeting that slug Basil Windermere this evening.'

'Look forward to tomorrow,' Paula told him. 'Santorini's will cost you a fortune. The lady would make an expensive girl friend. Lucky you can afford it,' she continued to tease him.

'I'm getting out of here. I'm Paula's target.'

He was walking to the door when it opened. Butler walked in, carrying a cardboard box with a pink ribbon round it. He handed the box to Marler.

'It works,' he told him.

'What works,' demanded Newman.

79

'It does.'

'I'll come with you, Bob,' decided Marler.

He walked out, carrying the box under his arm. Newman warned him again on their way down the stairs that there would be hell to pay if Windermere recognized him.

Inside the American Embassy, in the large room over-looking the square, was a conference table. At its head sat Jake Ronstadt. Only five foot four tall, his presence nevertheless dominated the eight Americans seated on either side. Clean-shaven, he had a large head, a thin mouth, a short thick nose and a lot of jaw. His chest was like a barrel but his legs were thin, his feet small. He shuffled a pack of cards as he gazed from one man to the next, his eyes hard, intimidating.

'You guys had better work a damned sight harder for the huge pay cheques you get,' he growled. 'I'm having to do everything myself. Met a guy who gave me the data on Strangeways. He wanted five thousand bucks for what he told me. He's at the bottom of the Thames now. Get the message?'

'Sure, Jake.'

It was a chorus from the eight men assembled around the table. A fulsome chorus, motivated by fear. Jake continued to shuffle the pack of cards. No one had ever seen him play a game. It was just a weird habit he had, part of his forceful personality. His accent was New York's back streets and he spoke in a deep rumble, spacing out his words as though addressing a bunch of morons. All his subordinates wore black English business suits. Jake was clad in a leather windcheater, leather trousers.

'Charlie says the operation is moving too slowly.'

'Who is Charlie?' asked Diamond Waltz.

'Hank.' Jake paused. 'I guess you kinda asked the wrong question. How cold do you reckon it is at the bottom of the river?'

'Sorry, Jake.' The bald-headed Waltz was shivering with fright. 'I'm very sorry. I made a bad mistake.'

'Don't hire guys to make mistakes. Keep your goddamn trap shut. Maybe then you'll live longer, Baldy.'

'Are we still working with Chuck?' asked another man. 'Just want to get the score clear.'

'Chuck Venacki wasn't invited to attend our little meetin' – you check everything you find out with me. Here are your targets.'

Jake stood up, holding a sheaf of papers. He walked slowly round the table. Behind each man he paused and the man he stood behind was careful not to look round. Then he laid a sheet of paper in front of each man. The sheets were white paper, blank except for the names typed on them. There was no identification that they had originated from the Embassy. Completing the job, Jake lowered his bulk into his chair, picked up the pack of cards.

'You guys all have different names on your sheets. Your job is to dig up any dirt you can on your names. All are prominent people in this country. Baldy, the first name on your list is important.'

'Paula Grey.'

'That's great, Baldy. Really great. You can read. She's to have the full treatment – unlike all the other names on the lists. Do it quickly.'

'I make her talk first?' Baldy said eagerly. 'Then she goes overboard?'

'You've got it. Charlie says it will break the morale of her boss. When she's fished out of the river.'

'Her address in Fulham is here. Should be easy.'

'Nothing's easy.' Jake waved a warning thick finger, taking in everyone round the table. 'I've trained you all

81

how to dig up dirt. Some guy with gambling debts, cheating on his wife, a pervert, open to a bribe. Anything that gives us a grip on them. So when we say dance, they dance. To our tune. You all have addresses of your targets. OK?'

'Very OK, Chief,' said a thin-boned man with a hard face who sat nearest to Jake.

'Not OK, Vernon,' Jake snarled. 'You need more.' He shoved a bulky envelop at him. 'Don't see why I should take another walk round this table. Inside that package is an envelope for each gentleman present. Has his name on it. Inside is a photo of each target, man or woman. Why not get on your feet and deliver the goods.'

Jake sat shuffling his cards while Vernon stood up, opened the package, walked round the table, dropping an envelope in front of each of his collegues. Baldy opened his, went through several photos, frowned.

'May I speak, Chief?' he suggested nervously.

'If you have anything to say.'

'No photo of a woman in my envelope.'

'So we didn't get a pic of the Grey twist. You've had to look before without a pic.'

'Sure, Chief. When I get her can I use the old warehouse in Eagle Street, down in the East End. Vernon showed me the place the day we arrived on Eurostar.'

'Sounds like a good idea. Wonder where that came from? Nobody will hear her screaming.'

'Paula,' Tweed suggested, getting up from his swivel chair, 'it has been a gruelling time. How would you like to join me for an evening at Goodfellows?'

'Lovely idea. Thank you. I could do with some relaxation – and Bob and Marler are off on a bar crawl with Windermere. I'll drive home to change, then come back here to join you.'

'I'm not changing. I put on a decent suit to see Strangeways,' Tweed told her.

He looked at Monica when Paula had left. She was talking to someone on the phone, making notes on a pad. When she put down the phone she nodded with satisfaction.

'That was a contact in Washington I was talking to. I'm still building up profiles.'

'I have an additional fact I'd like you to concentrate on. I need to know which of the profiles you're working on has a second name. Charlie. Or Charles.'

'English or American?'

'Could be either. I heard the name when I picked up a phone at the American Embassy and overheard a snatch of conversation. His identity could be the key to what is happening.'

'What is happening?'

'I'm not sure yet. I'm beginning to fear a gigantic operation is under way which bodes ill for this country. But Charlie can wait until the morning. Go home now and get some rest.'

'Not yet. The adrenalin is surging. I'm going to keep at it for a bit longer. You should enjoy Goodfellows. I hear it's a sophisticated nightclub. Expensive too. Nice for Paula.'

'I'm just hoping she won't be mad with me when she sees the clientele after we've arrived.'

'Why should she be?'

'Because it happens to be the in-place patronized by top Americans at the moment.'

Paula parked her car in the cul-de-sac off the Fulham Road. She was lucky – she had a permanent slot which went with her flat. She lived in the top half of a small elegant house divided into two flats.

She was standing under a wall lamp when she dropped her car keys on the cobbles. Swearing, she stooped to pick them up, then straightening up, she paused to smooth down her glossy dark hair. Then she ran up the outside staircase, paused again under another wall lamp to get out her two sets of keys to open the door.

Across on the other side of the Fulham Road, a man stood hidden in the shadows of a doorway. Baldy was dressed in an almost comic fashion. He wore a Borsalino hat, its wide brim well pulled down. It was partly a disguise and partly to shield his head from the intense cold.

'Got you, Paula Grey,' he said to himself. 'I guess you're not going to enjoy the last few hours of your life with me. Not one friggin' bit.'

8

'Cheers, my dear chap,' Basil Windermere called out.

Newman had just entered the ground-floor bar. He acknowledged the greeting with a wave of his hand. Windermere was perched on a bar stool. Walking slowly towards him Newman glanced at the couples dining at tables by the wall. No Marler. Quickly he averted his sweeping gaze. Marler was there, with a girl.

He's practically unrecognizable even to me, Newman thought. Marler was wearing a smoking jacket with a velvet collar. He also had a pair of large horn-rimmed glasses perched on his nose. It was the glasses which did the trick, Newman decided – he'd never seen Marler wear them before. For some reason his raincoat was folded over the empty chair next to him.

'Just finished a drink,' Windermere said as Newman sat on the stool next to him.

He wore his usual polka-dot bow tie, a pink shirt, a Prince of Wales check suit. It should have looked wrong but instead it looked smart. Windermere always took a lot of trouble over his appearance.

'Can you hold out a few more minutes?' Windermere said.

'Hold out?'

'Before you have a drink. This place is quiet tonight. I vote we go up the street to Goodfellows. Where the action is.'

'Where the rich ladies are?'

'Got it in one, chum.'

'Then we're leaving,' Newman agreed, raising his voice.

'At the double, as Rupert would say. Mockingly.'

Marler leaned across his table, spoke quietly to his companion, his wallet in his hand. He extracted a fifty-pound note, left it on the table as he spoke.

'Sorry. Warned you I might only have time for a drink. Have to rush back to the office. My pager just beeped.'

'I didn't hear anything . . .'

'You weren't supposed to. I'll call you.'

'Don't bother. You haven't even finished your food—'

She was talking to a blank space. Newman, trying to catch what Marler said, left his stool. Windermere was already on his way out. Marler slipped past Newman as though he didn't know him. He peered out while putting on his own coat, stiffened.

Looking down the narrow street he saw a small man wearing an old trilby hat, a shabby windcheater and denims, peering inside a dustbin. The Ear. As he watched, standing well back, Marler saw the small man start shuffling up the street at surprising speed. The little man passed him, Marler looked to his left. Basil Windermere was striding up the street, his long legs moving at an athletic pace. Marler was startled. The Ear was following Basil Windermere.

'I think this place is full of Americans,' Paula whispered.

They had just entered the luxurious interior of Goodfellows. Chandeliers were suspended from the ceilings. Each table was illuminated by a rose-coloured shade supported above an expensive, tasteful vase. Most of the tables were occupied and there was the sound of buoyant chatter mingling with the clinking of glasses.

'We have a table reserved. Name is Tweed,' her escort said to the head waiter.

'By a window, sir. I'm sure you will find it satisfactory.'

Paula sat in a chair facing in the distance the mahogany bar. She glanced round the restaurant, glad she'd taken the trouble to change. A lot of the men wore evening suits with black ties. Others were in smart business clothes. The women had all dressed up. She felt comfortable in her blue dress with its high collar and long sleeves. Round her slim waist she wore a thin gold belt. She looked at the bar again.

'I thought you were taking us out for an evening's relaxation.'

'That was the idea,' said Tweed, glancing up from the menu.

'The place is packed with Americans. That nice Ed Osborne is holding up one end of the bar. You brought us here to check up on who is in town.'

'Should I apologize?'

'Of course not.' Her tone softened. 'I'm sorry I talked like that. We have a job to do.'

'And there may not be much time left.'

Tweed returned to examining the menu, glancing down the wine list, turning pages of the leather folder. The waiter appeared quickly and Paula ordered a dry Martini. Tweed said he'd like a glass of dry white French wine. Paula stared again at the bar.

'When you can, look at the far end of the bar. Osborne is talking to a weird man, and gestured towards our table.'

'Wonder who he is? Not sure I like the look of him.'

The individual she had drawn his attention to was short, had wide shoulders, a large head and a barrel of a chest. His brown hair was cut short and he wore an evening suit. He left the bar, sidled his way between the tables and headed straight for them.

'Hi, folks. Ed Osborne suggested I came over to give you both a big hello. I'm Jake Ronstadt.'

'Paula Grey,' said Tweed. 'And to finish the introductions I'm Tweed.'

'You have a real good taste in beautiful ladies. I sure do envy you.'

He bent down, wrapped a bearlike hand and arm round Paula's shoulders. Inwardly she thanked Heaven she was not wearing an off-the-shoulder dress. Tweed was staring at Ronstadt. When he mentioned Paula's name the small, heavy-lidded eyes had flickered. Just for a millisecond, but the reaction had been strange.

'You sound to be from New York,' Tweed commented. 'What are you doing over here? You're a long way from home.'

'Right on the button. New York.' Ronstadt released Paula from his grip, stood up. 'I'm with the Embassy.'

'Really?' Tweed persisted. 'In what capacity? What job?'

'I guess you could say I'm in public relations.'

'And what does that involve, Mr Ronstadt?'

'Jake, please,' his voice rumbled. 'I smooth the way for making friends with people the Ambassador wants to meet.'

'Well, I don't see any reason why he'd want to meet me.'

'He sure does. That's why Ed sent me over to get to know you both. And I'll tell you something else.' He lowered his voice. 'Jefferson Morgenstern, our Secretary of State, is anxious to see you.' He placed a thick finger beside his stubby nose. 'That's off the record. Know what I mean? Guess I'd better leave you folk to get on with your dinner. Enjoy.'

'I don't like that man,' Paula said when Ronstadt had left. 'He radiates physical vitality and power – but he has the smile of a crocodile.'

'Someone else for Monica to profile,' Tweed said quietly. 'I see you've spotted someone at the bar, from your expression.'

'You're not going to believe it. Bob has just walked in with Basil Windermere. They're sitting at the other end of the bar from Osborne.'

'Guess I'll start with a Scotch,' Basil said as he settled on his stool.

'Do you ever sit on anything other than a bar stool?' Newman enquired.

'Not if I can help it. You'd be surprised at how many ancient dowagers think it's fun to perch on one with me. Makes them feel young again.'

'If you say so. I'll have a Scotch too,' he told the barman. 'Basil, you mentioned a Rupert who used the phrase "at the double". Rupert Who?'

'Rupert Strangeways, of course. There's only one

Rupert, son of *the* Strangeways. The old boy is loaded. Rupert's a drinking pal of mine.'

'On the Continent as well?'

'No.' A pause. 'Not on the Continent. Down the hatch!'

'Cheers. Do you still go to that shooting club down by the Thames?'

'Haven't been for ages. Got bored. No business there. No ladies dripping diamonds. Rupert used to come with me. He's stopped going.'

'Was he a good shot?'

'You must be joking. He hit everything except the target. I scored the occasional bull. Pure fluke. Talk of the devil – look what the tide washed up.'

A man in his thirties with a sneering expression had sat on the stool next to Basil. He wore a very expensive dinner suit, a jacket with silk-covered lapels. The barman came and stared at him.

'I'll have a double Scotch. At the double. While you're at it build me another as a reserve.'

The barman gave Rupert a look which was not friendly. Newman was trying to think of a way to get Basil out of Goodfellows. When they had come in Newman spotted Tweed and Paula at their window table. He was sure Basil, with the bar as his magnet, hadn't seen them. There had to be a ploy to persuade Basil to come with him elsewhere. Newman had also observed that Ed Osborne was occupying the far end of the bar. He wondered who the short, grim-looking individual with Osborne might be. He kept staring at Newman with his hard eyes. Newman thought it was a long time since he'd seen such a ruthless-looking man. His opportunity to shift Basil came unexpectedly.

'You shouldn't talk to the barman the way you do, Rupert,' Basil told him. 'He doesn't like it.'

'Who gives a frig for a barman?'

'Not the lord of the manor, the king of creation, God's gift to the casinos in Europe.'

'How would you like this drink poured over your crummy suit?' Rupert snarled.

'Time to go, find fresh fields,' Newman said firmly, gripping Basil's arm.

'I think you're right,' Basil agreed. He glanced at Rupert. 'You don't get the best type of person in here.'

Rupert was lifting his glass when Newman hauled Basil off the stool. Just in time. Rupert's double Scotch flooded the stool Basil had just vacated. Newman hustled Basil away from the bar, between tables and out of the entrance. The cold air hit Basil, who stumbled, swayed.

'Time to go home,' Newman insisted. 'We can have another drink there . . .'

An hour and a half later Tweed paid the bill and left the club with Paula. They had come by taxi and Tweed was looking for another cab. Of course, there was no sign of one.

'We'll find a cab and I'll see you safely home,' he said.

'That isn't necessary. It's out of your way. You can see me into a taxi and it will take me straight home.'

'Are you sure?'

'I'm certain.'

Tweed was in two minds. His instinct was to drop her off at her flat in the Fulham Road. On the other hand he wanted to go back to his office. He felt sure Monica would be working on her profiles into the early hours. He was impatient to see what she had come up with – and to add to her list the name of Jake Ronstadt. He had sensed something disturbing about the American's personality.

'That was odd,' Paula remarked, pulling her coat

more tightly round her against the chilly night, 'Rupert, of all people, turning up at the bar.'

'He probably haunts places like that at night. Especially a new one like Goodfellows, only opened two months ago. On the lookout for new girl friends. You told me Mrs Belloc, down at Irongates, made a reference to his harem.'

'He's a typical rich man's son. An idler and a wastrel. He seemed to know Windermere.'

'Like attracting like. Both of them are worthless.'

'At one moment it looked like turning ugly,' Paula reflected. 'Bob certainly moved fast, getting Windermere out of the club.'

'Here's a cab.'

Tweed flagged it down. He opened the rear door and Paula dived inside, glad to get into some warmth. Tweed gave the driver a banknote to cover the fare and the tip.

'It's your job to see my friend gets back safely to the address I've given you.'

'With a tip like that, mate, I'd take her safely to Singapore,' the driver assured Tweed.

'I must be tired,' Paula called out to Tweed after she had lowered the window. 'I forgot to thank you for a marvellous dinner. I feel so relaxed.' She leaned out, kissed him on the cheek. 'Thank you again.' She looked down at the pavement. 'And don't get wet – it must have rained when we were inside.'

'Good night. See you in the morning.'

Newman had two surprises when he steered Basil outside Goodfellows. His companion suddenly straightened up, walked a few very steady paces before he turned back.

'Aren't you coming? You know my flat is just off Regent Street. Takes only a few minutes to hoof it there.'

Newman's second surprise was when he looked across the street at another restaurant. Sitting at the window table by himself, still wearing the horn-rims, was Marler. What on earth was he up to?

'I said, aren't you coming?' Basil called out again. 'Bloody cold hanging around out here.'

'That flat of yours must be damned expensive,' Newman commented as he hurried to walk alongside his companion.

Basil, striding along, showed no sign that he was affected in any way by the amount of alcohol he had consumed. He was even humming a tune.

'Awfully damned expensive,' he agreed in a lordly way. 'What does it matter? I've borrowed it from a wealthy lady who has gone abroad.'

'Do you ever buy anything yourself?' Newman wanted to know.

'Not if I can help it. Here we are. Down this side street.'

Newman had the uncanny feeling they were being followed. He glanced back once. Couldn't see any sign of another human being. Odd. His instinct in that direction had always been right before. They walked rapidly down the narrow street. It was deserted. Basil stopped by his front door, felt for his keys. Newman turned to see if he could fit key into lock first time. He did without hesitation.

'Bob,' he said, turning on his heel. 'Now we've got here I'm feeling a bit tired.'

'Go straight up to bed,' Newman urged, relieved he wouldn't have to spend any more time with him. 'You look fresh but . . .'

'I was up till 4 a.m. last night – that is, this morning. Do you mind? And thanks for coming with me.'

'Off to beddy-byes.'

Basil disappeared inside, closed the door. Newman

felt spots of rain on his face. He swung round and Marler was only a few paces away. Newman grinned, punched Marler on his shoulder.

'Thought I had a tail.'

'You did. But it wasn't me.'

'Who the hell was it, then?'

'The Ear. He's been tracking Windermere all evening. I just wonder why.'

'Where is the Ear?'

'Ahead of us. He slipped past you when you watched Windermere opening his door. You never hear him. You rarely see him. And we're going to get soaked. Let's walk on, find a cab.'

They turned up the collars of their raincoats. It was very quiet. Only the patter of the rain and the squelch of their shoes on the pavement. Newman stopped suddenly, staring ahead. A small figure wearing a trilby hat appeared out of nowhere, shuffling away from them.

'I wonder who that is,' Newman mused.

'That is the Ear. Maybe he wants to talk to me. Now he is slowing down. Why?'

He looked up as he spoke and thunderclouds seemed almost to touch the top of the flat roofs of the terrace houses, most turned into flats, one of which was occupied by Basil Windermere. A brilliant flash of lightning was followed instantly by a deafening clap of thunder.

'Under cover,' said Marler. 'The Ear has darted into the shelter of a doorway.'

They had just reached their own shelter, close to a front door and under an overhang of a stone beam, when the cloudburst enveloped the street. Rain sluiced down at a slanting angle like a curtain of fine wires. Rivers of water ran down the street's gutters, the top of drainpipes overflowed, sending cascades of water down.

'That's why the Ear paused,' said Marler. 'He knew what was coming.'

Frequently he glanced out to make sure the Ear hadn't moved out of his shelter. The cloudburst ceased as quickly as it had erupted. They heard the storm drifting away to the east. Marler peered out again, stood stock-still.

'What's the matter?' Newman asked.

'The Ear is coming this way. I see now why he really paused.'

'Why?'

'Four men coming up the street this way. The Ear may be the target.'

It was the first time Newman had heard alarm in Marler's voice. He followed him, looked along the street. The small man was shuffling swiftly towards them. He must have recognized Marler, who had removed his glasses. He gestured over his shoulder, dived into another doorway.

Beyond him was a sinister cluster of four black opened umbrellas, feet walking under them. It wasn't possible when Newman first saw them to identify who was approaching – the cluster had the large umbrellas lowered, the feet steadily advancing beneath the shallow black cones. Then the front two umbrellas were elevated.

Each of the two visible men held handguns. Newman saw their weapons clearly as they passed under a street lamp. Soon they would reach the doorway where the Ear was hiding. He grabbed for his Smith & Wesson.

'Not wanted,' Marler snapped. 'Leave this to me.'

He took something out of his raincoat pocket. Newman saw it was a grenade. Marler waved a hand sideways at the Ear, who responded instantly, diving inside another doorway. Crouching down, Marler thrust his right hand, holding the grenade, behind him. Pressing a button, he rolled the object at high speed along the pavement.

It shot forward and the four umbrellas stopped moving. The object reached them, arriving in the middle of the group. There was a loud crack and the four men panicked, running along the pavement until they disappeared round a corner, their umbrellas waving madly.

'It was a dud,' Newman said. 'It should have killed them all.'

'Hardly.'

Marler was grinning as he stood up. He pulled his rain-covered coat away from his knees and waited for the Ear to reappear.

'What the hell was it?' Newman demanded.

'One of the new devices cooked up by the boffins in the basement back at Park Crescent. Looks like a grenade, it sounds like a grenade when it goes off. It explodes into tiny fragments you'd have trouble finding. It also contains a glue-like liquid which sprays all over the targets. They won't know what it is – probably be sure it's some kind of poison, which it isn't. I don't think we wanted dead bodies sprawled all over the pavement. We would have had a problem.

'Well, it worked. The thugs appear to have gone for good. They're probably rushing back to the Embassy to get checked by a doctor.'

'Here comes the Ear,' Marler observed. 'I'll introduce him as a friend.'

The little man was shuffling towards them. He glanced over his shoulder twice. A cautious chap, Newman thought – which was probably why he had survived so long. He was close to them when he crossed the street and looked back again to see round the corner where the attackers had vanished. A shot rang out. One single shot.

The Ear staggered, stumbled against the wall of a house, slid down the wall, his legs extended in front of him. He lay slumped there, very still, as Marler ran to him with Newman at his heels, the Smith & Wesson in his hand. Marler bent over the prone form. A red patch was blossoming on the forehead. He opened his mouth, staring at Marler. Blood gurgled.

'Basil . . .' Another grim gurgle. 'Schwarz . . .'

Then nothing. Marler checked his neck pulse. He stood up slowly, gazed at Newman. There was sorrow in his eyes – something Newman had never seen before.

'He's dead,' Marler said slowly. 'Not one of the thugs – he looked back towards us a fraction of a second before the bullet hit him. From the angle he was facing, the shot came from the roof of those houses. The Phantom.'

'I'll kill that bastard when the moment comes,' Newman said.

'No, you won't.' Marler placed a hand on Newman's arm. 'He's my meat.'

9

The taxi taking Paula home arrived close to the entrance to her flat. The driver had overshot the mark by a few yards. She got out into the quiet street, paid the driver, thanked him. She turned and walked the short distance back to the cul-de-sac.

Several cars were parked illegally by the kerb. It happened often at this late hour – wardens were rarely on duty at this time of night. An old lady approached her with a wrinkled hand held out.

'A fiver to save a soul,' she whined. 'I ain't eaten in two days. I'm droppin' with 'unger.'

The old woman had matted grey hair which hadn't been washed for Heaven knew how long. Her clothes were rags, held together in places with safety pins. Her beady eyes were pleading, at the end of their tether. Her thin lips trembled and her extended hand shook with the cold.

Paula tried to do two things at once. She pulled her shoulder bag in front of her, then used both hands to extract a five-pound note from her purse. Tired as she was she saw her shadow thrown by a street light on the damp pavement. Then she stiffened. There were *two* shadows.

With both hands holding her purse, she couldn't reach for her Browning in the special pocket. A rough hand grasped her throat. She lifted one foot to scrape it down the shin of her assailant. Then a pad was pressed against her face, covering her nose. She smelt chloroform. She tried to breathe out but the cold air had forced her to breathe in.

The old lady, bad teeth bared in an evil grin, blurred. Paula, as in a dream, was aware of the sound of a car door opening. Then she sagged, lost consciousness, knew nothing.

She was woozy, her eyes closed, her stomach threatening to erupt. She forced it to behave. She appeared to be sitting against some sort of couch. She kept her eyes closed. The fabric of the couch was well worn. She felt the hard edge of a wooden strut pressing against her back. It was icy cold. She forced herself to keep still.

She could hear the clump of hard shoes on a wooden floor. She opened one eye, then both eyes. A few yards away she could see who was making the clumping noise: The back of a short, thickset man with a bald head. The room was huge, like an old warehouse. She closed her eyes quickly as her captor began to turn round.

During her quick survey of her prison she had seen a large beam spanning the width of the warehouse, about ten feet above the floor. She felt sleepy, willed herself to keep awake. Something had been slung over the beam. She heard the clank of a chain.

That was what she had seen, a gleaming new chain with links about three inches wide. He was clumping about again, further away. Without moving her feet, she wriggled her toes. Anything to bring herself back to normal. The bald man had been holding something in his hand. A Colt automatic.

She became aware she no longer had her shoulder bag. He had her Browning somewhere. The feet came towards her. She knew when he stopped he was standing, gazing down at her. She kept her eyes closed, her body limp. He began to talk. Then she knew he was American, a coarse voice.

'Wake up, lady. You and I are going to have a fun time. You've got things to tell me. Questions to answer. What the hell is the matter with you? Wake up!'

He began to slap both sides of her face with his rough hand. She let her head flop from side to side with each blow. I have to get back to normal before he knows I'm conscious, she kept telling herself. The slapping stopped. He swore foully.

He was walking away from her again. She took in deeper breaths of the cold air without moving. Got to clear my head, get my strength back. I need more time. The clumping came back in her direction. She wasn't going to get more time. There was a musty smell which suggested a building that hadn't been opened for a long time. The heavy footsteps stopped in front of her.

'Wake up, you friggin' twist,' the coarse voice ordered. 'If you don't you'll get a bucket of cold water over you. You're going to be sodden wet soon, whatever you do or don't tell me.'

Inwardly she cringed. What was he talking about?

There had been something very sinister in those last words.

Then his hands grasped her shoulders and he was shaking her from side to side. She kept her eyes tightly shut. His grip was strong and painful. She kept her body loose, let him go on shaking her. She was breathing in and out slowly, clearing her mind.

'OK. You get the bucket of water . . .'

She moaned, moved shakily, opened both eyes. He was very ugly. His bald head gleamed in the light from the naked bulbs suspended from the rafters high above them. His eyes glittered with anticipation at some pleasurable experience. He hauled out the Colt from a wide leather belt under his windcheater.

'Try any funny tricks with me and you get a bullet in the head. Can you hear me?'

'Where am I? Who are you?'

'My bloody pals call me Baldy. Guess why?'

'I can't move.' She slurred the words. 'Can't see you. Where am I?'

'In a place where we won't be disturbed. You and I are going to have fun and games.'

'My head's swimming.'

She closed her eyes again. He administered several more hard slaps to both sides of her face. The pain was helping her to become more alert. She heard his feet clump a short distance, realized he was behind the couch. Then something cold and weighty was dropped round her neck. A chain. She fought down the terror which was threatening to overwhelm her. Now she was able to think, she realized her desperate situation. She was going to end up dead. Kidnappers who intended to release their victims were careful never to show their faces. Baldy hadn't even attempted to cover his face. She felt even more helpless with the chain round her neck.

'OK. You can get up now. Or I'll drag you up like a dog.' He giggled. 'Dawg on a chain. That's what you are.'

She opened her eyes. He was holding a length of chain in one hand. It must be attached to the collar of chain round her throat. She placed both hands on the couch as though for support.

'I don't think I can stand up.'

'So I'll drag you.'

'Give me a minute.'

'Get on your friggin' feet!' he screamed at her.

She stood up slowly, more slowly than she needed to. She stood still, bracing her legs to strengthen them. Now she could see far more. She appeared to be in an ancient warehouse used to dump unwanted furniture. There were a number of couches scattered round the planked floor. She saw her coat thrown carelessly over the back of a battered old wooden chair. Her shoulder bag dangled beside it. The clasp was still fastened. She felt sure he hadn't even bothered to rummage inside it. Which meant her Browning was still in the secret pocket. It could have been a mile away for all the hope she had of getting her hands on it.

'We are going for a little walk,' Baldy said, grinning.

'I may fall down . . .'

'Fall down, then!' he screamed. 'Then I'll drag you.'

'I'll try and make it.'

Baldy was holding a long length of chain. The end was attached to the part at the back of her neck. The links rested loosely on her skin, looped below her chin. She kept stopping as he approached the beam above them. During these brief pauses she stretched her legs without moving them, testing her strength.

'Keep going, little dawg,' he sneered. 'Haven't got all night.'

'My legs are going to give way,' she lied.

'So I drag you along the hard floor. Your choice, honey.'

She wished she could punch his leering face. She was feeling utterly humiliated. Then suddenly a cold fury took hold of her mind. *This wretched little thug from the back streets of God knows where!* She lowered her eyes so he couldn't see her change of expression. Which meant she was looking at the floor.

Stretching towards them from below the beam a section of the floor appeared to be a huge elongated panel, a closed trapdoor. At the far end, inset into the wood, was a small depression, and inside it, fitted level with the floor surface, was a wide metal lever. Terror returned again as she imagined what this might be. She suppressed the terror, concentrated on slowing him down.

'Come on, honey. Make with the legs.'

He jerked the chain and she nearly fell forward. Recovering her balance, she padded deliberately forward, her shoes clacking on the planks. She was almost under the beam when he moved behind her, still holding his long length of chain. Before she knew what was happening he had lifted the chain collar round her neck and inserted an extensive length under it.

'I'm not talking tied up like this,' she snapped.

'Shut your stupid female mouth. You'll talk your head off.'

Still holding the chain, he clumped over to a table. It supported a bucket of water and a glass. Dipping the glass into the water, he drank some, ran his thick lips slowly round the rim of the glass, then hurled the contents in her face. She had a double shock. The cold water dripped down inside the top of her dress. She shivered. The second shock was to have liquid in her face after he had run his foul tongue round the rim. He was behind her now. He was doing something with her ankles. She looked down. He had looped a section of chain round each one, with a gap between them of over a foot long.

She felt like a fugitive from a chain gang. It intensified her fury. I'd like to strangle him with my bare hands, she thought. Slowly. He appeared in front of her, holding a double length of chain. He grinned, touched her cheek.

'Cosy now, ain't it, my lovely?'

'I can do without the compliments,' she rapped back.

'Temper. Mustn't give way to temper,' he taunted her.

'I'm not talking trussed up like this,' she blazed.

'Let's work out how things are.' He was almost drooling with enjoyment. 'Chain round your neck is looped like a noose. Bit by bit it pulls tighter – till you choke to death. Better start using that spitting mouth of yours to answer my questions. That gives me an idea.'

He worked his mouth, then spat at her, hitting her on the chest. She just managed to stop herself recoiling with revulsion. *Don't give the little swine any satisfaction.* Standing back, he gripped the long length of chain, hurled it upwards. It swept over the beam, a length fell and he grasped the end. With horror, she knew what he was going to do. She gritted her teeth, clenched her hands.

'Let's start now,' he said. 'Quiz show. Like you get on television. Question, then answer. Get it? Question, then answer.'

'Put me back on the couch. Then we'll talk.'

'Listen to the lady! Giving me orders. Haven't you been listening, twist?'

He punched her in the ribs. Teeth still gritted, she didn't react. He'd used the hand holding the chain to deliver the punch so it had lacked a lot of his strength. Now he stood back from her and she tensed. While standing she had continued bracing her legs.

'Who's your boss?' he asked suddenly.

'Benson.'

'Wicked. Real wicked. Lying to Baldy.'

He hauled on the chain and she was elevated off the floor. Expecting this, her hands dived to her neck inside the chain, keeping it away from her throat. He went on hauling her higher until the top of her head was close to the beam. She found herself swaying, back and forth. She looked down and saw the top of his bald head.

'Swing 'igh, swing low,' he sang in his tuneless voice.

The strain on her hands was enormous. She knew she couldn't keep this up for long. Then he did something else which she had expected. He released the chain and she dived to the floor. She landed as she had been taught at the training mansion in Surrey, bending her knees to cushion the impact. She straightened up as his hated face peered round at her.

'You can't hold out for long. Who is your boss? Just the first question.'

'Benson.'

'Up you go . . .'

Again she was hauled upwards, held there, head almost touching the beam, but not quite as high as before. Again her body started swaying. She looked down. He was standing back a few feet from the beam. She forced herself to sway harder, hands protecting her throat against the chain. She was swaying back and forth through a greater arc, her knees lifted. She could never have done it without the aerobics and the exercises she had practised at the health club. She was beginning to sway back quite quickly when suddenly she dropped her legs to the fullest extent, opening them as wide as possible. She was staring at Baldy who gazed up at her in surprise. The chain round her ankles caught him under the jaw, round his thick neck.

He let go of the end he was holding, which she had

known he would if she could bring it off. Probably break my bloody back, she thought. The chain slithered over the beam, she plunged down behind Baldy, landed on one of the many old couches lying round the warehouse floor.

Positions reversed. Now she had him in a stranglehold, the chain tight round his neck as she clamped her feet together. He was on his back, hands clawing futilely at the chain cutting off his air supply. His heels hammered at the floor. One heeltip caught on the lever inset into the floor. The trapdoor he was sprawled along opened away from Paula. She whipped her feet apart. The ankle chain slipped up over his jaw. He was free. The trap slid downwards. Baldy let out a croaking scream. His body rushed forward, vanished into the gaping hole. Paula heard a distant splash, then silence.

Because she forced herself not to hurry, she released herself from the chain more quickly than she'd expected. She stood up off the couch, legs trembling. Cautiously she crept forward to the edge, looked down. Seeing nothing, she forced her aching limbs to take her across to the chair, took out her Browning, her torch. When she returned to the rim of the gaping hole she turned on her powerful torch. The tip of the beam just reached down to show her fast-moving water. The River Thames, she guessed. That was where she had ultimately been destined to go.

Forcing her arms into her coat, she picked up the chain, threw it down into the river. Behind her on the far wall was a closed door. She made herself walk quickly. An old key was in the lock. She had to use both bruised hands to turn it, to pull back a wooden bar. She had the Browning in her hand as she opened it and peered out. If any of Baldy's chums were waiting she was going to kill them.

She was gazing out into a deserted cobbled street, the

buildings looking fit only for demolition. A wall lamp cast an eerie glow over a street sign. Eagle Street.

To her left the street ended. Beyond it flowed the Thames, with wriggling lights reflected in its dark flow. She turned right after closing the door behind her. She emerged into a wider street which reminded her of the East End. Nobody about. A taxi came crawling along the street, its For Hire light on.

She flagged it down madly. The driver slowed, peered out to examine her. He looked surprised at her good coat and shoes, illuminated by another street light. He leaned forward.

'What's a lady like you doin' in a place like this?'

'A row with my boy friend. I just got out of his car and he drove off.'

'Better get yourself another boy friend. Where to?'

'Park Crescent, please. Facing Regent's Park.'

10

Paula was so relieved when she saw the lights in Tweed's office windows. She had guessed he might be working late. Entering his room, she found not only Monica but also Newman and Marler. Tweed took one look at her, jumped up, went to her.

'What happened?'

'I must look the most awful mess . . .'

She sank down behind her desk and told them about her experience. Reaction had set in. Her voice was shaky. Hidden beneath the desk, her knees trembled. She pressed them together, forced herself to go on talking. At an early stage Tweed asked Monica to fetch plenty of sweetened tea – he recognized that Paula was in shock. Later, while Paula continued, Monica checked her hands

– bruised where she had fought to hold the chain away from her neck. She brought the first aid kit, gently rubbed soothing salve on her hands, then on her neck.

Glancing at Tweed, Newman realized he was almost in a state of shock himself. Sagged in his chair, Tweed was appalled that he had let Paula go home by herself. He cursed himself for not insisting on accompanying her. At one moment, when Paula's head was turned away, he frowned at Newman and Marler, warning them not to mention the killing of the Ear. That could come later, when Paula had recovered.

'So that's it,' Paula concluded when she had described her ordeal. 'I think I'd like to go home now.'

'We'll come with you,' Tweed said instantly. 'Butler and Nield are still in the building. They will stay the night with you. I recall you have a couple of couches in the living room. Back in a minute . . .'

Paula was protesting it wasn't necessary as he disappeared. He came back a few minutes later, accompanied by Nield and Butler. Nield went over to Paula.

'Sorry you've had such a dreadful time. We have a plan. Harry and I drive ahead of the rest of you. Could you give me the key to your flat? We'd like to go through it with a fine-tooth comb before you arrive. You don't sound too good.'

'I haven't said anything. You used that phrase instead of saying you don't look too good. Which is the case. Thank you, Pete. Here is my key.

'I think I'd like to go to the washroom. I'm filthy,' Paula said when the two men had left.

'I'll come with you,' Monica told her.

'Jake Ronstadt is behind this,' Tweed said grimly when he was alone with Newman and Marler. 'I saw a peculiar, savage expression flicker in his eyes when I was dining with Paula and she told him her name.'

106

'When the opportunity arises I'll break every bone in his body,' said Newman.

'For starters,' Marler suggested.

There was silence in the room until, ten minutes after Butler and Nield had left, Tweed led the way downstairs with Paula. When she had returned with Monica, Newman noticed she had used a modicum of make-up and brushed her hair. Her complexion was still pallid.

They travelled back to the flat in the Fulham Road in the Merc with Newman behind the wheel. Marler sat beside him while Tweed occupied the back next to Paula. He put his arm round her, a gesture for which she was grateful. They were driving through deserted dark streets when Newman kept glancing in his rear-view mirror.

'We're being followed,' he remarked. 'A taxi cab. I'm pulling up here. Back in a minute.'

He walked back until the cab approached him. Only the driver behind the wheel. Newman flagged him down. The driver nearly didn't stop, then changed his mind. He stared unpleasantly as Newman opened his door.

'Been in this country long?' Newman enquired, smiling.

'Sure. What's it to you?'

The accent was coarse American. To talk to the driver Newman had run round the front of the stationary cab so he could open the door on the street side. He grabbed hold of the collar of the leather jacket the driver wore, hauled him out into the street. The American jerked away from Newman, his right hand slipping inside the jacket.

'Buddy, you sure shouldn've done that . . .'

He never completed his sentence. Newman's right fist collided with the American's jaw. A knockout punch.

As he was sagging to the ground Newman grabbed him again, heaved his unconscious body back into his seat. Unzipping the jacket all the way, he found a gun butt protruding from a shoulder holster. Searching in the other pocket he found an American diplomatic passport. Switching off the engine, he extracted the key, threw it into a garden, walked back to the Merc.

'We can now proceed,' he announced, seated behind the wheel.

'So we were being followed,' Tweed commented. 'They must have bribed a cab driver.'

'No.' Newman was still checking his mirror. 'The driver was an American.' He tossed the passport over his shoulder. 'See for yourself.'

'I wonder what happened to the real driver,' Tweed mused as he examined the passport.

'Probably at the bottom of the Thames,' Paula said vehemently. 'Where they dump all their victims.'

'Lew Willis is the name on the passport,' Tweed informed them. 'I think I'll phone Buchanan from Paula's flat, let him know there's a suspicious character in the cab back there. Without his passport he'll be in a real stew . . .'

Butler met them at the entrance leading to the flat. Nield arrived in their car, parked it, got out. Tweed told Paula to wait in the car until he'd spoken to them. Nield was jaunty, waving a hand.

'While Harry was checking the flat I patrolled the area in search of thugs. None about anywhere. All clear. What about the flat, Harry?'

'Clean as a whistle. The flat on the ground floor seems empty. No one inside. I've closed all the curtains in Paula's flat, switched on a few lights to welcome her.'

'Thank you, Harry,' Paula said with feeling. 'The woman downstairs is away. How did you get inside? I forgot to give you the key to the second lock.'

'Used one of my skeleton keys to get inside. You can't be too careful the way things are now.'

'Breaking and entering,' Paula teased him.

'That's right. One of my main occupations. It's cold out here. Better get inside. I turned up the heating.'

Once inside, Paula insisted on making coffee for everyone. Tweed made his phone call to Buchanan. When he put down the receiver he looked at Paula, who had just poured coffee.

'Do you feel like talking for a few minutes?'

'Of course I do. I'm tired but the brain is ticking over.'

'What happened at Eagle Street never happened. We've never even heard of the place. If we reported this to Buchanan we'd get bogged down in his investigation. We can't afford the time. The body of Hank Whoever . . .'

'Hank Waltz,' Newman said. 'Known as Diamond Waltz. I had a run-in with him months ago in New York when I was trying to interview Sir Guy Strangeways.'

'You mean a thug like that was protecting Strangeways?' Tweed asked in a tone of disbelief.

'So it seemed.'

'Before I force myself to take a shower,' Paula said, 'I'll get two pairs of blankets to make Pete and Harry more comfortable on the couches.'

'One pair,' said Nield. 'We'll take it in turns to stay awake while the other sleeps. God help anyone who tries to sneak in here.'

'Then I'll say goodnight.' Paula went to Tweed, hugged him.

'Now, don't brood over the fact that I came back to the flat from Goodfellows alone. I can look after myself. I did . . .'

'Earlier,' Tweed began after she had gone, 'I was going to say the body of Hank Whoever is likely to be washed up further down the Thames. Which is why we don't know anything about it. And how, Bob, did you know he was Diamond Waltz?'

'Two things. First from Paula's description of the thug. Also he happened to be in Goodfellows the night you were there with Paula and I was up at the bar with Basil and Rupert. Where to now?'

'Back to Park Crescent. It's going to be a long night . . .'

'I had sinister news when I talked to Buchanan on the phone,' Tweed told Newman and Marler when they were settled in his office. 'An American syndicate is bidding for control of two leading London daily newspapers. Plus bidding for one of the top TV stations and three key radio stations. They're offering so much money they're bound to succeed.'

'What's going on?' asked Monica, who had finished one phone call prior to making another.

'It's serious. The syndicate – when it gets control – will be in a position to start brainwashing the British public. There are shades of Dr Goebbels here.'

'Creepy,' Monica replied.

'The size of this gigantic operation is growing by the hour,' Tweed warned.

'How do we counter this?' Newman wondered.

'We need more men as tough as – or tougher than – the opposition,' Marler interjected. 'As you know, I've spent quite a bit of time in the East End. Just in case we ever needed reinforcements I've trained a team of cockneys. They're known as Alf's Mob. They're gut fighters.'

'They will never be a match for men with guns,' Tweed objected.

'Really?' Marler's expression was sardonic. 'They are lethal with their fists. In addition, in a remote spot in the countryside, I've trained them to use grenades – stun, smoke, the deadly variety. They're now familiar with automatic rifles and handguns. They're masters of stealth – they can creep up on me and have their hands round my neck before I know anyone is near me.'

'I'm impressed.'

'Don't forget,' Marler reminded him, 'if you read the history of the Burma fighting in World War Two it was cockneys who out-fought the enemy. Cockneys! In jungle warfare.'

'So we have a reserve. We may well need it. I'm working on a plan to go on to the offensive. We're not going to let these thugs have it all their own way. More details later.'

'About time,' Marler drawled.

'Tweed.' Monica leaned over her desk. 'I ought to alert you. Howard is back from his overseas visit. So he could be up here any moment.'

'We'll all go home and leave you to it,' Newman suggested.

'Hear, hear,' agreed Marler.

Howard, the Director, was not popular. A pompous man, he was always complaining that Tweed didn't keep him fully informed about what was going on. His complaint was not without foundation – Tweed had a habit of keeping progress to himself until he was certain he knew what was happening. The phone rang, Monica answered it, looked surprised, put her hand over the mouthpiece as she spoke to Tweed.

'There's a Denise Chatel on the phone. Says she's Sharon Mandeville's assistant. Asked if you were still here – she's speaking from a car phone. She could be here in five minutes.'

'At this hour? Oh, well, we need to find out all we can. What does she sound like?'

'She has a lovely voice. Enchanting.'

Tweed stared at Monica. He had never before heard

her refer to a woman with such words. Nodding, he indicated that the woman calling could come to Park Crescent.

'Now,' he began as Monica put down her phone, 'before Paula returned from her ordeal in Eagle Street we were talking about the Ear. You were telling me what happened to him.'

'I still feel rotten,' Marler said, 'leaving him there propped up against the steps, then making an anonymous call to Buchanan, telling him where there was a body.'

'Don't feel guilty,' Tweed assured him. 'The last thing we can cope with is getting caught up in an involved police investigation. Are you sure those men with umbrellas didn't kill him? You said they had guns.'

'Handguns,' Marler corrected. 'I should know enough now to recognize when a rifle bullet has hit someone. It has to be the Phantom.'

'And,' Newman pointed out, 'Basil Windermere had disappeared inside his flat a few minutes earlier. Plus the fact that the last words Kurt Schwarz grasped out were *Basil . . . Schwarz.*'

'Funny that he used his own name. Incidentally, I told you that when I was inside the American Embassy I saw Jefferson Morgenstern, accompanied by guards, putting a file in a safe. I'd like to get hold of that file. I think it's a job for Pete and Harry. They'll need a diversion. Heaven knows how they can manage it.'

'Set fire to the ruddy building,' Monica burst out.

'You know, that could be a good idea.'

'I was only joking,' Monica protested.

'I wasn't.' He paused while Monica answered the phone. She told him their visitor from the Embassy had arrived. 'Ask her to come up,' Tweed told her.

*

George opened the door, stood back, closed it when Denise Chatel had entered and stood quite still. Newman stared, then stood up. Marler leant against a wall, straightened up. He gazed at their visitor. Tweed was amused at their reaction.

Denise Chatel, thirty-something, was about five feet eight tall. She had a good figure, without being voluptuous. A brunette, her hair fell below her shoulders. She had a longish face, excellent features and the hint of a warm smile lingered on her mouth. Wearing a figure-hugging two-piece blue suit, she was enticing. Tweed stood up, held out his hand.

'Do sit down, Ms Chatel. I'm intrigued to know why you have called to see me in the middle of the night.'

She crossed her legs elegantly as she sat down. Neither Newman nor Marler could take their eyes off her.

'I'm an owl, like yourself, Mr Tweed. Which suits Miss Mandeville, who likes to work when most people have left the Embassy.'

'Would you like some coffee?' Newman suggested.

'I'll make it,' Monica said in a brittle tone.

'That would be most acceptable. And a glass of cold water – if that's not too much trouble.'

She had a cool American voice. Underneath it Tweed detected a very different accent.

'Denise Chatel,' he mused, scrutinizing her through his horn-rims. 'That sounds like a French name.'

'My father was French, my mother American. When I was almost thirty they moved to Washington – my father was offered a good job. I went with them.'

'Do you ever return to France?' Tweed persisted gently.

'Oh, frequently. My job takes me to the American Embassy in Paris. Sharon likes to keep herself well informed about what is going on in Europe.' She smiled. 'Are you interrogating me?'

'Just interested in your unusual international background. An American mother, a French father. What job does he have?'

'He was a diplomat.'

Tweed had not been looking at her as he talked. He was doodling circles on a pad, intertwining one with another. Something in her change of voice made him look up.

'Was?'

'He died a year ago. So did my mother. They were killed in a road crash outside Washington.'

He could have sworn there was a film of moisture in her eyes. She suddenly picked up her cup of coffee, drank some, put it down, stared round the room like someone hunted.

'My condolences. Not that words mean a thing when something like that happens. What happened to the other car – or cars? I hope you don't mind asking.'

'Of course not.' She swallowed more coffee. 'The police said there had only been one other car involved so far as they could tell. It vanished. They never found the driver.'

'I say,' Marler interjected, 'would you care to join me for dinner tomorrow evening?'

'May I think it over?' She had twisted round in her chair to address him, to look at him more carefully. 'Thank you for the offer.' She turned back to Tweed, leaned forward and whispered, 'Can you trust the people with us here? I know the woman who brought me coffee doesn't like me.'

'I could trust all three with my life,' he answered quietly. 'I have done in the past.'

'I'm frightened. Scared out of my wits.'

114

She was speaking again in a normal voice. But a transformation had taken place. When she had arrived she had been full of life, buoyant. Now her blue eyes appealed for help as she gazed at him. On the surface, she was indeed a very frightened lady. Newman refilled her cup.

'Is that the real reason you came to see me?' Tweed asked.

'Yes. I had an excuse to come – I can tell you that later.'

'Why me?'

'Cord Dillon said if ever I was in trouble you were the one man in London I could trust.'

Nothing in Tweed's expression changed. But she had shaken him. His mind was moving round at top speed – considering a variety of possibilities. All of them menacing.

'How did you come to meet this man, Cord Dillon?' he enquired carefully.

'Sharon used to ask him to come to her Washington office from Langley. I was always sent out of her office. Dillon struck me as a reliable soul. Once he arrived early and we were alone together in my office. I knew then that Sharon was due to come to London, that I'd be coming with her.'

'What is scaring you?'

'Well . . .' She paused. 'I saw some of the men who were to come to London. I've seen them since at the Embassy. They watch every move I make. I found my phone had been bugged. My apartment over here in Belgravia – close to Sharon's – was searched while I was at the Embassy. It was a highly professional job. Only a woman would notice that certain things were not quite as I'd left them.'

'What do you suggest I do to help you?'

'I want us to keep in close touch.' She turned to look at Marler. 'I'll be happy to have dinner with you tomorrow night. What is your name?'

'Alec,' Marler said instantly, using the first name to come into his head. 'We'll go to the Lanesborough. Can I collect you at your apartment?'

'No! Don't do that.' She was alarmed. 'They have someone watching my apartment whenever I'm there. I'll come to the hotel.'

'Eight o'clock suit you?' Marler suggested. 'I'll be waiting in the bar. I'll arrive early.'

'Thank you.'

'Maybe you'd better tell us why you were supposed to come here,' Tweed reminded her.

'My God, I nearly forgot that.' She turned to look at Newman. 'You're having dinner with Sharon tomorrow evening at Santorini's. She sent me over in a limo to say she'll be there at eight thirty.'

'She could have phoned,' Tweed pointed out.

'She told me she'd tried to get you but the line was always engaged.'

Tweed glanced across at Monica, who nodded agreement. She had tied up the lines, making calls to her contacts inside America. She was still building up her profiles.

'I'd better go now,' their visitor said, 'they may wonder why it took so long. And please call me Denise.'

'I'll see you safely into your limo, Denise,' Marler suggested.

'No! Don't do that. They may have followed the limo and then they'll see you. But thank you for the offer.'

'Keep in touch,' Tweed told her, standing up to shake hands. Her grip was firm. 'If you want to tell Marler more tomorrow evening he'll report it to me . . .'

Monica waited until she had gone. Then she began tapping her fingers on her desk to get their attention.

'You're all hooked on her.'

'I don't think so,' Tweed contradicted.

'Well, I do. I grant you she's a real looker.'

'Monica, maybe yes, maybe no. You've overlooked something.'

'What's that?'

'Your profile on Sharon Mandeville showed *her* parents died in a car smash in the States. Now we hear Denise's parents were also wiped out in another car accident, so called. That's too much of a coincidence – you know I don't believe in coincidences.'

'What are you suggesting?' she asked.

'One theory is the parents – in both cases – were killed so there was no risk of the daughters telling them something Washington didn't want spread around. I emphasize that is no more than my first thought. Have you identified Charlie?'

'Not yet. It's difficult,' Monica explained. 'I have to get copies of birth certificates faxed to me. A lot of people are given several names by their parents, then use only the one they like. I'll get there.'

'I know you will.'

Tweed began to doodle again. After a short time he looked at Marler.

'Basil . . . Schwarz . . .' he said half to himself. 'What nationality was Kurt Schwarz?'

'Swiss,' Marler said promptly.

'Which part of Switzerland?'

'The German-speaking part. His natural language was German.'

'Got it!' Tweed threw his pen down. 'Soon we'll all fly to Switzerland. Better get some warm clothes packed. There's heavy snow on the Continent.'

117

11

Jake Ronstadt sat at the head of the long table in the large room at the American Embassy. The blinds were closed over the windows. He was shuffling a pack of cards. Eight Americans sat beyond him, four on either side of the table. The Executive Action Department was in session in the middle of the night.

'Two of my guys went missin' last night,' Jake growled. 'I don't like two of my people to disappear. Which is why Brad and Leo have joined us.'

'What happened to them?' asked Vernon, the thin-boned man with the hard face.

'Shut your stupid trap. I was comin' to that. Hank Waltz was sent to deal with Paula Grey. Don't know whether he made it. Don't like what I don't know. Remember that. Lew Willis has also gone missin' – I heard from him on his mobile that after he hijacked a London cab he followed two men from Park Crescent. They drove like hell round all the friggin' side streets here. He loses them, drives back to Park Crescent. Next I hear he's following four people in a Merc. Then nothin' – friggin' nothin', so I try to call him on my mobile. No answer. You boys had better understand I'm good and mad.'

'We understand,' said Brad, a squat individual with large teeth.

'What you understand would fit into a pearl – but there'd be no value in it. Kinda shut your trap.'

Jake made them wait while he shuffled his pack of cards some more. It was important to make them know who was running this outfit.

'I figure it's time now we organize a reign of terror

for London. Show them our muscle. Show the people in this town their police are a bunch of kids. Get it?'

'Sure, Jake,' eight voices echoed in chorus. 'We got it.'

'No, you ain't. So I'll tell you. It's called destabilization. For you who don't know what it means – which means all of you – I'll explain. We'll leave bombs – big bombs with timers – in markets. Over here they call them supermarkets. We'll plant them in bars, restaurants – everywhere a lot of people gather. The Brits will get so they daren't leave their homes. Until bombs start exploding inside houses. Terror is a powerful weapon. Got it now? Great idea.'

'Terrific!'

'A winner!'

'A blaster!'

Every man tried to compete with his colleagues in thinking up a better superlative. Jake glowered at them, his mouth a thin tight line. He shook his large head, shuffled his pack a few times.

'You still ain't got it. When a load of bombs have gone off – with heavy casualties – the Brits will start shoutin' their heads off at their police. "Why can't you do something?" That's when we offer to send in an FBI unit. About a week after the FBI have supposedly gone for the tails of the bombers the explosions stop. Result? The Americans are much better at the job than the Metropolitan Police jerks. "Give the job to the FBI," the Brits will beg. We're in control. No more yapping. You had a trial run in Philadelphia when you planted dummy bombs all over the city. None were discovered.'

'When do we start?' asked Brad, daring to open his mouth.

'Soon. First I have to check with Charlie. Timin' is so goddamn important . . .'

*

119

Tweed had fallen asleep on the camp bed Monica had hauled out of a cupboard then made up with pillow, sheets and blankets. The phone began to ring at 4 a.m. and he was instantly awake as Monica answered it.

'Are you awake?' she called out softly.

'Yes.'

'I have Ed Osborne on the line. Wants to speak to you . . .'

'I'll take the call.'

Slipping on a dressing gown over his pyjamas, he sat behind his desk, picked up the phone.

'Tweed here, Ed. What can I do for you?'

'Hope you weren't asleep.'

'I was. What is it?'

'Think it's time you and I had a talk. Just the two of us. Do you know a pub called the Raging Stag in Piccadilly?'

'I do.'

'Can we meet there today? Say noon?'

'Can you give me a hint as to what this is about?'

'Sooner not, over the phone . . .'

'Noon at the Raging Stag, then.'

He told Monica the brief gist of his conversation. She raised her thick eyebrows, frowned.

'After his performance here I wouldn't have thought you would want another session.'

'The Americans can be a bit brash. Doesn't worry me. And the more I can find out what they're up to the better. We're very short of time, I sense.'

'You realize they are taking a great interest in us? Tonight Bob is dining with Sharon Mandeville at Santorini's. Then Marler is taking out Denise Chatel.'

'The same thought had occurred to me. Incidentally, I want you to book seats on the early morning Swissair flight to Basle for six people. Me, Paula, Newman, Marler, Harry Butler and Pete Nield. Not sure when we'll be going but it will be suddenly. So, each day book, then cancel, and immediately book for the next day. Keith Kent, the money tracer, called me to say millions of dollars have been deposited with the Zürcher Kredit Bank – confirming what Schwarz said. I wonder why.'

'Who knows? Millions of dollars. That's a vast sum. Going back to Osborne, I doubt he'll tell you much.'

'He might let something slip. Oh, at a civilized hour, get me Renée Lasalle, chief of the *Direction de la Surveillance du Territoire* – French counter-espionage in Paris – on the phone.'

'Will do.'

'Any luck with identifying Charlie?'

'No. As I told you earlier it's difficult, but I'll go on digging.'

The phone rang again. Monica pulled a sour face, took the call. She looked even more sour.

'Now we have Roy Buchanan on the line. Says it's urgent – at this time of night.'

'I'll speak to him.'

'I know you work all night,' Buchanan began.

'Sometimes I try to get a bit of kip.'

'Sorry, and all that. Something's happened. Can I come and see you now? I think you'd want to know about it,' Buchanan suggested.

'Can't it wait till morning?'

'It could, I suppose. When would suit you?'

'Eight o'clock. You sound worried. It's too early to worry. Wait a bit longer and then you'll have something to fret about. That is, if my present reading of the situation is correct.'

'I've got enough on my plate,' Buchanan snapped.

'Get a bigger plate. Goodbye . . .'

'And you'd better go to the office next door and get some sleep yourself,' Tweed told Monica.

'I think I will. You talk as though you're expecting a storm.'

'A gale. Force Ten.'

Tweed had two hours' sleep. He woke up, alert, hearing the door to his office open. His right hand slid under the pillow, gripped the 7.65mm Walther automatic under it. It was a measure of his estimate of the gravity of the situation that he had taken this precaution. He hardly ever carried a gun.

The light came on. Tweed, twisted on his right side, aimed the weapon at the door. Howard, the Director, stood framed in the doorway, looking startled. Tweed sighed, shoved the gun back under the pillow, got up, put on his dressing gown.

'Sorry if I wakened you,' Howard burbled. 'But George told me you were still here.'

'As you see, I am.' Tweed glanced at his wristwatch. 'I've had two hours' sleep and that will have to do. What are you doing, prowling about the place? I heard you'd returned from a holiday.'

He sat behind his desk while the Director flopped into the largest armchair. Howard was six feet tall with a plump, clean-shaven, pink face, and touches of grey in his neatly brushed hair. A large man in his fifties, he was immaculately garbed in a blue Chester Barrie suit from Harrods, a snow-white shirt and a Hermès tie. He rested one long leg over the arm of the chair, his usual posture. His voice was plummy.

'Hardly a holiday. I've just returned from Washington. I caught up on sleep by going to a hotel after the flight had landed. Had early breakfast, then came straight on here.'

'What's happening in Washington? Why go there?'

Tweed poured water from a carafe into a glass, left

for him by Monica. He sipped as Howard ran a hand over the dome of his head, a characteristic gesture when he was worried.

'I went there at the invitation of the august and influential Jefferson Morgenstern – only to find he had suddenly dashed off over here. He'd left some of his top staff to look after me. I was wined and dined at all the best places. Everyone I met made a big fuss over me as though I was the most important man in the world. Not the usual reception by a long chalk. All of which worried me. They wanted something – but never got round to saying what it was. Under their glowing greetings I detected tension. Something's rotten in the woodshed.'

Tweed was surprised. The pompous Howard often didn't grasp what was going on. But sometimes he had flashes of insight. Tweed drank more water before he began.

'The woodshed where there's something rotten is over here. I've got a lot to tell you . . .'

It was unusual for Tweed to tell Howard everything that had taken place. He did so now. If I don't survive, he thought to himself, someone had better be in the picture. Howard listened with great attention. He even removed his leg from over the arm of the chair, leaning closer to Tweed.

'So now you have the full story up to date,' Tweed concluded. 'Didn't they tell you anything in Washington?'

'They kept going on about the importance of the special relationship between Britain and America, the way things are in the world today. Each time I asked them to be more specific they changed the subject.'

'Interesting. Anything else?'

'They also kept asking if I knew where Cord Dillon might be. Told me he'd been sacked for embezzling funds.'

'Poppycock.'

'That's what I thought. I wouldn't have told them he was over here even if I had known. You said all the key personnel are down at the Bunker. I see why you had the place created now.'

'Not *all* the key personnel – but enough to make it an effective operational headquarters in a secret location.'

'What's this Ed Osborne you're having lunch with like?' Howard asked.

'What a lot of Americans would proudly call a tough guy.'

'Don't like the sound of him. Thank you, Tweed, for being so frank. You'll be wanting to take a shower and get dressed.'

'I will. One more thing before you go. I slipped over to see the new PM at Downing Street. Luckily I knew him when he was a Cabinet minister. He's playing the present situation softly, softly.'

'That wouldn't be your idea?' Howard enquired.

'I did make a few suggestions. Apparently Morgenstern keeps asking to see him urgently. The PM has fended him off, saying he'll see him as soon as he can but at the moment he's grappling with his new job.'

'Interesting, as you said a minute ago. Think I'll leave you to it for now. Anything I can do to help, you know where I am. Take great care.'

Which was another surprise for Tweed. He had never before known Howard to be so cooperative. When he returned to his office, fully dressed, Monica was already behind her desk, using the phone. When she had finished the call she looked at Tweed.

'I could get René Lasalle in Paris now. He gets in early to work, I remember.'

'Try him . . .'

'René, you old ruffian, how is life?'

'Life, Tweed, is pure hell. I was going to call you. What is on your mind?' the Frenchman asked in perfect English.

'I'm trying to get information on a Frenchman called Chatel. I haven't got his Christian name. He was married to an American, has a daughter called Denise. Your people sent him across to Washington as some sort of diplomat. He was killed in a car crash – along with his wife – about a year ago.'

'Is this line safe?'

'I met Harry Butler when I was coming into my office recently. He had just flashed the place. It's clean.'

'Good. Because this is highly confidential. Jean Chatel was posted to Washington as an attaché to the French Embassy. He was actually a member of the Secret Service. We'd heard rumours that Washington was considering mounting a major operation somewhere in Europe. Jean went to try to find out what it was. Before he could report he died, as you've just told me.'

'Probably murdered.'

'We were suspicious.'

'Any data you could collect on his daughter, Denise, would be helpful. When you can. Now, why were you going to call me?' Tweed asked.

'A small army of Americans has been passing through Paris from Washington, on their way to London. Not normal tourists – although they pretend to be. All carry diplomatic passports, look like tough professionals. Some fly on to Heathrow but more are coming to you via Eurostar. When I caught on I sent men to the airport. Passport officers signalled when a man showed a diplomatic passport and my people photographed him secretly. I have a collection of pics.'

'Could I see them? Urgently. I'd appreciate your sending them by courier to me.'

'Consider it done. What is going on? We don't like Americans too much.'

'I'm trying to find out. Let's keep in touch.'

'The courier will reach you today. Take care, my friend . . .'

Tweed sat staring into the distance. In his absence Monica had removed blankets, sheets, pillow and camp bed. She had also opened the curtains. In the distance trees in Regent's Park cringed under the onslaught of a bitter wind. Men hurried along the street, heads down. Women walked clutching their collars tighter, trying to keep in some warmth.

'Monica, could you please add Denise Chatel to your profile list? Sorry to burden you with more work. I gave you the gist of her life story so far last night before I went to sleep. Check it out.'

'I put her on the list myself.'

'Roy Buchanan is late. Not like him.'

'No, it isn't.'

'Thank you for the breakfast. I hope nothing's happened to Roy.'

At precisely 9 a.m. a long queue of people crowded into a large department store in Oxford Street. SALE EXTENDED. LAST-MINUTE BARGAINS. GREAT REDUCTIONS. Soon the ground floor was crammed. Shoppers sidled past each other, grabbed hold of goods, queued again to pay. They then had trouble leaving, so many people filled the place. There were several arguments as two women grasped the same bargain together.

The huge bomb detonated at precisely 9.15 a.m. There was a brilliant flash, a deafening explosion. Counters were lifted into the air. Shattered glass flew in all directions. Bodies slumped to the floor. Shoppers streaming with blood staggered about, their expressions dazed. Then the screaming started.

There was a powerful aroma of perfume on many people. The crowd surged towards the exits, stepping over bodies. Ambulance sirens in the distance came closer. It was a scene of havoc. Like a picture on TV of a foreign war.

12

'I think I should summarize what's happened so far. It might help us to get events into sequence – at the moment we're in a fog,' Tweed began.

In his office were Newman and Marler, with Monica and Paula behind their desks. Roy Buchanan had still not arrived and there had been no word from him. Monica had served everyone with strong coffee to increase their alertness.

'It began with the arrival of Cord Dillon, and Paula spiriting him out of a murder attempt. Cord, sacked from his job on the grounds of so-called embezzlement, is at the Bunker. Recently I hired Keith Kent, the money tracer, to check on American movements of money. He called me from Basle in Switzerland, suggested I went there. Then he tells me that huge sums in dollars have been sent from Washington to the Zürcher Kredit Bank – in Basle. Paula, give us your impressions of the characters we've encountered so far.'

'You're having lunch with Ed Osborne at the bar in Piccadilly today. At his suggestion. You went to see Sharon Mandeville. At her suggestion. Bob is dining with Sharon this evening. At her suggestion. Marler is taking out Denise Chatel, also this evening. It was at Marler's invitation, but she agreed immediately. All these people are key Americans. I get the idea they're trying to smoke us out.'

'You could be right,' Tweed agreed. 'Now give us portrait snaps of the characters involved.'

'Ed Osborne is tough, clever and dangerous. I'd say he's pretty high up in the opposition. Sharon I haven't met so far. Denise Chatel *appears* to be the nicest, but she's a mystery, so an unknown quantity who should be watched. Sir Guy Strangeways is also clever, but he's playing a peculiar game. Big question mark. Basil Windermere is a piece of social rubbish. Ditto for Rupert Strangeways, a worthless idler. Don't you agree?'

'Not entirely, but please go on,' Tweed urged her.

'Jake Ronstadt. I only saw him for a short time at Goodfellows but I feel he's very dangerous. He exudes dynamic energy. He was suave when he talked to us – I wonder how he talks to his staff. Hank Waltz tried to torture me to get information – he would have killed me later. I won't dwell on that episode. But it demonstrates the lengths to which they'll go. Then we have a horde of professional thugs entering the country via Paris. Why Paris? Because they hoped to get here secretly.'

'I spoke to René Lasalle of the DST this morning,' Tweed told her. 'He's very worried about the Americans – he's sending me by courier some photos discreetly taken of a lot of them. I'd like you to look at them when they arrive. What is really happening, then?'

'They're trying to increase their influence over Britain. At the least.' She paused. 'They could be planning to occupy Britain. You'll think I'm mad—'

She stopped speaking as the phone rang. Monica answered, told them Chief Inspector Roy Buchanan had arrived. Tweed told her to ask him to come up immediately.

When Buchanan entered they were all struck by how grim he looked. At Tweed's invitation he sat down, accepted Monica's offer of a cup of coffee.

'I need it.' He looked round the room. 'I trust everyone here, so I can talk freely. You've heard the news?'

'What news is that?' Tweed enquired. 'You look haggard.'

'A huge bomb went off this morning at a big department store in Oxford Street, when it was crowded with shoppers because of a sale. The bomb was planted under a perfume counter with a lot of boxes of stock. Casualties so far thirty dead and many injured. I've come from there – I closed off Oxford Street, which is why I'm late. It was horrific.'

'A rebellious IRA splinter group?' Marler asked.

'Absolutely not. The Bomb Squad arrived quickly. They found a second huge bomb which hadn't detonated. They locked the timer, dismantled it quickly. They told me it was such a sophisticated electronic device it couldn't be the IRA. Electronics suggests Silicon Valley in the States. Guess where the second bomb was planted.'

'Where?' asked Tweed.

'In the baby clothes and children's toys section. And there are dead children among the casualties.'

'Bastards,' snapped Newman.

'How did the bombers get in?' Tweed probed.

'No idea. The staff who opened the doors saw no signs of forced entry. In addition they had neutralized the alarm system, then re-set it so the staff wouldn't be alerted when they came in first thing.'

'Someone trying to cause panic?' Tweed mused.

'If it was, it worked. Oxford Street was deserted before I had it closed off. The news spread like wildfire. Thank you,' he said to Monica, who had brought him a second cup of coffee. 'It was an atrocity,' he concluded.

'Any idea who was responsible, then?' Tweed asked.

'None at all. It's early days.'

'Roy, you were coming to see me anyway. What was that about?'

'First, a body was washed up on a mudbank just south of the East End. A small, thickset man with a bald head. A Hank Waltz.'

'How do you know that?'

'Had a soggy American diplomatic passport in his pocket.'

'You're informing the American Embassy?'

'No, I'm not,' Buchanan said vehemently. 'And, would you believe it – I've lost the passport. Let the Yanks ask me – if they do. Then there was a second body.'

'Also dragged out of the Thames?' Tweed suggested.

'No. Had an anonymous call. For some reason I decided to go myself. Probably to see if it was another American. Found the deceased on some steps off Regent Street. This one had a rifle bullet through his head.'

'Any identification?'

'Yes. A Swiss passport with the name Kurt Schwarz.'

'He was murdered, then?'

'No doubt about it. Just one rifle shot. Why did I think of the Phantom?'

'Maybe because the PM, Keller in Germany and the Minister in France were also shot through the head with one rifle bullet. Any witnesses?'

'I had the team with me call at every house, waking people up. One of them was Basil Windermere. We know he lives off playing up to rich women.'

'And what did Basil have to say?'

'Said he'd been woken up by a faint crack! Thought it was a car backfiring, so he went back to sleep. He had no idea of the time when he heard the noise.'

'Was he sleeping alone?' Marler interjected.

'Yes.'

'Was he in his pyjamas?' Marler persisted.

'Yes. Why this interest in Windermere?'

'Suppose I just have the natural instincts of a detective.'

'I see.' Buchanan drank more coffee. 'You're not usually so vocal.'

'One more question, Roy,' Tweed said to divert the policeman from the subject of Windermere. 'The Chrysler in Strangeways' garage at Parham. Did you manage to check the vehicle?'

'Yes. I sent a team down to Irongates. They had a search warrant but they were careful. The entrance gates were closed. There were no lights on in the house – even though it was almost dark as night. They scaled the side wall. A locksmith released the padlock on the garage doors. There was nothing inside. No sign of a Chrysler.'

'They'd got out in time.'

'Seems so.' Buchanan took a folded sheet of paper from his pocket, handed it to Tweed. 'That is for your eyes only. Do you recognize any of the names?'

'Yes. Two Cabinet ministers. Several prominent MPs. And a number of well-known businessmen.'

'All of them have been bribed by the Americans. Given large sums in dollar bills inside executive cases. Special Branch officers have been watching the Embassy in Grosvenor Square. They have followed Americans coming out carrying executive cases. They meet the recipient of the bribe in out-of-the-way places. Obscure bars and pubs. They have a drink with the target, then leave alone, having propped the executive case against a bar or table leg. After they've gone one of the men on

131

that list leaves, after picking up the executive case. Three of them opened the case before they went off – produced several stacks of one-hundred-dollar bills and dropped them back inside the case. It's bribery of key British figures on a massive scale.'

'This is getting even more dangerous.'

'What I've told you all in this room is strictly confidential.'

'And will remain that way,' Tweed assured him.

Howard burst into the room at that moment. Seeing Buchanan he apologized. He spoke very quickly immediately afterwards.

'I think all of you ought to come to my office. There's a TV report on the bomb left in an Oxford Street department store. Have you heard?'

Paula led the way out of the room and upstairs to Howard's office. Newman and Marler followed her. Tweed turned to Buchanan, not sure whether he would spare the time.

'I think I'll come with you,' the policeman said. 'Sometimes whoever has committed a crime has an irresistible urge to revisit the scene of what he did . . .'

Inside Howard's room his secretary had arranged chairs and the TV was on. No one sat down. They stood in silence, waiting.

'How did the TV people get through?' Tweed whispered to Buchanan.

'I left instructions for them to be allowed in. The people who did this thing may rub their hands with glee, thinking it will terrify the population. I take a different view. I think it will cause universal outrage and fury. Here it comes . . .'

Unusually, there was no commentary, which made what followed more horrifying. The cameras panned round inside the store. The floor was covered with lethal shreds of glass. Paramedics were helping injured women and some men to leave. The counters and checkout points were shattered. No item of furniture remained undamaged. Bloodstained shoppers were still lying on the floor, attended by paramedics and doctors. One man had an arm missing. A prone woman's skirt was dripping with blood, her face slashed by flying glass. A number of bodies were lying very still, sprawled on the ground. The camera panned to the exit.

A woman, lying flat, her neck bandaged, blood seeping through it, was being carried out on a stretcher by two paramedics. She raised herself up, staring at the camera as though unaware of its presence.

'My husband. Where is my husband?'

Behind her, where she couldn't see, the paramedic carrying the rear end of the stretcher, shook his head. Paula gasped.

'Oh, my God,' she said half under her breath.

'It's like a battlefield,' Newman said to Tweed.

Paula stood up to leave. In the open doorway Monica stood staring as though she couldn't believe her eyes. She went down back to Tweed's office, followed by Newman, Marler, Tweed and Buchanan. The policeman tapped Tweed on the shoulder before they were about to enter the room.

'I'll have to go now. There was no one shown who wasn't with the ambulance men or paramedics. My men did their job. Try and keep in touch with me.'

'You do the same . . .'

There was complete silence when he went into his office, shut the door and sat down behind his desk. Monica sat stunned, her hands in her lap. Paula gazed at each of her colleagues, made no comment. Marler, leaning against a wall, was about to light a king-size, decided against it.

Tweed leaned forward across his desk. They all stared at him, knowing he was going to say something important. When he did speak his voice was calm, resolute.

'We use any devious ruthless method to defeat them.'

13

The Executive Action Department was again meeting in the large room at the American Embassy. Jake, at the head of the table, was again shuffling his cards. He made them wait before he spoke. Outside, beyond the windows, branches of the trees in the square shook under the onslaught of the late morning wind.

'Guess I ought to hand out half-congratulations to Vernon and Brad.'

'Why only half?' Vernon, the thin man with the boney face asked indignantly.

'Because the second bomb didn't go off. You must have fouled up the timer. If that bomb had detonated half the people in that store would have been killed. That would have been sensational.'

There were glum faces round the table. Jake Ronstadt was, as usual, in a bad mood. Brad, the squat man with shark-like teeth, risked opening his mouth.

'Which is the next objective? Maybe now we've started we oughta keep things movin' – scare the guts out of the Brits.'

'Maybe you ought to sit kinda quiet. I've sorta had enough of interruptions. In any case, it won't be Vernon and Brad who hit the next one. I handed out sheets of targets to you all. Raise your hands if you've now looked over those targets.'

Eight men raised their hands high in the air. They held them up until Jake made a gesture for them to lower them. He was shuffling his cards again. Vernon wondered if he ever played poker. He'd have liked to ask but knew that if he did he'd probably get Jake's fist in his face.

Leo, who had a head shaped like the moon, had once shot a baby in the back of the head. Afterwards he'd slipped away to down a couple of drinks in a bar. He was less afraid of Jake than anyone round the table. 'We haven't seen Ed Osborne at any of these meetings,' he remarked.

Ronstadt contemplated standing up, walking down the table and hauling the chair from under Leo. He knew Moonhead was independent-minded, that he was after his job. He decided to wait for a better opportunity to humiliate him.

'Ed is a very busy guy. Come to that, so am I. The idea to keep things movin' is crap. London will be swarming with cops hoping to get a clue, checking out their informants in the underworld. I'm sure Charlie will agree with me.'

He stood up in his brown leather jacket, his leather trousers. A man of limited height, it was his bulk, his large head, his personality, his expression which dominated the members of his team.

'Get the hell outta here,' he said, and left.

By lunchtime everyone except Monica and Paula had departed from Park Crescent. Paula had decided to skip lunch. After seeing the scenes on the TV newscast she didn't feel she wanted to eat anything. When the phone rang Monica spoke to the caller briefly, then said to Paula:

'It's Mrs Carson down at the Bunker. She's having trouble with Cord Dillon. Want to have a word?'

'Yes . . . Paula here, Mrs Carson. What's the problem?'

'Dillon is getting restless, feeling cooped up. He's even talked of coming up to London.'

'Can you hold him until I get there?' She had taken a swift decision. 'And have you see the news on TV? Heard it on the radio?'

'No. Dillon doesn't like either TV or the radio. Neither do I. Why do you ask?'

'I think Cord needs someone to talk to. Tell him I'm driving down there today, should reach you mid-afternoon. And both of you watch the next TV news broadcast. It's important you do.'

'I'll arrange that. And look forward to seeing you. It's quiet on the Romney Marsh.'

'Monica,' Paula said as she grabbed her fur-lined coat, picked up her motoring gloves, 'contact Pete Nield. Tell him I'll be back in time to accompany him to Santorini's this evening.'

'That's where Newman is having dinner with Sharon Mandeville.'

'I know. I've had a good look at Denise Chatel – seen enough of her to form a certain opinion. But I've had no chance to see Sharon. I'm not going to barge in on Bob, but I can observe the glamorous Sharon from a distance. Tell Tweed I've rushed off to the Bunker to soothe Cord Dillon. See you . . .'

Later, as she crossed the border into Kent, Paula took another quick decision. Parham was on her way. She could drop off at Irongates – in the hope of having a chat with Sir Guy Strangeways. She'd hardly exchanged more than a few words with the property magnate when she had visited the place with Tweed.

'Do come in, my dear. I'd love to see you.'

Paula stared at the speakphone outside Irongates.

Strangeways sounded exuberant, in contrast to the previous visit, when he had barked down the instrument. He was waiting for her when she parked below the terrace. She gave one last look back at the closing gates.

On her way down from London she had felt sure she was being followed. Try as hard as she could, she had not been able to identify a vehicle on her tail. It could have been imagination, but she didn't think so.

'Come inside. Mrs Belloc has prepared tea. A little early, I know, so just eat what you feel like and leave the rest.'

As he escorted her across the large bleak hall, into the library where she had waited on her last visit, Paula studied her host. Outwardly affable, she detected signs of strain. His eyelids were puffy, as though from lack of sleep. The crackling military-style voice she had heard before had disappeared. Instead, he spoke softly. He wore a sports jacket with leather patches on the sleeves, a heavy pair of beige slacks, gleaming brown handmade shoes. She waited until Mrs Belloc had poured tea, stared at her, then left the room.

'What do you think of this bomb in Oxford Street?'

'Dreadful. Truly dreadful.' His voice trembled. 'As you can imagine, when I was a soldier I stood on battlefields amid carnage. It didn't affect me. Can't do the job if you permit it to get to you. But those scenes on TV.'

'Who do you think is responsible? A splinter group of the IRA?'

'There are so many . . .' He paused. 'So many terrorist outfits in the world today. Could be any of them.'

Paula had the impression he wasn't happy with the subject. He drank tea, helped himself to a cake. Paula ate ravenously.

'I have another problem on my mind,' he began. 'Rupert. He's a terrible disappointment. I know he runs

137

after every pretty woman in sight. Don't mind that. He grew up late. It's his gambling.'

'With some people it's an addiction.'

'I'm not going to pay for his bloody addiction!' he stormed. 'Sorry. I raised my voice. Bad language. Not in the presence of ladies. I'm old-fashioned that way.'

'I appreciate that.'

'I've had a phone call from a casino in Campione. That's an enclave of Italy inside Switzerland.'

'I know. You get there by taking a steamer from Lugano.'

'Well, this blighter in Campione phoned me, demanding that I pay Rupert's debt. A hundred thousand pounds! I told him to go and jump in the lake. He said Rupert had referred him to me. I'm not paying a penny. I could afford it but Rupert can get out of his own messes. I told Rupert before he left the house. Called me a miser. I rang him at his London flat later to give him hell. The phone wasn't answered.'

'It must be very upsetting.'

'Sorry, I didn't ask you in to grouch about my small problems. Eat up!'

'You've got big property interests in the States. Will you be going back there?'

'I'm selling the lot, getting clear out of America.'

'You're a busy man. I think I should go now. Actually I did call in on my way elsewhere. Thank you for the tea – and your company, which I have enjoyed.'

'What a charming thing to say. I'll accompany you to your car.'

Paula reached down to adjust her right shoe. Something about it wasn't comfortable, and she used that foot for accelerator and foot brake. Strangeways helped her on with her coat and they crossed the hall. He opened the heavy front door and they stood framed in the doorway. Again Paula bent down to adjust her shoe. As she did so there was a *crack!*.

The bullet hit the side of the doorway where she had been standing. It ricocheted across the drive into the distance. Paula felt herself grabbed by Strangeways, pulled back inside as he used a foot to slam the door shut.

'Wait here,' he barked. He was taking keys from his pocket. 'I'm going to the gunroom. I saw the muzzle-flash. Came from the rooftop of the house opposite . . .'

Paula took several deep breaths. In no time Strangeways was back, holding a rifle. His eyes were blazing but his manner was controlled and calm. He was about to open the door again when Paula spoke.

'If you don't mind, I'd like to make a brief phone call.'

'Of course you can. The library. I'll wait here.'

Inside the room she took out a small notebook. She had written down certain phone numbers she had obtained from Monica. One of them was Basil Windermere's flat in London. She pressed numbers, listened. His cultured tones came clearly down the line on an answerphone.

'Dear caller, you have reached Basil. Ectually, I happen to be rather tied up at the moment. Sorry and all that. Do please leave your name and number. Then it will be my pleasure to return your call earliest possible. Cheerio.'

So Windermere was not at home. Paula put down the phone and went back into the hall. Strangeways gave her explicit orders in a commanding voice.

'Stay well back in the hall. I'm going out to investigate.'

Opening the door, he strode out. Reaching the drive he marched down it as though leading a division into battle. His rifle was elevated, aimed at the flat top of the mansion opposite beyond the rim of his wall. He stopped a few yards down the drive, called to her over his shoulder.

'Make a dive for your car. But first press the red button on the left-hand side of the door. Drive out fast. There's never any traffic in the square. Sorry about this. Keep moving . . .'

She obeyed him, pressing the button on the automatic security device. Throwing open the car door, she jumped inside, slammed the door shut. The gates were opening after she had pressed the red button. Strangeways moved on to the verge, his rifle still elevated as he continued to scan the rooftops. Gravel spurted up as she pressed her foot down. Then she was in the first deserted square, driving on into the second empty, larger square.

She slowed a lot to navigate her way through the village. As soon as she left it behind she rammed her foot down again. She was miles away when she reduced speed, continuing to check her rear-view mirror. No sign of any other vehicle. But she *had* been followed from London.

The heavy overcast dropped lower as she drove beyond Ashford and along a wide A-road. The massed black clouds made it almost as dark as night and she had her lights on. She was still on the almost deserted road when she first heard the distant sound of a helicopter approaching.

It was half a mile away when she glanced to the west and frowned. A Sikorsky. She couldn't see any identification signs on its fuselage. It was heading straight for her. She began to worry. If she continued straight ahead she would soon lead the machine to the secret Bunker.

To her left, a long way off across a vast field, she saw

a tractor dragging a harrow. A moment later, by the roadside, she saw an old barn, its doors yawning open; the home of the tractor, she imagined. She looked again at the helicopter. It had just disappeared inside a low cloud. She reacted quickly.

Slowing down, she swung the wheel, drove inside the large barn. An aroma of straw on the floor filled her nostrils. Switching off the engine, she looked back at the entrance. She was deep enough inside the barn to be totally concealed from the air. Then she heard the loud beat-beat of the chopper, flying much lower.

She lit one of her rare cigarettes. No chance of the smoke drifting outside the barn. She sat quite still, tense. The helicopter was now circling. At one moment it sounded to be just above the barn. Now she had no doubt that the crew on board were looking for her.

'I'm having a nice couple of days,' she said to herself. 'I had the fight at Eagle Street. Today someone tried to kill me at Irongates. There's no doubt the marksman was the Phantom – for no good reason, you idiot. Now you can just sit it out here.'

Sooner than she had expected the machine flew away, the sound of its engine fading. She still stayed where she was. Could be a trick – it might suddenly dart back. After ten minutes she decided it had gone and resumed her journey.

Turning off the road where a lane to the left was signposted Ivychurch, she followed the complex route down winding country lanes. She knew the way because Tweed had driven her to the Bunker when it was in the process of being constructed. Just before she reached the automatic gate which she knew Mrs Carson would open she stopped the car, turned off the engine.

She was listening for the helicopter. Instead, an oppressive silence she could almost hear descended on her. On all sides a flat plain of fields stretched away endlessly. Not a hill, not a tree in sight. Nor was there any sign of human habitation. The leafless hedges lining the lane on either side were grim networks of stark twigs and thorns, reminding her of barbed wire. No birdsong. She shivered. I might be in the middle of the Mongolian desert, she thought. This must be among the most desolate parts of England. Romney Marsh? You can keep it.

She turned on the engine, drove on. As she approached the automatic gate, she saw it opening. Mrs Carson must have used her binoculars, seen her coming.

'Welcome to Paradise,' Mrs Carson greeted her as she parked inside the courtyard and stepped out.

'I could think of another name for it. Don't know how you stand it down here.'

'I read a lot, dear. Come on in. Cord is a changed man . . .'

'Hi, Paula. Good to see you.'

Dillon stood up from where he had been sitting by a roaring log fire, rubbing his hands. The air outside was ice-cold, but the living room was so warm Paula slipped off her coat and gloves. Dillon looked anything but restless and his expression was grim. He wore an old polo-necked jersey and shabby corduroy trousers, obviously provided by Mrs Carson, and could have passed for a farm worker.

'How are you?' she asked as he took her right hand in both of his.

'Feeling pretty bloody-minded. Mrs Carson and I watched the TV programme. A Bomb Squad chief said the massacre had definitely nothing to do with the IRA. He mentioned a very sophisticated electronically operated timer he'd never seen before. Electronics. Silicon Valley.'

'What do you mean?' Paula asked.

'Shortly before I had to run for it I overheard a conversation between two scientists from Silicon Valley and a new man, a Jake Ronstadt. They were talking about a new device which had been perfected – an electronically operated timer for delayed-action bombs.'

'You think that links up with what you heard on TV?'

'Damned sure it does. It makes me sick to think my people could be responsible for the Oxford Street massacre. If I got hold of them I'd line them up against a wall and personally shoot them, one by one.'

'Who is this Jake Ronstadt you mentioned?' she asked cautiously.

'One of the new men brought in to the CIA. He passed all the tough training tests. Except one. I got hold of the report on him. The psychiatrist who checked him out wrote "psychologically flawed". That should have kept him out. It didn't.'

'Are you willing to stay here a bit longer? Tweed would be much happier if you did.'

'Sure I am. Guess Tweed has enough to cope with without worrying about me out in the open. He doesn't show it but he does worry about things like that. The guy is very human.'

Paula joined Dillon in drinking coffee, chatting as cheerfully as she could. She appreciated the fact that he made no attempt to extract information from her about what was happening. Then she said she must go back to London.

'This place is like a fortress,' the American commented as he accompanied her to the door. 'Tweed, and I guess Newman and Marler, really know a thing or two. The defences round the perimeter are diabolical.'

She didn't have time to ask him what he was talking about. As she drove back, her car heater turned up full blast, she found her mind jumping back and forth. She was keeping an eye open for the helicopter but the machine never reappeared. She was also thinking about the new timer device Dillon had overheard being discussed at Langley. Up to that moment she had found it difficult to believe Washington could really be behind such an attack.

She was also recalling what Dillon had told her about Ronstadt. As Tweed would have said, key pieces of the jigsaw were beginning to fit together. What she wasn't prepared for when she arrived at Park Crescent was that the last person in the world she would have expected was in a state of semi-shock.

14

'A letter from the dead.'

Entering Tweed's office Paula immediately sensed a strange atmosphere. Newman was sitting upright in a chair. Marler stood upright near a wall, no cigarette in his mouth. Monica's face had a frozen look. Tweed sat behind his desk, hands clasped on its surface, his expression neutral. Nobody said a word to her – until Marler spoke those five words.

He walked across to her slowly. His complexion was ashen. He handed her an envelope without saying another word. Then he walked back to his corner and stood very still.

Paula remained where she was, standing, her coat over her arm. She examined the outside of the envelope. It was addressed in a foreign-looking script to Mr Marler, c/o General & Cumbria Assurance, followed by the address. She noticed that it had been posted in London, carried a second-class stamp. Carefully she extracted the single folded sheet inside. It was written in the same script.

Dear Marler – Be very careful of the barges. You must locate the printing presses. Yours, Kurt Schwarz.

She looked round the room again, placed the letter, folded, inside the envelope. Then she walked across to Marler, gave it back to him. Dropping coat and gloves on her desk, she sank into her chair. She was worried about saying the wrong thing, was relieved when Newman began talking.

'The letter has naturally . . .' He had been going to say 'upset' but decided Marler wouldn't like that. '. . . disturbed Marler. As it has me. Marler had known Kurt for years. They were friends who trusted each other completely.'

'One more bullet for the Phantom,' said Marler in the same monotone he had spoken the first five words when she had entered.

'We both feel rotten,' Newman went on quickly, 'about leaving him propped up against those steps.'

'You couldn't do anything else,' Paula said quietly. 'And I'm upset . . .' She paused with a lump in her throat, forcing herself not to cry. 'He was such a nice man. I liked him from the moment he came to my flat. He joked with me, made me laugh. It's too cruel. So macabre . . .' She trailed off.

'Time for me to go,' Marler said, his voice normal. 'Must have a bath, smarten myself up. I have a date with Denise Chatel this evening. See you.'

Tweed waited until he had left. When he spoke his tone was offhand. He gave the impression that business as usual had now resumed.

'Kurt may have given us valuable information at some stage. I can understand Marler's reaction. He realizes Kurt wouldn't have sent that letter unless he thought he wouldn't survive long enough to pass on the message personally.'

'The barges,' Paula said, mystified. 'Does he mean barges on the Thames? And which printing presses was he referring to?'

'I have no idea,' Tweed responded. 'But we may understand in due course. You looked tense the moment you opened the door. How did you get on at the Bunker?'

'I'll have to learn to control my expression.' She paused, wondering whether to tell him about the attempt on her life, feeling sure he would go up in smoke. She decided she must give a complete report. 'On the way down to the Bunker I decided to call in . . .' she began.

Tweed sat like a Buddha, his eyes fixed on hers, listening. When she had finished he decided the last thing to do was rebuke her for taking chances on her own. She had gone through enough recently.

'You seem sure the bullet was intended for you,' he remarked.

'Why do you say that?'

'From your graphic description, Sir Guy Strangeways was standing beside you. Surely the bullet could have been meant for him?'

'I hadn't thought of that. Now you mention it, I don't know.'

'The Phantom has spoilt his record,' Newman commented. 'This time he missed his target, whoever it was.'

'Interesting that Basil Windermere wasn't at his flat when you called him. That was quick thinking,' Tweed remarked.

'As I told you, Cord Dillon seems content to stay where he is.'

'Pretty conclusive,' Newman said grimly, 'what he told you he overheard at Langley about the new timer. We know who we're up against now.'

'Up to a point,' Tweed told him.

'How did your lunch go with Ed Osborne?' Paula wondered.

'Never got there. I was leaving the building when a call came through from him. Full of apologies. Would I mind making our meeting this evening. Same rendez-vous. Nine o'clock at the Raging Stag in Piccadilly.'

'Shouldn't you have a bodyguard, after everything that's happened? And they did try to kidnap you outside the American Embassy. It was a good job Newman and the others were there.'

'Tweed gave us the signal that he was in trouble,' Newman explained. 'Standing at the top of the step on his way out he ran a hand over the top of his head as though smoothing down his hair.'

'I have to love you and leave you now.' Tweed stood up. 'I want to keep Howard up to date with the latest developments. Bob, enjoy your dinner with Sharon – I don't see how you can fail to do so. Paula, I suggest you go home early, get Pete Nield to drive you home, check out the area. Then cook yourself something simple and get an early night.'

Paula nodded, said nothing. She didn't want to refer to her intention to have dinner with Pete at Santorini's in front of Newman. He might not be best pleased with her idea of her checking up on Sharon from a distance. Monica waited until Tweed and Newman had left, the latter on his way home to get ready for his night out.

'Don't worry about Tweed,' Monica told Paula. 'I've fixed it up with Harry Butler to put on his best suit and to go to the Raging Stag discreetly – to keep an eye on him.'

Santorini's, the new in-place, was decked out luxuriously. One section even projected out over the river. The place bubbled with activity. Sharon, with Newman at her side, answered the maître d' when he immediately came up to them.

'Sharon Mandeville. You have a table reserved overlooking the river.'

'Good evening. We have indeed got your reservation. The best table, of course . . .'

Sharon wore a close-fitting, simply cut shift dress in purple which must have cost a fortune, with elegant court shoes. Her blonde hair fell in sweeping waves almost to her shoulders. As she preceded Newman men turned to gaze at her. Some to the amusement of their escorts, other women looking annoyed. She was undoubtedly, Newman thought, the most striking-looking woman in the place. And there was competition aplenty.

Their table was placed next to a large window looking out over the river. The water actually flowed below them. Sharon sat down and her hypnotic green eyes stared at Newman. She seemed unaware of the stir she was causing at other tables.

'I hope this suits you, Bob,' she said in her soft voice.

'Perfect. You must have clout to have secured this table.'

'Not really. I used the Ambassador's name. I don't really want to be well known. The waiter's here. Let's order our aperitifs.'

She was very calm, almost withdrawn, her movements slow and dignified. Her eyes held his, without in any way being aggressive or come-hitherish. They touched glasses when the aperitifs arrived.

'Here's to a memorable evening,' Newman said buoyantly.

'I'll drink to that,' she agreed quietly.

'How are you settling in at the Embassy? Must be a major change from Washington.'

'I prefer London. After all, my mother was English.

So I feel at home here. Washington is rather a bear garden. I have a nice house in Dorset.'

'And yet everything important in your life happened in America.'

'You're probably referring to my four husbands. Let's study the menu. This is my treat, by the way.'

'No, it isn't . . .'

'I hope you don't mind, but you can't do much about it. I have opened an account here.'

'Wicked of you.' He grinned. 'Next time it's my treat.'

'I'll look forward to that.'

They took time examining the large selection. Newman glanced out of the window and saw a massive barge tied up for the night. He stared. *Be very careful of the barges.* Kurt's warning in his last communication flashed into his mind.

'A penny for your thoughts,' said Sharon.

'Sorry. The reflections in the river look wonderful.'

'Dreamy . . .'

'Like the outfit you're wearing. Purple really suits you.'

'Thank you.'

He noticed there was not a trace of an American accent in her voice. She spoke as though she had lived all her life in England. He found her voice, her calmness very attractive. It was no effort to talk to her. He just felt comfortable. And her greenish eyes were remarkable, although she made no effort to use them as a weapon the way some women did. They said little as they consumed a magnificent meal. Looking round the tastefully appointed restaurant, he saw a lot of the in crowd were present, most of whom he disliked. Sharon brought up the subject when they were drinking coffee.

'I hope you don't mind but I'm also in the way of a messenger tonight. I've been asked whether you'd consider writing an article urging a closer special relationship between Britain and America.'

'May I enquire who asked you to do that?'

'I'm sorry, Bob, but I'm not supposed to say. It comes from someone very high up . . .'

Paula and Pete Nield had arrived at Santorini's a few minutes before Sharon and Bob entered. Paula had used Howard's name to ask for a secluded table. Howard, a member of several clubs, could get any table he wanted in London. Their table was in an alcove and Paula had a clear but distant view of the table over the river.

'What do you think of her?' Nield asked as they finished their main course.

'They seem to be getting on very well together. What do I think of Sharon? I'm not sure. She's beautifully dressed. Real taste in every way.'

'That's not what I asked.'

'She's poised. Quite at home in a place like this. She has an unusual technique for impressing a man.'

'Go on.'

'She's cool, very calm on the surface. A good listener – and that appeals to a man. She has control of the situation, without appearing to do so.'

'You used the phrase "on the surface".'

'I just wonder what she's really like under that appearance of unusual calm. I'm honestly not sure.'

'Not sure of what?' Nield smiled. 'Come on. Give.'

'I'm simply dist— puzzled. She's hard to read.'

'You were going to say disturbed and then altered it to puzzled. What is it about her that disturbs you?'

'Maybe a touch of envy.' Paula smiled. 'She's a very beautiful woman.'

'Be cagey, as you'd say to Tweed. And for my money you're looking like a present from Heaven.'

'Thank you, Pete.' She almost blushed. 'Do you want pudding?'

'I'm full up – this meal I've had will last me for days. But you go ahead.'

'I'm in the same state as you. Talking about Tweed, I know the Raging Stag stays open late. He may still be there. Do you mind if we have coffee there? I feel we ought to check there are no thugs in that area.'

'Good idea. I'll get the bill.'

They had chosen a moment when Sharon and Newman's table was masked by other guests also leaving. Nield drove them back towards Piccadilly, found the only empty parking slot in Mayfair and grabbed it. They made the rest of the journey on foot.

Paula clasped the collar of her coat round her neck. A wind which must have originated at the North Pole was blowing. Their natural route took them down Albemarle Street, which was deserted. It brought back to Paula the evening when she had bumped into Cord Dillon outside Brown's, the nerve-racking moment when a bullet fired from the Cadillac had smashed the glass behind them as they stood in front of it.

Nield made no comment on the incident but took Paula's arm and hurried her even more briskly. They slowed down as they approached the Raging Stag. Both their eyes were everywhere, checking for men waiting in the shadows. Piccadilly, also, was deserted.

Entering the expensively decorated pub-cum-restaurant, Paula scanned the place, saw Tweed among the crowd sitting at a table in the restaurant further in. He had his back to her and next to him sat Ed Osborne. Nield had also spotted them.

'Two stools free at the bar,' he said. 'I'll take them . . .'

He reached the stools seconds before two men, who

looked annoyed and tried to muscle their way in. Nield shook his head.

'Those are our places,' a large middle-aged man said aggressively.

'Sorry, but I have a lady with me. You wouldn't want her to have to stand, I'm sure.'

Paula backed him up by slipping past and perching herself on one of the stools. She turned, spoke to the aggressive man.

'Thank you so much. That was very kind of you.'

'You worked that well,' said Nield as the two men went away, muttering. 'What are you having to drink?'

'I'll stick to wine, I think. A glass of medium dry French.'

The place was as crowded, even at that hour, as Santorini's. Paula found she was in an ideal position to observe Tweed's table – she had a clear view of it reflected in the mirror behind the bar. She slipped off her coat, folded it in her lap as the drinks arrived, then she stiffened, held her glass motionless.

Tweed and Osborne sat on chairs close together. She had the impression they were having a friendly argument as Osborne waved his hands about and Tweed nodded. What had made her stiffen was the sight of a bulging briefcase perched against Tweed's chair.

'Something wrong?' Nield enquired.

'Nothing.'

She wrapped her scarf round her head to conceal her hair. A waiter had brought back the bill to Osborne, placing his credit card on it, which Osborne whipped up and slipped inside his wallet. Nield slumped further forward across the bar. He was wearing a new suit and he'd sensed Paula didn't want Tweed to see them. The two men who had tried to take their stools were standing behind them now, holding drinks, chatting. In the mirror it seemed to Paula they were concealed from anyone leaving. She saw Butler hidden in a corner.

Osborne was standing up. He slapped Tweed on the shoulder and made his way towards the exit, pushing aside anyone who got in his way by his sheer bulk. He wasn't even wearing a coat. It must be all that flesh on his large frame which enabled him to stand the arctic weather outside, Paula thought.

'We wait?' Nield asked.

'If you don't mind. Just a bit longer. It's only the second time I've been in this place. It's lively.'

Tweed waited at his table for a few minutes after Osborne had left. When he stood he was holding the briefcase in his right hand. Unlike Osborne, he threaded his way throught the crowd politely.

'Excuse me . . . thank you . . . excuse me . . .'

Paula felt a chill down her spine as Tweed walked out into the night, still carrying the briefcase. She had never seen him own anything like it. She waited a few minutes longer, then finished her drink.

'If it's all right by you, Pete, I think I've had enough.'

Something in her voice, in the way she held herself, caught Nield's attention. He waited until they were walking back to the car before he spoke.

'Is something worrying you?'

'Nothing at all. I've had a wonderful evening. I'm grateful to you, Pete . . .'

Nield had assumed he would be driving Paula back to her flat in the Fulham Road. She surprised him when they reached the car and had jumped inside it to escape the cold. He started the engine, turned up the heater.

'Be warm in a minute. Back to your flat?'

'No, Pete. I'd appreciate it if you dropped me at Park

Crescent. I've got some work I want to deal with. I can drive myself back in my own car later.'

'No good. You need a bodyguard.'

'Pete! I'm not a puppy that has to be kept at the end of the leash,' she snapped.

'You are worried about something. A worry shared is a worry halved.'

'I'm sorry, Pete – sorry that I flared up. That was awful of me after the marvellous evening we've had together. But I do want to call in at Park Crescent.'

'Fair enough. Why don't I drive on and check out your flat and the area round it? Someone very hostile knows where you live.'

'You're right, of course. And I'm grateful. Here's the keys to my flat so you can get inside.'

'If you don't mind I'll wait until you arrive.'

'Don't mind at all . . .'

She was silent during their drive. Furious with herself for the unjustified outburst, she couldn't think of anything to say. She gave him a kiss on the cheek, squeezed his hand before she got out at the entrance to Park Crescent. There was a light on in Tweed's office.

'Evening, Paula,' George greeted her. 'Mr Tweed's gone up to have a bath. Monica's still here.'

She went quietly up the stairs and opened the door. Monica wasn't there, she had probably gone upstairs to make herself a snack. She closed the door and stared. She almost trembled with trepidation. The bulging briefcase was propped up in the kneehole under Tweed's desk, the flap fallen open. Standing very still, she tried to make up her mind. She had never been one to snoop. But she felt she had to know the truth or the uncertainty would torture her mind.

Bending down, she carefully pulled out the case. She looked inside it and felt sick. It was stuffed with stacks of one-hundred-dollar bills. Each package had an elastic band round it. Taking one out, she quickly counted. One hundred US banknotes. With the number of packages there the case must contain thousands of dollars.

She replaced the case exactly where – and as – she had found it. Dazed, she stood up. She had to get out of the building before Tweed reappeared. She couldn't face him tonight. She ran down the stairs, paused to speak to George.

'Don't bother to tell anyone I was here. Tweed thought I was going to have an early night.'

'Very good, miss . . .'

She sat in her car after starting the engine, waiting to calm down. Then she drove back to her flat, thankful that there was no traffic, that the streets were empty – as empty as she felt.

15

At about the time when Paula and Nield were tackling their main courses at Santorini's, Marler was dining with Denise Chatel at the Lanesborough. The brunette, her long dark hair perfectly coiffeured, wore a silk trouser suit. He was immediately impressed by her stunning appearance and told her so when they'd sat down at their table.

'That's a nice compliment. I appreciate it,' she said with a warm smile. 'Thank you, Alec.'

Later he asked her to choose the wine and she selected a very good vintage in the medium-price range. They chatted easily and he found she was the sort of woman you quickly felt you had known for years in the nicest way. She gazed round the restaurant and her blue eyes stared into his.

'This is a wonderful place. No wonder it is full of people.'

'Used to be a big hospital before they converted it into this hotel. Have some more wine . . .'

They went into another room to have coffee and she crossed her shapely legs after sitting down on a couch. Alongside her, he thought about complimenting her on them, but decided it was a bit early in their acquaintance. It was a chance remark on his part which triggered off a development, the consequences of which he could not foresee.

'I remember you said you had a French father and an American mother. That's pretty cosmopolitan.'

'I was . . .' She hesitated. 'I was going to bring up that subject. I hope you won't regard this as trying to pump your business knowledge on the cheap.'

'Of course not.' He leaned forward. 'I'm interested in everything about you. Fire away.'

'When I was at Park Crescent I mentioned they had been killed together in a car crash. There was something mysterious about it and it still bothers me. They were killed just across the state line in Virginia at a small place I'd have to write down . . .'

'Here's a notebook,' he said, producing one from his pocket. 'I'd like all the details.'

'I called the sheriff in charge of the investigation. A man called Jim Briscoe. I'll write that down. He agreed for me to go and see him. He seemed nice enough but I sensed he was embarrassed. Which didn't make sense. He said these accidents unfortunately happened. I asked him if the accident had occurred at a black spot. He said it wasn't.'

'You didn't go out to view the location, I suppose?'

'Actually I did. Jim Briscoe took me there at my suggestion. There were no signs of skid marks near the bridge where it happened. I pointed that out. Again he seemed embarrassed, said a lot of traffic could have wiped them out. The only thing is it was a quiet road. I got the idea someone had rubbed out any skid marks.' She smiled ruefully. 'You'll think me paranoid.'

'No I won't. I believe you. What did you want me to do?'

'Well, Sharon said in passing that Tweed ran a special insurance outfit – that you insure prominent people against being kidnapped. Then, if they are, you negotiate their release unharmed. Which means you have investigators.'

'You could say that is our business.'

'Later, I tried to get in touch with Sheriff Briscoe again. A strange voice told me he'd retired early on full pension. I thought that peculiar – Jim Briscoe couldn't have been a day over forty. I said I wanted the FBI brought in – my parents had crossed a state line. The new sheriff was unpleasant – told me the investigation was closed for ever. He said I could be sued for wasting their time.'

'Odd, very odd. Can you describe the scene where this so-called accident took place?'

'Yes. A wide highway crosses a bridge over a deep gorge. Reluctantly, Jim Briscoe showed me a photo of the car my parents had died in. There was a huge dent in the side of the car – as though a heavy vehicle had driven into it. And at the exact point just before the bridge started, where they'd be sent straight down into the gorge.'

'It's a wonder their car didn't burst into flames – or did it?'

'No, it didn't. My father had quick reflexes. He'd obviously turned off the engine as they went over. I asked Briscoe about that and he confirmed the engine had been switched off.'

'Have you got Briscoe's present phone number?'

'No, I haven't. But the new man said he'd retired to a house in the same town. The unpronounceable one I've written down. I've also written down the name of the new sheriff and his phone number. Probably you can't do anything.'

'Don't be so sure about that.' Marler had had a bright idea. 'Give me the notebook and I might just find out what really happened. Something about what you've told me stinks.'

'I'm putting you to a lot of trouble,' she said, handing him back his notebook. 'I've also written down the address of my apartment in Belgravia – next to Sharon's. And a private phone number I've had installed. Ex-directory. On the quiet. I think the Embassy listens in to my calls on the phone that was there when I arrived.' She smiled again. 'Really, you must think I'm nuts.'

'I think you may have every reason to be worried. I'll see what I can do.'

'Let's talk about something else. This can't be entertaining conversation for you.'

'Actually, I'm intrigued.' She had checked her watch. 'You don't have to go yet, do you?'

'I really should. The limo driver who brought me must have been waiting outside for half an hour already . . .'

When they had put their coats on he accompanied her outside to the waiting limo. Before she got into the car she turned, kissed him gently full on the mouth. She gave him a very warm smile.

'Thank you for a really wonderful evening. I'd love it if we could keep in touch.'

'We'll do that.' He handed her a sheet from his notepad, kept his voice to a whisper. 'That's the phone number of my flat. There's an answerphone if I'm out. Just say Denise called and I'll call you back at the private number until I get you.'

'Take care of yourself, Alec. It's a dangerous world we're living in.'

16

Paula didn't sleep that night. She tried to but sleep wouldn't come. The briefcase stuffed with a fortune in dollars kept coming back into her mind. She had a long bath and that didn't help.

As she made coffee, knowing she would not get any rest that night, she kept recalling what Chief Inspector Buchanan had told them. How key figures in Britain were being bought with huge bribes. The technique used. How the Anti-Terrorist Squad officers, watching the Embassy, had seen Americans leaving, carrying executive cases, had followed them, seen them in pubs meeting their 'target'. Strictly speaking, in the episode inside the Raging Stag, it had been a briefcase Osborne must have propped against Tweed's chair leg.

Her mind moved in circles. Had Tweed decided they couldn't win? Had he gone over to the other side? It didn't seem to be possible when she recalled the years she had known him. It was far more likely there was another explanation – but she couldn't think of one.

'I'm bloody wrong. I have to be,' she said aloud.

But she was not convinced. Tweed had trained her always to deal in facts. And she had personally witnessed the 'transaction'. Edgy, she threw away half the cup of coffee, made herself some tea. Pacing round the living room, she smoked another of her rare cigarettes.

'I give up,' she said, again aloud.

*

She arrived very early at Park Crescent, was relieved to find she was alone. The briefcase with the dollars had disappeared. On Monica's desk a name was scribbled on a pad. *Keith Kent. Basle.*

She was seated behind her desk when they all arrived almost together. Monica came in first, settled herself behind her desk. She looked across at Paula.

'While you were down at Romney Marsh yesterday Keith Kent, the money tracer, called Tweed from Basle. Said he'd cracked the Zürcher Kredit account, wanted assistance urgently.'

'How did Tweed react?'

'Ask him yourself when he comes in.'

Paula welcomed the suggestion. It gave her something to say to Tweed. If she just sat like a dummy he'd quickly notice her silence. Newman came in. He was cheerful, positively buoyant. He grinned at Paula.

'Top of the morning. Isn't it a nice day.'

'It's a terrible day,' Paula replied. 'The temperature has gone even lower.'

'Helps to keep your wits about you,' he said with another grin, plonking himself into a chair.

Marler arrived, faultlessly dressed as always. He was wearing a new grey suit. He gave everyone a little wave. At that moment Tweed walked in, his step brisk, his manner businesslike as he settled behind his desk. He looked round the room.

'Monica has told me,' Paula began, 'that Keith Kent called you from Basle yesterday, said that he'd cracked the Zürcher Kredit account, whatever that means.'

'True. Everything is beginning to fit. Bob, how did you get on with Sharon Mandeville?'

'Fine. You know, she has no hint of an American accent. She struck me as a demure English lady.'

Paula stared at him, her lips pursed. Was Newman falling for Sharon? It certainly sounded so – from his manner and what he had just said. She lowered her eyes before he looked at her.

'Really?' Tweed paused. 'So you're getting on with her well. Any chance of a second meeting?'

'I would hope so. Yes, a good chance, I'd say.'

'Then you'll have another chance to try to extract information from her as to what is going on. If she has any, which she may not.'

'The lady asked me to write an article. Not her idea. Comes from someone higher up she couldn't name.'

'What kind of an article?'

'A plea for a much closer version of the special relationship between Britain and America.'

'Really?' A brief smile flickered across Tweed's face. 'The pattern is taking shape. Are you going to do it?'

'Haven't decided. If I do, I'll show you a draft first, of course.'

'And now we come to you, Marler,' Tweed went on. 'Did you enjoy your evening with Denise Chatel?'

'Very much. She's nice. She told me a very strange story. There's quite a bit to tell. It concerns the death of her parents . . .'

Marler had Tweed's full attention as the story began to unfold. From his excellent memory he reported every word Denise had said to him. Monica stopped using the phone and listened. Near the conclusion Marler waved a characteristic dismissive hand.

'I thought Cord Dillon was the man to make enquiries – that I could feed him the data and later he could phone America from the Bunker. Or you might think this is a diversion of energy.'

'On the contrary.' Tweed paused again. 'What I'm going to say is very confidential. René Lasalle of the DST in Paris told me recently – when I asked him – that Denise's father was officially sent out as an attaché to the

French Embassy in Washington. Actually he was a member of the Secret Service. He was trying to uncover details of some major operation Washington was planning. Before he could report back he was killed, with his wife, in a car crash. Sharon's mother and father were also killed in a car crash. As I said earlier, I don't believe in coincidences.'

'So I can get Cord to check this out?' Marler asked.

'You most certainly can. Tell him I want to know.' He leant back in his chair. 'Years ago, when I was at Scotland Yard . . .'

'As the youngest superintendent in Homicide up to that time,' Paula added.

'What I was going to say was – in more than one murder case I investigated I stumbled across the identity of the murderer by pure chance. But at least I recognized the significance of what I'd stumbled over. I think Marler has done the same thing. I regard what Denise told him as of great significance to what we are dealing with now.'

'Bully for me,' said Marler, mocking himself.

'Also yesterday, a courier arrived from Paris with photos of Americans passing through that city on their way here.'

He took an envelope from a locked drawer, spilled out a number of glossy prints. He spread them methodically over his desk.

'I want all of you to gather round and comment if you see anyone you recognize . . .'

They formed a half-circle behind him. Paula, glad of something else to think about, studied the prints with care. Then she pointed.

'That's Hank Waltz, the man who tried to kill me at Eagle Street.'

Tweed turned over the photo. On the back was written a date. He looked over his shoulder at her.

'He came in by Eurostar four weeks ago. Go on looking.'

'That is Chuck Venacki,' Newman told them. 'Smooth faced, smooth manner. Officially an attaché at the Embassy. A bit above people like Waltz in intellect.'

'I haven't seen him so far,' Paula commented.

'You may well. Yet.' Newman warned. 'He's intelligent, so could be dangerous.'

'Came in three weeks ago,' Tweed said, looking at the back.

'And that,' Paula pointed out, stabbing her finger at another of the prints, 'is Jake Ronstadt.'

'Came in five weeks ago,' Tweed noted. 'Which is interesting. He was in the vanguard, which suggests he came early to set up something. Maybe the Executive Action Department.'

'There are three people missing,' Paula observed. 'Denise Chatel, Ed Osborne and Sharon Mandeville. Maybe the French didn't photo them.'

'I don't think that's the explanation,' Tweed objected. 'I'd say they flew direct here from Washington to Heathrow. Just as Jefferson Morgenstern did.' He stood up. 'Which reminds me, I'm having dinner with Jefferson at the Ambassador's residence this evening. It's no more than a quick walk from here. Jefferson called me before I left my flat. I accepted immediately.'

'You need a bodyguard,' said Newman.

'I do not. Jefferson is one of the old school. A very devious man – has to be to do his job – and he has his own idea of honour. Monica, you're still booking seats for us on the Swissair flight, I imagine.'

'Day by day.'

'Since you're all here,' Tweed said, glancing round the room, 'I hope you have your bags packed with cold-weather clothing. You have? Good. Because we're leaving for Basle on the early flight tomorrow morning.'

'You're going somewhere?' Monica asked as Tweed put on his coat. 'It's much too early for your meeting with Morgenstern.'

'I know. I have somewhere else to go first.'

'I'd better warn Butler and Nield about the flight,' Monica said.

'Don't do that. They have a job to do back here. They'll come on to Basle when they're finished. So keep booking seats for them daily. I've got to go now. Everything is breaking loose.'

When he had gone Monica slammed down the pen she was holding. She sat behind her desk, arms folded, looking furious.

'What's the matter?' Newman asked.

'Tweed's always doing that to me recently. Says he'll be back as soon as he can. I ask him where I can contact him. So he simply says something like, "I have to be somewhere else in a hurry." No clue as to where he's gone.'

Back behind her desk, Paula's brain was in turmoil. She had felt better when Tweed seemed like his normal self, full of activity, carrying on as usual but with a hint of great urgency. Now Monica's grumble had made her wonder again. Why was he being so exceptionally secretive? Who was he going to see?

Marler sat behind Tweed's desk to call Cord Dillon at the Bunker. Mrs Carson answered, put Dillon swiftly on the line.

'Cord, Marler here. We have a problem which might just be up your street. If you're willing to go for it. There's a young woman, in her thirties, at the Embassy. Had dinner with her last night. She's called Denise Chatel. I'll spell that . . .'

With his notepad open in front of him, Marler

explained the problem, gave him all the data. He spelt out the name of the little town in Virginia where the fatal car crash had taken place over a year before and everything else Denise had told him. Dillon asked him to slow down so he could scribble on a notepad.

'Can you do anything, get some facts?' Marler ended.

'Sure thing. Glad to have a problem I can get my teeth into. This is just the sort of problem I dealt with sometimes, back at Langley – tracing a missing person or someone on the run. I'll get Jim Briscoe's number, wherever he's retired to. Virginia is on New York time, so they're five hours back. I'll wait for people to get to work, then go into action. Can I call you back at Park Crescent?'

'You can. And I'm very grateful . . .'

'Consider it done.'

In his usual abrupt way Dillon broke the connection. Marler took the envelope from Paris that Tweed had left on his desk. He spent some time examining each print, memorizing faces, recalling names that had been put to each one. Eventually he put them back inside the envelope.

'Enjoying yourself?' Paula enquired.

'It helps to know the enemy. Now I'm going back to my flat to collect a few more things for what Tweed keeps calling cold weather. I thought it was pretty nippy here . . .'

Marler did not drive straight to his flat. He had decided to look at the outside of the flat where Denise Chatel lived. Plus the fact that Sharon Mandeville lived next door. It was always useful to know the locations of people involved.

There was heavy traffic on the way to Belgrave Square. Marler knew he would have a parking problem so he drove slowly into one of the most expensive squares in London. Checking the numbers, he was close to where Denise lived when he saw a big truck pulled in at the kerb. The driver was changing a wheel. Marler played with his engine, causing it to make funny noises. He stopped near to the truck. The driver, stopping for a cigarette, saluted him.

'You got trouble too, mate?'

'Engine's playing up. It would. I'm in a hurry.'

'That's when they always let you down.'

Still seated behind his wheel, Marler was watching the entrance to the Chatel flat and hoping no police car came along. He was parked illegally. Then he sat up straighter, stopped playing about with the engine. It took a lot to startle Marler, but startled he was. The door to the flat on the ground floor had opened and Tweed walked out a few paces. He turned round and Denise appeared. They chatted for only a moment, then they shook hands and Denise closed the door.

Marler slumped down behind the wheel. An unoccupied taxi came along. Tweed flagged it down after glancing round the square. Saying something to the driver he climbed inside, pulled the door shut behind him. The taxi moved off, vanished round a corner.

Marler started his engine, backed, waved to the truck driver who gave him a thumbs-up sign. Then Marler drove back to Park Crescent in heavy traffic. For once he felt dumbfounded. What on earth could Tweed have been up to? He couldn't think of any explanation. He decided to keep quiet about what he'd seen.

'Tweed's with Howard,' Monica told Marler as he entered the office at Park Crescent. 'I expect he's telling him about your trip to Basle with the others. I've got your ticket, of course.'

'Thanks. 'Fraid I have to ask you to change that. Book me on the earliest possible flight to Geneva tomorrow.'

'What's the idea?' asked Tweed, who had just returned and heard Marler's request.

'Presumably we have to pass through all the usual checks at Heathrow before we board.'

'Actually, no.' Tweed was settled behind his desk now. 'I got in touch with Jim Corcoran, my old friend and Security Chief at Heathrow. We'll bypass Customs and Passport control so we get aboard the plane before anyone else.'

'But we'll still have to pass through the metal detectors,' Marler persisted.

'Yes, we do. Even Jim can't get us past that check.'

'So we'll arrive in Basle unarmed.'

'You have a point.'

'Which is why I'm flying to Geneva. I have a contact there who will supply me with an arsenal. For a price.'

'Then you travel the same day to Basle,' said Newman, who sat in one of the armchairs. 'By train – where there are no checks.'

'Got in one, chum,' Marler agreed.

'Don't forget my Browning automatic – and plenty of ammo,' said Paula.

'The lady will be equipped with her favourite weapon,' Marler promised.

'I should have thought of that myself,' Tweed admitted, 'but I have a lot on my mind. This evening I have dinner with Jefferson Morgenstern.'

'You'll tell him where we're going?' Newman teased.

'Of course not. Don't be so silly.'

Paula narrowed her eyes, then looked away. It was very rare for Tweed to have a flash of temper. Something must be putting him under immense pressure. Her mind flooded with doubts about him again.

'I was joking,' Newman said mildly.

'Sorry. I should have realized that,' Tweed said with feeling.

The phone rang. Monica answered, asked the caller to hold for a moment. She looked at Marler, her hand shutting off the mouthpiece.

'It's for you. Your girl friend, Denise Chatel.'

Tweed stood up, told Marler to take the call on his phone. As he picked it up, Marler noticed everyone else in the room was suddenly interested in what was going on outside the window, which amused him. Was this their idea of giving him privacy?

'Hello, Denise. Alec here. How is the desirable brunette?'

'All right. And thank you. I'm calling on my special line from my flat. Have you heard anything yet about Virginia?'

'Not yet. It may take a day or two. As soon as I have something you'll hear from me.'

'I'm afraid I won't. Which is why I'm phoning you. Sharon told me at lunchtime that we're flying to Basle in Switzerland today. We'll be staying at a hotel called the Three Kings. I'll call you as soon as I get back – although I don't know when that will be.'

'Did she give any reason for this sudden decision?'

'Not even a hint. But she works like that. I have to go. Take care of yourself.'

'You do the same. And don't mention the Virginia business to anyone.'

'I promise.'

Tweed returned to his desk. Marler walked over to the wall near Paula, leant against it. He took his time about lighting up a king-size. No one asked why Denise had phoned but Tweed sat looking at him.

'Denise is going abroad today,' Marler eventually announced. 'With Sharon.'

'So I can forget my date,' Newman commented.

'They are both flying to Switzerland today,' Marler

went on. 'Specifically, to Basle. They're staying at the Three Kings Hotel.'

'Which is where we'll be staying from tomorrow,' Tweed told everyone. 'Another coincidence? Probably. It is not only the oldest hotel in Basle, it's also the best.'

'So I may see Sharon again soon,' Newman said more cheerfully.

'Bob.' Tweed smiled. 'I foresee great activity in Basle. You won't have to much time to pursue your personal affairs.'

'You couldn't care to spell that last word?' Newman joked back.

'I wouldn't like to embarrass you.' Tweed smiled again. 'In fact, the closer you get to Sharon the more pleased I'll be. She's a beautiful lady – and men talk to lovely women. She may have heard something we need to know. If she has, sooner or later she may let something slip when you're together.'

The phone rang. After answering, Monica again looked at Marler.

'It's for you. Cord Dillon . . .'

Tweed again ushered Marler into his chair. He wandered over to the window, staring into the distance. Outside sleet was falling. Moving cars had their wipers going full blast.

'Marler here, Cord.'

'We may be on to something big, reaching right up to Washington. I found Jim Briscoe's phone number. Told him who I was, what my job was, omitting to say I don't hold the post any more. He'd had a few drinks, but his brain was ticking over. He's bitter as all hell. He has no doubt at all Chatel and his wife were murdered. A heavy truck or some other vehicle slammed them over the edge down into that gorge. He called in the FBI, wrote a report. Next thing he knows, he's been replaced by a new sheriff, retired on full pension. His report was shredded.'

'This is pretty sensational . . .'

'There's a bit more. A few weeks after his forced retirement Briscoe was drinking with a young deputy brought in at the same time as the new sheriff. The boy got talkative when Briscoe mentioned the Chatel case. His boss had told him the case was closed for ever – that if it was ever reopened someone back in Washington called Charlie would see they both disappeared for good. It stinks of a huge cover-up. Guess that's all I have to give you.'

'It's more than enough, Cord. I'm very grateful. You've been very quick.'

'You've got a job to do, damned well do it.'

The connection was broken without another word. Marler relaxed in Tweed's chair, recalled out aloud everything Dillon had said. As he went on, Tweed perched on the corner of his own desk, arms folded, his eyes fixed on Marler's. Eventually Marler spread both his hands.

'You've got the lot.'

'Charlie again,' Tweed said in a quiet voice. 'I know you're doing your best, Monica, but at the earliest possible moment we must identify Charlie.'

17

Halfway through dinner in a magnificently furnished room, full of antiques, Jefferson Morgenstern brought up the subject. Earlier he and Tweed had had drinks in a smaller room and the American Secretary of State had chatted about their previous meeting in Washington.

Morgenstern was about five feet eight tall, in his

fifties. He was clean-shaven with greying hair, plump-cheeked, had a longish face and a prominent nose and wore rimless glasses. His personality radiated self-confidence without arrogance and he spoke at speed in a deep voice. His mind moved like quicksilver and Tweed considered him one of the most intelligent men he had ever met.

He had the reputation of liking the company of beautiful women, providing they were also intelligent. His expressions were mobile – sometimes grave and on other occasions amiable. He was known internationally as a man who could charm the birds out of the trees and his diplomatic skills were awesome. Despite his long sojourn in the States he was far more European than American. His energy was legendary.

'You know, Tweed,' he began, 'today the world is changing, and to survive we must change with it.'

'Jefferson, what sort of changes had you in mind?'

Tweed finished his fourth glass of wine and out of nowhere an attentive waiter appeared and refilled his glass, then vanished. On the wine front Tweed was keeping up with his host. He had an unusual metabolism. He would drink hardly anything for months, then, when the occasion required it, could consume a large quantity without it in any way affecting his brain.

'For one thing,' Morgenstern continued, 'I believe we have to considerably strengthen the special relationship between our two countries. In every field – economically, socially and politically.'

'Why?'

'You haven't changed. You never hesitate to ask the leading question. Which is one of the many things I like about you. That and your global outlook.'

'So why?' Tweed repeated.

'From Washington's point of view – and the world's – we are the great superpower. Between us, I believe we have peaked. In the Pacific we face China. China is steadily building itself up into a monster . . .'

'So why,' Tweed interjected, 'is your President supplying the Chinese with advanced technology which will help them to build up a vast war machine?'

'At times he runs away with himself. But what he has done also serves the purpose of lulling the Chinese. Between us, we now have far more advanced technology in the missile fields than what we have given them. But China has a population of over a billion people. We have only approximately two hundred and sixty million. In a clash China could lose fifty million and think nothing of it. If that happens to the States it would be devastating.'

'I take your point . . .'

'When we look east we see Europe losing all its strength with their crazy idea of merging countries – nations, Tweed, all with different languages, histories, ways of life. Madness. History shows us the Austro-Hungarian Empire, also a hotch-potch of nations with different cultures, collapsed after the First World War. Yugoslavia, another mixture of nations who detested each other, was held together by Tito for a time. Tito dies. Yugoslavia, as a similar federation to the one proposed for Europe, collapses in a bloodbath. The Soviet Empire is another example of different nationalities which broke down into chaos. You see why Washington is so worried about Europe.'

'You've made a powerful case.'

The waiter appeared to fill their glasses. Morgenstern looked up, smiled.

'Thank you, but I will attend to the wine. We want to be alone. I'll press the bell when we need help.'

'I think you're leading up to something, Jefferson,' Tweed remarked.

'Then, beyond Europe, there are more menaces. Militant Islam is on the upsurge. Turkey, which could fall to

Islam, will soon have a population of a hundred and fifty million. Germany, the largest nation in Europe, has eighty million. It only needs a brilliant Muslim general to do a Mohammed. To sweep across Europe. Based in an occupied Britain, their missiles could annihilate the East Coast of the States – while the Chinese did the same thing to our West Coast. You agree it is possible? This dessert isn't bad.'

'It's the best I've eaten in years,' Tweed said.

'Then Iran is building nuclear bombs, has ballistic missile systems. Allied to Turkey, with Iran's huge population, nothing could stand in their way.'

'They sound pretty worried in Washington,' Tweed observed.

'With good reason, as I'm explaining. Britain, for a thousand years the bulwark against tyranny from Europe, is enfeebled in a military sense. It wasn't necessary. You have no army to speak of, a skeleton of an air force, a ghost of a navy. Yet not so long ago you were the main factor in destroying Hitler. How are the mighty fallen.'

'I find it difficult to argue against what you have said.'

'Why don't we adjourn to the smaller room for coffee and liqueurs?'

'Good idea.'

The 'smaller' room was also large, spacious and luxuriously furnished. They sat facing each other, on two couches, with a coffee table between them. Morgenstern's blue eyes were gleaming with vitality.

'With all these terrible forces soon to be so powerful,' Morgenstern continued, 'we have to adjust, adapt, be revolutionary.'

'I sense we're approaching the reason why you invited me to have dinner,' Tweed said, then sipped his Cointreau.

'You are a very intuitive man. I noticed that rare quality when we met in Washington.'

'Why didn't you ask Howard to meet you?' Tweed enquired.

Tweed was making no attempt to pretend to be running an insurance outfit. Morgenstern would know he was Deputy Director of the SIS, that Howard was Director.

'Howard is a nice man.' Morgenstern paused for the first time, choosing his words carefully. 'But he hasn't a fraction of your global outlook. We regard you as a key figure in the new system.'

'What new system are you referring to, Jefferson?'

'I said earlier we have to be revolutionary.' Morgenstern leaned forward. 'Britain and America have to merge in a new and much stronger relationship. That is why we are talking tonight.'

'Merge?'

'As I said earlier, economically, socially and politically.'

'Before you go any further I'd like to ask a few questions. I imagine you saw the TV pictures of the outrage in Oxford Street after the bomb detonated?'

'I did. I was appalled. Such savagery.'

'I think some of your people planted that bomb.'

'You think *what*?' Morgenstern sat back, appeared to be visibly shaken. 'You can't mean that, Tweed. It's crazy. I find it hard to believe I heard what you just said. We don't do things like that. Why would we, for God's sake?'

Tweed had been watching his host closely. He had a lot of experience in detecting when people were lying. He could have sworn Morgenstern believed what he had just said. He pressed on.

'We have evidence that a huge number of the worst American thugs – gangsters – have arrived in this country by devious routes recently.' He opened the executive case which he had brought with him, took the batch of prints from the envelope, spread them on the coffee table. 'These are the men I'm talking about.'

'They must be members of the Medellín drug cartel – or maybe the Mafia,' Morgenstern said as he looked at the prints. 'I can only assume someone has fed you with disinformation.'

'You've seen any of those men inside the Embassy at Grosvenor Square?'

'Heavens no! I most certainly haven't.'

'May I ask, do you know everyone who works at the Embassy?'

'Absolutely not. Why should I? My role is running foreign policy. I have a suite of offices on the second floor. And I always enter the Embassy by a side door – to avoid the press photographers.'

Second floor? Then Tweed remembered that in America the ground floor is called the first floor. So when he had seen the back of Morgenstern with two bodyguards at the time of his visit to Sharon Mandeville, on the first floor, the Americans would refer to that as the second floor. Which linked up with what Morgenstern was telling him. Again he had no doubt that his host was speaking the truth.

'You know Sharon Mandeville?' Tweed persisted.

'Yes I do. She has an office on the same floor as my suite. I don't know what her role is, but she has close connections with the White House. She's friends with the President's wife. You know something, Tweed? You make a good interrogator.'

'I've no intention of offending you . . .'

'That's enough.' Morgenstern smiled. 'You are someone who could never offend me. Very occasionally, you might be deceived by someone trying to make bad blood between us, but I make no claim to infallibility.'

'Would you like to explain in more detail this merger between our two countries you suggested a few minutes ago?'

'I said merge, not merger.'

'There's a difference?'

'I suppose there isn't. Have you read how when France was falling to Germany in the Second World War Churchill offered the French dual citizenship? The French would also have British nationality – and vice versa.'

'Yes, I have read about that. The French turned it down.'

'Let us suppose Washington made a similar offer to this country. All Britons would become American citizens – with all the huge advantages that would give you.'

'Is Washington going to make such an offer? Positively?'

'It has been discussed by the National Security Council. And I chaired the meeting.'

'You haven't answered my question. Positively,' Tweed goaded.

'Other aspects of the joining of our two nations have been discussed in great detail. The Joint Chiefs of Staff would welcome the establishment of further air force and naval bases in Britain. It would increase the reach of, say, missiles aimed from here at the Middle East by three thousand five hundred miles. And the East Coast of the States would be safe again – safe from the danger of an attack by Muslim powers from occupied Britain.'

'What else has been discussed behind closed doors in Washington?' Tweed demanded.

'A special Act has been drafted in secret for Congress – this would incorporate Britain into the American system.'

'What are the huge advantages to this country you mentioned a few minutes ago?'

'You have a population of about fifty million-plus. At the moment the largest state in the US is California – a population of roughly thirty million. Britain would be by far the most powerful element when it came to electing a President. You would have more electoral votes than any other state in the Union. From America's point of view it would greatly increase the Anglo-Saxon vote. You would be the powerbrokers. Who knows? In the not too distant future an Englishman, now an American citizen, might be elected President.'

'You always were very persuasive.'

'Emotionally,' Morgenstern leaned forward again, 'this merger would appeal to many Americans. They would feel they were coming home again. After all, the Republic originated in England, when the Pilgrim Fathers sailed across the Atlantic.'

Morgenstern refilled his liqueur glass with more Grand Marnier after topping up Tweed's Cointreau. He drank half of what he had poured, then continued, his energy undiminished.

'If you allowed yourselves to be dragged into the doomed federation of Europe you would be nobody, out-voted on every issue. And who would you be sitting with? Old enemies. Long ago you destroyed the Armada sent against you by Philip of Spain. One of your greatest generals, Marlborough, checkmated the power of Louis XIV of France in a series of military victories. You fought and defeated the Kaiser – and Adolf Hitler.'

'The dinner was excellent,' Tweed said suddenly. He suspected the chef was French. 'Thank you for a memorable evening.'

'You're not going? You haven't given me your reaction to all I've told you.'

'You propose to turn Britain into the fifty-first state of the United States . . .'

18

'They've all gone home,' said George when he opened the door at Park Crescent. He was blinking as though he'd just had a nap. 'Only Paula is still here.'

When Tweed opened the door to his office Paula was sitting behind Monica's desk. She checked her watch, looked at him as she made her comment.

'I persuaded Monica to go home, get some sleep. She's worked like a Trojan in building up her profiles. I said I'd wait to take calls. You've been a long time. It must have been a very long dinner with Morgenstern.'

'After I left Jefferson I got a taxi to take me to Downing Street. I had a chat with the PM, who is also working all hours.'

Removing his coat, he sat behind his desk. He poured water from a carafe into a glass that Monica, he felt sure, had left him.

'Roy Buchanan phoned,' Paula reported. 'When I told him I'd no idea when you'd be back he told me instead. He's heard a positive rumour that the American syndicate has bid for two leading daily newspapers, a key TV station and two important radio outfits. The money offered is so huge he's sure that a majority of shareholders will accept.'

'I know. The PM told me. It's a fact, not a rumour.'

'We're letting them get away with it?'

'The PM is still cleverly playing it softly, softly. He's allowing the bids to be made, then he'll refer them to the Monopolies and Mergers Commission. Meantime, he's going to watch how the Americans handle their new propaganda machine.'

'That is clever. How did you get on with Morgenstern – or shouldn't I ask?'

Paula was talking as much as she could. Anything to cover up her nagging doubts about Tweed.

'Paula,' he began, his expression grave, 'what I am about to tell you is for your ears only. I may tell Newman and Marler later – and anyone else if I feel they should know. Has this room been checked for bugs recently?'

'Only an hour ago. Harry Butler came in, checked everywhere – then he told me it was clean.'

'This is going to take awhile. I'm recalling everything which Morgenstern said to me . . .'

Paula found her confidence in him flooding back as he recited word for word the entire conversation over dinner. He ended by clenching his fist, banging it on his desk.

'Now you have the lot. Except I now believe the Americans are operating at two different levels.'

'What does that mean?'

'One is the diplomatic level. Morgenstern handles that. I'm certain he was telling me the truth when he vehemently would not believe any of his people could be involved in the bomb in Oxford Street. They're concealing the other level from him – knowing such a man would never go along with it.'

'And the other level?'

'The Charlie–Ronstadt level – the thugs and killers whose job is to destabilize Britain. I'm convinced now the two levels are operating in watertight compartments. One doesn't know the other exists. Someone – probably Charlie – is being diabolically clever. They're using every dirty method in the book – intimidation, bribery, mass murder, you name it. The object is to bring Britain to its knees, then the proposal that we merge with the US will seem attractive. We may see an FBI team arriving, "to clear up the mess".'

'Would the PM accept them coming?'

'I just don't know. Incidentally, when I was with the PM I suggested he take action in case they use logic bombs.'

'What on earth are they?' Paula wondered.

'New American expression. It covers advanced techniques for closing down phone communications and power supplies inside a country they want to destabilize. Imagine the breakdown if we couldn't contact anyone, if we had no power for heat and for lighting in present weather conditions. They could also insert misleading information into our computers. Hence the phrase, logic bombs. Logic would vanish.'

'Can't anything be done to stop them?'

'It can, provided we prepare for such an onslaught in advance. The PM has ordered troops to guard key exchanges in London – keeping out of sight. He's shutting down vital computers, fax machines. From now on communication is by a troop of army couriers on motorcycles.'

'That wouldn't be your idea?'

'Well, the PM and I did discuss the problem.'

'And we're still going to Basle tomorrow by early flight?'

'We most certainly are.'

'It will be interesting staying at the Three Kings Hotel – we stayed there once before. Remember?'

'Of course I do. Intriguing that Sharon and Denise are also staying there. I'd like another talk with Sharon.'

'I'm looking forward to this trip,' Paula mused.

'Maybe you shouldn't. My sixth sense tells me we're walking into an inferno.'

Tweed, Paula and Newman boarded the early morning flight to Basle. They were escorted to the plane by Jim

Corcoran, a friendly man in his late thirties. Later the other passengers took their seats. The plane was three-quarters empty and Tweed gave Paula the window seat, with himself alongside her. Behind them Newman occupied one of the two seats on his own. Even though no other passengers were near them, he was protecting the privacy of Tweed and Paula so they could talk freely.

Tweed was clutching an executive case which he kept in his lap. The plane was flying over France, heading for Germany where the pilot would turn south up the invisible Rhine. They both accepted the offer of drinks and Paula teased Tweed.

'You're getting to be a regular toper. Drinking on top of all that wine you told me you consumed last night.'

'You know I can turn it on and off like a tap. Like to see what I have inside this case?'

'I did wonder.'

Glancing over his shoulder, making sure the stewardess was busy at the rear of the plane, Tweed unlocked the case, raised the lid. Paula stared. It was neatly stacked with packages of one-hundred-dollar bills. He must have transferred the bills from the old briefcase, Paula thought.

'Should be enough to pay the hotel bill,' Tweed joked.

'I'll say. At a guess there must be a hundred thousand dollars you're carrying.'

'Nearer two hundred thousand.' He closed the lid, relocked the case. 'They're for Keith Kent, who is meeting our flight at Basle.'

'The brilliant money tracer. Why does he need them?'

'To pay into a certain account at the Zürcher Kredit Bank in Basle. No idea how he's going to do it, but he's going to manipulate the transaction so the millions of dollars paid in from Washington get lost in the system. That should help to stir things up a bit for starters.'

'They'll go berserk!'

'And that might cause them to make a big mistake. Doesn't look very wonderful out of your window.'

Paula felt a sensation of enormous relief now she knew what the huge sum of dollars was intended for. This was followed by a feeling of guilt that she could ever have doubted the integrity of Tweed.

She looked out of the window. Ever since they had left Heathrow there had been nothing but sullen dark overcast below them. It seemed even denser, the closer they approached Basle.

'I suppose that was one reason why you got Jim Corcoran to bypass most controls – all that money.'

'It was *the* reason. The case was specially designed some time ago at my suggestion by the boffins in the basement at Park Crescent. It looks normal but it hasn't a hint of metal in its construction. Plastic to look like metal was used. You noticed I carried it through the detector and there wasn't a hint of a ping. Because Jim was with us they didn't even ask me to open it. We've begun to descend.'

Five minutes later they broke through the overcast. Paula looked down at the ground and sighed heavily.

'Something wrong?' Tweed asked.

'There's a covering of snow, of all things. I didn't think Basle ever had snow.'

'It rarely does. It looks much heavier over there in Germany. That huge uplifted hump is the Black Forest . . .'

Tweed had asked Monica to arrange for two hire cars to wait for their arrival. Basle still had a very small, cosy airport, unlike Geneva and Zurich where once-compact airports had expanded into major terminals. Keith Kent was waiting for them when they walked outside.

'Welcome to Switzerland. The locals keep saying they

never get snow and are very indignant. Is it in that executive case, Tweed?'

'It is,' Tweed assured him, handing over the case. 'So how long before millions of American dollars vanish into thin air?'

'About a couple of hours from now.'

Keith Kent was of medium height, slim, clean-shaven, with a sharp-featured face and shrewd dark eyes. He had a ready smile and was dressed in a dark suit under a smart overcoat. Anyone who met him immediately had the impression of a businessman, probably the director of a firm.

'Don't wish to seem inhospitable,' he said, 'but I want to get on with this. Monica told me you were at the Three Kings. I'll come and see you there. Have a quiet stay.'

'I suspect,' Tweed told him, 'it will be anything but quiet.'

'Better watch my back, then.'

'And your front,' warned Newman, who had joined them. 'I'll drive one of the cars if you, Tweed, will take the other with Paula. Do we officially know each other at the hotel?'

'No point in pretending we don't – not with Sharon and Denise staying there.'

It took them only about fifteen minutes to reach their hotel. The first part of the journey was through open flat countryside, coated white. Then they started to enter the ancient city.

'I love this place,' Paula said. 'It's so very old. And it has narrow winding streets and alleys. And if I remember rightly, secret squares surrounded by massive buildings ages old.'

'You remember rightly,' Tweed agreed, behind the wheel.

Old stone buildings loomed on either side as they

183

drew near the Three Kings. On her left Paula caught glimpses of the Rhine at the end of short side streets. They parked in front of the hotel as Newman pulled up behind them. Tweed asked the doorman to have the cars parked as nearby as possible.

The first person he met as he entered was Sharon Mandeville.

'Are you following me?' Sharon asked with a smile.

'Hardly, since I thought you were still in London,' Tweed lied. 'I could hardly have hoped for such a pleasant surprise.'

'Wow!' said Newman. 'Great to see you again so soon.' He kissed her on the cheek. 'What brings you to Basle?'

'I have Swiss friends who invited me over. I grabbed at the chance to get away from the Embassy. I don't like some of the people there.'

'I'm forgetting my manners,' Tweed interjected. 'Sharon, this is Paula, my assistant. Paula, meet Sharon.'

'Hi there.' Sharon shook hands with Paula, smiling warmly. 'You have a wonderful boss to work for.'

'I think so,' replied Paula in a neutral tone.

'I'd better leave the three of you to register, get settled in your rooms. Maybe we could all have a drink before lunch. Oh, why did you say you were here, Tweed?'

'I didn't. I'm investigating the disappearance of one of my staff. The last I heard from him was when he called me from Basle.'

'Don't forget my offer for us to have a drink together . . .'

Newman had been studying her. As usual she was expensively and tastefully dressed. She wore a red two-piece suit with a Chanel scarf round her neck. She turned back as she was walking away.

'Isn't the weather hideous? I hear several roads in Germany are closed to traffic. Wrap up well if you go out.'

While Tweed was registering, Paula looked round the comfortable and spacious lobby, which she remembered. Towards the far end small tables were scattered and close to them were cosy armchairs and couches. The atmosphere was of quiet but not ostentatious luxury. The porter had taken their bags and they travelled up together in the small lift.

'I'm on the first floor,' Tweed said as the lift stopped.

'Bob and I have rooms on the second floor,' Paula said. 'I did hear your room number.'

'Come and see me later . . .'

Tweed had a large, well-appointed room which overlooked the Rhine. He unpacked first, using one cupboard and only a few drawers. It made repacking easier. Then he wandered over to the window. A few minutes later he heard a tapping on his door. Opening it, he let Paula into his room, returned to the window.

'Both Bob and I have rooms looking down on the river. I'd forgotten how wide it is, even at Basle, hundreds of miles from where it flows into the sea.'

She became aware he wasn't listening. Tweed was staring fixedly at an immense barge gliding upstream on his side of the river. He remembered that traffic on the Rhine had to use this side of the river when moving upstream, the far side when it was on its way downriver. The barge was so huge it seemed to take a minute to pass the window before passing under the arch of a big bridge to their right. At the stern a small car was parked.

'You're thinking about something,' she said.

'Just fascinated by the river. It's started to snow again – I suggest we stay inside the hotel, at least until Marler gets here from Geneva.'

'Suits me. I'm tired. I seem to have been on the go

nonstop recently. Do you mind if I have a bath and then take a nap?'

'I think you should. Oh, what did you think of Sharon?'

'On the surface she's elegant, reserved but amiable.'

'On the surface?'

'She struck me as being an enigma. Hard to sum up.'

The phone rang. Paula stayed by the window as Tweed went to answer it. He spoke in a very quiet voice and Paula made no attempt to listen. When he put the phone down she made for the door, deliberately not asking who had called.

'That was Arthur Beck, Chief of the Federal Police, as you know.'

'I've always liked Beck. And you call him the most able police chief in Western Europe.'

'He sounded grim. He's flying here to see me from his headquarters in Berne. He ordered me not to leave the hotel until he's arrived. He's never done that before.'

'You did say you might be walking into an inferno. I thought at the time you were exaggerating.'

'Maybe I was underestimating the danger.'

'How on earth did Beck trace us here so quickly?'

'He phoned Monica. Normally she wouldn't have told even him where I was. I'm going to ask him how he persuaded her. And it will be a few hours before he gets here.'

'Then I'm off to have my bath and some catch-up sleep.'

'Paula, under no circumstances are you to leave the hotel. That is an order.'

Newman, in cheerful mood, arrived soon after Paula had left. He followed Tweed over to the window. The first barge, which Paula had watched with Tweed, had been a bulk carrier. The new monster they stared down at was a tanker. Newman whistled.

'That's a huge job to travel as far as this up the Rhine. I asked the receptionist how far up they can go. Apparently there's a harbour where they dock on the outskirts of Basle, which *is* as far as they can go.'

'There's also another harbour further down to the left of us. That's where three countries meet – Switzerland, Germany and France. Better sit down. I've something to tell you.'

Newman listened while Tweed gave him the gist of the phone call from Beck. He whistled again. When he glanced at Tweed he thought his chief had never looked more serious. Tweed stifled a yawn, flexed his fingers.

'He didn't give you any hint as to what it was all about?' Newman asked.

'Not a dickey bird. I can't imagine what can have stirred up Beck to the extent of his flying from Berne to see me. On top of that he ordered me not to leave the hotel. Which reminds me. You're not to leave this hotel until we've heard what has so disturbed Beck. That is my order.'

'I'd better tell Paula . . .'

'I've already told her. Best to leave her alone. She's having a bath and then some sleep. I wouldn't mind some myself.'

'Oh, I have some news. Denise Chatel is staying here too. I was out of sight when I saw two people coming out of the lift.'

'Marler told us she'd be here – along with Sharon. Have you been downstairs, chatting up the cool Sharon?'

'No. I asked at the reception desk. She'd told them she was going out to meet some friends. The Swiss people she mentioned, I expect. She should be warm enough. When we dined together at Santorini's she had a sable coat.'

'Well, she can afford it, so why not?'

Newman had experienced this mood of Tweed's before, when he appeared to be taking in everything said to him and made replies which seemed to confirm this impression. But Newman sensed that Tweed's brain was racing, checking over in his mind what had happened, linking up sequences of events, forming a pattern.

This was waiting time. Waiting for Marler to appear. Waiting for Beck to arrive. And normally, the lull before the storm broke. He realized Tweed had heard every word he had said when he asked his question.

'You did say two people came out of the lift when you were out of sight and saw Denise. Yet you also said Sharon had left the hotel to visit friends. What I'm wondering is, who was the second person who came out of the lift with Denise?'

'I've been keeping that for last as a blockbuster surprise.'

'Then surprise me.'

'And he's staying at this hotel. It was Ed Osborne.'

19

Newman shook Tweed gently. Waking up instantly, Tweed sat up on the bed. He had taken off his jacket and shoes, had loosened his tie before lying down under the duvet hours earlier. Newman, who had said he didn't feel sleepy, had sat in a chair, insisting on acting as a guard. Tweed stared out of the window into the dark.

'What time is it?'

'4.30 p.m.'

'Lord, I've never slept like that before.' He hurried into the bathroom for a cold wash and to brush his hair. 'I've just never slept like that before,' he repeated.

'Showed how much you needed it. You've been on the go for ages, like Paula. She only woke a short time ago. She'll be down here any minute. Reason I woke you is Marler has just arrived. He'll be up very soon.'

'That's better. Think I can face the world now.'

He emerged from the bathroom, his tie neat, wearing his jacket and shoes. He sat in a chair and poured some of the coffee Newman had ordered after waking him. He drank two cups one after the other, the first black, the second with a helping of milk. Someone knocked on the door and Newman opened it cautiously, then let Marler in. He was carrying two large heavy-looking holdalls.

'Sorry I've been so long. Decided it was safer to hire a car at Geneva and drive here – considering what's in these bags.'

'What is in them?' Newman asked.

'Tell you later. More important information to impart.'

There was a tapping at the door and Newman let in Paula. She looked fresh and energetic. Ready to start a new day, Tweed thought. She greeted Marler who said he'd tell her about his trip later. Sitting alongside Tweed on a couch, Paula put a hand to her ear to show she was listening.

'The enemy has arrived in Basle in force,' Marler announced.

'Just what we need,' Tweed said ironically. 'Where are they?'

'Tell it to you in my way. I drove into Basle and parked near Hauptbahnhof. I was going to go into the station to stock up on cigarettes. I was still sitting in my car when who should I see coming out of the Euler Hotel, a five-star job? Jake Ronstadt and Chuck Venacki. Recognized Venacki from the Paris photos. They crossed the street, disappeared into the Victoria, a smaller hotel. I waited.'

'How was Ronstadt dressed?' asked Tweed.

'In an astrakhan fur coat with a hat to match. Strode across the street as though he owned Basle. Minutes later he comes out of the Victoria, with six more thugs in tow. All snapped in the pics from Paris. The whole gang walks down to the Hilton and disappears inside. To the bar, would be my guess.'

'We have a spot of trouble,' Tweed said.

'A load of it, I'd say. Missed out a vital bit. When he came out of the Euler, Ronstadt paid a quick visit to get something from his parked white Citroën. When they'd all trooped into the Hilton I darted across, fixed a little gizmo my supplier of arms had given me. Attached it underneath the chassis of the Citroën. We could follow him now.'

'How could we do that?' Paula asked.

'Good question. I've a good answer. There's a tracking device I can attach to your car, Tweed. Another for you, Bob. Range of ten miles. Incredible.'

'Where did you get this stuff?' Newman enquired.

'My chum in Geneva who gave me weapons and grenades has gone into business on another front. Tracking devices.'

'Where's my Browning?' Paula wanted to know.

'Eager, isn't she?'

Opening one of the holdalls Marler produced a .32 Browning automatic and spare ammo, handed it to Paula. Newman held out his hand and Marler placed a .38 Smith & Wesson and extra ammo in it. He also provided Newman with a hip holster.

Newman immediately took off his jacket, strapped on the holster, checked the action of the empty revolver, loaded it, slid it inside the holster, put his jacket on again and buttoned it up. He looked down at the holdalls.

'What other little treasures did you buy?'

'Besides the tracking equipment, Walthers for Harry

and Pete when they arrive, grenades, and smoke bombs. He even had the type of trick grenade I threw at those four thugs off Regent Street just before the Ear was killed. Can't keep a secret these days. I thought the Park Crescent boffins had come up with something no one else had. Oh, and a dismantled Armalite rifle with sniper-scope for myself.'

'You haven't forgotten the Phantom, then? Hence the Armalite.'

'I haven't forgotten the Phantom,' Marler agreed in a monotone.

'Better get those holdalls out of sight,' Tweed suggested. 'Arthur Beck is on his way here. With some bad news.'

'I thought Marler had brought us enough bad news,' Newman commented.

'Just information,' Marler replied, picking up the holdalls. 'And now I think I'd better get back to my room and hide these away . . .'

'Well, at least Ronstadt and Co. don't know we're in the same city,' Tweed remarked.

'Be nice to keep it that way,' Paula agreed.

Tweed answered the phone, which had started ringing. When he ended the brief call he looked at the others.

'Marler left just in time. Beck is here. On his way up.'

Arthur Beck entered the room with a smile. He went to Paula and hugged her. There had always been a warm rapport between them. The smile disappeared as he took off his snow-flecked overcoat. Refusing Tweed's offer to have fresh coffee sent up, he sat down in an armchair. Beck was in his late forties, a man of medium height, well-built, with a trim moustache, his thick hair greying. He had a strong face and a hint of humour in his penetrating grey eyes.

191

'I'll get straight to it. I've been in touch with Lasalle of the French DST. He told me a small army of American gangster types passed through Paris on their way to London. Some by Eurostar, some by plane. He sent me a number of copies of photos taken of them – sent them by courier. I distributed them to officers at three airports here – Zurich, Geneva and Basle. Just in case. A number of them flew into Basle yesterday. I have these photos of those we spotted.' He took an envelope from his pocket, handed it to Tweed, who took out the prints, glanced at them.

'These are familiar faces, Arthur. René also contacted me – or rather, I phoned him. He sent me these pics. By chance we know where they are here. Some at the Euler, others at the Victoria.'

'You do keep up with what is happening in this nasty world.'

'It's likely to get nastier.'

'The frustration is I can't do anything about it. Officers at Basle airport informed me they all carried diplomatic passports. Washington is beginning to worry me. What *is* happening?'

'Briefly,' Tweed began, 'America is the superpower on this planet. They're well aware of this. Sometimes great power increases a lust for more of it. History tells us this – Napoleon and Hitler are two prime examples.'

'Britain could be in big trouble.'

'We are. It's possible, from information received, to coin a cliché, we may be able to clip their wings here. We're certainly going to try.'

'Any help I can give, I am available. I'll be staying on in Basle. Police headquarters here is just across the street. Spiegelgasse 6. I'll make it my temporary HQ. I notice, Newman, you have a bulge under your jacket.'

'I twisted a muscle, didn't I? Had to have it bandaged.'

'Do take care of that muscle,' Beck said with a dry smile. 'I must be going now. I rely on all of you to take care of Paula,' he said standing up, putting on his overcoat.

'Thank you. Actually Paula can take care of herself,' Paula responded with a smile.

'I'm sure she can.'

'He really had a wasted journey,' Newman remarked when Beck had gone.

'I don't agree,' Tweed objected. 'He now has a hint of what is really going on. And if we need him he's close by. He's a powerful ally. I'm going out now to a public phone box to call Monica. I don't want the call going through a hotel switchboard. Plus the fact that occasionally lines get crossed and someone inside the hotel, one of the guests, might listen in.'

'You'll have company,' Newman told him. 'No argument.'

Marler returned at that moment, knocking on the door. Newman held his Smith & Wesson behind his back until he unlocked the door, saw their visitor.

'Tweed wants to make a phone call outside,' he told Marler.

'Feeling like a breath of fresh air myself. I've fixed those direction finders in your cars. The doorman showed me where they were after I'd described both of you, told him when you arrived. You can see them later.'

'We'll have a quiet walk,' said Tweed, putting on his coat. 'Lucky they don't know we're here.'

'It's bitterly cold out,' the concierge warned them as they arrived in the lobby.

'We're used to it,' Tweed joked. 'We come from England.'

The lobby was otherwise deserted. Whatever guests

193

were in the hotel would be in the dining room. Marler walked through the revolving door first, stopped in the street, his eyes scanning in all directions. As Tweed, Paula and Newman followed him out he raised a hand to hold them back.

'Thought I saw a shadow disappear behind that corner.'

'Probably your imagination,' said Paula. 'Lord, it's icy cold. And mind your footing – the pavement is slippery.'

One of Basle's small green trams came into view. They heard its rumble as it disappeared, crossing the bridge. Tweed led the way, his hands in his pockets. The air hit them like a blow in the face. Their exposed skin began to freeze as soon as they left the hotel.

'We'll walk up almost to Market-platz,' Tweed told them. 'I recall a phone box in a side street. Lucky I thought to bring plenty of Swiss coins with me.'

Once the rumble of the tram had died away a heavy silence fell. It reminded Paula of the silence of Romney Marsh when she had paused before reaching the Bunker. There was no one about anywhere. The street they were walking up was lined on both sides with old stone buildings. Paula felt hemmed in. She stopped suddenly.

'I can hear footsteps.'

'It's your imagination,' Marler said, repeating what she had said to him a few minutes before.

'Are you sure?' asked Tweed, who respected her acute hearing.

They had all stopped, between the glow of street lamps. She looked back, saw nothing. Marler shrugged impatiently.

'Can you hear them now?'

'No. They've stopped now we have.'

'I want to get to that phone,' Tweed said.

With Newman ahead of them, Paula and Tweed

walked beside each other. Marler brought up the rear on his own. They reached the beginning of the large open market square with the Town Hall, elaborately decorated with the symbols of Swiss cantons, behind the huge open space which was the Market-platz. Marler hitched up the strap of the canvas bag he was carrying higher up his shoulder. They walked a short distance and Marler glanced back again. But he was watching for shadows, not listening for footsteps.

'We turn up this side street,' Tweed told them. 'It's the start of a very ancient part of Basle. And there's my phone box.'

Going inside the glass box, he extracted coins from his pocket, then at the right moment pressed numbers to call Park Crescent.

'Monica, Tweed here. I'm calling from a public phone. More secure . . .'

'I'm so glad to hear from you. Happenings. The Bomb Squad checked a key telephone exchange, found two huge bombs, made them harmless. Same thing at Mount Pleasant sorting office. But another bomb had been placed inside a major Knightsbridge store. Blew the first and second floors to smithereens. At least fifty dead and many injured. The number of casualties is rising. That's it.'

'Thank you. I'll keep in touch.'

Outside the box he told the others what Monica had reported. Paula, particularly, was shocked. She stared at Tweed and had trouble getting the words out.

'When is this horror going to end?'

'When we've finished them off. Let's get back to the hotel. I am so cold I feel like a snowman.'

They had reached the end of the side street, had walked a few paces back the way they had come, when Marler held up a hand. He spoke very quickly.

'The Umbrella Men are back. *Drop flat!*'

Too close for comfort a cluster of four black umbrellas, held low so they concealed their owners, were advancing towards them. For a second Paula was hypnotized by the weird spectacle – the way the dark cones moved towards her, the rims just not touching each other, the umbrellas held quite still, not wavering an inch.

She dropped beside her three companions, who were already flat on the pavement. Fascinated, terrified, as though watching a macabre stage performance, she saw the four umbrellas elevate as one, with martial precision, exposing the four men beneath them. Each wore a dark overcoat, held their umbrellas with their left hands. Their right hands dipped inside canvas bags similar to Marler's, but larger. The hands emerged with astonishing speed, holding machine-pistols. The barrels of the deadly weapons elevated, again as one, again with military precision, aiming at their targets lying on the pavement. Paula was struggling to extract her Browning, knowing it would be too late. She saw all this as though her vision had quickened.

As he fell, Marler had dived a hand inside his holdall, the flap open. His hand came out holding a grenade. Newman hissed out the words.

'That trick grenade won't work this time. It's probably the same lot we met before . . .'

Paula stiffened. She was waiting for the thud of bullets into her body when a fusillade hammered them. Marler lobbed his grenade over-arm. It sailed through the night air in an arc, landed amid the group of men under the umbrellas. There was a brief flash of light, a loud *crack!* as the grenade detonated.

Two of their attackers staggered backwards, hit the pavement with heavy thuds. Another one tried to stagger into the empty street, fell forward. The fourth man slumped against a wall, slid down it. Paula had felt vibrations from the detonation passing under her. She stared again. Three of the umbrellas had shattered into shards, chips of stone from the nearby building had been hurled across the street. The man who had slumped against the wall had fired a short burst as he collapsed sideways, but his weapon had been pointed upwards. The burst had shattered a street lamp, showering the body with fragments of glass. What remained of the Umbrella Men were four still bodies.

'We'd better get out of this,' Tweed snapped, jumping agilely to his feet, slipping on ice, recovering his balance. 'Police headquarters are in the next street. The buildings may have muffled the sound but we'll take no chances. We'll go back down the opposite side of the street.'

He was walking down the opposite pavement, Paula by his side, when Newman and Marler came up behind them. Marler glanced at his companion.

'That, as you'll now have gathered, was the real McCoy. Have faith in me.'

'You certainly saved our bacon,' Newman said with feeling.

Ahead of them, Paula grasped Tweed's arm. She nodded her head in the direction of the other side of the street. The thug who had collapsed over the pavement edge was almost invisible. His umbrella, the only one to remain intact, had fallen over his prone corpse. It looked as though he was taking a nap and had used the umbrella to shelter under.

'It's surreal,' Paula whispered.

Then she saw on a shop window they were passing a huge smear of blood. The temperature was so low it had congealed in the shape of a hand. She shuddered. Tweed hurried her back to the Three Kings. They paused outside to brush snow and dirt off their coats, then walked into the warmth of their hotel.

'Heavenly,' Paula said to herself.

The concierge came from behind his counter to press 'one' by the side of the lift. All four of them were just able to squeeze their way inside.

'We'll all go to my room. Have a drink,' said Tweed.

He poured wine from an ice bucket into four glasses. Before the others sat down they took off their coats. Tweed sat on a couch next to Marler, so they faced Paula and Newman on another couch. Tweed raised his glass.

'Here's to survival.'

'I'll drink to that,' said Paula with enthusiasm.

'I must apologize to one and all,' Tweed began. 'For being an idiot. I said something like, "It's lucky they don't know we're here." They do. Very significant.'

'You're not going to tell us why, of course,' Paula teased.

'I have other things on my mind.' He smiled to take the edge off ignoring her question. 'When Bob went to fetch his coat Keith Kent phoned me. He's coming to see us in the morning.'

'My tummy's rumbling,' Paula remarked.

'Bob,' Tweed requested, 'could you phone down and make sure they'll serve dinner for us? It's a bit late.' He drank some more of his wine. 'Well, that's four of them disposed of, thanks to Marler. A long way to go yet.'

'They'll serve dinner when they see us,' Newman reported, returning from the phone.

'Tweed,' Paula pointed out, 'you're still wearing your overcoat.'

'So I am. Mental concentration,' he explained, taking off the coat. 'I want us to get cracking tomorrow. I sense we have very little time left. Oh, Paula, could you tell us the three different names for this city?'

'I suppose I could,' she said, puzzled. 'first, Basle, which is the English version. Then Bâle . . .' She spelt it out. 'I just gave you the French version. Third, B-a-a-sel.

198

I have just pronounced the German version.' She spelt it out.

'B-a-a-sel,' repeated Tweed. 'Exactly. The German pronunciation. Sounds rather like Basil – especially the way Windermere pronounces his name in his high-falutin' voice.'

'What's the point?' asked Marler.

'*Basil . . . Schwarz*. Isn't that what you heard the Ear say as his last words?'

'Yes, it was.'

'You overlooked the fact that when a man knows he is dying, is desperate to get a message across to you, he's likely to revert to his natural language. Which was German. Poor Kurt was pointing his finger at this city. Which is the main reason we're here when I'd realized what he'd really tried to say.'

'But why use his real name? Schwarz?'

'For the same reason. He'd reverted to German. In that language *schwarz* means black. Hence the Schwarz-wald – the Black Forest. There was mention that the Americans had a secret base outside Basle. I think it's somewhere in the Black Forest. So our next job is to locate it – bearing in mind it's likely to be heavily protected.'

20

In the morning Marler was early down to breakfast. He had called on Tweed first, but his chief was studying a large map of the Black Forest. He told Marler to go down and he'd join him later. The dining room was almost empty at that early hour. Seated by herself at a table, Marler saw Denise Chatel.

'May I join you?' he suggested. 'Or if you're one of those people who prefer to breakfast alone I'll understand.'

'Please sit down, Alec. Sharon went out somewhere, said she'd be back later. And I do prefer company at this hour.'

'Then I'll join you.'

He ordered a full English breakfast. The pleasant waitress was pouring him coffee as he broke a roll and began eating. He was famished. Denise, he noted, had contented herself with coffee and croissants.

'Are you alert?' he asked quietly.

'You have news for me?' she reacted eagerly. 'If so, I want to hear it. I'm a lark, on top of everything as soon as I get out of bed.'

'It's rather grim.'

'Just tell me, please. All the details you have.'

She was dressed in a thick beige two-piece trouser suit with a poloneck. He thought she looked very smart. Her blue eyes were fixed on him and she stopped eating as he recounted what he had learned from Cord Dillon. There was still no one else in the dining room as he concluded and his bacon and eggs had just been put before him.

'I'm sorry,' he said, 'but there seems little doubt that it was cold-blooded murder. And it was covered up by Washington. Possibly on the orders of the mysterious Charlie. I must have given you a shock.'

'You haven't. It just confirms finally what I suspected. I wish I knew who Charlie was,' she said vehemently. 'I have heard his name mentioned just once at the Embassy.'

'Who mentioned it?'

'A very unpleasant-looking man. Someome told me he was called Jake Ronstadt. I was walking along a corridor in rubber-soled shoes when he came out of a

200

room with another man. I heard him say, "I told you. First I have to check it out with Charlie." Out of the corner of my eye I saw him stare at me but I kept on walking.'

'Any idea at all who he was referring to?'

'None at all. It's the only time I've heard the name. What made me remember it was the venomous look Ronstadt gave me as I passed him.'

'Well, have you any idea what Ronstadt's job is?'

'None at all. He was pointed out to me by a friend when we were in the Embassy canteen. My friend told me to keep well away from him. She'd heard he was dangerous. That's all I know about him.'

'I think I've upset you. You haven't eaten a thing since I started talking.'

'Don't worry, Alec.' She gave him a radiant smile. 'It's a kind of relief to know my suspicions were justified.' She began eating again. 'And thank you very much for finding out what really happened to them. I was very fond of my parents, especially of my father.'

'Does Sharon know I'm here?'

'No. I didn't even know until you walked in to the dining room. She doesn't know you exist. I'll keep it that way.'

'Please do. Has she any idea that Tweed is staying here?'

'Oh, yes. She mentioned to me she'd seen him arrive with Robert Newman.'

'Oh, of course. Tweed told me she'd been in the lobby when he arrived. Have you any idea how long Sharon plans to stay here?' Marler asked casually.

'None at all. I get on very well with her, but she's rather reserved. Very English, is how she strikes me. I hope you'll excuse me, I have to go now, get some work done. Maybe, if you're free one evening, we could have dinner together outside the hotel?'

'That is something I'd look forward to. Trouble is I'm pretty busy myself. Working on an investigation job with Tweed. If I get the chance I'll certainly contact you.'

'It's been lovely talking to you.' She took out a small notepad and scribbled on it, then tore out the sheet and handed it to him. 'That's my room number. I really do have to dash now . . .'

Marler was facing the exit. As Denise reached the door Tweed appeared on the other side, opened it for her. He smiled and Marler heard what he said.

'Good morning.'

He had spoken rather formally, as though his only contact with her had been when she had come to his office. Marler smiled to himself, recalling how he had seen Tweed leaving her flat in Belgrave Square.

'Newman will be joining us in a minute,' Tweed said as he sat down opposite Marler. 'Paula's coming too.' He lowered his voice. 'Sorry I've been awhile. Beck paid me a quick visit. Armed with the photos, he'd sent a couple of his men in a car to watch the Euler. Early this morning two of the thugs came out, got into a car and drove off. Beck's men followed them to the border. They drove on through the checkpoint along the autobahn into Germany.'

'Which leads to where?'

'A small town called Breisach, if you turn left off Autobahn 5. On the other hand, if you turn right you arrive in Freiburg.' He paused. 'That's the route into the Black Forest.'

'Pity we couldn't have followed them. But the tracking signal is under Ronstadt's car. You could be right about the Black Forest. Maybe we ought to take turns in driving up close to the Euler, standing watch on Ronstadt's car. Newman and I would be the best bet, taking pre-arranged watches.'

'I don't think so.' Tweed shook his head. He looked

up. Paula and Newman had entered the restaurant, came to join them. 'I've something to tell you while this place is quiet . . .'

Tweed then repeated what he'd told Marler about Beck's visit to him. He also told them about Marler's suggestion, that he had turned it down.

'Why?' asked Paula. 'If we're not careful we'll lose Ronstadt. Then we have no way of locating their base.'

'Yes, we have. Beck is very clever. He gave me this.' He took from his pocket a small mobile phone of a type Paula had never seen before. 'I vetoed Marler's suggestion because I'm sure we need a large force when we do locate that base. All of us, in fact.'

'So how on earth do we manage that?' Paula persisted.

'I said Beck was clever. He'd heard about the bomb outrages in London and he takes as savage a view of them as I do. He has arranged for a succession of his own men – in unmarked cars – to watch the Euler. The ones on duty will carry a mobile like this one. It's specially coded and can't be intercepted. The moment Ronstadt leaves in his car they'll inform Beck, who will immediately inform me.'

'We might still miss Ronstadt,' Paula objected.

'Wait, please, until I finish. If Ronstadt takes the same route as his two thugs did earlier, he'll have to pass through the checkpoint on the Swiss side before you drive through on to Autobahn 5. Beck will instantly phone the officer in charge of the checkpoint, giving him the number of the Citroën. He will stop Ronstadt.'

'Stop him? What's the good of that?' Paula wondered.

'You really are in an argumentative mood this morning,' Tweed chided her.

'Very sorry. Please continue.'

'As I said, the officer will stop Ronstadt at the checkpoint. He will take his time searching the car, explaining

203

that they conduct random searches for drugs. Briefly, he will delay him until we arrive. You and I, Paula, have to be in the lead car. I will be driving. As we approach the checkpoint you take out a cigarette and make a big fuss of lighting it. The checkpoint officer has a clear description of both of us – given to him by Beck.'

'This is clever of Beck,' Paula agreed. 'We'll have to stay out of sight of Ronstadt – that villain met both of us briefly at Goodfellows.'

'I think I can manage that. Marler, you'll follow in your car. Bob, you bring up the rear in your car. I wish Butler and Nield were with us. Butler could have travelled with Marler while Nield came with Bob . . .' He paused briefly. 'This investigation is going to take longer than I'd expected,' he said in a louder voice, sitting erect in his chair.

Paula glanced over her shoulder. Sharon Mandeville had entered the dining room. She headed straight for their table.

'I thought I could rely on you, Tweed,' she said in a quiet voice. 'Yesterday we were going to have drinks.'

'I'm so very sorry, Sharon,' Tweed responded, standing up. 'I was caught up in a business meeting I couldn't get away from.'

'You're forgiven. Thank you, Bob. Or am I interrupting?'

Newman had jumped up, brought her a chair which he placed next to Tweed's. When Sharon sat down she was facing Paula.

'I feel out-gunned,' Sharon said with a smile. 'So many men.'

'I'm here,' Paula reminded her. 'I'll give you moral support.'

'That's very sweet of you.'

'You look dressed magnificently,' said Newman. 'Ready to set the world on fire.'

He was referring to the smart red trouser suit she wore. She gave him a warm smile of appreciation, then frowned before she spoke.

'Talking about setting the world on fire, somebody tried to do just that last night to the American Embassy in London. Smoke and flames were pouring out of a window, the fire brigade was called, Grosvenor Square was in chaos.'

'How do you know this?' asked Tweed.

'I called the Embassy this morning. What is happening? I don't know.'

'Which part of the Embassy was set on fire?' Tweed enquired.

'The office next to the Security room on the first floor. My office is OK, thank Heaven. I'm glad I wasn't there.'

'So am I,' said Newman.

'Hi, everybody. Mind if I join the party?' a voice boomed behind Newman.

Tweed was looking up. He smiled ironically. The large figure of Ed Osborne had come into the dining room. Dragging a chair from another table, he placed it at the end, eased his bulk into it, clapped his large hands together, a grin on the outsize face above a bull neck.

'Great to see you guys again,' he said, looking at Paula and then Tweed. 'What brings you to this hick town?'

'First of all,' Newman rapped back, 'it's not a hick town. It is a more ancient and interesting city than you'll find in the whole of America.'

'Naughty.' Osborne slapped a hand against the wrist of the other hand. 'Keep your big mouth shut. Trouble is,' he went on, leaning forward, 'the mouth opens and it all hangs out. Coffee, *garçon*,' he demanded, addressing the waitress. 'PDQ. And since I guess you don't understand the lingo, that means pretty damned quick.'

'And for breakfast, sir?' she asked quietly.

'Just the coffee, honey. Didn't get that it was a girl at first,' he remarked as the waitress moved away. 'Her hair is trimmed so short.'

'Men don't wear skirts,' Paula snapped.

'They sure do – when they're transvest—' He broke off. 'Guess that's not a subject for breakfast.' He gazed at Paula. 'You enjoying a holiday out here?'

'We were. Until you arrived.'

'Great!' Osborne grinned broadly. 'I like a lady who answers back. You and I must get into a huddle soon as we can.'

'Don't go in for huddles,' Paula told him. 'And what are you doing in Basle anyway?'

'I get around. Why I am here?' He gave a belly laugh. 'Business, honey. Monkey business.'

Tweed pushed back his chair. Before he could stand, prior to leaving, Sharon leaned over, whispered in his ear.

'Now you won't forget we're having a drink together. Would noon in the bar behind us suit you?'

'Perfect,' Tweed whispered back.

'Hey!' Osborne boomed out. 'You two got a thing going together?'

'You'll excuse us,' Tweed said, standing up. 'We have an appointment to keep. We enjoyed your company, Mr Osborne.'

'Ed! I keep tellin' you, it's Ed . . .'

They were on their way out of the restaurant. Tweed had Paula by his side while Newman and Marler followed behind them. As the door to the restaurant closed behind them Paula exploded.

'What a coarse man!'

'Don't underestimate Osborne,' Tweed warned. 'Under that brash manner I suspect is a shrewd operator. Ruthless, too. I bet he could recite how all of us were dressed. His eyes were all over the place.'

'Well, he could do with a few lessons in how to dress. That loud jacket, striped shirt, flashy tie, dingy corduroy slacks. It was all wrong. Like his conversation. If you can call it that.'

'Can we all have a quiet word?' Marler had caught up with them. 'Maybe over there in that far corner?' he suggested.

'Since you want to,' Tweed agreed.

They sat in a circle round a small corner table in the lobby, well away from the reception counter. Marler was about to explain when he stared. Pete Nield had appeared from the direction of the lift. He fingered his moustache as he greeted them.

'Harry and I just got here from the airport.'

'Enter the Knife Man,' Marler commented.

'And what does that mean?' demanded Tweed.

'Pete has added to his talents. During the past month or two he's been practising knife-throwing,' Marler explained, keeping his voice down. 'He's become fantastic. He invited me to go with him to a low-down pub in London. They were playing darts and Pete bought drinks all round, then asked if he could use a knife instead of darts. Everyone thought he was a lunatic but let him have a go. He stood well back from the target, threw his knife six times. Result? Six bull's-eyes. I lost a packet. I'd bet him he couldn't do it from that distance.'

'Could come in useful,' Tweed commented. 'Now what were you going to tell us, Marler?'

'It's about the Ear. Poor Kurt. He gave me an address where I could meet him in Basle in an emergency. Drew a map.' He produced a folded sheet of paper from his pocket. 'As you'll see it's a five-minute walk from here – as long as you're good at climbing steps.'

'So what is your idea?'

'That we go there and check out this place. It's not

where he lived, wherever that might be. There might be a note left for me there.'

'Who is going?' asked Newman, studying the map.

'All of us,' said Tweed.

'Any thugs in Basle?' Nield enquired.

'The place is crawling with them. They appear to be based at the Euler with more at the Victoria. Two hotels close to the Hauptbahnhof.'

'I know where those hotels are. I came to Basle for you once before,' Nield said. 'I know the place pretty well. And after what you've told me I don't think it's a good idea you trooping up to this place *en masse*.' He took the map back from Newman.

'Then what do you suggest?' Tweed asked.

'I'm going up to have a quick look at this address by myself. I can be back in a few minutes. I'm off now. Harry will be down soon.'

Before Tweed could protest Nield, taking the map with him, had walked away. Prior to going through the revolving door he slipped on the coat he'd held over one arm. Then he was gone.

'Do you think that's a good idea?' Marler queried. 'I don't. I just hope he'll be all right. He's got the map, so we'll have to sit here and hope for the best.'

Even though it was morning it seemed like night to Nield as he headed along the pavement. The heavy overcast appeared to be almost touching the tops of the old buildings, making the atmosphere even bleaker. There was no one about. All the workers would be thankfully inside their centrally heated offices. Anyone who could would stay in their apartment. It was very quiet. The only sound was the crunch of a tram's wheels as they passed over ice.

Nield had turned left after leaving the hotel. The map

was in the breast pocket of his jacket now – having once seen it he knew where he was going. He passed the steps leading down to where, in summer, ships took tourists on short cruises up the Rhine, crossed the street, came to the entrance to the Rheinsprung, a steep street leading upwards for pedestrians and cyclists only. He knew that if he followed that eventually it would lead him to the Münster, a great feature of Basle overlooking the river from a considerable height. Instead, he was treading carefully on the icy slope, looking to his right. He saw what he was looking for very quickly.

A plate on a wall identified it as a *gässlein*, a narrow alley of endless steps leading up between two high vertical walls. The plate gave the full name, a trainload of German letters. Nield, skilled in speaking and reading German, translated it.

'Alley of the Eleven Thousand Virgins. Sounds hopeful,' he said to himself.

It was a stone staircase mounting upwards into the distance. Very dark, very lonely. Remembering to bring his coat from his room, he had forgotten his gloves. His fingers were beginning to tingle with the cold when he thrust them into his coat pockets. He started climbing his staircase to heaven.

Despite the icy surface of the worn steps he climbed steadily. One advantage of the eerie quiet was he would hear anyone who might be about. He counted as he climbed. It was sixty-eight steps to the top. He paused on the last step, listening, looking. A brand-new Yamaha motorcycle was perched against a wall. A BS registration number – Basle.

Nield knew he was gazing into Martins-platz, a small cobbled square enclosed by old buildings, hidden away from the city. He walked into the deserted but claustrophobic square. No sign of anyone. He knew the address he was looking for was just beyond where the motorcycle with the large saddle had been left. The heavy wooden door was closed, but when he turned the handle slowly it opened. Warmth flooded out to meet him. He pushed the door open slowly, soundlessly. The hinges were well oiled. A dim lamp illuminated the interior. He walked in a few paces and then stopped.

An old woman wearing a dark ankle-length dress sat in a chair, her grey hair tied back in a bun. An ape of a man had been holding a lighted cigarette close to her right eye. The ape was very big, very fat, clad in a black anorak, black slacks, a black beret on his melon-like head. He spun round, holding in his other hand a Magnum pistol, pointing it at Nield. The end of the muzzle seemed like the mouth of a cannon. Like so many fat men, the ape moved swiftly. Dropping the cigarette on the stone floor he leapt forward. The barrel of his weapon struck at Nield's head. He moved slightly so the barrel slid off the side of his face, but the force of the blow made him dizzy. The ape grasped him by the collar, threw him back with a vicious shove. He went backwards, dipped his head at the last moment so his shoulders took the impact of colliding with the stone wall. His legs gave way and he sank down, back resting against the wall.

He felt groggy, but was aware of the ape's hand feeling under his armpits, sliding down his sides, then down his legs, searching for a concealed weapon. Nield was not carrying a gun. Dimly, he saw the ape straighten up, his body enormous. He spat at Nield.

'Whoever you are, you can have the pleasure of watching me torture this stupid woman.' The accent was heavily American. 'I will then deal with you after she's talked – which she will.'

Nield tried to straighten up, sagged again. His vision was beginning to clear. He was in a square stone-walled room. The warmth came from an old ceramic wood-burning stove in a corner. The ape grinned, sharp teeth showing behind his thick lips. He lit a fresh cigarette, held it between his fingers, went over to the old woman, the burning end pointed towards her. On his way, he shoved the door closed.

21

Rage was growing like a fire inside Nield. It started the adrenalin flowing. The burning end of the cigarette was close to the old woman's eyeball. He eased himself a little higher up the wall. He dared not move much – it would attract the attention of the ape. His right hand crept up over his side. He leaned forward a few inches. His hand was behind his back. The ape became aware of movement. He turned round. In one hand he was still holding the huge gun.

Nield withdrew the stiletto-like knife from the sheath strapped round the top of his back. The stiletto flew across the room with great force and speed. It embedded itself in the throat of the ape. For a moment nothing happened. Then the ape dropped the cigarette, followed by the gun. One hand reached up to the knife, then fell to his side. He gurgled. Blood began to stream down his neck. His massive weight fell forward, his head and neck striking the stone floor. The hilt of the knife was rammed upwards, the point of the stiletto projected out of the back of his neck. He lay still.

Nield let out a deep breath of relief. The door opened. Marler came into the room, Walther automatic in his hand. He was followed by Tweed, Newman and Butler. Newman took in the situation in a glance, ran to help Nield who climbed shakily to his feet. He stiffened both his legs as Newman held on to him. He managed a weak smile.

'In the films they'd say, "What kept you?"'

'Who is this lady?' Tweed asked quietly, going to her.

'No idea.'

Tweed looked at her carefully. In her seventies, he estimated. Her face was lined, her hair was thinning. But her hazel eyes were clear as she looked back at him. He laid a gentle hand on her shoulder. He smiled sympathetically.

'It's all right now. Do you understand me?'

'I understand.'

'What's happened?' Tweed asked Nield.

Clearing his throat, Nield told them, in as few words as possible, his experience since reaching the top of the stone staircase. As he listened, Tweed bent down, checked the neck pulse of the body on the floor. He turned round, mouthed the word 'Dead' without saying it aloud.

'Good,' said Nield with grim satisfaction.

He then continued telling them what had happened up to the moment his knife had flown through the air like a dart. Marler whispered to him, 'Bull's-eye.'

'So,' Nield concluded, 'after the ape hits the floor you lot come charging in when you're not needed.' He grinned. 'I'm joking.'

'Could you tell me, please, who you are?' Tweed asked, turning back to the old woman, still sitting in the chair.

'You haven't said anything to me,' she told him in a clear voice.

'General Guisan,' Marler said suddenly.

'So, you are the right man,' the old lady replied. 'Kurt said you would come. You have come.'

'I come with bad news,' Marler said quietly.

'I know.' The old woman put a hand on her heart. 'I felt it here. Kurt, my husband, is dead.'

'I am sorry. He died very quickly.'

212

'I am Helga Irina,' she went on. 'Many years ago I was Russian. I met Kurt in the cheap bar. We fell in love then. He was clever man. He helps me to escape from Moscow. Terrible life. He takes me out to Finland. Secret route. To Helsinki. Then to West Germany. We come here, his home. We marry. He was the great man. He tell me if he loses his life his friend, the Englishman, comes. I know him if he says General Guisan. This KGB kind of man on floor follows Kurt. One day in a bar Kurt talks to his Swiss friend. This KGB man sees them. When Kurt goes his friend is made drunk by this man. Barman tells Kurt later. In his drink friend tells Kurt has wife, Irina. Me. Must be how torture man found me. The week later, after friend of Kurt is dragged from river, his head smashed.'

'Can I make sure you get home safely?' Tweed suggested. 'You have had a terrible time. I am sorry.'

'No!' Irina jumped up from the chair quickly, looked at Marler. 'Kurt tells me give the little black book to the Englishman who says General Guisan.'

She staggered as she began to walk. Tweed grasped her arm, helped her to walk. After a few paces her legs moved normally. She went to the wall to one side of the stove, her gnarled right hand reaching up to a section of the wall. Her fingers worked with surprising agility, Tweed noticed, as she slowly eased out a stone which appeared to be firmly embedded in the wall. She seemed to read Tweed's thoughts.

'I was seamstress in Russia. I am seamstress in Basle when Kurt has married me. It gives me good money to live with.'

She had released the oblong stone which Tweed took from her. Behind where the stone had rested was a cavity. Reaching inside, she brought out a small black book with a faded cover. She walked across the room, handed it to Marler. Behind her back Tweed took out his wallet, extracted ten one-thousand-franc Swiss bank-notes, put them in his coat pocket.

'Thank you,' said Marler, taking the notebook from her.

'That is what I would never give to the torture man – no matter what he does to me. Kurt says it has important information.'

'I must pay you the fee Kurt earned.'

'No! It is his gift for you.'

Staring at Marler, Tweed jerked his head towards the door. It was a gesture Marler grasped immediately.

'Now I will take you safely home,' Tweed said.

'It is not needed,' Irina protested. 'I know the way.'

'There may be more bad men outside. I will take you home,' insisted Tweed.

'The stove!' Irina turned, walked to it, bent down and turned something. 'Now it goes cool, then out.'

'We'll deal with that,' said Marler.

'Get out of here as soon as you can,' Tweed whispered to Newman. 'If the police arrive that dead body would take some explaining.'

'Will do . . .'

Irina had picked up her coat which lay in a heap behind the chair she had sat in. Marler presumed the thug had torn that off her, thrown it down before he began his foul work. He waited until Tweed had escorted Irina halfway across the square and then slipped outside. It was his job to shadow them, then keep out of view while he followed Irina to her home – to make sure she arrived there safely.

'You said at one moment your name was Helga Irina,' Tweed began. He was steering her mind into another direction, hoping it would help her to forget the dreadful ordeal she had suffered. 'Irina is Russian,' Tweed went on as they continued walking. 'Helga is German. I do not understand.'

'You are the boss? The Englishman's boss?'

'Yes, I am.'

'Thank you for what you save me from. I did not thank that nice young man who save me. Please give him my love.'

'I will do that.'

'You were asking me about Helga.' She had slipped her arm inside Tweed's, so he knew he had at last established her confidence in him. 'My mother was Russian,' she explained. 'She met a German prisoner-of-war who escaped from Stalin's gulag. They fell in love and were married secretly by a priest who had an underground church. So I am Irina for my mother, Helga for my father. They worked for the anti-Communist opposition. I was told by a friend they were trapped trying to escape from the meeting in a cellar. Both were shot dead. I was ten years old.'

What hellish lives some people have led, Tweed was thinking. They had crossed another deserted silent square and eventually walked into the Rheinsprung, high up and close to the Münster. Irina slipped her arm free of Tweed's and stopped. As she did so he pushed the folded banknotes into the pocket of her coat. She frowned, slid her hand inside the pocket, feeling what he had put there.

'This is a lot of money. Too much. The black book was a gift from Kurt. I leave you here, but I give back the money.'

Tweed moved away from her so she couldn't hand him anything. He spoke briefly before he began to make his way back down the Rheinsprung, knowing it would lead him to the hotel.

'Kurt earned a big fee. He gave us very valuable information. You cannot give back what Kurt earned. Take care . . .'

Then he was walking carefully down the steep

215

cobbled slope, wary of its icy surface. He knew that Marler would be somewhere close by, the Invisible Man making sure Irina reached her home safely. Arriving at the bottom, passing the Alley of the Eleven Thousand Virgins, he stopped as Newman appeared out of nowhere.

'She's on her way home,' Tweed told him. 'Marler is secretly following her to make certain she gets there.'

They were crossing the empty street, stepping over the tramlines, when Nield and Butler appeared, also out of nowhere. Tweed spoke rapidly before they entered the hotel.

'Pete, you did a great job, saving that poor lady from hell. Now, all of you, we must keep away from that area.' He took a notebook from his pocket, opened it at a certain page, handed it to Nield. 'Pete, that's the phone number of Beck's temporary headquarters. Could you call him, disguise your voice, give him the address? Tell him he'll find a corpse there. Be brief – so he can't trace where you're calling from.'

Entering the hotel, he met Paula who had just emerged from the lift. She lowered her voice.

'Keith Kent has arrived. He's in your room. He told me the Americans are going berserk.'

22

Paula unlocked the room door with the key Tweed had left with her. He had asked her to stay behind in case Kent arrived during his absence. They all followed her inside, with the exception of Nield, who said he was going to his room to make a phone call.

Keith Kent was sitting in an armchair. In his hand he nursed a glass of brandy. Introductions were not necessary. They all knew the visitor. Kent lifted his glass.

'With the compliments of Paula. Central heating to warm me up. At least, that's my excuse.'

'I hear you have news,' Tweed said, taking off his coat while the others did the same. Paula took them to hang them up. 'I'd like to hear it,' he said, occupying an armchair close to Kent.

'And I expect you'd all like some hot coffee,' said Paula as she picked up the phone without waiting for a reaction.

Keith Kent was the soul of relaxation. No matter how tense a situation might be, he never showed any sign of nerves. As usual, he was smartly dressed, clad in a dark blue suit, pale blue shirt and a Chanel tie with a motif of peacocks.

'I expect Paula has told you,' he began, 'that the Americans are in an uproar. Behaving as though they don't know what to do next. And don't like it.'

'How do you know all this, Keith?'

'This morning I called in at the Zürcher Kredit Bank again – to check that my transaction with the fortune in dollars had been completed. Turned out I didn't even have to speak to the teller. She was occupied – in a big way. A couple of Americans, one of them banging his ugly fist on the counter and shouting at her.'

'Could you describe him?'

'Not very tall. He has a very big head, clean-shaven, with a boxer's face – slit mouth, tough jaw. Very wide across the chest, tapers down to small feet. Hair brown. He glanced at me once – eyes hard as diamonds.'

'Jake Ronstadt,' Paula said to herself.

'Would he recognize you?' Tweed asked.

'Doubtful. I wore a scarf pulled up over my chin, a hat with the brim pulled down. Normal wear, considering the weather.'

'Go on.'

'As I said, he was shouting at the girl. "There was a

fortune in this account and now you show me a balance sheet with zero funds." Then he lowered his voice but I have acute hearing, as you know. He went on raving. "I want to see a friggin' director. I want to see him now. Got it?" That was when he started crashing his fist down on the counter. What the girl said next didn't help.'

'What did she say?'

'That there wasn't a director on the premises. They were away, holding an executive meeting. He really blew his top at that. "Get on that friggin' phone and tell a director to get back here before I bust this place to pieces. Millions and millions of dollars can't vanish, you stupid twist." That was when I quietly left the bank.'

'You said there were a couple of Americans. Can you describe the other one?'

'A tall thin man with a hard thin bony face. I heard the short one call him Vernon.'

'Sounds like that could be Vernon Kolkowski,' Newman interjected. 'I was shown photos of various thugs when I was in New York. The police captain said he was called the Thin Man, a notorious killer. They could never get him. If there were witnesses willing to testify they ended up floating down the Hudson River.'

'Sounds like a suitable candidate for the people we are up against,' Tweed commented.

'After I left the bank,' Kent went on, 'I sat in my parked car to see if anything else happened. It did. About five minutes later the short man with the big chest stormed out of the bank. He walked straight across the street. A car had to come to an emergency stop to avoid running him down. The American crashed his fist down on the car's bonnet, swore foully at the driver and went on to his car. Vernon followed more slowly, as though he didn't want to be too close to the other one. He had to dive into the car as it started moving off.'

'Paula told me the Americans had gone berserk. Probably your word.'

'It does mean,' Kent pointed out, 'that my conjuring trick has worked. Their millions have disappeared into thin air. Could take them weeks, even months, to trace them.'

'Thanks, Keith. You've really achieved something. Don't forget to send me a bill.'

'Oh, I'll bill you.' Keith finished off his brandy and grinned. 'Should I hang around a bit longer?'

'Yes. Where are you staying?'

'At the Hilton.'

'That's fortunate. The thugs are at the Euler, more at another hotel, the Victoria.'

'I'll show you out,' said Paula as Kent stood up. She fetched his coat. 'Yes, I'm coming down in the lift with you.'

'Let's keep in touch,' said Tweed. 'And thanks again . . .'

Less than a minute after they had left Nield arrived. He accepted Tweed's offer of coffee, settled himself on a couch next to Newman.

'I waited until Kent had left. I made the call a while ago. I had to slam down the phone when Beck tried to ask me questions. He was trying to keep me on the line while he had a trace put out.'

'You kept it brief, then,' Tweed said.

'Simply asked him to take down an address as soon as he came on the line. Then told him he'd find a body there. I had a silk handkerchief over the mouthpiece. Then Beck started to ask me something. I slammed the phone down. Couldn't have been on the line more than thirty seconds.'

'Good.' Tweed looked up as Paula let Marler into the room. 'I trust Irina got home safely – and without your being seen?'

'Of course she did.' Marler went across to a wall, leant against it. 'And of course she didn't see me.'

'What was that General Guisan business? I gathered it was a password.'

'Exactly that. Kurt once told me that if he went down and later I could get here, I should meet someone in that room. He said if I used "General Guisan" I'd get some valuable information.'

'General Guisan,' Tweed mused. 'The C-in-C of the Swiss armed forces during World War Two. He stopped the Nazis from invading Switzerland by clever threats.' He stopped speaking as the phone rang. Paula answered it. She put it down quickly.

'Beck is here. On his way up.'

Tweed braced himself for an aggressive Beck. Instead, the Swiss police chief came into the room with a quizzical expression. He accepted Tweed's offer to sit down, refused his offer of coffee. He gazed round at them all, one by one.

'All present and correct. I think that's the English phrase.'

'It is,' Tweed agreed.

'In case it's news,' Beck continued, his tone ironic, 'four corpses were found in a street near Market-platz early this morning. All Americans. All with diplomatic passports. All blown to kingdom come by a grenade.'

'Disturbing,' said Tweed.

'So, well before dawn, I phoned the Euler. The night receptionist knows me, recognized my voice. I asked him to read out a list of Americans staying there. Recent arrivals. Only one had a suite. I guessed he was the top man. A Jake Ronstadt.'

'We met the gentleman briefly in London.'

'So,' Beck went on, 'I asked to be put through to him.

220

He was not happy at being woken at that hour. He was even less happy when I gave him the news, read out the names of the deceased. He admitted they were members of his staff, as he put it. Had to. They were registered as staying there.'

'What was his exact reaction, Arthur?'

'Thunderous! Had I caught the villains who committed this foul crime? I hadn't? Why not? He was reporting this to the American Embassy in Berne. I told him it would take time, that I had only just begun the investigation. He swore at me. I asked him what their profession was.'

'That must have foxed him,' Tweed commented.

'It didn't. He repeated he was getting in touch with Berne. I said I thought that was his best move. He slammed the phone down on me.'

'He sounds to have been disconcerted.'

'He was in a towering rage. I had to phone him again a short time ago. Another body was discovered after I received an anonymous phone call. Wonder who that could have been? This corpse was in a ground-floor room near the top of the Alley of the Eleven Thousand Virgins. Had a knife through his throat. It had penetrated through the back of his thick neck.'

'Who was this one?' Tweed enquired.

'Another American. Another with a diplomatic passport. A Rick Sherman. Also registered as staying at the Euler.'

'How did Mr Ronstadt react to this further news?'

'He was apopoplectic. Raved on about how I was the Chief of Police and Basle was becoming the murder capital of Europe. He slammed the phone down on me before I could advise him to get in touch with his Embassy in Berne.'

'Things do seem to be warming up,' Tweed remarked.

'I know these men are gangsters,' Beck said, his tone grim. 'I still have to investigate.' He paused, looked at Newman and then at Butler, both of whom sat with their legs crossed. 'I wondered whether you had been outside this morning. I notice that Newman's shoes are drying out in this warmth, but the soles are still damp. As are Mr Butler's.'

'We went for a breath of fresh air along Blumenrain,' explained Tweed. 'Very fresh it was. I noticed your river police still have that boathouse under the lee of the promenade.'

'We have to watch the river. Along Blumenrain? Well, that is in the opposite direction from the Alley of the Eleven Thousand Virgins.' Beck stood up. 'Thank you for allowing me to question you.'

'Any time, Arthur,' Tweed replied, standing up. 'Any time.'

Paula was about to open the door when Beck turned back. He smiled at Tweed.

'Incidentally, whatever the plans of the Amerians were they seem to have put them on hold.'

'How do you mean?'

'Well, the car with two Americans which drove them through the checkpoint towards Freiburg – and possibly on to the Black Forest – has returned here. The officer at the checkpoint has told me he had the impression they have been recalled in quite a hurry. Take care of yourselves, everyone . . .'

When they were alone Tweed rubbed his hands. Paula poured him more coffee, then looked at him as she spoke.

'You look pleased with yourself.'

'Pleased, but not with myself – and not complacent. I

just knew Ronstadt would be checkmated, at least temporarily . . .'

'Knew?' queried Paula.

'Wrong word, my sixth sense told me.'

'And how did you know the boathouse for police launches is still there?' she asked. 'We never walked along Blumenrain.'

'If you lean out of my window, as I did when we arrived, you can see it. You're interrogating me,' he joked. He looked at Nield. 'Pete, I meant to ask you earlier. Did you think to do something about your fingerprints on the handle of that knife you threw at Sherman?'

'Naturally. It was a bit of a job with Sherman in that position, but I managed it.'

'While I gently lifted the corpse,' Butler added.

'Thank heavens for that,' Tweed told them. 'Then there was that brick Irina removed from the wall.'

'Which we carefully put back in place,' Newman confirmed.

'You seem to have thought of everything.'

'That is our job,' Newman remarked.

'I'm sure that sooner or later Ronstadt and his thugs will drive to the Black Forest – Kurt did tell us with his last word that the base is there. But recent events have thrown Mr Jake Ronstadt off balance – the loss of the money at the Zürcher Kredit, plus the loss of five of his men within hours. It does give us a breathing space.'

'I have something for you,' said Marler.

He handed to Tweed the small black book with a faded cover extracted from the cavity behind the brick. Tweed was about to examine its contents when Nield spoke.

'And I've got something for you. I'll fetch it from my room. Back in a minute.'

Tweed had started to read the brief notes in English

in the notebook when Nield returned. He handed Tweed a file. Tweed's mind flashed back to the American Embassy in London, when he had seen Jefferson Morgenstern placing a file into a safe which had looked like a bank vault. He looked up.

'Pete, is this what I think it is?'

'It's the file you asked us to grab from the safe inside the Security room at Grosvenor Square.'

'How on earth did you manage it. I thought afterwards I'd given you an impossible task.'

'Simple, really,' Nield explained. 'Most of it was down to Harry, expert locksmith and safe-cracker. We went in late evening by a door in a side street. Harry spotted it was equipped with a concealed alarm. Took him no time to deal with that, to open the door. There were still people in the building. We crept up a side staircase, got into the room next to Security, left a special firebomb with timer under the window, then Harry unlocked the door into Security . . .'

'Pete did act as lookout,' Butler added, 'so I could concentrate on my bit.'

'His bit involved opening the safe. Biggest job I've ever seen.'

'The more complex they try to make them,' Butler remarked, 'the easier they are to get into. I closed it after we'd got our hands on the file.'

'About that time the firebomb went off,' Nield continued. 'It gave off a lot of heat, which cracked the glass of the window. Important, that. The bomb contained a huge amount of smoke which flooded out of the window. We heard alarms going off, people rushing up and down the corridor outside.'

'How on earth did you get out?' asked Tweed.

'Simple. Opened the window when the fire brigade arrived – in no time at all. Saw them using a telescopic ladder to rescue a few people from another window. We waved like mad, they moved the ladder along, sent it up to us. Helped by a chap in a helmet, we climbed down the ladder, walked away. We wore charcoal black business suits – the type Americans pretending to be English are wearing at the moment. Walked to where we'd left our car, drove back to Park Crescent. Simple.'

'Nothing like as simple as you make it sound, I'm sure.'

Tweed opened the file. He sat back to read the first typed sheet. He read it again. Then he sat up straight.

'Oh, my God.'

'What is it?'

Paula had asked the question. She had rarely heard Tweed use the words he had just uttered. He sat rigid. He handed the file to her.

'Read that first sheet. The Americans are moving much faster with their operation than I'd anticipated. Which means we may have very little time left to stop them . . .'

The vast task force sailed on into the night, leaving behind Newport News, the naval base on the east coast of America. The centrepiece of the force, a main asset of the United States, was the gigantic 110,000-ton aircraft carrier *President*. The colossal ship had a crew of 6,500 men aboard, was armed with a devastating collection of nuclear missiles. Such ships do not put to sea without a fleet of powerful escorting vessels – distributed at a distance to port and starboard, way behind the stern, way ahead of the immense bow. No nation in the world could have mustered a fleet as advanced and numerous as the escorts.

Aboard one escort vessel was a unit of SEALs. These were naval men trained to be the toughest fighters on the planet. On the same vessel were new fast-moving amphibious craft which could carry the SEALs to land them on any beach, put them ashore so they could drive inland to destroy their target.

Perched on top of the endless deck of the aircraft carrier, reared the Island – the control tower, over forty feet high and composed of several different levels. The *President* was one of the jewels in the crown of American world power. The movements of this terrible weapon of war were controlled by Rear Admiral Joseph Honeywood. Six feet two tall, he was built like a quarterback and had a craggy face, which was why he was known throughout the US Navy as Crag. He sat relaxed in his chair at a lower level inside the Island. His eyes were blue, his hair dark, his movements slow and deliberate.

Outwardly he was a calm man. He had never been known to allow a crisis to disturb him. He issued orders tersely, in a quiet voice. He abhorred anyone showing excitement on the bridge and an offender would be demoted on the spot. Which is why it was surprising that he had been startled when he had opened his sealed orders. Not that anyone observing him would have known his reaction. He read them twice, then handed them to his Operations Officer.

'Say, Bill, you might like to take a look.'

It was the opening, brief paragraph which caused the officer to muster all his self-control not to show surprise. That paragraph was followed by route instructions, ordering them to steer clear of all shipping lanes and flight paths of commercial airliners. As the Rear Admiral had done, the officer read the opening paragraph twice.

Objective: Great Britain. The English Channel off Portsmouth.

'I reckon, Bill,' Crag said in an offhand way, 'it should take us no more than seven days to reach our objective.'

226

23

'It's time we killed some of Tweed's people.' Vernon grunted, then continued. 'Better still, wipe out all the m★★★★★★★★★★★★ with one bomb. Put them underground for good.'

'Or underwater,' Ronstadt said viciously. 'You've given me an idea.'

He had called a meeting in his suite. Only three people were present, Ronstadt, Vernon and Brad. Recently Ronstadt had promoted the two men to be his deputies. He played with his pack of cards. That had been a smart move, he was thinking. If he gave them a task which was dangerous they'd go for it, puffed up with pride by their new status. Which left him in the clear if anything went wrong.

'Underwater?' queried the squat Brad. 'Don't get it.'

'Wouldn't expect you to – otherwise, feller, you'd be sitting in my chair. Like this suite?' he asked suddenly.

'It's great, Jake,' Vernon said quickly.

'It's really great,' Brad agreed.

'Play your cards right and maybe – just maybe – you'll have a suite like this one. Play your cards,' he repeated, then held up his pack. 'See what I mean, dopes?'

'Sure, Jake,' they both said at the same time.

'It was a joke, morons,' Ronstadt snarled. 'Trouble with you guys is you ain't got no sense of humour. Remember what we pulled off outside Paris last year? You do? Amazing. Guess we could do the same thing here. We need a whisperer. Has to convince that bastard Tweed. Guess I know who could do it for us.'

Standing up, Ronstadt left the table, walked over to a window, gazed at the traffic outside the Euler. He was turning the idea over in his mind. He suddenly returned to the table, where his two deputies were waiting for him.

'I've got it, you guys. We use the bar here at the Euler. I hope you brought back the explosive when I recalled you from Höllental on my mobile. Höllental!' He grinned nastily. 'I've heard that's German for Hell's Valley. That's what we're going to give them. Hell.' His tone became savage. 'Tweed's mob has eliminated five of my men. I always pay back. And do I have to ask you again? Did you bring back the explosive?'

'We did,' Vernon said hastily. 'Enough to blow the Three Kings Hotel sky-high.'

'We'll need that kind of amount for this job. Give you details later. Stay in your rooms. Don't drink. Why are you still here? I have phone calls to make.'

'We're going now,' Vernon said, jumping up, followed by Brad.

Alone in the room, Ronstadt shuffled his cards, almost without realizing he was doing so. He'd had to tell his deputies about the five dead men – they'd soon notice they were missing. What he had kept to himself was the disaster at the Zürcher Kredit. He'd threatened Vernon with mayhem if he mentioned the scene he'd witnessed. In any case, what did Vernon know about money?

The one thing Ronstadt had hated doing was having to explain to Charlie what had happened. On top of that he'd had to ask Charlie to have more funds transmitted electronically from the US to the Zürcher Kredit. Charlie had given him a roasting.

Standing up again, he went back to the window. He'd better make that phone call, get the show on the road.

He grinned as he visualized what was going to happen this evening. He waved a hand behind the net curtain.

'Bye-bye, Mr Tweed . . .'

Paula stared with shock at the document, the typed sheet Tweed had passed to her. She could hardly believe what she had just read.

THE COMMONWEALTH OF BRITAIN.

Governor – Tweed.

Following Tweed's name was a list of other positions. One was Chief Medical Examiner. Each position had the name of a well-known Englishman or Englishwoman shown. She stared at Tweed as he spoke.

'Hand it round to everyone.'

'What does it mean?' she asked, passing the sheet to Newman. 'Why is the word Commonwealth used?'

'Because in America a number of states are called by that name. The Commonwealth of Virginia is one example. You're looking at a blueprint of Britain to be absorbed into the United States. If they pulled it off we'd be the fifty-first state.'

'You really think they're going to try and do this?'

'I know they are. Morgenstern practically said so when I had dinner with him. Gave me a lot of plausible reasons why they had to do it – from America's point of view. I just listened most of the time, to find out what they were up to. For some reason Jefferson has great faith in me. Hence my appointment to the top job – Governor.'

'You'd make a good one,' Newman commented.

'Except I'd slip abroad rather than have anything to do with their plan. When you've all seen that sheet you'll realize what a supreme effort we have to make to defeat them. And I have a horrible feeling we're up against a tight deadline.'

'So how do we hit them?' asked Marler, who had just read the sheet.

'In Kurt's black book he mentions a place called St Ursanne. I happen to know it. It's an attractive village, or small town, south of here, in Switzerland, the French-speaking part, and close to the border with France. That's where we're going this morning.'

'Why?' asked Paula.

'Because in his little book Kurt has written after St Ursanne the Hôtel d'Or, in La Ruelle. And a name, Juliette Leroy. He has scribbled after that General Guisan. I assume I have to use the same password when I meet Leroy as Marler used when he met Irina. I think Kurt Schwarz had great faith in women keeping secrets – providing he chose the right women.'

'He could make friends with women easily,' Paula said. 'I was very taken by his gentle personality when he had dinner at my flat.'

'Hold on,' said Marler. 'We all come with you? I think we should after what's happened. But what about the Black Forest? If Ronstadt and Co. take off for that area we won't be here to follow them.'

'Ronstadt isn't going anywhere at the moment. He's waiting for more funds to arrive after Keith's conjuring trick at the bank.'

'You sound as though you know,' Paula said.

'I'm betting on being right. I'll cover the Black Forest before we go, by phoning Beck. No, I'll pop across the road, hope he's in, and see him. I think I can persuade him to get two off-duty officers to stand by the check-point in an unmarked car. If Ronstadt leaves they can follow him. We have to find out what there is in St Ursanne. I have great faith in Kurt Schwarz.'

'When are you going to see Beck?' Newman asked.

'Now.'

'Then I'm coming with you.'

'I welcome your company. The rest of you get ready for this trip. Incidentally, we're going by train. Paula, find out train times to St Ursanne. We have to change at a place called Delémont.'

The phone rang, Paula answered it, asked the caller to hang on just a minute. She extended the phone to Marler.

'It's for you. Denise Chatel. She says she has urgent news. She wants to meet you immediately. She's in the hotel.'

'Ask her to go to my room. Give her the number. Tell her I'll be waiting for her . . .'

'I wonder why he gave her his name as Alec,' Paula remarked when Marler had gone. 'Good job he told us all.'

'Probably the first name that came into his head,' Tweed surmised. 'Bob, we'll wait until Marler gets back. I'm intrigued by what Denise calls urgent.'

'Come in, Denise,' Marler said at the open door of his room. 'I must say you look great in that outfit.'

She wore a navy blue trouser suit, a colourful scarf at her throat. She looked pleased at the compliment even though she dismissed it.

'It's just workaday clothes, but they're warm. I'm in a rush.'

'Well, at least you can sit down. Care for some coffee? I think it's probably still fairly hot.'

'No, thank you.' She was breathless, sat down in an armchair. Her small hands twisted in her lap. She was nervous. 'I can't really understand what I'm going to tell you, but it sounded threatening.'

'I'm a good listener.'

'I had a phone call in my room here a little while ago. It was from a man. I didn't recognize his voice. An

American. I'm not telling this very well. He said he had a message from Sharon who had had to leave in a hurry. She wanted to meet me immediately at the bar in the Hotel Euler. So I grabbed a cab and went there.'

'What sort of voice did the caller have?'

'Oh, very polite and smooth. He talked quickly. An educated voice. I should have asked his name but it all happened so quickly.'

'I understand. Do go on.'

'Outside here I was lucky. I grabbed a passing cab and it dropped me outside the Euler. I found the bar quickly. It was almost empty and there was no sign of Sharon. I ordered coffee and sat in a booth. I thought she'd been held up. Soon afterwards two men came in and sat in the booth behind me. Americans.'

'Ever seen them before?'

'No, never.'

'Can you describe them briefly?'

'Up to a point. They walked past where I was sitting to get to their booth. Funny pair. One was quite short, squat might be the right word. The other was very tall and thin. I didn't like the look of either of them.'

'What happened next?'

She was still tense, nervous. She unconsciously ran her fingers through her long dark hair.

'They ordered drinks. As soon as they'd been served they started talking quietly, but I could hear every word. The thin man said a meeting of everyone, including Charlie, had been arranged for later today. It would take place aboard a barge on the Rhine called the *Minotaur* . . .'

'Are you sure you got that name right?'

'Certain, Alec. *Minotaur*. Like the legend about the monster on Crete thousands of years ago. He said they'd cruise down to the harbour before dark, about four in the afternoon. They were meeting to work out a plan to destroy Tweed and his whole organization. That's why I used the word threatening. I just wouldn't like anything to happen to you, Alec.'

'I really appreciate your concern. Hear anything else?'

'Yes. Incidentally, the thin man is called Vernon. The squat man used his name once. He went on to say that at long last they'd meet the mysterious Charlie. Then they got up and left. I was lucky again outside the Euler. I grabbed a cab and came back here to tell you. Heaven knows what happened to Sharon.'

'Will you tell her about this experience of yours?'

'No, I won't. She has her own problems. The Swiss couple she goes to see are thinking of separating. She's known them for years. She's trying to persuade them to stay together while they give it some more thought.'

'I'm very grateful to you, Denise, for passing on this news.'

'I must go now. Sharon has given me a ton of backlog work she brought from London.' She had stood up, was near the door when Marler gave her a hug. She smiled. 'You take good care of yourself.'

'I've had a bit of experience at doing that.'

'Oh, I forgot something.' She paused before he had opened the door. 'The thin man said Jake was organizing the meeting on the *Minotaur* . . .'

'Quite a bit to tell you after listening to Denise,' Marler said after returning to Tweed's room.

'We have time,' said Paula. 'I phoned the station. We've just missed a train to Delémont. The next one is not departing for an hour.'

'We've still a lot to do,' warned Tweed. 'We have to see Beck before we leave. Paula phoned the Spiegelhof – Basle police HQ, just across the road. Beck is waiting until we arrive. Now, Marler, I'm listening.'

There was complete quiet in the room as Marler

recalled every word Denise had said to him. Tweed sat back in his chair, his eyes half-closed as he absorbed the information. Marler waved a hand when he had finished.

'Interesting that Charlie will be aboard that barge. And now we have even more to tell Beck,' Tweed remarked. 'You get on rather well with Denise, don't you, Marler?'

'She's a nice lady.'

Something in the way he'd said the words made Paula glance across at Marler. Was he falling for Denise? Then she also wondered about Newman – who seemed so enthusiastic about Sharon. Newman spoke just after the thoughts had passed through her mind. He addressed Marler.

'Could you repeat Denise's description of the man she heard called Vernon?'

'First, she called him very tall and thin. Later she referred to him simply as the thin man.'

'And she said his name was Vernon. I think we're encountering at a distance – which is safest – Vernon Kolkowski. He was the man in the Zürcher Kredit Kent described as accompanying Jake Ronstadt. We'd better watch out for him – I told you I saw his mug shot when I was in New York. He's already killed several times and got away with his murders.'

'Time to go and see Beck,' Tweed said briskly, standing up. 'I will take Bob with me. Paula, I've made a note of the train time you gave me, the one to St Ursanne, while Marler was out talking to Denise. Scribble those details down on a bit of paper and give it to Marler.' He looked round the room at Butler and Nield. 'You go with Paula and Marler so you're at the Hauptbahnhof in good time. It's a weird set-up – you go to the section known as the French station. Make sure you have your passports. Bob and I will get there as soon as we can – we have a lot to discuss with Beck, including that meeting on board that barge. The tram stop is near where we had the episode with the Umbrella Men. A No. 1 or a No. 8 will get you there.'

With his coat on Tweed paused at the door. He looked back at Marler.

'You called Denise Chatel a nice lady. You'd all better get it through your heads we can trust no one. No one at all.'

Jake Ronstadt, in his suite at the Euler, made a phone call to another room standing up. Ronstadt had always disliked sitting down – it made him restless. Ever since he was a kid in Hoboken, not the best district in New York, he liked to keep moving. When his number was answered he was cautious. Wouldn't do to have someone listening in to what he was going to say.

'That you, Leo?'

'Operator!' he snarled suddenly. 'Something wrong with this goddamn line.'

He waited for a reply. Nothing. The line was clear, safe.

'Leo, you have started sending down men in relays to watch the Three Kings Hotel?'

'Sure, boss. Got a man on duty now. Just about to drive down myself and take his place.'

'This is a smart mob we're watching. Would they spot the guy there now – or you?'

'No way. We're dressed as Swiss. We pretend to be waiting for a tram. There's a stop close to the hotel. Don't matter that we don't get aboard one. Looks like we're waiting for another one going to a different destination.'

'Sounds like you've got it tied up,' Ronstadt agreed reluctantly. 'Get on down there. You've all got mobiles. You see any of them, report back to me instanter. I gave you a description of Paula Grey and Tweed. You have pics of Newman from the reference library back in London. Get off the line. *Move!'*

24

Paula boarded the tram for the station first, followed by Nield and Butler. Butler chose a seat by himself, as though they didn't know each other, and Nield followed suit. The tram was made up of three green cars, joined to each other. It was only about a quarter full.

Marler was the last to mount the steps. He was checking the other passengers who had been waiting at the stop. They all seemed to be local Swiss, wearing heavy winter clothes. Ahead of him a moon-faced man made his way to the very back of the car. Marler decided to join Paula.

'What I can't understand,' she said as he settled beside her, 'is why Tweed thought it necessary to give the train details to you. I've got them.'

'He was being clever. When we get to the station you can buy tickets for yourself and Nield. I'll buy them for Butler and myself – in case any of the opposition are watching the Hauptbahnhof. Don't forget it's very close to the Euler.'

'Of course. I must be half asleep. I must get my wits about me.'

'You'll be all right if we run into a spot of trouble.'

'What's in that holdall on your shoulder?'

'A flask of coffee sticking out, oranges and other food. In case we have to picnic.'

'Heaven forbid. In this weather.'

Earlier Paula had stared straight ahead. Marler knew why – they had been passing the scene of the massacre

236

of the Umbrella Men. The tram swayed round corners, climbing all the time. Basle, Paula remembered, sloped down from the station until it reached the Rhine.

They stopped briefly at Bankverein. Looking out of the window she saw the Zürcher Kredit Bank. Then they were moving on.

She glanced back once at the other passengers. They all had a glazed look as they stared out. It must be even colder than they were used to, she thought. She looked again at Marler's canvas holdall.

'Is that all you've got inside there? Food and drink?'

'Well,' he drawled, lowering his voice as she had done, 'there is the odd weapon at the bottom, including a .32 Browning so you won't feel naked.'

'We may have to pass through French Customs. Let's hope you make it.'

'Another reason for separate tickets. If I don't you'll get through – and so will Tweed and Newman.'

'We're nearly there. You do think of everything.'

'I try.'

At the rear of the car the moon-faced man had slipped his phone out of his coat pocket. Well away from any other passengers, he whispered into it. He kept his message brief, then put his instrument away. It was Paula he had recognized – from the careful description Jake had given him.

'Who is it?' Ronstadt rapped out on his mobile.

'Leo Madison here . . .'

'How goes it, Moonhead?'

'I just said it was Leo here.'

'Heard you, Moonhead. Get to it. Any news from the Three Kings?'

'Paula Grey, Newman, Tweed and some other people

237

are leaving the French station for some burg called St Ursanne. They change on to a local train at a place called Delémont. I bought myself a ticket—'

'Hold it. Where's this friggin' place, St Whatever?'

'Down in the Jura. To the south. French-speaking Switzerland.'

'Got it.' Ronstadt had looked at the map of Switzerland spread out on a table. 'Tear up your ticket.'

'Do what?'

'You heard. On a train – two trains – they'll spot you. Get a cab to the airport. We have a chopper there, as you know. I'm calling the pilot. He'll fly you – he can follow that train, see them change at Delémont. You've got that fancy disguise?'

'With me. The telescopic stick is down my belt, with the dark glasses.'

'Use them when you track them to where they're going. My guess is they're meeting someone. Whoever it is, wipe them out. Got it?'

'The train leaves in five minutes—'

'Moonhead, tear up your friggin' ticket. Get to the airport. Last time you called you said you're on the tram with them. They're smart. They'll spot you. Grab a cab. For the airport. *Now!*'

'The name is Leo. Next time you call me Moonhead I'll headbutt you in your face. On my way. Airport—'

'You talk to me like that again you won't have any head!'

Ronstadt slammed the phone down. Moonhead had disconnected. 'I am going to kill that guy,' he said to himself. Moonhead was the one member of his team he couldn't tame. Then he remembered it was Moonhead who had once shot a baby in the back of the head. Ronstadt shuddered, called the pilot at the airport.

*

There was Passport Control before they passed through on to the platform of the French station, but no one behind the Customs counter, which was a relief to Marler. Tweed and Newman arrived to join the others minutes before the train was due to depart. Paula had given them their tickets, then the three of them ran. Nield and Butler had boarded the last coach, which was empty when they entered it. Marler had followed them and was leaning out of the window when Paula and her two companions jumped on to the train.

'That was a near-run thing,' Paula commented as the train moved off.

'As Wellington said about Waterloo,' Tweed replied.

Marler had continued leaning out of the window until the train was clear of the platform. As he sat down Tweed asked him what he had been looking for.

'I memorized the faces of all the passengers on the tram which brought us here. None of them has boarded this train.'

'So we've given them the slip,' said Paula.

'We *hope* we've given them the slip,' Tweed corrected her.

'You're never sure of anything,' she chided.

'Which is why I'm still alive.'

'Let's be positive,' she responded. 'How did you get on with Beck?'

'We made a lot of arrangements. We have to be back at police headquarters before four this afternoon. Beck was very helpful.'

'We should just make it, with a bit of luck,' she said after consulting a timetable.

'From the station at St Ursanne it's a good ten-minute walk down to the village.'

'Then we'll make it, with a lot of luck. I sense you're very anxious to meet this Juliette Leroy at the Hôtel d'Or.'

239

'I have great faith in Kurt Schwarz.'

'What was the outcome of your talk to Beck?'

'A very important decision concerning that barge, the *Minotaur*. I learned from Beck the vessel isn't used for transporting cargo any more. Some Swiss entrepreneur has converted it to a floating hotel for business conventions. It has conference rooms, a bar, a restaurant and all modern communication facilities. Today an American called Davidson phoned the owner, hired the *Minotaur* for a week.'

'Davidson?'

'I think Mr Davidson is really Jake Ronstadt. Beck has laid plans to follow the vessel, to board it from police launches, then to arrest everyone on board for interrogation. He's going to use the dead Umbrella Men as a lever.'

'How?' she wondered.

'They were all carrying guns. They were all staying at the Euler. That's enough for starters. He thinks he'll find the people at that meeting are also carrying weapons.'

'Pity we aren't going to see it happening.'

'We are. He's loaning us an unmarked launch. I asked him to let me have a loudhailer, which he did. I dashed back to the hotel with it, left it in my room before Bob and I raced up to the station in a taxi.'

'What do you want with a loudhailer?'

'Might come in useful . . .'

Tweed lapsed into a brooding silence and Paula looked out of the window. They had left Basle behind and it was a bright sunny day with a crystal-clear sky. She felt relieved to be away from the city. She liked Basle, had loved it the last time she had been there with Tweed, but this time she was depressed by the grim ancient buildings looming over her everywhere, like being inside a sinister fortress.

She decided her reaction was partly due to the weather – and to the events which had occurred there. The Umbrella Men, then Nield's description of the last-minute rescue of Irina, of the ghastly ape man who had come so close to torturing Irina. The train entered a deep gorge. On either side rose sheer walls of jagged limestone. Peering out, her face close to the window, she could just see the crests, tipped with snow. It was so warm inside the train they had all taken off outer clothes.

'We're in the Jura Mountains,' Tweed remarked. 'Nothing like the enormous heights of the Bernese Oberland but I'm fond of the Jura. You don't feel a million tons of rock is going to fall on you.'

The train emerged from the gorge and open fields stretched away into the distance. Here and there was an isolated wooden farmhouse, sometimes with a ramp at its side leading up to a storage barn attached to the house. They were seeing the Switzerland so liked by more sophisticated tourists.

'Looks like we got clean away from Ronstadt and his thugs,' remarked Newman.

'There aren't any on the train,' Marler agreed.

'I feel safe,' said Paula. 'At peace with the world. The sun is wonderful.'

She had just spoken when she saw the helicopter, flying on a course parallel to the train, about a quarter of a mile away. She stared at it, all her misgivings returning. Tweed caught her change of expression.

'It's probably just a traffic helicopter. The Swiss use them a lot.'

'That reminds me,' Paula told him. 'I forgot to tell you that when I was driving to the Bunker on Romney Marsh I heard a chopper. It was flying straight towards me. I was still some distance from the Bunker when I saw an open barn by the roadside. The chopper was temporarily hidden in a cloud so I drove inside the barn out of sight. I had to wait a while. The chopper came closer, sounded to be circling above the barn. Then it went away and I didn't see it again. I drove on to the Bunker.'

'You are wise to take precautions,' Tweed assured her. 'The Bunker has become our main operational centre. Before we left I sent down more personnel. There's only a skeleton staff left at Park Crescent. Howard agreed it was a good idea. He'll keep in touch with the Bunker.'

'Pretty drastic,' Paula commented. 'Why did you do it?'

'I think you all realize now we're up against the most powerful state on earth. America has limitless resources, vast sums of money. It took me a while to grasp that it was really planning on taking over Britain. The idea seemed so momentous. I'm convinced now – after my dinner with Morgenstern – and after reading that file Pete and Harry grabbed from the Embassy in Grosvenor Square. We can only stop them by superior cunning and a certain amount of luck. Don't look so serious, Paula. We're coming into Delémont, where we change trains. You're really going to like St Ursanne.'

Aboard the helicopter Leo Madison – or Moonhead, as Ronstadt sneeringly called him – grasped hold of the powerful binoculars hanging from a strap round his neck. He glanced at the pilot in the seat next to him.

'From now on we must change our flying tactics. Don't want to make the targets suspicious. Train's comin' in to Delémont. Can you hold us still while I check the platforms?'

The pilot slowed the machine, hovered. Through his binoculars Leo clearly saw Paula Grey, Tweed and Newman alight. Two more men appeared to be with them but they were strangers to him. In the lenses he could

242

see the faces of the trio he recognized. He saw them hurry across the platform, climb aboard a smaller train. He lowered his binoculars, waited until the little train started moving.

'Now you follow that little job. But do change your angle of flight.'

Again they had a coach to themselves. As the small train moved on into open country Paula had her eyes glued to the window. The scenery was superb, with large fields showing a froth of green sweeping up the slopes of high, hump-backed hills. She was looking out at a panorama as far as the eye could see – with here and there a lonely village of wooden houses clustered together and the tiny spire of a church. The helicopter had disappeared.

'You see,' Newman reassured her, 'that machine in the sky has gone.'

The next moment they entered a long tunnel. The wheels of the train made a quiet drumming sound. The lights had come on, Paula relaxed, looking forward to seeing the village Tweed had recalled with such enthusiasm. Her eyes closed and she almost fell asleep. Suddenly they emerged from the tunnel. She was alert instantly.

In the near distance the hills were higher, the slopes steeper. There were no villages anywhere. She saw a car driving along a road which seemed to follow the railway. They were climbing.

'It's back,' she said.

'What is?' Marler asked.

'The chopper. Can't you hear the beat-beat of its engine? I think it's flying directly above the train.'

'And I think you're right,' Marler agreed.

'I don't honestly see how they could have known where we are going,' Nield interjected.

'Pete has a point,' Tweed agreed.

He was anxious to reassure Paula. But he didn't believe what he said. He was beginning to think that it had been a good idea of Marler's to distribute weapons from his canvas satchel earlier. A chopper near Romney Marsh. Now another one out in the wilds of the Jura. The Americans, as he'd pointed out earlier, certainly had unlimited resources. He checked his watch. They were almost arriving at St Ursanne.

'We'll soon be there,' Tweed said. 'A good job it's such a perfect day. As I mentioned earlier, we have a good ten-minute trot along a road before we reach the village. Maybe fifteen minutes . . .'

The helicopter swung away from the train after climbing directly above it. By this tactic the pilot hoped the targets aboard the train would not think he had been following them. A minute before giving the pilot his instructions Leo had focused his binoculars on the small station – just one platform – the train was nearing. The signboard read St Ursanne.

'Let's get clear away from the train,' he began. 'See that small village in the distance?'

'Got it.'

'I want you to land me as close to it as you can – within close walking distance of the place. You should be able to drop me somewhere. Then wait until I return to take me back to Basle.'

'Will do.'

The chopper was already climbing vertically. The pilot became aware that his passenger was wriggling around a lot, that he had removed his safety belt. He had no time to look at him as he concentrated on his manoeuvre, then high in the sky swung away from the

244

railway. Now he was searching for a landing point. He saw one at the edge of the village.

'Here we go.'

'Try and land before the train stops at the station. I'll tell you when.'

'Will do.'

It was then that he glanced at his passenger and had a shock. He would never have recognized the man seated next to him as Leo.

25

'Back of beyond out here,' Tweed remarked as they alighted on the deserted platform.

'Nobody else has got off except us,' Paula observed.

'Who would? At this time of year? At this time of day?' Marler replied.

Tweed was hurrying. They followed him as he went down a ramp and started walking along a narrow road alongside the station. The road led steeply downhill with a high rock wall on one side. No traffic. They turned a bend and for a moment Tweed stopped and pointed.

'St Ursanne.'

Paula almost gasped with pleasure at the beauty of the scene in the sunlight. In the distance, where Tweed had pointed, way below them, an ancient village was huddled inside a valley, the old houses close together, with the spire of a church spearing up amid the dwellings which must have existed like this for centuries. It was idyllic. To their left, beyond the empty road, the ground fell steeply for quite a depth. At the bottom a small river meandered through meadows until it passed the edge of the village. Paula gestured down.

'Any idea which river that is?'

'The River Doubs,' Tweed told her. 'It figures in the famous and controversial novel, *Le Rouge et Le Noir – The Red and the Black*, by Stendhal. Now we must keep moving. I have a growing sense we have very little time left.'

Almost before he had finished speaking Tweed was hustling ahead down the road which had become even steeper, his legs moving like pistons. The others had to increase pace to keep up with him.

'Where's the fire?' called out Nield.

Tweed didn't reply. He seemed intent on reaching their destination in the shortest possible time. Lower down there was a pavement on the left side but he ignored it, keeping to the road. Paula caught up with him. If she had to move any faster she would be running. It was only when they were very close to the village, and old houses appeared to their right, each with plenty of land and perched on a slope, their entrances small gates in their garden walls positioned well below them, that Tweed stopped.

'We'll be cautious now,' he said as the others arrived.

'Well, at least the chopper has vanished,' Paula remarked. 'And I am wondering whether we ought to have phoned Juliette Leroy before coming all this distance.'

'That would have been a mistake. Like Irina, I think Leroy has to see us before she will talk.'

'Hear it?' Marler asked. 'Behind us?'

Tap . . . tap . . . tap . . .

It was a weird sound in the serene silence of the sunny afternoon. As one, they all turned to look back. A man was emerging from one of the gardens they had passed, his stick tapping on the stone steps leading down from the house. Arriving at the gate, he fumbled with the catch, opened it, came out slowly, closed the gate and came trudging slowly towards them.

Tap . . . tap . . . tap . . .

He wore an old coat, which Paula thought must be too heavy for a sunny day. But he was old. He wore a floppy brimmed Swiss hat and beneath it very dark glasses were perched on the bridge of his nose, his head bent. In his right hand he carried a white stick, ringed at intervals like a bamboo cane. It was tipped with a rubber at the end. He was tapping the stick against the edge of the pavement.

'Poor devil. He's blind,' Paula whispered.

'Better let him pass us,' Tweed suggested. 'We'll move out of his way.'

They crossed to the far side of the road and waited. The man with the dark glasses trudged on. They kept quiet as he passed them, seemingly unaware of their presence.

The handle of his white stick was curved like a shepherd's crook. Paula noticed it was flexible, moving in the hand which gripped it as the cane tapped. Immediately ahead of him was an ancient stone tower with an archway below it, high and wide enough to let a farm cart pass through. They watched the man raise his stick to tap at a side wall of the archway, then make his way through it.

'Must be a local,' Paula mused. 'Probably knows his way about the place better than we ever shall.'

They waited while the man tapped his way carefully along the street beyond. He was some distance away when he paused with his back to them. Taking an old pipe out of his pocket he half-turned, used the side of a lighter to tamp the bowl, then lit it. He resumed his slow progress away from them.

'Let's get on with it,' said Tweed.

Walking through the archway, Paula noticed the street ahead had a plate on the side of a wall. *Rue du 23 juin.* Tweed had stopped by her side, looking to his left.

Steps led up to the Hôtel La Couronne. The door at the top was closed.

'We might enquire here,' he suggested.

'I don't think so.'

Paula pointed to a small notice in the window near the door. It had a simple message. *Fermé*. Closed. Tweed shrugged. Paula was gazing down the main street, fascinated. On either side ancient houses, joined together, had tiled roofs at different heights. Like something out of a child's fairytale. The walls were covered with plaster, each house painted a contrasting muted colour – yellow, ochre, cream and other attractive tones.

'It's like Paradise,' she said. 'And so quiet. Apart from that blind man there's no one about anywhere. I wonder how we're going to find that street?'

'La Ruelle. Look at that plate on the wall over there. It's in this side street.' He peered down it. 'There's the Hôtel d'Or. Not twenty yards away.'

They walked down the street and Paula followed Tweed up stone steps to a landing on the first floor. It had a door with a window masked by net curtains. Tweed pressed a bell by the door's side. The door opened and a tall attractive slim woman in her fifties stood looking at them, as she quickly removed an apron.

'Do you speak English?' Tweed enquired.

'I do, Monsieur. How can I help you?'

'I have come from the late General Guisan, so to speak.'

'Please to come in.' She peered down the steps. Newman was waiting with the others, not wishing to crowd the flight of steps. 'Those are your friends?' she asked.

'You are Juliette Leroy?'

'I am.'

'Yes, they are my friends, but there are rather a lot of us.'

'Please to ask your friends to join you.'

They walked into a large room which was obviously a dining room with a bar at the back and the kitchen in the rear. The walls and ceiling were covered with pinewood, which gave the place a cosy atmosphere. Extending close to the kitchen area paintings of scenes in the Jura hung from hooks and with very heavy-looking gilt frames. One long table was laid for a meal with ten places but the other tables were bare of cloths.

'I have waited for you,' said Leroy. 'I have something for you from Albert.'

'Albert?' The surprise showed in Tweed's voice. 'My friend is called Kurt.'

'Please to excuse me. That was a little test. I will get it for you now.'

She hurried to the kitchen, hauled out a drawer full of cutlery. Balancing it on a work surface, she detached an envelope taped to the underneath. She handed it to Tweed.

'There you are. You will see Kurt signed it on the back with his Christian name. You are hungry?'

'We can't impose on your hospitality . . .'

'I ask if you are hungry.' Her blue-grey eyes held his and he had the impression of a forceful personality. At the same time she gave him a radiant smile. 'You like *Filets des Perches* with the *pomme frites*? Most Englishmen do. The table is already laid, as you see.'

'For someone else, I suspect, Mademoiselle.'

'I am a widow. The table is laid for a group of farmers – they will not be here until this evening. I have plenty of food for them and for you and your friends.'

Tweed glanced at his watch. He suddenly felt terribly hungry. And what she had offered was one of his favourite dishes.

'We have to leave in an hour at the latest – to catch a train back to Basle.'

'Then please sit down, everyone. You have plenty of time.'

She was already returning to the kitchen. She produced several pans, opened the large fridge-freezer. Everyone was sitting down when Paula noticed the entrance door had not been closed properly. She went to shut it and thought she caught sight of someone moving in the street.

Opening the door wider, she went out on to the landing. There was no sign of anyone. Nearby several narrow alleys led off the street. Must have been my imagination, she thought. She closed the door and sat next to Tweed at the table.

The plates of food, which smelt wonderful, were placed before them more quickly than Tweed had expected. Juliette sat down opposite him, noticing he had already broken some crusty bread. She smiled.

'You were hungry. You have started eating the bread.'

'It's some of the best bread I've ever tasted,' he answered honestly. 'This is very good of you, Madame Leroy.'

'I enjoy this.' She looked round the table at Newman, Nield, Butler and Marler, then at Paula. 'It gives me much pleasure to watch you eating. You are all most hungry.'

What a nice woman, Paula thought. She radiates good humour. She loves to see people having a good time. What a pity there aren't more like her in the world.

'I fear we must go now,' Tweed said a short while later. 'I don't want to but, as I said, we have to catch that train. Something important waits for us in Basle.'

They stood up from the table, their plates cleared of food. Then Tweed had a friendly argument when he insisted on paying. He became emphatic.

'You are running a business here. I must pay.'

'You come here for holiday with me. All who can. All, I hope.' She laughed. 'Then you pay through the nose. Is that correct?'

'Perfect English.' Tweed reluctantly put away his wallet. He could argue all night and she wouldn't give way. He made a gesture of resignation.

'Madame Leroy—'

'Juliette. Please.'

'Juliette, we will come here on holiday – to your beautiful village. To sample your superb cooking. You gave us a meal to remember.'

'Go and catch your train. And may God go with you.'

When they reached the archway under the ancient tower Paula paused and they waited for her. She was looking back at the beauty of St Ursanne. She wanted to be able to visualize the village later when they were gone. Then she forced herself to turn round and they started to hurry up the road which seemed steeper climbing it. They were halfway to the station when Newman stopped, swore under his breath.

'Something wrong?' asked Paula.

'I've left my gloves, my motoring gloves in the restaurant. I'm going back to get them. They're the ones you gave me for Christmas, Paula.'

'You'll miss the train,' Tweed warned.

'No, I won't. Remember, I came in the first ten in the London marathon.'

He began to hare off down the hill. Paula paused briefly to take one last look at St Ursanne. Soon the sun would drop behind a nearby mountain and the village would be swallowed up in shadows. At the moment she could see every detail in the crystal-clear light.

'It's a dream village,' she said as she resumed climbing upwards alongside Tweed. 'I'm looking forward to a wonderful holiday.'

'So am I,' Tweed agreed.

Behind them Newman, running, was about halfway to the old stone tower. His right foot slipped on a large stone and he sprawled full length. He took the worst of the impact on his forearms. When he began to get up he realized his right ankle was hurting. He sat up in the road, pushed down his socks, examined it. Wiggling his foot, he was relieved to realize he had neither broken nor sprained it. The only sign of his minor accident was a faint bruise.

He stood up, tested the foot. When he glanced back up the hill the others were tiny figures approaching the bend below the station. He was glad they hadn't seen him fall and he found he could move at a brisk pace back to St Ursanne.

Tap . . . tap . . . tap . . .

Juliette Leroy frowned as she heard the strange sound coming closer and closer, mounting the steps outside. She went to the door and opened it. A man with very dark glasses, holding a white stick, stood motionless.

'I am sorry to disturb you,' he said, his accent American. 'I am very thirsty. I have walked a long way. Could you give me a glass of water?'

'Of course. Please come in.'

Juliette was disappointed. She had just found a pair of gloves on a chair. She had hoped it was one of her new friends returning to collect them. At the same time she felt sorry for the blind man. He had looked so lonely. It must be awful to go through life like that.

Tap . . . tap . . . tap . . .

She turned and saw her visitor coming across the room, his stick guiding him between the tables. She remembered reading somewhere that the blind developed a keen sense of hearing. He must have picked up the sound of her footsteps walking across the floor to the kitchen.

With her back to him, she took a clean glass from a cupboard. She wiped it carefully on a clean cloth although it had been washed recently. Juliette was a stickler for all forms of hygiene. She turned off the tap when the glass was three-quarters full.

Behind her, Leo moved swiftly. Reversing his stick, he held it close to the tip. Elevating it, he hooked the flexible handle round her neck and throat, pressing a button which tightened the grip remorselessly. Juliette dropped the glass, tried to scream. Her air supply was cut off and she managed no more than a gurgle. The rubberized handle tightened. She reached up with both hands, trying to insert her fingers inside it. This was the moment when Leo jerked her backwards.

She toppled, hit the side of her head on the edge of a wooden working surface, sagged to the floor. Leo pressed the button again, releasing the grip of the handle. Bending over her unconscious form he checked her pulse. It beat steadily. He swore foully.

He glanced round, saw the heavy framed pictures hanging from the wall. Moving with great speed, he lifted one of the pictures, surprised at its weight. But that meant the hook left on the wall as he propped the picture against a cupboard was more than strong enough for his purpose.

From his pocket he pulled out a coil of thin strong rope – as strong as wire. Holding on to one end, which had a small wooden handle, pencil-thin, he whipped out the rope. The other end had a curved hook firmly attached. Bending down, he fashioned the first end into a loop with a hangman's knot. Slipping the loop over the unconscious woman's neck with the knot at the back, he used one strong arm to lift her. When he had her pushed close to the wall he slid the curved hook over the hook high up on the wall which had held the picture. Then he let go.

He had calculated the length of the rope perfectly. She was hanging with her feet well clear of the floor. That was when consciousness briefly returned to her. Leo stood back as her eyes opened, her heels thudded against the wall, then the rope tightened round her neck. The thudding of her heels ceased. Her eyes stared out of her head. She hung motionless.

Leo grabbed his stick, twisted a band round it, closed it with a telescopic motion, thrust it down inside a pocket. He opened the door slowly, peered out. No one anywhere.

He ran down the steps, along the street. Reaching the archway exit he paused, looked round it. He saw Newman running towards him, then collapse, stretched out in the road. He waited. He chose the moment when Newman glanced back up the road to dart across the arch, then down a side street opposte La Ruelle.

Above this part of St Ursanne a steep slope climbed behind the buildings. Its crest was topped with a dense palisade of leafless trees. The helicopter which had brought Leo had landed on a wide secluded plateau. From there he had found a way into a large garden of a house which appeared unoccupied. He knew he must not go back the same way. At the end of the street he found a footpath climbing up. It should not be difficult to find the plateau where the chopper was waiting to take him back to Basle airport.

26

Paula had the train door open. Newman hurtled up the ramp into the station, dived inside the coach, Paula shut the door as the train started moving. Newman, streams of sweat pouring down his face, sank into a corner seat, stared round. They were now all aboard.

Tweed sat opposite him, next to Marler. Butler and Nield were in seats on the other side of the central corridor. Once again they had the coach to themselves. Gradually Newman's breathing became normal. He took out a handkerchief, wiped his face and the handkerchief was sodden.

He had never run so fast in his life. Not even for the marathon. And all the way it had been uphill. Everyone was staring at him. He didn't like it. He'd sooner have been alone. Paula was the first to speak to him. Quietly.

'I see you got your gloves back.'

He looked down. His right hand was still clutching the motoring gloves he had picked up. He had forgotten about them. He wasn't really in the train carriage at all. In his mind he was back at the Hôtel d'Or in St Ursanne. He had been suspicious when he saw the door was half open. He had crept silently up the steps, his Smith & Wesson in his hand. When he had walked in, seen what was there, he had automatically closed the door behind him.

He could see it now vividly. Juliette's body hanging from the picture hook like a side of beef. Her body limp, her eyes wide open, lifeless. His training had asserted itself. He had forced himself to search the place first, checking to see if the killer was still there. Then, futilely, he had reached up and checked her neck pulse. She was

255

dead. Dead as anybody could be. He remembered thinking he should have checked her pulse first.

Holstering his gun, he had reached up again, one hand round her body, the other lifting off the hook. He was surprised at how light she had felt. Tenderly, he had placed her on a couch. Finding a knife in a kitchen drawer, he had carefully cut through the hangman's knot, removed the rope from round her neck, which was already swelling up.

He had thought of calling the local police. He had rejected the idea quickly. He could be held there for days. As a witness – more probably as a suspect. And there was work to do in Basle. Tweed needed him. That was when he had seen something lying on the floor under a table. He had picked it up, examined it for only a moment. Then he had known who the brutal killer was.

He had gone back briefly to the couch where she lay. He put a hand on her face. It had felt so cold. Then he had moved like a robot, using his handkerchief to wipe his prints off the handle of the knife, to open the door to the outside world, his gun by his side in his left hand. He hadn't thought he would see the murderer in the street but he had looked anyway. Nothing. Nobody.

He had checked his watch. He would never make the train. He had walked to the arch, had taken a deep breath, had begun running up the road beyond nonstop. His brain had dulled, all his concentration on running. Now the shock was receding, he was thinking clearly.

'Let's change seats, Paula,' he said in a normal voice. 'You like to look out of the window.'

They had changed seats but she hadn't looked out of the window. She was looking at him. Newman didn't realize that his complexion was ashen. Except for Tweed, the others were now being careful not to look at him. They were giving him time.

'You look washed out, Bob,' Tweed said casually. 'Has something happened?'

'You could say that.'

'I'd like to hear about it. When you're ready.'

Aware of Paula beside him, Newman phrased it carefully. He kept it simple. She had gone through enough already with her experience in Eagle Street – and then, more recently, the Umbrella Men.

'It's not good news, I'm afraid.'

'I didn't think it would be,' Tweed said in the same casual tone.

'It's about Juliette Leroy?' Paula whispered.

'When I got back I found her – strangled.'

'Oh, no . . .'

Paula tightened her lips. Newman had decided to give no details. They could come later. Any description now would be too horrific. He felt in the pocket of his coat. He had the attention of everyone now. He took the coat button he had picked up off the floor, handed it to Marler.

'Recognize that?'

'Can't say I do.'

'For once you slipped up.'

'I'm not with you,' said Marler.

'The killer walked past you before we went into St Ursanne. A fake blind man. Put on a clever show. As I think Tweed once said, we're up against professionals.'

'I'm still not with you,' Marler repeated.

'He wore an old coat with unusual buttons. They almost merged with his coat. But I noticed them because the symbol on them is unusual. Couldn't identify it at the time. Look at it again. Looks like the torch held up by the Statue of Liberty outside New York.'

'So it does.' Marler handed back the button. 'Where did you find it?'

'Under a chair in the room where we had a meal at

the Hôtel d'Or. There must have been a struggle. Or maybe the thread holding it was hanging loose.'

'And we saw him walk past us,' whispered Paula. 'And I thought, poor old thing.'

'Which was what you were intended to think,' Tweed remarked.

'Poor Juliette,' Paula went on. 'She was such a nice kind person. And I was looking forward to seeing her again. Dream village? It's turned into a nightmare.'

She stared out of the window. Sunlight still shone brilliantly on the greening landscape. She wasn't taking it in. Her mind had gone back to their lunch at the Hôtel d'Or. Tweed and Juliette had got on well together, their conversation easy. Maybe if they had returned for a holiday the two of them would have struck up a warm companionship. Years before, Tweed's wife had run off with a Greek shipping millionaire. He had never bothered to divorce her.

Tweed was also gazing out of the window, his expression pensive. The sunlight vanished. They had entered the tunnel. When they emerged from the other end Marler spoke.

'A second before the train left I thought I heard a chopper taking off.'

'You did,' agreed Newman.

'Probably the machine which brought the assassin, then flew him out afterwards.'

'That's what I thought,' Newman agreed again.

Arriving back at the Three Kings, Tweed followed Paula inside and stood stock-still. Standing by the reception desk was the last person in the world he expected to encounter. Sir Guy Strangeways.

'Hello, my good friend,' Strangeways greeted him. 'Small world.'

'As you say.'

'I'd appreciate a word with you. The writing room opposite the lift do you?'

'Just for a short time.'

As Strangeways disappeared into the room Tweed joined the others waiting for the lift. He kept his voice down.

'In half an hour's time we have to be in Beck's office across the street. You go on ahead when you're ready. I'll follow you. Guy has something on his mind.'

The door to the small room was closed. When Tweed opened it, shut it behind him, Strangeways was seated at a desk, writing furiously. There was no one else in the room as Sir Guy, hearing the door close, dropped his fountain pen, twisted round in his chair with a worried expression.

'Good of you to come so quickly. Please do sit down.'

'How did you know I was here?' Tweed demanded, still standing.

'That's hush-hush. Sorry, I gave my word.'

'What was it you wanted to see me about? I haven't much time.'

'I have problems.'

'We all have. What are yours, Guy?'

'Rupert, for one thing.' Strangeways grimaced. 'I told you – he owes that casino at Campione a packet. They're turning nasty. They even had the nerve to call me at Irongates.'

'So where is Rupert?'

'I do wish you'd sit down, Tweed.'

'I can only give you a few minutes just now.'

'Rupert's here. With me.'

'In this hotel?'

'Yes. Situation being what it is, thought I'd better keep him under my wing, so to speak.'

'He may sneak off,' Tweed warned. 'To borrow more money.'

'He's tried that back home. No one will give him a *sou*. Didn't know I was going to have to buy three tickets when we came out here.'

'So who is the third party?'

'Basil Windermere.'

'And has he a room in this hotel?' Tweed asked, suppressing his annoyance.

'He has. Not the sort of chap I want within a thousand miles of me, but I hadn't much choice. They're close friends. I know at one moment they'll be snarling at each other, then the next they're bosom pals. I thought Rupert needed someone of his own age to keep him company.'

'Where did you think I come in on this domestic problem?'

'Well . . .' Strangeways capped his pen, began twirling it between his fingers. 'I thought maybe Bob Newman could phone the boss at Campione, threaten to write an article exposing him.'

'Threaten? He doesn't know anything about the place.' Leaning on the edge of the desk, Tweed folded his arms. He stared down at the worried man.

'I don't think that's the real reason that you – somehow – found out where I was and hopped on a flight to see me.'

'There was something else.'

'I've got a couple of minutes left before I have to go.'

'Morgenstern called me, urged me to come and see him right away at the Embassy. You know what he's like – wants everything yesterday, if not sooner. I drove up for the meeting. His one theme, hammered away nonstop, was that the special relationship between Britain and America must be enormously strengthened. And quickly. He thinks you're a key element in the plan. He said he'd seen you once. Now he wants to see you again. I'm worried.'

'Why?'

'As you must know, recently American companies have taken over electricity companies in Britain. Also water supply companies. Soon they'll control our country. Do we resist – or do we go along with them?'

'Guy, you were in the Gulf War. Did you ever wonder whether to fight the enemy or to go along with him?'

'Put that way, we have no alternative. I'd still like to talk to you about what Jefferson Morgenstern said later.'

'Later, we will. I must go now . . .'

Tweed had just entered his room, the coat he had taken off earlier over his arm, when someone tapped on his door. It was Paula. He had called her from the reception desk before coming up in the lift. She carried her own fur-lined coat over her arm, had her gloves in one hand, and was wearing knee-high boots. She went straight to a table, poured a glass of water from a bottle on the table, took it to him. She had dropped her coat on a chair and held out the other hand.

'Take this now. We have fifteen minutes. You should have had it earlier. A Dramamine tablet. Don't look out of the window but the river is rough. You know you hate being on water.'

'Thank you.'

He swallowed the tablet, drank the whole glass of water. Then he sat down. Paula noticed he looked grim, sat beside him on the couch.

'Want to tell me about it?'

'First, we can expect Keith Kent very shortly. I phoned him to come over from downstairs. I want to show him what was inside the envelope Juliette gave me which I opened in the taxi on our way from the station.'

'I didn't see what it was. I knew you'd tell me if you wanted to.'

'These were inside. No note. Just these.'

Taking the envelope from his pocket, he extracted two banknotes. He handed them to Paula. She stared at them, examined them, then looked at him with a puzzled expression.

'One English twenty-pound note, one English ten-pound note. I am mystified. Why would Kurt travel all the way to St Ursanne to see his friend, Juliette, just to leave these with her? And then put her details in that little black book Irina extracted from behind the brick in the wall?'

'He was leaving us a secret paper trail for us to follow. I imagine he knew he had a tail. That's a guess. So he evades the tail and goes to St Ursanne.'

'Just to hide two ordinary banknotes? Why?'

'I haven't a clue.'

'Was there anywhere else written down in the little black book?'

'Yes, but we haven't time to follow it up at the moment. Now, I had a chat with Strangeways . . .'

He told her all about their conversation. She listened, memorizing every word. When he had finished she sat lost in thought before she reacted.

'Something very weird's going on. And I could have told you Rupert is here. He's on the same floor as me.'

'He saw you?'

'No. I dodged back in my room until he'd gone off down the corridor. He definitely did not see me. And how, in Heaven's name, did Strangeways find out you were here? Monica would never tell him.'

'I told you what he said. I don't like his finding me any more than you do. There's a leak somewhere.'

He stopped talking as the phone rang. Paula jumped up, answered it. She called out to Tweed.

'Keith Kent's in the lobby.'

'Ask him to come up immediately.' He checked his watch. 'We have about five minutes before we rush across to Beck. I see Marler remembered what I asked him to do. He must have given it to a maid and asked her to use her pass key.'

He walked quickly to where a canvas holdall was perched by a settee. Picking it up he opened the flap, turned it upside down to show Paula it was empty. Wondering what the deuce he was up to, she watched as he unlocked a cupboard, took out a powerful cone-shaped loudhailer, slipped it inside the holdall, closed the flap.

'What do you want that for?' she asked.

'I hope you'll never know. If you do, it will save lives.'

Before she could ask him what he was talking about someone knocked quietly on the door. Paula, shoulder bag over her arm, took out her Browning. She opened the door a few inches, then threw it wide. Keith Kent strolled in.

'Warm in here,' he remarked, taking off his overcoat. 'Don't go out. You'll freeze to death.' He smiled at Paula. 'Normally the service here is first rate. I get a cup of steaming coffee.'

Paula went to the largest table, felt the silver pot, took her hand away quickly. One of the staff must have brought up a fresh pot with new cups when they had seen Tweed return. The service at the Three Kings *was* first rate. They had noticed the amount of coffee Tweed consumed. She poured a cup for their guest.

'Thanks.' Kent had sat down. He drank half the cup. 'Makes really good central heating. Now, what can I do for you?'

'These mean anything to you, Keith?' Tweed asked.

He handed him the two British banknotes. Kent felt them with his sensitive fingers. Standing up, he took

263

them over to the window, held them up to the light. Returning to the couch, he sat down, took an eyeglass from his pocket, screwed it into his right eye, examined the banknotes again. Then he removed the eyeglass, put it back in his pocket.

'I'm sorry, Keith,' Tweed said, 'but we do have to leave here in about three minutes.'

'That's all right. Where did you get these?'

'Can't tell you that. Does it matter?'

'Not really.' He drank more coffee. 'I just wondered.'

'Have you any comment?' Tweed persisted.

'Yes. They're fakes. Paper they're printed on seems OK. Can't imagine how whoever printed them got hold of it. But they are quite definitely forgeries. Some of the best I've seen. But they do have an error.'

'Would it be spotted by a bank teller?'

'Yes. Especially if someone walked into a British bank with a wad of them. As the teller riffled through them the error would jump out at him. If a lot of these were in circulation they'd be detected very quickly. Good as they are.'

'Thank you. It's a breakthrough. Keith, would you mind moving from the Hilton to this hotel? They're more than half empty. Time of the year.'

'I'll go and collect my things now.'

'Thank you again.' Tweed was putting on his coat, picking up the canvas holdall. 'We have to rush now. Book yourself a room here on your way out. Get one overlooking the Rhine, if you can.'

'All mod. cons. I do like the life of luxury,' Kent said.

27

They were transported in unmarked police cars from headquarters to the far side of the river. The route took them over the bridge Tweed could see when he looked right – upstream – from his bedroom window. Beck drove the first car with Tweed sitting next to him, nursing the canvas holdall in his lap. In the rear sat Paula and Newman. The others were in a similar car following behind them.

'The *Minotaur* will come downriver on this side,' Beck explained. 'I've had a report from my officer watching the vessel that a number of people in cars drove into the yard, then when they came out they only had the driver in each vehicle. So the party is aboard.'

'Did your officer wait – to see if those cars returned?' Tweed asked.

'No, he didn't. Why would the cars return so quickly?'

'I just wondered.'

A strong wind had blown up suddenly. Crossing the bridge, Paula noticed wavelets ruffling the surface of the Rhine. She hoped the tablet she had given Tweed would work. It was likely to be choppy aboard a launch. Added to the wind, an army of low dark clouds swept over the city, creating a heavy pall. Beck had driven into the city on the other bank and then turned right along a course parallel to the river.

'You have your own launch, as requested,' he told Tweed. 'I am in the big one brought out of the boat shed. There will be three other launches, packed with my men. One of them has boarding equipment – just in case we meet resistance when I order the *Minotaur* to heave to. I shall do that further downriver, near the harbour.'

'I have a loudhailer here. If I order all launches to speed away from the barge they must do so very quickly.'

'What would cause you to do that?' Beck asked in surprise.

'An emergency. A dangerous one.'

'If you say so. You usually know what you're doing. All launches have wireless communication, but the skipper of each one also has a mobile phone, as I have.'

'If it comes to it, use the mobile. It will be quicker.'

'I should have checked earlier. You do have someone experienced in handling a high-powered launch?'

'Two,' Tweed replied. 'Newman and Marler.'

'We have cordoned off a section of the riverfront with police tape,' Beck went on. 'To keep the public away from where our launches are assembled.'

'You seem to have thought of everything.'

'I believed so – until you made your remark about your loudhailer. I expect this to be a straightforward operation. We shall arrest everyone on board, saying we have been tipped off that the barge is carrying drugs. They'll wave their diplomatic passports, particularly if Ronstadt is aboard. I'll say I think they are producing phoney documentation and have to check with their authorities. Ronstadt will think I mean their Berne Embassy, but in due course I'll contact Washington. Meantime we interrogate the passengers.'

'You've thought it out well. Have you had a complaint from the Berne Embassy?'

'Not a cheep, as I think you sometimes say. Obviously he was bluffing. Rather a giveaway.'

'It's after 4 p.m.,' Tweed said. 'If they stick to their timetable the *Minotaur* is coming.'

'And here we are at the landing stage.'

*

To Paula's surprise Tweed hurried aboard the large launch allocated to them. He then made his way to the bow, one hand holding on to the gunwale, the other gripping the loudhailer.

Even while berthed at the landing stage the launch was swaying. The motion seemed to have no effect on him. He gazed back upriver for his first sight of the barge. The other four launches, crammed with police, were waiting to take off.

Beck's very large launch had a bridge at a higher level. The word *Polizei* appeared on its sides and stern. Above the bridge was mounted a large searchlight and a prominent horn. Beck came back from his vessel to Tweed's launch.

'The plan is to let the *Minotaur* pass us, then we go after it when it has gone under the bridge. The current is flowing stongly, so you may be surprised how quickly it will reach the bridge. Good luck . . .'

The wind cut through Paula's coat like a knife. She was hoping the barge would appear soon. Then one of the policemen from Beck's launch appeared, carrying an armful of oilskins. Handing them to Newman, who had been experimenting with the engine, he called out above the wind.

'All of you put these on. Extra warmth. Stop you getting soaked.'

'Thanks a lot,' said Newman.

'This is better,' said Paula, putting the oilskin over her coat.

Tweed sat down to put on his oilskin, then immediately stood up again. There were no other craft on the Rhine and no public to gawk at them from behind the distant tape. The weather had kept them indoors.

'Here she comes,' Tweed called out.

Round a bend in the river a massive barge loomed

into view. The conversion to a passenger craft had been extensive. Huge portholes like giant eyes had been cut out of the hull. Tweed noticed that curtains were closed across all of them. Behind each one a light glowed.

'They've got music,' he called out.

'Didn't expect this,' Paula responded.

'Well, it's supposed to be a pleasure craft,' Newman remarked as he turned off the engine.

He had been surprised at the power it generated. These launches could really move, he decided. The strains of the 'Blue Danube' waltz grew louder. Hardly appropriate for the Rhine, Paula was thinking. There was no sign of anyone on board, but she wouldn't expect passengers to be flaunting themselves on deck in weather like this.

'I can see the helmsman,' Tweed called out. 'In the cabin at the stern.'

'Appears to be by himself,' Marler commented.

'Only takes one man to hold the wheel,' Newman told him.

None of the launches had started their engines. Tweed guessed that Beck had ordered them to maintain silence until the huge barge had passed them. He wouldn't want to alert the people on board to his flotilla waiting to pounce.

Even though she was wearing her gloves Paula's hands were beginning to chill. Butler and Nield, standing up, were slapping their arms vigorously round their bodies. Despite the cold, Paula sensed an air of tension, of suppressed excitement aboard their launch. They were within a few minutes of rounding up the whole American gang which had descended on Basle.

Coming closer and closer, the barge seemed even more enormous than she had expected. Its bow wave swept out like a minor tidal wave, causing their launches to rock madly when it reached them. Tweed remained standing up, still gripping the gunwale, staring fixedly at the monster.

As far as Paula could tell, he seemed focused on the shadowy silhouette of the burly helmsman inside his cabin. He was standing stock-still, his hands moving the wheel slightly for a moment. He never glanced to port or starboard. His whole concentration was ahead, on the bridge where he would soon pass through one of the large arches.

Beck, inside his own bridge, was equally motionless. He did not give the barge a glance as its immense hull started to sweep past. The *Minotaur* was so long it seemed to take ages to pass them, even though travelling at speed with the current. There were a number of dinghies, powered by outboard motors, on the main deck. A poor substitute for lifeboats, Paula was thinking.

Eventually the stern of the *Minotaur* loomed above them and the vessel approached the arch under the bridge. Paula saw Tweed had put his loudhailer down at his feet, and was now using a pair of binoculars to scan the barge. As far as she could tell, he was focused on the cabin and the helmsman inside.

The barge passed under the bridge, was now opposite the Three Kings. It struck her that anyone sitting by the windows at the rear of the lobby would have a ringside view. Beck was still erect and still as a statue, his eyes glued to the receding barge. Once he glanced at his watch. Paula guessed he had estimated the barge's speed, was waiting for it to reach a certain point on the river.

Looking back onshore, she noticed the cars which had brought them had disappeared. She wondered where they would eventually land. Then she remembered Beck had said something about ordering the barge to heave to further downriver, near the harbour. Maybe the cars had been driven there, waiting to pick them up as passengers again.

The stern of the barge had vanished from sight. Surely Beck was cutting the timing a bit fine? As though he had read her mind, he raised his right hand, held it aloft, staring at his wristwatch. The engines of the launches burst into action, but remained at the landing stage. Then Beck dropped his hand.

The launch he was aboard moved off when one of his men freed the rope holding it to a bollard. Marler unleashed them in the same way and they sped out on to the Rhine. Paula noticed that the strong current was giving them extra speed. Tweed, the binoculars dropped from a loop round his neck, the loudhailer gripped in his hand, turned to shout at Newman, who was gripping the wheel.

'Bob! Get ahead of Beck. Get this damned launch moving!'

'Doesn't expect much, does he?' Newman said to Marler.

He opened full throttle and the launch soared forward while Tweed gripped the gunwale with both hands. They were skimming over the waves as Beck passed under the bridge. Newman was still behind him as their launch sped through the arch under the bridge. In the distance Paula could see the *Minotaur* again. The barge was about to pass under another bridge. Tweed again turned round to shout a fresh order at Newman.

'Keep us as close to the shore as you safely can. Do get a move on!'

'What does he think I'm doing!' Newman snapped to Marler. 'Paddling across the Serpentine?'

He changed course to obey Tweed's command. Paula couldn't understand what Tweed was up to. Beck's craft was in the middle of the Rhine – or as close as he could be without leaving the official channel for vessels moving downstream. Paula was so intent on watching what was happening ahead she forgot to glance at the Three Kings as they passed it.

Newman was coaxing an extra burst of speed out of his engine after changing course, which had lost him a few seconds. Seated, as everyone else was, except Tweed and Newman, Paula looked back quickly. The other police launches were racing close behind them. It was then that she remembered Newman had once taken part in a powerboat race off Cannes. Up against some well-known names, he had won the race.

Beck's launch passed under the second bridge. Newman, with a determined look on his face, roared through the arch, was now almost alongside Beck with a safe distance between the two craft. Beck was waving him back but Newman thundered on, inched his way ahead. Paula, who had been gazing back at Newman, turned to face the way they were going and was taken aback when she saw how close they were to the *Minotaur*, passing a well-known pharmaceutical firm's headquarters on the opposite bank.

Now they were a short distance ahead of Beck. In the bow Tweed was hanging on to the gunwale with one hand. With the other he had the binoculars pressed against his eyes. He saw the helmsman leave his cabin, throw overboard a dinghy attached to the barge with a tow rope. He followed this by throwing over the side a rope ladder, was starting to descend it when Tweed dropped his binoculars, snatched up the loud-hailer.

'Everyone get away from that barge. Move away at top speed as far as you can. MOVE!'

'*Flee for your lives . . .!*'

To Paula, his thunderous commands reminded her of

recordings she had heard of Churchill speaking. The moment he began his warning she saw Beck using his mobile. The helmsman from the barge had landed in his dinghy, cut the rope linking him to the barge, started his outboard, moving towards the shore.

'Hang on like grim death!' shouted Newman.

Paula, one hand already holding the gunwale, used the other to grip the underside of the plank she was sitting on. She leaned back. Newman swung his wheel hard over. The launch swung in a violent U-turn, so fast, so suddenly, Paula knew they were going to capsize. For the first time Tweed had sat down, had both hands gripping the gunwale.

The launch swung over at an angle of almost forty-five degrees. Vaguely, as in a film speeded up, Paula saw Beck's craft heading back upstream. The other police launches were also swinging round, speeding away. She shook her head to clear her vision, looked back, froze, still looking back.

The *Minotaur* exploded like a giant bomb. The *boom!* echoed down the Rhine. A huge piece of the hull rocketed across the water, struck a large craft anchored to a buoy near the opposite shore. The craft, fortunately empty, disappeared altogether. Another section of the hull broke off, elevated high above the river, then plunged downwards, landing in the river at the very point where Newman's launch had been. It plunged below the surface. Half the stern broke away, skidded across the water, dived out of sight where Beck's launch had been a few seconds earlier.

Newman had just successfully completed his manoeuvre, was racing upriver in the wrong channel, when the shock wave from the explosion hit them. Like a blast of hot air from a furnace it hit their launch when it had just stabilized. They were rocked from side to side but Newman continued speeding them away from the inferno. The other police launches had escaped certain destruction.

Paula's teeth were chattering – whether from fright or the cold she wasn't sure. Then Beck's calm voice was carried over the water through his loudhailer.

'Everyone follow me. I'm taking you in to a landing stage.'

'I could do with a bit of *terra firma* under my feet,' called out Tweed, his voice as calm as Beck's.

When they climbed, stiff-legged, out of the launch, Beck's craft was already moored to the other side. As he walked across to speak to Tweed Paula looked back down the Rhine. From what remained of the wrecked barge flames were blazing upwards, a glare in the near-dark. Fire-boats, which had appeared from nowhere, were directing great jets of water from hoses onto the fire.

'What about the passengers?' she asked.

'There weren't any,' Tweed told her. 'Otherwise we'd have seen at least a few of them on deck. Only the helmsman was aboard. I think he fixed the wheel to keep the barge on course before he escaped in his outboard. I caught a glimpse of him diving into a waiting car after he'd reached the shore. The bomb, I feel sure, was detonated from a distance by radio – once the helmsman got clear.'

'You expected something like this?' demanded Beck grimly.

'I didn't know what to expect – whether, in fact, to expect anything. I was just suspicious of the way the information reached us.'

'You can see your cars have arrived. I called them on my mobile. We'll drive you back to your hotel. Paula, are you in shock?'

'No. But thank you for asking. What I do need is a cup of something hot to drink.'

'You'll get that at the hotel. Tweed, I'll want to talk to you later,' Beck snapped.

28

Arriving back at the Three Kings, they climbed out of the two unmarked police cars. Tweed bent down to speak to Beck, behind the wheel, through his open window. The second car deposited Marler, Butler and Nield, who waited.

'Thank you for the lift,' Tweed said. 'I'm sorry it turned out to be such a grim fiasco.'

'We'll talk later,' Beck replied abruptly.

Newman was the last to enter the hotel. He had hung around outside, on the lookout for hostile watchers. There didn't seem to be any. He went inside and bumped into Basil Windermere, as always smartly turned out. He wore a new camelhair coat.

'How are you, Bob?' he began. 'Just the chap I was hoping to meet. Tell you what, we'll go into the bar, have a drink and a chinwag.'

It was on the tip of Newman's tongue to refuse. But he was startled to see Windermere in Basle. Tweed had not had time to tell him of the presence of Rupert and Windermere. He decided he'd better find out what was going on. Reluctantly, he agreed. They took off their coats on the way to the bar, which was beyond two restaurants adjoining each other.

'What are you having to celebrate?' Windermere enquired.

They were sitting in two comfortable seats upholstered in red leather. No one else was in the bar except for an attractive blonde waitress, who immediately came to them. Windermere looked her up and down appreciatively. Newman sensed the girl did not like the way he looked at her.

'I'll have a double Scotch,' he said.

After what's just happened I think I need it, he was thinking. And I'm not staying here a moment longer than I have to. Not with this piece of rubbish.

'Cheers! To eternal friendship, my dear chap,' said Windermere, raising his glass.

'What are we celebrating?' Newman asked without enthusiasm.

'The fact that we're together again, of course. I must say you're looking chipper.'

'Why are you here?'

'Just like the old Newman, foreign correspondent *extraordinaire*.' Windermere gave a saturnine smile. Newman realized he'd never before noticed how like a handsome fox the playboy was. A smile which probably had rich dowagers swooning. 'Always digging for info,' Windermere went on.

'You haven't answered my question. Why?'

'To keep dear Rupert company, of course.'

'Rupert is in Basle?'

'Ectually, like me, he has a room in this hotel. Sir Guy also is here.'

'I get it. He's paying for you both.'

'You could be a little more diplomatic at times, Bob.'

'When it's staring me in the face, I tell the truth.'

'See you've finished your drink.' Windermere summoned the waitress. 'Same again?'

'I'll have a single this time, thank you.'

'You know, Bob,' Windermere remarked when they were alone, 'at times life can be hard. A chap doesn't know where the next penny is coming from.'

Windermere was wearing a new blue Armani suit, an

expensive starched white shirt, a Valentino tie. He sat with his long legs sprawled out, crossed at the ankles. His feet were clad in handmade shoes.

'From the way you're dressed I'd say you were doing all right.'

'Ah! Appearances can be deceptive.' He placed a finger along the side of his Roman nose. 'Not a word to Betty. At the moment I haven't a bean. Thought you might help me out. Twenty thousand pounds would help me to get by. Just as a loan,' he added hastily. 'Pay you back as soon as I get on my feet.'

'I know. This year. Next year. Sometime. Never.'

'You know you could afford it – never even notice a difference in your bank balance. You did write that book – world bestseller. *Kruger: The Computer That Failed*. Must have made you independent financially for life.'

The book had done just that for Newman. He had no intention of confirming the fact to Windermere. He finished his drink, turned in his chair to face Windermere.

'Basil, I never borrow, I never lend. A maxim you might like to think about.'

The waitress had placed the bill on the table. It was left there for Windermere to sign. His expression turned ugly. He lifted his glass, drank the contents quickly, hammered down the glass.

'I thought you'd get me out of a hole. I've got back rent due on my flat . . .'

'You will live just off Regent Street. Move to Clapham.'

'You know I couldn't possibly receive my friends in Clapham . . .'

'Your rich widows. Ever thought of getting a proper job?'

'If you don't mind my saying so,' Windermere said with an edge to his voice, 'I don't too much care for what you're saying.'

'It's not an ideal world, Basil.'

Newman stood up to leave. Windermere caught him by the sleeve. The smile was a memory. Newman was surprised at how vicious Windermere looked.

'You've forgotten the tab,' he said, pointing to the bill.

'And you've forgotten you invited me to have a drink.'

Without waiting for a response he left the bar. On his way up in the lift to his room Newman had a thoughtful expression. He was recalling his conversation with Basil Windermere. He was also remembering the vicious expression which had crossed Windermere's face at one moment. It didn't fit in with his previous impression of a playboy who preyed on rich woman. He'd have to see Tweed a little later.

Tweed was alone in his room. He had taken his time having a hot bath, changing into fresh clothes. His mind was racing round in three or four different directions. He was just about to call Newman, Marler and Paula when the phone rang. To his surprise the hotel operator told him Beck was waiting downstairs to see him.

'Please ask him to come straight up . . .'

It was a solemn-faced Beck who entered. He accepted Tweed's invitation to sit down, refused his offer of coffee. Crossing his legs, he sat quite still, as though gathering his thoughts, or wasn't sure how to start. Tweed sat opposite him and waited.

'That was a grim business,' Beck began. 'Fortunately there were no casualties, which was a miracle.'

'You know what it was all about? A determined attempt to wipe out me and my team at one blow. I doubt if you would have survived.'

'I'd worked that out for myself. I've just had a stormy

phone conversation with Jake Ronstadt. I called him. I told him what had happened, that I was just about to report the incident to Washington – together with the fact that five of the men staying with him had been killed in Basle, that all were found to carry weapons. He didn't like it at all.'

'What was his reaction?'

'Oh, what I expected. Raved on, saying it was nothing to do with him, that he had diplomatic status. I interrupted him, said that after I had spoken to Washington I would want to see him here at police headquarters. He erupted.'

'In what way?'

'He said he'd not stand any longer being harassed by Swiss police. In any case, he was leaving Switzerland for good during the next two or three days. And he'd be taking his staff with him. Then he slammed the phone down.'

'So you got what you wanted.' Tweed smiled ruefully. 'What you are after.'

'I'm not sure I understand you.'

'Arthur, you understand me only too well. Your phone call was intended to drive Ronstadt and his men out of the country. And you succeeded.'

'I must admit I'm sick and tired of the violence the Americans are causing.'

'And,' Tweed said quietly, 'you'll be glad to see the back of us.'

'I don't remember saying that.'

'Because you're tactful. But you know when Ronstadt and Co. do leave – probably to Germany – we'll go after them.'

'My job is to protect Swiss civilians,' Beck admitted. 'Luckily, so far there haven't been any casualties among our people. But if what has happened continues, then it's only a matter of time.'

278

'I think you're absolutely right. You said Ronstadt told you he would be leaving in two or three days. I think he may slip away tomorrow.'

'I'm still keeping officers on watch at the exit to autobahn 5. When Ronstadt and his thugs do move they'll be detained at the border; as I said before, on the pretext that we suspect they're smuggling drugs. Then I'll inform you, give you time to get there and track them.'

'For that, I'm very grateful. Over the years you have always been a reliable ally.'

'That has worked both ways. I'd better go now. You take care of yourself.' Standing up he took a compact mobile phone out of his pocket, placed it on a table close to Tweed. 'I know you mistrust these things, but it will let me contact you urgently – wherever you may be at the time. Incidentally, I think Ronstadt is tricky. Don't overlook the possibility he might leave in the middle of the night . . .'

When Beck had gone Tweed used the phone to summon everyone to his room. Paula arrived first, followed almost immediately by Newman, Marler, Butler and Nield. Tweed had also ordered three pots of coffee and cups for seven people. Afterwards he had called Keith Kent and asked him to come and see him.

Tweed was standing by the window, hands behind his back as he gazed into the night. It was a stance Paula recognized – he had at times done the same thing at Park Crescent when he was working out a problem.

'Coffee!' she called out with enthusiasm. 'How about the rest of you?' she asked when they had all arrived. 'Put a hand up if you want a cuppa.'

Six hands rose in the air. She started pouring as they found somewhere to sit or perch. Keith Kent looked round, saw he had met everyone present in London, clasped both hands and made a shaking motion. Unusually, it was Marler who spoke first.

'Tweed, when we reached safety on the landing stage, I heard you say to Beck that you were suspicious of the way the information reached us. You were referring to the earlier news that Ronstadt and his gang would be holding a meeting aboard the *Minotaur*. So you had to be talking about what Denise Chatel told me.'

'I was,' Tweed agreed.

'You think she made up the story?'

'I'm not sure. But it all seemed rather neat. Denise being called by an unknown American. Then told that Sharon wanted to meet her at the bar in the Euler.'

'So we can't trust her?' Marler remarked, now leaning against a wall.

'We can't trust anyone,' Tweed said emphatically.

'I have good news for you,' Newman said ironically. 'Dear Rupert is here. Staying at this hotel.'

'I know,' Tweed replied. 'Sir Guy told me.'

'And he has his pal Basil with him,' Newman went on. 'Also staying in this hotel. I had a drink with Basil, the ladies' dream. You'll never guess what he wanted to cadge off me . . .'

He relayed what had happened in the bar. He abbreviated their conversation but gave them the flavour of it. Paula gasped.

'Twenty thousand pounds! The nerve of the pimp.'

'He wasn't best pleased,' Newman told her, 'when I told him to go jump in the Rhine, or words to that effect. I was surprised at how ugly he turned.'

'Must be desperate,' Paula commented.

'Desperate men are dangerous,' Tweed mused. 'What I can't understand is how Guy found out we were here. And he wasn't prepared to tell me.'

'Could Ronstadt have told him?' Nield wondered. 'It

stands out like a sore thumb that Ronstadt has known we are here for a while.'

'Why would he do that?' asked the normally taciturn Butler.

'Possibly to confuse me,' Tweed suggested. 'Have me looking in all directions so I'd miss something obvious.'

'That would mean Strangeways is one of them,' objected Butler.

'I did say a few minutes ago we can't trust anyone,' Tweed reminded him.

'Not even Denise Chatel,' said Marler.

'Beck has been over here to see me,' Tweed began. He told them everything the Swiss police chief had said. 'So if he's right,' he concluded, 'we had better be ready to leave at any time. Better get some packing done when you leave here.'

'You still think it's the Black Forest?' Newman queried.

'You should know. Kurt's last word was Schwarz, which, as I remarked earlier, is German for black. If I had to gamble I'd say it will be the Black Forest.'

The phone rang, Paula answered, told Tweed Beck was on the line for him.

'Yes, Arthur . . .'

'Just heard a weather report. Thought you ought to know there's been a heavy fall of snow in the Black Forest. More on the way. Unusual for this time of year, but occasionally it does happen. Excuse me now, I'm up to my neck in work.'

Tweed put down the phone. He told them what Beck had said. Paula sighed.

'Just what we needed. If I have time I'm going to shop for warmer boots.'

'Incidentally, Keith,' Tweed said, 'I'd appreciate it if you would come with us when we leave here.'

281

'Go to Singapore as long as you pay me. If you don't need me I'd better go and start packing.'

'Good idea.'

'What sort of game do you think Strangeways is playing?' Newman asked when Kent had gone.

'I wish I knew,' replied Tweed. 'But I'll tell you one thing. As soon as I can I'm going to make him tell me how he knew we were here. I think I can get it out of him. He's in a highly nervous state. When I went into the writing room the hand holding his pen was trembling. Then later he started fiddling with it.'

'I think,' said Newman, standing up, 'we'd all better get back to our rooms and start packing. Beck could be right. Ronstadt might try and do a moonlight flit.'

Paula waited when everyone except Tweed had gone. She was curled up like a cat in an armchair. Tweed refilled her cup before he spoke.

'You have something on your mind.'

'Yes. Don't worry about my being ready if we have to leave at a moment's notice. I'm half-packed already.'

'Knowing how methodical you are, I thought you might be. Now, what's bothering you?'

'Not bothering. I admit it's sheer curiosity. But why is Keith Kent coming with us when we leave?'

'I told you in the car on our way to the launch what he had said.' Tweed produced an envelope, took out the two banknotes, a British twenty-pound note, a ten-pound note. 'Fakes. Good ones. They really worry me.'

'Why?'

'Remember that letter from the dead, as Marler called it – from Kurt Schwarz? The wording was brief. *Be very careful of the barges*. At Park Crescent I thought he was referring to Thames barges. When we arrived here and I saw barges on the Rhine I began to think they were what Kurt had referred to. We now know it was. We'll never know how he suspected what might happen.'

'But he was right. So what about the banknotes?'

'The second sentence in Kurt's letter said: *You must locate the printing presses.* So what prints banknotes? Printing presses. I think Washington has devised a diabolical plan to destabilize Britain. There may not be much time to stop them. And I think the secret lies at their base in the Black Forest.'

29

Tweed received the invitation soon after Paula had left him. When he picked up the phone it was Sharon Mandeville. He remarked he hadn't seen much of her since arriving in Basle.

'Well, some people would say that's your fault,' she chided him gently in her soft voice. 'You stood me up for drinks.'

'I was about to apologize for that. Something I couldn't ignore turned up. And I had to rush out.'

'You're forgiven. I'm calling you because I thought it might be nice if you and Bob Newman had dinner with me this evening. Here at the hotel, if that suits you.'

'Suits me down to the ground. What time?'

'Would eight o'clock be all right? Maybe afterwards we could all adjourn to the bar.'

'Sounds like a great programme. I could phone Bob Newman to save you the time.'

'Would you? I'm about to dash out to see my Swiss couple again. They're getting wearing, but I agreed to go. See you tonight . . .'

Instead of phoning Newman, Tweed called him to ask him to come to his room. He was staring out of the window when Newman arrived. Then he told him about the invitation.

'I hope you don't mind,' he said, 'but I accepted on your behalf.'

'I'm glad you did. I'm just wondering what she's up to.'

'She sounded a bit fed up. I got the impression she's in need of some company. I'm hoping to lever information out of her.'

'What could she possibly tell us?'

'Maybe something she's observed while at the Embassy in London. Now, I'm popping down to the reception desk. There's something I want to ask whichever girl is on duty.'

'I'll continue with my packing, then.'

'Hurry. As I told you, Beck phoned to say there's been a heavy fall of snow in the Black Forest, with more to come.'

'In that case we're going to need cars with snow tyres. I'll call in on Marler to give him the good news. He won't find a car hire place open now, but he can organize things in the morning. We'll just have to hope Ronstadt and Co. don't leave tonight. Oh, what time is the dinner?'

'I should have told you. Eight o'clock in the main restaurant downstairs. Don't forget to put on your best suit for Sharon . . .'

Tweed walked down the wide flight of stairs instead of taking the lift. The lobby was empty. No one was sitting at any of the tables overlooking the Rhine. He smiled at the receptionist, kept his voice quiet.

'I expect you've heard about the barge disaster near the harbour?'

'Yes, sir. Everyone is talking about it. Apparently it exploded but I heard no one was hurt.'

'That's right. No one was. And the trouble was one of the boilers blew up.'

'Oh, that is what caused it.' Tweed guessed that at the earliest opportunity she would pass his fictitious explanation down the grapevine. Which would soften rumours. 'Anyone sitting by the windows over there must have seen it pass,' he suggested.

'Two guests did. One was Ms Mandeville. She was sitting by herself at the corner table when the barge passed us. Then there was Mr Osborne, sitting in a chair near the restaurant. Both of them had binoculars. We all heard the sound of the explosion – of the boiler blowing up. It's never happened before. Someone's coming,' she ended in a whisper.

'Hi, there, Tweed!' Osborne's very American voice boomed behind him. 'Been lookin' for you, feller.' A strong hand grasped his arm. 'Time we had a drink together. Mebbe more than one. Nobody over by those windows.'

'I haven't a lot of time,' Tweed warned.

'Always time for a drink – or two.'

Osborne guided Tweed to the corner table he had sat at before. He boomed across to the receptionist.

'Send a waiter, would you? Toot sweet, as the French say.'

'They do speak excellent English,' Tweed remarked as they sat at a table next to a window.

'Guess I like to try out my foreign languages. When in Rome . . .'

'I'll have a glass of French white wine, medium dry,' Tweed ordered as a waiter appeared swiftly.

'You ain't got Bourbon. Don't know why,' Osborne complained. 'I guess I'll settle for a double Scotch on the rocks.'

'You know about the barge which blew up?' Tweed enquired.

'Sure. No bodybags needed, so I heard.'

'Ed, why are you here in Basle?'

'*Ed*. That's better, much better. Why am I in this weird town? Embassy sent me to check on a Swiss PR firm. See if they know their stuff. I guess they're OK. We might pick up their key people. Take them to New York. Boy, here are the drinks. Your good health, Tweed.'

'Yours too.'

'Now the job's done, guess I may soon move on. To Freiburg – near the Black Forest. They tell me there's a nice place there. Hotel Schwarzwälder Hof. Some street called Konvikstrasse. I like that. Convict Street.' Osborne gave a belly laugh. 'Just the place for me.'

'When are you thinking of going there?'

'Haven't decided.' He paused. 'Could be in the next few days.'

Osborne shifted his large bulk. His chair creaked under the weight imposed on it. He was wearing a cream jacket with orange stripes, pale yellow slacks and a white shirt with a flashy tie. His outfit struck Tweed as loud, the kind he'd seen in California.

'What made you choose this hotel?' Tweed asked.

'There's an interesting story behind that.' Osborne had lowered his voice. 'Back at the Embassy in London I hear Sharon is also comin' to Basle. So I ask her where she's stayin' and – without much enthusiasm – she tells me about this place. Thought I'd have a bit of company. I can be a naive guy. Hardly seen sight or heard sound of her since I got here. That's the way it goes.'

'Do you mind if I ask what exactly is your job?'

They were both talking quietly now. Osborne took out a cigar case, offered it to Tweed, who refused. The American took his time clipping off the end, lighting it with a match, moving it round the exposed tip.

'I'm forming a propaganda outfit,' he said. 'A team

of spin doctors and all that crap you have in Britain at the moment. I guess the purpose is to fool the voters, brainwash 'em, repeat the same line over and over again. Sounds like Dr Goebbels, doesn't it? Smells like him.'

'This outfit is for Washington?'

'Sure.' Osborne turned to Tweed, smiled drily. 'Where else?'

'Wasn't it Abraham Lincoln who said you can't fool all the people all the time? Something like that.'

'It was.'

'You like doing this?'

'Sure.' Again he smiled drily. 'It's a job. Until something else comes along.'

'Thank you for the drink,' Tweed said, getting up. 'Excuse me, I have work to do.'

'Let's have another drink tonight,' Osborne called after him.

Angled in his chair so he could see the whole lobby, Tweed had seen Denise Chatel emerge from the lift. She had walked into the writing room. At the same moment Paula was descending the flight of stairs behind him. Tweed walked to the writing room door, opened it and Denise swung round in her chair in front of a desk as he shut it. Her expression was startled, uncertain. Tweed wondered whether the psychiatrist who had said she was highly strung was right.

'If I'm disturbing you I'll leave,' he said.

'Of course you're not. Please sit down,' she said stiffly.

She was tense, almost had a hunted look on her attractive face. He sat in a chair close to hers, smiled.

'How are you getting on? That file in front of you isn't more work, I hope.'

'Yes, it is – a whole load of work I have to finish

287

before I have dinner.' She was rattling out the words. 'Sometimes I've got the impression Sharon invents work to keep me busy. Don't tell her I said that, will you?'

'Of course not. Tell her you're tired, that you need a break.'

'She doesn't believe in breaks. She never stops working herself. Even going out to see someone she takes a file with her so she can work on it while she's in the car. She always has a driver to take her round. She's a fanatic for work. The ultimate career woman.' She was rattling on again. 'At times I admire her incredible drive. She gets by on hardly any sleep.'

'Have you talked to anyone this afternoon? To give yourself a bit of variety?'

'I've chatted to quite a few of the staff, including the duty manager. They're very sociable here. I think they've noticed I'm on my own a lot.'

'Have you seen Marler this afternoon?'

'Only briefly. I passed him in the hall on my way to my room.'

'Well, I've given you a little break.' He smiled again. 'But I think I'm interrupting your work.'

'I should get on if I'm to get through it.'

'Don't push yourself too hard. I'll leave you to it.'

He was walking back upstairs to his room when he met Marler on his way down. They were alone on the staircase and no one was within hearing distance.

'Marler, I gather you saw Denise briefly after we'd got back from the barge disaster.'

'Briefly is the word. She just said, "Hello, there," and kept on walking to the lift. Struck me she was pretty busy.'

'I'm sure you're right. No luck with cars equipped with snow tyres at this time of day, I imagine.'

'I did get lucky. I phoned the hire people who had cars waiting for us at the airport. They were just closing.

I managed to persuade them to deliver cars with snow tyres – a couple of white Audis. They're in the garage here. They took the other cars back.'

'So we can leave at any time. That might be soon. Good work, Marler.'

Tweed continued on up to his room, thinking. His thoughts disturbed him. Denise had warned Marler about the supposed meeting aboard the *Minotaur*. Denise had talked to staff inside the hotel since they'd got back from the Rhine. It was obvious their main topic of conversation was the explosion aboard the huge barge. Denise had since met Marler briefly. *Yet Denise had made no mention of the barge to Marler – or to himself.*

30

At about seven in the evening Paula was wandering around the hotel on her own. She wanted to see what, if anything, was going on.

'There are two hostile elements in this place,' she said to herself. 'Ed Osborne and Denise Chatel. On someone's instructions – maybe Ronstadt's – Denise made up that story about a so-called meeting on the *Minotaur* to lure us into the trap. When the barge exploded we'd all be killed.'

She had descended from the second floor and started walking down the corridor on the first floor. Suddenly a door further along opened, Denise came out of Tweed's room, turned to say something and closed the door. She walked towards Paula with a blank look. Then she walked straight past her as though she didn't exist.

'What the hell's going on now?' Paula said to herself.

The hotel was strangely quiet and there was no one

else about. She continued prowling. Downstairs there was no one in the lobby and the restaurant wasn't open yet. She opened the door to the writing room, peered inside. No one there. She went back upstairs to see Tweed.

For a moment she thought the same scene was being replayed – like a film turned back and then run forward again. The door to Tweed's room opened, Sharon came out, turned to say something, then closed it. She began to walk in her elegant way towards Paula.

'Just the person I was hoping to see,' Sharon greeted her with a warm smile as she stopped. 'I'm organizing a small dinner in the restaurant here this evening. Bob Newman and Tweed have agreed to be my guests. I'd like you to be there.'

'Well . . .'

'Don't think about it, just say yes.' Sharon smiled more radiantly, her green eyes holding Paula's. 'Take pity on me. One woman and two men doesn't work. I'll be outgunned. You can give me moral support. Please!'

'I'd love to come. Thank you so much.'

'Eight o'clock. In the main restaurant – not the Brasserie next door to it.'

'I'll be there.'

Paula watched her walk away. Sharon almost glided, her figure erect, the waves of blonde hair just touching the top of her shoulders. Then she was gone. Paula frowned, then remembered a friend who had told her she'd develop creases in her forehead. Turning round, she went to Tweed's door, tapped on it, he called out, 'Come in.'

'It's just me. I was passing so thought I'd see how you were.'

'I'm fine. You know I like to get ready for a meal in good time. A little while ago Sharon phoned me, invited

Bob and me to have dinner with her tonight. Here in the hotel, bless her – considering what it's like outside.'

He'd put on his best suit, a blue bird's-eye. Now, seated on a couch, he was bent over, buffing his shoes. He seemed very relaxed.

'I've just bumped into Sharon in the corridor,' she said, perching on the arm of the couch. 'She's invited me to join the dinner party. I accepted.'

'I'm glad. That makes us a foursome. You know something? Apart from Sharon's call a while ago that phone hasn't rung once. Peace and quiet. It seems a novelty.'

'I think I'd better go to my room and get changed. Competing with Sharon takes some doing.'

'Oh, I don't know. You always look so perfectly turned out.'

'Thank you, sir.'

She bent down, kissed him lightly on the cheek, then left as she checked her watch.

She'd had a bath earlier but decided she'd have a quick shower.

They kept it very warm in the hotel. She was on her way to the bathroom when she paused before a large wall mirror. She looked at her dark, glossy hair, her large blue-grey eyes, her thick brows, her well-shaped features, her good complexion.

'I'm a brunette, Sharon is a blonde,' she said aloud. 'What is it about that lady which makes her so striking? I'll study her over dinner. No! Admit it – you're an envious witch.'

There was a knock on the door. When she unlocked it Newman was standing outside. She invited him in with a smile. He had on his best suit and a brand-new tie she hadn't seen before, a Valentino. How *was* Sharon able to mesmerize such different men?

'I just called in to let you know Sharon has asked Tweed and me to dinner at the restaurant downstairs.'

'She's just asked me to join the party. I said I would.'

'That's great, really great. I was getting bothered you'd feel left out when you saw us.'

'That was nice of you, Bob. Now you can stop getting bothered.'

'I rather think you'll be changing, so I'm holding you up.'

'That's all right. But I was about to dive into the shower.'

'Then I'll leave you to it.'

'Bob, just before you go. Have you noticed Tweed often seems to know what's going on in the enemy's mind? Calls it his sixth sense.'

'Yes, I have.'

'Well, I think he has an agent inside the American camp.'

Newman headed for the ground floor after he'd left Paula. Unusually for him, he stopped for a moment to check his appearance in a mirror on the corridor wall. It was seeing Windermere's Valentino tie, when they had a drink in the bar, which had caused Newman to dig out his own new tie. He walked downstairs, looked in the lobby, wished he'd stayed in his room. Seated by himself at a table overlooking the river was Rupert Strangeways.

'I say, Newman, do trot over and join me for a drink. A chap gets lonely, don't you know.'

'And what brings you to Basle?' Newman asked as he sat down.

He had been told by Tweed what Sir Guy had said, but he wanted to see whether the stories of father and son tallied. Rupert waved a commanding hand.

'First things first. A waiter chappie is coming. What's your tipple?'

'I'll have a double Scotch, no ice.'

I'm going to need it to get through this, he thought. Rupert, heavily in debt, wore an expensive dark smoking jacket, a pair of dark trousers with a razor-edged crease, a crisp white shirt and a polka-dot bow tie. Newman had always mistrusted men who sported bow ties.

'Mine is a very dry martini, shaken, not stirred,' Rupert ordered with a dry smile. 'I was always a follower of James Bond,' he told Newman when the waiter had gone. 'Poor joke, I know. Maybe I'll sparkle after a few drinks.'

'I think I asked you what brings you to Basle.'

'You most certainly did. Amazing memory you have.' Rupert grinned. 'I'm not being sarcastic. Meant to be a joke. Not doing very well, am I?'

'You'll liven up. I'm listening.'

'Pater put on his military uniform, in a manner of speaking. Told me to come with him. The idea, I'm sure, was to keep me out of mischief. And here I was, waiting for a pair of gorgeous female legs to appear, and what happens? You turn up. Again, no offence meant.'

'None taken. I had a drink with Basil earlier. I suppose that he came along for the free ride.'

'You've got it.' Rupert snapped his fingers, grinned wolfishly. 'Literally.'

'I think I missed something there.'

'Pater's paying for all Basil's expenses, including the air ticket. The idea is I need someone to keep an eye on me. Basil was elected.'

'As a nursemaid,' Newman joked.

'Can't say I find that tremendously funny. Comes from being one of those reporter chappies, I suppose. They all develop a rather weird sense of humour. Of course you made a mint out of that huge bestselling book you wrote, *Kruger: The Computer That Failed.* I've met reporters who failed – ended up behind some crummy desk subediting other people's stories. On a clerk's pay.'

'So what are you going to do when you get back home?'

'I rather fancy the idea of becoming manager of a mutual fund.'

Newman could hardly believe his ears. He had never heard Rupert talk like this before. He'd always thought the prospect of doing a proper job had never occurred to him. That was for the peasants.

'I'm surprised,' he said.

'Thought you might be, old boy. Oh, is the divine Paula about?'

'Yes, she is.' Newman became wary. 'She's very booked up now. Tonight she's having dinner with a party of us. Think I'd better make a move.' Newman reached for the bill the waiter had left so he could sign it. 'I'll handle this.'

'No, you won't.' Rupert's hand grabbed the bill. 'I invited you for a drink.'

Newman got up to go. He had left the table when Rupert called out to him. He swung round and Rupert was smiling sardonically.

'Bob. Give my love to Paula when you see her . . .'

Jack Ronstadt sat at the head of the long table in his suite at the Euler. He was in a towering rage. He spoke very quietly, which alarmed everyone sitting with him. They knew when he was quiet it was a very bad sign.

'You bombed,' he began, using the American expression for falling flat on your face. 'First, four of our guys are blown to hell by a grenade. Second, Rick Sherman, sent to torture information out of the Irina

294

crone before he breaks her stupid neck, ends up with a knife in his throat.' He looked round at the tense faces. 'Any more contributions? What about you, Vernon?' he asked the thin man.

'Well, Chief . . .' Vernon cleared his throat. 'Guess you're talkin' about the barge.'

'You're goddamn right I am.' His fist crashed down on the table. 'I put you in charge of organizing what should have been the end of Tweed and his mob. What friggin' happens?'

'It kinda didn't work out . . .'

'*Kinda?*' Ronstadt was going full throttle now. 'Don't mess with me. It was a friggin' catastrophe.'

He bunched his fist. It moved so quickly no one saw what was coming. The large fist connected with Vernon's jaw. He fell over backwards, taking his chair with him, lay sprawled on the floor. Vernon kept his eyes lowered, concealing hatred welling up inside him. He clambered to his feet, lifted up the chair, resumed his place at the table.

Ronstadt's expression was passive, as if nothing had happened. He had hit his subordinate with only half his strength. If he had really hit him Vernon's jaw would have been broken – and he needed Vernon.

'So we move on,' he continued quietly. 'First thing tomorrow Vernon and Brad are turning in all our cars. They're gettin' vehicles with snow tyres for us. There's been a big snowfall in the Black Forest. My idea is we leave tomorrow night. I do mean in the middle of the night. We collect a big cargo waitin' at the base. It has to reach Britain very fast.' He smiled for the first time. 'Any questions?'

There was silence. No one felt like opening their mouths after witnessing the punishment meted out to Vernon. Ronstadt sighed. He started shuffling the pack of cards he'd picked up.

'Some smart guy might have asked, "What about weapons?"'

'What about weapons?' Vernon asked obediently.

'Vernon, you'se comin' on.' Ronstadt reached out a hand, grasped Vernon's shoulder, squeezed it in a friendly way. 'You'll make it yet. Tomorrow mornin' all weapons and explosives left are to be dumped in the Rhine. That officer at the checkpoint close to the autobahn is a nosy bastard. When we're on the way, across the border, a car from base will meet us with more weapons. Don't no one go to bed tonight. I may call another meeting middle of the night. After I've contacted Charlie, got the OK . . .'

Paula was ready early for the dinner. In her room she began thinking about Denise Chatel. It struck her Denise was lonely. She might be upset if she saw the dinner party to which she had not been invited. She picked up the phone, spoke to the operator.

'Could you put me through to Denise Chatel's room, please.'

'Sorry. I can't do that. Ms Chatel has checked out.'

'Checked out? What do you mean?'

'She asked me to have her car brought to the entrance about three-quarters of an hour ago. Then she checked out. Left the hotel.'

'Did she leave any forwarding address?'

'No, she didn't.'

'Thank you.'

Paula hurried along to Tweed's room. He opened the door and she waited until she had sat down. She was feeling stunned. Normally she was quick when it came to working out relationships between people. Now her mind was circling round at speed like a whirlpool.

'I've just heard that Denise Chatel has checked out of here,' she announced.

'When?' Tweed rapped out.

'Over three-quarters of an hour ago. Had her car brought to the entrance, then she was off.'

'Any idea where to?'

'None at all. She didn't leave a forwarding address. Tweed, I just don't know what's going on any more.'

'Have some more coffee . . .'

'No! I don't want any more coffee. I'm up to here with it. And I think you're drinking too much of the stuff. Caffeine sets your nerves on edge.'

Tweed sat down in a chair opposite her. As he poured himself another cup he glanced across at her, then concentrated on what he was doing. Sitting back, he sipped at his cup.

'I'm sorry,' said Paula. 'That outburst was very rude. Don't know what's got into me.'

'Too much coffee,' Tweed said with a smile. He put down his cup. 'Newman and Marler will be arriving in a minute. I want a word with them before our dinner. And I want to tell them while you're here. It's important you're fully in the picture. I'm not surprised you felt confused. So did I – until I realized certain people are feeding me with smokescreens. Verbal camouflage is a better description. They're trying to conceal from me who is who – and what is really about to happen.'

'I feel better. I thought it was me.'

She had just finished speaking when Newman and Marler came in. Paula decided to speak up first when she saw Marler. He stood against a wall, lit a king-size.

'Marler,' she said, 'Denise checked out of the hotel less than an hour ago. Drove off by herself . . .'

'What?'

It was rare to be able to gauge his reactions from his expression. Now he looked staggered, mystified.

'She didn't leave a forwarding address. So we have no idea where she's gone, why she left so suddenly, anything.'

'And she didn't say a word to me. Don't understand it.'

'There may be quite a simple explanation,' Tweed interjected. He looked at Marler. 'Paula, Bob and I are having dinner with Sharon downstairs this evening. I'd like everyone to leave this to me,' he warned. 'At a suitable moment I'll bring up the news about Denise. Incidentally, I shall be playing a power game, so don't be surprised when I say something odd to our hostess. My objective now is to disturb the enemy. I think I can use Sharon without her realizing it.'

'Shouldn't we pass on this strange business about Denise to Pete Nield and Harry Butler?' Marler suggested.

'I was going to ask you to do just that. At the moment they're testing out the new Audis with their snow tyres. I had an interesting chat, by the way, with Ed Osborne down in the lobby.'

'You must have enjoyed that,' Paula commented.

'He apparently let slip that soon he's moving on to Freiburg at the edge of the Black Forest. He even gave me the name and the address of the hotel he'll be staying at. The Schwarzwälder Hof.' He looked at Paula. 'Before dinner could you phone up the place, book rooms for all of us? I've scribbled details of the hotel and its address on that pad over there.'

'Book rooms? In our own names?'

'Yes. Exactly. Tell them we may arrive tomorrow, but they're to hold the rooms until we do arrive. We'll pay for them even if they're unoccupied for a day or two.'

'Is this a good idea,' Paula questioned, 'all of us in the same hotel in the Black Forest area?'

'Yes. I think we'll need as heavy a force close together as we can muster.'

'Before I forget,' Newman began, 'I had a drink with what sounded like a reformed Rupert . . .'

He went on to describe his conversation with Rupert Strangeways. They all listened with a mixture of surprise and disbelief. As he finished Paula burst out.

'Do you believe a word of this? Rupert getting himself a proper job? The mind boggles.'

'It could be,' Newman speculated, 'that Rupert wants to get into his father's good books. After all, Sir Guy is a millionaire.'

'What do you think?' Paula asked Tweed.

'I don't think anything.'

'Going back to Osborne,' Newman said, 'you used the words "he apparently let slip" when you told us about Freiburg, the hotel he's staying at, the address. Did it occur to you he might have deliberately told you this?'

'Indeed, it did.'

'Then I vote that Paula does nothing about booking rooms in the hotel he mentioned.'

'Sorry, Bob, you're outvoted. By me. I want Paula to do what I requested.'

'I don't understand it.'

'I thought I'd made myself quite clear.'

'It's a trap,' Newman told him vehemently.

'So we walk into their trap.'

When Tweed, Paula and Newman arrived in the dining room Sharon was already waiting for them at a table by a window. There were place cards and Tweed sat next to Sharon by the aisle. Paula's card put her by the other window, facing Sharon with Newman alongside her.

'I think we're dead on time,' Tweed had greeted his hostess.

'Dead on time,' Sharon agreed with a smile.

'Don't use that phrase,' Paula whispered under her breath.

Only Newman heard her. He realized Paula was tense, on edge. Outwardly she was the model of composure. She smiled at Sharon.

'I think your ensemble is one of the smartest I've seen this season.'

'Thank you, Paula. That is generous of you.' She looked at two waiters who had arrived. 'Let's get the party going. What are you all going to have for aperitifs?'

As they ordered Paula found herself studying Sharon, despite her previous determination not to. She wore an emerald-green dress with a high collar. Round her slim waist was a gold belt. It was all perfect. She sat very erect, very much in control of herself but without a trace of arrogance.

She exudes an air of complete calm, Paula thought. She moved her head constantly, but slowly. Her green eyes also swept the table slowly and Paula had the impression she was taking in every little detail about her guests. She didn't fiddle with her magnificent mane, as so many women do. Her white, beautifully moulded face would attract the attention of almost any man the first moment he saw her. But there was not a hint of flirting with the men as she chatted in her very English accent.

'I propose a toast,' Tweed said, raising his glass and turning towards Sharon. 'To our hostess, Sharon, one of the most remarkable women in the world.'

'I'll second that,' Newman said instantly.

'I'm going to blush,' Sharon replied, then sipped her drink. 'I've dined with Heaven knows how many people in America,' she went on, 'but I haven't, until tonight, been honoured with a group of such talent and dynamism.' She looked straight at Paula. 'And what I have just said very much includes you.'

'Thank you. I fear you exaggerate.'

'No. It is the Americans who exaggerate.'

Paula had listened carefully to Sharon when she was speaking in her soft voice. She had also been watching her. As far as she could tell Sharon spoke with absolute sincerity. It was at this moment that Newman said something Paula thought would ruin the pleasant, relaxed atmosphere.

'I imagine you should know, Sharon. About exaggeration. After all, you have been married to four Americans.'

'Oh yes, I have.' Sharon broke into peals of laughter. Then she concentrated on Newman, her wide mouth smiling. 'It would be you, Bob, who brings up the subject of my adventures – experiments is a better word – with four American husbands. I was very young when I was first taken to the States. I was dazzled. Then after a year I realized I couldn't stand my husband. Always boasting about his big deals, running after other women. I left it to my lawyer to arrange the divorce settlement. I was staggered when he told me what he was going to get me. It was then it dawned on me.'

'What did?'

'Bob, do go ahead and have a cigarette.'

Paula realized that Sharon had noticed Newman reach for a packet in his pocket, then think better of it. He nodded, took out the pack and lit a cigarette.

'What did?' Sharon repeated. 'It dawned on me that in America the only people looked up to are the rich. So I thought, if this is the game over here, I'll play it. I was still very young. I had been elevated by my first husband into the world of country clubs, top hotels, Cadillacs, you name it. Which is how I fell for my second husband.' She burst out laughing again. 'I'll go on in a minute. We must study the menus.'

Paula was fascinated. Sharon's personality had

suddenly – at the mention of husbands – become amazingly animated. She glowed with life and Paula realized even more why men would, at their first meeting, be hypnotized by her.

Once everyone had decided on their main courses, refusing starters, Sharon consulted Tweed about the wine list. After telling the wine waiter what they wanted, she looked at Tweed.

'I've been chattering on too much. Your turn now.'

'Did you know that Denise Chatel has booked out of this hotel – and driven off in her car? Someone told me before dinner.'

'Yes, I found that out too.' The animation was replaced by her deep calm. 'She didn't say a word to me. I can't understand why she did it. Or where she's gone.'

'So she's disappeared?'

'Vanished into thin air. And after working for me for two years. I'm puzzled – and worried.'

'Would it be worth informing the police?' Tweed suggested.

'I thought of that, then rejected the idea. After all, she's a free soul. She was a good worker, but often I was never sure what was going on in her mind.'

'Sorry to bring that up,' Tweed replied. 'Let's settle down and enjoy ourselves, as we were doing.'

'Husband Number Two,' said Newman.

'He doesn't let go, does he?' Sharon put her hand across her mouth to suppress a giggle. 'I really did fall for him. After we became engaged he took me to Hawaii. Before I knew what was happening we were married – on the beach. It all seemed very romantic. Then after six months he was running after other women. By then my lawyer, Joshua Warren, had become a friend. After a year I'd had enough of it. Joshua again took over – and again I was astounded at the size of the settlement. I won't bore you with Number Three, which followed the same pattern.'

'Where were you by then?' Newman asked.

'Washington. The trouble there is a single woman is suspect – the wives of high society men think you're after their husbands. So you don't get invited anywhere. I'm all right on my own – I love reading, but there's a limit to the number of books you can occupy yourself with. Then Joshua introduced me to Number Four. I admit I married him so I could lead a more social life. When my fourth husband went off the rails Joshua was in attendance to handle the divorce.' She paused. 'I was rather naive. It was only then I understood the enormous fees Joshua was making out of my divorces. Enough to set him up for life.' She went very quiet, staring at the table. 'I began to feel like a high-class call-girl – with Joshua manipulating me like a pimp. That's the way it goes in America – they're all corrupt. Which is why I hanker for England.'

She looked up as the wine waiter showed her a bottle. He waited while she looked at it, then at him.

'I ordered 1992 – that's 1994,' she said sharply.

'I'm sorry, madame. I must have misunderstood you.'

'I spoke clearly enough.'

Tweed glanced down towards the main entrance. Rupert and Basil had just come in together. They strolled along the aisle and then Rupert paused by their table. He was staring at Sharon.

'I can recognize Venus-like beauty soon as I see it.'

Sharon glanced up with a blank expression. She stared at him, then lowered her eyes, her mouth tight with annoyance.

'Bob, aren't you going to introduce me?' Rupert persisted.

Basil stood by his side, smiling blandly. He adjusted a silk handkerchief in his top pocket.

'No, I'm not,' Newman told Rupert brusquely. 'And for your information this is a private dinner party.'

'I say, I say. A *cordon sanitaire*, as the French would say. Excuse me for being alive. Basil and I are on the way to the bar.'

'Your usual watering hole. I suggest you shove off there now.'

Newman had pushed back his chair. If necessary, he was ready to grab Rupert by the scruff of the neck and escort him through the Brasserie next door into the bar beyond. At that moment the head waiter, sensing trouble, appeared.

'Is everything all right – to your satisfaction, I hope?'

'It's tewwific,' Rupert told him. 'They want the same all over again.'

Before Newman could intervene Basil pulled at Rupert's sleeve. He said something in an undertone and guided Rupert away from them into the Brasserie.

'Everything is perfect,' Tweed told the head waiter. 'You have served us a meal to remember.'

'Thank you, sir . . .'

By then they were well into their main course. Tweed and Newman had chosen fillet of turbot. Sharon and Paula were both eating skewers of scallops and lobster on a bed of mashed potato with diced vegetables. During brief pauses in her conversation Sharon had delicately devoured large portions of her meal. Now she put down her knife and fork and looked at Paula.

'Who was that silly schoolboy?'

'Oh, that was Rupert Strangeways. His father is Sir Guy Strangeways.'

'I met him several times in Washington – Sir Guy, I mean,' Sharon explained. 'A nice man. I shouldn't say it, but he deserves a better offspring.'

'If you hadn't said it,' Newman told her, 'I would have done. Anyway, he's gone now . . .'

There was silence for a while as they concentrated on the meal. After dessert had been served and consumed Tweed posed his question to Sharon.

'Have you encountered a man called Jake Ronstadt?'

A heavier silence descended on the table. Sharon was dabbing at her lips with her serviette. She turned to look at Newman.

'Tweed is an interesting man. He fires intriguing questions at the most unexpected moment.' She smiled warmly at Tweed. 'Like a detective. Yes, I have encountered Ronstadt twice at the Embassy in London. Briefly on both occasions. I think he's a horrible man. Like a gangster. I can't imagine what he's doing at the Embassy.'

'He's not there now, Sharon,' said Tweed.

'Oh, have they sent him back to Washington?'

'No, he's at the Euler.'

'The Euler?'

'It's a top hotel here in Basle, no more than a mile from where we are sitting.'

'I find that very peculiar. Why here in Basle?' Sharon asked.

'I've no idea. Someone who knows him by sight spotted him, told me. I was just curious.'

'So am I,' she said. 'Well, I'll be moving on soon. Not sure exactly when.'

'Moving on?' Tweed queried.

'Yes.' She turned, gave him her full attention. 'I was going to suggest we have coffee in the bar with a liqueur. That's when I was going to tell you.' She looked up as the waiter appeared. 'Can we have coffee in the bar? A quiet table if you can manage that.'

'Certainly, madame.'

Newman had turned round in his chair to survey the restaurant behind him. There were just a few couples here and there. He then saw Ed Osborne sitting at a table by himself. Osborne had a grim look on his face. Newman gave him a small salute. Osborne pretended not to see it, bent his head over a newspaper. What has disturbed him? Newman wondered.

Earlier, when Basil guided a wobbling Rupert through the Brasserie, the second restaurant in the hotel, and on into the bar, he had to hold him up. He had found Rupert at a table in the lobby. There were several empty glasses on the table Rupert was sitting at.

'Need another drink,' Rupert mumbled.

'Are you sure?'

'When I say need 'nother drink, I need 'nother drink. Wha's the matter, Basil? Don't understand the King's English?'

'It's the Queen's English these days. Has been for long as I can remember.'

'Basil!' Rupert said aggressively. 'You tellin' me how you want me to speak my own language? 'Nother Scotch. Wanna sit down.'

The bar was empty. For the moment there was no one behind the serving counter. Basil guessed the girl had taken an order into the restaurant. He kept Rupert moving. There was another exit which led out straight on to the street.

'You need some fresh air first,' Basil said firmly. 'Then we can come back and get something to drink.'

'Fresh air? Can't drink fresh air. Didn't you know that?'

'I'll bring you a drink outside,' Basil lied.

'Against Swish law. Drinkin' in the street. End up in pokey, we will.'

'Almost there.'

Basil was anxious to get Rupert out of sight before someone returned to the bar. He got a strong hold on

Rupert, propelled him to the door at the rear. He opened it with his back, hauled Rupert out with him. The outside air hit them like a blast from the Arctic. Rupert's legs gave way. Basil let him slide down until he was slumped with his back inside the alcove. Then he left him there, confident he would recover swiftly. He had no doubt Rupert would go straight back inside the bar to order another drink.

Basil hurried the short distance along the road, entered the hotel by the main door, took the lift to his room. He reappeared very quickly. He was wearing a long black overcoat which almost came to his ankles. He walked off into the night.

When Sharon's party walked through the Brasserie Tweed saw Nield and Butler having dinner at a table on their own. Neither of them looked up or said a word as they walked past. At another table, by himself, sat Marler. When he saw them coming he picked up his newspaper and began studying it.

'I'll go in first,' Newman said to Sharon. 'See if it's all clear.'

'I'm coming with you. People like that schoolboy don't worry me.'

A little distance behind them Tweed followed with Paula by his side. She kept her voice down.

'Rupert seems to have reverted to his normal obnoxious self.'

'I was sceptical about what he said to Newman. No more than a pipe dream, I'd say. He probably believed what he was saying at the time.'

'You really think so?'

'You sound dubious.'

'I think he was putting on an act. Here we are. And no sign of either of them, thank heavens.'

They ordered liqueurs from the girl who, at that moment, took up her position behind the bar counter. As soon as she saw them she came over and took their orders.

'Sharon,' Tweed began, 'I got the impression from what you said in the dining room that you are really fed up with the Americans.'

'I am. Which is why I'm out here. I was appalled to hear Ronstadt is in town. I can't stop myself working, but officially I'm here on holiday. I'm floating around while I take a big decision. I'm getting away from it all so I *can* think. I'm playing with the idea of moving to living in Britain permanently. Down at my manor in Dorset.'

'So you're staying on in Basle?'

'No. I need different surroundings. I'm soon going to Freiburg, staying at the Hotel Colombi, which has five stars. You know, you look very smart in that blue bird's-eye suit. Pity that pocket bulges.'

Tweed put his hand in his pocket, brought out Beck's mobile. He smiled with resignation.

'Should have left it in my room. Picked it up automatically.'

He had hardly spoken when the mobile started buzzing. He stood up, shrugged, looked at Sharon apologetically.

'Excuse me. I refuse to use these things when I'm with guests in a restaurant or bar. I'll be back in a minute . . .'

He walked over to an empty table well away from anyone else. Only then did he answer the mobile phone. It was Beck on the line.

'Tweed, where are you now?'

'Just finished dinner in the hotel.'

'Please get over here quickly. It's an emergency.'

Tweed returned to the guest table, apologized,

thanked Sharon for a marvellous evening, explained he had to rush off to a meeting. He then walked swiftly into the Brasserie. Marler, drinking coffee, looked up as Tweed swept past him. Tweed was about to step in the lift when he found Marler behind him. As they ascended he told Marler what had happened.

'I'm coming with you. No argument . . .'

31

'All hell has broken out in London,' Beck said grimly.

Tweed was taking off his coat. A uniformed policeman took it and also Marler's. Beck's office at police headquarters was bleak. The police chief was sitting down at a large wooden desk, its surface empty except for two phones and a pad with scribbles on it. Tweed sat down facing him, with Marler by his side.

'Tell me,' Tweed said.

'Late this morning a huge bomb exploded inside a store in Regent Street. There was a sale on. Crowded with shoppers. Reports say there are at least a hundred dead, many more injured. I had all this from Chief Inspector – now Superintendent – Roy Buchanan. Monica had phoned Berne. Luckily spoke to my assistant, who knows her. He gave her my number here. She passed it to Buchanan, who has phoned me, wants you to call him.'

'Then I'll do that from here, if I may.'

'There's more. Buchanan said an American syndicate has bought the *Daily Despatch*. One condition was they took over as soon as the deal was signed. An American editor has arrived. His first edition has a huge splash headline – FBI MUST TAKE OVER.'

'The net tightens,' Tweed said quietly.

'I can get Buchanan for you now.'

'Do it, please . . .'

Marler was looking round the office. The walls were painted an uninviting green. Two metal filing cabinets stood in one corner. The room was illuminated by fluorescent tubes suspended from the ceiling. The blinds over the windows were closed.

'Tweed here, Roy.'

'Beck has told you?'

'Yes. About Regent Street. The American takeover of the *Despatch*. Its damnable headline.'

'So you're partly in the picture. At lunchtime the Commissioner asked me to take over as head of the Anti-Terrorist Squad. I told him I must have full powers. He said the PM had already agreed that.'

'Sounds as though the PM's backbone has stiffened.'

'Regent Street was the last straw. They also tried to blow up a major power station. We had it covertly guarded. Two cars drove up close to it. They were stopped. The driver in the first car dived out, ran back to the second vehicle, dived into it. The second car took off, a policeman stood in its way to stop it – the car drove over him. He's dead. The first car was a mobile bomb. The radio device which would have detonated it from a distance was dismantled.'

'You've got a big job on your hands.'

'The one I wanted. I sent you a tape recording of my TV broadcast to the nation this afternoon. Has it arrived?'

'Not yet.'

'It will do any moment. Forget vanity. I want you to see how I'm going to handle the situation. How are you doing?'

'We've got a bunch of them out here. We may be on the eve of a major battle.'

'Good luck. I must go now.'

'Take care.'

Tweed put down the phone. He stood up, hands in his pockets, staring into space. Marler thought he had never seen him stand so motionless, with such an expression on his face. It reminded him of a picture he had once seen of Bismarck. Tweed came out of his trancelike stance.

'Thank you, Arthur. Can I ask you a favour? When we cross the border into Germany could you be sure Marler's car isn't searched?'

'I'm sure Marler wouldn't be carrying anything I would disapprove of,' Beck smiled drily. 'And I'll warn the officer at the checkpoint to leave him alone. How many cars have you?'

'Just two,' Tweed replied.

Beck tore off the top sheet of his pad. He pushed it towards them. Then he rolled a pen across the table.

'Could you put down the registration numbers of your cars?'

'I can do that,' Marler told him, reaching for pad and pen.

'I'll pass those on to the checkpoint officer,' Beck told them.

'One final point, Arthur,' Tweed interjected. 'I'm assuming the same arrangement applies. You'll call me on your mobile as soon as you know Ronstadt is on the move?'

'I was going to do that anyway. Strictly between us, I have installed a new plain-clothes officer from Berne as a guest at the Euler. He'll inform me the moment he sees signs the Americans are leaving.'

'I'd like to thank you for your very thorough co-operation,' Tweed said. 'If there's what I think there is in the Black Forest you will have played a key role.'

'Nonsense.' Beck paused. 'I hope you approve, but I took it on myself to phone your old friend, Otto Kuhl-mann, chief of the Kriminalpolizei in Wiesbaden. He promised me he wouldn't get in your way, but he might just come in useful.'

'Ronstadt is not the only man who can close in a net. Thank you again. I'd better get back to the hotel. I have to brief my people.'

Ronstadt sat in the bar at the Euler with Vernon. They were the only two people in the place, except for the barman, who was a long distance from their table. Ronstadt was wearing his favourite outfit, a heavy brown leather jacket with leather trousers of the same colour, and rubber-soled shoes which made not a sound when he was moving.

'You and Brad dump all the weapons, the rest of the explosives?' Ronstadt asked.

'Sure, Chief.'

'Had to be in daylight, I guess,' Ronstadt said casually.

'No. After dark. We drove up the river. Got well out of Basle, found a quiet place. No houses. No people. Nothin' at all. Backed the car up to the river's edge. Brad handed me the stuff, I dumped it in the river.'

'You know somethin'? Go on like this and you'll make deputy.'

'Thought I was that now.'

'*Temporary* deputy – until I see how you make out. Say, Vernon, you see a big snake. Whaddya do?'

'Run like hell . . .'

'So, mebbe, Vernon, you won't make it. You cut off its head.'

'I don't get where you're comin' from.'

'Tweed. He's the head of the snake's causin' me trouble. So I made arrangements. Can't risk him messing with us where we's goin' any time now.'

'That's smart, Chief. Very smart.'

312

'I thought it was.' Ronstadt chuckled, an unpleasant sound. 'I thought it was . . .'

Tweed and Marler left Spiegelhof, police headquarters, for the short walk down Spiegelgasse to the Three Kings. A tram, empty except for the driver, trundled along the street they had to cross. As the rumble of its wheels disappeared the cold silence they had come to associate with Basle descended.

Marler was looking up, staring at the tops of the buildings they passed as they reached the other side. They were close now to the main entrance to the hotel. Tweed was deep in thought, his feet moving mechanically, his mind on what Buchanan had told him. He arrived at the revolving door. Suddenly Marler grabbed hold of him, shoved him forcefully into a compartment of the door which caused him to slam into it and be pushed inside. At the same moment a bullet hit the stone floor where he had been standing a millisecond before. The bullet ricocheted into space.

Glancing up at the building opposite, Marler followed him into the lobby. Tweed was waiting for him. He spoke calmly.

'What was that?'

'A bullet with your name on it.' Marler kept his voice down as the receptionist was coming towards them from behind the counter. 'I'd go after him but he's like a cat burglar. I'd say he's long gone already.'

'The Phantom?'

'No doubt about it.'

'Don't mention it to the others.'

The receptionist reached them. She was holding an addressed package. She was holding it out towards Tweed when Marler took it.

'This arrived by courier for Mr Tweed. He said the plane was late. Something about ice on the runway.'

'Thank you,' said Tweed.

'I'll take this to my room, check it carefully before I open it,' Marler said when they were inside the lift.

'Come straight to my room as soon as you can. I'll have everyone else there when you arrive. I want to ask some questions first. You're ready to leave at the drop of a hat?'

'Before the hat hits the floor.'

Tweed gave Paula some instructions when she arrived in his room first. As he was speaking she listened, then stared in disbelief.

'I want you to do the same thing with the Hotel Colombi in Freiburg that you did with the Schwarzwälder Hof. Book rooms at the Colombi for all of us. Give them my credit card number and tell them we'll pay for any unoccupied rooms. Not sure when we'll get there.'

'What on earth for?' she wanted to know. 'Sharon is staying there.'

'I know. That's not the reason. This way we have two different bases in Freiburg. We may find it useful to flit from one to the other.'

'I'll call now . . .'

Tweed waited until everyone was settled in the room. When Paula completed her call, he used the phone to contact Keith Kent.

'Keith, like you to be here in my room to hear what's going on.'

'First of all,' he said, seated on a hard-backed chair, 'Paula, I would be interested in your impression of Sharon. You did sit facing her during our leisurely dinner.'

314

'She's enigmatic.'

'That doesn't tell me anything. Be more specific.'

'She's very experienced in the company of a lot of people, I'd say. But she doesn't hold the stage. I can't quite penetrate what's under that deep calm. On the other hand she can be very buoyant and great fun. I think she's tugged this way and that as to whether to stay in America or move to Britain for good. I sense she's leaning towards the latter. Sensibly, she's moving to different locations to get a perspective on her life.'

'What do you think, Bob?'

'I don't believe one word she says.'

There was a hush. Paula looked quite taken aback at his reaction. So much so, she began smoking one of her rare cigarettes.

'What do you base that on, Bob?' Tweed asked.

'I was joking. I think she's great.'

'What is it about her that makes her so attractive to men?' Tweed enquired.

'I can tell you that,' Paula replied. '*Personality*. She's a mix of the cool and the exciting. This intrigues men. They're not sure where they are with her. Outcome? They want to know her better.'

'That's pretty shrewd,' Newman agreed.

'I've got grim news for you,' Tweed said suddenly. 'It came to Marler and me via Beck and Roy Buchanan . . .'

He told them about the horror which had taken place in London. They listened in complete silence. Butler bunched a fist as though he wanted one of the opposition present to slam it into. Nield closed his eyes, then opened them, his expression one of fury.

'We've got to bust these bastards,' Butler exclaimed.

'I agree with you one hundred per cent,' Tweed assured him. 'I want you all now to watch a tape of Roy

Buchanan broadcasting on TV this afternoon. Marler, could you oblige?'

'Right now,' Marler said.

He inserted it into the video recorder. Picking up the remote control, he backed away, perched on the arm of Paula's chair. The red light was already glowing on the set. He pressed the button and a BBC news bulletin was showing. Scenes of carnage far worse than those seen earlier of the bombed store in Oxford Street were preceded by an unusual warning from the newsreader.

'Before we show the following pictures we would advise anyone who is squeamish not to watch. We especially suggest children should not see what follows.'

Paula gasped, wanted to close her eyes. She forced herself to go on viewing. They reminded her of scenes of the war in Vietnam. The pictures were a tangle of horribly injured victims, of stretcher after stretcher being brought out with the bodies on them showing no signs of life. Chaos and blood were everywhere. A woman staggered out of the ruined entrance. A paramedic appeared, took hold of her gently, removed her from camera range.

The scenes of carnage gave way to the reappearance of the newsreader, his voice solemn.

'There will now be a short broadcast by Superintendent Buchanan of the Metropolitan Police.'

Roy Buchanan's image appeared, a view of head and shoulders. He stared straight at the camera, his expression grim, his voice calm and determined.

'Ladies and gentlemen, the Commissioner of the Metropolitan Police has just appointed me as Head of the Anti-Terrorist Squad. I have also been given full powers to call on the help of any other unit I may deem to be necessary. We know that the atrocity you have just seen – together with the bombing of two other department stores in the capital – is not the work of the IRA. Nor is it the work of any ultra-extremist Muslim sect. I shall be working day and night to hunt down these vile murderers. I have given orders that when they are encountered by my men, if they open fire, we shall shoot to kill. Let there be no doubt about that. Thank you for giving me your attention.'

'That was pretty tough,' Newman said as Marler switched off the TV. 'Thank God. He really means it.'

'So do I,' Tweed said very quietly. 'We will exterminate these vermin.'

Marler remained behind when the others had left, after a warning from Tweed that no one should contemplate going to bed. That they must be ready to leave at a moment's notice.

'After we got back from Beck's place,' Marler said, 'and you missed death by inches, I went up to my room. I immediately phoned Windermere's room. There was no reply. I then phoned Rupert's room. Again there was no reply. So both were out.'

'You think one of them is the Phantom?'

'Don't you?'

'It could be a third person who hasn't yet appeared on the scene,' Tweed mused.

'The Phantom is a crack shot, although twice he's just missed. Once with Paula at Irongates in Kent, the second time with you tonight.'

'You don't think they could have been deliberate misses, to unnerve me? And why has it to be a man. These days there are some women who are as expert shots as men,' Tweed speculated.

'I'll get him – or her – in my sights sooner or later. I still have my Armalite.'

'By the way,' Tweed said, 'when we drive to Freiburg, which I'm convinced will be the case, we'll be staying at the Colombi to begin with. I remember it – a first-class hotel not far from the railway station and fairly close to the outskirts. We have the Schwarzwälder Hof as an alternative base. It's deep inside the old city. We may even dodge backwards and forwards. And don't be surprised if, when we do arrive at the Colombi, we see Sharon. She told me at dinner she's going there.'

'What is that woman up to? I saw her when you came through the Brasserie on your way to the bar.'

'She's trying to decide whether to leave America for ever, to settle down in England.'

Someone tapped on the door. When Marler opened it Paula walked in. Without sitting down, she stopped uncertainly.

'Is this the wrong moment for me to turn up? I can always go back to my room. I was restless. The waiting.'

'Stay,' Tweed told her. 'Sit down.' He turned to Marler. 'I was wondering why you asked about Sharon.'

'I doubt if instructions to kill you were transmitted over the phone. Which suggests to me they were given by someone inside this hotel.'

'What are you talking about?' Paula demanded. 'Instructions to kill Tweed?'

'I was going to tell you later,' Tweed said quickly. 'On our way back from seeing Beck across the road someone took a pot-shot at me. Missed by a mile.'

'A short mile,' Marler corrected.

'So why query Sharon?' Tweed asked him. 'There are other people in the hotel.'

'Who, for example?'

'Ed Osborne.'

It was in the middle of the night when Jake Ronstadt called the members of his outfit to his suite. As ordered, they were all fully dressed. Unusually he stood at the head of the table.

'Who the hell gave you permission to sit down?' he snarled when they had automatically occupied their chairs. 'Get on your feet.'

'Anyone gettin' old and tired?' he sneered as they jumped up.

'Sorry, Chief. We're OK,' said Vernon.

'You'd better be – otherwise you'll find yourself with a bullet in the head, dumped in a ditch.' His voice changed, became dangerously wheedling. 'Has everyone packed, like I said? If you ain't raise your right hand.'

No hands were raised. Ronstadt stared slowly round, his hard eyes glaring at each man. They waited, not daring to move a muscle. Ronstadt spoke again, this time in a calm voice.

'We're leaving – for Freiburg first, then the Black Forest. I've told you before. But in case you've got short memories I'm goin' to repeat myself. I'll drive the lead car. Vernon comes up behind me. When we're on the autobahn, Vernon, I'll signal where you turn off – with a wave of my arm. You go up the slip road, meet the two cars waiting, transfer the weapons into your car, then drive down to rejoin me. Is that too difficult for you?'

'Piece of cake.'

'Then ram it down your throat. The bill's paid, so why are you all hangin' around here?'

'So Denise never called you after leaving?' Tweed asked.

'No. Why would she?' Marler said. 'I'm the last person she'll want to see again. She must have concocted that whole yarn about the *Minotaur*.'

'Seems she did.'

Tweed was trying to think up things to say. In his

room everyone was gathered, including Keith Kent, who seemed the most placid. In the middle of the night there was an air of unspoken tension. Everyone was waiting to get on with it, knowing that nothing might happen. Paula sat in an armchair, swinging her crossed legs. She reached for her pack in her shoulder bag, then decided she didn't want a cigarette. Newman, seated on a couch, kept checking his watch. Marler was leaning against a wall. The other two who were most patient were Butler and Nield, chatting quietly to each other.

'Anyone like some more coffee?' Tweed enquired. 'Helps to keep you alert.'

No one did. Newman was thinking he could have had a nap in his room. Paula got up, went over to the windows, carefully peeked through a gap she made in the closed curtains. On the opposite bank of the Rhine a few lights gleamed in the old houses, their reflections trembling in the river. Insomniacs, she thought. They existed all over the world.

The mobile phone on the table began buzzing. Tweed forced himself not to grab. Picking it up, he was aware of six pairs of eyes watching him intently.

'Hello?'

'They're on the move. Must be close to the border.'

'Thank you.'

Beck's distinctive voice had come clearly across. Tweed put the mobile into his pocket. He spoke offhandedly, as though they were going on a day trip to a resort.

'Time to go. I suspect we have very little time left.'

In the Atlantic, well clear of the American coastline, Crag – Rear Admiral Joseph Honeywood, in command of the huge naval task force – settled into his seat in the Island of the *President*. It was night and he liked to be at control after dark. That was when you could get an unpleasant surprise. He looked at his Operations Officer.

'We're making good time. We should be on station in the English Channel less than four days from now.'

'No doubt about it, sir.'

'And so far, Bill, we've been lucky. We haven't been spotted by any other ship or a commercial airliner.'

'I have a feeling that will go on. The Brits will wake up to find us off their shores.'

'The SEALs are ready for action?'

'They are. If they have to land they'll sweep over anything that gets in their way. They're rarin' to go.'

32

Driving through Basle at night was an eerie experience, Paula was thinking. She liked the city, but in the dark the medieval buildings, illuminated only by street lanterns at intervals, had a majestic – and sinister – atmosphere. There were no trams running at this hour, the streets were deserted, the shadows deep and menacing.

She sat beside Newman, who was driving the first car. In the rear seats Tweed was alongside Keith Kent. Tweed was sitting up erect, his eyes everywhere. The adrenalin was flowing and he was very alert. He knew the layout of the city well and was on the lookout for anything unusual, which should not be there.

'We're getting close to the border,' he warned after a while.

'Marler's keeping up with us well, not too close, not far behind,' Newman commented after checking his rear-view mirror.

Tweed glanced back through the rear window. Marler

was driving the second Audi. As passengers he had Butler and Nield in the back. The seat beside him was unoccupied – for a purpose. He slowed as Newman's car lost speed, then the two cars stopped.

In the near distance was the checkpoint at the border. Paula could make out the heavy figure of Jake Ronstadt behind the wheel of a black Audi. He had his window down and appeared to be arguing with the duty officer. Another officer searched the interior of the car while three men in dark coats stood outside.

'What the hell is this all about?' Ronstadt was demanding for the third time. 'I've shown you my diplomatic passport. You have no right to stop us – let alone search the car.'

'Information received, sir,' another officer replied.

'What information might that be, buddy?'

'We are not allowed to disclose our sources. Would you mind stepping out so I can check the front?'

'I damned well would. I'm reporting this to Washington. And I'd like your name.'

'As Chief Customs Officer at this crossing point I have sole authority . . .'

He paused as another officer pulled at his sleeve. They walked a short distance from the car. They conversed briefly and the Chief Customs Officer was careful not to look to where Newman's car was waiting with Marler's, parked in the shadows. He returned to the Audi.

'If it was a large consignment we would have found it by now. You are free to proceed.'

Ronstadt started his engine. He lowered his window. The moment he had crossed the border he shouted back, 'You can stick your sole authority.'

He pressed his foot down, increasing speed as he drove onto the autobahn. Behind him three more black

Audis followed. In his own Audi, Newman commented while he waited a little longer.

'Four cars. I counted four men in each – that's sixteen. We're outnumbered.'

'That worries you?' Tweed enquired from the back.

'Not at all. We've been outnumbered more heavily before. Time to go.'

The officer waved them through. He even saluted them. Then they were on the wide autobahn. It had two lanes in both directions, separated by a metal crash barrier and hedges. They drove on through the night and there was no other traffic as Newman held back from the convoy ahead. He drove so he could always see the red lights of the rear-most vehicle. Paula was shielding a pocket torch as she examined an ADAC map she had purchased of the Schwarzwald area.

'We turn off at junction 63 to get to Freiburg,' she called out. 'It's quite a distance yet.'

'We'll get there.'

In Ronstadt's car Leo Madison, the man who had murdered Juliette Leroy in St Ursanne, sat beside Ronstadt. He kept looking back down the autobahn behind them. He was trying to decide if it was wise to speak. He decided it was.

'Every time we go round a big curve I see two white cars behind us.'

'So?'

'When you speed up, they speed up. When you go slower, they do.'

'So?'

'Reckon it could be Tweed and his mob. I've heard German drivers love overtaking.'

'That worries you, Moonhead?'

'The name is Leo Madison. They may tail us to where we're goin' and that could be a problem.'

323

'Moonhead, I expected Tweed to follow us. What do you think that crap at the checkpoint was about? Holdin' us up so Tweed could get there. A little idea of that nutter Police Chief Beck. I'm happy if that is Tweed behind us. Wait our opportunity and wipe out Tweed and his boys off the face of the earth. Any more comments floating round in that thing you call a brain?'

'Nothin' I can think of, Chief.'

'Well, we're comin' up to junction 66. That's where Vernon peels off up the slip road, collects the weapons, brings them back to us. We wait.'

A few minutes later he slowed, lowered his window, reached out an arm and made a circling gesture. He continued to slow down and then parked at the side of the autobahn, which was illegal.

Tweed had taken from his pocket a pair of night glasses. He was focusing them on the lead car of the convoy of black Audis as they swept round a curve. He grunted.

'They're slowing down a lot. More than they have previously.'

'They're testing,' Newman suggested. 'To see if we do the same thing, which we have to. Maybe Ronstadt suspects we're following him.'

'I'm sure he does,' Tweed replied. 'At least I hope so. I want to keep up the pressure on him. Keith, you saw him when you went into the Zürcher Kredit Bank. What was your impression of him?'

'Very confident, quite dynamic, impatient and with a short fuse.'

'Which is the picture I got of him when he came over to see Paula and me when we were dining at Santorini's. That short fuse may blow – when it does he's liable to make a mistake. And now the whole convoy has stopped.'

'So I'll park here until we see what they're up to,' Newman remarked. 'Except it's totally illegal and we'll be caught if a patrol car comes along.'

'If it does,' Tweed assured him, 'I'll ask them to use their radio transmitter to put me through to Otto Kuhlmann in Wiesbaden. That will stop them searching Marler's car . . .'

'Marler wouldn't like that,' said Marler at the open window. 'I pulled up and came along to see what's happening.'

'No idea. It's possible they may be picking up some weapons. They wouldn't risk carrying them through the checkpoint.'

'Then now is the time to take them,' Marler urged.

'It is not. We shoot down unarmed men – with diplomatic passports – and we haven't a leg to stand on. Even Kuhlmann would have to arrest us.' Tweed had pressed his night glasses to his eyes after removing his spectacles as he spoke. 'The second car is moving off by itself. What's up there?'

'From my map,' said Paula, 'I'm pretty sure they're stopped just before junction 66.'

'I think you're right. The second car has disappeared up a slip road. Yes, that must be it, they're collecting a load of weapons. We'll just sit it out here until they make their next move.'

'Meantime,' Marler said, 'I'll hand you back your ironmongery.'

He gave Newman his Smith & Wesson, his holster and ammo. Then he returned to Paula her Browning and ammo. Diving his hand inside the canvas holdall slung over his shoulder, he produced two stun grenades, passed them to Newman. Taking out another grenade, he extended it to Paula.

'I don't think I need that.'

'Take it. They're not Pekinese waiting a bit further up

the autobahn. They're the most cold-blooded and pro-fessional killers we have met so far. That's better.'

He looked at Keith Kent. The money tracer was sitting relaxed as though half asleep.

'I think, Keith, you should have a Walther automatic.'

'Thank you. It's a little while since I used one of these.'

'We'd better keep you locked up safely in a cupboard somewhere, then,' Marler commented before returning to his car.

'While we're waiting,' Tweed said, 'you may be inter-ested to hear that Sharon checked out of the hotel an hour before we left. She drove off in a Mercedes.'

'She must have made up her mind quickly to go on to Freiburg,' Paula remarked.

'She must indeed. I found that out at the last moment when I paid the bill at the Three Kings. I also heard from the receptionist that Ed Osborne also had checked out and taken off in his own car.'

'Again to Freiburg, I imagine,' said Paula. 'That town is going to be rather crowded. I meant to ask you earlier: any word from Monica about the identity of Charlie?'

'Monica did call me. Very discreetly. In words no one except me would understand she did inform me that so far she has found no trace of anyone called Charlie. She's still digging.'

Five minutes later Tweed was again gazing through his night glasses. Paula had closed the window to stop any more of the night air freezing them. Newman had kept the engine on, so the heating was beginning to warm up the interior again. Tweed lowered his glasses.

'That second car which drove off up the slip road has appeared again. All four men got out carrying suitcases. They deposited two cases in the first car and then one in each of the last two cars. They must have an armoury now.'

'So Marler was right to hand out grenades,' Newman said. 'And they're on the move again.'

He waited a short time, then drove on with Marler following behind him. Paula started checking her map again. Ahead of them the autobahn stretched away into the distance. A moon had risen, casting a milky glow over the empty countryside on either side. They had passed junction 65 when Newman reduced speed. Paula looked up, saw a faint covering of snow on the autobahn. The convoy in front of them slowed seconds later.

'Here and there are patches of ice under this snow,' Newman explained.

'I wouldn't want to skid at the speed you were going,' Paula remarked.

'It would be all right if there was ice all the way,' Newman told her. 'Then I'd know how to handle it. But they are random patches. You hit them without warning. Ronstadt has obviously come to the same conclusion. I will give him one thing – he's an expert driver.'

'He probably started out his career driving get-away cars in the States,' interjected Keith for the first time.

'Just the type,' Newman agreed. 'Then worked his way up over a pile of bodies.'

They drove on and on through the night. The black Audi convoy had slowed down. Newman guessed Ronstadt was no keener on racing across ice patches than he was. The moon was now illuminating the light covering of snow on the fields stretching away. In the rear of the car Paula was once more studying her map.

'We're just about to pass junction 65. Then it's a longish run to junction 64. When we eventually reach 63 we can drive straight into Freiburg.'

'Can I look at that map?' Tweed asked her.

Using the torch, he examined the map carefully. He was relying partly on his memory, but the Germans might well have changed the road layout since his previous visit. Holding on to the map, he called out to Newman.

'When we've passed junction 65, could you pull up? I need to have a brief word with Marler.'

'Will do . . .'

'We have just passed junction 65,' Paula reported a few minutes later.

'I know.'

Newman reduced speed, then pulled over and parked. Marler had stopped close behind them. Without being summoned he appeared at the window which Tweed had lowered. He smiled as he leant inside.

'So far, so good. What's the next move?'

'Look at this map.' Tweed used the torch so Marler could see clearly. 'If Ronstadt turns off at junction 63, which I think he will, we're then on route 31 leading direct to Freiburg. But here, close to the city, the road splits. Right fork leads to the Münster – close to the Schwarzwälder Hof where we have rooms booked. Left fork will take us in close to the Colombi, where we also have rooms booked. I just have a feeling that several of the cars behind Ronstadt will peel off, taking the right fork. If that happens Paula will flash her torch three times through the rear window. That means you leave us, take the right fork, follow any cars which do peel off. Wait till the occupants have booked in at the Schwarzwälder Hof, then book in yourselves.'

'Clear enough,' replied Marler. 'What are you going to do?'

'Follow Ronstadt – if he does take the left fork. You can always communicate with me at the Colombi in that eventuality.'

'I'll get back to my car.'

'And I'd better get moving,' Newman said as Tweed closed his window. 'There's continuous ice now under this snow, so hold on to your seat belts. I have to catch them up.'

Once moving, he increased speed. Now and then he could feel thinner ice crunching on his wheels. He kept up his speed. Paula was tense. Tweed, having given his instructions, leant back and closed his eyes for a brief nap. There was only one moment, as they charged forward, when the car began to skid. Newman went with the skid, hands relaxed on the wheel. He came close to the steel barrier, then straightened up, slowed.

'That's fortunate,' he remarked, 'I can see their red lights. Relax, everybody . . .'

'We're very close to junction 64,' Paula reported a while later.

'Coming up now,' Newman replied. 'There, we've passed it,' he said a few minutes later. 'So we're now heading for the vital junction 63.'

'Which isn't too far ahead,' Paula warned.

'The decisive moment,' said Tweed, who had opened his eyes.

'Be funny if Ronstadt just keeps on and on,' Newman reflected. 'We'd find ourselves heading for Mannheim.'

'Then I'd be lost,' Tweed admitted. 'All my thinking in ruins.'

'The junction beyond – 62 – also leads to Freiburg,' Paula said optimistically.

She sensed that the tension engendered by doubt was present in the car now. Newman had tightened his grip on the wheel. When she glanced back Keith Kent was leaning forward, staring ahead. Tweed, on the other hand, appeared to be the soul of relaxation, leaning back against his seat, his eyes half-closed.

'I daren't get any closer,' Newman said. 'They'd be sure we are following them.'

It was a pointless remark. Paula realized that, unusually, Newman had felt he had to say something.

'They will be sure by now,' Tweed said quietly.

'Junction 63 is coming up,' Paula said quietly.

'I *can* read the signs,' Newman snapped back at her.

A gloomy silence descended inside the car. No one spoke another word. They were staring ahead.

33

'We're really goin' to fool 'em good,' Ronstadt gloated. 'Poor old Tweed. He ain't gonna know what to do.'

'If he falls for it,' warned Leo Madison, by his side.

'Moonhead, ain't it occurred to you? I could open the door on your side and shove you out. I reckon the best you could hope for is a cracked skull.'

Madison decided it would be best not to answer back. Ronstadt had a revolver tucked down inside his belt behind the smart suit he was wearing. Madison also recalled how Ronstadt had smashed his fist into Vernon's jaw during the meeting in his suite at the Euler. Ronstadt was a very unpredictable man.

Some distance behind the black Audi convoy, Paula had heaved a sigh of relief when the cars ahead turned at junction 63 onto the road to Freiburg. She relaxed and Tweed squeezed her arm.

'It's going to work out all right.'

'I don't know how you do it. You seem to read Jake Ronstadt's mind. And I have known you do that before, with other people.'

'There's no magic about it. I just try to put myself into the shoes of the enemy. You've got a torch ready to signal to Marler when – or if – it's necessary?'

'I'm ready.'

She settled down to look at the moonlit landscape. The road they were now travelling on was narrower than the autobahn but it had a good surface. It was elevated above the surrounding white fields below them and leafless trees, like sentinels, stood at intervals on either side. It was rather like driving along a tree-lined boulevard. Then she leaned forward, peering ahead. In the mid-distance reared up a brooding white massif, a range like a huge frozen wave.

'What's the grim-looking thing in the distance?' she asked.

'That,' Tweed told her, 'is the Black Forest.'

'Looks pretty sinister.'

'In winter, after a heavy fall of snow, it can be beautiful.'

'I'll take your word for it.'

She concentrated on checking her map. They were not too far from where the road forked. When she looked ahead again the massif seemed much higher and menacing. Nearer to them she saw a wall of buildings huddled together. Above them glowed a faint halo which, she assumed, was street lights. She sat up and gazed steadily at the receding red lights of the convoy.

Then she saw the lead car disappearing to the left. Behind it three cars turned to the right. She twisted round in her seat. Marler's car was fairly close. Lifting the torch, she carefully switched it on and off three times. She thought she saw, behind the wheel, Marler's head nodding in acknowledgement.

'You predicted again what they were going to do,' she said to Tweed.

'I don't always get it right.' He leaned forward. 'When you've taken the left fork, Bob, I'll try and guide you to the Colombi. Let's just hope they haven't moved it,' he added with a touch of humour.

'Won't Ronstadt guide me there if I follow him?'

'If I'm right, yes he will. If you're getting too close call on my help. And, everyone, when we get to our rooms, unpack the very minimum of clothing. We may have to leave the hotel very quickly . . .'

They waited ten minutes parked in a dark street after Ronstadt and the three men with him had entered the Colombi. A uniformed employee took his car away. By night the dark buildings on both sides cast black shadows. In contrast, the illuminated entrance to the Colombi looked warm and inviting. Tweed checked his watch.

'Time to go inside. Let's hope Ronstadt and his thugs have gone to their rooms. If they're hungry they'll probably have to use room service . . .'

When they alighted from their car, porters took their bags. The same employee who had driven away Ronstadt's car attempted to do the same thing with their Audi. Newman intervened.

'I may have to drive off quickly soon. Please leave it where it is.'

'That would be most unusual, sir.'

'I'm an unusual man.'

Newman smiled at him. He handed him a hundred-mark note. There was no further argument. Tweed and Paula had walked inside. While Tweed was registering Paula glanced round. The hotel reeked of luxury and taste. Leaving the reception area, Tweed glanced into a lounge, stood stock-still.

'What is it?' whispered Paula as Newman joined them.

'Come in and see for yourself.'

Tweed walked in, his coat over his arm. It was like a replay of their arrival at the Three Kings. The first person he saw, leaning forward in an armchair, was Sir Guy

Strangeways. In another chair, facing him, with a table between them, Sharon sat with a glass in her hand. She looked up. She raised her eyebrows, then smiled invitingly.

'What an unexpected pleasure. Now you can host a dinner for me here tomorrow evening. No, it's almost 6 a.m. I should have said this evening.'

'Are you following us?' Strangeways demanded abruptly.

'You arrived together, then?'

'No, we didn't,' Sharon said quickly. 'I drove myself here in a Merc. I told Guy where I was going and he said he'd be coming too. I thought he was joking. But, as you see, here he is. Do sit down. Paula, how nice to see you. And, Bob, you have completed the party.'

'A party? At six o'clock in the morning?' Newman queried.

'Why not?' Sharon gave him an inviting smile. 'It's the serene time of the day. I love it. No one up yet in the hotel. Just the five of us. Champers, Paula?'

'Not for me, thank you.'

Sharon was holding a bottle she had taken out of a silver bucket of ice. From a side table she had picked up a fresh glass.

'You'll join me, won't you, Bob?'

'Just one glass. Might keep me awake. Or put me to sleep.'

'And, Tweed, you'll join me. Tell me, how much sleep have you had in the past twenty-four hours?'

'I had a couple of brief naps in the car on our way here.'

'I thought so. I'm sure you and I have one thing in common.' She gave him a ravishing smile as she poured him a glass. 'We are both blessed with immense stamina. I get by on four hours a night. Less, if I have to.

'More for you, Guy?' she suggested.

'No, thank you. Think I'll have to crawl up to bed soon. I did ask you a question, Tweed. Why are you following us?'

'You've just rephrased the question, Guy. And I was going to ask you just the same question. First you arrive at the Three Kings in Basle, just before I do. Now you turn up here.'

'I think I must get up to bed now.' Guy dragged himself out of his chair. 'I'm dropping. Goodnight . . .'

Tweed was mentally contrasting Guy with Sharon. The man who had just left them had had puffy eyes, a strained look, almost haggard. On the other hand Sharon looked fresh as the proverbial daisy, ready for anything. He looked at her and the green eyes glowed back.

'I got the impression Guy is very worried about something. Did you?' he asked her.

'Yes, I did. Ever since he sat down, which was quite a while ago, he's been crossing and recrossing his legs. Then he kept shifting round in his chair. I asked him point-blank. He wouldn't even give me a hint. He drank a lot of champagne and I had to order another bottle. Mind you . . .' She smiled again. 'I contributed to killing that first bottle. He's definitely got something on his mind, but won't come out with it.'

'Might depend on what it is,' Tweed mused, sipping at his glass.

'I suppose it might.' Sharon looked at Paula. 'You're awfully quiet. Hardly said a word since you sat down.'

'Sorry. Excuse my bad manners. The fact is I need some sleep. It's been a long day.' She smiled. 'And a long night. I hope you don't mind if I go up to my room.'

'Think we could all do with a bit of kip,' Newman said, standing up at the same moment as Paula. 'Look forward to seeing you later.'

'You're not going to leave me on my own, are you?' Sharon asked, gazing at Tweed.

'I'm afraid I am. I have some papers I have to go through. As Bob said, we'll see you later.'

'You're abandoning me,' she said with mock disappointment.

'Not for long. How could I?'

'Tweed,' she called out as he was leaving, 'that awful man Ed Osborne is staying here. Thought you ought to know . . .'

'The eagles gather.'

'I'd like both of you to pop along to my room with me. Just for a moment,' Tweed said as they were going upstairs. 'We have to plan for any emergency.'

Tweed unlocked the door to his room and let Paula go in first. She looked round and gave a sigh of pleasure.

'What a lovely room. Pure luxury.' She sat on his bed and bounced on it. 'If you're not careful I'm just going to drop off here.'

'Then I'll have to move all my stuff to your room. Not that I'll unpack much.'

'What do you think of Ed Osborne being here? We knew he would be coming, but he gave you details of the Schwarzwälder Hof. Not this place.'

'You heard my comment when Sharon warned me.'

'Which tells me a lot. You mentioned planning for an emergency. I took that to mean a sudden take-off. I've already decided I'll have a very quick shower, change into fresh underclothes, sleep in them. When we leave I'll be in my warm clothes, leggings and boots. I think it will be cold.'

'It will be freezing,' Newman told her.

'Paula has put her finger on the basic plan,' Tweed said, sitting in a chair. 'Ready to leave at a moment's notice. I think we'll get warning that they're on the move from Marler. There are a lot more of them at the

Schwarzwälder Hof. Here there's only Ronstadt and his three thugs.'

'So you're relying on Marler to call you?' Newman suggested.

'Yes. When he came to the car window to return your weaponry I slipped him Beck's powerful mobile phone.'

'What if Beck happened to call you?' Paula enquired.

'Then Marler would pass onto me whatever message Beck wanted to pass on. Incidentally, Ronstadt will probably leave tomorrow – that is, today – unless something happens to upset him.'

'Let's hope it does,' said Paula as she got up to leave. 'I'm not too keen on an early departure. I've got some sleep to catch up on. And I get the impression you're all falling for Sharon.'

'What man wouldn't?' Tweed said with a dry smile. 'She really is the most amazing woman.'

'Don't expect me down to breakfast. I'll have it in my room. I really couldn't stand seeing Ed Osborne at another table. He looked so grim when we left the bar at the Three Kings.' She made a face. 'As though he was expecting the heavens to fall.'

'Perhaps they will,' replied Tweed.

'Any idea where we're going when we head into the Black Forest?' she asked as she reached the door.

'In Kurt Schwarz's little black notebook, which I have with me, he mentioned Höllental. Which, as you know, is German for Hell's Valley.'

'You're so good for my morale. Give my love to Marler if he does call . . .'

Earlier, after turning down the right fork, Marler had found it easy to follow the three black Audis. Not that the route was easy. They soon plunged into a one-way system which twisted and turned. It wasn't long before

Marler realized they had entered the Altstadt – the Old City of Freiburg, built centuries ago.

Ancient stone buildings lined either side of the narrow streets. The lighting, from old street lanterns, was dim but adequate. They kept moving into shadows, then briefly into an illuminated area. The streets became cobbled, the car rocked as Marler kept down to a slow pace, imitating the red lights of the three cars ahead. There was hardly any other traffic, which was a blessing, but cars were parked everywhere, which was a curse.

Suddenly he caught sight of the moonlit towering spire of the Münster. Nield, sitting beside him, stared fixedly ahead.

'I reckon we must be nearly there. I think they're parking in that big open space by the Münster.'

'I think so too,' Marler agreed.

'So we wait until they've pushed off to the hotel.'

'Seems sensible. We'll give them time to register, get up to their rooms. If possible, I'd like both of you to keep under cover. It probably means going straight up to your rooms while I register, then having something to eat in the rooms.'

'Suits me,' said Butler.

'Good strategy, I'd say,' Nield agreed. 'What will you do?'

'Eat in the restaurant. I think those thugs will do the same. I want to memorize their faces.'

'Not an enjoyable pastime, I'd imagine,' commented Nield.

Having parked their cars, all twelve occupants walked out of the Münsterplatz and down a side street. Marler waited a little longer, then drove his car into the square and chose a place to park some distance from the three black Audis. He checked his watch, waited a minute or two longer, then they left the car, carrying their bags and walking down the side street.

It was very narrow, cobbled and black as pitch. Emerging at the other end they saw to their left the bright lights of the hotel. They entered, were met by a wave of warmth as they opened the door. Marler made straight for the reception desk.

'I'm sorry, but we are rather late,' he said to the man behind the counter. 'We have bookings.' He gave their names. 'My two friends are very tired. Could they go straight up to their rooms while I register?'

'Yes, sir. Here are their keys. Now, if you will register . . .'

'I'd like something to eat,' Marler told the receptionist. 'Any chance that the restaurant is still open?'

'Of course. You go through there. I can take your case to your room.'

'Thank you. I'll keep my holdall.'

The restaurant was large and inviting. It was constructed almost entirely of pinewood. It had panelled walls of pine, here and there were square pillars of pine, the woodblock floor was pine. They have an awful lot of timber in the Black Forest, Marler thought. On one side of the restaurant were banquette booths, each large enough to seat six people. He checked the menu, ordered one substantial dish when the waiter came.

He was alone in the spacious restaurant, but not for long. He was drinking a glass of wine, eating bread, when twelve tough-looking men trooped in. After looking round, a tall thin man ushered them into the booths. Several carried black anoraks and most wore thick woollen sweaters and heavy dark trousers.

Without appearing to do so, he kept an eye on them as he hurried through his meal. Next to the tall thin man sat a smaller man who was also not carrying much weight. Marler caught the small man staring at him. As soon as he looked up the man looked away, started talking to the thug who seemed to be the boss.

'Vernon,' he said quietly. 'That guy over in the corner with the smart clothes. I've seen him before.'

'And where would that be, Bernie?'

'Once when Jake put me on watch duty, checking out the Three Kings Hotel. Jake had given me a description of the girl with Tweed. Seem to recall her name was Paula Grey.'

'So what? Get to it.'

'I saw the Grey girl comin' out with another guy – and with the guy over there. My bet is he's here to spy on us.'

'You're sure?'

Bernie looked across at Marler again. He looked away quickly. Marler had glanced at him again. Bernie was hungry. He stuffed bread in his mouth.'

'Don't do that,' Vernon snapped. 'I asked were you sure.'

'I'm certain.'

When he had finished his meal Marler called out to the waiter. He raised his voice so it carried.

'Is it much colder outside? I feel like a breath of fresh air before I go to bed.'

'It is very cold,' the waiter replied.

'I still feel like a short walk.' He scribbled on the bill given to him by the waiter. 'Put the meal on my room number.'

With the holdall slung over his shoulder, he walked out of the restaurant into the lobby. Climbing a curving staircase he soon located his room. He looked round for a hiding place. Then he explored the bathroom. He put the holdall inside a linen bin, roughed up some towels, shoved them on top, replaced the lid. He left his coat in a cupboard. Marler could stand a lot of cold weather and a coat restricted his movements.

Returning downstairs, he walked through the restaurant. He had earlier spotted another door which led to the outside world. He closed the door after stepping into a narrow street, little more than an alley. In the restaurant he had left, Vernon put his face close to his subordinate's.

'Bernie, go after him. Waste him. Not too close to the hotel.'

'Not my job, Vernon. I'm a printer.'

'Bernie, listen. Listen good. When you joined this outfit I remember Jake sent you to Philadelphia to eliminate a certain guy. It was a test. Jake likes all his people to handle a gun when it comes to it. You killed the guy in Philadelphia. You got a gun on you now.'

'I know. Do I get more bucks for doin' this?'

'That we can discuss later. Get after him.'

When he had closed the restaurant door behind him Marler looked up at a street sign, which was illuminated. *Munzgasse*. The alley was cobbled – and deserted. He started walking along it to get an idea of his surroundings. Knowledge which might come in useful later. It was very cold, very silent.

Near the end of the long alley he paused. To his left there was a café, Wirschaft. It was closed, as everywhere else would be now. He had heard footsteps behind him. Slow, cautious footsteps. Whoever he was, the damned fool had metal studs in the soles of his shoes. When he paused he no longer heard the footsteps. He was careful not to look back.

He walked out of the alley and stared ahead in surprise. Ahead was the last thing he had expected to see in the Old City. A weird complex of very modern concrete houses were stepped steeply up the side of a hill. They appeared to be detached residences and were the sort of structures he'd have expected to find in America.

The complex – with houses on either side – was divided into two sections by a long flight of wide concrete steps. Apart from those at street level, you had to climb the steps to reach the houses, which were on different levels. Behind them, higher still, loomed dense tree-clad slopes. He imagined this was the verge of the Black Forest. He could hear the footsteps behind him again, moving more rapidly.

He began climbing the steps quickly. The footsteps hurried now. Suddenly turning round, he looked down. It was the small thin man, wearing an anorak. Marler was almost at the top level. In his right hand his tail carried a gun. Marler smiled.

'What's all this about?'

'We kinda don't like spies.'

'What makes you think I am a spy?'

'Saw you leavin' the Three Kings in Basle. With your friend, Paula Grey.'

'You're not threatening me?' said Marler, still smiling.

'I'm kinda goin' to kill you.'

Marler stared down behind the gunman. It was the oldest trick in the world. He smiled again as though he hadn't a care in the universe.

'I like to know who's pointing a gun at me. You got a name?'

'Bernie Warner. Guess you might as well know the name of the last guy you'll ever see in this world.'

Marler was still staring fixedly behind Bernie. The thug was beginning to notice this. Also the fact that Marler kept smiling bothered him. You don't keep smiling when you're expecting a bullet in the chest. Marler nodded his head.

'Take him, Mike,' he called out.

Bernie swung round, saw there was no one behind him, turned back to shoot. In the two seconds it had taken him to check his rear Marler jumped on to the top step, dived sideways behind a concrete pillar. Crouched down, he found himself hemmed in by a collection of large, filled rubbish sacks with a sheaf of folded spares under his knees. Obviously when it became daylight the dustcart was due.

Jumping up the last few steps, Bernie stopped, swivelled the muzzle of his gun to where Marler crouched. A shot rang out. A red spot like an Eastern caste mark appeared on his forehead. Still gripping the Walther automatic in his hand, Marler watched Bernie collapse backwards, sprawling down the top steps.

Standing up, he walked down a couple of steps, checked the neck pulse. Nothing. Marler then became very active. He took one of the large spare sacks, walked down the two steps to where Bernie's head rested. He eased the head inside the sack first, then manoeuvred the shoulders inside. He had trouble getting the arms in but he managed it. Then he lifted the sack carefully and the rest of the corpse slithered in, leaving space at the top.

'Lucky he was a small man,' Marler said to himself.

He used a handkerchief to pick up Bernie's Beretta pistol, which still had his fingerprints on it, then dropped it into the sack. He next went back to the piled sacks, opened one, took out rubbish, stuffed it inside Bernie's sack. Fastening it, he heaved it over his shoulders, dumped it with the other sacks awaiting collection. His last precaution was to use his handerchief to remove the few spots of blood on the steps.

For the third time he glanced quickly round the concrete villas. No sign of lights, of life. It would be daylight soon. If anyone had heard the shot they'd probably thought it was a car backfiring.

He hurried down the steps. At the bottom he turned left and soon saw a main highway. He guessed that would be the route they'd take when they left Freiburg. Then he saw what he was looking for – a street drain.

Screwing up the blood-stained handkerchief, he pushed it down into the drain. He had once bought it while in Berlin, as one of a set. There was no way it could be traced back to him.

Turning back, he walked down Munzgasse to the hotel. He entered by the door leading into the restaurant. Five of the thugs were still seated in their booth – with the thin man Marler had picked out as the boss. Then he recalled Keith Kent's description of the man with Ronstadt in the Zürcher Kredit Bank. A tall thin man with a hard, thin bony face. The description fitted. And Newman had identified him as Vernon ·Kolkowski. Vernon had two empty steins in front of him and was halfway through a third. He was glowering when Marler walked in. His expression changed to one of disbelief when he saw Marler.

'Goodnight,' said Marler as he passed close to their table. 'Or, rather, good morning.'

Vernon's glower returned. He said nothing as Marler walked on, went up the curving staircase to his room. As soon as he was inside, the door relocked, Marler sat on his bed. He took from his pocket the small mobile, pressed numbers without consulting the piece of paper Tweed had provided with the number of the Colombi. When the night operator came on he asked to be put through to Tweed.

'Marler here. There were twelve little black men. Now there are eleven. And I'm coming to the Colombi – to attach another tracking gizmo to Ronstadt's Audi. Earlier in Basle he had a Citroën.'

'Thank you for keeping me informed . . .'

Tweed, still up, making notes on a pad, knew what Marler had meant. The twelve men in black Audis had now been reduced to eleven.

34

The repercussions of Marler's encounter with Bernie Warner were far more widespread than he could ever have anticipated. Jake Ronstadt, unable to sleep in his luxurious bedroom at the Colombi, was still up long after a grey and gloomy dawn light had spread over Freiburg. He sat in a chair, wearing an oriental dressing gown with dragons rampant. He was trying to make up his mind whether to move on to Höllental that day, or whether to wait for twenty-four hours.

On the one hand he was very short of time. On the other he knew his troops were fatigued, and by no means at their fighting best. The short, barrel-chested figure wedged in the armchair was also not in good shape. The fact that he had been drinking generous slugs of the precious bourbon he kept in a hip flask had not helped.

He'd had a shock earlier when, hidden in the bar, he'd seen Tweed, Newman and Paula Grey sitting with Sharon and Sir Guy. Where were Tweed's other men? He'd expected they would all head for the Schwarzwälder Hof. They appeared to have split into two forces, which worried him.

He was helping himself to another slug of bourbon when his phone rang. He clambered out of his chair, picked up the instrument.

'Yeah?'

'It's Vernon, Chief. We have a problem.'

'That I could do without. What problem? Spit it out.'

'Bernie has gone missin' – we've looked everywhere and he's just gone . . .'

'*I don't believe you!*' Ronstadt yelled down the phone.

'He has to be with you. Goddamn it, he's the printer. I need him as a double-check.'

'I don't get that.'

'You're not supposed to. What the hell are you talkin' about?' he raved. 'Maybe you'll get around to tellin' me what's goin' on.'

'Give me a chance, Chief. We're eatin' in the restaurant here. Bernie recognized one of Tweed's men. Saw him comin' out of the Three Kings place. I thought it was a good moment to cut down the opposition. This guy goes for a walk in the night, I send Bernie after him. The guy comes back! About half an hour later. Bernie never comes back.'

'You shouldn't have sent Bernie, you friggin' idiot.'

'He was the one who recognized him.'

'You said you'd looked everywhere. What in hell does that mean?' Ronstadt snarled.

'Six of us went out. I went myself. Brad nearly got knocked down by a dustcart collectin' rubbish.'

'Pity you weren't knocked down.' Ronstadt took a deep breath to get himself under control. 'Here's what you all do for today. Nothin' at all. Get it? You stay in your rooms and wait there for me to call.'

'OK, Chief. We need the rest.'

'Stick your rest. Why you had to send the printer on a job like that I don't know. Bernie was important. A damn sight more important than you!' he shouted, then slammed down the phone.

He went back to his armchair, slumped into it. He had a lot to think about. Should he try and contact Charlie? No! Charlie would crucify him. He had a deadline to keep and, in his fury, he had thrown away twenty-four hours. Unusually for Ronstadt, he wasn't sure what to do. His mind whirled. Should he ask Charlie to find a substitute for Bernie? No! Even if he risked Charlie's wrath there wasn't time. He reached for his hip flask, then left it in his hip pocket.

He'd have a bath, get dressed, then go down for breakfast. He might get an inkling of what Tweed was up to. Then he had a bright idea. They'd leave for Höllental in the middle of the night. The decision taken, he felt better. He decided a shower might help to clear his brain. He had the mother of all headaches.

Paula woke, felt her normal alert self. She checked the time. It was only 9.30 a.m. Maybe they would still be serving breakfast in the dining room. She disliked room service. An American habit. Showering and dressing quickly, she went down and paused at the entrance. They were still serving breakfast.

Ed Osborne, big in a thick white polo-necked sweater and grey slacks, sat at a table by himself from where he could survey the whole room. At a remote corner table Sharon also sat by herself, eating buttered toast with one hand, marking up a file with the other. That woman never stops working, Paula thought. Osborne saw her, looked at her with a forbidding expression, then bent his head over a newspaper.

At another table for four Tweed sat with Newman. He caught her eye, gestured for her to join them. She sat down so she was facing the distant Sharon.

'When I came in,' Tweed said, 'I went over to her and suggested she'd probably sooner be on her own at breakfast. She thanked me for my intuition and consideration.'

'She's a slave-driver,' said Newman, 'the slave being herself. We didn't expect you down so early. You got some sleep?'

'I crashed out. It may not have been for long but I feel I've had the best sleep for days.' She looked up as a waiter stood by her. 'I'll have coffee, a glass of orange juice, and also croissants. Nothing else, thank you.' She looked at Tweed. 'Any idea of what we're doing today?'

'None at all. I'm waiting for Marler to press the button. Look who's just arrived.'

She stared at the entrance. Jake Ronstadt was standing there as she had, scanning the restaurant. She was staring because of the way he was dressed. Granted it was breakfast time, so she wouldn't have expected guests to dress up. But Ronstadt was wearing a brown leather jacket, heavy brown leather trousers and thick-soled shoes. Over his arm he carried a black overcoat and his left hand clutched a baseball cap.

'Looks as though he could be leaving,' Paula whispered. 'Oh, Lord, I think he's coming over to us.'

Before he started moving towards their table Sharon had glanced up, then immediately looked down at her file. Osborne, also, had seen his arrival. He gave the newcomer one bleak stare, then resumed reading his newspaper.

'Hi, folks,' Ronstadt greeted them. 'What a big surprise. You're a long way from Goodfellows back in London,' he said addressing Paula. He held out his large hand and she felt compelled to shake it. 'Say, you've got quite a grip there.'

'It comes in useful on occasion,' she replied, staring straight into his hard eyes.

'I guess it does.' He chuckled, a deep rumble which seemed to originate deep down in his chest. 'Fending off unwanted admirers. I guess there must be quite a few of 'em.' He turned his attention to Tweed. 'You sure get around.'

'So do you,' Tweed replied bluntly. 'Where exactly have you come from to get here?'

'I was in Basle. Nice peaceful city. Nothin' ever

347

happens there.' He paused, as though expecting a reaction. 'Now I'm tourin' Germany. Kinda restin' up. Got a big job in London when I get back there.'

'What kind of a job is that?' Newman rapped out.

'Settlin' in new staff. We're enlarging the Embassy. London is becomin' the key city in the Western world.'

'London could do without the bombs,' Paula said, lifting her voice. 'And the hideous casualties caused by mindless terrorists.'

Out of the corner of her eye she saw both Sharon and Osborne look up, startled by her vehemence.

'You're sure right there,' Ronstadt agreed equably. 'Think I've disturbed you folks enough. Have a nice day.'

He walked off to an isolated table. On the way he called out in a rough manner.

'Waiter! Over here! I'm hungry.'

'Aggressive, callous bastard,' Paula hissed quietly, her hand gripping the napkin in her lap to regain self-control.

'Oh, he was deliberately being provocative,' Tweed said calmly. 'I liked your reference to bombs and terrorists, Paula. He didn't linger after that. I don't think he was very happy about the whole restaurant hearing you.'

'Did he hurt your hand when he shook it?' Newman enquired. 'I saw he exerted all his strength.'

'No, he didn't. My grip is as strong as his. My aerobics. And I wanted to test his strength. I might come up against him later on my own.'

'Don't,' Newman warned, keeping his voice down. 'He's probably packing a gun at this moment.'

'And I'm packing my Browning,' Paula retorted. 'It does look as though he's leaving after breakfast, doesn't it?'

'No,' said Tweed.

'What makes you say that?' she demanded.

'The fact that he was putting on a demonstration for our benefit.'

'What kind of a demonstration?'

'Rather an obvious ploy. To give us the impression that he is leaving shortly. Hence his clothes, his overcoat and baseball cap. If he was on his way he'd attempt to conceal it. I think he's had enough of us. And something Marler phoned me about will, I'm sure, have upset Mr Jake Ronstadt. Thrown him off balance. Tell you later.'

'So we're here a bit longer?'

'At least for the rest of the day would be my guess. I see Sharon is leaving. She's gone now.' He drank more coffee. A short while later he stared. 'Well, look who's arrived.'

Paula and Newman stared across the dining room. Standing in the entrance, looking round the room, dressed in a dove-grey two-piece suit, was Denise Chatel. She was clutching a large handbag. After swiftly checking out who was having breakfast she vanished.

35

Newman was getting up from the table when Tweed glanced across at Ronstadt. It seemed obvious he hadn't seen Denise. Crouched over a mobile phone, he had his head down, concentrating on his conversation.

'I'm going after her,' said Newman.

'Good idea,' said Tweed.

He doubted whether Newman had heard him. Without appearing to hurry, he was moving at speed out of the restaurant. He found no trace of Sharon outside. She must have gone straight up to her room. He saw Denise at the *garderobe*, collecting her coat. He went over in time to help her on with it. She nearly jumped out of her skin until she saw who it was. She moved towards the exit and Newman walked alongside her.

'Someone in the restaurant you didn't like the look of?' he asked cheerfully.

'Yes.'

'Ronstadt? Osborne?'

'I don't want to talk about it.'

'But you do want breakfast. We can find a café outside. Plenty of them in Freiburg.'

'I'm ravenous, Bob.'

They were already outside in the street. She was becoming more confident about him, he sensed. They turned left and, walking fast, she almost slipped on a stretch of ice. He grasped hold of her, saved her from falling.

'Loop you arm through mine,' he said firmly.

She did so. She was trembling, and not with the cold. She was wearing a thick overcoat with a high collar. He smiled at her as they continued walking.

'People will start talking if they see us like this.'

'That's not funny.'

'Just a joke.'

'Bob.' She looked at him. 'You haven't got a coat and it's freezing. Should we go back so you can get one?' she suggested without any enthusiasm.

'The cold doesn't worry me. It's the great heat – with humidity – which I find trying.'

He was telling the truth. In this respect he was like Tweed, who also could stand any amount of cold, but he had to push himself hard in hot, humid weather. They arrived outside a large café-cum-restaurant. Denise tugged at his arm.

'Let's check out this place. I want to get you inside into some warmth.'

It was an old place, with huge dark wooden beams across the ceiling. There were several couples inside, dressed like locals. Denise nodded, guided him inside, made for a remote table near the back. He helped her off with her coat and felt the warmth on his face and bare hands. They sat facing each other.

'When did you last eat?' he asked, picking up the menu.

'I had a snack yesterday afternoon in my room at the Three Kings.'

'Nothing since? I see. How about a whopping great omelette?'

'Sounds wonderful. Mushroom, if they've got it. Otherwise plain would do fine. And a lot of coffee, with milk.'

The waitress, with a checked blouse and a dark skirt, appeared. He ordered a large omelette for Denise, a small one for himself. He had already had breakfast but he thought it would make her feel more comfortable if he ate with her. He didn't look at her. Instead he looked round the restaurant.

'Is Alec with you?' she asked suddenly.

'Alec?'

'Marler.'

'Of course. I was dreaming. He's in the city, but he's some way off. I'm afraid you'll have to put up with me.'

'I'm sorry, Bob. I didn't mean it like that. I feel perfectly comfortable with you.'

'Thank you. Good . . .'

He said no more until they were served. Then he waited until she had eaten every scrap of her huge omelette, plus quite a lot of bread, drinking her milky coffee between bites. Her face had been ashen, but now her high colour had returned. She leant back in her chair, laid a hand on her tummy.

'Not very elegant, but I do feel better.'

'You drove here from Basle?'

'Yes, I did. It was very tiring. When I appeared in the

restaurant I registered, had my bag taken up to a room, was given my key.'

She produced it from her handbag. Holding it, she let him read the number, then dropped it back into her handbag. He asked her if she'd mind if he smoked one cigarette.

'Not if you give me one too. Thank you. Did Alec tell you what I'd told him? About my parents in the States?'

'Yes, he did.'

'You probably wonder what I've been doing. First I disappear, then I reappear.'

'Tell me only if you want to.'

'I didn't tell Marler. I kept it as a secret from everyone. I felt I didn't know *who* I could trust. I recently hired another top private investigator in Virginia to check out my parents' so-called accident at that lonely bridge. A man called Walt Banker. He's visited that retired sheriff, Jim Briscoe, the man who took me to the site of the tragedy, then was retired quickly. Banker told me Briscoe has changed his story, says it was an accident. Banker was sure he was lying. Somehow he checked his balance at the local bank. Recently he paid in fifty thousand dollars. My investigator said it had to be a bribe paid to Briscoe, which is why he now says it was an accident.'

'Did this Banker go back to see Briscoe to ask him about this big sum of money?'

'Yes, he said he did. Briscoe hit the roof. Said it was a legacy from an uncle. Banker asked for the uncle's name. Briscoe flew into a rage, threw him out. A couple of days later Banker was nearly killed. A car tried to run him down. Banker got the registration number of the car, checked it out.' She paused. 'He found it had been hired. In Washington.'

'Interesting. Very. And what are you going to do now? Go back to the hotel?'

'I'm scared, Bob. What do I tell Sharon? After I left the Three Kings I took a room in a small hotel so I could phone the investigator safely. She'll go stark raving mad if I tell her. I'll be fired and I'll never get another job. She pays me very well.'

'Why wouldn't you get another job? There must be plenty available in Washington for someone with your experience.'

'Because it will be passed down the grapevine. I'll be blacklisted. That's how it works in Washington.'

'Just exactly how does it work in Washington?' Newman asked.

'Employers at Sharon's top level form a kind of club. They tell each other about their employees. You get blacklisted, and every door is closed to you.'

'Really. And Sharon would blow the whistle on you?'

'I know she would.'

'Then here's what you tell her.' Newman drank more coffee while he worked it out, checking to make sure it was watertight. 'You went out for a walk in the evening – to freshen up for more work. You were followed by a tall thin man with a thin bony face. Can you remember that?'

'Yes, he doesn't sound very nice.'

'He isn't. He exists. Sharon may well have caught sight of him back at the Embassy in London. The tall thin man was very close to you – he wore a black overcoat – when a cruising police car approached. You crossed the street, hurried back to the hotel. You were just going inside when you saw the same man coming towards you from the opposite direction. You rushed up to your room, packed, asked the doorman to bring your car. Then you drove off, stayed for a few hours at the small hotel in Basle, the one where you did stay. When you'd recovered you drove to the Colombi. Have you got that?'

'Every word. I was imagining it happening while you were talking. Sharon may start questioning me. She's like that.'

'Just stick to the same story. Don't embroider. No more details. If necessary blow your top, tell her you were scared out of your wits. Tell her you're still thinking of phoning the police in Basle to report the incident.'

'It might work,' Denise said.

'It will work. Now go back to the Colombi on your own. When you arrive ask for Sharon's room number. Find her at once.'

'I'm very grateful to you, Bob . . .'

'Just go. Now.'

When he was alone Newman drank more coffee. He decided that he would try and contact Marler. The intense cold hit him when he left the café. Walking a short distance, he found a smart-looking men's clothier. Going inside, he bought a German coat, a pair of gloves. Resuming his walk, he passed locals muffled up, treading warily on the slippery pavements. Overhead a low grey bank of cloud pressed down on the city like a lid. He stopped to study a big map of Freiburg, located Konvikstrasse near the Münster.

Threading his way through a network of alleys, he was guided by the looming spire of the Münster. More people were about as he entered Münsterplatz. Hurrying, to get out of the cold, a few bumped into him. Apologizing, they hastened on. Then he saw Marler. Newman siffened. Locals pushed past Marler, who was walking slowly. Behind him a hatless man in a black coat was only three people away from Marler's back.

Newman himself began hurrying, bumping into people. Then he stopped at the edge of the crowd. Marler had also stopped, glancing over his shoulder. The hatless man in a black coat had turned away, was hustling off towards the edge of the square. Newman saw him enter a narrow alley, stop, then he turned round and waited as though observing Marler.

Newman had had a better look at him in profile. Tall, thin with a hard bony face. It was the man he had described to Denise. Vernon Kolkowski, the man Keith Kent had seen with Ronstadt inside the Zürcher Kredit in Basle. Kent's description fitted perfectly. Newman joined Marler.

'You had company.'

'Mornin' to you, Bob,' Marler drawled. 'And I knew I had company. He's standing in an alley leading to the Schwarzwälder Hof, watching me – while I watch something else.'

'Which is?'

'Look across the square. Three black Audis parked close together. Four of Ronstadt's men getting into one car.'

'They're on the move . . .'

'Are they? Where are the rest of them? Eight more men – seven, now. I had an arument with one of them early this morning. He won't be arguing with anyone else ever again. There they go, driving off.'

'Did they have luggage?'

'Yes, each man carried a bag.'

'Then we'd better break all records getting to the Colombi so we can warn Tweed. Won't take us long to get there.'

'My idea too!'

In his room at the Colombi Jake Ronstadt was sprawled along an expensively upholstered couch. He had his back against one arm, his body and legs stretched out. He hadn't bothered to take off his boots, which rested on a decorated cushion. His mobile phone had started buzzing.

'Yeah?'

'Vernon here. It worked like a dream.'

'Get your head screwed on, Vernon. I do like specifics.'

'Your plan. The guy who went out early this morning – and Bernie follows him – was eating a late breakfast. I sent out four of my guys with bags through the restaurant. The guy leaves the rest of his breakfast, follows my four to their Audi. Another guy – one of them – joins him. They stand in the square, watch the Audi take off, then they move like hell away from the square. Could they be comin' to your place?'

'Of course they are, Brainless.'

'So I tells the six still here to pack and we all move off with Brad in the Audi that's just left?'

'Brainless, you stay exactly where you are until you hear from me. Are you listenin' with both your thick ears?' Ronstadt snarled.

'Sure, Chief.'

'When I say you stays there you all stays in your rooms. Got it?'

'Sure, Chief.'

'Miracles sometimes happen. Brad and his three men don't go to the base. They waits at the point I tells you about earlier.'

'Brad knows. I marked the place on a map, the place you described to me. Brad said looks like they's gonna have to drive up a bloody mountain,' Vernon warned.

'That's his problem. They got food and drink? They's gonna have to wait a long time. Till after dark. Till a coupla white Audis follow me along that road into Höllental. Did Brad get the crowbars?'

'Sure, Chief. Sent him out early this mornin' and he finds a car spares shop. He buys three crowbars, has 'em well wrapped, and he locks them in the Audi. He said it sounds like a long wait and a lot of hard work diggin' out boulders. If there are any.'

'There are. I noticed them last time I visited the base when I flew over earlier in the year. Can't start an avalanche without a bit of work. Go back to your room, Brainless.'

'That's where I am now.'

'Get some sleep, if you want to. Keep the phone close to your thick ear. Get the kitchen there to make up food packs for all of you. With drink,' Ronstadt demanded.

'Sure, Chief.'

'Another miracle. You musta eaten a lotta fish. Good for the brain. Eat a whole lot more . . .'

Ronstadt cut the connection. He stretched out a bit further on the couch. This was an unusual experience. Enjoying a bit of comfort. He grinned savagely and said the words aloud.

'Good place for you to end your career, Tweed. In the dark of the Black Forest.'

36

'No! Definitely not!' said Tweed.

Ten minutes earlier he had listened in silence while Newman and Marler told him what they had seen close to the Münster. In his room, when they had arrived, were also Paula and Keith Kent. Newman let Marler speak first. Then he reported what Denise Chatel had told him when they'd breakfasted together in the café further into Freiburg. Tweed stood as he listened, close to a window with hands clasped behind his back, his eyes fixed on whichever man was speaking. It was after Newman made a suggestion that Tweed spoke so emphatically.

'So,' Newman had remarked, 'we think the best thing

is to leave here now, follow that Audi – I'm sure we can catch them up on the main route into Höllental.'

'What's your objective?' Newman persisted in response to Tweed's vehement rejection. 'Or perhaps I should say objection? They have made a fatal mistake. They've split their forces. We can destroy them piecemeal.'

'My main objective is to destroy their base.' Tweed took from his pocket an envelope, extracted the two fake British banknotes they had obtained in St Ursanne. 'I'm convinced the Americans have devised a deadly plan to destabilize Britain.'

'I don't see their significance,' said Paula.

'Oh, you will, you will. Marler, you've just told me about how you dealt with Bernie Warner, whoever he was. Did you notice whether the tips of his fingers were dirty?'

'Yes, I did. At the time I didn't think anything of it. They were stained black.'

'Printing ink,' said Tweed. 'You probably exterminated one of Ronstadt's key men.' His voice took on a grimmer note. 'But we must destroy that base. And the only man who'll lead us to it is Ronstadt. So we have to wait until he leaves here on his way to Höllental. Have you a good supply of explosives, Marler?'

'Enough to blow half Freiburg sky high.'

'Good.'

'What Bob is worried about,' Marler explained, 'is that the Audi which has left with four men inside could be setting up an ambush.'

'I'm sure it is,' Tweed agreed equably. 'I'm sure you can deal with that, Marler, while we keep after Ronstadt.'

'They may be using something like bazookas,' Paula warned. 'You know what the Americans are – they think anything big is better, whether it's a battleship or a weapon operated by one man.'

'We do have smoke bombs, a lot of them,' Marler reminded her. 'A man using a bazooka has to see his target. Smoke bombs land all round him. He's in a fog. Target disappears. I'll give you a few more.'

'Another point,' Newman pressed, 'is how can we be sure we'll know when Ronstadt is leaving?'

'I've attended to that,' Tweed told him. 'I phoned Kuhlmann, head of the Federal Kriminalpolizei in Wiesbaden, as you know. Also a close friend. He has phoned the manager here, saying he is tracking terrorists. He's asked the manager to inform me of any sign that Ronstadt is leaving.'

'Point covered, then.'

'Reverting to that intriguing story Denise Chatel told you: if it's true, wouldn't it be strange if the key to the momentous events we're caught up in lies in the car accident, so called, which killed both her parents in Virginia?'

'It would be very strange,' Newman agreed. 'But I don't see how.'

'It's just a glimmer of an idea which flashed into my mind as I listened to you. And we still don't know who the mysterious Charlie is. Charlie's identity is possibly the real key.'

A little later Tweed told Marler to go back to the Schwarzwälder Hof and to keep him informed. He then looked round at the others and said he wanted a private meeting with someone, so would they mind leaving him until he phoned them in their rooms? As soon as he was alone he picked up the phone and asked Guy Strangeways to come and see him for a chat. While he waited Tweed took out a recording device, tested it to make sure it was in working order.

'Guy, do sit down. Would you like some coffee?'

'No, thank you. Drank too much of it already at breakfast.'

'You don't look your normal self, you know.'

Strangeways had seated himself in an armchair, slumped against the back. Tweed sat in a chair opposite him with a small table between them. His guest showed every sign of nervous exhaustion. He kept pulling at his moustache, staring at Tweed. When he did speak his voice almost quivered.

'What is this all about?'

'It's about you. You've got something on your mind and it is tearing you to pieces. We've known each other a long time, off and on, so maybe you can help me.'

'God knows, I'm the one who needs help.' He paused, then it all came tumbling out. 'I've besmirched the family name. That must sound pretty old-fashioned.'

'Not to me, it doesn't. What happened?'

'I took a gamble in business in the States and I was short of money. Only for a while but my competitors were closing in on me. Tweed, to cut a long story short, I accepted a bribe from the Americans of half a million dollars.'

'Anyone operating in the States can get caught up in the corrupt atmosphere that prevails over there. You must have promised something in return for the bribe.'

'The Yanks are planning on converting Britain into a colony of America,' he burst out. His voice grew stronger. 'We will become a state of their bloody Union. Hawaii was the fiftieth state. We would become the fifty-first state. The condition of the bribe was that if you refused to become Governor – they were very keen for you to accept – then I'd assume the post. If you accepted I'd get another big post running Britain.' He stood up, began marching round the room as he talked. 'I feel better now I've told you. Ironically, I didn't need the half a million. I tried to give it back. It's still in a special account I had set up in London.'

'What happened when you attempted to return the half a million?'

'They showed me a photo – taken secretly – of my opening their executive case with the money inside. They said they'd send the photo, and the story, to tabloids in Britain and to top newspapers in New York. My reputation would be ruined.'

'Guy, who handed you the money?'

'That vile creature Jake Ronstadt. A man I wouldn't have inside Irongates. In the photo he's smirking. I'm going to return the money anyway. I had put a codicil in my will that it was to go to a charity.' His voice had become vibrant. 'Now I'm going to return it and damn the consequences.'

'How will you do that?'

'I've asked Sharon if she knows the private address of the Secretary of the Treasury in Washington. She does. I didn't give her any idea what I wanted it for.'

'But by accepting the money you were able to gain information as to what they intended,' Tweed said quietly.

'That's true.'

'So that's why you accepted the supposed bribe. Guy, we have to defeat them, even at the eleventh hour. I have a recording machine here. I want us to start the conversation all over again. You answer my questions, explain that you accepted the so-called bribe to find out what they were really up to. So you could tell me. If you do this it will help me enormously.'

'It will?'

'Enormously. Let's start now . . .'

Tweed put the same kind of questions, Guy answered them as Tweed had suggested. The answers came in a strong clear voice. Watching him, Tweed was startled by the transformation which had come over Guy Strangeways.

He looked years younger, totally alert, his blue eyes fiery. When they had finished Tweed switched off his small recorder.

'Are you expecting a firefight with the enemy?' Guy asked suddenly.

'It could be on the cards.'

'Got as many men as they have?'

'No. We are outnumbered, but that doesn't worry us.'

'Take me with you, to help even things up.'

'Can I think about that?' Tweed suggested.

'Don't think I'm up to it, do you? I am armed.'

Guy slid a Smith & Wesson .38 revolver out of a shoulder holster under his jacket, the weapon favoured by Newman. He began unloading the gun, placing six bullets on the small table.

'Why are you carrying that?' Tweed asked quietly.

'Like to be able to look after myself in a tight corner. See that picture of a man over there? That's the target.'

Guy loaded and raised the revolver, aiming at the picture. Tweed watched him closely. Guy held the revolver in one hand, pulled the trigger six times in rapid succession. The gun was steady as a rock. No sign of even a hint of a quiver. The demonstration impressed Tweed far more than he'd expected. Guy talked while he reloaded the weapon, returned it to his holster.

'I did manage to cope in the Gulf War. As you know, I was a general. Part of the sweeping left hook which raced across the desert to cut off the whole of Saddam's Presidential Guard. Then the damn Yanks stopped us. In another twenty-four hours we'd have destroyed Saddam for ever.'

'I know,' said Tweed. 'I'd like first to get in touch with one of my team. Then could I phone you in your room?'

'Of course. Incidentally, when you speak to your chap stress I take orders from him. I serve as a simple foot soldier. Won't make any suggestions unless I'm specifically asked for them.'

'I'll tell him. Going back briefly to that silly business about the money. Did you tell Sharon?'

'Good God, no! Thought I'd made that clear. Wouldn't dream of it. I've told no one except you, and I'll keep it that way. Just before I leave you alone, there is another problem.'

'Which is?'

'The usual one. Rupert. He's traipsing round with that swine, Basil. Windermere is a bad influence on him.' He smiled grimly. 'And probably Rupert is equally a bad influence on Basil.'

'You don't mean they're here?'

'They are. Both have a room in this hotel. They were passengers when I drove here from Basle. Found myself between the devil and the deep blue sea. Didn't want them with me. Didn't want to leave them behind. Thought it best to keep an eye on them. At this moment they're in the bar downstairs, of course. Saw them a few minutes before I went back up to my room in time to take your phone call.'

'You'll have to leave them on their own if you should come with us – if we're going anywhere.'

'Trouble is Basil has hired a car here in Freiburg. So they're mobile. But there are more important things than those two. I'd better go now. I'll wait for your phone call . . .'

Alone in his room, Tweed called Monica on Beck's mobile phone. He could tell from her voice the moment she answered that she was excited.

'Tweed, is this line safe?'

'Yes, it is. You have news?'

'Roy Buchanan called me, wanted to speak to you.

363

When I said you weren't available he gave some data to pass on. No more bombs have exploded. You know why?'

'I will if you tell me.'

'Well—'

'Monica, could you hold on? Something I have to check. Back in a moment . . .'

Tweed had started calling Monica as soon as Guy had left the room. He had vaguely been aware of some kind of commotion outside in the corridor. Running to the door, he opened it. Paula stood there. Her expression was strange. He went into the corridor. To his right stood Osborne, smoking a fresh cigar.

'Hi there, Tweed. Time we had that drink in the bar.'

Osborne seemed the jovial hail-fellow-well-met type he had been when he had visited Tweed in his office at Park Crescent. He waved his cigar in greeting.

'What is it, Paula?' Tweed asked, irritated.

'I was coming along to your room when I heard an argument. Two voices. One was Sir Guy's. He was shouting, sounded furious. I couldn't see who the other person was. The argument sounded vicious. I was a little way round a corner, so I couldn't see anything. When I got here I saw Sir Guy disappearing. Mr Osborne was standing where he is now . . .'

'The name is *Ed*,' Osborne called out amiably. 'OK, Paula?'

'The name is Miss Grey,' she shot back. 'Did you see who was in the corridor with Sir Guy Strangeways?'

'Nope. I just came outta my room. What's the problem?'

'There isn't one,' said Tweed. 'Paula, come in. I'm talking to somebody.'

He locked the door when they were both inside, ran back to the phone he'd left on a table. He explained briefly to Paula over his shoulder.

'I have Monica holding on. Be with you soon . . .

'Monica. Sorry about that. Turned out to be nothing. Now I can give you my full attention.'

'Well, Buchanan is using to the full his new powers. He's ringed the American Embassy in Grosvenor Square with a large team of plain-clothes officers, all armed. When anyone comes out they're followed – on foot if they're walking, in a car if they drive away. Since he employed these tactics no more bombs, as I told you earlier.'

'Any protests from the Americans?'

'You bet. Buchanan happened to be there in a car with a team when Morgenstern came out, was driven off in a limo. Buchanan followed him. Morgenstern stopped his limo, demanded to know what was going on. Buchanan explained they'd had a tip-off that terrorists were going to bomb the Embassy, so he was providing protection.'

'Clever. Significant that the bombings have stopped.'

'Earlier someone had placed a bomb – a big one – inside a key telephone exchange. The Bomb Squad found it, defused it.'

'Any other developments?'

'I was just going to tell you. An FBI team flew in, offered their services. Buchanan said he didn't need an alien force to help. They didn't like that at all. The situation appears to be under control. For the moment.'

'Thank you, Monica. Make a note of this hotel's name and my room number. I may not be here long. And I'll give you the number of my mobile phone . . .'

He gave her the data, thanked her again, ended the call, turned to look at Paula. She was sitting down, listened intently as he asked the question.

'Something very weird went on in that corridor a few minutes ago. I even thought I heard the sounds of a

365

struggle. Were you able to identify the second voice – the voice of the person arguing with Guy?'

'No. It was a voice I haven't heard before. Strident. Using filthy language.'

'Voice of a man, a woman?'

'Sorry, Tweed, but I couldn't tell. I thought I caught the tone of a very American accent, but I could be wrong. I was still a distance along the other corridor, which muffled things a lot.'

'But you could hear Sir Guy's voice?'

'Definitely. His is so distinctive. I thought I heard him shout, "Don't you damned well talk to me like that." But again I'm not sure. When I turned the corner he was just disappearing round a corner in the distance. Ed Osborne wa standing outside his room.'

'How long do you think he'd been there?'

'No idea. It looked as though he'd just come out of his room. His cigar had been trimmed and was alight.'

'I don't like it.' Tweed stirred in the arm chair he had sat in. 'Something very weird is going on, as I said a few minutes ago.'

Paula, sitting in an armchair opposite him, the one Guy had occupied, reached out and felt the coffee pot on the table. She reached for a clean cup and saucer.

'This coffee feels fresh. Drink some. It will help you to get the brain racing.'

She watched while he drank slowly. He was staring at nothing, as though his mind was miles away. He put the cup down and spoke slowly.

'Guy was with me before he left this room. He's offered to join us as a reinforcement. He knows roughly what they're up to and thinks they should be stopped. Incidentally, regarding what happened in the corridor you used the word "vicious". Were you referring to Guy?'

'No, to whoever he was arguing with. I've just had a

thought. Osborne was in the corridor. Could he have been the person Guy was having a verbal battle with?'

'Wouldn't you have recognized his voice?'

'Not necessarily. I've never heard Osborne in a towering rage.'

'Voices do change according to the mood a person is in.'

'You said Guy was going to join us. Is that a good idea?'

'I came to the conclusion he would be an asset. But if he does come he'll have to travel in Marler's Audi. There's space for a fourth person there. I must phone Marler, put the idea to him. If he doesn't agree, Guy doesn't come.'

Tweed took the mobile out of his pocket. He called the other hotel, explained the position to Marler vaguely, not using Guy's name. Then he put the phone on the table.

'Marler's phoning me back from an outside phone. We'll have to wait.'

They waited ten minutes. During that time they didn't speak a word to each other. Paula deliberately kept silent. Tweed was frowning, had a look of intense concentration. When the phone rang he explained the idea in detail, emphasizing it was up to Marler whether he agreed. When he broke the connection he smiled at Paula.

'Marler agrees we take Guy. It was Guy's reference to his being treated as a foot soldier which convinced him. And Guy knows something about war. Which is what I foresee we'll be engaged in during our trip to the Black Forest. All-out war.'

'Any chance of a quick lunch downstairs?' Paula suggested. 'I had a good breakfast but I'm hungry again. Must be the cold.'

'We'll go down now.'

It was when they arrived in the lobby, bustling with staff, all moving about in a chaotic state and apparently to no purpose, that they received a dreadful shock. The chief receptionist ran up to Tweed. His hands were trembling.

'Mr Tweed, Sir Guy Strangeways has been shot. He's dead. He went out for a walk and left his gloves on the counter. I ran out and saw him fall. I heard the shot.'

37

Paula stood very still, hardly able to take in the news. Tweed also froze, his expression blank. But not for long. He spoke quietly to the receptionist to calm him down.

'Did you see anyone, or anything, else while you were outside?'

'No one. I thought I saw the rear of a brown Opel disappearing round a corner. But I can't be sure about that.'

'Where is the body?'

'With the help of some of the staff I put it in that room over there. The one with the closed door.'

'Thank you,' Tweed said as Newman appeared.

He heard Paula telling Newman what had happened as he walked towards the closed door. He had his hand on the handle when Rupert arrived, grabbing his arm.

'You can't go in there,' Rupert growled.

'Don't ever take hold of me again!'

Tweed heaved his shoulder against Rupert. The impact sent Rupert staggering back. He recovered and was advancing again on Tweed when Newman grasped hold of Rupert from behind, twisting up his arm.

'You're hurting me,' Rupert snarled.

'Make any more wrong moves and I'll break your bloody arm.'

Tweed had opened the door and walked into a sitting room. Over a couch a sheet had been drawn. He lifted it, looked down at the body laid on its back. Guy, eyes closed, looked very peaceful, except for one blemish. In the centre of his forehead was a ragged hole with congealed blood where the bullet had gone in. He replaced the sheet, left the room, closed the door, walked over to the receptionist.

'How long ago did this happen?'

'I suppose it must have been at least half an hour ago, sir.'

Tweed turned to Paula. He guided her away from the staff milling round in the lobby. He spoke to her in a quiet corner.

'Could it really have been half an hour?'

'Easily – or longer. After we heard Sir Guy arguing with someone in the corridor you took a while drinking coffee and thinking. Then you called Marler,' she went on, keeping her voice low, 'and we had to wait for him to call us back. Afterwards, when he did call back, you spent quite a bit of time explaining things to him about Sir Guy's offer to come with us. Time can pass more quickly than we realize. Now I come to reckon it up, it could have been well over half an hour before we came down to get some lunch.'

'What's happening now?'

Paula turned round and saw men in white coats and trousers come in carrying a stretcher. Rupert guided them to the room where his father lay. Tweed strode forward with Paula at his heels until he reached Rupert.

'What's going on?' Tweed demanded.

'I called them after consulting the receptionist. They're taking him to the airport just outside Freiburg, if you must know.'

'The airport? Why, in Heaven's name?'

'Because – ' Rupert's manner became sarcastic – 'at airports they have planes. I've hired a private aircraft to fly him straight home. I know that's what he would have wanted.'

'You must be mad. Your father was murdered. There'll have to be an autopsy here.'

'I'm not having foreign doctors cutting up my father's body. In case you haven't grasped it, I'm his next of kin. It's nothing to do with you.'

'It has a lot to do with the German police.'

'Oh, I fixed that. I phoned Chief Inspector Kuhlmann at Wiesbaden. I told him you agreed the body should be flown straight back to Britain.'

'You told him *what*?' Tweed was in one of his rare rages. 'How dare you use my name without my permission? And what exactly did Kuhlmann say?'

'Something about in view of the present situation he'd make an exception and waive the normal formalities. Reluctantly, I believe he said – providing he received a full report from London.'

'And where is this private aircraft flying your father to?'

'Heathrow. Kuhlmann also agreed that under the circumstances he'd phone the airport controller here to authorize the flight. Some such bull.' Rupert adopted a sneering tone. 'Don't know why you're fussing like an old woman. You were supposed to be a friend of my father's.'

'You're flying home with the body?'

'Glory, no. Think I want to put myself through that? Because I don't – and won't.'

Newman made a move to grab hold of Rupert. Paula grasped his sleeve, held him back, whispered something. While all this was going on the stretcher-bearers were carrying the body outside to a van waiting at the kerb.

'I've a good mind to call Kuhlmann, tell him the truth, and make him reverse his decision,' Tweed rasped. 'Let's get just one thing clear. If you ever use my name again without coming to me first I'll have you arrested and charged with deception of the authorities.'

'Do what you bloody well like!'

'You mind your filthy mouth.' Newman snapped. 'Or I'll close it for you.'

'Toodle-pip. I have to go with the van to the airport.'

'I'm going to tell the driver he's acting illegally,' Tweed said in a cold voice.

'Wait a minute,' Paula said urgently, again keeping her voice low. 'You don't want to get involved. Haven't you enough on your mind? Far more important things to attend to?'

'You're right, of course.' Tweed was suddenly calm. 'And now look what we've got on our doorstep. I think I'll have a word with him.'

Basil Windermere, sporting a cashmere overcoat, had appeared at the entrance. He walked in, stared round at the air of chaos. Tweed went up to him.

'I say,' said Basil, 'what's the party in aid of? All the staff standing round. And didn't I see Rupert getting into the front seat of a van? Having fun, are we?'

'Hardly,' Tweed replied. 'Rupert's father has just been murdered. Shot down in cold blood in the street outside.'

'You don't say. Of course the old boy was getting on a bit. But to go like that. Not cricket.'

'Where have you been?' Tweed asked through gritted teeth.

'Doing the Grand Tour of Freiburg. Parked by an expensive fashion shop, watched some nifty fillies going in. And a few older ones. Must be rolling in it.'

'I heard you'd hired a car. Is it outside?'

'Think so. Unless the hotel attendant chappie has taken it to the garage.'

'Show me. What's the make?'

'An Opel. Nothing to top up the image.'

'Let's have a look now.' Tweed beckoned to the chief receptionist. They walked outside. The Opel was still there, it's colour blue. 'Was this the car you saw disappearing?' Tweed asked the receptionist.

'I do not really know, sir. It all happened so quickly.'

'You said a brown Opel,' Tweed reminded him. 'This is blue.'

'I only saw it for a second, sir. I was really looking at the body.'

'Anyone mind telling me what this is in aid of?' Basil demanded.

Tweed looked straight into the pallid eyes of Basil Windermere. He could detect no sign of any kind of human feeling, no reaction at all to the news Windermere had just heard. He went on staring into the eyes while he answered.

'We're looking for a serial murderer.'

Then he turned away and joined Paula and Newman. He led them up to his room and sat down in a chair, telling them to make themselves at home. He took Beck's mobile from his pocket.

'What does it all mean?' Newman asked. 'Was it the Phantom?'

'I'm sure it was. Guy had a bullet dead centre in his forehead. Wasn't that the case with Kurt Schwarz?'

'Yes, it was.'

'Why would they kill Guy?' Paula asked.

'I think it was triggered off by the argument you and I heard outside in the corridor. I think that after a while in his room Guy decided to go out for a walk to calm down. By that time arrangements had been made to kill him. Someone moved very fast.' As he spoke he was pressing numbers on the mobile.

'Marler? You recognize my voice? Good. The extra asset we thought we'd have with us is no longer available.'

'Understood,' Marler acknowledged.

'I had to be careful,' Tweed remarked, 'since I was phoning him at the Schwarzwälder Hof. Now I'm going to try and get hold of Roy Buchanan. I can remember his mobile number.'

'Why Buchanan?' Paula asked.

'Listen and you'll see – if I get him . . .'

Buchanan responded very quickly and Tweed explained that Sir Guy Strangeways had just been murdered, most probably by the Phantom. He told him of the arrangement to fly the body to Heathrow, asked if he could arrange to have the private plane met, then for an autopsy to be performed.

'When they've taken the bullet out of Guy,' Tweed continued, 'I suggest it's compared with the one which killed our Prime Minister, the one which killed a man found dead off Regent Street, the one which killed the German, Keller, and the one which killed a French Minister . . .'

Tweed listened for a few minutes, replied briefly, listened again and then thanked Buchanan before he broke the connection.

'Any news from Roy?' Paula enquired.

'Yes. He was on his way to Heathrow. They had an anonymous call that a bomb has been placed aboard a plane bound for the Western hemisphere. That covers a lot of territory. Umpteen planes are grounded. Chaos at Heathrow. A fresh ploy to destabilize us. Roy is going to wait to meet the plane flying in Guy's body. I think that tells you all we said to each other.'

'I forgot to mention it earlier,' Newman said. 'Just before we came up here I noticed someone come back into the hotel from outside. It was Ed Osborne.'

'Interesting,' commented Tweed. 'Now let's go down and see if we can get a late lunch. I think zero hour is very close.'

When they entered the dining room waiters were clearing away the empty tables. But the maître d' told Tweed that of course they could have lunch. The only other guest in the room as they made their way to their table was Sharon.

She raised a hand, waved to them, then returned to checking a file. A waiter brought her a fresh pot of coffee, removed an old one. Paula sighed after they had ordered.

'That woman never stops working. She has a pile of files on a chair.'

'She's dedicated,' said Tweed.

'I wonder if she's heard about Guy.'

'Paula, if she has, she has. If she hasn't she'll hear sooner or later.'

'You're in a hurry, aren't you?'

'Yes. It will be dark soon. It would be anyway at this time of the year, but with this heavy overcast it will come quicker.'

Like Paula, Tweed was eating quickly during gaps in their conversation.

'Which means?' she asked quietly.

'I think Ronstadt will be leaving any minute. I'm surprised I haven't heard from Marler. I'd expect activity over where he's staying.'

'We've finished dessert. We could skip coffee.'

'I think we should.'

Newman looked up as someone appeared at the entrance to the restaurant. A tall smooth-faced man wearing a good suit. He glanced across at Sharon. She was so absorbed in her file she didn't see him beckon briefly to Newman.

'Excuse me,' said Newman. 'Back in a minute.'

The tall man had disappeared. Newman found him waiting at the entrance to the bar. Inside Basil Windermere sat with his back to the entrance, nursing a glass. The tall man moved a few feet along the wall as Newman approached him with a smile.

'Well, if it isn't Chuck Venacki. Last seen with a car parked outside Park Crescent, watching the place.'

'And then Bob Newman rams me up the rear in his four-wheel drive. You pulled that job pretty smartly.'

'What is it, Venacki?'

'You can call me Chuck. Tell Tweed to go to his room now. I do mean now.'

'Why?'

'He'll find out why very quickly. You're short of time.'

'Can you tell me why?'

'Make with the feet, Newman, for God's sake.'

Newman walked back into the restaurant. He sat down, pushed his dessert dish away. While he did this he leant close to Tweed.

'I suggest you go to your room immediately. It could be urgent.'

'I'll come with you, if that's all right,' Paula said.

'Yes, come with me.'

'I'm going to my room,' Newman said. 'So you know where to get me.'

Tweed, with Paula by his side, strolled out of the restaurant. He looked across at Sharon, but she was so absorbed in working on her file she didn't notice them.

'That woman,' Paula remarked on their way up, 'has extraordinary powers of concentration.'

'A real brainbox,' he agreed.

They were inside his room, the door relocked, when she asked a question. Perched on the arm of a chair, she was wearing her outdoors outfit, complete with leggings and a strong pair of boots which would grip firmly on rough ground.

'I wonder who that man was, the one Bob went out to talk to? He seemed to know him.'

'Maybe an old contact from his days as an active journalist.'

'You don't really believe that.'

'Frankly, at the moment I don't know what to believe.'

'And why, I wonder, was it so important that you came up here?'

'No idea. I just do what I'm told – when it's Bob who tells me.'

A minute or two later the phone rang. 'Maybe it was this. We'll soon know. Yes,' he said, 'who is it?'

'Ronstadt left a few minutes ago. With his bag. He checked out.'

'You'd sooner not give me a name?'

'Right on the button. Good luck.'

Tweed put the phone down. He spoke as he went to a cupboard to fetch his packed bag.

'We're on our way. Whoever phoned had a smooth American voice. And I have to call the others.'

Paula was already on her way to the door, heading for her room. She stopped as Tweed's mobile started buzzing. He snatched it out of his pocket.

'Yes. Who's calling?'

'Me.' Marler's voice. 'Activity here. Drive over. Tell Bob to park at the edge of the Münsterplatz. He knows where . . .'

'That was Marler,' Tweed said and Paula left the room.

Tweed picked up the phone after dumping his bag

close to his feet. He called Newman and Keith Kent. His
message was the same to both of them.

'Now! Meet you with your bag outside the hotel. On
our way to the car. I've kept the bill up to date, so paying
won't take a moment.'

38

It seemed almost night as they drove away from the
Colombi. In the white Audi they occupied the same
positions as they had when driving from Basle. Newman
was behind the wheel with Paula beside him, a map
open on her lap. In the rear Tweed sat with Keith Kent.
The traffic was light amid the gloom and soon Newman
was approaching the Münsterplatz. He slowed down,
dimmed his lights, stopped. Out of nowhere Marler
appeared. He spoke quickly but concisely through Newman's lowered window.

'You got here just in time, I reckon. Ronstadt's black
Audi has just left. Four men inside, including nice Jake,
who's driving. The two Audis parked here also left, with
seven men inside them. They're in front, with Ronstadt
following. Bob, haven't you turned on the gizmo I
bought in Geneva? The tracking device.'

'No, I forgot. I've switched it on now.'

'How does it work?' Tweed asked, leaning forward.
'I hadn't even noticed it.'

Below the dashboard, Marler had earlier attached,
with magnetic grips, a circular screen about six inches in
diameter. Illuminated now, the glow showed it was
divided by thin lines into the points of the compass. A
round red light, about the size of a British five-pence
piece, was moving very slowly in an easterly direction.

'That red light,' Marler explained, 'is Ronstadt. Earlier,

377

Bob and I slipped back to where the Colombi parks cars. The signal-sending device was still on the roof of his car. It's about as big as one of those buttons you see on camelhair coats. The signal travels up to a satellite which instantly returns it to your receiver, which you're looking at. To mine also. Luckily the device is black, so it merges with the colour of Ronstadt's car. Got it?'

'Just assume we do,' pleaded Paula. 'No more technicalities.'

'He can't move all that fast,' Marler went on. 'Heard a forecast. There's been another heavy fall of snow in the Black Forest. Before we move off I'm Father Christmas.' He hitched up a long canvas holdall, started handing weapons through the window.

'One machine-pistol with ammo.'

'I'll take that,' said Paula. 'I've practised with them a lot recently down at the mansion in Surrey.'

'Walther 7.65mm automatics with spare mags.'

'I'll take one of those,' said Tweed, his voice grim. 'I remarked earlier we must exterminate this vermin.'

Keith Kent accepted a Walther as Marler went on producing more.

'Grenades, smoke bombs . . .'

'Some for me,' called out Paula.

She stuffed them carefully inside her shoulder bag. She had already loaded the machine-pistol, laying it at her feet, the muzzle pointed at the door. Marler emptied his holdall, then said:

'Tweed, do you agree I drive ahead, Bob follows? Then if there's an ambush, which I think there will be – remember one Audi left hours ago – I'll deal with it. Bob drives on to maintain contact with Ronstadt and his convoy. If they reach their base wait until I catch you up. Four men went ahead earlier, there are seven with Ronstadt, which makes eleven thugs. You'd be outgunned.'

'You might have trouble finding us,' Newman warned.

'No, I won't. I'm attaching another gizmo to your roof. It will show a blue light on my screen so I'll find you. That is if all this lot works. Modern technology. Dicey business.'

'I agree your strategy,' said Tweed.

'Then I'm off to the killing ground, as they say. The Black Forest.'

Marler reached up. Paula heard the magnetic clamps of the gizmo attach to the roof of their car. Marler ran off to where his white Audi was parked. Nield was already waiting in the front passenger seat. Butler sat hunched in the rear. Then Marler ran back to Newman's car.

'I forgot,' he told Newman through the window which had been lowered again. 'When that red light starts flashing you're almost on top of Ronstadt. Now I really must get moving . . .'

'Paula,' said Tweed, 'sometimes Marler does have a grisly way of putting things.'

'You're referring to his use of the phrase "killing ground",' she replied. 'I don't care. I was thinking of poor Guy. I want to send the lot of them to where he's gone.'

They left Freiburg behind more quickly than Paula had expected. Soon they were driving over thick snow. As darkness fell the moon had risen, casting its vaporous glow over the lonely countryside. They entered a world of steep rolling hills covered with dense masses of fir trees, marshalled trunk to trunk like an invading army about to overwhelm them. Their branches and foliage, holding the snow, glittered like Christmas trees in the moonlight.

'You see now,' Tweed said to Paula, 'why I said it can be very beautiful. Are you listening to me?'

She was staring at the red light on the glowing screen. Her expression was almost brooding as though her thoughts were miles away. She shook her head, looked at Tweed.

'Sorry, I didn't catch what you said.'

'Doesn't matter. What were you pondering?'

'A lot of things. For one, why didn't the manager of the Colombi warn us Ronstadt had checked out? Especially after Kuhlmann had spoken to him.'

'Could be he was away from the hotel at the time. Or, if he was there, he might not have wanted to report the movements of one guest to another. If that was the case, I don't blame him. He has the reputation of the hotel to think of.'

'I was also wondering about the three thugs who travelled with Ronstadt. We never saw them while we were there.'

'He probably confined them to their rooms.'

'I do remember what you said now.' She looked out of the window. 'It is beautiful – but also sinister. And we haven't seen any traffic since we started out. Except for Marler's rear lights in the distance.'

'Something's coming towards us now in the opposite direction,' Newman remarked.

'What on earth is it, Bob?'

'Giant snowplough, clearing the snow. You have to give it to the Germans. They don't waste any time keeping the highways clear.'

'It's the first one we've seen,' she objected.

'Not surprising. It's out of season. Tourists – the skiing type – don't expect snow here as late as this. It's a really huge machine.'

'Bob, slow down,' Tweed ordered.

'Marler didn't.'

'I said slow down until we've passed it. Ronstadt is capable of any trickery.'

Tweed had lowered his window. He had his Walther in his hand. Paula automatically picked up the machine-pistol, laid it on her lap. The machine came closer, Newman had obeyed Tweed's command to slow down. Paula took a firmer grip on her weapon. The snowplough was moving very slowly and now the driver was visible. He appeared to be operating his machine innocently. Newman slowed down even more, cruising across the snow.

'Can you see anyone else other than the driver?' Tweed asked.

'Not from where I'm sitting,' Newman replied.

Paula gently pushed Tweed back against his seat. She elevated her machine-pistol, aiming it through the open window. It had been so warm in the car before the window was lowered she had begun to feel sleepy. Now, with the ice-cold air pouring in, she was totally alert.

The rumble of the big snowplough was very loud as it came on, much closer, spewing great quantities of snow off the highway. Just before it drew level the driver took off his peaked cap, waved it to them, then proceeded past them as Paula swiftly dropped her weapon out of sight. She let out her breath.

'Now we can relax.'

'No, we can't,' Tweed warned. 'Somewhere ahead I anticipate a major attack. So stay at the ready.'

Newman increased speed – the gap between his and Marler's car had grown. Tweed closed the window and Paula started gazing out. Here and there she saw an isolated house made of wood, standing well back from the road, with welcoming lights. The houses had very steep roofs, presumably to slough off an accumulation of heavy snow.

In the distance was a sweeping panorama of far-off

summits, white with snow, of deep valleys inside which she saw tiny colonies of houses huddled at the bottom. One panorama succeeded another and in the moonlight it looked like paradise.

'It's so peaceful,' she commented.

'It is, so far,' Tweed warned.

'The red light is growing fainter,' called out Newman. 'Same direction, but for some reason Ronstadt has speeded up.'

'So has Marler,' Keith Kent said, speaking for the first time.

'I'm doing the same,' Newman replied as he accelerated.

'We're getting close to the Höllental,' Paula announced after checking her map with the aid of her torch. 'Very close, I'd say.'

A few minutes later they entered a vast gorge. On both sides steep rugged slopes closed in on the highway. Paula felt a return of a sense of tension. The slopes, almost vertical in places, seemed to hem in the car. And now their height hid the moon, still shining on the upper slopes, but plunging the gorge into deepest shadow. No more cosy little houses with their welcoming lights. Just the dark remote gorge, cutting off all contact with the outside world.

'I wonder how Marler's getting on?' Newman speculated. 'For some reason he's slowed down again.'

'Keep a close eye on the heights,' Marler said to Nield.

'I am doing just that.'

'If they're up there they have to have found somewhere they could drive up. I don't think they'd go in for any mountaineering if they could help it. In any case they'd have to park the car on the highway.'

'Why are we going so slowly?' Butler called out from the back.

'So we can see if they have turned off,' Marler told him.

He had his lights on full beam, so he could look as far ahead as possible. Glancing up, he detected enormous snow-covered boulders poised high above them. Not a sight he welcomed. He checked his screen. The red light, which was Ronstadt's car, was fainter, telling him the American had increased his speed considerably. Why?

He leaned forward, staring at the precipitous slope to his left. Could he be wrong? He drove on, still staring hard. Then he saw it wasn't his imagination. Ahead, climbing up the slope to his left, he made out the double tracks of a car's wheels, deep ruts in the otherwise virgin snow. He increased his speed.

'Hold on to your seat belts. We're going up that slope. That's where they are. Lord knows how high above us.'

Butler held his breath as Marler swung the car at speed – skidding as his rear wheels swung round. He rammed his foot down and began climbing what turned out to be a curving gulley with high banks of snow on either side. The snow tyres gripped the hard-frozen ground as he plunged higher still.

Perched on the heights way above where the gulley left the highway, Brad, squat and ugly, but powerful, had earlier watched the highway far below through his night glasses. He had seen Ronstadt's convoy of three black Audis pass, heading deeper into the Höllental. Brad was in charge of the unit of four men, given the task of destroying Tweed and his team.

'Dan,' he called out to a big man with a down-curving

moustache, 'you've got an automatic rifle. Climb that tall tree over there. Do it now – before the bastards arrive.'

'Buster,' he shouted to a fat man with a face like a slab of stone, 'you've got your machine-pistol. Get down behind that boulder so's you can cover the exit from the gulley. Just in case.'

'And you, Bruce,' he shouted again, 'you got your boulder ready to go down with mine?'

Bruce, heavily built with a scarred forehead, like Brad stood at the edge of the ridge with a steep rolling slope below, but further along. He held a crowbar he'd used to lever the rock loose. Now he only had to heave on the crowbar inserted under it to send it down at murderous speed onto the highway.

Brad was standing behind an enormous snow-covered boulder. It had taken all his considerable strength to lever it out so now it was poised on the brink. He stood with his crowbar shoved well underneath it. Like Bruce, he had only to exert enough pressure to send it flying into space. He called out again to Bruce.

'T'ain't just the boulders which will kill Tweed's cars and everyone inside them. When the boulders go down they'll start an avalanche. Slope below us is unstable . . .'

When Marler suddenly swung off the highway up the gulley at speed he had no way of knowing he had averted – at least temporarily – their doom.

About to lever the boulders, Brad was taken by surprise at Marler's unexpected and swift manoeuvre. Earlier he had used his glasses to check who was in Marler's car. No sign of the girl Ronstadt had described to him, no sign of Tweed, also described to him. He decided to take the car out anyway – until the last second.

'*Bruce!*' he screamed. 'Not yet! They're in the gulley, comin' up.' He switched his attention to the man with the machine-pistol behind a boulder. 'Buster! They's drivin' up the gulley. Blast the car to hell soon as it appears . . .'

Marler was making steady progress, swinging the wheel quickly as one curve succeeded another and blotted out any view of the top. The snow tyres saved him, kept the car moving up and up and up. It was still deep in the gulley with the high snow-covered banks on both sides.

'Damned gulley goes on for ever,' Butler called out.

'It has to end somewhere,' Marler called back.

He had just spoken when the car swung round another curve and he saw, beyond a very steep stretch of track, moonlight glowing at the top.

On the highway Newman, worried that the red circle on the screen which was Ronstadt's car was fading, had accelerated. He was now moving at speed as Paula looked up at the steep slope on her left. High up along the rim in the near distance she saw boulders perched – boulders which had been there probably since prehistoric times.

'We're catching up with Ronstadt,' Newman told them. 'The red light is stronger. Can't see any sign of Marler's rear lights. Don't understand that.'

'Just keep moving,' Tweed urged.

'What do you think I'm doing!'

Near the top of the gulley Marler braked at the foot of the last steep stretch. He left the engine running. No profit in finding themselves without transport out here in the middle of nowhere. His mind was racing as he tried to put himself inside the head of the enemy – what he would have done had he been in his position. He decided quickly.

'This is where we get out. I don't like what might be waiting for us at the top.'

'We scatter,' said Nield.

'That's right.'

'I'll climb the left bank,' said Butler, already opening the door.

'Pete, you and I'll take the right bank. Don't peer over the top too quickly . . .'

The verbal exchange had taken only seconds. Marler carried his Armalite in his left hand, a Walther automatic in his right. Butler started climbing the left bank, digging his feet into the snow. His right hand was gripping a Walther. Cautiously, he peered over the top, blinked in sheer astonishment.

He was only feet away from Brad, who was standing with both hands gripping the crowbar, his eyes on the second white Audi approaching at high speed. He had no fewer than three pistols shoved down inside the belt round his anorak. A flicker of movement caught his eye. He turned to his left, saw Butler, did all the wrong things. He let go of the crowbar, desperately tried to haul out one of the pistols from his belt.

Butler shot him three times. Blood spurted, a pool of it staining Brad's anorak. He staggered to the side of the huge boulder, grabbed at it for support, slipped, fell forward, began sliding down the slope. Grabbing at the boulder had upset its delicate stability. It began to roll down, gathering momentum. Brad had fallen in its path. It rolled over him. By the moonlight Butler saw one large arc of the boulder had turned red, was smeared with parts of the body it had crushed. It thundered on down towards the highway.

*

Inside their Audi, Paula saw the massive boulder roaring down. She calculated it would hit the highway just ahead of them – or hit them.

'*Brake!*' she screamed.

Newman reacted, not knowing why. He brought the car to an emergency stop. In the back Tweed and Kent had braced themselves but they were thrown forward against their seat belts, which saved them. The boulder hit the highway, bounced, seemed to pass across their windscreen. It continued its passage of tremendous velocity across the highway, dived down into a gulch, clear of the other lane.

'Thank you,' said Newman.

'Any time,' said Paula.

He began moving forward at speed. Paula peered out of the window again, gasped. Ahead of them another huge boulder was starting to come down. For a moment she was stupefied, unable to speak. Then she screamed again.

'*Speed!* As fast as you can!'

Newman pressed his foot through the floor. The Audi took off as though flying, sending up bursts of powdered snow. Paula, hands clammy, gripped together, watched the projectile coming. She also saw that the whole slope now was on the move, a tidal wave of snow and rock descending. The second boulder had triggered an avalanche. She prayed, which she rarely did. Newman was fighting to keep the car on the road.

Looking back, she saw the boulder hit the highway behind them. Like its predecessor, it bounced, then tore across the other lane and disappeared. The avalance had now landed on their lane of the highway, quietened down suddenly, leaving the lane in the opposite direction comparatively clear.

'You'd better take over the bloody wheel,' Newman told Paula amiably.

'We must be getting close to Ronstadt,' Tweed's calm voice called out. 'The red light is very strong now . . .'

Bruce, the man with the scarred forehead, had levered down the second boulder and immediately snatched a pistol from his belt. He had heard Butler's three shots. He could see no sign of Brad, but he could see two men crouched in the snow on his side of the gulley. He raised the pistol, gripped it in both hands. There was another shot. Marler had had the cross-hairs of his Armalite aimed, had fired. A red disc appeared on his forehead in the middle of the scar. He stood quite still for a moment, his arms falling, letting go of the pistol, then he fell over backwards, staring sightlessly at the moonlit sky.

'Be careful,' Marler warned. 'There are two more of them somewhere.'

'I thought I saw movement in the forest. I'm going to fan out,' Nield replied in a whisper.

'Good idea.'

Marler began crawling along a dip in the ground towards where the gulley they had driven up ended. Nield moved in a different direction, crouching low and running in spurts from boulder to boulder. He'd noticed one of the tall trees had dropped some snow. Why this tree?

In a roundabout way he approached closer, went into the forest. The particular tree which had caught his attention had a thick trunk with small lower branches which provided a natural ladder for anyone who wanted to climb high. He found his own tree trunk, not too close, not too far away from the tree attracting his curiosity. He saw Marler beginning to get exposed in the open. Three huge clots of snow fell from the tall tree.

Now he was sure, and with Marler in the open he had to act at once. He studied the tree, took a grenade from his pocket, lobbed it about fifteen feet up through a gap in the snow-covered foliage. The grenade denotated, Nield thought he heard a muffled scream. Then the body fell, Dan catapulting from branch to branch until he hit the ground and lay still. His rifle came down a second later.

At almost the same moment Buster stood up from behind his large boulder, swivelling his weapon for a quick burst. Marler shot him twice. Buster sagged to the snow, on top of his gun.

'That's four of them,' Nield called out. 'I've found their car.'

'Lose it,' Marler ordered.

'Both of you get down into the gulley near our car, then.'

Nield had found the car easily. He had simply followed the twin tracks of wheel marks in the snow. Ronstadt's thugs had parked it out of sight behind a large copse of frosted shrubbery. Above it loomed a large tree.

Nield found a deep dip in the ground behind one of the boulders strewn everywhere. He stood in the dip, took out a grenade, lobbed it carefully so it would land under the car's petrol tank and dropped behind the boulder. He heard the grenade detonate. Then there was a roar. The petrol tank had blown. A spectacular shaft of flames soared up. Snow on the tree melted instantly. He peered over the boulder. The black Audi was a total wreck, looked as though it had been through a car crusher. He walked down the gulley and Marler was behind the wheel of the white Audi with Butler in the back. Nield sat again in the front passenger seat and Marler revved up to take it to the top, turn it round and drive back down the gulley.

'Funny,' Butler said, 'we could all be dead by now.'

'Not really,' Marler replied, 'not when the Americans are such amateurs when it comes to tactics.'

39

'We're in danger of losing Marler,' Newman warned, 'moving at this speed.'

'We'll have to risk that,' Tweed replied from the back of the car. 'The man we mustn't lose is Ronstadt. If the Americans are planning what I suspect they are, then they'll win. Britain will be plunged into turmoil – from which it may not recover.'

'There are four of us, eleven of them,' Newman persisted. 'The odds are lethal.'

'Keep going,' Tweed ordered. 'What I can't understand is that we've passed the Höllental. The base has to be somewhere else. Kurt Schwarz missed something. At least, I think he did.' He took out the little black notebook they had found behind the loose brick when Irina had been rescued in Basle. 'Paula, let me borrow your torch.'

'What's worrying you?' she asked.

'Kurt wrote down Höllental on one page, then that was followed by a blank page. I don't understand it.'

'The explanation could be very simple,' said Paula, handing him her torch. 'I've done it myself. Turned over two pages without realizing it, leaving one page blank.'

'I hope you're right. Let me check what's on the following page. I see. Just one word. *Schluchsee*. Sounds like a lake.'

'Give me back my torch. I want to check the map.'

She studied the map, looked quickly at the screen with the red light showing Ronstadt's convoy ahead of them. She watched the light for a few minutes. Then she spoke rapidly.

'We were moving south-east through the Höllental.

Now we're heading east towards Titisee, which has a smaller lake and is a famous resort. But soon there's a big junction which turns us southwest and soon runs alongside Lake Titisee . . .'

'Which we don't want,' Tweed protested.

'If you'd just let me finish,' Paula snapped. 'There is a Schluchsee, a much bigger lake, and it looks remote. After passing Lake Titisee we come to another junction on the way to Feldberg.'

'Highest point in the Black Forest,' said Tweed. 'About four thousand five hundred feet high. Sorry,' he concluded.

'I can do without any more interruptions until I've finished. At the junction we turn left and then we're heading due southeast – straight for Schluchsee.'

'If the blue light on Marler's screen which is us vanishes, he will never follow such a complicated route,' Newman objected.

'We'll have to take that risk,' Tweed repeated.

'I don't like it. I should slow down, give Marler time to catch up with us,' Newman insisted.

'I'm not going to keep giving the same order,' Tweed told him. 'Your job is to keep Ronstadt in sight. That's a direct order.'

'Might be a good idea if we all calmed down a bit,' Keith Kent suggested.

'You're right,' Tweed agreed. 'Tension will get us nowhere.'

'So,' said Paula, 'let's all relax – including you, Tweed.'

'We're losing Tweed,' said Marler, driving his Audi at speed. 'The blue light is fading. We'll just have to go faster.'

'And end up going off the road,' Nield warned.

'I don't think so,' Marler drawled. 'I used to be a racing driver.'

'But this isn't Le Mans,' Nield remarked as Marler accelerated even more. 'Strange that we've left the Höllental behind. I thought that's where their base was. And you're not flying a plane, Marler.'

'And there could be ice under this snow,' called out Butler, which was the first time Nield could recall him ever showing nervousness.

'I'm not going to let Tweed down,' Marler informed them. 'Did you,' he began, changing the subject, 'notice that amazing complex of buildings in the Höllental – the Hofgut Sternen?'

'Wouldn't have minded stopping there for a bite to eat,' Butler remarked. 'Place was enormous and a blaze of lights.'

'I was surprised to see a number of parked cars,' Nield replied. 'And I caught sight of people eating in a pretty good-looking restaurant.'

'Germans,' Marler said, 'coming from not too far away. The cars had skis attached to their roofs. A few hoping to take advantage of the falls of snow.'

There was silence for a while. Marler refused to moderate his speed. To their left a dense forest of firs stretched endlessly up a slope. Still no other traffic on the road. Thank heavens for small mercies, Nield thought.

'Tweed's blue light is growing stronger,' Marler said suddenly. 'We're catching him up. Half a mo' – he's changed direction. He's going due southwest now.'

'We're coming up to a junction,' Nield told him.

Like Paula, he had a map open on his lap. He had been studying it with a small torch. He stared fixedly ahead for signs of a turn.

'Newman's now heading for the Feldberg,' he

announced. 'That is the highest point in the whole of the Black Forest.'

'Deeper snow up there,' Butler commented, half to himself.

'Slow down, for God's sake,' Nield pleaded.

Marler, content now that he was much closer to the other Audi, reduced his breakneck pace. Nield leaned forward even more, stretching his seat belt.

'Turn here. We're on our way to Titisee.'

Marler obeyed his instructions. He pressed his foot down again. A short while later on their right they had glimpses of Lake Titisee, gleaming in the moonlight and utterly deserted. Close to the far shore Nield caught sight of colonies of holiday cabins. Marler checked the blue light again.

'Now Newman's turned due southeast,' he remarked.

'He's not heading for the Feldberg,' Nield reported after checking his map. 'There's another junction ahead. He appears to be heading instead for a big lake, Schluchsee. I wonder why?'

'Still no sign of Marler,' Newman commented to Paula.

'The red light which is Ronstadt flashed once,' she warned. 'So we must be closing on him.'

'Drop back a bit, then,' Tweed ordered. 'But don't lose him.'

'I've got it – do two things at once,' Newman cracked back at him.

But he did slow down. Everyone in the car noticed that now they had begun to descend and kept on doing so. Paula checked her map again.

'Soon the road zigzags a lot,' she warned.

'Well, I have slowed down,' Newman reassured her.

'Good job you did.'

As she spoke Newman was guiding the car round a

steep bend and then immediately afterwards he was swinging round another. By his side Paula was staring through the windscreen, hoping to catch sight of the mysterious lake. The atmosphere inside the car was now far more relaxed, Tweed was thinking. Which he welcomed. Lord knew what was facing them ahead, if they were able to track Ronstadt to his base.

'I can see something now.'

As Paula spoke Newman stopped the car. The red light on his screen was flashing madly. He had almost overtaken Ronstadt's convoy. Paula raised a small pair of high-powered night binoculars she'd had looped round her neck. She thought she had never seen anywhere so lonely and forbidding.

They were still high up and she was looking down on a small section of the long lake way below. She felt she might have been in a remote region of Canada. The moon kept fading as transparent drifts of cloud crossed beneath it. The lake was still as death and black as pitch. Its surface was so unruffled it gave her the impression it was covered with ice. The opposite shore was banked by steep hills choked with fir forest.

'See anything?' Tweed asked.

'Nothing. No sign of life, of human habitation. Just nothing.'

'Very promising.'

'Marler has caught us up,' Newman called out, unable to conceal his relief.

'I'm getting out of the car for a closer look,' said Paula.

She had got out, closed the door quietly, when she found Marler standing beside her. A few yards behind Newman's Audi, Marler's was parked, lights dimmed, as were Newman's.

'Well, I gather Ronstadt's base wasn't in the Höllental,' Marler remarked.

'No, it wasn't,' Paula replied. 'Tweed has an idea it has to be somewhere near here. That weird lake down there is called Schluchsee.'

'Tweed is sure the base is in this area,' Tweed called out through a window he had lowered. 'Kurt Schwarz has a reference to this place in his little book. I missed the significance of the name – a blank page followed his note on the Höllental.'

'Let's get closer,' Paula suggested to Marler. 'I think there's a track beyond the verge.'

Newman had switched off his engine. They had been so close to Ronstadt he'd felt it was a wise precaution. The enemy could have had the same idea and switched off their engines to listen. Walking a few paces along the track, Paula was struck by the incredible silence which added to the sinister atmosphere of this place out in the wilds. She sensed they were waiting for something terrible to happen.

For a short time she welcomed the bitter night air, well below zero. It was a pleasant contrast to the fetid air which had built up inside the car. She'd left her gloves in the car so she could manipulate the binoculars more easily and already her face and hands were beginning to feel frozen.

'Marler, I should have asked first what happened when you vanished off the highway. Are Nield and Kent OK?'

'In the pink. We had a bit of a dust-up. Four down, eleven in front to go. Tell you about it later.'

Moving a short distance down the track gave her a far more panoramic view, no longer obscured by a copse of firs at the roadside. The lake was wide but seemed immensely long – far longer than Lake Titisee which she had caught sight of earlier. She scanned it through her binoculars. Still no sign of a single building, or even a landing stage. The silence, lack of movement, the absence of even a small wooden house with lights in it was getting to her.

'Lake surface looks as solid as slate,' Marler commented. 'A perfect setting for a horror film. Subhuman giants with huge axes creeping out of the woods.'

'Stop it,' Paula protested. 'I have a vivid imagination. I'll be seeing them now.'

'Any data?' asked Tweed behind her after getting quietly out of the car.

'Not a damned thing. Look for yourself.'

'No thanks. I can see with my own eyes. As desolate a spot as I've seen for a long time. We'd better get back in the car. The red light has stopped flashing. Ronstadt's on the move.'

40

'We're nearly there, Moonhead,' Ronstadt said to the man beside him.

Ronstadt was behind the wheel of the third Audi, following the two cars ahead of him as they bumped over the wide track round the tip of the lake. The moon had temporarily been blotted out by a dark cloud and the cars had their headlights full on. He suddenly let out a belly laugh of pure pleasure.

'What is it?' asked Leo Madison.

'Moonhead, it's turnin' out great. No sign of Tweed and his miserable crew. Brad and his boys must have made hash browns of them back in Höllental. With ketchup for the blood.' He laughed again, a raucous sound. 'Think of the avalanche hittin' those two white Audis. Think of what the people inside look like now. Hope that Paula Grey was with 'em. It's great.'

'Funny Brad and his boys haven't caught up with us,' Madison commented.

'Takes time to cook a dish like that.' He laughed again. 'I like it. Cookin' a dish like that. The dish is Paula Grey.'

'I just hope you're right.'

'You know your problem, Moonhead?'

'I guess you're gonna tell me.'

'You ain't got no sense of humour. Better roll up your sleeves, feller. Lot of work to do.'

'What kinda work?'

'Loading cartons – heavy ones – on to three trucks. I guess Bernhard Yorcke will have loaded one truck ready for the go. Makes four truckloads. What's in 'em will destroy Britain.'

'Who is this Bernhard Yorcke?'

'Came from Luxembourg years ago. He's a printer. Moved on to Switzerland as a youngster. Stayed there ever since. Just where he shoulda gone, being a printer. Swiss, I'll give 'em that, are best printers in the world.' He peered up through the windscreen. 'Nearly there. Trouble with Bernhard Yorcke is he can be a very nasty piece of work.'

Coming from Ronstadt, Madison wondered what on earth this Yorcke could be like.

'What's he print?' he asked.

'See when we gets there, won't you?'

'There is a base,' Paula said, 'and that has to be it.'

'I agree,' said Tweed.

They had driven down and down from the point where Paula had surveyed Schluchsee through her binoculars. Newman's car had progressed first, with Marler's following close behind. The red light on Newman's screen

397

had glowed so strongly he had driven at a slow pace. Gradually the red glow had dimmed. Newman had had his lights dimmed when he'd stopped suddenly for two reasons. They were now on the level and he'd caught sight of an open stretch of road running next to the lake. They parked the cars on the left-hand verge, under cover of a copse of trees. Then they had cautiously walked into the open.

To their right was a shoulder-high wall between the road and the lake. All seven of them had kept out of sight behind the wall, peering over it. Paula had perched her elbows on top of the wall and stared through her binoculars. Immediately opposite them on the far side of the lake was the base.

A very large and old two-storey building stood on top of a bluff at the lake's edge. It had huge and very steep gables, was built of wood as far as she could see. It appeared to be a cross between a farmhouse and a private residence. It had been masked from her previous survey, much higher up, by the fir forest which extended forward almost to the brink of the bluff. Tweed had borrowed Marler's binoculars and now Newman spoke urgently.

'Tweed, loan me those glasses for a minute.'

'Take mine,' said Paula and handed them to him.

Newman swiftly focused them. His target was not the house. He was aiming them at the string of red lights from the three black Audis retreating round the tip of the lake. As he spoke he followed them through the lenses.

'They're driving along a wide track which leads round the end of the lake. That's where we'll follow them when they've reached their base. I can drive along that track without lights.'

'And with luck,' Tweed commented, 'driving in white

Audis they won't see us coming. We'll merge with the snow.'

'Is that why you asked me to get white cars?' Marler enquired.

'Yes. I'd heard about the first snowfall. It struck me white cars would be less visible, which might come in useful.'

'It will,' agreed Newman, still staring through the binoculars. 'We'll just hope the moon stays the way it is now. Not too strong but with a bit of light. They've reached the end of the track, turning away from the lake. Now they're half-hidden so the track must lead up through a gulley.'

'Which will help us too,' Marler remarked.

Paula was standing with her arms folded, trying to keep in a bit of warmth. The well below zero temperature was gradually penetrating the extra clothing she was wearing. Her head was perched on the wall top as she crouched to keep hidden.

'It reminds me of that house in *Psycho*,' she said. 'It has a flight of railed steps leading up to the front door. The main difference is that large ramp to the right. Frightening.'

'It's just a house,' said Newman.

'That ramp is interesting,' Tweed observed, his binoculars still trained on the house, 'because it would be possible for two cars to drive down it at the same moment – or a very large truck.'

'Why would they want trucks?' Kent asked.

'To transport what I think they've produced inside that building. If I'm right, it's far more deadly than bombs. That edifice beyond the top of the ramp looks like a huge garage. I'd swear the door is modern – unlike everything else about the place.'

Paula was staring round the shores of the lake in the

ghostly light. The moon came out from behind a cloud briefly and she saw she was right.

'There are sandy beaches here and there along the edges of the lake. But I can't see any sign of holiday chalets.'

'They all go to Titisee in the season.' Tweed told her. 'The convoy has almost arrived.'

'The track forks three ways when it gets close to the house,' Newman reported. 'One route up to the bottom of the flight of steps, another proceeds on to the foot of that ramp. The third leads to somewhere behind the house – and that's the route they are taking. Time to go?'

'Let's wait a little longer,' Tweed suggested. 'Give them time to settle in.'

'No lights at all in the place,' Paula pointed out.

'There are several,' Tweed corrected her. 'Difficult to see because they're low down – must be a basement. I think there are curtains drawn across them.'

'You mean there's someone there already?' Paula asked.

'I'm sure there is. In the basement. Now, I wonder? Yes, it might well be in the basement – if it's big enough.'

'What might?'

'What we've come to destroy.'

'Which is?'

'A fortune,' replied Tweed, and he smiled. 'Time to find out.'

The moon obliged. It cast no more than a half-glow as Newman, in the lead, turned off the road and down onto the track. Behind him Marler's Audi followed. They drove without lights and Newman, having studied the track, found he could see where he was going without difficulty.

'What were you and Tweed discussing with Marler before we left?' Paula, seated beside Newman again, asked him.

'We were planning tactics for the assault,' Tweed answered her from the rear of the car. 'We had several options.'

'Which did you choose?' she asked.

'I was just going to tell you when you spoke. It's important you know as much as the rest of us. Bob, do you want to start putting Paula in the picture?'

'There are seven of us,' Newman began. 'We thought there'd be eleven of the enemy but that light in the basement Tweed spotted means there will be at least twelve of them. At least,' he repeated. 'The obvious point of attack is to follow their cars round the back. Maybe a bit too obvious, wouldn't you agree?'

'Yes, I would,' replied Paula. 'I'd have thought we have to split up a bit – so we have the place surrounded.'

'Which is exactly what we decided,' said Newman. 'Keith, I'd like you to get out when we reach the house, so you can creep up that staircase to the main front door. I don't think this will happen, but they may all come out there. Marler gave you an extra Walther – you may not have time to reload. Shoot them down as they emerge.'

'I think I can manage that,' Kent said easily. 'Tweed must have told you I'm what they call a shooter back home. Belong to a club.'

'What about the rest of us?' Paula pressed.

'Marler and Butler take up the best positions they can find at the back of the house. Tweed and Nield follow Keith when we drop him off, then they go further along to take up positions on the ramp side of the house.'

'What about you?'

'I've got a roving commission. I'll be circling the house – as reinforcement wherever I'm needed.'

'You've left someone out,' Paula said coolly. 'Me.'

'No, I haven't. You'll come with me.'

'As protection?' she asked not so coolly.

'Of course not. As backup – for me.'

'The essence of our strategy,' Tweed intervened, 'is to entice them out of the house. By now they'll be getting to know its layout. We haven't the faintest idea of that. So we bring them out to us.'

'And how exactly do we do that?' Paula wanted to know.

'You've noticed lights are starting to come on inside the house. So we—'

'Shows overconfidence,' Newman interrupted. 'That's helpful.'

'I was going to tell Paula that Bob will throw grenades inside the house through the windows. That will shake them up, bring some of them outside where we'll be waiting for them.'

'That's clever,' Paula replied.

'We'll soon be there,' Newman warned.

The track had now entered the gulley, which was steep and wide. Newman felt relieved. There was no sign so far that the thugs inside had noticed their approach. He reached the top of the gulley and then the point where the track forked in three directions.

'They may not hear our cars coming,' said Paula. 'As you know, I have acute hearing, and I can hear machines whirring inside the place.'

'This is where Keith and Tweed drop off,' said Newman. 'In the rear-view mirror I can see Nield leaving Marler's car ready to join you.'

'Keith,' Newman called out, 'I suggest you crouch against the wall of the house – between the front door and the ramp. Less of a target.'

'I'm going to do just that,' Kent replied.

Both Tweed and Kent were careful not to slam their doors as they left the car. Tweed had his Walther in his right hand, spare magazines in his left. The moonlight did not reach the outside of the house and the two men disappeared like wraiths. As Newman drove on at a slow pace Paula bent down, picked up her machine-pistol.

'We'll make a good team,' said Newman.

'If you say so,' she snapped, still annoyed.

They were moving along the track which ran past the side of the large house. In the distance Paula could just make out the silhouettes of three parked black Audis. All of them were turned round for a swift getaway. They were crawling past the side of the house when she called out.

'Stop!'

'Why?'

'Stop! Damn you! There's a side door at the top of a flight of steps. I'm getting out. No bloody argument.'

Newman sighed, stopped. It was no use arguing with Paula once she'd made up her mind. And she had a point. They hadn't expected a side entrance. She opened the door, smiled at him, slipped out, closed the door. He drove on with Marler following him with only Butler in his car now.

The first thing that occurred to Paula as she stood for a moment, adjusting to the huge drop in temperature, was the extent of the flight leading up to a closed door. At least a dozen steps. Her eyes were becoming accustomed to the pitch darkness and she saw the ground was littered with boulders.

She crouched behind one, then decided crouching would restrict her movements. It would all happen so quickly if some of the thugs did emerge from the side door. She found a flat-topped rock in the shadows. She checked behind her, listening for the sound of someone prowling. Maybe they had posted sentries outside. No one had thought of that. Satisfied with the heavy silence, she perched on the rock, putting spare mags in her lap. Then she elevated the machine-pistol until the muzzle was aimed at the platform outside the door. She lowered it swiftly, repeated the exercise.

'This is a damned quiet forest,' she said to herself. 'No bird song. No sign of night birds.'

She had removed the glove from her right hand – her trigger hand. It would freeze but she'd have to put up with that. She kept flexing the finger round the trigger.

'Come on, you swine,' she said under her breath. 'Your lot has killed enough people with the bombs in London . . .'

More lights had come on in the house, Newman observed as he began circling the building. He had another reason for choosing his role. He wanted to check that everyone was in as safe a position as possible. He saw Paula sitting erect on her rock and he sighed. He was going to go to her to say something, decided not to. Paula had come a long way, knew what she was doing. He recalled how she'd dealt with Hank Waltz in the Eagle Street warehouse in London's East End.

He went in the opposite direction to the rear of the house. He found Marler behind a tree, his Armalite at the ready. Beyond was Butler, crouched behind a shrub. Both were watching yet another exit – this door level with the ground. He continued walking round the far side of the house.

Nield peered out from behind a small wooden hut. He waved his Walther at Newman. Further on, closer to the ramp and under its slope, Tweed stood waiting, unconcerned, staring upwards. He didn't even look as Newman passed him and reached the front.

As he'd suggested, Keith was beyond the top of the staircase leading to the massive front door. He was crouched with his back to the wall of the house. He must have heard Newman. He suddenly swung round, Walther aimed. Then he lowered it. Time, he decided, to wake up the thugs inside, to throw a few grenades through the lighted windows.

When the three black Audis arrived at the parking place, Ronstadt was first out of his car. As he hurried towards the door at the back of the house he was accompanied by three men – Leo Madison, Chuck Venacki and Vernon Kolkowski. They had all travelled in his car.

'Moonhead,' he warned, 'you've seen a few tough guys in your time, but prepare yourself for Bernhard Yorcke . . .'

'Guess I've seen all the tough guys,' Madison said dismissively.

'You keep your big mouth shut. I hadn't finished. Yorcke is about five foot three tall. He's a gnome – and a hunchback, and strong as an ox. He gets very nasty if you says the wrong thing. Admire his work. Tell him what a great guy he is.'

'OK. If you say so.'

Ronstadt pressed the door bell three times slowly, then twice, then three times again.

They waited. Madison shuffled his feet. Behind him the other three thugs stood back. Ronstadt liked men to observe the courtesies where he was concerned. Which meant he led the way and the others followed like hired lackeys.

'Where the hell is he?' snapped Madison. 'Friggin' cold stuck out here.'

He had just spoken when they heard the door being unlocked from the inside. When it opened a strong light shone from the large room inside. Madison sucked in his breath. Standing crouched in the doorway was the ugliest, most evil-looking man he'd ever seen.

Bernhard Yorcke had a high forehead and lank, greasy dark hair. His nose was hooked and the dark eyes which stared out strangely were black and menacing. Below the nose a wide, thin-lipped mouth was twisted at an odd angle, which gave the impression he was smiling permanently in a sneering way. A most unpleasant smile. Clean-shaven, his long face tapered to a pointed chin which increased his gnomelike look. His fingertips were black. They would always be black – with printer's ink.

'You are late,' he said nastily.

'Sorry 'bout that,' Ronstadt replied, smiling. 'Difficult drivin' conditions. A lot of snow and ice.'

'You're still late. You had better come inside with your men. There will be no food for them. I cannot waste my valuable time looking after strange visitors.'

Yorcke spoke English slowly, with great precision, emphasizing syllables. His voice was high-pitched, which added to the sinister aura of his personality. He stood to one side as Ronstadt's thugs filed in, then locked the door with his left hand. In his right hand he held a long black iron bar which terminated at one end in a sharp point. At the top a small bar extended at right-angles. It gave Madison the feeling of a vicious dagger.

'You are wondering what I am holding in my hand,' Yorcke said to Madison. This horrible guy misses nothing, thought Madison, who had been glancing at the bar. 'It is an instrument of my trade.'

'Bernhard is the greatest printer in the whole world,' boomed Ronstadt. 'He gives you a date and the work is finished by that date.'

'Everything is ready now, Ronstadt,' Yorcke confirmed. 'I have even printed a greater quantity. It is running on the machines now. For that, of course, I expect a bigger fee.'

As he spoke he advanced very close to Ronstadt. The spiked bar was raised to his chest level as though about to strike. He stared hard at Ronstadt, who answered quickly, trying not to look at the nearness of the spike.

'You'll get a big extra fee. And I won't pay you in what you've produced.'

'Don't do that,' purred Yorcke. 'Life can be short.'

'It was a joke,' Ronstadt assured him hastily. 'Can we start loading the trucks?'

'One truck is already loaded. The driver is waiting to leave.'

'Tell him to get moving, please.'

His men were exploring different rooms as Yorcke went to an old-fashioned phone attached to the wall. He used a turn-handle to ring the bell in the garage.

'Dave, take the truck to its destination. Yes, now.'

Newman, with a holdall he had borrowed from Marler, was starting his tour of the house. He grabbed a grenade from the holdall, hurled it with great force through an illuminated window. Glass cracked as the missile landed somewhere inside. It detonated. The window shattered, scattering glass all over the snow outside. Newman had already moved on, hurled another grenade. He continued throwing the grenades almost nonstop as he ran.

Below the wide ramp Tweed was crouched against the wall, Walther in his hand. He suddenly heard the sound of a powerful engine starting. Looking up, he saw the huge door of the garage elevating swiftly, automatically. A large white Mercedes truck roared out, sped down the ramp. He aimed his gun, fired. A useless shot. The driver inside his cab was way past him, had swung the vehicle round at the bottom, accelerated, headed for the track and thundered down it. Nield was by his side.

'We've lost it. I fired but hit nothing. Where could it be going?'

'Tell you in a minute . . .'

He watched the truck rushing along the track. In no time at all it reached the road, swung left, heading back the way they had come. Then it was gone.

'Freiburg for starters would be my guess,' said Tweed. 'There may be a way of stopping it later.'

Newman dashed past them. He was running round the house, hurling more grenades from the holdall slung over his shoulder. He aimed one well clear of Kent, crouched by the front wall at the top of the steps. There was a fresh detonation. More glass sprayed the outside, none of it coming near Tweed and Nield. He didn't stop running.

Half a minute earlier, the door at the top of the steps at the side of the house where Paula waited, was thrown open. Three thugs rushed out, down the steps, firing at random. Paula elevated her machine-pistol. She fired one long burst, lowering the weapon. The thugs on the steps tumbled over each other, fell in a heap, very still. She was reloading, expecting more, when Newman rushed round the corner, took in the situation at a glance.

'Great work. Don't go inside!'

He ran on. Paula waited. No one else emerged. She laid her machine-pistol on the ground. It would be difficult to manipulate inside the confines of the house. Holding her Walther gripped in both hands, she walked to the foot of the steps. Slowly she began to climb them, threading her way between the strewn corpses. Then she disappeared inside.

At the rear of the house Marler waited well back at the edge of the trees, holding his Armalite. Butler was standing nearby, crouched low behind some wild shrubbery.

'Keep your eyes on that door,' Marler called out.

'They're doing that.'

When the assault came it was in an unexpected way – and from an unexpected direction. Without warning –

they had heard, had seen, no sign of activity – a hail of smoke bombs arrived from inside the shattered windows. Marler and Butler were lost in a dense, choking fog.

The door opened quietly. Ronstadt led the way out, followed by Leo Madison, Chuck Venacki and Vernon Kolkowski. They had guns in their hands but they did not fire them. Instead they ran for Ronstadt's Audi, now parked in front and facing the track. Ronstadt opened the driver's door quietly, sat behind the wheel as he was joined by Chuck at his side with Madison and Vernon in the back. He started the engine, accelerated.

Marler, coughing, emerged from the smoke. He saw Newman appear round the side of the house. Ronstadt drove the car straight at him. Newman jumped clear just in time. Then the car had gone, vanishing down the gulley.

Newman clambered to his feet, realized he had sprained his ankle. He stared at the flat-topped rock where Paula had been sitting. He looked quickly up at the open door at the top of the steps, beyond the piled bodies.

'Marler!' he shouted. 'Paula's gone inside. Up those steps. For God's sake go after her.'

'On my way.'

When Paula reached the open doorway she paused, listened, then peered inside. She was looking up and down a lighted corridor. Deserted. She frowned. She could hear a strange noise. Clatter ... clatter ... clatter ...

It went on and on and was coming from an open door further down the corridor to her right. As she walked down the corridor the noise became louder and louder. A slablike door was open, pushed back against the wall. As she came closer she saw it was made of solid steel. She peered round it and suppressed a gasp of surprise. She was looking down into a vast basement which must run under the entire house.

She understood the noise now. The basement was occupied by an array of machines working like mad. Illumination came from fluorescent tubes suspended from the ceiling. Beyond the door a flight of concrete steps led down into the basement, with a metal rail on one side. She scanned the area as far as she could. No sign of anyone. Step by step she began to descend the flight. The noise of the clattering machines was hellish, trapped inside the basement.

Walking down stealthily, she caught glimpses of the battery of machines. At one end large reels of paper were being fed in. They became perfectly flat sheets as the first machine carried them along. Then they passed under a series of huge revolving rollers. They emerged, still flat, but now printed with what, at first, she thought were outsize postage stamps. A moment later she realized they were banknotes, row upon row of them. They continued their journey until they reached a series of very large metal plates which jumped up and down, slicing them.

She had almost reached the bottom step when she slipped on some spilt oil. Her legs collapsed under her as she grabbed for the rail. The hand was still holding the Walther and she bruised herself, dropping the gun. Picking herself up, she flexed her hands and legs. No damage – she always fell limply. But where was the Walther?

The light was bright enough for her to see clearly but there was no sign of the weapon. It must have slid under one of the machines. She swore. Shaking her head to clear her mind, she began walking towards where the printing process started. Near the end was a concrete platform, elevated about a foot high. She assumed it was an observation platform so a printer could check to make sure everything was functioning properly.

Suddenly she sensed a presence behind her. She swung round and let out a gasp of fear. The most hideous man she had ever seen was close to her. A gnome with a hunchback, his evil face twisted in a leer of anticipation of a pleasure to come. In his right hand, raised high, he held a ferocious-looking black spike.

'I am Bernhard Yorcke,' he called out above the noise of the machinery. 'The greatest printer in the world. You have come to sabotage my beautiful work.'

'I think your work is the most beautiful I've ever seen,' she said quickly.

'No, you don't. You have been sent to destroy it. So I will destroy you.'

'You're a genius,' she babbled.

'I am the greatest genius of them all,' he said, coming closer.

'That's why I came here. To see your wonderful work.'

'You lie,' he snarled. 'You came to destroy. Instead, I am going to destroy you.'

She knew he was going to drive the dreadful spike into her face. As she backed away her right hand was feeling desperately inside her shoulder bag. Her fall had pushed it behind her back. She missed the special pocket sewn in which held her Browning. Her hand plunged deep, felt a canister of hair spray. He was very close to her as she brought out the spray, aimed it, her own eyes closed, ejected the spray.

'You foul whore.'

She opened her eyes, then realized the spray had only hit his left eye. His right eye stared into hers as he lifted the spike higher to jab it forward. Backing away from him she had come up against the wall. There was nowhere to go, to escape.

Marler came bounding down the steps like a rocket, Armalite in his right hand. He hadn't been able to shoot from the top for fear of hitting Paula. He saw the oil on the step which had brought down Paula, leapt over it.

'You ugly deformed little bastard!' he shouted.

The insult had the effect he had prayed for. Yorcke, about to jab the spike forward, turned round. Marler used the barrel of his Armalite like a club, smashing it across Yorcke's forehead. Yorcke staggered back, still clutching the spike. He felt his legs press against the concrete platform. With incredible agility he jumped up on to the platform to give himself extra height. He was waving the spike when the Armalite hammered into him again, catching him across the hooked nose.

He lost his balance, fell backwards on to the moving machine. Sprawled on the paper, he was carried along to the rollers. They had a safety device, jumping up when something large hit them. The large object was Yorcke's head. The roller came crashing down and Marler turned Paula away so she couldn't see. Yorcke let out a ghastly scream, heard clearly above the noise of the machinery. His shoulders reached the roller which jumped up again, then down. There was no further scream and the rest of his body swept under as the immensely heavy roller crashed down again. The paper was stained with a spreading pool of blood. Marler spoke quickly.

'Don't look.'

He heard someone call down from the top of the steps. Newman stood there with Tweed. Newman, followed by Tweed, hobbled down the steps, stopped when Marler warned him about the oil. Marler, his arm round Paula, guided her to Newman.

'Take her to the car. Stay with her.'

'You've hurt your foot,' Paula observed. 'I'll tend to it in the car. I've got a first-aid kit. Let's go. Take your time.'

Tweed stared at the printed sheets still proceeding along the battery of machines. Then he looked at Marler.

'British twenty-pound notes, ten-pound notes and fivers. It was Lenin who said, "If you want to destroy a country debauch the currency." Something like that. It's quite fiendish. The Americans were going to flood Britain with forged banknotes. We'd lose all faith in the pound. Then the Americans would persuade the population to switch to dollars. Then they would have taken us over.'

He looked up. At the top of the staircase Kent, Butler and Nield were gazing down. He shouted up to them.

'The three of you move as a unit. Check every room in this house. Make sure no one else is here. If it's all clear come back and tell me. But be careful.'

'I imagine you'd like all this to be wiped out?' Marler suggested.

'As soon as possible. Trouble is, the ceiling's concrete.'

'I think not.'

Marler climbed a ladder perched against a wall. Reaching up, he tapped at the ceiling. Looking down he shook his head.

'Not concrete at all. Some kind of polystyrene – to match the concrete floor. Above it will be wood flooring. And wood burns. I need to go back to my car for extra supplies. Don't go round the end of this battery of machines. Something very unpleasant will be there.'

When Marler had gone Tweed started to walk to the end of the conveyor belt of machines. He had a Walther in his right hand. Seeing what the last machine had spewed out onto the floor he skirted the remains of Bernhard Yorcke. His stomach churned. He walked on,

413

past large packed bales piled to the ceiling, reaching a very wide door which was open. Beyond the door steps led up to a lighted area. He found himself inside the huge garage with the automatic door at the front still open.

It was freezing cold. He saw a switch on the wall, pressed it. The automatic door lowered swiftly. More fluorescent tubes lit the interior of the garage and three more white Mercedes trucks stood parked, replicas of the truck he had seen driven away. He looked inside the open backs. Empty. He went back down the steps into the machine room.

Inside a drawer he found a collection of knives. Selecting one, he bent down to rip open one of several bales on the floor. He stared at its contents – stack after stack of British twenty-pound notes, each neatly held together with an elastic band. He heard footsteps running down the steps from the house. Kent was in the forefront with Nield and Butler behind him.

'Come and look at this,' Tweed called out. 'But when you reach the end look at the wall.'

'All's clear,' Nield reported. 'No one else in the house.'

'Oh, my God . . .' gasped Kent. 'What is it?'

He had overlooked Tweed's advice. Now he was staring at what had seeped out of the last machine onto the floor.

'Don't ask,' Tweed snapped. 'I told you not to look. Instead, come and look at this.'

Kent came round the corner, bent down. He extracted a stack of the banknotes, took off the elastic band. His expression was grim.

'More forgeries. I don't need to use my eyeglass. They are very good, but once you know what to look for you can see at once they're fakes.'

'So once the knowledge spread like wildfire every bank teller, every shopkeeper, every shopper in Britain would know they were holding useless money?'

'That's how it would work,' Kent agreed. 'Then panic.'

Picking up the knife Tweed had used, he ripped open another bale. This one was brimful of stacks of fivers. He opened a stack, glanced quickly at several banknotes, shook his head.

'Again, at first glance they're the real thing, but they're not.'

Kent ripped open several more bales. He found stacks of ten-pound notes, fifty-pound notes. Tweed then led him up the steps into the garage. He pointed at one of the trucks.

'How much of the faked currency do you reckon that could contain?'

'Millions and millions,' Kent replied. 'It's a big truck. It would contain enough – if distributed – to start a run on the pound.'

'Worse than I thought. Much worse. One loaded truck got away.'

They returned to the machine room as Marler appeared, lugging a very heavy holdall. He dumped it on the floor, well clear of the spreading reddish pool. He glanced round the huge basement.

'I imagine you'd like me to lose this lot?'

'Yes. And the whole house. Can it be done?'

'Without difficulty. I've got thermite bombs which will turn the place into an inferno. Plus high explosive – just to make a professional job of it. If you've finished here, I suggest you leave me to it. Everyone returns to the Audis, then drive down to the end of the gulley. I'd appreciate it if you'd wait for me to arrive.'

'How does it work?'

'With this.' Marler took a small black object smaller than a matchbox from his pocket. It had a shallow depression on one side.

'I press that,' he explained, 'and the world blows up. It works rather like the gizmo you press when you drive home, pause at the end of your drive, press your gizmo. Hey Presto! The garage door lifts automatically. Based on a radio signal with a code. Same thing here. I've laced the rooms in the house with thermite and high-explosive bombs. All have a signal receiver. The whole shooting match goes up when I press this gizmo.'

'Put it away in your pocket,' Kent suggested. 'We don't want an accident.'

'Then clear off now and leave me to it,' Marler repeated.

With their two Audis parked beyond the bottom of the gulley, they waited. They had a clear view of the strange house perched on its bluff. Also they were close to the road running alongside the lake. They seemed to wait for ever but, by Tweed's watch, it was only five minutes later when they heard two dull explosions.

'It's started,' said Paula. 'Oh, Lord, where's Marler?'

'Hasn't started yet,' Tweed assured her. 'And here comes Marler like a rocket.'

When he reached the two cars Marler was out of breath. He stood still for a moment. Then he took the small black object he had shown them from his pocket. He looked at Tweed.

'Ready for the fireworks?'

'We are.'

Marler pressed the device. They all stared fixedly at the weird house. They had left all the lights on. Paula could make out the broken windows. There was a simultaneous roar blasting out across the forest – accompanied by a searing sheet of fire. At first flames shot out of the windows, then the house began to come apart. The garage elevated. A truck rocketed into the air, on fire. It shot forward in an arc, descended into the lake. Flames fizzled, the truck sank. Within seconds there was an even more deafening roar. The house came apart. The front section elevated, was lifted bodily forward like the removal of a stage façade. It fell forward, dived off the bluff, landed in the lake. For a moment it floated, burning, a bizarre sight. Then it sank below the surface with a sinister sizzle. It created a small tidal wave which rushed forward, hit a long beach, sent up high a cloud of spray which settled.

'Those are banknotes,' shouted Paula.

She snatched up the binoculars she had focused on the house before Marler arrived. Above the crumbling side and rear walls of the house was a snowstorm. In her lenses she could see she was right. They were banknotes. Then a sheet of flame soared up, consumed the snowstorm. A strange large object was carried forward by the shockwave. She caught it in her binoculars. It was a huge section of a printing machine with a slab of concrete attached to its base. It dropped into the lake with a tremendous splash, sank instantly without trace. The flames, which had become an inferno had reached the nearest trees, setting them on fire.

'The forest is burning,' cried out Paula.

'Won't get far – not when they're saturated with snow,' Tweed remarked.

Slowly the wall of flames became less ferocious, suddenly no more than a series of flickers. They could see now that the house had vanished, reduced to a pile of ashes. The crackle of the flames had been loud as the wood burned but now there was a deathly silence. It was as though the *Psycho*-like house had never existed.

'We'll get moving,' Tweed decided. 'Back to Freiburg.'

41

The black Audi was driven at speed through Höllental. Ronstadt was behind the wheel with Chuck Venacki by his side. In the back Madison sat with Kolkowski. No one had spoken since their wild departure from the base at Schluchsee. They had sensed that their driver was in a very bad mood.

'We'll put those guys under ground for good later,' Ronstadt said suddenly. 'The main thing is one truckload is on the way. Should just meet the deadline. That will mess up the British currency real good. There's millions aboard it.'

'Where are we goin' to now?' Madison called out.

'Listen, fellers. Moonhead wants to know where we's goin' now. Maybe I'll tell 'im. Moonhead, we're on our way back to Freiburg. When we gets there you three guys have dinner. I'll book my room again.'

'We're stayin' there for the night?' Madison enquired.

'Sure. That's why I just booked one room. Friggin' idiot. I need the room so I can contact Charlie. For that I needs privacy. I likes to let Charlie know where we are in the game.'

'Say, where is this Charlie?' Madison went on. 'Washington? No. I got it. Charlie's in the London Embassy.'

'You keep on with that guessin' game and I'll put a bullet in your head.'

Ronstadt stared at Madison in his rear-view mirror. He gave him a look of pure venom, then increased speed. When they arrived at the Colombi everything went according to plan. Ronstadt collared the receptionist while his three men marched into the dining room. They were halfway through their meal before Ronstadt joined them. Madison noticed Ronstadt was ashen-faced.

'Charlie give you a hard time?' he enquired.

'All of you finish your food quick as you can. We have to get on the road again fast. You can fill your bellies at the Petite France in Strasbourg.'

'Petite France?' Madison queried. 'Is that a hotel?'

'No, Moonhead, it's a district of Strasbourg. We'll stay at the Hôtel Regent. Now, shut your mouth – or I'll shut it for you.'

Ronstadt's impatience to get going was so obviously mounting that they all stopped eating. Before getting up Ronstadt piled meat between two pieces of bread, making himself a sandwich which he wrapped in a napkin.

'I've got to go to the men's room,' said Venacki.

'Hurry it up. Car's waiting outside.'

The two white Audis raced through Höllental at a speed Paula was hardly able to believe. She kept glancing at the speedometer. Tweed was driving the first Audi. He had insisted on taking over when they left Schluchsee. He had pointed out that Newman must rest his damaged ankle.

Paula had used ointment on the ankle, then wrapped it in a bandage before they started out. Tweed enquired how bad it was.

'Not too bad,' Paula told him. 'With the ointment I've used the swelling will have gone away in three or four hours – maybe less. But he can't drive yet. I could.'

'I'll drive,' Tweed said firmly. 'I have the stamina.'

He now had Paula beside him with Newman and Kent in the back. Behind them Marler drove his Audi, again with Nield next to him and Butler in the back. He'd almost had trouble keeping up with Tweed.

'We're really moving,' Paula ventured as they were passing through Höllental.

'Don't worry,' Tweed assured her. 'That snowplough we saw has cleared this lane of snow. I'm anxious to get to Freiburg, back to the Colombi as soon as possible. There may be a message for me.'

'Who from?'

'Monica, of course.'

'I suppose we botched it back at Schluchsee,' Paula mused. 'We let one truck get away.'

'Oh, come off it,' Newman called out. 'Ronstadt started out with twelve men when he left Basle. Now he's down to four, including himself.'

'And,' Tweed pointed out, 'we have destroyed a fortune in forged banknotes, plus the machines for producing more, plus the base. When we reach the Colombi I'll try again to reach Roy Buchanan to deal with that single truck.'

'You tried earlier a way back,' Paula reminded him. 'You made no contact.'

'I think the Feldberg was in the way.'

'Why Buchanan when Otto Kuhlmann would do everything he can to help?'

'Because I think Otto would find himself in an impossible position politically. I'm convinced that truck is on its way to one of the American airbases in Germany. I think they have a transport plane lined up to take the truck aboard, then fly it to one of their bases in East Anglia. There should just be time for Roy to stop the truck – providing we keep moving. I have a feeling we're now desperately short of time.'

'Incidentally,' Newman said, 'those two small explosions we heard before the house went into the sky were Marler throwing a grenade under each of the two remaining black Audis. He aimed them under the petrol tanks. Told me while we were watching the fireworks.'

'We'll get a meal at the Colombi,' Tweed announced. 'An army marches on its stomach, as Napoleon once said.'

'Then what do we do?' Paula asked.

'No idea. That's why I hope there'll be a message at the Colombi.'

When the two cars were parked outside the hotel Tweed succeeded in contacting Buchanan on Beck's mobile. He explained the problem tersely. Buchanan listened without saying a word until Tweed finished: 'I do think, Roy, it's important to locate that truck.'

'Tweed, it's not important, it's absolutely vital. If the forged money is as good as you say it is we must do everything we can to stop it getting into circulation.'

'I just hope you have time.'

'I have. By chance I'm in Norwich. I'm going to use all the power I've been given to ring every possible American airbase. You said you thought it might well come aboard a C47 transport. That needs a long runway, which cuts down the number of airbases I have to think of. I'm getting on it now.'

Tweed and Newman, with Paula, were the first to enter the lobby. The receptionist leaned over the counter.

'Mr Newman, I have a message for you. In case you came back.'

Newman looked surprised. He took the sealed envelope. Tweed was about to head for the dining room when the receptionist called out again.

'I also have a message for you, sir.'

Tweed took the sealed envelope, put it in his pocket. Then he questioned the receptionist, phrasing his words carefully.

'A close friend of mine might still be in the hotel. A

Sharon Mandeville. You probably saw us together in the lounge.'

'Yes, sir, I did. Ms Mandeville checked out a good few hours ago. She drove off with her secretary, Ms Denise Chatel.'

'Did she leave a forwarding address?'

'No, sir, I'm afraid she didn't. We've had a bit of activity this evening – and now you turn up.'

'Mind if I ask who else has been here? It couldn't be my old friend, Jake Ronstadt?'

'I'm only here temporarily, sir.' The receptionist lowered his voice. 'Yes, Mr Ronstadt was here with three other men. They had dinner and then left.'

'Thank you. So I've missed him. Can't be helped . . .'

They left their coats, followed Tweed and Paula into the dining room. There were only two couples having dinner. Waiters made up a large table and they settled down to study the menu. When they had ordered, Tweed took out the envelope, opened it. The wording, like his name on the front of the envelope, was in ill-formed block letters.

REGENT HOTEL, PETITE FRANCE, STRASBOURG.

Newman had at the same time opened his envelope. He frowned as he reading the wording, written with a pen in a strange script.

Hôtel Regent, Petite France, Strasbourg.

'What on earth can this mean?' he asked, handing the letter to Tweed. 'And I most certainly don't recognize the handwriting.'

'I'd say you weren't meant to,' Tweed commented after scrutinizing the communication. 'It's educated, but awkward handwriting. My guess is it was written quickly by a right-handed man – using his left hand. Now look at my message.'

'This is incredible,' Newman exclaimed. 'What does it mean?'

'The version you're looking at was probably written by a less-educated man. Also, notice the different way the hotels are named. I've stayed there. I know in France it's called Hôtel Regent. Which again suggests a well-educated person.'

'Is someone going to let me in on the secret?' Paula pleaded.

They both handed her their letters. She studied them, took her time. Then she looked up.

'This is crazy. Same address, but apparently provided by two quite different people. Why?'

'It's a mystery,' Tweed agreed. 'And here's our meal. I'd like everyone to get on with it. I'm sure we're very short of time.'

'I know,' said Paula, 'gobble it down even though we haven't eaten for hours. Then we all get indigestion.'

'No need to do that,' Tweed assured her.

Marler finished first. Like Tweed and Paula he drank only water, avoiding wine. They didn't believe in touching alcohol when it came to driving.

'I told you about our brief confrontation with those four thugs in Höllental,' he began. 'I also mentioned the landslide. I was worried that when I drove to the bottom of the gulch that the exit would be blocked. Luckily, the landslide which covered the highway had not reached the right-hand lane. So we just drove straight off.'

Soon afterwards Tweed summoned the waiter, paid the bill. He pushed his chair back, anxious to leave.

'Just a moment,' Paula said. 'It would be nice to know where we're going.'

'To Strasbourg, of course.'

'It could be a trap,' Newman warned.

'I agree. Only way to find out is to get there. As I mentioned earlier, I once stayed at the Hôtel Regent. It's a very good hotel.'

'I'll take over the driving,' Paula offered.

'Thank you. But I'm just waking up,' said Tweed, 'so I'll go on driving.'

'And I'll continue behind the wheel,' Marler chimed in.

'Oh, well,' Paula sighed. 'Strasbourg here we come.'

Paula was certain she would never forget the headlong drive up the autobahn heading for Strasbourg. They were all seated as they had been during the drive from Schluchsee. She was next to Tweed, with Newman and Kent in the back. She had her map in her lap and referred to it frequently with the aid of her torch.

There was no longer any trace of snow and the moon glowed down brightly. Ahead she could see nothing but the endless stretch of the autobahn going on for ever. Tweed kept overtaking huge trucks lumbering along. One moment they saw red lights, the next, so it seemed to Paula, they had whipped past the vehicle. Hedges on the central reservation whipped past in a blur. She glanced at Tweed.

He was sitting quite still, his hands on the wheel relaxed as he continued staring into the distance. Her next glance was at the speedometer. Oh, my God! she thought. But of course there was no speed limit on German autobahns. There was also no speed limit for Tweed as the Audi devoured the miles.

'Are we trying to break some record?' Newman called out.

'We have so little time left,' Tweed replied.

As if Newman's comment and his own reply had

alerted him he pressed his foot down even further. Paula suppressed a gasp. She thanked Heaven they had left the snow behind long ago. Red pinpoint lights appeared in the distance. Another truck. Then Tweed was overtaking. The juggernaut whizzed past, was gone. Paula realized she was pressing her feet hard against the floor, that the palms of her hands were damp. Surreptitiously, she wiped them on her trousers.

'We're getting there,' said Tweed cheerfully.

'I'd already gathered that,' she replied.

In the second Audi, some distance behind them, Marler kept up his speed. Once he glanced at his speedometer. He raised his eyebrows.

'You know something,' he said to Nield next to him, 'this is North Pole or bust. In other words, Tweed has really got the bit between his teeth.'

'Oh, is that what is happening,' Nield answered, suddenly aware that he was sitting very tensely.

'I think he's in a bit of a hurry to get to Strasbourg,' Marler remarked.

'And I think he believes he's flying Concorde.'

Paula was studying her map again. She looked up as something flashed past. She cleared her throat to warn Tweed she was going to say something. He glanced at her.

'Comfortable?' he enquired.

'Oh, very. Would you mind if I suggested you slowed down just a bit?'

'We've got to get there.'

'I know. But we're approaching junction 54. That's where we'll turn off the autobahn and head for Kehl.'

'But we just passed junction 55,' Tweed objected.

'Yes, we did. And at the rate we're moving we'll overshoot 54.'

'Not a chance.'

They overtook a convoy of three huge trucks. Paula

looked up at the roof. It had been like watching a video on fast-forward. They had to be very close to 54 now. Then she realized Tweed was slowing – at least they were not travelling quite at supersonic speed any more.

'We have to be extremely close to it now,' she warned.

'I'm sure we are.'

She glanced at him again. For the first time she realized that mixed with his sense of anxiety about time was a sense of pure enjoyment. He felt he was achieving something. Which, she supposed, he was – if they got there in one piece.

'We're nearly at junction 54,' she said. 'And before you slap me down may I remind you I am the navigator?'

'Best in the world, I'd say.'

'Flattery will get you nowhere!'

Tweed had reduced his speed a lot. Turning off the autobahn at the junction he proceeded at a more sedate pace. Paula checked her map again.

'Soon we'll cross a bridge over the Rhine. After that we're in Strasbourg in no time.'

'Look for the spire of the cathedral,' Tweed suggested. 'It is immensely high. From the top on a clear day you can see the Vosges Mountains and the Black Forest, and they're a long way off.'

'What's Strasbourg like?'

'The centre, crowded round the cathedral, is a labyrinth of streets and alleyways. The buildings are as old as the hills. They're crammed together and their rooftops are all different heights, a lot of them lopsided and odd-looking. The best part is where we're going – Petite France.'

'And what do you expect when we reach the Hôtel Regent?'

'Something unpleasant, but we're getting used to that.'

42

Paula almost purred with delight as Tweed, deep inside Strasbourg, drove across an old bridge lined with elegant iron railings and she saw the Hôtel Regent. A large old four-square building, it was illuminated with tinted floodlights. She stared down beyond the railings at its reflection in the water under the bridge.

'We seem to have crossed a lot of bridges to get here.'

'The waterways are an essential part of Strasbourg,' Tweed explained. 'It's a very complex system and eventually you can sail in boats which take you on to the Rhine. Pleasure boats operate a lot in the season. I'm just hoping the hotel has rooms for all of us. The European so-called Parliament is here and when in session European MPs with fat expenses grab all the best accommodation.'

Paula glowed as they walked into a very modern and palatial reception area. The floor was paved with light green marble and the sides of the reception counter were also faced with marble. Round white pillars supported a high ceiling where the illumination was provided by recessed spotlights.

'We'd like rooms for seven people if that's possible,' Tweed said to the woman behind the curved counter. She was attractive, very fashionably dressed and had an air of authority. 'We have driven a long way,' Tweed added.

'No problem,' the woman said with a welcoming smile. 'We can give you all very nice rooms. If you could register, sir.'

Tweed dealt with the formalities, then looked at the woman as he returned her smile.

'If the porters could take our coats, some of us would like to go straight to the bar.'

'Certainly. Let me show you the way.'

Paula and Tweed were followed by Newman and Kent. Tweed heard Marler say the rest of them would like to go straight up to their rooms. Like the reception hall, the bar was modern but tasteful. In the manner of certain high-class cocktail bars it had comfortable arm-chairs upholstered in purple.

Tweed smiled to himself as they walked into the bar. By herself, seated in one of a series of banquettes facing each other, was Sharon Mandeville.

Marler was on his way upstairs to his room when a woman rounded a corner and started to descend. Denise Chatel. She looked harassed and had a briefcase tucked under her arm. She stopped dead when she saw him.

'Hello, Denise,' he greeted her. 'You'll think I'm fol-lowing you.'

'Are you?' she snapped.

Then she hurried past him down the stairs. Her expression was bleak and completely lacking in warmth. Marler shrugged.

'I think,' Nield whispered, 'she's gone off you . . .'

In the bar Tweed walked straight over to Sharon. She looked up and gave him a smile of extreme pleasure. Putting down her file, she stood up so he could hug her.

'Just when I was getting so bored with all this work you walk in, so now I can look forward to a really entertaining evening.'

'Rather a late evening,' he said sitting down facing her.

428

'Oh, the night is young. Who knows? We may be here at dawn.'

'This is Keith Kent,' Tweed introduced. 'Keith, Sharon Mandeville.'

'How nice to meet such a competent-looking man for a change. I am wondering what you do for a living.'

'I'm a banker.'

'A moneyman. Well, they say money makes the world go round.'

'Except,' Tweed said, 'at times the lust for money, when satisfied, is sometimes succeeded by the lust for power.'

'Tweed, you are a cynic.' She laughed. 'A dyed-in-the-wool cynic.'

'Or maybe a realist.'

'Paula.' Sharon focused her attention on her. 'I'm so glad you're here. Otherwise I'd feel outgunned. Why don't we go shopping together? There are some marvellous shops here if you know where to go.'

'I doubt if my bank balance would come up to yours,' Paula said with a smile.

'Nonsense. It would be a change to have some female company. I'm drinking champagne. I'll order another bottle.'

'Not for me,' Tweed said hastily.

'There's Paula and Keith. May I call you Keith? Good. And now, Bob, I noticed you were hobbling. You've been in the wars?'

'Slipped on a flight of stone steps in Freiburg. It's nothing.'

Sharon waved to a waiter. She ordered two more bottles of Dom Perignon. Then she leaned towards Tweed, speaking quietly.

'Talking about company, have you seen who is at the bar?'

429

Tweed turned round. At the bar, which had a pale yellow front, two men were perched on bar stools, their backs to the room. Rupert and Basil Windermere. He looked back at Sharon.

'What are they doing here?'

'Lord knows. They're a nuisance. Both of them, separately, have pestered me. I gave them a very cold shoulder. I can't imagine why they turned up here – unless they followed me on the autobahn. But why would they do that?'

'Your guess is as good as mine.'

'Then, to cap it all, you haven't noticed who is at a corner table by himself over there. That boor, Ed Osborne.'

Tweed again twisted round on his banquette. At that moment Ed Osborne looked up, caught his eye, stood up and lumbered over to their table between the facing banquettes. He slapped Tweed on the back, grinning, slurring his speech.

'Hi, feller! Great to see you again. You folks mind if I join you? Guess it's OK.'

As he sat down next to Tweed he looked across at Sharon and winked. She ignored him and started chatting with Newman. Osborne had a glass of Scotch in his right hand. Waves of the drink were drifting into Tweed's nostrils.

'What brings you all, as I believe they say in our Deep South, to this part of the world?'

'What brings *you* here?' Sharon asked sharply, her expression cold.

'Good question. Very good question,' Osborne mumbled. 'Guess I can give you a good answer. Had a hard time in Washington, then in London. So I'm takin' a few days off. Kinda holiday – just roamin' around, roamin' where the spirit takes me.'

'Then I hope you're enjoying yourself,' Sharon replied, her manner still cold.

'What gets me,' Osborne went on, 'is how we all keeps turnin' up in the same places. First there was Basle, then Freiburg and now, believe it or not, Strasbourg. I reckon it's a case of who is following who?'

There was a silence. Sharon busied herself pouring champagne into glasses. Paula shook her head, thanked her. Kent leaned forward, his voice crisp.

'Maybe if we started with leaving London we'd know what is going on. Would you agree, Sharon?'

'Sorry, Keith, but you've fogged me.'

'Well, take myself. I travelled to Basle to check a bank account. Then I moved on to Freiburg because a man called Jake Ronstadt was going there.'

'A horrible man,' Sharon exclaimed. 'No manners at all.'

'I agree with you,' Paula joined in. 'He kills people – like all those victims in Britain when bombs went off in department stores. Random massacres.'

'I can't believe that, Paula,' Sharon flared up indignantly. 'You will have gathered Ronstadt is not a man I want anything to do with from what I said earlier, but the idea that he could in any way be involved with those horrific outrages is absurd. Damn it, he has a big job at the American Embassy in London.'

'What sort of job?' Paula asked.

'I'm sorry, but I have no idea.' Sharon had calmed down. 'At the Embassy we function in watertight compartments. It's the new Ambassador's idea. Something to do with security, as far as I can gather.'

'So he wouldn't be running the Executive Action Department, then?' Newman suggested. 'The EAD for short.'

'I've never heard of it.' Sharon sipped champagne,

frowned. 'If it exists it sounds like a section directly controlled by the Ambassador – to ensure his decisions are carried out. He's more corporate than diplomatic, came after resigning as president of a big oil company.'

'Ruthless people,' Osborne commented, 'bosses of big oil outfits. Get up to a lot of skulduggery. Stuff the public never hears about. Washington shouldn't bring big business into diplomacy.'

'He – the Ambassador – has always been perfectly charming to me,' said Sharon. She looked up as Denise Chatel appeared, holding a file. 'Not now, Denise. Can't you see I've got company?'

'You said it was important,' Denise began.

'Well, it will have to wait. I don't get much chance of relaxation for a change. We'll deal with it later. Understand?'

Denise, looking humiliated, started leaving. On her way out she was passing close to the bar. Rupert's hand came out, wrapped itself round her waist.

'Let go of me.'

'You all play hard to get. Think I don't know that by now?' he sneered.

Newman stood up, walked over, still hobbling slightly. Reaching the bar, he laid a hand on Rupert's shoulder. He was smiling when he spoke.

'Lady doesn't want your attentions, Rupert. Doesn't like being touched by you.'

'And I'm fussy about who touches me. So kindly remove your hand from my shoulder. I never hit cripples,' he sneered viciously.

'Very wise of you.'

Newman removed his hand. In a blur of movement he bunched his fist, slammed it into Rupert's jaw. Rupert came off his stool, just managed to grab the edge of the bar to stop himself sprawling on the floor. Denise had gone as he lifted his hand, felt his jaw, glaring at Newman.

'I'll get you for this. That's a promise.'

'I say, chaps,' Basil broke in, 'we do have an audience. Best to preserve our dignity in such situations, don't you think?'

'Couldn't agree more,' said Newman, and he returned to his banquette seat.

'They really are a most unpleasant couple,' Sharon commented. She looked at Newman. 'I like a man who can take care of himself.'

'You know something,' Tweed said, speaking for the first time, 'I've done a lot of driving. I feel like stretching the limbs. I think a little walk might do us good, freshen us up.'

'Good idea,' said Newman. He looked at Sharon. 'I hope that you won't think us rude.'

'Not at all. When you get back I'll be here going through my work. Must make up for lost time. Then you can come in and rescue me and we'll kill the rest of the champagne.'

Tweed was helping Paula on with her coat in the lobby while Kent and Newman collected theirs from reception. Marler appeared, already attired in his coat. Tweed told him what they proposed doing.

'I've just come back from checking where they park guests' cars. Ronstadt's black Audi is there.'

'I thought Ronstadt and his thugs might be hidden away inside this hotel,' Tweed remarked as they wandered outside. 'It is high time they were taken off the face of the planet.'

'Setting yourself up as bait?' Marler suggested.

'I'm worried about the passage of time. I want us to

be able to stop having to think about Ronstadt and his lethal tricks. And look who we have here.'

Butler and Nield, muffled in coats, stood just out of sight of the hotel entrance. Marler told them to follow a little way behind them.

'Ronstadt and Co. are probably going to put in an appearance,' he warned.

'Can't wait,' said Butler.

Paula slipped her hand inside her shoulder bag, withdrew her Browning .32 automatic, slipped her hand under her coat. Again the arctic air hit them after the cosy warmth of the interior of the Hôtel Regent.

They walked past a waterway and Paula paused to peer down over a steep wall. The water was about fifteen feet below here. She glanced back, saw a flight of steps leading down to a small landing stage. A small open launch was tied up to the foot of the steps. She thought she saw movement, then decided it was her imagination. They walked on, trailed by Marler with Nield and Butler.

'You really have to see this part of Strasbourg by night – this way you appreciate its beauty, its strange character,' Tweed said.

'Strange is the word,' Paula agreed, huddled in her coat.

Their footsteps were the only sounds in the dark of the night. No traffic anywhere. No people at this hour. Paula was fascinated by the architecture. Hulking ancient buildings leant out over cobbled streets. She saw that many of them had pointy gables, that the roofline went up and down and in the walls was embedded a crisscross of old wooden beams. Most of the buildings were four storeys high with an endless variety of tiny dormer windows in the ski-slope roofs above, dormers perched so precariously they seemed to be on the verge of sliding down into the streets below. One grotesque old house was so crowded with dormers on its roof and looked like Gothic gone mad. She was reminded of a scene from Grimm's *Fairy Tales* – with the emphasis on grim.

'It gets claustrophobic,' she said, 'with the narrow streets and the buildings looming over us.'

'It's unique, as far as I know,' said Tweed.

They had followed a complex route, turning into different streets at almost each corner. Always, to their right, the stone wall rose above the pavement and, beyond it, another waterway. She was beginning to feel lost.

'I hope someone knows the way back,' she remarked.

'I do,' replied Tweed.

'A stranger would need a map.'

'I've got one in my head from the last time I was here. And I noticed in the hotel they have another kind of map – one showing the network of waterways for people hiring boats.'

Paula was disturbed by the areas of dark shadow where the moonlight couldn't penetrate. At intervals there were street lamps and then more shadows. She kept looking back and always Marler and his two friends were a short distance behind them. Marler waved at her encouragingly. She waved back, then stopped.

'We've actually walking in a circle to take us back to the hotel,' Tweed told her.

'I can hear a strange noise. Water rushing.'

'That is the sluice, which is quite spectacular. Heaven help anyone who takes the wrong turning on the waterways and finds himself being carried down it. They do have notices on the walls warning sailors. And we're nearly at Pont St-Martin. That's the bridge nearest the sluice. We might take a look at it.'

Tweed had started walking again and the sound of water rushing at immense speed grew louder. Paula stopped again.

'What is it now?' Tweed asked gently.

'I can hear a different sound. Chug-chug. Like the motor of a launch.'

'You're right. And it's coming closer. *Don't* look over that wall,' he warned.

'I'd take his advice,' said Kent. 'Stay where you are now.'

They had all stopped. Paula looked back. Marler held up a hand to keep her where she was. She watched him as he conferred with Butler and Nield briefly. Perplexed, she watched as Butler took a beret from his pocket. He placed it at the end of his Walther. He was standing by the wall.

Paula took her Browning from under her coat as the chug-chug grew nearer and nearer. Keeping his head well clear of the far edge of the wall, Butler eased the beret forward until it perched over the brink. There was a shattering rattle of machine-pistol fire. The beret was shredded, disappeared. Marler, dipping his hand into the holdall slung over his shoulder, took out one of his remaining grenades.

Butler had taken off his scarf. He wrapped it round his Walther. He had twisted the scarf so in the gloom it looked almost like a man's head. Again he eased his weapon close to the edge, then a few inches over the brink. A fresh murderous rattle from a machine-pistol ripped the scarf to bits. It was a long burst and when it stopped Paula guessed the unseen weapon needed reloading.

Immediately Marler looked over the top of the wall, dropped the grenade. Ignoring Tweed's warning, Paula was peering along the waterway. Illuminated by a street lamp she saw the small launch she had seen much earlier, tied to a landing stage. In the launch stood Ronstadt, fiddling desperately with the machine-pistol. With him was a moon-faced man and a third man with a hard bony face. She saw Marler's grenade dropping and jerked her head back. The detonation, although muffled by the walls, still sounded very loud in the silence of the night. Looking back over the wall Paula saw the half-wrecked launch racing towards her. Moonface had been at the controls and had kept the engine running. Now it proceeded along the waterway without any human guidance. Tweed, Newman and Kent were also gazing at it as the launch passed below them. Three crumpled bodies lay in it, motionless.

'It's taking in water,' said Tweed. 'And it's near the sluice.'

They watched, hypnotized, as it entered the narrow sluice of churning, foaming water. The launch slid downwards, toppled over sideways, casting its cargo into the maelstrom. In seconds the corpses had disappeared, swallowed up by the wild water.

'I hope no one has unpacked,' Tweed said as they approached the entrance to the Hôtel Regent.

No one had. Tweed was walking quickly as they reached the hotel. He paused for a moment while they were still outside.

'We're leaving immediately,' he told them. 'We're driving now to Paris, then on to London. Get your bags and we meet in the lobby. I'll pay for the rooms.'

Paula waited with him while he explained to the receptionist he had received an urgent message. If any-one wanted to contact him would she please tell them they were on their way to Paris, that they might stay a few hours at the Ritz before going on to London.

He was walking along the first-floor corridor when they heard voices behind a closed door as Newman joined them. Tweed put a finger to his lips and they stopped to listen. Denise's voice was clear and very loud.

'I won't take any more from you. You were a horrible person back at the Embassy . . .'

'Don't you dare talk to me like that, you friggin' little traitor,' an unrecognizable voice shouted and roared. 'You've had enough money out of the Embassy funds to put Versace on your rotten little back.'

'You're always pestering me!' Denise screamed back. 'Back at the Embassy I avoided you whenever I could.'

'I'll kill you if you say any more. I'll push you out of a high window, watch you fall, hit the street with a splash of blood!'

'No you won't,' Denise shrieked back. 'From now on I'll take good care there's always a witness with me!'

'A witness! What are you insinuating, you ignorant wretch? You think the organization can't do without you? Who are you, anyway? A small-time adventuress!'

Tweed started walking swiftly towards his room with Paula and Newman. No one said anything until he reached it.

'They were having quite a party, weren't they?' Tweed remarked.

43

Tweed again insisted on driving and Paula was beside him as navigator, a new section of map open on her lap. In the back Newman sat with Keith Kent. Behind them followed Marler, with Nield and Butler as passengers. If Paula had expected Tweed to take it easy along the autoroute to Paris she was soon disillusioned.

He rapidly built up speed until Strasbourg was just a distant memory. Newman leaned down against his seat belt, removed his bandage, felt his ankle, flexed it this way and that. Kent asked him how it was. Newman replied it was OK.

'Tweed,' he called out, 'my ankle is normal now. I can take over the wheel whenever you want me to.'

'Maybe later.'

'Maybe never,' Paula said under her breath. She looked at Tweed. 'I was surprised at the twists and turns of our conversation with Sharon and Ed Osborne in the bar. You came out with some pretty blunt remarks,' she continued, glancing over her shoulder.

'They did so at my suggestion,' Tweed informed her. 'I had a few words with Bob and Keith at the reception counter. They reacted splendidly. And you, Paula, caught on quick and added your own loaded comments. You sensed the rhythm of how things were going very skilfully.'

'Did you learn something from that conversation, then?'

'Let's say I found it intriguing.'

'I thought Sharon held her own very well, bearing in mind that Osborne was present. Who knows how much power that man wields,' Paula said thoughtfully.

'That's what all this spilt blood and upheaval is about,' Tweed told her. 'Power. It's all about power, which can intoxicate people.'

'The only thing you said during the conversation referred to power,' Paula recalled. 'Apart from that you kept absolutely quiet.'

'I was listening, watching.'

'Why,' she asked, 'did you leave details of where we're going at the Hôtel Regent reception? Not like you.'

'So that anyone who wants to follow us knows where to head for. We might as well flush out as many of them as we can.'

'So Paris may not be safe.'

'Nowhere is safe now.'

'You're really stepping on the gas,' she said.

'I'm convinced we're almost fatally short of time.'

Rear Admiral Honeywood, known throughout the naval service as Crag, settled himself into his chair on the control deck of the immense aircraft carrier, the *President*. The vast array of escorts were way ahead of their bow, way behind their stern and spread out to port and starboard.

'We'll be on station in the English Channel, I reckon, about two days from now,' he remarked to his Operations Officer.

'That would be my estimate.'

'And so far,' Crag reflected, 'we haven't been seen by anyone.'

'Correct, sir. No submarines have been detected by sonar. We have seen not a single ship which might have reported our presence. And no commercial airliner has passed over the task force.'

'Let's hope it continues that way. The Pentagon is counting on our surprise arrival on their doorstep to stun the Brits out of their skulls.'

'Maybe it's time to report our situation back to the Chairman of the Joint Chiefs of Staff. He gets restless if he isn't kept regularly in the picture.'

'Old Stone-Face does just that. Send him another report. Include that worn-out phrase "proceeding according to plan". He'll like that.'

'Can't this buggy move any faster?' Osborne demanded.

'The chauffeur is doing very well. We're going at high speed now,' replied Sharon acidly.

She was sitting in the back of the stretch limo with

Osborne by her side. In the front Denise Chatel sat next to the chauffeur, her head down as she studied a file open on her lap. The limo streaked along the autoroute to Paris.

'Guess I could drive the jalopy faster myself,' Osborne grumbled.

'I don't know why you had to come with me as a passenger,' Sharon retorted.

'Simple, lady. Your limo was just leavin' when I needed to. I want to reach the Ritz before Tweed does, to be waitin' for him.'

'Well, I would appreciate it if you would leave the driver to do his job – which he's doing very well.'

'We gotta keep movin', baby.'

'And please do not call me baby. I really have no idea what your position is at the Embassy.'

'Call me an expediter. Hi, Denise,' he called out, 'how is the world goin' with you?'

Denise Chatel kept her head bent over her file. She made no reply. With one hand she shut the half-open section of the glass partition dividing the front of the limo from the rear. Osborne shrugged, waved both large hands in a gesture of resignation.

'If I'm not being nosy,' said Paula, 'why are we going to Paris?'

'I want to see René Lasalle, head of the DST. I think face to face, as opposed to talking on the phone, René may tell me more about the father of Denise.'

'Her father who was killed with his wife in a car crash somewhere in Virginia a year or so ago?'

'That's right – Jean Chatel. Sent over officially as an attaché, but really a member of the French Secret Service.'

'Why are you so interested in him?' she asked as Tweed overtook a convoy of three large trucks.

'Because he was sent to find out what the Americans were up to – and especially because Jean Chatel and his wife died in a car accident at exactly the same bridge where years before Sharon's parents died in a car accident.'

'I don't see the connection.'

'Neither do I,' admitted Tweed. 'But I have a feeling there is a connection – and that it might be the key to what is going on now. I'm hoping René will be able to give me more information.'

'Does he know you're coming?'

'Yes. I called him briefly on Beck's mobile from my room when I went to collect my case before we left the Hôtel Regent.'

'We're getting low on petrol,' Paula warned.

'Yes, I had noticed. And I think I see the lights of an all-night service station ahead. While we're filling up I want to call Roy Buchanan.'

'I'll deal with the petrol,' Newman called out.

'I can do that myself,' said Kent. 'I feel like stretching my legs, making myself useful.'

'You've been of invaluable help already, Keith,' Tweed assured him. 'But if you feel like that you can tank us up. Here we are.'

While Kent was filling up the tank Tweed used the mobile to try to contact Buchanan. He was lucky. The familiar voice, taut and grim, answered immediately.

'Who is this?'

'It's Tweed. Roy, if you can, I'd like you to do something for me. I'm going to see Jefferson Morgenstern when I get back to London. Have you any evidence that the Americans were behind the bombings in London?'

'Yes. A security video in the Oxford Street outrage survived the blast. We have a very clear picture of the man who planted that bomb. A very tall thin man with a hard bony face . . .'

'A very tall thin man with a hard bony face,' Tweed repeated, looking back at Newman.

'Vernon Kolkowski,' Newman said promptly.

'We know – knew – him,' Tweed reported to Buchanan 'He's dead as the proverbial doornail. Name of Vernon Kolkowski. I'll spell that . . . Got it? Good. He was probably based at the American Embassy while I was still in London.'

'He was. We secretly photographed him when he re-entered the Embassy. Couldn't do a thing about it. They all carried those diplomatic passports.'

'What I'd like you to do is to compile a file of evidence – including what you've told me, with pics. I'd like as fat a file as possible to show Morgenstern when I get back.'

'Consider it done. No more bombings. Our drastic security precautions are working. Touch wood,' he added. 'When will you be back?'

'At a guess, within the next twenty-four hours.'

'The file will be waiting for you.'

The connection was broken and Tweed sank back with relief. He smiled as Paula asked the question he'd been expecting.

'Why do you want to talk to Morgenstern?'

'I said quite a while ago that I was convinced that the Americans are operating at two different levels, in watertight compartments. Sharon confirmed that. I don't think the diplomatic side has any idea of what the Executive Action Department lot have been up to, the crimes they've committed. And Morgenstern is greatly respected not only globally but also inside the States. To the American public Morgenstern *is* Washington.'

He glanced in his rear-view mirror. Marler's Audi was parked behind them while Butler filled up its tank. Kent reappeared out of a large café attached to the petrol station. Paula lowered her window as he handed her two large paper bags. He leaned into the car.

'Mineral water in one bag, fresh croissants in the other. Most of the customers sitting inside are truckers. Their vehicles are parked out at the back. In France bakeries work through the night to produce fresh croissants. The French insist on them, as you may know. In the morning housewives make a trip to the nearest source of supply. Must have fresh croissants for breakfast.'

'Keith, you're an angel,' Paula purred.

She leant out of the window, kissed him on the cheek. At that moment Marler strolled up to Tweed's window. He was stretching his arms.

'Got a moment?' he asked.

'A few minutes only. Think I'll get out and flex my muscles . . .'

Paula was drinking water out of the bottle. When she'd quenched her thirst she wiped the neck of the bottle with a clean handkerchief. Then she handed the bottle to Newman.

'Excuse my unladylike manners. When you've had a drink I'll pass you some croissants. Don't forget Keith,' she went on as Kent got back in beside Newman.

'While I was marooned back at the Schwarzwälder Hof in Freiburg,' Marler began, 'I went out, found a public phone, called Alf.'

'Alf?'

'Alf Rudge. Top man in that cockney mob I once mentioned to you. In my spare time, for several weeks I've been training them as a reserve. Tough lot. All cab drivers. Took them out into the wilds of the Chiltern Hills. Seven of them, including Alf. Set up a makeshift shooting range in the middle of nowhere. Trained them with handguns, grenades, and machine-pistols. Three of them already knew their stuff – veterans of the Gulf War. They're all pretty much crack shots now.'

'Could come in very useful,' Tweed mused. 'The Americans have unlimited manpower. How can they afford the time if they're cab drivers?'

'Easy. They all own their cabs. Alf has one or two Americans as friends, but like the rest of his mob he does not like the Yanks. Can I tell you quickly a story about Alf?'

'In five minutes – at the outside – we must head for Paris again.'

They were walking about, working their legs in the glare of lights. Nield, a grenade concealed in one hand, his Walther in the other, was outside, watching the highway.

'Alf,' Marler explained, 'flew to LA for a change. One night he's out for a walk when three thugs approach him, demand his money. He takes out his wallet, shows them it has only a single one-hundred-dollar bill. Tells them he has more back where he's staying nearby. If they promise not to harm him they can have all the money. Leads them back to the rundown hotel where he's staying, up to his room. The chief thug has a gun barrel pressed into his neck, the other two stay downstairs in case police appear. Alf says if the chief thug takes the gun off his neck he'll tell him where to get the money. The thug obliges, Alf tells him to open a heavy drawer. The thug does so, Alf jams his hand inside, ramming the drawer shut. Alf slams him one on the jaw, the thug collapses, semiconscious. Alf calls down to the others. They arrive, Alf uses the chief thug's gun to hammer their heads. He topples all three down the stairs, out into the street. Sleazy owner turns up, Alf pays his bill, tells him he's going to Malibu. Packs his case, flags down a cab, goes to the airport, catches the first flight home.'

'Alf can take care of himself,' Tweed commented. 'I

445

see Butler, like Kent, has taken a bag of goodies to your car. Now, we get moving. Fast.'

'Shove your ruddy foot down,' snarled Rupert. 'This car's moving like a snail.'

'Some snail, my dear chap,' replied Basil, behind the wheel. 'I'm driving right on the speed limit.'

'To hell with the speed limit. I wanna get to Paris.'

'That's where we're going, dear boy.'

'Don't you "dear boy" me. We're the same flaming age. Thirty-two. In case you've forgotten,' he sneered.

'I had not forgotten. Exceed the speed limit and a patrol car nabs us. We end up in the Santé Prison in Paris. Heard of what it's like inside there, have we? They shove you inside and throw away the key.'

'I'll take over the wheel. Stop the car,' Rupert raged.

'Not sure that would be a frightfully good idea. Not after how much you consumed in the bar at the Hôtel Regent. What's all this hurry to reach Paris?'

'I wanna drink.'

'I think you want to have a go at Newman. Not a good idea. He can look after himself in a mean way.'

'Not interested in Newman. A has-been fifth-rate reporter. I wanna drink. Couldn't get one to bring with me at that crazy bar. Closing as early as that.'

'It was the middle of the night,' Basil pointed out.

'What's that got to do with it? I should have brought a bottle.'

'Well, I fear you didn't – because you couldn't. You did drink five times as much as me.'

'You were counting, were you?' Rupert sneered once more. 'Just the kind of thing you would do.' He waved his hand about. 'I know you won't mind if I say you're one lousy driver.'

'We're getting closer to Paris now. Why don't you have a nap?'

'Don't wanna a nap. Wanna a drink.'

'While I think of it, Rupert. You phoned your late father's lawyer from the Colombi in Freiburg,' said Basil in a perfectly sober voice. 'You told me he'd agreed to advance you some money. I'm desperately short of that commodity. I could do with a loan very urgently. I'm sure you could spare ten thousand pounds.'

'I suspect we're not too far from Paris,' said Tweed.

'You're right,' Paula agreed. 'We'll soon be seeing the outskirts. Why? Are you getting tired?'

'No, just impatient. I have a feeling we should get back to London as fast as we can, that time is running out.'

'I've just remembered something important,' Newman called out from the back. 'Back at Schluchsee, when I was nearly knocked down by Ronstadt when he was fleeing in his car. There were *four* men in that car. But when Marler dropped his grenade into the launch in Strasbourg there were only *three* men in it. One is still missing.'

'Maybe the Phantom,' Paula joked. 'He seems to live a charmed life.'

'You could be right,' Newman replied seriously. 'So far as we know he's still on the loose.'

'If he isn't dead,' Tweed remarked. 'I hope he appears sooner or later. He has to be wiped out – the number of people he's killed up to now.'

'When you've finished your business in Paris how do we get home?' Newman enquired.

'It all depends on which is the quickest way back,' Tweed answered. 'It could be by Eurostar or flying back from Charles de Gaulle airport. Lasalle will know the answer.'

'It's beginning to get light,' said Paula. 'With a bit of luck we'll reach the Ritz before the horrendous rush hour starts in Paris.'

A faint glow of light was rising in the east. Gradually it spread across the cultivated fields on either side of the autoroute. The clear sky was a pallid blue. There was a promise of a fine day on the way.

'A bit different from the Black Forest,' Paula said cheerfully.

'The weather forecast predicted a brighter fresh day for this area,' Tweed recalled. 'Makes a change. And I was just wondering how Howard is coping. He's had to run the whole show himself under very difficult circumstances . . .'

Many hours earlier – it was midafternoon of the previous day – Howard had decided he must drive down to the Bunker to see for himself how they were getting on. It was a gloriously sunny day but Howard had to force himself to make the trip. He'd had hardly any sleep for the past forty-eight hours and was concentrating as best he could behind the wheel of the car.

By himself, he had passed through the village of Parham. He had given a brief thought to calling at Irongates on Sir Guy Strangeways, but had decided he'd better keep going while he was still awake.

His eyes kept wanting to close and he nearly missed the turn-off from the road south of Ashford to Ivychurch. Now all his concentration was called for as he negotiated the narrow, twisting lanes. Half the time, the spiky hedges, waiting for spring to come into leaf, blotted out his view of what lay beyond the next bend.

'I'm driving a lethal weapon,' he said aloud. 'I must look out for other people.'

Normally he would have been alerted by the *beat-beat* of a helicopter approaching. In his exhausted state he assumed it was a traffic-checking machine. He drove very slowly as he approached the automatic farm gate which would be operated by Mrs Carson. He could still hear the chopper when Mrs Carson ran out into the yard and gestured to him furiously to drive on inside a large barn with its door open. He did so. Getting out of the car, he nearly stumbled. As soon as he was outside Mrs Carson slammed the barn door shut.

'Get inside the house. Quick!' she shouted.

Once he was inside she shut the door immediately. He slumped into an armchair. He knew that if he wasn't careful he'd fall fast asleep.

'Black coffee, please,' he mumbled. 'A litre of it.'

'That chopper circling above us,' she said. 'It hasn't got any kind of markings. You should have waited further up the road.'

'Sorry. Could I have that coffee, please?'

Inside the helicopter the co-pilot held a powerful camera, aiming it down at the farmhouse. As the machine circled he took pictures from every angle. His tone was exultant when he spoke.

'Gene, we've just located the Brits' secret communications centre. I've gotten some great pictures.'

'That's great, Lou. What about the exact location?'

'I've marked that clearly on my detailed map of Romney Marsh. Guess we should get promotion for this.'

'What about those hedges surrounding the perimeter?'

'They're just hedges. I've got all we need.'

449

'OK, Lou. Then it's back to base. The pics and the map can be sent back to Washington. Guess they could go right up to the Chairman of the Joint Chiefs of Staff.'

44

'René Lasalle is out,' Tweed said as he put down the phone in his bedroom at the Ritz. 'He left a message that he'd call as soon as he returns.'

'This is a lovely room,' Paula enthused, 'with a wonderful view out over the Place Vendôme. It looks marvellous – especially as the day is so glorious.'

Tweed joined her, gazed at the famous column erected to Napoleon in the centre of the many-sided square. The superb architecture of the stone buildings enclosing the *place* had been cleaned. He had always thought this was the most magnificent square in the whole of Paris.'

'You'll never guess why René had to rush off,' he remarked.

'Tell me, then.'

'A bomb has exploded in a big department store. Quite a few casualties.'

'You mean the Americans are now turning their attentions to France? More work by the Executive Action Department?'

'No, I don't think so for a minute. The deputy of René's to whom I spoke said it's the work of Algerian extremists. The world is in a wild state.'

'So the Cold War is over and now we have an equally sinister Hot War? Worse, in a way, because it's so difficult to locate the fanatical killers.'

'I want to phone Monica later, maybe have a word

with Howard. Meantime I feel like a full English breakfast. What about you?'

'I've got a void in my tummy. Full English will do me.'

Emerging from the lift at ground-floor level Newman, who had joined them, rubbed his hands in anticipation. He looked around as they walked to the dining room.

'You know something? I've learned to enjoy luxury. I even think I've earned it – when I think of some of the hovels I tried to sleep in overseas as a foreign correspondent.'

'The pack has followed us,' Paula whispered to Tweed.

Running down the stairs, with surprising agility for so big a man, was Ed Osborne. At the same moment, as they approached the entrance to the restaurant, Rupert came out with Basil Windermere. As they reached the couple Rupert had paused. He bowed with mock courtesy to Paula.

'We've beaten you to it. Early bird catches the worm.'

'I've no intention of trying to catch you,' she replied tartly.

'One in the eye for you, Rupert,' Basil commented.

Rupert gave Paula a venomous look. As the two men strolled on Newman caught Tweed's arm to get him to pause. No one else was about and he could hear what the two men were saying.

'I'm off out to get something from my car,' Basil said.

'And I,' Rupert said in a loud voice, glancing over his shoulder, 'am going to get a shower. It's fun to have company in a shower,' he went on, staring at Paula. 'Maybe you'd consider joining me sometime soon.'

As they continued strolling away Paula flushed. She gritted her teeth. Had Rupert been close enough she'd have slapped his face. Newman took her arm, guided her into the restaurant, followed by Tweed.

'No point in exchanging more insults with such trash,' he advised her. 'And surprise, surprise, look who is here.'

Sharon sat at a large table by herself, breaking a croissant between her elegant hands. She waved to them, an invitation to share her table. Tweed walked to her table, waited for Paula and Newman to join him.

'Paula, do sit by me,' Sharon suggested. 'Gentlemen, choose your seats.'

'I thought you were going to say choose your weapons,' Newman joked.

'Are you following me, Bob?' Sharon enquired as Newman sat down. 'If so, I take that as a great compliment. Or maybe, Tweed, you are the one who is pursuing me?'

'That's right,' Tweed replied, glancing at the menu, 'divine inspiration told us you'd be staying here.'

'Is there anywhere else to stay in Paris?' she retorted.

'Mind if I join you folks?' a deep American voice rumbled. Ed Osborne had a hand on the back of an empty chair facing Tweed. 'Guess we're gettin' to be a family – the way we keep meetin' up.'

'You're welcome, of course, Ed,' Sharon replied unenthusiastically.

'Great. I'm a sociable guy. Like company. What are you guys havin' for breakfast?' he enquired.

'We're having the full English,' Tweed told him. 'Here's the waiter.'

'Guess I'll go along with that,' Osborne agreed.

After they had ordered Sharon concentrated her attention on Paula. Putting a shielding hand to her face, she raised her eyebrows and glanced to her left at Osborne, as much as to say 'Here we go again.' Instead she said something else.

'When I've finished breakfast I'm off to the hairdresser. They have a good one here.'

Paula looked at Sharon's blonde waves, sweeping down gracefully to her shoulders.

'You look as though you've just come from the hairdresser,' she remarked.

'That's the nicest thing anyone's said to me for a while.' Sharon extended a hand across the table, clasped Paula's. 'Thank you. Tweed, why are you in Paris?' she asked suddenly.

'I'm investigating the probable murder of Denise Chatel's father and mother at a lonely bridge in the state of Virginia.'

Osborne spilt coffee from the cup he was holding on his napkin. A waiter hurried forward, checked to make sure no coffee had stained his smart beige suit. Presenting him with a fresh napkin the waiter took away the spoilt one.

Paula was stunned by Tweed's unusual candour. She stiffened but managed to avoid a startled expression.

'Murder?' Sharon looked puzzled. 'I thought they died in a road accident.'

'You got something wrong there, brother,' said Osborne. 'It *was* an accident, according to the official report.'

'I have a witness who says otherwise,' Tweed told him.

'A witness?' Osborne was incredulous. 'Who is this so-called witness?'

'I don't think I can reveal a name at this stage.'

'This is Paris, France, not Virginia,' Osborne protested.

'The long arm of retribution sometimes stretches across continents.'

'I'm stupefied,' said Sharon. 'Stupefied and shaken. If you're right, does Denise know about this?'

'By the way, where is Denise?' Tweed enquired, evading a direct answer.

'In her room here. Working. She had a very early breakfast.'

'Talkin' about breakfast, here it comes, praise the Lord,' said Osborne. 'Everybody here probably thinks with my weight I'd be better off with just grapefruit. Fact is, I'm in good shape. Keep myself in good shape at the gym. Slam at punchbags, lift weights. All that stuff.'

'You must have good reflexes, then,' Newman suggested.

'He has,' Paula confirmed. 'I saw him coming downstairs this morning like a ten-year-old.'

'In a hurry for my breakfast,' said Osborne, and he chuckled.

'I have to go upstairs to make a phone call,' Tweed announced after finishing his meal.

He glanced round the restaurant. Marler, as instructed, sat at a table by himself some distance away. At another table, again as instructed by Tweed, Butler and Nield sat at their own table. No point in identifying all his people to anyone in the restaurant who might be interested.

'I hope you'll excuse me,' Tweed said to Sharon.

'Of course. I'm just going to have another cup of coffee and then I'll be working too.'

As Tweed left the restaurant Marler stood up, strolled casually after him. En route to the lift with Newman, Tweed felt like a breath of fresh air. As Paula, following behind them, had said earlier, it was a glorious day.

Walking the full length of the wide corridor Tweed approached the main exit leading out onto the Place Vendôme. He reached the door and no one else was about. He stepped forward into the open and was forcefully jerked backwards by Marler. A bullet struck the exact point where he'd been a second earlier. The bullet ricocheted out into the *place*. The uniformed doorman on duty outside ran up to him.

'Something wrong, sir?'

'Caught my foot on a stone someone must have kicked into the entrance.'

'I thought I heard a noise.'

'Car backfiring.'

Marler had run out into the *place*. The doorman saw nothing of what he was doing as he was talking inside to Tweed. Marler was circling the empty *place*, a Walther in his hand. He had it pointed upwards along the rim of the mansard rooftops opposite. He didn't expect to be fired at – he was a moving target. His reaction was a warning to the invisible marksman who had aimed to kill Tweed. Again from a rooftop, as had been the case in Basle.

Inside the reception hall Tweed was viewing the potentially lethal incident calmly and philosophically. Which was not the case with either Paula or Newman. She kept her voice down but didn't mince her words.

'You must be crazy to walk out of that door by yourself. It was only due to Marler that you weren't killed. What were you thinking of?'

'Paula's right,' Newman agreed. 'What the hell were you thinking about – taking a risk like that?'

'Yes, you are both right,' Tweed responded. 'I was thinking about something that happened at breakfast – or rather something that didn't happen. I'll express my gratitude to Marler when I see him.'

'It means,' Newman pointed out grimly, 'that the Phantom tracked you to this hotel.'

'It means just that,' Tweed agreed.

Earlier, en route to the lift, before he had decided to sample some fresh air, Tweed had paused to take a good look at the patio beyond some windows. He had recalled this was where, in summer, society women gathered for tea and an exchange of the latest scandal. Osborne had passed them on his way out from the restaurant, hurrying to the exit.

Now it was Paula who paused. She was examining the contents of a glass showcase displaying *objets d'art* sold by a famous shop in the rue St-Honoré. The prices were sky high.

'Some valuable stuff there,' Tweed commented.

'You're far more valuable than anything in that showcase,' she reprimanded him. 'In future you don't go out unless Bob and I are with you.'

'Well, you know I always do as I'm told,' he replied with a smile.

'I'm not joking,' she snapped. 'I want you to promise us.'

'I promise. Now I'm going up to my room to make a phone call.'

He had just spoken when Osborne came in through the front entrance. The American was breathless, waited a moment before he could talk.

'Hi, folks. Just been for a quick jog. Told you I kept in shape. Don't tell on me – I've just committed a crime.'

'What was that?' Newman asked.

'Fed a parking meter. It was way over the top. Parked my car in a side street just off the rue St-Honoré last night. No space left in the Ritz garage. See you.'

Paula watched him run nimbly up the stairs he had earlier descended on his way to breakfast. He took the steps two at a time.

'He's recovered quickly from his jog,' Paula observed.

Tweed had gone up in the lift by himself. Paula had paused again to take another look at the showcase. A diamond clasp shaped like the wings of a bird was fascinating her. Newman had waited with her. Marler returned through the front entrance and strolled up to them.

'Like a word. Up those few steps is a small lounge. No one in it.'

'Find anything?' Newman asked when they were settled on a couch.

'I found the bullet intended for Tweed. Here it is.'

He took from his pocket an old tobacco tin with the lid fixed on. Paula stared at it. Then she remembered the time when Marler had smoked a pipe before he switched to king-size cigarettes. He removed the lid. Inside the tin rested an ugly-looking bullet.

'Evidence of a sort,' Marler commented.

'Any sign of the assassin?' Paula asked.

'No. At first I assumed he'd fired from a rooftop. After I hauled Tweed inside I was out there like a rabbit. I scanned the entire square. Then I realized even a cat burglar could never have scaled those roofs. And no window was open. Had one been pulled shut I was out there so fast I'd have noticed it.'

'Then where did he shoot from?' Newman enquired.

'Had to be from ground level, from behind a corner. A bit further along to your right, as you leave the entrance here, there's a large arcade. It was deserted. We had a very late breakfast. All the workers are in their offices. The ladies who shop are still in front of their mirrors, applying make-up and Lord knows what else.'

'You're a cynic, Marler,' Paula teased him.

'I'm wrong, then?'

'No, you're right. I was just amused at your perception about the habits of some women. Comes from experience, I suppose.'

'Where else?' Marler replied.

*

Flight BA 9999, bound for New York, was well out over the Atlantic. It was temporarily flying an unusual course to avoid turbulence. The captain had handed over control to his co-pilot for a few minutes to refresh himself. He was gazing down through a window.

At thirty-five thousand feet there was a sea of endless cloud below them, masking any sight of the ocean far below. The forecast had been for a continuous overcast all the way to their destination, many hours away. Captain Stuart Henderson was sucking a sweet provided by his chief stewardess, Linda. On a shelf, securely wedged in, was his video camera. Henderson had promised his wife that he'd try to get a series of shots of the approach to New York. Linda had agreed to operate the camera. Not that Henderson thought they'd have any luck – not at this time of the year. The overcast would stay with them all the way to JFK.

Henderson glanced at his watch. Time to take over from the co-pilot – he'd had his break. He took one final look down, stiffened, stared in sheer disbelief.

'Give me the video camera, Linda,' he called out. 'Quick.'

Below there was an enormous break in the clouds. Below that he saw a gigantic aircraft carrier. Spread out well beyond it to port and starboard were escorts of heavy cruisers. While Linda patiently held the camera Henderson used a pair of high-powered binoculars. He could just make out it was flying the Stars and Stripes. Guided-missile cruisers were protecting the carrier. Midway between the two destroyers sailed on a parallel course.

'Linda, take these, give me the camera. There's a ruddy great American task force down there. At a guess it's heading straight for Britain.'

He was operating the camera as he spoke. He swivelled it at different angles, trying to take in the whole of the vast battle fleet. Then the overcast reappeared, blotted out everything. Henderson stood motionless for a minute, his index finger tapping the side of the camera he was no longer operating.

'Frank,' he said to the co-pilot, 'have you heard anything about a major American task force heading for British waters?'

'No.'

'Neither have I,' said Linda. 'And I read the newspapers from page to page. Nothing on the radio. Nothing on TV.'

'I think I'm going to send a detailed and urgent radio signal to the Ministry of Defence,' Henderson decided.

45

Tweed first attempted to call Monica, using Beck's mobile. He had to give up eventually – the line was constantly engaged. Instead he called Roy Buchanan, reaching the Chief Inspector immediately.

'Tweed!' Buchanan sounded triumphant. 'The bullet matches.'

'Pardon?'

His mind had been elsewhere, replaying the breakfast conversation in the Ritz dining room when Osborne had joined the party.

'The bullet!' Buchanan repeated. 'Remember? You called me from Freiburg, told me to have the plane carrying the body of Sir Guy Strangeways met here. I personally was on the spot when the machine landed at Heathrow. I had a top doctor standing by, had the body rushed to him. He performed the autopsy, dug out the bullet which killed Strangeways. I had it compared with the bullet which assassinated our Prime Minister. Both bullets matched up perfectly. Which means the Phantom shot both the PM and Strangeways.'

'He has a lot to answer for . . .'

'Haven't finished yet. I've sent the Strangeways bullet to René Lasalle in Paris by courier. He'll have it by now. So he can compare it with the bullet which assassinated the French Minister.'

'Very good work, Roy.'

'More yet. I had patrol cars waiting in secret just outside all American airbases in East Anglia. One of them grabbed the big white truck flown in from Germany. Also its driver. You know what was inside that truck?'

'Money.'

'Enough brilliantly forged British banknotes to cause a financial panic here if they'd been distributed. I've got them under heavy guard. Have sent specimens to the Bank of England. They are in a state of shock.'

'This is wonderful news, Roy. Congratulations.'

'We've beaten the so-and-sos,' Buchanan said jubilantly, a man Tweed had never before known to show emotion.

'Hold on, Roy,' he warned. 'I think the monster crisis is yet to come. How about the bombings?'

'None since I surrounded the American Embassy with plain-clothes men.'

'Thank Heaven for that. Just don't relax your efforts one inch.'

Tweed had just put down the phone when it started ringing. He picked it up quickly.

'Hello, who is it?'

'René. I'm back. Could you come now to rue . . .' Lasalle paused. 'Is this phone safe?'

'Yes. I'm on a hacker-proof mobile.'

'Then could you come now to rue des Saussaies? I have news for you.'

'Can you dig out your file on Jean Chatel?'

'It will be waiting for you, my friend.'

'I'm on my way. Oh, can I bring Paula and Newman with me?'

'They will be most welcome.'

Tweed kept his word. He phoned Paula and Newman, asked them to come to his room immediately.

Very few people know about – or notice – rue des Saussaies, the headquarters of the *Direction de la Surveillance du Territoire*. In other words, French counter-espionage. A short narrow street almost opposite the Elysée Palace, it is passed by without so much as a glance by tourists. The entrance to the nondescript building is halfway along on the left, approached from the Elysée end. Newman stopped the car at the entrance and Tweed showed the guard his passport. The guard waved them inside.

'M. Lasalle is expecting you, sir.'

Newman parked the car in the small cobbled courtyard at the end of a short stone tunnel. An officer in plain clothes led them inside and up an old stone staircase to an office on the first floor. Lasalle rose from behind an old wooden desk to greet his guests.

'Coffee?' he suggested.

'It would help,' Tweed agreed.

René Lasalle, in his fifties, was small and slim and sported a neat moustache. He was dressed in a dark business suit and he pulled out a chair for Paula, then returned to sit behind his desk. A shabby green file was the only object on its surface apart from a telephone.

'The bullet arrived from Chief Inspector Buchanan some time ago,' he began. 'I'm sure you know which bullet I'm referring to.'

'I know very well,' Tweed assured him.

'We have had time,' Lasalle explained in his excellent English, 'to compare it meticulously with the bullet extracted from our late French Minister. It is a perfect match.'

'Then it's the Phantom again.'

'I would like your permission to send this bullet to my colleague in the German police at Wiesbaden, Otto Kuhlmann. For comparison with the bullet extracted from the body of Keller, also assassinated, as you know.'

'Send it by all means,' Tweed urged. 'Is that the file on Jean Chatel?'

'It is. I would ask you to treat its contents with confidentiality. In fact, officially you have never seen it. The Secret Service is very prickly about its documentation. Rightly so, you might agree.'

'Of course.' Tweed read the first few paragraphs, typed in French, then began to comment. 'This states that the real purpose of Jean Chatel's assignment to Washington is illumination. Specifically, is it true the Americans are preparing a plan which would change the geopolitical balance in Europe? Important that this includes the state of Great Britain . . .' Tweed went on reading.

'It was just over a year ago roughly when Chatel went to Washington, wasn't it?' asked Newman.

'No. Twenty months ago. But it was just over a year ago when he and his wife were murdered in the fake car accident in Virginia.'

'Murdered? You have evidence?' Newman queried.

'Let Tweed read on. You will see then.'

'This,' said Tweed, 'is a summary of a report sent to Paris by Chatel fifteen months ago. Chatel has reported he is followed everywhere by a team of American agents. He fears for his life, but asks to be allowed to continue his investigation.'

'It's getting grimmer,' commented Paula.

'It gets even grimmer,' Lasalle told her.

'The next report from Chatel,' Tweed went on, 'states that there is a highly detailed plan for the Americans to occupy Great Britain by subterfuge, employing every ruthless technique which will help to bring this objective about.'

'Why didn't you warn us?' Newman demanded.

'I wished to do just that,' Lasalle said bitterly. 'But it was argued by my superior that we had no concrete evidence, no documentation. He said the British would simply think it was a device by the French government to drive a wedge between Britain and the United States. I protested vigorously. The issue went up to the President in the Elysée. He agreed with my superior's decision.'

'Here we come to it,' said Tweed. 'Chatel reported that the momentous operation had been devised and was being directed by an individual called Charlie . . .'

'My God,' exclaimed Paula.

'Let me go on,' said Tweed. 'Chatel reported that he had made all efforts to identify the individual, Charlie, but so far had had no success. He ends by saying he thinks he is very close to locating Charlie.' Tweed looked up at Lasalle. 'How recent was this final report?'

'One week before he was killed in the so-called road accident.'

'Would it be possible, René, for me to have a copy of this final report? If so, I suggest you do so in a way which eliminates the printed reference to your department at the top of this sheet?'

'You ask a lot.' Lasalle paused, clasped his hands, stared up at the ceiling. 'But you deserve a lot,' he decided eventually. 'Considering we did not warn you earlier. Ah, at long last, we have coffee.' He spoke in French to the officer who carried a tray. 'Have you had to fly to Brazil to get the beans? Just put it down on my desk and leave us alone.'

463

He picked up his phone and spoke rapidly in French. Almost at once when he had ended the call an attractive girl came in, took the sheet he had extracted from the file handed back to him by Tweed. Then he poured coffee, handing the first cup to Paula.

'I have it on my conscience that I did not contact you to warn you. We have worked so well together in the past it seemed to me I was guilty of a kind of betrayal.'

'Nonsense,' replied Tweed, after sipping coffee, 'and it is very possible your President was right. Our late Prime Minister was not strong on international politics. He might well have thought it was all more French trickery to undermine our relationship with the Americans.'

'I comfort myself with the fact that I did report to you that a horde of strange Americans were infiltrating Britain by air and by Eurostar.'

'Also, René, the photos you sent enabled us to identify some of the most villainous types – most of whom are now dead.'

'Dead?' Lasalle's grey eyes twinkled as he glanced at Newman and Paula. 'I expect you have all been very busy.'

'There has been a certain amount of activity,' Newman replied.

The four of them chatted for a few minutes about times when they had cooperated during a crisis. The attractive girl came back, handed several sheets to Lasalle, who thanked her. Lasalle took the original sheet, carefully inserted it back inside his file. He then folded three other sheets, inserted them into a thick white envelope which he handed to Tweed.

'There are three excellent photocopies of the vital page. You are most welcome.'

The phone rang. Lasalle answered, listened, took a pad from a drawer, scribbled on it. At one stage Tweed heard him asking the caller to spell a name. He then ended the call.

'Tweed, this information may – or may not – be of interest to you. A Mlle Sharon Mandeville left the Ritz a while ago to catch a flight back to London. Shortly afterwards, in another car, a M. Osborne also left to catch the same flight. A M. Basil Windermere with a M. Rupert Strangeways left earlier to board the Eurostar for London.'

'Yes, the information is useful,' Tweed replied. 'May I ask, how do you know this?'

'Because I had one of my men staying as a guest at the Ritz to see what was going on. The information does not involve the staff of the Ritz in any way.'

'Thank you, René, for everything. We had better get back to the Ritz ourselves now. Would you know the quickest way we can get back to London?'

'Yes.' Lasalle checked his watch. 'You have two to three hours. The next Eurostar will get you back to London most quickly.'

In the lobby of the Ritz Tweed quietly gave Newman some instructions.

'Please contact Marler, Nield and Butler. Also Keith Kent, of course. Tell them to be ready to leave with us in precisely ninety minutes from now. And book seven first-class seats on Eurostar through the concierge. Also we shall need two hotel cars to take us to the Gare du Nord, where we board Eurostar. Finally, hand in to the nearest relevant car-hire outfits the two Audis we drove here in. Now, I'm going to my room to make a phone call.'

'Can I come with you?' Paula asked. 'I'm ready to leave now.'

'Yes, you can.'

Once inside his room Tweed hurried to the desk, sat down, used Beck's mobile to call Monica. Paula wandered over to the window to take a last look at the Place Vendôme.

'Tweed!' Monica sounded so relieved. 'I've been trying to call you but the hotel operator said you were out.'

'I was. What is it?'

'I've got a whole load of data for you, on all the profiles I've been working on. Birth certificates sent to me by courier from the States. giving most of the profiles' full names, et cetera. Are you ready?'

'Hold on just a moment.' Tweed called out to Paula, 'Get me the pad out of the zipped-up pocket in my suitcase.'

She found the pad, ran with it, placed it in front of him on the desk. Then she returned to the window.

'Fire away, Monica.'

Tweed began scribbling away, using sheet after sheet, keeping all the data on each name on a separate sheet. When Monica had come to the end he stared at one sheet, then closed the pad.

'Howard wants to speak to you very urgently. He's here now,' Monica said quickly.

'Tweed, when are you going to be back at Park Crescent? It's vital you arrive here within hours. A monster crisis has arisen. Defeat is staring us in the face. A hideous defeat.'

There was no element of panic in Howard's voice. He sounded to be in command of himself. But, underneath, Tweed detected a terrible anxiety.

'Tell me about it,' he said quietly.

'Not over the phone.'

'This line is safe. Perfectly safe.'

'No phone line is safe. I can't risk going into any detail. I have to wait until I see you. When will that be?'

'Today. Definitely. At a guess, midafternoon.'

'I can't wait to see you.'

When the connection was broken Tweed decided he wouldn't mention what Howard had said. What was the point in unsettling his team, even causing an atmosphere of alarm? He swung round in his chair.

'I now know who Charlie is,' he told Paula.

'Who?'

'I'm not saying yet. Before you accuse me of being cryptic, it's unlikely you'll meet Charlie, but you might have trouble keeping a blank expression, behaving normally. I think I'd like us to get to Gare du Nord early.'

Settling himself once again in his chair on the control level of the *President*, Crag opened the signal which had just arrived from the Pentagon. It was a long signal and was accompanied by a map. As he finished reading it once he sat up straighter, his mouth tightened. He looked at his Operations Officer.

'Bill, we have to hit the Brits.'

'What?'

'Not with missiles, Bill. This is a job for the SEALs.'

'What's their objective, sir?'

'A main and secret communications centre. Situation between a funny little place called Dungeness and another one called Hythe. The actual area of attack is Romney Marsh. It's almost on the coast – there are smooth sandy beaches the SEALs can land on, then they move a short distance inland, locate the installation, destroy it.'

'Won't it cause an international crisis?'

'The Chairman usually knows what he's doing and this operation has top sanction. The map is good – pinpoints the exact location of this communications centre. Contact the Mission Controller aboard the vessel carrying the SEALs. I reckon the attack ought to go in at midnight tomorrow. Get the Commander's opinion – after he's received this signal and the map. Have a look at it yourself first.'

'So this is going to be more than a demonstration of power?'

'Kind of looks that way.'

46

Arriving at Park Crescent, Tweed first ran up the stairs to his own office with Paula and Newman. Monica beamed with relief when she saw him. She pointed to his desk.

'The fat envelope came in from Roy Buchanan.'

'Good.' Tweed opened it, glanced quickly at its contents. 'Now, Monica, try and get Jefferson Morgenstern on the line.'

'I'm sorry. That's one thing I forgot to tell you. Morgenstern wants to see you. He must have called me eight times.'

'Tell him I'm now available to meet him within the hour. At any place of his choosing. Now I have to go up and see Howard.'

He left his office, ran up the stairs, followed by Paula and Newman, who waited outside Howard's office. Tweed walked straight in. Howard, as always impeccably dressed, was seated behind his desk. He showed signs of strain but his voice was firm.

'Am I glad to see you,' he greeted Tweed, standing up to shake his hand. 'Do sit down.'

'I have Paula and Bob outside. Could they join us?'

'I think they'd better.'

When everyone was seated Howard clasped his hands on top of his desk. He leaned forward.

'Briefly, a vast American task force is approaching our shores. No warning from Washington that it was on its way here. We'd never have known until the bastards showed up – except for the captain of a BA jet flying to New York. He saw it through a break in the clouds, even took video pictures of the damned thing, which was smart of him. The pics were flown back here on the next flight from New York. See for yourselves.'

Howard pushed forward a number of large colour prints across his desk. Tweed was surprised at their clarity. He looked at Howard.

'How high up was the aircraft?'

'I spoke to the captain myself over the phone. He was flying at thirty-five thousand feet. Apparently photography is his hobby. Told me he'd spent a mint on his camera. As soon as he'd taken his pics he sent a signal to the Ministry of Defence. A high-ranking pal of mine contacted me. The originals are with the MoD. Those are copies.'

'Amazing detail. What's that microscope you've got on your desk?'

'The most advanced version in the world. Loaned to me by my naval pal. Use it.'

Newman reached for the microscope. Under its lens he studied a warship sailing to port of the aircraft carrier. Then he whistled quietly.

'I'd say there are a load of SEALs aboard that ship. And they appear to be exercising for a landing. They're lowering small motorized amphibious landing craft over the side.'

'That's what my naval friend said,' Howard confirmed. 'Sinister, don't you think?'

'Any idea of their course, of when this battle group arrives?' asked Tweed.

'The captain of the aircraft told me that, as far as he could tell, it is headed straight for Britain. Time of arrival? The naval people tell me that, if it continues on course, they estimate the task force should appear in the English Channel after dark. Tomorrow.'

'Engagement possibly imminent.'

'Tweed . . .' Howard paused, appeared embarrassed. 'I have to tell you I made a real botch-up. I was tired out, hadn't slept for forty-eight hours – but I wouldn't take that as an excuse from a subordinate. I was driving down to the Bunker in daylight, middle of the afternoon. I was vaguely aware of a chopper hanging around. Took no notice. Drove straight into the courtyard of the Bunker. Mrs Carson tore me off a real strip. Deservedly so. The damned machine then circled over the complex for several minutes, flew off. Mrs Carson said the helicopter had no markings. I'm sorry, very sorry. Let the side down in a big way.'

'Don't be sorry.' Tweed smiled. 'No one is infallible. I have made some pretty stupid mistakes myself in the past. Do you mind if I leave now? I had a lot to do anyway, but after what you've told me I must move like Concorde.'

'I feel better now you're back.'

'I'll keep you fully informed about developments. Everything is going to happen very quickly now.'

He was on his way when Howard jumped up, followed him to the door. Howard almost whispered.

'One more very important point. The PM is anxious to see you as soon as possible.' He smiled ruefully. 'I think he regards me as second best.'

'Nonsense . . .'

Returning to his office, Tweed found an impatient Monica waiting for him. She waved a bit of paper.

'Jefferson Morgenstern says he'll see you at his office in the Embassy. He'll wait for you. Any time this afternoon.'

'Good. Now I want you to get me Sharon Mandeville on the phone. She's probably at the Embassy.'

Paula was behind her desk, Newman had settled himself in an armchair, Tweed was just about to seat himself in his own chair when the door opened. Marler walked in, an unlit king-size in his right hand.

'Sorry to barge in but I have someone downstairs I think you'd like to meet. Alf Rudge, boss of my cab-driver mob.'

'Ask him to come up now.'

When the door opened again everyone stared at the figure Marler ushered in. Alf Rudge was at least six feet tall, in his fifties, with a burly figure. In his hand he held one of the old-fashioned caps many cabbies used to wear. His blue eyes scanned the room quickly.

'Pleased to meet you, Alf,' Tweed said, extending a hand. 'I am Tweed. Make yourself at home. Try that armchair.'

'Hold that call for the moment,' he called across to Monica.

Tweed then introduced Alf to everyone in the room. Alf got up, shook hands with them. He struck Paula as being rather shy – or reserved – as his large paw squeezed hers. The big man then sat down in the armchair again, looked across the desk.

'I've 'eard a lot about you, Mr Tweed. No one except an idiot tries any monkey business with you.'

His cockney accent was very pronounced. Tweed immediately warmed to Alf. The salt of the earth, he thought. The backbone of England which really counted.

'Anything we can do to 'elp,' Alf went on, 'we'll do. Marler 'ere has knocked 'ell out of us in his trainin' out in the country.' He looked over his shoulder at Paula and Monica. 'Excuse me, ladies.'

'We may need you as reinforcements at a moment's

471

notice,' Tweed told him. 'Tomorrow at the latest, I would guess. How can we have your people close at hand?'

'Easy, Mr Tweed. I've got my mobile and the boys 'ave got theirs. Tell you what, if you agree – from this evening I'll have all of 'em patrolling the streets near here. They won't pick up no customers. Don't think they should be parked – make 'em obvious.'

'They'll patrol throughout the night – without sleep?'

'Won't worry 'em one little bit. They can always park for forty winks if they feels they needs it. Shall I lay it on?'

'Yes, please, Alf. Keep in touch with Marler. And thank you for offering to help us.'

'It's nothin', Mr Tweed,' Alf said, embarrassed as he stood up to leave. He turned at the door. 'If this means we 'ave a go at the Yanks the boys will love it . . .'

Marler returned almost immediately after escorting Alf to the front door. He looked round.

'Well, what's the verdict?'

'If all Alf's friends are like Alf,' Tweed said, 'then we have the equivalent of a very tough army platoon at our disposal.'

'They're all like Alf,' Marler declared.

'I really took to him,' Paula enthused. 'I was touched by his shyness, but I detected underneath it a man who would never let us down, however desperate the situation.'

'I'm on the side of Alf,' Newman agreed.

'But what about weapons?' Tweed queried.

'You know me,' Marler said, leaning against a wall, 'I break all the regulations. For training purposes I had a whole armoury of weapons sent up from the Surrey mansion a few weeks ago. Alf and his mob are armed to the teeth. Including bazookas.'

'You trained them to use bazookas?' asked Tweed.

'Yes. And they really know how to use them.

Especially the three who were in the Gulf War. Alf will have thought of weapons. His boys will be carrying them secreted inside their cabs. Now, I'll love you and leave you. Things to do.'

'Make that call, please, Monica,' Tweed requested when Marler had gone.

'Tweed!' Sharon's soft voice purred with delight over the phone. 'You're back in London? Wonderful. You have neglected me, you know. You can't deny it.'

'I wouldn't even try, Sharon. Good to know you are safely back. If possible, I'd like to come and see you this afternoon. The answer is yes? Splendid. Oh, do you mind if I bring Newman and Paula with me? You'd love to see them. Sometime this afternoon, then.'

As he put his coat on he gave Monica an instruction.

'Please inform Howard where I'm going. Tell him Paula and Bob are coming with me. Then Howard won't worry.'

'Who do we see first?' Paula asked.

They were sitting in the back of the car Newman was driving towards Grosvenor Square. The good weather was lasting. It was a brilliantly sunny afternoon with not a cloud in a duck-egg blue sky. The air was fresh and pedestrians were walking briskly as though enjoying the return of the sun.

'The sequence is important,' Tweed said. 'First we see Morgenstern. Afterwards we call in on Sharon.'

'So you can ask her out to dinner,' she teased.

'I thought I came first,' Newman called out. 'Am I supposed to stand in line?'

'We'll see,' Tweed replied.

'And you are clutching that package of evidence from Buchanan as though the fate of the world depended on it,' Paula commented.

'Maybe it does,' Tweed told her.

'What's inside it?'

'Among other things, photos of the dead Umbrella Men who tried to kill me in Basle near Market-platz. With their names.'

'How on earth did you get hold of them?'

'Reliable Arthur Beck again. He omitted to mention it, but he sent the material to Roy Buchanan at New Scotland Yard. The two men met at an international police conference a few months ago. Roy told me they got on very well together.'

'I can spot some of them already,' Newman reported as they neared Grosvenor Square.

'Some of who?' Paula wanted to know.

'Buchanan's plain-clothes sleuths. Stationed to keep a close eye on who comes and goes from the American Embassy. I think he's told some of them to make their presence obvious – to act as a deterrent. Roy Buchanan really never, under any circumstances, misses a trick.'

For Tweed, as they mounted the steps and walked inside the spacious entrance hall, it was like a replay of a film he had seen before. The girl who had treated him so offhandedly on his previous visit was behind the reception desk. But this time when he gave his name her attitude was very different. Standing up, she gave him a beaming smile.

'Mr Tweed, Mr Morgenstern is waiting to see you. His suite of offices is on the first floor. Here is the number,' she said, handing him a plastic disc. 'And could you please take this card? There are a lot of guards about who may stop you. If you show them this they will let you straight through.'

'Thank you,' said Tweed.

He led the way to the elevator, pressed the button. The door opened and inside he pressed the first floor button. The elevator ascended, the doors opened and they stepped out into the wide corridor. Tweed stopped, smiled.

Denise Chatel had been walking towards the elevator. For once, Paula noticed, she was not carrying a file. More than that, she was stylishly dressed in riding kit, complete with jodhpurs and gleaming riding boots.

She gave them a great big smile. Coming forward she hugged Paula, kissed Tweed on the cheek and then gave Newman the same attention. To Tweed she seemed a different woman. Her attitude was buoyant and cheerful and warm. What could have happened?

'How do you like my outfit?' Denise asked.

She swivelled round in a circle. Her brunette hair swung over her shoulders. Her face was pink and full of life.

'Very fetching,' said Paula.

'The picture of happiness,' said Tweed.

'You look just terrific,' Newman told her. 'What have you been up to?'

'I've just come back from a ride in Hyde Park. It's a wonderful day. I even managed a gallop, which may be illegal, but I just didn't care. I was on top of the world.'

'Hence your high spirits,' Tweed remarked.

'You've hit the nail on the head,' Denise responded.

'And what else?'

'Why?' She hesitated. 'Nothing else.'

'You'll excuse us. We've come to keep an appointment.'

'What was all that about?' Paula asked as they proceeded along the corridor.

'No idea.'

A tall, smooth-faced man came out of a room, closed the door behind him. Dressed in a smart blue pin-stripe suit, he strode confidently towards them. Then he stopped, gave a broad grin.

'Chuck Venacki,' greeted Newman. 'The great survivor. How do you do it?'

'Do what?' Venacki asked amiably.

'Survive. The catastrophe at Schluchsee.'

'Where's that?' Venacki enquired, still amiable. 'Sounds as though it could be Austria, Switzerland, Germany?'

'Give the man the money,' Newman went on. 'Even though he didn't get it until his third try. Come off it, Venacki. You remember when we last met.'

'Sure I do. Outside Park Crescent a hundred years ago. When you rammed the Lincoln Continental with your four-wheel drive.'

'Nice try. At Schluchsee Ronstadt drove his car straight at me. Four men inside that car. You were sitting with Ronstadt in the front. Ronstadt, by the way, is dead, but you survive.'

'Guess you mistook me for someone else, wherever this dramatic car incident took place. Now, I have to get going.' He looked at Paula, then at Tweed. 'Enjoy yourselves. We try to make visitors feel at home here.'

'And that,' said Tweed quietly, 'sounded like the voice of the anonymous American who phoned me in my room at the Colombi. The call which told me Ronstadt had left.'

'I don't get it,' Paula commented. 'He seemed nice enough.'

'And this,' Tweed said in the same quiet voice, pointing to a door they were passing, 'is where Sharon lives. We'll come back later. The critical interview is the one with Morgenstern.'

47

'Do come in. Good to see you. I've had fresh coffee delivered. The receptionist told me you were here.'

In response to Tweed's knock Jefferson Morgenstern himself opened the door, ushered them inside. He locked the door, then gazed at his visitors with a smile. Tweed introduced Paula as his assistant and confidante. Morgenstern smiled even more broadly as Tweed turned to Newman.

'No introduction necessary here, Tweed. Bob Newman once interviewed me. And I don't give many interviews.' He shook Newman's hand warmly. 'You're looking great and maybe a bit tougher. Experience does that to us all – if we have the fibre. Come and sit down. I'll serve coffee.'

Paula had been studying Morgenstern closely. He was shorter than she had imagined, but his figure in a grey Savile Row suit was well padded. She had the impression of a man of great intelligence who enjoyed the good things of life – especially wine and food. His hair, neatly brushed, was greying and he emanated an aura of supreme self-confidence and dynamic energy – of power.

His large desk was a genuine antique, Chippendale, she thought. On it was a silver engraved tray with a silver coffee service. Three comfortable upright chairs were arranged in front of the desk and Morgenstern dragged his swivel chair round to join them. Not a man to flaunt his importance.

'You were looking at my coffee service,' he said to Paula after she had seated herself, which made her realize this man didn't miss a thing. 'When I was a poor student in Europe I was once invited to a mansion where they had such a service. I decided then,' he continued as he poured coffee, 'that one day I'd have one like it.' He smiled. 'It was a long journey before I was able to purchase one.'

His face was long, Paula noted. His nose was long, his features strong, and beneath his American accent she detected a trace of some European accent. When he had served coffee he sat down near Paula, drank half the contents of his cup, folded his arms.

'Tweed, I've been giving a lot of thought to what you said to me when we last met. At the time I was dismissive. Since then I have given your accusations more thought. I admit I'm a troubled man.' He looked at Paula, then at Newman. 'May I take it that anything we talk about today will be in complete confidence?'

'Quite definitely. These two are my right and left arm. I said recently I'd trust them with my life. That I had done.'

'Good enough for me. The weak link in what you said is a complete lack of evidence.'

'That is what I have brought with me. Overwhelming evidence. In photographs and documents. Some of it was supplied by Arthur Beck, Chief of Swiss Federal Police. I can supply you with his number in Berne if you want it later. While in Basle recently four of the men attached to this Embassy tried to murder me – along with Paula and Bob. Instead, they were killed. They all carried American diplomatic passports. Here is a photograph of the dead killers, supplied to me by Beck. Their names are on the back. And here are photocopies of the passports they carried. Beck has the originals.'

Morgenstern studied the photo of the dead Umbrella Men. He looked at the back, where their names were given. Placing it on his desk, he looked at the photocopies of the passports. His mouth tightened. He placed them on his desk.

'There's worse to come,' Tweed warned. 'There's a clear video picture of the man who left the bomb in the Oxford Street department store.'

'His name is Vernon Kolkowski,' Newman said quietly. 'He also had a diplomatic passport. Once, in New York, the police chief told me he was a professional who had murdered at least six men. They could never indict him. No witness dared testify. If one was willing to testify he'd been found dead in a side street.'

'Then,' Tweed continued, 'we rescued a poor woman who was being tortured by another American with a diplomatic passport. Name of Rick Sherman. He's dead too.'

'Could you pause?' Morgenstern requested. He took from his pocket a leather-bound notebook. 'I'd like to note down some of these names. What was that last one?'

'Rick Sherman.'

'Thank you. And Vernon someone. I'd like the surname.'

Newman spelt it out carefully. Morgenstern wrote it down in his notebook. Then he looked again at the video print of the man who had planted the bomb in the Oxford Street department store.

'As far as I can gather,' Tweed went on, 'I know you are handling the diplomatic side of this huge operation. But there is another secret section inside this Embassy called the Executive Action Department. That is staffed by what I would call the gangster level – and all the members have been given diplomatic passports.'

'How can I phrase this?' Morgenstern wondered aloud. 'While you were away I made certain enquiries here. I had the impression certain people evaded giving me answers to my questions.'

'Have you heard of the Executive Action Department?'

'No.'

'I'm certain it's located in this building. That it is responsible for the outrages. Individual murders and wholesale bombings.'

'I am good at assessing character, Tweed. I am sure you would not ever invent such horrific stories.'

'Is there any way you could check the names of everyone who has been issued with a diplomatic passport over, say, the past seven weeks?'

'I was thinking of that. Yes, there is. But first I must refresh your cups.'

Paula glanced round the large room while Morgenstern manipulated the silver coffee pot. The room was furnished in expensive but restrained taste. Heavy floor-to-ceiling curtains flanked the windows, curtains with a Regency stripe. The wall-to-wall carpet was a pale mushroom colour. The few pieces of other furniture were also antiques. The room had a restful atmosphere. On another desk the Stars and Stripes was suspended from a bronze column.

'I'm going to ask the Ambassador's personal assistant for the record of all diplomatic passports issued recently,' said Morgenstern.

'Mrs Pendleton,' he said on the phone, 'I require urgently the list of all personnel working here issued with diplomatic passports over the past seven weeks.'

Mrs Pendleton had a loud raucous American voice. Tweed could hear her end of the conversation clearly.

'Well, the list exists, but I can't supply it to you without the consent of the Ambassador.'

'Ask him now, then.'

'I can't. He is out.'

'Mrs Pendleton, do you recognize my voice?'

'Of course, sir.'

'Then kindly remember you are talking to the Secretary of State.'

'I do know that, sir.'

'Then I expect you to deliver the list to me within two minutes.'

'Some people,' Morgenstern smiled briefly, 'who have held down a job for years develop delusions of grandeur.'

Paula was struck by the brief smile. Since Tweed had started to produce his evidence a change had come over Morgenstern. Instead of his earlier amiability his expression had become one of gravity. He's taking this very seriously, she thought.

There was a tap on the door, Morgenstern called out to come in. A plump self-important looking woman in her late fifties entered. She was holding a green leather-bound ledger which she placed on the desk.

'I'm afraid I need a receipt before I release that ledger,' she said, producing a small pad.

'Really?' Morgenstern stared at her. 'Have you a short memory? If so, something could be done about that. Only minutes ago I reminded you I am Secretary of State.'

'I suppose I could make an exception.'

'Mrs Pendleton. Do you see the handle of that door you opened to come in here?'

'Yes, sir.'

'Go over it, take hold of it. That's right. Now turn it to the left.'

'I'm sorry, sir, if . . .'

'Now you keep hold of the handle. Pull the door open towards you. I see you've managed it. Now, walk into the corridor and close the door quietly behind you. It's not too difficult.'

Tweed smiled to himself. It was notorious that Morgenstern had an acid side to his nature. He couldn't suffer fools gladly.

'Now, we can do our homework,' said Morgenstern. 'Excuse me if I go and sit behind my desk for a moment.'

Taking his chair back to its original position, he sifted through the photos and documents he had quickly arranged in a pile before Mrs Pendleton arrived, so she couldn't see anything. Taking out his notebook, he then opened the ledger. He had perched it on an inkstand so his visitors could not see its pages.

Using a pen as a pointer, he began to check the names provided by Tweed with the list inside the ledger. It took a while but often he stabbed at a name in the ledger with his pen. His expression became grimmer. When he had closed the ledger he sat staring at Tweed. Then he hauled his chair back to join his visitors.

'I have decided,' he said.

'What is your decision?' Tweed enquired.

'Can you leave with me all the items you have given me?'

'Certainly.'

'I have a Gulfstream jet standing by permanently at Heathrow. I like to be mobile. Soon after you have left me I shall drive to Heathrow, board the jet, and fly immediately to Washington. If you want to contact me, call this number.' He took a pad from a drawer, wrote on it, handed it to Tweed. 'I shall inform all my aides that if you call you are to be put through to me – even if I'm at the White House.'

'Sharon Mandeville next,' Tweed said when they had left Jefferson's lair. 'Might as well tie the lot up at once.'

'Do come in.' Sharon, like Jefferson, had opened the

door herself to welcome them inside. 'What a pleasure to see you all again.'

She kissed Tweed on the cheek, shook hands with Paula and Newman. Then she escorted them across the spacious room towards a desk which was even larger than Jefferson's. As they followed her Paula glanced round the room. It was very expensively furnished – money had been no object – but unlike Jefferson's office, it was very modern.

Sharon's enormous desk was made of gleaming white wood, all the chairs were upholstered in white leather, the carpet was white and scattered across it were tiger-skin rugs. The coffee service on a tray on her desk was almost surreal in design. And the rims of the cups were six-sided, which made them very difficult to drink out of without the contents ending up in your lap.

Three chairs were arranged in front of the desk. Behind it was a high-backed chair which reminded Paula of a throne. Sharon gave Tweed a ravishing smile.

'Do sit down, all of you, please. Coffee for everyone?'

'Not for me,' said Tweed as he sat down.

'Me too neither, thank you,' said Newman.

'I'll also pass,' said Paula.

Sharon was wearing a navy blue trouser suit which suggested the high-powered businesswoman. Newman thought she had never looked more attractive. She was pouring herself a cup.

'Excuse me, but I need an ocean of caffeine to keep me going.' She sat in the chair behind the desk. 'Well, Tweed, I suppose we can say we have completed the Grand Tour of Europe.'

'Something like that.'

'Oh, come – ' she gazed at him over the rim of her cup – 'no call to be so serious. It isn't the end of the world.'

'Isn't it?'

Sharon's nails were painted blood-red, a varnish which Paula hated. She had a high collar, buttoned up to her neck. She went on gazing at Tweed, as though assessing his mood. He had taken off his glasses and was cleaning them on his handkerchief. He put the glasses on again.

'Now you get a clearer view of beauty,' Newman joked.

'I have a clearer view of a lot of things now,' Tweed replied.

'So why have you come to see me?' Sharon asked in her soft voice. 'How can I help you?'

'You can confirm certain information I have received.'

'You sound just like a policeman.'

'I was once a policeman,' Tweed told her. 'A century ago.'

'He was the youngest superintendent at Scotland Yard,' Paula explained. 'His speciality was Homicide.'

'What information are you referring to?' Sharon asked.

She was still her calm self. She was leaning back upright in her chair. Her half-closed eyes, glowing greenly, were fixed on Tweed.

'I have here a certain document.' Tweed took a thick envelope out of his breast pocket, extracted a sheet. 'This is a copy of your birth certificate.'

'Really? Isn't this rather personal? How, I wonder, were you able to obtain it?'

'By perfectly legal means. Such certificates are in the public domain, as you must know.'

'Oh, come on, Tweed.' She smiled, still leaning against the back of her upright chair, her body very erect. 'All the way across the Atlantic?'

'Precisely. All the way across the Atlantic.' Tweed

unfolded the sheet of paper. 'You were born in Washington, DC. You are forty-two years old.'

'Not very gallant of you, to broadcast my age.'

'On this copy of the certificate it gives your full names. Sharon Charlotte Anderson.'

'So?' Her eyes were almost closed now. 'Where does this lead us to?'

'*Charlotte.* Sometimes abbreviated to Charlie. Even with a woman. You are Charlie.'

Paula had difficulty suppressing a gasp. She glanced at Newman. He looked stunned. She switched her glance to Tweed, sitting next to her. He looked very relaxed. Still holding the document, he was gazing back at Sharon.

'Charlie,' he said, 'we know masterminded the gigantic operation under way to absorb Britain into America as the fifty-first state. Do you deny you are Charlie?'

'*Damn you!* Nosy, insignificant little man. Friggin' two-bit so-called detective!' Sharon was standing up now, leaning over her desk as though about to leap at Tweed. 'You don't know what the bloody hell you're talking about!'

She continued screaming at the top of her voice, uttering a foul stream of obscene abuse. Her voice had completely changed. Her lung power was awesome. Suddenly she grabbed the certificate out of his hands, tore it to shreds, threw the pieces over her visitors.

'I do have other copies of that birth certificate,' Tweed informed her quietly.

'Much good they will do you. You can't prove any of this friggin' nonsense you've been spouting at me. How dare you?' she yelled.

'Imminent events will prove me right.'

'Imminent events,' she screamed, 'will see you out of a job, you friggin' nobody. You'll be lucky to stay alive.'

'Is that a threat?' Tweed asked quietly. 'The kind of order you gave to Jake Ronstadt? Because he is no longer available.'

'What do you mean by that?' she raged.

'Jake Ronstadt is dead.'

'Dead?'

'He tried to kill me in Strasbourg – under your orders, I'm sure. One of my people dropped a grenade into the launch Ronstadt was guiding along a waterway. Result? Ronstadt and the two men with him vanished when the launch sailed on into a wild sluice.'

'Tweed, you are a very inventive man,' she spat at him.

'Then there was Rick Sherman. He was torturing the wife of Kurt Schwarz – again on your orders, I'm certain. He's dead – with a knife through his throat.'

'You're lying, Tweed,' she said in a deep voice full of hate. 'You always lie.'

'I'm sure, when it is checked, that it will be found you organized the recruitment of this large gang of thugs from the back streets of New York. You must have sanctioned the issue of diplomatic passports to an army of killers. There has to be a record of who did that.'

'You're crazy,' she went on screaming. 'Stark raving mad. That is something which will be proved. Do you hear me? Do you hear me? *Do you hear me?*'

'I can hardly avoid hearing you, Sharon.' Tweed stood up. 'I suggest this interview is over, that it is time for us to leave.'

She picked up a cup, threw it at him. Tweed ducked. The cup hit the white wall on the far side of the room, broke into a dozen pieces. Tweed led the way to the door, opened it, stood aside as Paula and Newman walked into the corridor, then walked out himself, closing the door with never a backward glance.

'I'm breathless,' said Paula.

'I'm staggered,' said Newman.

'And you, Bob, once described her as a demure English lady,' Tweed recalled as they headed for the elevator.

'Is Sharon really Charlie?' asked Paula.

Tweed hadn't the opportunity to reply. Walking briskly towards them was a familiar figure, a large man. Paula never ceased to be surprised that big heavyweight men often had small feet and moved with such agility.

'Hi, folks,' called out Ed Osborne. 'Great to see you paying us a visit. That's what I call real friendly.'

'Do excuse us, Ed,' responded Tweed, 'we're late for an urgent appointment. See you sometime.'

'Sure thing.'

'We have to keep moving,' Tweed warned as they approached the lift. 'Howard said the PM wants to see me. So, Bob, drop me off at Downing Street before you go on to Park Crescent.'

'We'll drop you off – then wait for you,' Newman said firmly.

When they stepped out of the lift on the ground floor the receptionist rose to her feet and called out to them, 'Have a nice day.'

48

Arriving back at Park Crescent from Downing Street, Tweed dashed upstairs to his office. Besides Monica in her usual post behind her desk Marler was waiting for him. Paula and Newman came in, sat down.

'I've just come back from a record-breaking trip to the Bunker,' Marler said.

'What sent you down there?' Tweed asked from behind his desk.

'Howard had briefed me after you'd rushed off to the American Embassy. Told me about the American task force, what Newman had observed from the pics about the SEALs and their exercises. He also told me about his own trip, how a chopper circled above the complex. I have a suggestion.'

'Fire away.'

'Howard told me that everything that mattered here is now down at the Bunker. I reckon one of the prime targets of that task force will be the Bunker. So I went down there to check out the defences. They seem OK to me.'

'Good. What is your suggestion?'

'I think we ought to send Alf's mob down there. I can contact Alf.'

'I agree. They won't travel in convoy, I hope?'

'No. Alf has his head screwed on. Also, if they drive down just after dark no one will spot them.'

'I agree. Monica, phone Mrs Carson and warn her seven men with their cabs will be descending on her. You can explain to her about Alf's mob.' He looked at Marler. 'They'll have to find somewhere to hide all those cabs – so they won't be seen from the air.'

'Alf will think of that himself. He does have all his marbles.'

'One more thing.' Tweed opened a drawer. 'Give him this map, otherwise he'll never find the place.'

'I was about to ask you.' Marler looked out of the window after taking the map. 'Talk of the devil. Alf's cab is parked on the main street. I think he's stopped to light a fag. I can tell him now if I move. See you all later. Things to do.'

'Blow!' said Tweed. 'One thing I forgot to tell him. When I've finished, Monica, phone this data to Mrs Carson. Tell her to warn Alf and his mob as soon as they arrive. I've warned everyone else down there, including Cord.'

'Warn him about what?' Paula enquired.

'When Marler was supervising the construction of the Bunker he found there were a number of very deep shafts in the grounds. He guessed, as they looked so ancient, they were ventilation shafts. They're like vertical tunnels which lead down to horizontal tunnels the smugglers used in the old days. Marler had metal gratings put over the top of each shaft so nobody would ever fall down one. They already had ancient grilles over them but they were crumbling with the passage of time, so he had them renewed. I worry he might have missed one.'

'I'll make it all one call to Mrs Carson,' Monica promised.

'So you're sure Sharon is Charlie?' Paula remarked. 'If we've time to relax for five minutes.'

'We not only have the time – we need it.'

'Were you suspicious of her earlier?' Paula suggested.

'Yes, up to a point. Who was always on the spot when attempts were made to kill us? In Basle? In Freiburg? In Strasbourg? Sharon Mandeville. Someone had to be instructing Ronstadt and his thugs.'

'Monica,' Paula went on, turning in her chair, 'while building up your profiles did you ever fill in those long strange gaps in Ed Osborne's life?'

'No, I was never able to fill one of them. A mystery man.'

Paula turned back to Tweed. 'I noticed that Sharon never admitted she was Charlie. And Osborne was always on the spot. In Basle. In Freiburg. In Strasbourg.'

'You are a very observant lady,' Tweed told her.

'And I was also struck,' she said, 'by Chuck Venacki,

the smooth-faced man we met in the corridor. He was so much more polished, spoke very well, an educated man who was very well dressed.'

'A lot of Americans are,' Newman said. 'We've been meeting the dregs of American society. We do have the same type over here.'

'Are you sure,' she pressed him, 'that you saw him in that car by the side of Ronstadt at Schluchsee?'

'I am sure. I know I was jumping for my life out of the way but I saw him clearly. Don't ask me who the other two were.'

'It's weird,' she said. 'And when do we all go down to Romney Marsh?'

'That reminds me,' said Tweed. 'I have to phone a friend of mine at the MoD. What he tells me will answer your question.'

Paula got up to stretch her legs. She gazed out of the window. Marler was still talking to Alf. As she watched he got into the cab as though he were a passenger. Alf had not got his light on. Not available for taking fares.

'Philip,' Tweed began, using Beck's mobile, 'Howard has told me about—'

'Hold it, please,' a cultured voice interrupted. 'Is this a safe line?'

'Absolutely. I'm on a hacker-proof mobile, advanced Swiss version. Can I go on? Good. Philip, I need to know the progress of that American task force – how close it is.'

'You're talking to the right chap, Tweed. I'm in charge of monitoring it. It's still heading straight for us. We estimate it will be well inside the English Channel late tomorrow night. I can keep you informed of its progress, if that would help.'

'It would be a life-saver. A plan I'm working on depends on my knowing their timetable. If I'm not here could you give the latest news to Monica? You know how reliable she is.'

'Think I'd trust Monica before I trusted you,' Philip joked. 'I'll keep you in close touch with developments. Let's have a drink when this is all over.'

'Time you paid for your round. Bye . . .'

'There's something else,' Newman remarked.

'And I thought we'd got enough on our plate,' Paula chided him.

'We mustn't forget the Phantom is still on the loose,' Newman warned.

'Oh, he'll turn up again,' Tweed assured him. 'Maybe next time he will make a fatal mistake. I wonder who's paying him.'

'Sharon?' Paula suggested.

'Possibly.'

'So when is zero hour? I imagine you know, after talking to your old chum, Philip.'

'At a guess I'd say between 2200 hours and midnight. So it will be dark, which worries me.'

At that moment Marler returned. He gave Paula a little salute and took up his favourite position. Leaning against a wall he looked at Tweed.

'Alf is all clued up. He's gone off to meet his pals one by one. He'll brief them. He's going to photocopy that map in some small all-night shop he knows about. Alf knows where to get anything done.'

'I'm glad you came back so quickly, Marler. A friend of mine at the MoD has warned me that task force will arrive after dark tomorrow. That's when I think they will launch their attack on the Bunker. The dark will make it difficult to see them coming.'

'Problem solved. I'll go back to my office now to call down to the mansion in deep and darkest Surrey. They have a collection of mobile hand-operated searchlights.

And a goodly number of star shells would come in handy. I'll talk to the one man who knows where the Bunker is, tell him to load up a van immediately, to drive it himself through the night to the Bunker.'

'You're a genius,' said Tweed.

'Oh, I know. But it's nice to have it confirmed. See you.'

'Why didn't I think of that?' Tweed asked when Marler had gone.

'Because you're not a genius,' said Paula. 'Incidentally, I'm not going to ask you what you discussed with the PM. Out of bounds. But what was your objective during our visit to those people at the American Embassy?'

'To destabilize them, the way they're trying to destabilize us. It worked better than I'd hoped. Morgenstern is the kingpin.' He looked at his watch. 'By now he should be airborne in his Gulfstream jet, heading for Washington.'

'You certainly destabilized Sharon.'

'A trifle dramatic, wasn't it? I'd wondered what lay under her deep calm at all times. Now we know. A volcano. And I managed to trigger it off. A real eruption.'

'What do you imagine she's doing now? Checking out the first flight back to the States in the morning?'

'Maybe. And maybe not.'

In her white office at the Embassy Sharon Mandeville was her normal cool self. Leaning back in her tall chair she was on the phone to Washington.

'Hi there, Senator, this is Sharon. How goes it?'

'Great. Just great, honey. You'll be needed back here soon to start your campaign. All the posters are printed for the billboards. You look a winner on them. You will be. I'm banking on it.'

'I'm very grateful to you, Grant. I hope you know that.'

'Hell with that. I'm looking forward to retiring, to putting you in my place. Don't forget this is a big state, a key state when it comes later to the nomination for a presidential candidate. A whole load of electoral college votes in your pocket.'

'I've got to get there first, Grant. To become a senator as a springboard for the big one.'

'You'll walk it. Both elections. For senator. For presidential candidate. Lord knows you've made enough speeches so far. And everywhere you spoke the crowds went wild. I know it hasn't hit the press or TV yet, but that's the way we want it. You come out as the big surprise. Is this phone OK?'

'Totally OK.'

'Got a bit of great news. Keep it quiet. Your nearest rival for senator is withdrawing from the race.'

'He is? How the hell did that happen?'

'Wise old me made it happen. Had him investigated. He's taken bribes from the Chinese. Needed a whole load of dough and Beijing coughed up. Needed that dough to try and keep his companies afloat. He's still bankrupt. Nobody knows, but I got hold of documents. Went to have a chat with my old enemy at that palatial house of his. Told him to announce his withdrawal – for reasons of health – or I'd send the documents to CNN and the *New York Times*. He's making his announcement tomorrow.'

'You're wicked. That's blackmail.'

'Aren't you glad I'm on your side? You know what?'

'Do tell, Grant.'

'I'm looking forward one day to telling my grandchildren how I propelled the first woman in history into the White House.'

'Thank you, Grant.'

493

'With your money and my know-how you're home and dry.'

'Thank you again, Grant.'

'When can I expect you to reach Washington?'

'Soon, very soon now. I'll let you know when I'm flying over, give you my ETA.'

'I'll be there to meet you. With flowers.'

'Anybody ever tell you that you're a great guy? I'm telling you now.' She paused. 'I've some unfinished business to attend to.'

'Goodnight, Madame President.'

Crag had sat immobile in his chair as the task force headed at speed for its objective. A few minutes later an aide appeared, crossed the deck, saluted, handed the Rear Admiral an envelope.

'New maps, sir. Just transmitted to us from Washington.'

'Thank you.'

The aide saluted again, left the deck. Crag opened the envelope, extracted several maps. An attached signal explained the aerial photos the aide had called maps had been taken by a helicopter flying over the vital section of the Kent coast. Crag reached for a powerful magnifying glass resting on his work table.

He grunted as he studied the photos carefully. Then he looked up. He handed the photos to his Operations Officer.

'Bill, I guess we ought to rush these over to the SEALs commander. Seems to me the operation will be a piece of cake. They land on a flat beach of pebbles just east of some place called New Romney. Then they strike inland over territory as flat as a pancake. Only a short distance to that communications HQ.'

'I'm worried, sir, that the Brits may know we're

coming. That commercial airliner which flew above us just when there was the only break so far in the overcast.'

'I wouldn't worry.' Crag stretched his long arms, suppressed a yawn. 'Passengers on those flights soon get tired of looking out of the windows. They'd either be tired or drunk – or both. And it was at pretty high altitude. We estimated thirty-five thousand feet.'

'I'd better report to the Chairman that we've received the signal and the maps.'

'Aerial photos, Bill. Hold on sending a report. Let's first get the reaction of the SEALs' commander aboard the warship he's travelling on.'

Crag sat thinking. In his mind he was checking over the sections of the task force he'd contacted recently. Some admirals in his position, he knew, had a written list they ticked off. Crag carried the list in his head.

Fifteen minutes later – ten of which had been taken up lowering the fast boat over the side which had taken the data and its racing to the warship – his Operations Officer returned with a signal in his hand.

'May I read this to you, sir? I emphasize I'm using the words used by the SEALs' commander.'

'Let's hear it, Bill.'

'"To hell and high water in fifteen minutes." That must mean the time he estimates to complete the whole operation.'

'It must.' Crag allowed himself one of his rare smiles. 'I always thought that commander was a top gun.'

49

It was the middle of the night. Tweed was asleep in his office. Monica had hauled out his camp bed from a cupboard, had then made it up for him. Tireless, she watched over him from behind her desk. The door opened and Marler walked in. Monica put a finger to her lips.

'Progress to report, Marler?' enquired Tweed.

He had lifted his head off the pillow, was now sitting up in his dressing gown, with the vivid Oriental design. Marler hesitated, worried that he had woken Tweed.

'Well?' prodded Tweed, who had put his glasses on. 'I'm only taking catnaps. I like to be kept informed.'

'Progress, yes,' Marler replied. 'First, the van from the Surrey mansion reached the Bunker two hours ago. They now have a large collection of searchlights and star shells. I gather Alf and his mob have been practising with them.'

'So Alf is down there already?'

'He's been down there with his chums for at least three hours.'

'I find that very satisfactory,' said Tweed, stretching himself higher up. He checked his watch. 'I was going to wake up now, anyway. As you know, I have an alarm clock in my head. Monica, get me Philip at the MoD. I'd like a word with him.'

Tying the belt round his dressing gown, he padded over to his desk. He smiled grimly as he addressed Marler.

'At times likes this the essential thing is to stay calm. Did I detect a note of subdued excitement in your voice?'

'You might have done,' Marler admitted.

'Wait until I've taken this call and then go to your office and bed down on your couch.'

'Don't feel sleepy.'

'Irrelevant. We all need a little sleep to keep us on our toes.'

'If you insist,' grumbled Marler.

'I'm giving you a direct order.'

He picked up the phone as Monica gestured to him madly. He was still using Beck's mobile. He asked Monica to tell Philip he'd call him back immediately, which he did.

'Tweed here. Yes, Philip, again on a very safe line. What news?'

'The task force continues to head straight for the English Channel. We've sent special high-flying planes out with the latest radar. So the Yanks don't catch on, as soon as the planes have located its present position they fly back here.'

'Time of arrival in the Channel?'

'No change. Between 2200 hours and midnight tonight. They are getting pretty close.'

'No rumours of their presence?'

'None that have reached me. And any would. I'll go on keeping you in touch. Or tell Monica. Do you ever sleep?'

'I've just had forty winks.'

'Some people have all the luck.'

Tweed pushed the mobile across his desk. He was wide awake and looked very fresh. He spoke to Marler.

'I've been thinking – probably in my sleep. I do that. Before you get some kip – which you must do – could you call Paula, Newman, Nield and Butler from your office? Tell them we leave from here ten o'clock sharp in the morning – to drive down to the Bunker. At that time the traffic may be quieter, as far as it ever is quieter.'

'I'll do that right away.' Marler smiled. 'I'm going to

497

be so popular, waking them up in the middle of the night.'

'I wouldn't worry. As soon as you've called they'll swear at you, then they'll fall fast asleep again. They've had a really exhausting time of it recently. So have you, Marler, so don't forget my order.'

'There's one thing I've forgotten,' he said when Marler had gone. 'Food. Down at the Bunker.'

'Two cooks went with the staff when they moved down there from here,' Monica informed him. 'I hope you don't mind, but it occurred to me the arrival of Alf and his men might strain the situation to the limit. I phoned the mansion. Their best cook, Mrs Payne, travelled to the Bunker in the truck when the driver took the star shells and searchlights. She makes giant shepherd's pies. She's taken ingredients and cooking utensils with her.'

'You're an angel. Shepherds pie? You're making my mouth water.'

'I can probably get you one now. There's a place that stays open all night not far from here.'

'Wait until I've had a shower and got dressed,' he said, collecting his clothes.

'For when you drive down there your warm coat's on that hanger. I got it out for you. It will be chilly on the coast – after dark it could be freezing.'

'Again, you're an angel. Shepherd's pie.'

Tweed had a dreamy look at he left his office.

When Tweed returned, fully dressed, he had a shock. Sitting at her desk was Paula, also fully dressed, wearing the same outfit, complete with leggings and boots, she'd worn in the Black Forest. Her jacket hung from the back of her chair. She gave him a great big smile.

'Good morning, Tweed. You're up early.'

'So are you. And you look fresh as a daisy, a very fresh daisy. Couldn't you sleep after Marler called you?'

'I was awake when he did call. Have you forgotten? I'm like you. I can get by with a few hours' sleep. Monica's gone out to fetch the goodies. I told her I'd look after the phone while she was gone. Trust Monica to know probably the only food shop round here open all night.'

She had just finished speaking when the door opened and Monica walked in carrying a tray. Arranged on it were two large plastic cartons with covers. She placed the tray end on, so one end was in front of Tweed's chair, the other facing it.

'Now how did I know, Paula, you'd be here? Fancy shepherd's pie?'

'I'm so hungry,' Paula told her, 'I could devour it. I hadn't the patience to make myself something at the flat.'

'Bring your chair over this side,' Monica ordered.

She waited until they were settled, facing each other across the desk. Then she bent forward.

'Have to do this properly like they do in posh restaurants,' she announced.

Monica grasped the covers of each carton, paused, then with a flourish she removed the covers. Tweed realized he was famished as an appetizing aroma drifted into the room.

'Thank you, waiter,' said Paula.

'There'll be a pot of tea shortly. Don't wait for it – your food will get cold.'

'I have things to tell you,' Tweed said between mouthfuls.

He told her about his conversations with Philip at the MoD, about the arrival of Alf's mob at the Bunker, about the delivery of the searchlights and star shells. They were still eating when Howard came into the room, a rather dishevelled Howard. His shirt collar was open at the neck, his hair was only roughly brushed, his jaw whiskery.

'Excuse my appearance. I fell asleep for hours in my office. Pardon me, Tweed.' Taking a spoon, he scooped up a helping of shepherd's pie. 'That's very good. Why don't I get service like this?'

'Make passionate love to Monica,' Paula suggested.

'I'll get it for him anyway,' Monica said hastily.

'Howard,' said Tweed, 'we drive down at ten o'clock on the dot this morning. I'll keep you in touch as far as I can.'

'Please do that. I'll be thinking of you all.' He put his hand on Paula's shoulder, squeezed it. 'You take care of yourself.'

'I don't think I'm too bad at doing that. But thank you for the thought.'

'I'm going off now to make myself respectable. Good luck to you all.'

He left quickly. Paula had the impression he was on the verge of getting emotional. As they finished their meal Monica was working away at her desk. She was checking the profiles again.

'Sharon Charlotte Mandeville,' she called out suddenly. 'Charlotte. I suppose she couldn't be Charlie.'

'Tweed thinks she is,' Paula replied. 'I'm not one hundred per cent certain.'

At precisely 10 a.m. two cars drove away from Park Crescent. In the lead car Paula was behind the wheel with Tweed by her side. In the back Newman relaxed, legs crossed as he gazed out of the window.

Behind them Marler drove the second car. Next to him sat Nield and in the back Butler sat very upright, scanning the traffic, looking frequently back through the rear window to see if there was any sign they were being followed. There wasn't.

'Thank you for letting me take the wheel,' Paula said as they left London behind.

'I thought it was your turn,' Tweed replied. 'And I know that you love driving. You realize you're humming a tune?'

'I know. It's such a lovely day. Not a cloud in the sky and the air is so crisp and fresh.'

'It will be a different atmosphere after dark,' Newman commented. 'Might be a bit too fresh for you, Paula.'

'Now don't you get fresh with her,' Tweed joked. 'I think she's safer with you in the back.'

'So she's safe with you in the front?'

'So far she is. I'm not making any promises about later.'

Tweed continued keeping up a bantering conversation. He knew that they wouldn't be able to avoid the growing tension once they had reached the Bunker. For as long as possible he wanted to create a holiday mood. The atmosphere changed when they were driving slowly through Parham.

'Sir Guy's village,' Paula recalled. 'And the poor chap will never again see Irongates. What guts – the way he offered his help when we were going on to the Black Forest. You know something? I could strangle the Phantom with my bare hands. And slowly.'

'He was a remarkable man,' agreed Tweed, 'both in his military career and in business. I share your sentiments, Paula.'

There was a brooding silence in the car as they continued on their way, south through Ashford, then the turn-off from the highway to Ivychurch. Paula had slowed down, was driving carefully as she negotiated the twists and turns of the narrow lanes.

She was approaching the farmhouse where the Bunker was located when she suddenly stopped, staring to her left. Tweed and Newman looked in the same direction.

'What is it?' Tweed asked.

'I think I saw something. Back in a minute.'

Before Tweed could protest she had jumped out of the car and plunged along a track leading to a large copse of evergreen trees, a rare sight on Romney Marsh. Newman dived out to follow her, his Smith & Wesson in his hand.

'What the hell are you doing?' he hissed as he caught up with her.

'I thought the sun flashed off something. Look.' She stopped. 'See where Alf parked all his cabs? That was clever. They can't be seen from the air.'

Newman stared. The cabs were arranged laager fashion, left in a small circle. All were sheltered from observation from the air under great evergreen spreading branches.

'No flies on Alf,' he said.

'I think he's a very astute man. Better get back to the car or Tweed will fret.'

Once inside the car, they told Tweed what they had found. He was intrigued. He agreed that Alf knew exactly what he was doing in any given situation. Paula lowered her window, switched off the engine. She had repeated this performance several times after leaving Parham behind.

'Why do you keep doing this?' Tweed enquired.

'Listening. For any sign of a chopper. Not a whisper. So we can drive on. We're nearly there.'

'I know,' Tweed said quietly.

She was crawling as the farmhouse came into view. Deliberately to give Mrs Carson time to observe them, then to open the automatic gate.

Tweed stared hard at the frmhouse. He kept his expression neutral to conceal his reaction. He spoke to himself without letting anyone hear a word.

'The battlefield.'

50

Paula was amazed by the complexity and the global reach of the communications system which had been created. Mrs Carson was taking her on a conducted tour. They had reached the underground rabbit warren of offices by first descending into the cellar beneath the farmhouse.

'We enter through here,' Mrs Carson explained.

She opened a slablike steel door and they entered a long tunnel. The concrete roof above them was arched, illumination was by a series of fluorescent tubes suspended from above. She opened one door and Paula peered inside. A large number of men in shirtsleeves sat behind computers and radio terminals. All wore earphones and most were scribbling like mad on yellow pads.

'Coded messages coming through from all over the world,' Mrs C. explained.

'I didn't see any masts with aerials when we arrived,' Paula commented.

'Wait till we get back upstairs. Alf and Marler have redesigned the whole reception before you got down to see us. Staggering what those two men – with helpers – achieved. This is the decoding room.'

She opened another door further along the corridor. Inside there were more men in shirtsleeves. They were working at desks with codebooks open while they deciphered messages, writing on more yellow pads.

Paula noticed that in both rooms no one had looked up when they stood in the doorways, such was the concentration on the work.

Mrs C. led Paula into another tunnel, running at right angles to the main one. Opening another door they peered inside a vast canteen. Paula recognized Mrs Payne, wearing whites and preparing large quantities of food. Guiding Paula further down the tunnel, Mrs C. opened yet another door. Beyond was a large, very clean and modern washroom.

'I think you've seen enough to give you the general idea,' Mrs C. decided. 'If you stay down here too long and you're not used to it you get a feeling of claustrophobia. And the rattle of the teleprinters gets on your nerves.'

'How can Mrs Payne possibly cope on her own?'

'She won't have to. Other cooks on the staff come on duty shortly. She was preparing lunch for you and the people who drove down in your two cars.'

'And all this converted out of what was once a major smugglers' haunt, ages ago.'

'Yes. And the main tunnel extended to close to the sea. They must have worked like madmen with the most primitive of tools.'

'Imagine the number of casks of brandy which must have travelled along these tunnels at one time.'

'Makes me feel tiddly just to think of it,' said Mrs C. leading them back into the farmhouse's cellar. 'Now I've shown you the system I can get back to reassembling my machine-pistol. I dismantled it this morning to clean it.'

'Machine-pistol?' Paula queried as they mounted the steps and arrived back in the farmhouse.

'Yes. Tweed phoned me earlier to warn me what's coming. It will be all hands to the pumps. I was trained by that nice man, Sarge, at the mansion in Surrey. Wonder why they call him Sarge?'

'He was a sergeant at one time, SAS I believe.'

Tweed sat drinking tea by himself at the large old wooden table in the living room. He put down his cup when they arrived.

'Well, Paula, what do you think?'

'They have much more space down there than in the second building they normally occupy in Park Crescent. Would it be an idea to keep them down here?'

'We're considering just that – if we survive tonight.'

'Of course we will,' scoffed Mrs C. 'We'll blow hell out of them.'

Paula stared at Mrs C. Plump-figured, her apple-cheeked face was smiling. She was actually looking forward to what was coming.

'I'll go now,' she said.

'Put your coat on,' called out Mrs C., disappearing into another room. 'It's pretty nippy out there.'

She must have eyes in the back of her head, Paula thought. She was slipping on her coat as she went out into the farmyard. Newman, standing at the entrance to a narrow passage between two old barns, beckoned to her. She followed him, emerged at the other end into the open. She gazed around. As on her previous visit, she thought she had never seen bleaker terrain.

To the south, until the ground belonging to the farm terminated at a hedge, the land was almost completely flat, covered with miserable tufts of grass. Like a desert, she said to herself. A chill wind, freezing her face, made her glad she'd taken Mrs C.'s advice.

'This way,' said Newman.

He was leading her to a copse of very tall leafless deciduous trees. Thick, black, skeletal branches extended out way above her. Marler was standing next to a large thigh-high wooden box which had a pyramid of thick wires over it. From the tip of the pyramid a pulley was attached. A cable, extended high up, was looped over two heavy branches, then its remaining length dropped to the ground. Marler was wearing motoring gloves.

'What on earth is all this?' Paula asked.

'Observation point. One of Alf's Gulf War veterans said we needed one. And that box he's standing by is like one of those cat's cradles window cleaners are suspended from to clean the windows of high buildings. Care for a ride up?'

'On my own? Who made the box?'

'Alf, with the help of Marler and some of Alf's men. When this place was built the builders left behind a workhouse complete with tools in one of those barns. And you won't be on your own. I'm coming up with you.'

Newman had a powerful pair of binoculars slung around his neck. From the pocket of his weather-proof jacket he produced Beck's mobile, loaned to him by Tweed. Marler had his own mobile suspended from his neck.

'Communication,' said Newman. 'All aboard.'

He helped her climb inside the cradle, then joined her. There was plenty of room for both of them. She heard Marler shout to one of Alf's men to come and give a hand. Hypnotized, she watched the two men, both with gloved hands, haul on the wire cable. She gripped the side of the cradle with both hands as it began its ascent. It moved upwards faster than she had anticipated, swayed a little. She gritted her teeth, refused to look down. Newman put an arm round her waist.

'Safe as houses.'

'I'll have to take your word for that.'

She experienced an unexpected change of mood as the ascent continued. As a vast panorama of Romney Marsh spread out she experienced a sense of exhilaration. They were very high up when their cradle stopped moving. She stared at a large wooden platform, constructed of wooden planks, situated between heavy branches.

'Time to disembark,' said Newman. 'Don't look down.'

He helped her to leave the cradle. Then she was standing on the platform. Her nervousness disappeared as she gazed into the distance.

'You can see far out into the Channel.'

'That's the idea. Like to use my binoculars? I'll hold on to you,' he said, clasping her round the waist.

'I can see a ship sailing up the Channel.' She focused the binoculars. 'I can read its name. The *Mexicali*. This is wonderful.'

'Get the idea?'

'We'll see them coming. No, it will be dark.'

'So we use night glasses. And we have communication.' He took out Beck's mobile. 'Marler, they're here.'

'*What? Where!*'

'Just joking.'

'Bob, don't do that again. I was about to raise a general alarm.'

'Sorry. That was stupid of me.' He looked at Paula. 'At least it proves the communication works. Time to go down.'

When they had climbed back into the cradle Newman called Marler on the mobile. The two men waiting on the ground released the wire cable from a large iron hook driven deep into the ground they had wrapped the end round. As it descended Paula noticed a thin black cable attached to the tree trunk. She pointed to it.

'What is that?'

'The cable from the underground complex up to a camouflaged aerial at the top of this tree. We had a normal thirty-foot mast sticking up out of the ground, thought it was too prominent, so we substituted that.'

'Clever.'

The cradle landed gently and Paula stepped out with Newman. She was surprised to realize her legs felt stiff. With tension, she assumed. They next showed her how to operate one of the compact mobile searchlights which manoeuvred easily on thick rubber tyres. At Newman's suggestion she aimed it at the copse of evergreens concealing the taxi cabs. She switched it on, was startled by the intensity of the device even in daylight. The evergreens glowed in the glare. She switched if off quickly. Mrs C. appeared.

'I've slowed down lunch,' she called out. 'You're busy. Tweed said he'd like you to join him. He's way over by the perimeter.'

It was quite a walk over the open ground but Paula welcomed it. A chance to stretch her legs, get them moving. Tweed stood, hands in his coat pockets, waiting for them.

'See anything wrong with this hedge?' he asked her.

'No,' she replied, after studying it. 'Just a very prickly hedge.'

'Very prickly,' he told her. 'We've entwined coils of barbed wire inside the whole length of hedge round the perimeter. The wire was painted the same colour as the twigs. Anyone trying to get through it will be ripped to pieces.'

'Diabolical,' she said.

'We're playing for keeps,' Tweed said grimly. 'Time for lunch, I'm sure. Let's get moving. I'm hungry again.'

The afternoon dragged by on sluggish legs. Waiting was always the worst part. Weapons had been distributed. Everyone was issued with a large shoulder-slung canvas holdall, packed with deadly material.

'I'll take a machine-pistol and extra ammo,' Paula said at one point to Newman.

'You've got your Browning and loads in the holdall.'

'Have you lost your memory, Bob? I used a machine-pistol back at Schluchsee to take out three thugs emerging from a side door of that *Psycho* house.'

Paula was given her machine-pistol. Unloading it, she went outside to practise, to get the feel of it again. In the late afternoon it was still a brilliantly sunny day. Tweed and Newman joined her, strolled across the flatlands.

Without warning a low-flying light aircraft appeared from the direction of the Channel. It swooped low over them, circled as Tweed looked up. Marler came running out, gripping his Armalite. The plane flew off inland, vanished.

'You think it was them?' Newman asked.

'I'm sure it was,' Tweed replied. 'Lucky you weren't up the tree, Marler, and that the mobile searchlights are hidden in a barn. So it won't help them – the fact that the passenger had a camera. I suggest we keep under cover inside the farmhouse.'

Night came suddenly like a black menace. Inside the farmhouse Mrs C. served supper at six o'clock. To her disappointment they ate only half of what was on their plates, except for Paula, who was famished again. By now they had all been issued with mobile phones which would be worn slung from their necks. The mobiles had special amplifiers, so everyone would hear what was said no matter how much noise was generated by weapon fire. The amplifiers had been designed by the boffins in the basement at Park Crescent weeks before.

'Don't forget,' Newman warned, 'that the whole perimeter is split up into sectors A, B, C, D, E, F and G.'

'That's the third time you've told us that,' Paula complained.

'I want you to remember it,' Newman told her.

'We ought to have had music to see us through the evening,' said Marler.

'What would you have suggested?' enquired Newman.

'The end of the *1812 Overture*. The crash of the guns.'

'I don't think that's funny,' snapped Paula.

'Wasn't meant to be,' Marler rapped back.

Tweed again checked his watch. He pursed his lips, glanced at everyone round the table.

'That's the fifth time you've checked the time,' said Paula.

'Who's counting?' Newman snapped back.

'I am.'

'It's nine o'clock,' Tweed said in a bored voice.

He had just spoken when Mike, one of Alf's Gulf War veterans, got up from the table. He put on a short sheepskin coat. His night glasses were slung round his neck.

'Time I went up that tree. It is the observation point. Come and haul me up to heaven.'

Newman and Marler stood up, accompanied Mike outside. Paula, on edge, frowned.

'He'll freeze to death up that tree. It's too early.

'Never too early,' said Alf, who rarely spoke. 'And he'll be all right. Once trained for three months in the Arctic.'

'I could put the radio on,' Mrs C. said brightly. 'That is, if anyone wants it on.'

No one wanted the radio. The silence was oppressive. But the radio squawking away would be even more irksome. Tweed again checked his watch. Paula bit her lip to stop herself protesting. With Tweed it was not nerves – he was probably the coolest person sitting at the table. But he knew how time could suddenly flash by.

Paula got up, went outside. The moon was high and brilliant she was thankful to see. They would need its pallid light to detect signs of movement. She took a deep breath, almost felt giddy. The temperature had dropped below zero. She hurried inside again.

'What is it like out there?' Tweed asked casually. 'I know I could find out for myself, but why should both of us freeze?' he asked humorously.

'It's godawful cold. But the moon is up and casting plenty of light.'

'Couldn't be better. Just what I ordered from the weather man.'

'Any more coffee for anyone?' asked Mrs C.

'Have some, Paula,' Newman urged. 'Keep you alert.'

'For your information, *Mr* Newman, I have never felt more alert.'

'Suit yourself.'

'That's exactly what I propose to do. Thank you, Mrs Carson, but I've had enough for now.'

'It's fairly near ten o'clock,' Tweed announced, after checking his watch. 'Bob, could you describe again – for everyone's benefit – the small advanced landing craft your American friend showed you when you visited that naval base in the States six months ago?'

'Very hush-hush,' Newman began. 'Had to sign a document that under no circumstances would I publish anything. These vessels, for use by the SEALs, are about the size of a small country bus – but they have no roof. They're amphibious, very stable on water. But also when they reach land huge wheels like snow tyres project underneath the craft. Driver just pulls a lever. On land they can move at about forty miles an hour.'

'How many occupants?' asked Tweed.

'Maximum of ten SEALs per craft. Three doors on either side – so they can get out fast. On land the powerful engine makes a gentle purring sound.'

'We have to call them something,' Tweed said. He gazed into space. 'Got it. Something that's at home in water and on land. Crabs. That's what we'll call them.' He pressed a button on his mobile. 'Tweed here. If the enemy has landing craft we're going to call them crabs.'

'What's that?' Mike's voice queried. 'Got it. Crabs. Like the name, matey.'

He came back on the line less than five minutes later. A cool voice. Everyone had switched on their mobiles.

'They're coming now. Enormous ruddy fleet. Stretches back miles down the Channel. Wait a minute.' At the table they all sat upright in silence. 'Now I can just make out a ruddy great aircraft carrier, big as a football pitch. Hang on, one warship well ahead is turning this way, belting towards the coast at a rate of knots. Hang on a mo.' Round the table they seemed to wait forever this time. A crackle on the mobiles. 'Looks like they're coming for us now. Lowering crabs over the side Hang on.'

'How many crabs?' asked Tweed.

'Three in the sea now. I think that's it. Three crabs coming.'

'I suggest we all take up battle positions now,' said Tweed. 'Do not forget my earlier order. No one opens fire until – or unless – they start shooting at us, or try to break through the wired hedge. I want to be able to say later they opened hostilities first.'

'Matey, another crab lowered,' Mike warned. 'Following the first three heading for the shore now. Fast.'

'That's forty men,' Tweed said coldly. 'We're outnumbered. So the first shot they fire, we all open up. When we see a target.'

'Matey, another crab lowered over the side. Now following the others.'

'Fifty men, then,' Tweed said. 'Same instruction as before . . .'

512

51

Paula was first outside. She had slipped on her warm coat earlier while Mike was still talking. She wore surgical gloves. They'd keep out a bit of the cold, but she needed flexible fingers to press triggers. Over one shoulder hung her shoulder bag with her Browning inside, over the other was looped the heavy canvas holdall. She'd grabbed her machine-pistol and extra ammo off a couch.

Mrs C. followed her. She had the same equipment. She caught up with Paula and chuckled, brandishing her weapon.

'Used this to shoot rabbits. They were overrunning us. Men are bigger than rabbits. We're both Sector A.'

'Centre of the hedge where they'll probably attack,' Paula replied drily. 'Some kind of a compliment, I suppose.'

'I'll be with you,' said Newman as he joined them. 'Paula, you take A. You took your searchlight out there earlier?'

'Of course.'

They walked quickly across the flat earth, but refrained from running. With what they were carrying that could be fatal. Paula had lost her edginess. She was now cool, determined, alert. In the moonlight they could see the distant hedge they were advancing towards clearly. It had a blurred look at night, more like a wall. Paula revelled in the ice-cold air. It had become stuffy inside the farmhouse.

To their left and right shadowy silhouettes of men moving quickly were ahead of them. Alf's mob were swift on their feet. Hunched forward with the weights they were carrying, they reminded Paula of the opening scene in *Silas Marner*. There a shadowy figure moving through the night had been laden down.

'Rabbits,' said Newman, who had heard Mrs C.'s earlier remark. 'That means rabbit holes, risk of twisted ankles. We'd better be careful.'

'No need,' Mrs C. replied, moving quickly. 'They're all in that southeast corner – and beyond the hedge.'

Tweed was the only man who had not joined the relentless march to the southern hedge. After putting on his coat, he had gone out and climbed a wooden staircase Mrs C. had shown him. It was attached to the side of the farmhouse and led to a platform at the top. Standing on it, he could see clearly over the top of the roof. It did not give him the panoramic view from the observation post, but it did provide an uninterrupted view over the hedge and Romney Marsh beyond. He focused his night glasses on the hedge.

'Matey, four crabs landed on beach. Crossing it. Heading inland at speed towards us. Crab number five now beaching . . .'

'Everyone,' said Tweed into the mobile slung close to his mouth, 'get into position as soon as you can. You heard the latest report. Keep your heads down.'

Tweed, who normally mistrusted mobiles, thought the communication system was excellent. Everyone could hear him. Everyone could hear the reports from the observation post. Knowledge was power. Could make all the difference to the outcome.

'Matey, four crabs approaching. Number five coming up behind. Fast.'

Tweed refocused his glasses to see a low ridge on the marsh. Within a minute he saw four of the strange vehicles poking their snouts over the ridge. They came over it. They were advancing towards Sectors A. B and

514

C. A frontal attack. Just like the Americans. Get up and go.

'Matey, count ten men in each crab. Number five a weirdo. Seems only to have the driver. No other men aboard it.'

Tweed frowned. He could see No. 5 now. Heading for the centre of the hedge. The first four crabs stopped suddenly. About one hundred feet from the hedge. Large men, uniformed, wearing helmets, jumped out from the four stationary crabs, spreading out, weapons gripped in their hands. No. 5 continued advancing, stopped no more than thirty feet from the hedge. What the devil was its purpose?

'Everyone in position?' Tweed asked into his mobile.

'Yes . . . Yes . . . Yes . . .'

The stream of replies continued. Paula's voice first, Mrs C.'s next, then a jumble as confirmations overlaid each other. Tweed was satisfied that everyone was where they should be. He spoke into his mobile.

'They've left their crabs. Forty men advancing. Objective appears to be Sectors A, B and C. Close in on those sectors.'

Any moment now, he thought. Would the invaders open fire? Or would they try to keep advancing through the hedge? He couldn't guess this one.

Sharon was driving the limo at manic speed. She had just left Ashford behind. She accelerated. The speedometer climbed. By her side Denise Chatel was petrified. She crouched back in her seat. Sharon sat very erect.

'Where are we going?' Denise asked.

'To check that a key installation has been destroyed.'

'What key installation?'

'Shut your stupid mouth.'

515

'But where are we going?' Denise repeated.

'If you want to gab, we'll gab. For starters, how did you get hold of that file I found you reading?'

'You sent me to fetch you a file. I must have picked up the wrong one.'

'Crap.'

'It was all about the investigation into my father's death in a so-called car crash in Virginia.'

'It was a red file.'

'I found it on your desk.'

'You're lying. Most of my files are green. The one I sent you to get was on my desk. You poked your nose into my filing cabinet. I'd forgotten to lock it. That red file was in front of the cabinet.'

'I don't know what you're talking about. And I did read some of that file, which reported doubts as to whether the so-called car crash was an accident.'

'You shut your mouth! If I didn't need both hands for the wheel I'd slap your idiotic face. And,' Sharon sneered, 'you've no idea how stupid you look in that riding outfit.'

'You wouldn't give me time to change. Look out!'

Sharon had swung off the highway where a signpost pointed to Ivychurch. Before leaving she had attached to the dashboard a map showing the route to the Bunker, a map radioed to her from Washington. Instead of a main road, she was now driving along a winding lane at speed. Denise had called out because as they rounded a bend a single light rushed towards them. The motor-cyclist was only moving at thirty miles an hour. Before Sharon could brake the limo swept past, its side brushing the motorcycle. The machine toppled over, hurling the rider into a ditch. Denise just had time to stare back – to see the inert body in the ditch, the machine on its side, its wheels still revolving futilely.

'We may have killed him,' Denise gasped.

'Killed who?'

'That motorcyclist you hit.'

'What motorcyclist are you talking about? Must be your imagination. I haven't seen anyone.'

'You're dangerous.'

'Don't talk to me like that,' Sharon responded, her voice and her expression now very calm.

The eerie silence of the night on the Romney Marsh was broken only by a single eerie sound. The purring of the engines which had not been turned off, the engines of the motionless crabs. To Paula it sounded like the purring of some monstrous and evil cat. She was crouched down, as were all the others. She had no idea what was happening and the tension was growing.

It was broken by one powerful shout of one word. She thought the American accent was Texan.

'Barrage!'

The night came apart. A thunderous fusillade of gunfire coming from automatic weapons shot at the same moment caused her to press her head into the earth. The commander of the invading SEALs was a Texan. He was also not a man to take any chances – even though there was no sign of life from the invisible installation. It was the American way – equivalent to the battleships far out at sea which had once bombarded the Vietnam jungle, killing no one.

The fusillade had been aimed at the middle of the fields beyond the farmhouse. The rain of bullets spurted up tufts of grass, pellets of soil. The barrage, deafening, continued for a short time, then stopped as abruptly as it had started. The SEALs were reloading.

From his platform Tweed observed all this, realized

517

that there had been no casualties among his own troops, who were too far forward. He spoke quickly into his mobile.

'Shoot any target you can see.'

Marler, stationed in Sector C, to Paula's right, aimed his Armalite. A heavily built SEAL, confident he could take on anybody, swaggered forward as he reloaded his automatic rifle. Marler's bullet hit him dead centre in the chest. The SEAL stopped, let out a strangled yell, dropped, lay still.

Alf aimed his automatic rifle at two SEALs standing too close together. He fired twice. Both men sank to the ground. Then a fresh fusillade was let loose, aimed at the same area as its predecessor. More grass tufts, more soil jumped into the air. Tweed spoke again.

'Wait till they've stopped . . .'

The Texan commander, who believed in barrages, as opposed to any individual shooting, waited for his men to reload. One six-foot SEAL had had enough. The guys should be breaking through the friggin' hedge. He had reloaded quickly. Now he ran forward, plunged into and across the hedge. His body fell onto the hedge, onto the concealed barbed wire. He screamed, then stopped moving.

Mrs C., close to Paula, saw an even taller, heavier SEAL rushing forward. He'd realized he could use the prone body as a bridge. Mrs C. hissed at Paula.

'Use your searchlight. Quick.'

A second SEAL followed the first, with the same idea in mind – they had a bridge. Paula swivelled the light, aimed it just above the prone body, now dripping blood. The incredibly powerful glare shone at the moment the first SEAL was treading on the body, standing upright. Mrs C. let rip with her machine-pistol. The SEAL remained upright briefly, his arms shot up, releasing his weapon, which curved in an arc, landing on the far side of the hedge. Mrs C. continued blasting, bullets thudded into the second SEAL. The first SEAL toppled over backwards as the SEAL behind him staggered, moved a few steps as though drunk, then sagged to the ground.

'Barrage!' roared the Texan.

'Cease fire for a moment,' Tweed ordered.

'Barrage!' shouted the Texan.

This new fusillade came closer, but it was still a dozen yards beyond where the defenders lay still. Three more SEALs, who had ignored their commander's order, rushed forward, guns blazing, to use the prone body as a bridge. Mrs C.'s machine-pistol chattered as they ran into the glare of Paula's searchlight. All three fell beyond the hedge, tumbling on top of each other.

On his platform, Tweed was intrigued by the motion-less crab – No. 5. Then it struck him what it might contain. He spoke.

'Marler, bomb that forward crab. Everybody flatten yourselves.'

Paula glanced to her right as Marler glanced at her. While he felt in his holdall for a grenade with his right hand he saluted her with his left hand, grinning. She nodded her head, acknowledging. Then she wriggled herself a couple of yards closer to Mrs C. She was moving away from the glaring searchlight, an obvious target.

She glanced sideways again at Marler, realizing he'd had something in his left hand when he'd saluted. It was a wide-mouthed short-barrelled pistol. She had forgotten the star shells.

As the fresh fusillade died away Butler and Nield, both holding machine-pistols, suddenly stood up. Marler waited. Beyond the hedge four SEALs, not too far apart, were reloading. Nield and Butler opened fire, swinging

519

their weapons slightly. All of the four SEALs dropped, lay still. Marler watched Butler and Nield as they kissed the earth, waited. This was the moment.

Marler jumped to his feet. His right arm, holding the grenade, swung in a high arc, then he flattened himself. In the glare of Paula's searchlight Tweed saw, from his platform, the grenade land inside crab No. 5. A second later Paula's searchlight went out, hit by a SEAL's bullet.

Synchronizing with the flight of the grenade, Marler began firing star shells, his body still flat with the earth. White, and then green bursts, illuminated the scene from high up. The grenade detonated. The world went wild. The crab burst as a tremendous explosion echoed across the marsh. Tweed saw between ten and fifteen SEALs hurled into the air, thrown sideways over the marsh. Where the crab had been was a deep hole. The star shell illumination was blotted out by the flash of the explosion.

As Tweed had guessed, No. 5 had been filled with explosives intended for the destruction of the complex. More star shells burst high above the marsh, green, red and white. They showed Tweed a scene of utter devastation. Bodies lay everywhere. A few injured SEALs staggered, limped towards the two crabs still intact, their engines still purring, the only sound in a sudden deathly hush.

Tweed, who had been counting enemy casualties as far as he was able to, estimated more than half the enemy's attack force had been wiped out. Men were carrying injured comrades towards the remaining two undamaged crabs. There were no more shouts from the Texan commander – if he was still alive. Tweed watched for a few minutes longer. There was no more sign of aggression on the part of the SEALs. Those who had survived were concentrating on limping, hobbling, dragging themselves to board one of the intact crabs. Other SEALs, who had taken no punishment, were carrying their injured and dead comrades to the second intact crab.

'Cease fire,' Tweed ordered. 'Marler, shout at the top of your voice the two words I just uttered.'

'*Cease fire!*' Marler bellowed.

His words galvanized the mood of the enemy. The SEALs moved more quickly, more confidently. Two came up to the hedge, began wrestling free the prone SEAL impaled on the wire. Paula turned her head away. When she looked again the body had gone but that part of the hedge was tainted a dark red colour.

The next sound she heard was an increase in the purring noise of the crabs' engines. From his platform Tweed saw the two crabs turn round, start to move away, circumnavigating the enormous hole left when crab No. 5 had blown up. Tweed still waited to be sure. The crabs disappeared beyond the slight ridge.

'Matey, they're going home, heading for the beach and then their mother ship.'

'Everyone return to base – with your equipment,' Tweed ordered.

Tweed, Paula and Newman stood on their own in the open air a little distance from the farmhouse. Everyone else had gone down into the washroom under the farmhouse. Mrs C. was the last to leave.

'Well at least the staff stayed under ground, as they were ordered to. Think I'll go down and reassure them. They must have felt and heard the explosion when that ammunition dump inside the crab went up.'

'Good idea,' said Tweed.

'I think I'd sooner stay out here in the fresh air for a bit,' Paula said.

'Me too,' Newman agreed.

'Sensible,' said Tweed. 'After a period of tension –

mental and physical – it helps to have a period of relaxation. Doing nothing, saying nothing.'

They stood quietly. No one spoke. A couple of times Paula walked a few paces backwards and forwards to stretch her stiff legs. For once she welcomed the dead silence of Romney Marsh. It was peace. Then her mouth tightened.

'I can hear a car coming at speed. Not more, please.'

A black stretch limo, with Sharon behind the wheel, braked with an emergency stop, inches from the closed gate. Newman sighed, ran to the farmhouse, reached inside the front door, pressed the switch which opened the gate. He ran back outside. Sharon was turning the car, ended up with it pointing back to London. Then she alighted, walked towards them.

She was wearing a mink coat and slung from her right shoulder was the largest white leather handbag Paula had ever seen. It was like a huge envelope. Paula blinked as Denise followed her. She was still clad in riding kit. Most peculiar. Her knee-length boots gleamed in the moonlight. To Paula, the silence suddenly seemed menacing as Sharon continued walking towards them. She stopped about fifteen feet from them.

'What brings you down here, Charlie?' Tweed began.

'*Charlie!*' gasped Denise.

'Yes, Charlie,' replied Sharon, moving a few paces, putting space between herself and Denise. 'My middle name's Charlotte, as Tweed was clever enough – and foolish enough – to discover. Don't you reach for that gun, Newman,' she snapped.

As she spoke, Sharon's right hand emerged from her handbag holding a Magnum revolver. Paula gazed at the large weapon, surprised that Sharon's small hand could level it so easily. She swivelled it in an arc between Tweed, Paula and Newman, covering them all.

'Spread out your hands,' she screamed suddenly.

'Well away from your bodies – or I'll shoot you in the stomachs. You'll take a long painful time to die. Such a long-painful time . . .'

They spread their hands, stretched them outwards. To Paula the end of the Magnum's muzzle looked like the mouth of a cannon.

'The report in that red file said my father was killed on the orders of Charlie,' Denise screeched.

Sharon slipped closer to Denise. With a movement almost too quick to follow she slashed at Denise's face with the barrel of her gun. Denise moved her head quickly. The barrel barely scraped her but she slipped on a smooth stone, toppled backwards, saved her head striking the ground with her hands. Then she sat there, her right leg turned at an awkward angle.

'I've twisted my leg,' she yelped, rubbing her boot with one hand.

'Stay down there,' Sharon snarled. 'A twisted leg won't kill you. I will.'

The Magnum had instantly been swivelled back to cover the trio with outstretched hands. She's quick, too damned quick for me to haul out my Smith & Wesson, Newman thought. Before I grabbed the butt all three of us would be dead. Sharon knew exactly what she was doing. She stood too far away to be rushed, but near enough to shoot them all.

'I'll ask you again, Charlie,' Tweed said quietly. 'What brought you down here?'

'To make sure your bloody stupid communications centre has been destroyed.'

'It hasn't. The Americans who tried it are on their way back to their task force ship, those who survived.'

'You're lying! You always lie! Damn your soul to hell, Tweed,' she went on screaming with fury. 'You always lie, you friggin' little nobody! You're trying to trick me. Me! Of all people!'

Newman simply gazed at her in disbelief. An extra-ordinary transformation had taken place. Her face was so contorted with insane rage she was hardly recognizable. Jekyll had become Hyde. She suddenly moved sideways on to a small elevated piece of ground. It gave her greater command of the situation. Denise, moaning, still sitting, was rubbing her hand over the boot on her twisted leg.

'You said, Charlie,' Tweed remarked, 'a moment ago, "Me! Of all people!" Where do you think you're going? As President in the Oval Office?' he suggested sarcastically.

'That's exactly where I'm going, you not-so-clever little nobody! You think I'm going to let any of you stop me? You'll all be dead and buried while I'm starting my campaign to be senator. I won't let any of you get in my way! Hear me! I won't!'

Her face was still hideously contorted, still hardly recognizable. She kept swivelling the Magnum to cover them. She was breathing deeply now, working herself up to press the trigger.

'You killed my dear father,' Denise bleated.

'Sure I gave the order to waste your late father. Another friggin' nobody who was getting in my way. Nobody gets in my way and survives!'

Paula had dropped her eyes briefly. The mound Sharon stood on had a rusty grating like a drain cover. She raised her eyes quickly. Tweed had glanced at Denise's right hand. It was levering something from inside her boot.

'Can't we compromise in some way, Sharon?' he suggested.

'So it's gone back to Sharon now, has it? You're trembling in your shoes, aren't you, Tweed! And with good reason!'

Distracted by her venom for Tweed, Sharon had

Epilogue

It was early morning in London. Some time after dawn the sky was once more a cloudless blue. Very little traffic at that early hour. This time Marler, with Butler and Nield, had taken the lead car, had gone on ahead.

Newman, behind the wheel, slowed to a crawl as he approached the entrance to Park Crescent. Tweed was beside him, with Paula in the back. Newman turned the corner into Park Crescent, driving at no miles per hour. He continued crawling forward. The left-hand side of the windscreen was blurred with mist. The shot pierced the glass, the windscreen crackled. The passenger by his side slumped.

Stopping the car, Newman jumped out. A second rifle shot rang out. Paula, crouched down a few seconds earlier, had left the car, followed by the man who had crouched beside her. They were just in time to see the figure perched on the roof above their entrance rear up, as though subjected to a high-voltage electric charge. Then the figure plunged down vertically, landing on the steps leading up.

'Not on my doorstep,' said Tweed, running forward with Paula.

Newman had got there first. He waited for them. The body of a man wearing a balaclava lay very still. Newman bent down, checked the neck pulse, shook his head. He then took hold of the balaclava, gently pulled it back to reveal the face.

Rupert Strangeways stared up at them, the eyes open, the mouth twisted. Paula had the grisly impression he was sneering at them. Newman stepped back as Marler, who had raced round the Crescent, arrived.

'And I thought it was Basil,' said Paula. 'The Phantom.'

'Good shot,' said Newman.

Marler's bullet, fired from his Armalite, had made a smudged red hole in Rupert's forehead. George, their doorkeeper and guard, came out of the front door. He stared down.

'My Gawd, who is that?'

'A phantom,' said Tweed. 'Cover it with a sheet. We don't want passers-by gawking.' He ran upstairs, with Paula at his heels. 'I must phone Roy Buchanan at once, ask him to send an ambulance.'

Inside his office he stared at the empty desk on his left. The cover was still on Monica's computer, her chair pushed under her desk.

'Where is Monica?'

Paula picked up a hastily scribbled note. It was an apology from Monica. Despite her allergy to shellfish, she'd indulged in a shrimp cocktail for supper. It had upset her and she wouldn't be in for the day.

'I'll call Buchanan, explain the position,' she said. 'And I'll sit at Monica's desk, look after the phone today.'

A few minutes later Newman and Marler came in. Newman sat down while he explained.

'Marler and I think it best to leave the car you travelled up in where it is until Buchanan arrives. Then he can see the dummy Tweed for himself. Rupert's bullet would have hit you in your head – if you'd been sitting beside me. The bullet penetrated the dummy and is lodged in the padded head rest I reinforced.'

They had created the dummy to look like Tweed before leaving the Bunker. Mrs C. had helped – supplying pillows to pad out a jacket she had borrowed from one of the staff. The upper part of the top pillow had been squeezed into the size of a head. Marler had provided a pair of horn-rimmed glasses with plain lenses he'd used in the past for disguise. Mrs C. had used safety pins to attach the glasses to where Tweed's eyes would have been. As a final precaution, Newman had carried Mrs C.'s hair spray. He had stopped the car a short distance before they reached Park Crescent, had used the hair spray on the dummy's side of the windscreen to blur the image.

'Well, it worked,' said Marler. 'And we were right in thinking the Phantom would be waiting for Tweed's arrival here. Now, I'm going up to my office.'

'Now, I'll make us all some coffee,' said Paula.

Buchanan, with Sergeant Warden, his wooden-faced assistant, was standing in Tweed's office fifteen minutes later. Looking out of the window, Paula saw two men carrying a stretcher with the body covered with a sheet. They hoisted it inside an ambulance.

Buchanan listened without interruption while Tweed and Newman explained what had happened. They kept their statements terse and made no reference to either Sharon or Denise.

'Marler is waiting in his office upstairs,' Tweed went on, 'so you can take a statement from him.'

'I prefer it that way,' Buchanan agreed. 'Having a separate interview with him. I have only one question. Who fired first?'

'Rupert Strangeways did,' Newman confirmed. 'Marler will tell you he was crouched with his Armalite behind his parked car. It was only when he saw the muzzle flash from Strangeways' shot that he located where he was.'

'Glad you left the Tweed dummy in the other car,' Buchanan said. 'Before we go and have a word with Marler we'll take a look at that, then leave a couple of policemen on guard. We'll get moving.' He paused by the door before opening it. 'Tweed, you'd like to know, I'm sure, that bullet I sent by courier to René Lasalle not only matches the bullet which killed our late PM, it also matches the bullet which killed that German, Heinz Keller. Otto Kuhlmann, your friend and the police chief from Wiesbaden, happened to be visiting Lasalle. He brought the Keller bullet. That also matches. Rupert Strangeways was not only a hired hit man – he was also a mass-murderer.'

'It's dreadful,' Paula said when the policeman had gone, 'when we realize Rupert also murdered his own father in Freiburg.'

'As cold and greedy as they come,' replied Tweed. 'Doubtless he hoped to inherit his father's fortune. I have a feeling he would have done no such thing when the will is read. Changing the subject, I think Denise will keep quiet.'

'She promised me she would off her own bat when we left her at that flat in Belgravia,' said Paula.

She was referring to the fact that they had driven back from the Bunker in three cars. Wearing gloves – to avoid fingerprints – Newman had driven the stretch limo, with Denise by his side. In the car following him, Tweed was behind the wheel with Paula and Newman as passengers. Behind them, Marler had driven the third car, which contained Butler and Nield.

There had been no one about when Newman dropped off Denise at her Belgravia flat. He had then driven the limo to Mayfair and, unseen, had parked it in a mews. He had then transferred to the car with the dummy while Tweed and Paula had crouched low in the rear.

Howard then stormed into the office, his normal self. Wearing a grey Chester Barrie suit, he was freshly shaved, pink-faced and with neatly brushed hair. He assumed his favourite position, sitting in an armchair, one leg perched over an arm.

'Sensational news from Washington. Morgenstern has resigned as Secretary of State. His action has hit the States like a thunderbolt. He's holding a press conference later today.'

'That's due to Tweed's final interview with him,' Paula said.

'Really?' Howard stared at her before going on. 'And thank you, Tweed, for calling me on your mobile on your way back here in the car. Just afterwards Philip, your naval pal at the MoD, phoned me. That American task force has left the Channel, is steaming back at a rate of knots towards the States. Another sensation. A rumour is circulating the US that a SEALs landing exercise went horribly wrong. Dummy ammunition should have been issued. SEALs were divided into two forces, one attack, one defence. But the ammo issued was the real thing, due to some cock-up. SEALs have twenty-five dead. Combined with Morgenstern's action, all hell has broken loose.' Howard jumped up. 'Must go. Tweed, we will have lunch at my club.'

Paula had answered the phone just before Howard finished. She waited until he had left, her expression bleak.

'Tweed, you have visitors downstairs. Ed Osborne and Chuck Venacki. What shall I do?'

Newman reached inside his jacket. He was grabbing his Smith & Wesson.

'Don't do that, Bob,' said Tweed. 'Paula, ask them to come up.'

Ed Osborne entered, quietly and smiling. Behind him Chuck Venacki was also smiling. Tweed stood up, shook their hands, invited them to sit down.

'Everyone here,' he began as he sat down, 'must treat what they listen to as top secret for ever. Meet Ed Osborne who, as far as he could, kept me informed about what Ronstadt was up to.'

'My mother was English,' Ed said, his manner now pleasant. 'So I always had a soft spot for this country, totally disagreed with their plan. But the man you should thank is Chuck Venacki, my confidant. He put his life on the line, travelling round with Jake Ronstadt, keeping me in touch when he could.'

'We have you both to thank,' said Tweed.

'That's nice. I can't linger. Felt I just had to come over to see you. Washington is in a state of chaos. The Ambassador here has been recalled – he'll be replaced. And I'm resigning as Deputy Director of the CIA. There's a new director at Langley. Old friend of Cord Dillon's. Guess who's going to get my job.' He stood up. 'Great to see you all survived.' He went round, shook everyone by the hand. 'Take care. I'm off with Chuck.'

'I'm staggered,' Paula said when they had gone. 'But I suspected you had someone on the inside. Incidentally, who was the Phantom's paymaster?'

'Paymistress. Sharon, I'm sure. She must have disguised her voice, phoned Rupert about the targets. She'd guard her identity.'

'And I've wondered about a coincidence. Sharon's parents were killed in a car crash. Years later poor Denise's parents are killed in a car crash on the same bridge.'

'I'm sure Sharon gave orders for Denise's father to be murdered by staging a fake collision on that same old bridge in Virginia. The bridge would linger in her memory as a place where accidents did happen. Never prove it, of course.'

'Another thing,' Paula went on. 'Monica struggled like mad to fill in those mysterious gaps in Ed Osborne's life. She never could find out where Osborne was when he seemed to disappear off the face of the earth for longish periods. Where on earth was he during those long disappearances?'

'That,' said Tweed, 'is something I'd decided to apologize for to Monica. During those gaps he was working for me, so any record was carefully erased. So, that's it. Although I do have one more problem.'

'What's that?' enquired Newman.

'Paula,' Tweed pleaded, 'can you think of some way I can decently avoid that lunch with Howard? I can't stand the food at his club. And I can't stand the other members – they sit there like waxworks.'

TRAMP IN
ARMOUR

To Jane

Author's Note

I wish to record my thanks to Mr M. J. Willis and to Mr P. Simpkin of the Imperial War Museum for their invaluable technical assistance.

France, May 1940

General von Bock's
Army Group
B –
Start line

General von
Rundstedt's
Army Group
A –
Start line

Dover
Calais
Boulogne
Dunkirk
Lemont
Gravelines
Etaples
St. Pol
Lille
Béthune
Arras
Cambrai
Abbeville
Amiens
Beaucaire
St. Quentin
Laon
Sedan
Luxembourg
Antwerp
Brussels
Etreux
Paris

*Parachutist
lands*

The attack

Sergeant Barnes' route
Front line of the French Armies in the South
B.E.F. Front Line
Route of General Storch's 14th Panzer Division

50 mls
80 kms

N
W   E
S

Chapter One

Thursday, 16 May

The war had started.

'Advance right, driver. Advance right. Two-pounder, traverse left, traverse left. Steady . . .'

The tank commander, Sergeant Barnes, thought that should do the trick – when the tank emerged from the ramp on to the rail embankment, in full view of the German troops of General von Bock's Army Group B, the turret would rest at an angle of ninety degrees to the forward movement of the vehicle, the two-pounder and the Besa machine gun aimed straight at the enemy. The tank crawled upwards at a steady five miles per hour, still invisible to the German wave advancing across open fields to assault the embankment behind which the British Expeditionary Force waited for them, while overhead the sun shone down on Belgium out of a clear blue sky, the prelude to the long endless summer of 1940.

Barnes' squadron of tanks was positioned on the extreme right of the BEF line, and the troop of three tanks which formed his own unit was stationed on the extreme right of the squadron. Somewhere beyond this troop the French First Army, the next major formation which faced the attacking German army group, reached out its left flank to link up with the BEF, but this vital link was not apparent, which was why Barnes had just received his urgent wireless instruction from Lieutenant Parker, his troop commander.

'Find out where the hell the French are, Barnes, and report back immediately, if not sooner.'

The natural route to the French, the road below the embankment, had been blocked by dive-bombers, and now what had once been a road was a barrier of wrecked buildings, so Barnes decided there was only one way to go – up to the top of the embankment and along the rail track in full view of the enemy. The prospect of exposing his tank like a silhouette on a target range didn't greatly worry him: the armour on the upper side of the hull was seventy millimetres thick and none of the light weapons the German advance troops carried could do more than scratch the surface. As for the big stuff farther back, which was already lobbing shells into the BEF rear areas, well, he'd be off this embankment before they could bring down the range of their artillery. Any moment now, he told himself, pressing his eye to the periscope.

Four men crewed the tank: Trooper Reynolds inside his own separate driving compartment in the nose of the tank, while in the central fighting compartment Barnes shared the confined space with his gunner, Trooper Davis, and his loader-operator, Corporal Penn. The fighting compartment in the centre of the tank was shaped rather like a conning tower, the upper portion protruding above the tank's hull; the floor, only a few feet above the ground, comprised a turntable suspended from the turret, so that when the power-traverse went into action the entire compartment rotated as a single unit, carrying round with it the guns and the three men inside, the traverse system controlled by the gunner at the commander's instructions. They were very close to the top of the embankment now, but still the view through the periscope showed only the scrubby grass of the descending slope, while outside all hell was breaking loose, a hell of sound infinitely magnified inside the confines of the metal hull: the horrid crump of mortar bombs exploding, the scream of shells heading for the rear area, while the permanent accompaniment to this symphony of death was an endless crack of rifle shots, a steady rattle of machine-gun fire. It was only possible for the crew to hear Barnes' sharp instructions because he gave them over the intercom, a one-way system of communication through the microphone hanging from his neck which transmitted the words to earphones clamped over the crew's heads. Barnes screwed up his eyes, saw the wall of embankment disappear. They were over the top.

The view was much as he had expected, but there were many more of them – long lines of helmeted Germans in field grey advancing like the waves of a rising tide, running towards him across a vast field. Some carried rifles, some machine-pistols, and there were clusters with light machine-guns. The tank had reached the embankment at the very moment when the first assault was being mounted.

'Driver, straight down the railway – behind those loading sheds. Two-pounder. Six hundred.' Davis set the range on his telescope. 'Traverse left.' With a hiss of air, turret and crew began to swing round, the tank still moving forward. 'Traverse left.' The turret screamed round faster, the guns and the fighting crew now at an angle of forty-five degrees to the tank hull. 'Steady,' Barnes warned, his gaze through the periscope fixed on the anti-tank gun in the distance as a fusillade of bullets rattled on the armour-plate. 'Anti-tank gun,' he snapped, pinpointing the target.

'Fire!'

Davis squeezed the trigger. The tank shuddered under the recoil, the turret was swamped with a stench of cordite. Barnes didn't hear the explosion but he saw it – a burst of white smoke on the gun position, a brief eruption of the ground. Then they were moving behind the loading bays which the ramp served, out of sight of the enemy for swiftly passing seconds, emerging again as Barnes gave fresh orders.

'Besa . . .'

The destroyed anti-tank gun was the only immediate menace to Bert, as they called their tank. Now for the German troops. The tank had scarcely moved beyond the sheltering wall of the loading bays when the Besa opened fire, the turret traversing in an arc from left to right, pouring out a murderous stream of bullets which cut down the first wave of Germans like a scythe. The turret began to swing in a second arc, the Besa elevated slightly to bring down the second wave, and all the time the tank moved forward down the rail track while Penn, who had already re-loaded the two-pounder, attended to his wireless. Parker, the troop commander, was speaking to Barnes now.

'What's the picture, Barnes?'

'German assault waves just coming in – they'll be over the top in your sector any second now. They stretch as far as I can see, sir. Over.'

He pressed the lever on his mike which controlled wireless communication and waited. Parker sounded exasperated.

'But the French, Barnes – can you see the bloody French?'

'Nothing so far, sir. I'll report back shortly. Off.'

All the way up the ramp and along the embankment so far the turret lid had been closed down, so Barnes had relied on the periscope to let him know what was happening outside, a method of sighting which he found restricted and unsatisfactory. Now that he could no longer hear the clatter of bullets ricocheting harmlessly off the armour-plate, he risked it, pushing up the turret lid and lifting his head above the rim. For once, he was wearing his tin hat. A quick glance told him that no Germans were close to the section of the embankment they were advancing along. Instead, the troops in that area were running back across the field away from him: they had seen what had happened to their mates. To encourage their flight he gave orders to fire the two-pounder twice and then called for a burst from the Besa. If he was really going to see what was going on he would have to lift his head well out of the turret. He clambered up and stood erect, half his body above the rim, gazing all round quickly as he gave Reynolds instructions automatically.

'Driver, full speed ahead down this railway. All the speed Bert will give.'

The tank began to pick up speed, one caterpillar track outside the railway, the other travelling midway between the two iron lines, while inside the driving compartment Reynolds had his eyes glued to the slit window in front, a window protected by four-inch armoured glass. Normally, he sat on his jacked-up seat with his head protruding clear of the hatch in the front hull, but now this seat was depressed so that he sat inside the hull and a steel hood was closed over the hatch above his head. He vaguely wondered what Barnes was going to do next, a line of thought which was occupying Barnes himself at the same moment.

To the left the fields of Belgium stretched away to disappear inside a curtain of black smoke, the result of RAF bombing and BEF heavy artillery fire. In front of the curtain small figures moved like the inhabitants of a disturbed anthill, but always the apparently chaotic movement was forward, except in the sector ahead of the tank. They were now perched a good twenty feet above the surrounding countryside and to

Barnes' dismay he realized that the embankment was gradually rising all the time the farther south they progressed, the sides growing steeper, making their descent from the railway more difficult every yard they moved forward. His eyes scanned the ground on the Allied side of the embankment and saw nothing which comforted him. As he had anticipated when he had decided to mount the embankment and make a dash along the railway, it gave him an excellent view of the battle area. The outskirts of the Belgian town of Etreux had been badly battered by the Stuka raids, but even at this early stage of the campaign he was becoming used to these scenes of devastation. What he had not expected was that the desert of rubble would be *unoccupied*, and as his eyes searched and searched again for signs of life a chill began to crawl up his spine. The wireless crackled: someone was coming on the air again.

'Hullo, hullo! Troop calling. Parker here. Anything to report, Barnes?'

'Barnes here, sir. No sign of our friends yet. Repeat, no sign of our friends. I am a quarter of a mile out and no sign of them yet. Repeat, at least a quarter of a mile. Over.'

'Are you quite sure, Barnes? I've got to report to Brigade at once. I must be quite sure. Over.'

'Quite sure, sir. I'm twenty-five feet up here and the place has been flattened, so vision is good. I'm a quarter of a mile out at least and there's no sign of them ahead. Do I proceed farther or return? Over.'

'Proceed a farther quarter of a mile if you can, then report again. Over.'

'Barnes OK. Off.'

At least it was a convenient distance. The tank was still moving ahead along the railway line, the embankment straight as a ruler, and about a quarter of a mile farther along the line disappeared into a steep hillside. Barnes could see the arched opening of a tunnel clearly now. So the distance was all right, but the timing probably wasn't. He glanced at his watch and caclulated that within the next two or three minutes the Germans would have wirelessed back for artillery support to lay down a barrage along the top of the embankment. Soon the first ranging shots would be falling, a spotter would be reporting their fall, and unless Barnes was very much mistaken they would hardly have completed their quarter-mile run before the shells began to bracket the tank. The fact that the embankment was so damned straight would make the German gunners' work that much easier. He wondered how the others liked being stuck up silhouetted against the skyline and glanced down inside the turret. Davis had the shoulder-grip tucked into position and he couldn't see the gunner's expression, but Penn happened to look up and on his thin, intelligent face Barnes thought he detected signs of worry, but then it would always be Penn who worried first because Penn had the imagination to think of all the things which might happen. Too much intelligence could be a distinct disadvantage when you were locked up inside a tank. He spoke briefly into the mike, urging Reynolds to keep up the speed.

Below him the ruins of Etreux glided past while he continually watched for the first sight of a gun position, for French troops. There had been a muck-up, the certainty of this was growing on him. First, there had been the hectic rush forward on 10 May when news of the German invasion of Holland and Belgium had come in, a rush from behind prepared defences on the Franco-Belgian frontier out into the open to meet the German onslaught in head-on collision. And now it was Thursday, 16 May, only six days later. To Barnes it felt more like six weeks later, but at least they were stuck into them. For a brief moment he glanced back to where the line of German dead lay, victims of the Besa's murderous sweeping arcs. He felt not a trace of pity, but he also felt no exultation, only perhaps a certain satisfaction that one of the few British tanks with the BEF was already proving its worth.

The railway tunnel was very close now, barely two hundred yards away, the black arch coming closer every second as the tank ground forward. And still no sign of the French, no sign at all. He'd have to report back soon now. Even in this sector there was a lot of noise – the heavy boom of the big artillery, the whine of shells – and this was why Barnes failed to detect the arrival of the enemy. Also, in his concentration on Etreux, he had neglected to search the sky for the past minute. It happened with terrifying suddenness – the appearance of a plane above his head screaming down in a power dive. He looked up as he dived inside the tank, saw the Messerschmitt hurtling earthwards, its guns blazing straight at Bert, and rammed down the lid, almost crushing his fingers in his haste. But he was just too late – one bullet whistled in under the closing lid, missing Barnes by millimetres, and terror entered the tank.

With the driver's hood closed and with the turret lid down, the occupants of a Mk II Matilda tank in 1940 could feel themselves reasonably secure against everything except a direct hit. On the other hand, if by some mischance a bullet from a rifle or a machine-gun were able to enter the armoured confines of the tank, then what had once been a haven of comparative safety immediately became a death-trap. Entering the mobile fortress under the impetus of its own tremendous velocity the bullet has to spend its velocity somewhere, and it does this by ricocheting back and forth off the armour-plate hull of the *interior* of the tank, flying about unpredictably in all directions until its force is spent – normally by its entry into human flesh. As soon as the bullet entered, the three men knew what they were in for, and knew that there wasn't a thing they could do about it – except to wait and pray. The biting sound of bullet tearing from one metal surface to another only lasted for a brief period in time, but nerves stretched to breaking-point by the wear and tear of battle reacted to screaming pitch as the danger flashed into three battered minds, drawing from them in seconds reserves of physical and mental strength they would normally have expended over hours. Then there was a momentary silence while Reynolds drove at top speed towards the tunnel. Penn was the first to speak.

'I think it went into the wireless set.'

Barnes checked his communications and banged the microphone while he looked at Penn, who was examining the set. Then suspicion flooded into his mind and he scrambled up the turret, pushing the lid back and staring up into the clear morning sky. The clever bastards! They'd sent the Messerschmitt down not hoping to hit anybody but to get him *to close the turret*. In this way his vision would be restricted and he wouldn't see what was coming next, but he could see it now coming from the east – an arrow-shaped formation of ugly, thick-legged birds – Stuka dive-bombers coming for Bert. He spoke into the mike, his voice dry and harsh, using his driver's name.

'Reynolds, we're going to be dive-bombed unless you get us into that tunnel first.'

He stayed in the turret to check the course the Stukas were taking, remembering that these were the planes which had battered Poland. He might well die in this war, he knew that, but not yet, not yet! He wanted to see Germany smashed first. With narrowed eyes he watched the tunnel draw closer as the Stukas came over at a bare thousand feet. Yes, he'd been right – they were coming for Bert. They'd change direction now and he waited for the first one to peel off, waited for the hair-raising shriek of those screaming bombs which would put fear into the dead.

'Lights on,' he ordered, automatically as Bert thundered towards the tunnel.

The first Stuka was peeling off now, falling sideways, ejecting black eggs from its belly. Barnes slammed down the lid, dropped to the turntable floor and rotated the periscope so that he saw the tunnel moving towards them.

'Wait for it,' he warned the others, but mainly to warn Reynolds who was driving.

They heard it coming, a high-pitched whistle growing to a piercing shriek which easily dominated the engine sound, penetrating the armoured walls as though they were papier mâché. It's a direct hit this time, thought Penn. He looked at Davis but the gunner's eyes stared fixedly at the turntable floor, his jaw muscles clenched, his forehead moist with sudden sweat. Penn looked at Barnes, but the sergeant had his eyes glued to the periscope as he watched the tunnel coming closer. God, thought Penn, he's got no nerves at all. The thing was screaming like a banshee now. Would it never land? Up in the nose of the tank Reynolds could hear it coming, too, but he was wrestling with two separate fears. Reynolds had no imagination but as he saw the mouth of the tunnel looking towards him through the slit window he remembered a story he had once read in a newspaper. It had happened in Spain during the Civil War – a scout car racing towards a tunnel to escape bombing

12

had met an express train coming out of the tunnel at high speed ... But nobody would be running trains in the battle area. The tunnel mouth yawned towards him and the bomb exploded.

The shock wave dealt the armour-plating such a blow that it rattled the plates, seeming for a moment about to blow the tank off the embankment. Fitments clattered down on to the turntable floor and the detonation reverberating inside the metal room was so loud that they were all deafened. Then they heard the next one coming. First the whistle, then the scream. This time Barnes felt fairly sure they were going to get it: the scream was much louder, its aiming point seemed to be dead down the turret. It had to happen to someone during the war – a bomb dead centre through the lid, exploding inside that confined space ... The bomb hit, detonated. It rocked the tank like a toy, smashing at the plates with a hammerblow, the acrid smell of high explosive seeping inside the fighting compartment. That one had been close! He glanced at Davis, who still stared at the floor as though his life depended on it. Penn had gone as white as a sheet, his small neat moustache quivering before he clenched his lips together and then unclenched them to speak.

'Knock, knock. Who's there?'

Nobody laughed, nobody smiled. They just looked at each other strangely, as they heard the next one coming. In the driver's seat Reynolds kept the tank going full out, conjuring up reserves of speed from

Bert that even he hadn't known existed. The tunnel mouth now filled the breadth of his slit window. He had forgotten all about trains coming out of hillsides. His hands holding the steering levers were as wet as though he had dipped them in water. Sweat streamed off his broad forehead and dripped into his eyes, but he kept them open, seeing the beams of his headlights inside the tunnel now. Then the third one started to come down. The tunnel rushed closer and closer as the bomb fell lower and lower, louder than its predecessors. Please, Bert, *please*! Reynolds whispered to himself. The walls of the tunnel rushed forward and they went inside as the bomb detonated. The force of the explosion seemed to take hold of Bert's rear and shove him inside the hill, followed by an appalling clattering sound, a low rumble behind them, then the ground under the tracks shook and they felt the vibration inside the tank. Barnes swore, swivelled the periscope through one hundred and eighty degrees, and stared back to where should have been an arched frame of daylight, seeing nothing but pitch blackness. The last bomb had caught the top of the entrance, blowing the hillside down over the track and sealing off the outside world.

'Halt,' Barnes rapped out into the mike, 'but keep the engines revved up.'

The last thing he wanted inside this tunnel was an engine failure. He looked at the others and they stared back, stunned now by the nerve-racking silence. Except for the engine sound it was uncannily quiet.

No shells whining past, no projectiles screaming down from above.

Cautiously, he climbed into the turret and pushed back the lid on its telescopic arms. It was like emerging into an underground cavern, a subterranean cave weirdly lit by Bert's headlights. Barnes felt a tightening of his stomach muscles as he swivelled his torch beam into the dark corners, moving it slowly over the enormous rock pile. Through the intercom he told Reynolds to switch off the headlights and at the same moment he doused his own torch. Not a glimmer of light anywhere: the entrance was well and truly blocked. He climbed down off the tank and used his torch to guide him to the rock wall. Still no sign of daylight. The only way out was forward to the far end of the tunnel. When he climbed back into the tank he found Penn was still examining the wireless set. He put on his headset and ordered Reynolds to switch on the headlights. The corporal looked up and pulled a wry face.

'It's hopeless. Two valves went when the bullet charged in. Mind you, I'd sooner have it nestling in there instead of in my pelvis, but I haven't any spares so we'll have to wait till we get back to squadron HQ.'

Barnes tested the intercom again. At least that was still working, but being cut off from Parker was serious. Thank God, he had sent out one warning about the gap in the French lines. Taking the map case out of the rack he climbed down on to the hull and

15

Penn followed, watching over his shoulder as he spread out a large-scale map of Belgium and Northern France over the engine covers at the rear of the tank. His torch focused on the area round Etreux.

'This tunnel's a damned long one, Penn. We'll just have to jog through it and then make our way back as best we can, Jerry permitting. At least we'll have a pretty good report on the area when we do eventually land back.'

'It's going to be a long way round, isn't it?' queried Penn. 'As soon as we get out of the tunnel that canal bars the route back for miles. We'll have to go over that bridge, then follow this road . . .'

His finger traced a wide semi-circular course which would take them back into the rear outskirts of Etreux. Barnes agreed that this was the only way and he cursed inwardly at the breakdown in wireless communication. Parker would be wondering what on earth had happened to them and meanwhile he'd have to fight the German onrush with two tanks instead of three. It couldn't be helped, but they'd better get cracking. Climbing back inside the tank he explained the position to Reynolds and Davis, giving Reynolds a word of caution over the intercom.

'This tunnel won't be straight, you can bet your life on that, so keep your speed down to five miles an hour or less and watch for bends. I'm going up into the turret to help guide you. What's the matter, Davis?'

The burly gunner with the squarish face and red

hair had a hunted look and an air of tension radiated from him. He opened his mouth and closed it again without speaking.

'Come on, spit it out, man,' snapped Barnes.

'You'll think it's stupid, Sergeant, but I've always had a horror of tunnels. I was a miner once, as I told you. I was in a colliery disaster in 1934 – we were locked in for five days and we thought we'd been buried alive . . .'

'Well, Davis, this happens to be a railway tunnel and we'll be through it in ten minutes, so get your mind on your guns. You never know,' he smiled grimly, 'we might meet a Panzer division coming up from the other end.'

He had reached the turret and given the order to advance when the hollowness of his joke struck him. If the Germans had just happened to break through at the other end, it might seem a very good idea to send tanks along the tunnel in the hope of taking Etreux on the flank. He decided that he'd better keep a close lookout ahead and his mind began to calculate the possible effect of two-pounder shells exploding inside the railway tunnel. The powerful headlights penetrated some distance into the tunnel and soon Barnes was warning Reynolds of a curve in the line. Now that they were away from the battle area the driver had rolled back the hood from the hatch and jacked up his seat so that his head protruded above the hull like a man in a Turkish bath cabinet. The journey along the tunnel was eerie and strange, the grind of

17

the tracks and the throb of the engines echoing hollowly, probably very much like riding through a mine shaft, Barnes thought, and he glanced down into the compartment below. Penn was still fiddling with the wireless set as though hoping to perform an act of faith, but Davis sat rigid as a stone behind his guns, his body thrust hard into the shoulder-grip, his hand on the two-pounder's trigger. Undoubtedly, Trooper Davis' idea of a private hell was meeting a Panzer column deep underground.

The engine noise sounded far too loud with its reverberations hemmed inside the tunnel and the grind and clatter of the steel tracks conjured up the advance of the biggest tank in the world. Barnes looked at his watch again and then gazed ahead. They should be seeing daylight soon now if the map was anything to go by, and leaving the tunnel was going to call for some pretty careful reconnaissance. Barnes had absolutely no idea what the position might be on this sector of the front: what he had seen from the embankment gave him little cause for optimism as to what might face them once they reached the far end. One part of his mind concentrated on the probing beams while another considered the various possibilities they could encounter – calling on the one hand for a swift dash out into the open or, on the other, for a more cautious passage. As far as he could tell from the map, the railway emerged into open country with no sign of an embankment; there should be fields on both sides with the canal barring the way to the west, the way they wanted to go. They'd just have to see. The headlights were now beginning to sweep round a gradual bend. Somewhere round this bend they should see daylight, probably a first glimmer, then a distant archway. When that happens, Barnes told himself, I'll halt the tank and go on foot for a recce. Just so long as we don't have any trouble with Davis. He glanced down again and saw that Davis was sitting in exactly the same position, gripping the two-pounder as though his very life depended on it, a posture of such implacable rigidity that Barnes was none too happy about his gunner's likely reactions.

'We'll soon be there, Davis,' he said down the intercom. 'Penn, get back to your seat just in case. Be ready to halt, Reynolds, as soon as I give the word.'

The tank ground on, the left-hand track rumbling over wooden sleepers while the right-hand track scattered pebbles, so that the tank was tilted very slightly to the right, the three sounds complementing each other – the throb of the engines, the grumbles of the tracks, and the slither of pebbles. Abruptly, Barnes gave the order to halt, saying nothing more while he wondered how to break it to them. The headlights penetrated the darkness and then halfway along the full extent of their beams they splashed out over solid surface, a wall surface with boulders protruding from a scree of soil and rubble which resembled a landslide.

This end of the tunnel was blocked, too. They were sealed off inside the bowels of the earth.

On 10 May the BEF had moved from France into Belgium and Barnes' unit had moved with it. On 10 May, four hours earlier at 3 a.m., General von Bock's Army Group B had advanced across the frontiers of Holland and Belgium with the express purpose of tempting the BEF and three French armies to leave their fortified lines. Before the end of the day the movement of these vast forces was quite apparent to London and Paris, but a third movement of even more massive forces had so far gone unnoticed.

At the point where Belgium, France and Luxembourg meet lies one of the least known areas of Western Europe – the massif of the Ardennes range, a remote zone of high hills enclosing steep wooded gorges along which snake second-class roads. This was the sector of the huge front from Belgium to Switzerland which the French High Command had long ago declared 'impassable', and it was opposite this sector that they had placed their weakest forces.

During the early hours of 10 May General von Rundstedt's Army Group A began its secret forward movement through the 'impassable' Ardennes, an army group more powerful than any the world had ever seen. It comprised a force of forty-four divisions, including the main mass of the Panzer divisions which contained over two thousand armoured vehicles. All

night long the army group penetrated into the twisting defiles, drawing ever closer to the French border.
The tanks drove in close formation, each vehicle
guided by the hooded rear light of the tank ahead, an
exercise they had practised over and over again. Seen
from the air through the eye of an infra-red camera
the German host would indeed have resembled a
snake, or rather a series of snakes – armoured snakes
threading their way through the darkness towards the
Meuse near Sedan.

The leading Panzer division was commanded by a
thirty-two-year-old general who had won his spurs –
and his promotion – in Poland. His unit had led the
Wehrmacht into burning Warsaw and now he looked
forward to leading it into burning Paris. Without
aristocratic connexions, on sheer ruthless ability, the
general had risen in a few brief years to command the
very tip of the spearhead aimed at the heart of
sleeping France. His was, in fact, the first tank, and
now he stood in the turret erect as a fir tree, night
field-glasses dangling over his chest, the Knight's
Cross suspended from his neck, his eyes fixed on the
motor-cycle patrol ahead.

Under his high-peaked cap his hawk-like face was
calm and without a trace of emotion. His gloved hand
rested lightly on the turret rim, without tension, to
correct his balance as the huge vehicle made its way
along the insidious road. He might well have been on
manoeuvres, looking forward to the congratulations
of the umpires later and a drink with his fellow offiers

in the mess. Except for the fact that the general neither smoked nor drank, and except for the further fact that he was leading the advance guard of the coming onslaught, confident that he was about to play a decisive part in the total annihilation of the British and the French.

The tip of the German spearhead reached the Meuse on 12 May, crossed it on 13 May, and by Thursday, 16 May, the general was in Laon, deep in the heart of France. He led the advance still erect in his tank, still wearing the peaked cloth cap in spite of the earlier entreaties of Colonel Hans Meyer, his GSO1, to exchange it for a steel helmet.

'It won't be necessary, Meyer. You will see,' the general had said, 'we shall cut through them like a scythe.'

Meyer withdrew the helmet as he sourly recalled a conversation he had had with the general a month earlier during the final war manoeuvres near Wiesbaden. To Meyer it now seemed that the conversation had taken place at least a year ago since already the Panzers were pouring over the pontoons across the river Meuse.

'There will be two or three major battles,' the general had said, 'and these will take place soon after we have crossed the Meuse. We can expect the fiercest resistance for two or three weeks and then a total collapse of the enemy.'

'I wonder,' Meyer had replied dubiously.

The general was a little too confident for Meyer's

liking, particularly when he remembered that his commanding officer was a nobody whereas Hans Meyer was descended from one of the oldest families in East Prussia. One must move with the times, of course, and Meyer was only forty-three years old. As he watched the endless Panzer column advancing into the fields of France, Meyer reminded himself that he expected high promotion in this war and that this largely depended on the general's goodwill. So he must compromise, keeping his doubts about the general to himself.

Once beyond the Meuse the Panzers met with only sporadic resistance – the frantic firing of a few shells from artillery pieces, a rattle of machine-guns, an irregular thump of mortar bombs falling somewhere. The general drove his division forward non-stop along the main road, thundering across France in a cloud of dust while the early summer sun beat down on the iron column. Away from the road, women working in the fields stopped to watch that dust cloud which rose like a smokescreen against the hot blue sky. It was a beautiful morning, the sky cloudless, the sun building up the intense warmth which suggested leisured ease rather than total warfare. Some of the women thought that the dust cloud marked the progress of a French column, although it was travelling in the wrong direction. Others stood and wondered, a feeling of depression and fear clutching their hearts, but still not able to accept the fact the the German army had broken through.

For this is exactly what it had done – it had broken clean through the French lines where the Ninth and Second armies met – the least defensible point along any continuous front. And so far, since the dive-bombers had smashed all resistance on the west bank of the Meuse, there had been no fierce battles, none at all. Because the general was young, in the prime of life and endowed with enormous funds of energy and optimism, his sixth sense was beginning to tell him something. It was a matter of keeping going, of not stopping for anything. This mood was not shared by Colonel Hans Meyer.

There was an ugly scene when the general's tank halted briefly in the centre of a French village. Behind him four more heavy tanks rumbled into the square and halted, their huge guns revolving slowly round the upper windows of the old square, menacing even the thought of resistance. Meyer climbed down from his tank and approached the general who remained in his turret, still standing erect, his face expressionless as he handed down his map.

'Meyer, the patrol has taken that road,' he pointed with his gloved hand, 'but is it the right one? They have assured me that it is – what do you think?'

Meyer examined the map quickly, looked round at the exits from the square, consulted his own map, and handed the other back to the general.

'I'm sure they are right, sir.'

'We'd better check with the locals. You speak French. That man over there – ask him.'

The general took off his glove, unbottoned his holster flap, extracted his pistol, and pointed it at a middle-aged man with a grey moustache. It was an astonishing scene: the sun shining down so that it was almost hot, the inhabitants standing in the old square rigid with fear, like waxwork figures out of a tableau. Only five minutes earlier they had been going about their daily routines with a touch of anxiety but with no real fear. Then it had happened – the scared boy running into the square shouting something about a huge dust cloud. He had hardly finished telling his story when the motor cyclists had flashed across the square, tryes screaming at the corners, vanishing as they raced off to the west. People had come out of their houses at the commotion, completely bewildered. A woman had seen German soldiers in the side-cars, helmeted figures carrying machine-pistols. Arguments had broken out. She must be mad, must be seeing things. And while they argued and wondered the general had arrived with five tanks. The village was paralysed as he unsheathed his pistol and aimed it.

The man with the moustache stepped forwards and sideways, presenting his body to the pistol muzzle, shielding a woman instinctively. His wife. A hush of horror fell on the sunlit square. Even Meyer was disturbed. He spoke quickly.

'That won't be necessary.'

'Ask him, Meyer.'

The gun remained levelled at the man's chest.

Meyer stepped forward, his face stiff with anger. He even placed his own body between the man and the pointed muzzle as he addressed him in excellent French.

'Which is the direct route to St Quentin? You see what we have with us, so think carefully before you reply. The direct route to St Quentin.'

The Frenchman moistened his lips and glanced sideways as an Army truck drove into the square. Before it had pulled up men were jumping out of the back, German soldiers armed with rifles and machine-pistols. Their sergeant held a map in his hand, a detailed map of the district. He glanced around quickly, pointed, and a detachment ran into a building. Outside in the square, the moustached Frenchman had taken his decision: he had his wife to consider, and the other villagers. He pointed in the direction the motor cyclists had taken, his hand wobbling.

'That is the way to St Quentin – the only direct way. I swear to God.'

Meyer nodded and turned round, his body still shielding the Frenchman while the general put away his pistol.

'He says the route is down that street. He's telling the truth, I'm sure of it.'

'Good, good. As long as we're sure.' The general turned round in his turret and called out to the sergeant who stood by the truck with several of his men.

'Tell them we come as liberators. Tell them also that at the slightest sign of resistance they will all be shot.' He broke off impatiently. 'You know what to say, I should hope. We are pressing on.'

He issued the order to his driver and the tank rumbled away from the square, leaving Meyer to scramble up inside his own vehicle while the villagers stood perfectly still, not yet able to grasp the nightmare which had arrived in brilliant sunshine.

I'm right, the general told himself as the tank advanced into open country beyond the village, I do believe I'm right. He allowed a little of the exultation to well up inside him. *There isn't going to be any real resistance.* Those people in the village were symbolic: the shock of the armoured hammer had smashed French morale, had brought on a state of psychological paralysis. We must keep moving, on and on. And on and on raced the German spearhead, a spearhead tipped by the 14th Panzer Division, commanded by General Heinrich Storch.

The tank crew had been entombed inside the tunnel for over twenty-four hours and the strain was telling. In spite of the fact that they had spent over two-thirds of their time in back-breaking toil, removing large boulders with their bare hands, carting away hundredweights of debris with the shovels they carried on the tank, their state of near-physical exhaustion still couldn't prevent them from thinking, and the longer they remained trapped inside the hill the more they began to wonder whether they would ever leave the tunnel alive. Barnes paused to lean on his shovel, wiping sweat from his dripping forehead as he looked at his watch in the headlights. Seven o'clock in the evening of Friday, 17 May.

They had driven into the tunnel at eleven o'clock on the morning of the previous day and there was still no sign that they had more than scraped the surface of the landslide. At the rock face, its impenetrable solidity, only too apparent in the pitiless headlight beams, Davis and Reynolds wrestled to haul out a massive boulder from the left-hand side of the wall. The two men were working together as a team while Barnes and Penn wielded the shovels – a sensible division of labour since the two troopers were easily the strongest men in the crew. Barnes stood back and watched them working while he began his fifteen-minute break. They had fifteen minutes off in every hour, and he had further arranged that the breaks should be taken in pairs, so that each man had someone to talk to, but at the same time he was encouraged by still seeing the work in progress. Four men resting at the same time, all voicing their fears, could have a disastrous effect on morale.

'Time for a break, Penn,' he called out.

'In a tick – I'll just finish shifting this lot.'

Thirty-four years old, Barnes was not only the oldest member of the crew, he was also the smallest.

Barely five foot seven inches tall, he was small-boned and slim, but his frame was wiry and on a long-term endurance basis he could probably outlast the other three on sheer will-power alone. His face was lean, clean-shaven, and above prominent cheekbones his brown eyes were still alert and watchful as he studied Reynolds and Davis. In size there wasn't a great deal to choose between them; they were both large, heavily-built men, but there was an enormous difference in temperament. Whereas Davis, the ex-miner, was subject to moods of melancholy, Reynolds could be relied upon to carry out any task he was set until he dropped, showing neither enthusiasm nor depression at any stage. As for thirty-year-old Corporal Penn, he was easily the most intelligent and best-educated of the four men. At the outbreak of war he could have obtained a commission but he had turned it down for reasons which were never quite clear. Slim and tall, he was the most light-hearted of the crew, and at the same time the most sensitive. Dropping his shovel, he wobbled over to Barnes in an exaggerated manner.

'There should be extra pay for this, there really should. Working underground doesn't come within my agreed sphere of duties, you know. I'll have to look it up in King's Regs. Mind if we take a stroll along the promenade?'

Along the promenade was Penn's version for walking through the tunnel, so Barnes got up off the hull where he had been sitting and walked with Penn, his torch beam showing the way. As soon as they were out of earshot of the other two men Penn began talking.

'I don't like the look of Davis. I don't think he can stand much more of this.'

'He'll have to – it's the same for all of us and we may be through to the other side any moment now.'

'Do you really think so? That wall could be twenty feet thick. I imagine the Germans blew in the entrance.'

'It looks like it – or they might have been bombing the open country beyond the railway and dropped one which started a landslide. It doesn't make much difference now – we've just got to get far enough through to be able to use the two-pounder.'

'The two-pounder?' Penn stopped in the middle of the rail track. 'You're joking, of course?'

'Look, Penn, by the time we see daylight we're going to be pretty tired. And in any case we've been away from the troop for well over twenty-four hours. God knows what's been happening on the outside but our job is to get back as fast as we can – and the way to do that is to shoot our way out when we can. We'll wait until we have a hole big enough for me to crawl through and do a recce. Then Davis can take his mind off things by shelling the rest out of the way.'

'Just so long as Davis lasts out the course – and always assuming we ever reach your little hole.'

'Now you're beginning to talk like Davis. It doesn't seem to have struck any of you that being cooped up inside here is a damned sight safer than being bombed by Stukas.'

Penn glanced at Barnes in amazement. He had really meant what he had said, Penn felt sure of it. The idea that they might be trapped inside this tunnel until they were out of water, out of food, out of lighting when the batteries ran down – none of this seemed to have crossed Barnes' mind. In his usual way he just assumed that they would make it, that it was only a matter of time before they broke through that terrible wall. Well, if faith moved mountains, Barnes was likely to move that wall, and their tank commander had a habit of backing up his faith with planning and forethought: they were still enjoying meals of bully beef and biscuits because of Barnes' insistence that they should always carry provisions for one week. He turned and followed Barnes back to the rock face, sensing trouble as soon as they arrived. Davis had apparently been waiting for their return and now the burly gunner was glaring at his sergeant, his voice an insubordinate growl.

'We'll never get through this bloody wall.'

'No, we won't – not if you just stand there,' Barnes agreed mildly. 'So get on with it.'

'We're wasting our time . . .'

'No, Davis – we aren't. At the moment you are the one who is wasting time, so get on with it.'

Barnes' voice was still very mild. He stood close to his large gunner with a relaxed air, his eyes never leaving Davis'.

'We're going to die down here – *die*, did you hear me? And one day they'll open up this bleedin' tunnel and find four corpses – four skeletons.' His voice was close to hysteria now, his mouth and hands working as though on the edge of a complete breakdown. 'I'm a miner – I know what this means. I've . . .'

'Davis!' Barnes' tone was sharper now. 'You haven't by any chance thought yourself into thinking that this *is* a mine shaft, have you?'

'No, but . . .'

'So, instead of being hundreds of feet below the surface we're actually at ground level – right? The fact is, Davis, that your being a miner is just about as relevant as the fact that Penn was once a draughts-man. Now, do you expect Reynolds to shift that boulder all by himself or are you going to give him a hand?'

'It may take a fortnight to shift that lot,' Davis persisted stubbornly. 'There could be hundreds of . . .'

'Davis, I'm beginning to lose patience with you. It's just possible that it will take all four of us to break through, so we can't afford any spare wheels round here, and that's what you are at the moment. For the third time, I'm ordering you to get on with it.'

'Why not have a go at the other end – the wall may be thinner there.'

Barnes' face tightened. He prodded a stiff finger hard into Davis's chest, punctuating his words with prods.

'You have been given an order three times and

three times you have refused to carry it out. As soon as we get back you're on a charge. In the meantime you will do your bit with the rest of us, and since you've wasted five minutes gassing, your next break period will be ten minutes instead of fifteen. Give Reynolds a hand with that boulder at once.'

He turned away and went back to sit on the tank hull, checking his watch to see whether his fifteen minutes was nearly up, putting his hands flat on either side of his body as he watched Davis start work again. Beside him Penn grinned and whispered, 'He thinks he can be Bolshie now we're on our own.' But Barnes made no reply and his face was grim. It had been a close run thing. They only needed one rotten apple in the barrel for the infection to spread, and the most contagious infection of all is fear. Outwardly, Barnes remained perfectly confident, his every word and gesture indicating clearly that it was only a matter of some hard slogging before they reached the outside world, but inwardly he didn't like the look of it. They were marooned in the centre of a battlefield and the war could rage backwards and forwards over the front for weeks as it had done a quarter of a century earlier. While that went on there would be a certain shortage of people to go round digging out buried tunnels, even supposing that the idea seemed important to them. There was no real problem of air – the tunnel was long enough for them to breathe inside it for weeks – but their water and food supplies would only last for several days, to say nothing of Bert's batteries. And when the batteries went they would be plunged into darkness, which would make working on the wall face almost impossible. For the first few hours of their entombment Barnes had mainly fretted about being cut off from his troop, but as the hours passed and they entered on a new day he found his mind beginning to think like Davis', and the analogy of the mine disaster was only too apt, which was why he had shut up Davis at the earliest possible moment. He glanced at his watch again, nodded to Penn, and went forward to pick up his shovel.

Twenty-four hours later, in the evening of Saturday, 18 May, they had removed an incredibly large mass of rubble and rock, but still the wall face was intact. They worked now by the light of the oil lamp which Barnes always carried inside the tank, and the reason for this was not only to save Bert's headlights: Barnes foresaw that later, when morale was sagging, switching on the headlights again might just keep them going a while longer, but he kept the real reason for this decision to himself. In the middle of the afternoon there had almost been a fatal accident when part of the wall suddenly came away and slid forward of its own momentum. Only Reynolds' speed and strength had saved Davis when he had grabbed the gunner's arm and hauled him sideways out of the path of the tumbling boulders. It was a measure of their anxiety that even when Davis had just experienced this shock he was the first to recover, running away from Reynolds to gaze up at the centre of the wall in desperate hope, his voice hoarse and strained.

'Maybe we're through now.'

'Keep back. I'll see,' snapped Barnes.

Gingerly, he had climbed up the rubble slope, expecting at any moment a fresh fall, but when he had reached the rock face and pushed it was like leaning against the side of a fortress. So they had started again, Barnes and Penn working furiously with their shovels to remove the fresh rubble so that the other two could reach the rock face with their crowbar. It was just after seven o'clock in the evening when Penn made his remark during their rest period. Barnes sat alongside him on the tank hull, watching Reynolds prising out a fresh boulder while Davis sought to give extra leverage by pulling with his bare hands.

'It's funny, but ever since we've been in here we haven't heard any sound of the battle.'

'We've probably driven them back a bit – besides, there wasn't so much going on this side of Etreux.'

He left it at that, wondering why the obvious and macabre conclusion had not been drawn by the others long ago. The fact that they could not hear even faint sounds of the huge bombardment taking place in the outside world demonstrated more clearly than anything the immense thickness of the wall which barred their escape. The thought had occurred to Barnes twenty-four hours earlier and had so worried him that he had waited until the others were asleep before walking back down the tunnel. When he reached the far end he had listened carefully at the blocked entrance but no sound had penetrated from the outside world. They were well and truly sealed in at both ends. Taking a sip of water from his mug, he frowned. Then, very carefully, he put the mug down on the hull and walked over to where Reynolds and Davis were working. He faced the wall and then turned sideways as though listening. It was a dramatic moment and Penn instantly guessed that something had happened because he got down off the tank and walked forward. Something in Barnes' attitude had attracted the attention of Reynolds and Davis and they stopped working.

'What is it?' asked Penn.

Barnes shook his head and faced the wall again, his hands on his hips, his eyes searching the surface carefully. When he spoke his voice was quiet.

'I think we're nearly through.'

'Why?' Penn asked quickly.

'I can feel a faint current of air – come and stand here.'

'My God! You're right! You're right!'

They began to work feverishly at the point where Barnes had traced the air current's entrance, a point about four feet above the level of the tunnel floor. A quarter of an hour later they experienced another heart-lifting moment when Barnes told them to stop working for a minute while he put out the lamp. For a short time there was no sound in the darkness of the tunnel while four pairs of eyes strained to see any sign of daylight in the wall. It was Barnes who spotted it first – a narrow, paper-thin slit along the upper surface of one large boulder.

'We're through,' shouted Davis. 'We're really through. Dear Mother of God, we're through.'

'Take it easy now,' warned Barnes, 'this could be tricky. There's still a solid mass of rock up there.'

He relit the oil lamp and when he turned round Davis was already inserting the crowbar into a corner near the end of the slit they had seen, his hands gripping the iron with a ferocious intensity as he drove the end deeper into the wall and began to twist and turn for leverage. Barnes opened his mouth and closed it again without speaking. The poor devil must have gone through even greater agonies than the rest of them with his memories of the mine trap he had escaped from. Barnes had realized this when he had treated Davis roughly, but any display of sympathy at that time could have destroyed the morale of all of them, and Barnes never forgot the dictum of Napoleon – morale is to the material as three is to one. So now he let Davis loose as he dug and rammed the bar into the remaining barrier, punishing his hands with the force of his efforts and never even noticing the punishment. Penn spoke as he shovelled debris to expose the base of the remaining rocks.

'I'll tell you now, I never thought we'd make it.'

'We'll face tougher things than this before this war's over.'

Within ten minutes Davis had prised the boulder loose and Reynolds was helping him to haul it back out of the wall, a boulder as large as the oil stove they carried inside Bert for emergency cooking arrangements. It came away suddenly. One moment Davis was leaning his full weight against the crowbar, sweat streaming down the sides of his face, and then the rock was shifting inwards, swaying gently before it toppled back into the tunnel, so unexpectedly that the two men had to jump sideways to avoid it. Picking up the oil lamp, Barnes held it behind his back and they all stared at the oblong of daylight. It was a memorable moment. Four men, each of whom had secretly felt that they would never make it, knew now that they would live. There was a pause when no one spoke, no one moved. Then Davis went berserk.

Seizing the crowbar which had fallen with the boulder, he rammed it behind the rock above the opening and began heaving and twisting with all his strength. Barnes shouted a warning, but Davis either didn't or wouldn't hear him. He felt the rock moving easily and dropped the crowbar. Reaching up to his full height he pushed, both hands flat against the rock, which fell outwards, enlarging the window considerably, enlarging it enough for Davis to climb up into it, crouching inside the alcove on his knees as he pushed with his hands at the loosened rock above. Barnes was still shouting when disaster struck.

The upper rock was held in position over the opening by ledges on either side of the aperture, but it moved loosely on the ledges so that when Davis again pushed his full strength against it the rock wobbled and then fell outwards under the fierce pressure of Davis' hands. As it fell away it unhinged the centre of gravity of the wall above. Davis was still crouched in the aperture when there was a low rumbling sound. The whole upper wall began to quiver and disintegrate. Barnes was running forward to grab Davis when Penn grasped his arm firmly and hauled him back against the side of the tunnel. A second later an avalanche of rock and rubble poured down over the floor where Barnes had been standing, spilling tons of debris along the centre of the rail track, filling the tunnel with a roaring sound which deafened them. Then they were bending over and choking and spluttering as the dust invaded their lungs and blinded their eyes.

It was only when the dust began to settle that Barnes saw what had happened. On the far side of the tunnel, his back against the wall, Reynolds was safe. Beside Barnes, Penn was wiping his eyes to try and clear his vision. But it was the entrance to the tunnel which was the most awe-inspiring sight. The new landslide had completely cleared the upper part of the tunnel, leaving a great gap above the rubble slope which now stretched deep inside the tunnel, a gap through which they could see the blessed evening sky, a gap through which Bert could be driven once he had mounted the slope.

It took them several minutes to locate Davis, and they found the gunner only a few feet away from where Barnes had been standing after Penn had jerked him back out of the path of the falling wall. At least, they found Davis' head. The rest of his body was buried under the fall and it needed only a second's examination for them to realize that he was dead.

Chapter Two

Saturday, 18 May

Something very strange had happened to the world in this part of Belgium. The war had gone away.

Before they drove the tank out of the tunnel, up the rubble slope, and down the other side, Barnes had made a personal reconnaissance in the brilliant warmth of early evening. The first thing that struck him was the incredible silence, a silence which was intensified by the only sound, the peaceful twittering of an unseen bird. Beyond the tunnel the railway stretched away across open country, the track empty, the green fields deserted, not a sign of life anywhere. Etreux, or what was left of it, must have petered out farther along the hillside, because over to his right there were no buildings, no people. Only the still waters of the broad canal which barred their easy way back to Etreux.

He found the silence, the absence of gunfire, so disturbing that he climbed a little way up the hillside above the wrecked tunnel entrance, but still he heard nothing, saw nothing. The war had gone far away – to where? And which way? He sat down for a moment on the grass, his nerves strangely on edge as though the peaceful landscape were full of sinister meaning. He sat there blinking against the strong sunlight, drinking in the fresh air, then he got up quickly, went back to the tank, and gave the order to advance.

There had been no question of burying Davis, for Davis was already buried under a ton of rock, so they wrote his name, rank and number on a piece of paper and left this under a rock close to the head. Then they drove away, too exhausted to feel much emotion other than shock at the suddenness of the gunner's death. The thought uppermost in Barnes' mind now was that his crew was reduced from four to three. They were all capable of firing the guns in an emergency and he told Penn that when the need arose he would act as gunner. As they moved along the rail track Barnes stood in the turret, map in hand, and his mind weighed up the situation grimly. At least they had almost full fuel tanks, which meant that they could travel one hundred and fifty miles along the roads, a distance which would be reduced by fifty per cent once they began moving across country, but this was the only credit point he could muster. One crew member short, the wireless out of action, no knowledge of where Parker might be: they almost resembled a warship sailing into uncharted seas with no means of communicating with its base. Half his mind pondered the dubious likelihood of rejoining his troop while the other half toyed with the glimmer of an idea which was to grow. *Whatever happened, they must find a really worthwhile objective.*

A mile from the tunnel the track reached a level crossing and it was at this point where they turned off the railway line and began to move along a second-class road which ran between low hedges bordering fields of poor grassland. Six miles farther on they should turn right along a road which would take them into the rear area behind Etreux. But where were the armies?

Standing upright in the turret Barnes strained his ears for sounds of gunfire, strained his eyes for sight of smoke or planes. The fields stretched away, empty; the sky, a vault of pale blue, stretched away uninhabited. The uncanny feeling grew, a feeling of men moving into unexplored territory. The tank tracks ground forward at top speed, the engines throbbed with power, as though determined to enjoy to the full this race across open country after the confinement inside the tunnel, and then Barnes saw the first traces of battle – the faint marks of tank tracks in the fields, the occasional crater where a shell or bomb had exploded, and as they proceeded along the deserted road the traces became more frequent, less reassuring. At one point Barnes ordered Reynolds to halt while he got down to examine wrecked vehicles by the roadside. They were burnt-out tanks, five of them, and they were French Renault tanks which looked as though they had fought the entire German Army on their own. A little farther along the road he stopped again and Penn climbed out with him to look at a mess of French equipment. In the ditch, rifles lay there as though they had been thrown down in panic flight from something awful and overpowering. When Barnes picked up one he found the weapon was still loaded. A few yards farther along there were abandoned Army packs, abandoned helmets, all French. Search as he might, Barnes could find no German equipment. Two of the helmets were occupied, the bodies lying on their backs facing the sky. Then more rifles, all of them loaded.

'I don't like the look of it,' said Barnes, 'The loaded rifles, I mean. It looks as though they just ran for their lives. Tanks against men, probably.'

'They've retreated, then,' remarked Penn quietly.

'Looks like it. A helluva lot must have happened while we were bottled up in that tunnel. According to the map there's a village about five miles farther on – we should get news there. I may halt Bert outside and go in on foot. I don't like the look of this at all.'

'It could be Jerry who had retreated,' said Penn thoughtfully. 'Parker may be on the Rhine now.'

'Wars don't move at that speed, Penn, not in either direction. As to Jerry retreating, I still don't like the look of those loaded rifles in the ditch – they smell of French retreat. We'd better get on.'

As they moved along the road Barnes saw more and more evidence that the scythe of war had passed that way, more and more burnt-out Renault tanks, smashed guns, still figures lying sprawled in the fields, helmets. And always they were French helmets. He was still waiting to see even one sign of German casualties in either men or machines, and he had not found it when he saw in the distance the first indication of life in this eerily empty landscape – a horizontal line of smoke. The line crossed the sky just above the ground and it hung perfectly still as though drawn in with charcoal. But at one end, the end which was approaching the road half a mile farther on, the line was growing and he realized it was smoke from a train's engine, a train which was still invisible below the level of an embankment. He scanned the sky and stiffened, his hand tightening on the turret rim. High up in the blue vastness a formation of planes was flying on a course which seemed to parallel the direction of the train. It was impossible to be sure but they looked like a squadron of British Blenheim bombers and his heart lifted at the sight of them.

As the tank trundled forward he watched the planes coming closer and then, focusing his glasses along the road, he saw the level crossing which the train would pass over within the next minute. He swivelled his glasses back to the aerial formation and caught his breath. They were moving into line now – *coming in for a bombing run.* He gave the order to halt and warned his crew over the intercom.

'I think there'll be some bombs dropping in the vicinity shortly. Don't laugh – but they'll be coming from our chaps.'

No one laughed as they waited in the stationary tank, the engines still ticking over. Should they reverse, wondered Barnes, and then he rejected the idea. They might just as easily reverse into a bomb. He prepared to slam down the lid but for the moment he waited, curious to see whether the Blenheims hit their target.

'What are they after?' Penn called up.

'A train, I think. It's just about to cross the road farther along, so get ready for it.'

His glasses brought up the road ahead now and he saw the smoke line emerge from behind the embankment. The train began to move across the road into the fields beyond. Two engines, drawing a line of goods coaches. He sucked in his breath as he saw tiny figures clustered round a long barrel on a flat truck. A Bofors? He could hear the gun now as it began pumping shells into the sky. When he looked up the first bombs were falling, small black dots against the warm blue, too far away to menace Bert, thank God, but they were going to be close, mighty close, to that train. The stick of dots vanished behind the smoke and he waited for the detonations. As he stood there, his eyes glued to the smoke line, a colossal explosion murdered the evening, far more enormous than it should have been. The first shock wave swept along the road as a coach went hump-backed. The wave buffeted against the tank hull and Barnes started to scramble inside, the words screaming through his brain. Ammunition train! The second, more devastating shock wave hit the tank when he was halfway down, his hand inside the turret, the lid still open. The tremendous force of the wave unbalanced his

46

footing and his head smashed back against the steel rim. At that very moment the undetected Messerschmitt swooped in a power dive, all guns blazing, but Barnes was already unconscious.

Saturday evening, 7 p.m. The 14th Panzer Division was racing deeper into France, now well beyond Laon, coming close to the Somme. General Heinrich Storch not only had the nose of a hawk, he also had the eye of that predatory bird, and this eye was now fixed on a hump some distance away across the fields. Whipping up his glasses, he focused on the object, letting out his breath in a hiss. He spoke briefly into the microphone hanging from his neck as a shell screamed across the field towards the tank column. A 75-mm gun, Storch told himself, the best artillery piece in the whole French Army, probably the only gun capable of taking on a German heavy tank. He looked back as the shell exploded over the road and in the field beyond. A ranging shot. The column was already obeying his command.

Storch's tank increased speed, rumbling along the road like an angry dinosaur while the gunner followed Storch's orders, traversing the turret which carried the barrel of his heavy gun towards the French artillery position. Behind him four tanks were moving at different speeds, so that in less than a minute they were well spaced out, making the French gun-aimer's task infinitely more difficult. He could now aim at only one target, while at the same time four tanks were firing back without fear of retaliation. The Panzer column stopped, five long barrels aimed across the field towards the camouflaged hump. A second shell screamed towards them, fell just short of the centre tank, and exploded in the grass, scattering a rain of soil over the hull. The Panzers replied.

One hand gripping the turret rim, the other holding his field-glasses, Storch felt the recoil of his own heavy cannon. This shell also fell short of its target, sending up a cloud of smoke in front of the 75-mm position. Storch spoke briefly, confident that the next shot would be on target, but his gunner never had the opportunity to fire because a shell from the tank behind landed squarely on top of the French position. It exploded, smoke blotting out the target, then there was a second explosion as the 75-mm ammunition went up, hurling the mangled bodies of the gun crew across the field. Two more tanks fired, as though encouraged by the marksmanship of their neighbour, both shells landed inside the billowing smoke, scattering the relics of the smashed gun. Storch issued the order to cease fire, his field-glasses on the target, his voice quiet.

'Congratulations, Meyer. Your duck-shooting experience is bearing fruit.'

Inside his own tank turret Meyer tightened his lips. It was typical that Storch could not pat him on the back without in the same breath digging him in the ribs. The duck-shooting remark was a slighting reference to his aristocratic background, he had no doubt about that. While they waited, Meyer polished his monocle and screwed it back into position. He wore it on every possible occasion simply because he knew that it annoyed Storch, who regarded the eye-glass as a badge of caste. Then he heard the general's high-pitched voice through the crackle of his earphones. They were on the move again.

Storch's sense of exultation was growing. In his mind's eye he was already racing ahead to the distant objective of Amiens, only twenty-five miles from the sea. His Panzer division was in the lead of the extraordinary advance and he was determined that it should maintain that position. Speaking into the microphone, he ordered the driver to increase speed, even though there was a danger that they might overtake the motor-cycle patrols, but the spotter plane had just radioed back to say the road ahead was clear.

Following up in the second tank, Meyer wiped his face clean of the dust kicked up by Storch's vehicle, his mood very different from that of his commanding officer. Soon they were passing through yet another French village without stopping, witnessing once again the same astonishing scene: another church, another village square, the inhabitants standing petrified against the walls, too scared or too astounded to rush indoors as the Panzer column thundered past. This can't go on much longer, Meyer told himself grimly. They had already far out-distanced the infantry and he was going to have a word with Storch about that at the next stopping point. All Meyer's professional instincts revolted against this wild headlong rush into the blue.

They left the village and emerged once again into the open French landscape, a sea of fields stretching away for ever, the sunlight shining down on dry pasturelands. And whereas Storch saw every evidence of a French collapse in the deserted view ahead, Meyer saw a panorama full of hidden dangers. He was well aware that the Manstein Plan envisaged a tremendous encircling sweep which would cut off the northern group of Allied armies from the French forces in the south, a sweep which would be completed when they reached the sea, but it seemed to Meyer that this plan was based on the extraordinary assumption that the Allies would sit back and let this happen. From his Great War experience Meyer knew this to be the assumption of a madman. At any moment the enemy counter-attack would erupt, rolling like a tidal wave against the armoured columns stretched out far ahead of the main German army. He only hoped to God that the counter-attack would not materialize *behind* them. Another instruction came as they approached a crossroads. Storch was waiting in his stationary tank as Meyer arrived. Climbing down out of his own vehicle he walked over and stood looking up at his general, who spoke first.

'The spotter plane reports something on the road ahead – it's investigating.'

'I know.' Meyer took a deep breath, wishing that

Storch would come down out of his turret. 'I've been expecting this – there'll be a heavy counter-attack at any moment. May I suggest that we wait here until the infantry catches us up? It might even be wiser to withdraw a few miles – to consolidate.'

'Why?'

Storch's voice was silky. He leaned over the turret to examine Meyer, who was at a further disadvantage because the general's peaked cap shaded his face and he couldn't see his expression.

'Because we have no supporting troops to hold the ground we have taken.' He took another deep breath. 'In fact, what we have taken may mean very little without troops occupying the ground we are rushing over like the Berlin Express.'

As soon as he had spoken he felt that he had gone too far, but having spoken he was determined not to back down and he prepared to defend himself. In any case, if things did go wrong this might well be a useful conversation to repeat at a military court of inquiry. The general did not reply immediately. Instead, he turned his head sideways, cocking his ear as though listening to something almost beyond the range of human hearing. Storch did have exceptional hearing powers and he attributed these to his total abstinence. Looking up, squinting against the sun's glare, Meyer had a view of Storch's profile now – an arrogant curve of nose, the thin wide mouth, the sharply pointed jaw-line.

'It sounds like bombing,' the general commented.

'Our Stukas must be taking out the next town. So, you think we ought to stop here do you, Meyer?'

'Or withdraw to a less-exposed . . .'

'May I remind you, Colonel Meyer,' Storch paused, still listening, 'that this Panzer division is under my command, and I, in turn, am responsible to the Corps Commander, General Guderian, who takes his instructions from General von Rundstedt?'*

Meyer was appalled. What on earth was coming? Surely Storch was not contemplating sending him back to base? He stood stiffly as the awful realization of his tactical error dawned on him. For Storch could easily interpret what had just been said as faint-heartedness in the face of the enemy. Meyer said nothing as Storch continued in the same silky tone.

'And may I also remind you of General Guderian's orders that the Panzers are to be let off the leash – to push forward as far and as fast as they can while their diesel lasts out?'

For the first time the general looked down at his GSO1 as he pulled down his earphones in position, listened, and then lifted them again. His voice was harsher now.

'It may interest you to know that the spotter plane has located and identified the obstacles in our path – two French farm carts. I don't imagine, Colonel

* General Guderian, who had carefully studied General de Gaulle's work, 'The Army of the Future', was chiefly responsible for the development of the Panzer divisions. Guderian later took the armoured host to the southern approaches of Moscow.

Meyer, that we should allow ourselves to be troubled by such opponents.' He stood up in his turret, erect as a ramrod. 'Meyer, please return to your tank – the advance will continue in the general direction of Amiens.'

Barnes sensed that something was wrong, that this was no normal waking, so he resisted the temptation to open his eyes immediately. He listened. His mind felt muddled and he was vaguely aware that he had been dreaming, dreaming something unpleasant, something to do with the war, but it had receded from his realms of consciousness. He always woke up quickly and now he pushed the dream, the nightmare, away, struggling to grasp where he was.

Where the hell was he? It was very quiet inside the building and he was lying stretched out on his back staring up at a beamed and raftered ceiling far above his head, alarm gripping him as memory surged back. The Blenheims, the long smoke line, the ammunition train, the terrible explosion, a feeling of something tearing into his right shoulder, then oblivion. Still lying on the blanket, his fingers reached up and explored the shoulder, contacting a thick dressing, sticky plaster. Yes, they'd got him, all right. But where was he now – and where were Penn and Reynolds?

He tried to sit up on the blanket and flopped back as a wave of dizziness rolled over him. His head was aching horribly and he felt weak and washed-out, hardly able to concentrate. Under the dressing his shoulder throbbed and at the pit of his stomach was a sensation of sickness. Tentatively, still lying down, he tested his legs by crooking them at the knee; first the right knee, then the left. They seemed to be in one piece. Now for the arms. He worked them round over the blanket, clenching and unclenching his fingers. As far as he could tell his main handicap was an appalling weakness which had reduced his normally wiry frame to the consistency of a jelly. Turning his head to one side, he saw his boots standing a few feet away, placed neatly together, the toecaps gleaming like black glass. He knew they were his own boots because he recognized a tiny scratch on one toecap, and the sight of these boots heartened him because they had recently been cleaned with great care, which meant that Reynolds must have cleaned them. To take the weight off his shoulder, he moved his body over sideways, lifting his head to examine his quarters. He was inside some kind of outbuilding, probably part of a farm. Yes, in the far corner he could see an old plough and beside it some of their Army kit – a dixie supported on an improvised tripod, suspended over the ashes of a fire, and two enamel mugs. Then he saw something standing against the wall which gave him a bad turn. A German machine-pistol with the magazine protruding below the barrel, its strap coiled in a neat loop.

He tried to stand up to reach the loaded weapon but his legs gave way, so he crawled from under the blanket over his body and wobbled his way across the wooden floor on his knees, naked from the waist upwards. He collapsed as he reached the weapon. Gritting his teeth, he forced himself up on to his knees again, grabbed the pistol by its long barrel and then crawled back to his blankets. Sitting up, he began to examine the machine-pistol, extracting the magazine before he fiddled with the firing mechanism. As he found out how the gun worked it came back to him. Someone had attended to his wound, a man with red cheeks and a bushy white moustache. The same man had given him an injection, he could remember the prick of the needle in his right arm, and later the stranger had come back to re-dress his wound. He could remember that very clearly because he had resented being woken up. But how long had they been inside this place? Six hours? Twelve hours? He looked at his watch and the face was cracked, the hands stopped at 7.45. That would be about the time when the ammunition train blew up. Through a window high up in the wall he could see that it was broad daylight, another glorious day with the sky blue and hot. It must be Sunday morning or afternoon, Sunday, 19 May. Then he heard someone coming. Re-inserting the magazine, he pulled a blanket up over him and sat still, the gun concealed under the blanket, his left hand under the barrel, his right hand round the trigger guard.

Two men walked in through the huge door at the far end of the building. Penn and a stranger, a lad no older than eighteen, who wore a blue denim jacket and trousers, his shirt open at the front. He looked the picture of health, tall, well built, his manner radiating an air of vitality. His fair hair was combed neatly back over his head and his blue eyes looked down at Barnes with curiosity. Penn looked surprised as they stopped near his bedside.

'You're awake, Sergeant.'

'What did you expect to find – a corpse? Who's this?'

'This is Pierre. He speaks English. Pierre, meet Sergeant Barnes.'

'I am happy to meet you, Sergeant.'

The lad bent down and to Barnes' embarrassment he solemnly shook hands. Then he stood up and waited without saying a word.

'Where's Reynolds?' demanded Barnes.

'He's on guard outside.'

'Guarding Bert, you mean?'

'Yes, Bert's in the next shed. Don't worry – he's well out of sight.'

'And what does that mean – why should I worry?'

'How are you feeling?' Penn inquired. 'You've had . . .'

'Well enough to wonder what the devil is going on. How long have we been in this place, Penn?'

'You've had concussion. When the Jerry fighter dived at us you caught a bullet in the shoulder and banged your head a fourpenny one on the turret.'

'I can remember that,' Barnes snapped irritably. 'Do get to the point and answer my question. How long have we been here?'

'Four days.'

The answer hit Barnes like a thunderclap. For once in his life he was speechless as the implications of Penn's statement raced through his brain. Where was the troop? Come to that, where was the BEF? Sitting up was making the throbbing of his shoulder wound worse: he would have loved to lie down again but that was out of the question. He blinked away the muzziness of his vision as Penn spoke again.

'You'd better listen to what Pierre has to say – he knows more about it than I do.'

Barnes looked up at the lad, his voice polite but firm.

'Pierre, would you mind going outside and staying with Trooper Reynolds for a few minutes?'

He saw Pierre's face drop and Penn frowned. When the lad had gone out and shut the door Penn protested.

'I wish you hadn't done that – we may need him. You don't know the position here.'

'And I won't until you tell me,' Barnes dropped the blanket and laid the machine-pistol on its side.

'What did you want that for?' asked Penn.

'I'd no idea what was happening when I woke up – a couple of Jerries might have walked through that door. Now, what's the position?'

Penn paused and then burst out with it. 'We're a helluva long way behind the German lines. Maybe twenty miles or more.'

'We can't be . . .'

'The Germans have broken through along the whole front. They've torn a tremendous gap in the lines and it's a bloody great mess – just how great it's hard to tell because there are so many rumours . . .'

'It could be a rumour that they've broken through, then.'

'No chance of that – I heard this morning that the Panzers have reached Arras. The Luftwaffe has the whole show to itself – our lot and the French Air Force were shot out of the sky in the first few days. The Germans have hundreds of tanks and thousands of planes. You've got to face it – we're miles and miles behind the German lines.'

'Today is Thursday, then?'

'Yes, Thursday, May the twenty-third.'

'And where exactly are we?'

'Just outside a place called Fontaine. We're fairly close to the French frontier.'

'What?'

For the second time in five minutes Barnes was staggered, but this time he simply stared at his corporal grimly as he climbed to his feet. He felt his legs giving way at once, but sheer will-power stiffened the flagging muscles. Leaning a hand against the nearby wall, feeling the sweat trickling down his back with the effort of staying upright, he smiled wintrily.

'Penn, if I haven't gone potty I seem to recall that when the ammo train went up we were a good forty miles from the French frontier.'

Penn's moustache quivered and then his sense of humour got the upper hand and he spoke lightly.

'Sergeant Barnes, you have been away from this wonderful world of ours for four days – in other words you've been out cold, so it was up to me to see you home safe and sound, if you can call this home, although personally I've known better ones. Supposing you just let me tell you what's happened and then you'll feel a lot happier. You won't,' he added with a grin, 'but you know I always phrase things in the most tactful way.'

'The floor is yours.'

'When the train blew up we were attacked by a Messerschmitt and you collected one in the shoulder. You managed to smash your head good and hard at the same time. On the way down you did get the lid shut and that's why I'm talking to you now – I heard half a beltful of bullets rattling on the turret before Jerry pushed off. When I checked the state of your health you were dead to the world and bleeding like a stuck pig, but I managed to get a dressing on.' He took a deep exaggerated breath to illustrate the drama of it all. 'For the next few hours, till well after dark, we were dodging Jerries. It was a sheer fluke that we got away with it – mostly by driving across open country. Eventually, hours later, we ended up here and here we've been ever since.'

'You drove through the night?'

'Yes, there was a moon, which helped, considering we daren't use the headlights. When we got here I hadn't the slightest idea where we were. And before you blow my head off about that, you can't read a map at night when you're travelling across country, keeping an eye open for Jerry, and popping down to see whether your tank commander is still in the land of the living. At least,' he ended with a grin, 'I can't.'

'You did damn well, Penn. Thanks. What made you stay in this place?'

'I found a Belgian doctor who was willing to look after you without letting anyone know we were here. These buildings are outside Fontaine and the village still don't know about us. The doctor's a nice old boy called Lepin and the last time he called he said it was just a matter of changing your dressing and waiting till you came round. I doubt if he'll be back again – he could be shot by the Germans for treating you. The main thing is we haven't been spotted yet . . .'

'Pierre has spotted us.'

'I'll come to him in a minute. How are you doing?'

While they had been talking Barnes was testing himself, walking slowly round the floor and keeping close to the wall as he forced his reluctant legs forward. The wound was thumping him good and proper now but the dizziness was receding.

'Fine,' he said quickly. 'Go on.'

'Lepin was a godsend. You probably don't remember it – and that's your good luck – but while you were drugged he took out the bullet. He said you'd need at least ten days' rest – that's a week starting from yesterday.'

'Arras – where did you get that news about Arras?'

'It came through on the radio bulletin. I go into Fontaine once a day to listen in. Lepin's house backs on to a field and he leaves the wireless set in a shed for me.'

'The French radio may not be reliable.'

'I'm talking about the BBC.'

A chill ran down Barnes' spine. Arras was halfway to the sea. He still found it difficult to grasp the extent of the catastrophe and he still held on to the hope that the reports were wildly exaggerated.

'We must have some idea of how far behind the German lines we are,' he said sharply.

'I've no idea at all.'

Barnes paused to hold himself up against the wall. 'Look, Penn, there must be a front line somewhere. Don't the radio bulletins give any indication at all?'

'Sergeant, you still haven't grasped it. The French to the south of Etreux took an awful bashing. The whole weight of the German armour was thrown against them from what I can make out, and there isn't a front line down here any more. Everything's all over the place. Jerry has torn a bloody great gap in the line and it's getting bigger every day. And the BEF is a long way west of Brussels now.'

'There are no Germans in Fontaine?'

'Not up to this morning. A column of tanks went

through two days ago but that's the way they seem to be operating – they didn't leave a single soldier behind.'

Barnes found that interesting. He thought about it while he picked up his clothes and started dressing with difficulty. At least he was still wearing his battledress trousers so he wouldn't have to struggle with them. Then he resumed his cross-examination.

'The tank's next door, you said. In what condition?'

'Engines are in full working order. The Besa's OK. So is the two-pounder. The wireless is still US but the intercom's OK. We can talk to each other but we're cut off from the outside world. Reynolds and I have spent most of our time on maintenance while you were playing Rip Van Winkle.'

'One thing bothers me, Penn. This lad, Pierre. How does he come into the picture?'

'He's helped us enormously. He saw us coming into this place when we first arrived and he's been around ever since. He knew we were here so I thought the best thing was to make friends with him – and the fact that he speaks English as well as his native French is a godsend . . .'

'He's Belgian?'

'Yes, his parents come from the north and he's lost touch with them. He was visiting an uncle in Fontaine when the war started.'

Barnes asked a lot more questions while he finished dressing and among other things he learnt that it was now two o'clock in the afternoon. At the end of the conversation he returned to the subject of Pierre.

'You said he was visiting an uncle here when the war started – you mean way back in September last year?'

'No, I meant when the Germans attacked Belgium a fortnight ago. I still say Pierre could be useful. We both know a little French but if we're going to get out of this we'll need someone who can talk to the locals, and he's as keen as mustard to come with us. How the hell will we know where we are if . . .'

'Bring him in to me.'

Barnes picked up the machine-pistol, extracted the magazine again and began testing the mechanism.

'Pierre brought that . . .' began Penn.

'I said send him in.'

Barnes went on fiddling with the gun after Penn had brought in Pierre and he kept him waiting while he went on examining the weapon. He was looking down at the gun when he fired his question at Pierre.

'Where did you get hold of this?'

'I found it on the road outside Fontaine. I saw a car stop and the driver threw it into the ditch. Then he drove away very fast. It is in good order, Sergeant Barnes.' He pronounced it 'Burns'. 'I tested it myself. After first taking out the magazine,' he added proudly.

'I see. Where did a lad of your age learn about things like this?'

'My father works at the Belgian small-arms factory at Herstal. He can fire all the pistols and machine-guns.' Again the hint of pride. 'Including your own Bren gun. They call it by that name because it was first made in the city of Brno in Czechoslovakia.'

'You have an uncle living in Fontaine?'

Barnes looked directly into the lad's blue eyes and his gaze was returned steadily. Pierre's eyebrows were so fair that he almost appeared to have none, which gave him a curiously older appearance.

'Not any more,' he replied. 'My uncle fled from the Germans three days since.'

'I see. Why didn't you go with him?'

'Because I am not scared. I am going to fight the Germans.' He went on talking quickly. 'I shall be eighteen years of age by July so I am quite old enough and my knowledge of weapons means that training is not necessary. Corporal Penn said that I could come with you.'

'Steady on, laddie,' Penn interjected. 'I said you'd have to ask Sergeant Barnes and that isn't the same thing at all.'

Barnes opened his mouth to say that he couldn't come under any circumstances and then he changed his mind. There was no point in antagonizing the lad before they left Fontaine. Instead, he asked a question.

'Where did you learn to speak such good English?'

'Thank you, Sergeant.' Pierre glowed with pride. 'My father sent me to spend six months with the

British firm of Vickers in Birmingham so that I could learn about British weapons. They tell me that I have a Midland accent.'

'You'd better go and talk to Trooper Reynolds, Pierre, while I have a look at the tank with Corporal Penn.'

Barnes started to explain to Penn how the machine-pistol worked, handing the weapon to him to demonstrate a point while Pierre was leaving the building.

'The temptation with this gun is to hold on to the magazine, but you've got to grasp it higher up just under the barrel ... That doctor, Lepin, did you talk to him much while he was here looking after me?'

'Hardly at all – he's a very quiet type and I left Pierre to interpret for me.'

'You've been into Fontaine yourself?'

'No, I kept well clear of it except when I visited Lepin's garden shed to hear the news. I thought the Germans might occupy the place at any moment and I wanted to lie low till you were better.'

'Who owns these buildings – they belong to some farmer, I imagine?'

'Yes, they do, but he's cleared out with the refugees so we should be all right here for a while until the roads are quieter. The main one through Fontaine is still crammed with refugee traffic and the place itself is lousy with them. We may have to sit it out here for several days.'

'Get the map for me, Penn. Staying in one spot

behind the German lines for four days isn't a healthy idea at all and I'd say our luck is due to run out at any moment. We must get moving.'

'You've only just got up . . .'

'And I intend to stay up. Warn Reynolds to make any last minute checks he thinks necessary so that we're ready to move at a moment's notice. And I could do with something to eat if there's anything left.'

The atmosphere was changing already with every word Barnes said, and Penn could sense it. A feeling of urgency had begun to animate Barnes and that feeling communicated itself to Penn, but he made one last effort.

'I still think you ought to rest up at least . . .'

'I'm going into Fontaine with Pierre to see for myself. When I get back we must be ready to move. Make no mistake about it, Penn, we'll be out of this place well before nightfall.'

The feeling that they ought to be on the move, away from this place, tugged insistently at Barnes as he marched steadily along the road to Fontaine with Pierre. The afternoon sun shone down brilliantly over the fields of France, beating down on their faces and warming their hands, a physical sensation of pure heat. Barnes had two reasons for his reconnaissance: he wanted to smell the atmosphere for himself and he wanted to test his own staying power. The blazing sunshine added to the discomfort of his wound, so that now as well as the throb-throb he could also feel a pricking sensation round the edges of his dressing, a sensation which made him want to tear off the bandage. His head was aching and he walked rigidly, forcing himself to take long strides, each footfall thudding up into the sensitive shoulder like the impact of a small road-bumper. But he was still on his feet, so he was all right. In his holster he carried the Webley .455 revolver and the flap was unbuttoned.

'There's the village, Sergeant Barnes.'

'What on earth is that lot on the road?'

'They are the refugees. They go through Fontaine all day and all night. It is difficult to cross the main square.'

A grey slate church spire rose up from a huddle of stone-walled buildings and from that distance they could see on both sides of the village a road which ran at right angles to the road they were walking along. The main road was packed with an incredible congestion of traffic, a slow-moving column which travelled at such a snail's pace that it hardly seemed to move at all. Barnes turned off the road and began to cut across the fields diagonally along a course which would take them to the eastern outskirts of the village.

'Are we not entering Fontaine?' inquired Pierre.

'I want to have a look at that column. Later, I want to go in to buy some food.'

'You will not get any – the village store is empty

and the storekeeper left two days before. He was very frightened and said it was time to go.'

'Frightened of the Germans?'

'No, of the villagers. He said that soon they would take what they wanted without paying him a franc. One man did call him a robber – I saw it myself. Other people in the store were threatening him.'

The incident had an ugly ring and Barnes began to feel alarmed. The sooner they got out of this area the better, but he must check the state of the roads first. We're in a jam, all right, he told himself. If all the main roads are like this we'll have to move across country, and that will slow us down and double our fuel consumption. They were approaching the refugee line broadside on, a line which stretched as far as the eye could see. A dozen yards from the roadside they stopped in the field and watched the spectacle. The road was crammed from verge to verge with a swollen river of fleeing humanity – several cars, a large number of horse-drawn carts piled high with bed linen, mattresses, and a jumble of household goods. On one cart he saw a brass-posted bed which threatened to lurch over the edge at any moment. But above all the road was congested with people on foot and Barnes had never seen more pathetic faces, the faces of men and women at the end of their tether, their expressions weary and despairing, their eyes fixed dully on the vehicle ahead as they trudged along under the merciless heat of the sun.

'We'll never get through that lot,' he said eventually.

'There is a road which turns off over there.' Pierre pointed across the fields to a low hedge. 'You could take your tank along that road. No refugees have come from that direction since the Germans attacked.'

'Do you know where it goes?'

'Of course. It leads to Arras. I have never been there but my uncle has told me. I have been along it for many miles and it is wide enough for a tank.'

What Pierre was saying agreed with the map Barnes had studied and he found his thoughts turning more and more towards the town of Arras. Penn had told him that a news bulletin that morning had reported an Allied counter-attack developing in the area of Arras, a counter-attack of British tanks, and the town was the one fixed point where the Allies seemed to be engaging the Germans. He looked to the right as he heard a car coming closer, its horn blaring persistently. It was an open touring Renault, a green four-seater, and superficially it had the appearance of a military staff car. For one split second Barnes throught he might have re-established contact with the Allied forces, and then he saw that the only occupant was a woman. The horn blared again and again as she stopped and then edged forward a few more yards. Barnes felt that she must be crazy, but as he watched her he was filled with a sense of unease, an odd foreboding. To add to her idiotic behaviour she had not even offered a lift to any of the exhausted wretches who trudged in front of her on foot.

'How provocative can you get?' growled Barnes.

'Pardon?'

The German attack came without warning, without mercy, came out of clear blue sky from in front of the sun so that it was almost impossible to detect their approach, but Barnes heard them coming.

'Down!'

He shouted the word again and again to the bewildered crowd and then dropped flat on the grass beside Pierre as the first Messerschmitt swooped along the column, its engine screaming, its machine-gun blazing non-stop. The crowd was dazed, stunned with terror, unable even to attempt to run for safety in the shock of the sudden onslaught. In front of him Barnes saw an old man turn and stare at the plane as it came straight along the road with a scream and a stutter. He must have taken a dozen bullets in the chest before he crashed back against a cart. As the first machine screamed past, Barnes tugged out his revolver and waited for the next one, steadying the gun barrel across his arm. The second Messerschmitt pulled out of its dive and sped over the procession almost immediately. Barnes saw the outline of the pilot's helmet, the black cross on the fuselage, the swastika on the tail. He fired three times in rapid succession, knowing that it was hopeless. Unless a .455 bullet burst through the petrol tank he might just as well be armed with a bow and arrow, but he had to try something. The third machine was coming now, its nadir so low that it almost skimmed the heads of the panic-striken refugees. Barnes fired, swearing foully as he switched his eyes to the west where another one was coming, and at that moment a horse went berserk, dragging its cart off the road as people scrambled desperately to escape this new menace.

There were six machines altogether, and when they had flown away from the carnage the afternoon was suddenly horribly quiet. Only the heart-broken cries of sobbing women disturbed the stillness as Barnes clambered to his feet and ran over to the stationary Renault. When he reached the car and looked inside he clenched his teeth; the woman in the Renault had taken the full blast of the machine-gun and now she was hardly identifiable even as a blood-soaked corpse. The engine was still running so he leaned over and switched off the ignition. He would give these refugees what help he could and then head for Arras nonstop.

The tank rumbled southwards at top speed and the road ahead was clear as far as the eye could see, another panorama of Belgian pastureland spreading away with hardly a tree anywhere, which meant no cover from air attack.

Standing in the turret, Barnes concentrated on keeping all-round observation: the deserted road ahead, the road behind, the fields on either side where people worked a long way off and never seemed to notice the passage of a British tank and, above all, the sky overhead where the most instant danger could strike without warning. Below him Penn occupied Davis' old position behind the guns, while in the nose of the tank Reynolds sweltered as he handled his driving levers, his head thrust up through the open hatch, relieved that once again they were on the move and that Barnes was in command. To Reynolds, all was well with the world so long as Barnes was in command. Behind the turret sat Pierre. He was perched outside the tank on the engine covers and already had grown accustomed to the gentle wobble of the hull as the huge tracks ground farther south with every revolution. There had almost been a row between Barnes and Penn over taking the Belgian lad. At first, Barnes had refused point-blank.

'We need him for information,' Penn had protested. 'He knows the country and we don't. Supposing we're inside a town close to the battle area – accurate information will be vital. Our lives may depend on it and the only one who can get it quickly from the locals is Pierre. He's taken some chances with us already – he was with us in the building all the time the Panzer column was moving through Fontaine. We didn't know it at the time but if he'd been caught with us they'd have shot him. And he brought food for us.'

It was probably the gesture of bringing food which had finally persuaded Barnes to let Pierre travel with them until he could drop him off in an area more peaceful than Fontaine. They were on the point of departing when Pierre had come running back from the village with sticks of French bread under each arm and a satchelful of tinned meat hanging from his shoulder. He even had a packet of coffee in his pocket. No one had inquired too closely as to how he had obtained these provisions: after all, there was a war on.

And now, as the tank left Fontaine far behind them, Barnes was weighing up many things. It was pleasant to have the sun shining down on them, but it was from the sun that the Luftwaffe made its sneak attacks, so frequently he shaded his eyes to scan the sky, straining his ears for the first warning sound of approaching engines. The landscape ahead was beginning to undulate and he kept a careful observation along the ridges to detect any signs of gun positions which might lie in ambush. So far they had only met Belgian horse-carts on this lonely road which seemed to go on for ever, horse-carts which plodded past while their drivers stared at the tank as though hardly able to believe their eyes. As he kept up his vigilant watch Barnes was also trying to locate on the map the road they were travelling along and he was puzzled. There was a road from Fontaine which led south-west in the general direction of distant Arras, but this road had gradually turned until they were heading due south. Without mentioning his discovery he kept an eye open for landmarks.

They were going to run into trouble soon now,

Barnes could feel it in his bones. They were travelling with their guns loaded and the power-traverse on, and Barnes had given Pierre strict instructions that in case of trouble he must immediatelly leave the tank and take cover. The farther they moved along this peaceful road, the only witnesses to their progress cows grazing in the fields, the tauter Barnes' nerves became. It was only a matter of time before they met something big and when that happened he'd have to take a lightning decision. He only hoped that he was up to that. He had reached the stage where he accepted the throbbing and pricking of his shoulder as a permanent burden, as much a part of himself as breathing, but he did wish that the dreadful pounding headache would go away. Under the circumstances it was remarkable that he reacted at all when the emergency arose, and the fact that he reacted instantly was little short of a miracle.

At the time they were travelling at reduced speed on his instructions because they were approaching a hump-backed bridge. The character of the countryside had changed again and now there were low hills close to the road. Even from the elevated vantage point of the turret he found it impossible to see the stretch of road immediately beyond the bridge, so as they drove forward his gaze was fixed on the crest which was still a hundred yards away. Instinctively, he didn't like the look of the bridge. He began to give precautionary orders, just in case.

'Two-pounder. One hundred. The bridge ahead.'

Below him, Penn's head was pressed hard against a padded bracket, his eye peering steadily through the telescope at the small circle of countryside which centred on the bridge crest. The two-pounder's leather-bound grip was fixed tightly round his shoulder, under his armpit, so that only the slightest movement of that shoulder automatically raised or depressed the muzzle of the gun. His left hand gripped the power-traverse lever while the other hand gripped the trigger handle. Now the cross-wires inside the glass circle were aligned dead centre on the bridge crest. The range was set, he was ready, and all this had taken only a few seconds.

Barnes had hardly completed giving the orders, Penn had just completed obeying them, when it happened. Straight over the crest of the hump-back, travelling at high speed, recklessly high speed, hurtled a large covered truck. Barnes registered its identity in a flash – even to the soldier peering round from the back, leaning well out, a pudding-shaped helmet set squarely on his head. A German detachment of motorized infantry.

'German truck! Fire!'

The barrel dropped slightly, because now the truck was over the hump, still tearing towards them. Knowing what to expect, Barnes gripped the turret rim. The tank shuddered under the stomach-jerking spasm of the recoil, the shell screamed forward, its target rushing to meet it. The two missiles met in frightful collision, the shell smashing into the truck just above engine level, exploding with a roar, ripping apart metal, canvas, flesh. Inside the turret the air reeked of cordite fumes as Barnes, who was now behind the gun, re-loaded, flipping in a fresh round with a certain force to make the breech-block close. Then he scrambled back to the top of the turret, the tank still trundling towards its target. In the nose of the vehicle Reynolds stared at the truck with grim satisfaction. God, that had been a close one!

The truck was pulverized, but the force of explosion plays strange tricks and this explosion had hurled from the open back several German soldiers still clasping their machine-pistols, throwing them out on to the grass verge where they lay stunned for a second. But when Barnes looked out from his turret they were recovering, jumping up off the grass, the reflex of fear speeding their movements as they darted into the field, spreading out the target. In a matter of seconds, if they were well trained, they would be circling round the tank. Barnes gave instant orders.

'Driver, right, off the road, right. Besa. Besa. Right. Well right. Fire!'

Penn's trigger hand jumped to the Besa. Reynolds swerved off the road, through a low wire fence, over the grass, heading straight for the running men. The Besa began to stutter, a hail of bullets catching the man on the right-most flank, catching him in mid-stride, in mid-air as he began to flop, his body hiccupping convulsively, the machine-pistol falling from his grip.

'Besa. Traverse left, left . . .'

Coolly, without panic, Penn's mind and hand paralleled Barnes' intentions and the turret began to swing, taking the flail of bullets with it. Get the one on the far right first, then sweep left against the forward movement of the running men, catching all five men as they desperately tried to spread, depressing the Besa to sweep it at ground level over those who had dropped to the grass. In half a minute it was all over and Barnes gave the order to take the tank back on to the road.

The smashed truck sagged grotesquely to one side, still on its wheels but keeled over at a crippled angle, flames licking over the bonnet, the torn canvas at the back catching alight. Then the petrol tank went up, a dull thump. Flames soared up and the canvas flared, burning rapidly, exposing the metal framework. Halting the tank, Barnes waited until the conflagration had died down, his eyes scanning the summer sky constantly for aircraft, but it was empty of any sign of war. Only on the ground death disfigured the gloriously sunny day. As soon as the flames began to peter out Barnes gave the order to move the tank forward. The shelled truck now blocked the way, the wreckage standing in the middle of the road. Carefully he guided the tank along the grass verge, turning it so that the front hull faced the truck broadside on.

'Driver, move forward slowly and tip it over the edge.'

The tank crawled forward, its tracks bumping the

side of the truck. Foot by foot, it thrust the truck backwards towards the slope at the end of the bridge, a slope which Barnes now saw led down to the canal. From the turret he could see over the hump of the bridge and the road beyond was clear for miles. He could also see on the floor of the cab and inside the truck itself a huddle of clothes which bore little resemblance to uniformed soldiers. The truck was almost on the brink now, pushed backwards by the tank which was manoeuvring the vehicle like a bull-dozer shifting waste material. As the truck began to topple a helmeted figure scrambled out from under the bodies, dropping to the roadway and swinging his machine-pistol round in one movement. God knew how he had managed to survive the holocaust but now he survived only seconds. As the machine-pistol came round Barnes fired his revolver at the same moment as the Besa began to stutter. The German fell back over the edge a few seconds before the truck toppled, crashing down the slope on top of him with a jarring grind of crumpling metal as the vehicle landed on the edge of the canal, settling like a crushed concertina. There was an unpleasant smell of burnt rubber as Barnes gave the orders to reverse, drive forward over the bridge, and halt on the far side. Then he clambered down into the road and went back over the bridge.

He saw Pierre in the distance, climbing up out of the ditch where he had jumped as soon as the truck appeared. Now he walked slowly along the road as

Barnes scrambled down the slope to investigate the carnage. It was like a miniature battlefield. In its fall down the slope, the truck had thrown out its grisly load, scattering bodies along the canal bank. One man lay half in the canal, face downwards. The smashed and twisted bodies were all dead, all except one. Grimly, Barnes walked over to the moaning man, the moans reminding him of an animal in mortal pain. Both his legs had been blown off and he lay on his stomach, the lower part of his body a blood-stained stump. He had lost his helmet and appeared to be biting the ground. It was quite clear that in a short time, half an hour at the most, he would be dead, but during that half an hour he was a creature who would be racked by unendurable agonies. Christ, thought Barnes, why didn't you have the sense to die too? He clenched his teeth bitterly. You poor bastard. He mouthed the words silently for fear that the man might hear him, might even manage to turn his head. Leaning down, unaware that his teeth were locked rigid, he held the muzzle of the revolver within an inch of the man's head and before he could think about it he pulled the trigger. The German gave a quick convulsive movement and lay still. Barnes let out his breath. As he straightened up he sensed that he was not alone and he turned round. Over the parapet of the bridge two faces stared down. Penn and Pierre.

'Pierre,' shouted Barnes, 'come down here a minute.'

The lad came down slowly, watching his feet as he

slithered down the slope, not looking at what lay beneath him. Up on the bridge Penn still looked down, his face like stone. When Pierre reached the bottom he stopped and looked at Barnes, his hair freshly combed, his expression blank.

'Take a good look, Pierre,' invited Barnes. 'This is the war you were so eager to get mixed up in. When you reach your age group you'll get called up – and it's my bet the war will last long enough for that. But don't ever think that it's going to be fun.'

Pierre's eyes wandered over the bodies, his face still devoid of all emotion. He stood very erect.

'Take a good look,' went on Barnes, watching him closely. 'These are the bastards who machine-gun women from tanks and planes.'

'Can I go now?' Pierre asked coldly. He omitted to add the word 'sergeant'.

'Yes, go straight back to the tank and wait there with Trooper Reynolds. Penn, come down here a minute.'

He waited. Pierre had disappeared over the bridge when Penn reached the tow-path, his eyes blazing, his voice sharp-edged.

'Did you have to do that to him?'

'I had my reasons. Now find two machine-pistols in working order and as many spare magazines as you can. That'll give us one each and they may come in handy.'

They worked in silence. Barnes counted the bodies and as far as he could make out the truck had carried a complement of twenty men including those lying in the field on the other side of the road. He would have liked to search the clothes of the officer who had undoubtedly sat in the cab beside the driver, but in this jumbled horror such a search would have taken hours. Instead, he went back to the man without legs, felt under the body, and extracted his Army pay-book. Gustav Freisler, the 75th Field Regiment. At least what's what he thought the long German word identifying the unit meant. He put the pay-book in his pocket. It would positively identify the unit when he reached the Allied lines and also he wanted the report of this poor devil's death sent back to Germany via the Red Cross as soon as possible.

When they returned to the tank, Barnes spent a short time explaining to Penn and Reynolds how the German machine-pistols worked and he made them practise using them without magazines. While this was going on Pierre sat on the engine covers and gazed up at the sky without taking the slightest notice of Barnes. Penn practised with his pistol diligently and said hardly a word, climbing up into the tank when the exercise was over with an expressionless face. Only Reynolds seemed unaware of the coolness in the atmosphere and he spoke with conviction as he turned to get down inside his hatch.

'Good old Penn. He can really use that two-pounder.'

'Good job he can – there were twenty of them inside that truck.'

Good old Penn. Reynolds was right there. If he hadn't clobbered that truck with his first shot, the dead German officer might well be examining their pay-books now. But it was what lay ahead of them that was occupying Barnes' thoughts now, and as he screwed up his eyes to check the late afternoon sky he felt sure that they couldn't hope to get through the coming night without very serious trouble.

There was an element of danger in his decision, but Barnes took a calculated risk when he decided to spend the night by the river bridge. Since leaving the shelled truck by the canal they had experienced an evening of tension which had played havoc with their already strained nerves, and since both Penn and Reynolds had taken it in turn to mount guard during the four nights when Barnes lay unconscious at Fontaine, all of them were in a state close to physical exhaustion. Probably the factor which more than any other drained their resources was the knowledge that they were moving behind the enemy lines, that at any moment they might encounter an overwhelming German force which would easily annihilate them in a matter of minutes. Most of all, Barnes feared that they would meet a Panzer column head-on.

The rising tension made itself felt in different ways. Two hours had been wasted by the roadside when the engines broke down and they struggled to find and repair the defect. During this time Pierre, who had to leave the tank when they pulled open the engine covers at the rear, sat on the grass verge without speaking. Barnes suspected that even Penn was beginning to wish that he hadn't been so keen to bring the Belgian with them, but he couldn't be sure because the corporal himself was unusually silent. Reynolds worked stolidly on the engines, noticing nothing wrong, but then Reynolds was never over-sensitive where atmospheres were concerned. They found the cause of the trouble eventually, repaired it, had a drink of water and then moved on, leaving the road to circle round a town. So far they had avoided three towns by moving across open country in wide sweeps, returning to the road well beyond each town. This tactic, too, had caused an argument with Penn.

'Why don't we risk it?' he had pressed. 'We have Pierre and one of us can sneak in with him to get some news.'

'We may have to do that later, but not yet,' Barnes had replied firmly. 'I want to have some better idea of where we are first.'

'Doesn't the map tell you that?'

The engine had just been repaired and before starting out again Barnes and Penn had wandered off into a nearby field as Reynolds made his final checks.

'No, it doesn't, Penn. We'll go round this place like we went round the last one.'

From where they stood they could see the town in the distance. A tall church spire, several factory chimneys, a long line of buildings. A flight of Stuka dive-bombers crossed the sky very high up, heading for the north-west. Since leaving Fontaine they had stopped four times while enemy planes flew out of view. Irritably, Penn persisted.

'But if you just trace the road down from Fontaine . . .'

'Penn, the road we're travelling on doesn't correspond with the road we thought we were taking. It doesn't correspond with it at all. We're travelling south-west now, I know, but for a long time we were heading due south.'

'The compass may be playing up. It does sometimes with all that metal . . .'

'I'm going by the sun – that isn't affected by the metal, is it?'

'You mean we may have got back on to a different road when we made one of our detours?'

'I mean there's something damned peculiar about the whole business. So,' Barnes spoke emphatically, 'we're not going near any town today. We'll go round this place, wherever it is. We'd better get moving.'

It was very close to dusk when Barnes saw the bridge, a large stone affair with a broad span which could easily take two lanes of traffic. They were in the middle of open country miles away from anywhere and within half an hour they wouldn't be able to move without putting on the headlights, a course of action he was anxious to avoid at all costs. As they came closer he noticed a copse of trees to the right of the bridge. He stopped the tank and went forward with Penn to investigate.

'This might be a good place,' Penn suggested. 'Bridges are lucky for us. We could park Bert in these trees.'

But the copse was a hopeless cover. It was simply a handful of thin-trunked saplings staggered at intervals through the grass. No matter how they parked the tank, Bert would still be visible from the road, and it was the road which worried Barnes. Penn thought differently.

'This is an ideal spot, particularly at night.'

'Not correct, Penn. Any vehicle coming over that bridge from the south will swivel its headlights straight over this spot. We've been lucky so far – I think the German invasion had cleared all normal traffic off this road but that doesn't mean Jerry won't be sending more troops this way. We've got to find somewhere we can park Bert completely out of sight. Under that bridge might do the trick.'

'*Under* the bridge? . . .'

But he was talking to himself. Barnes strode off back to the road and scrambled down the bank by the side of the bridge, pushing his way through thick brambles to the river at the bottom. Yes, there was ample room under the high stone arch, but how deep was the river? Bert could comfortably wade through three feet of water providing the fording flap was closed over the rear air outlets. He found that under the bridge the water was less than a foot deep and blessed the fact that it hadn't rained for over a fortnight. Even better, the bed of the river was surfaced with smooth rocks and between the rocks was a fine gravel.

An old footpath ran along the north side of the river, a footpath half-submerged under weeds and tall grass, and this would give them a place to sleep close to the tank. Looking up under the arch he judged that there was sufficient clearance to take Bert's overall height of eight feet. Now for the question of concealment. He walked along the footpath under the bridge, pacing out the distance. Twenty-six feet. Bert's overall length was eighteen feet so he would rest well inside the archway. The only problem lay in getting the tank down to the river bed – the banks were at least twelve feet high and steeply inclined, their slopes covered with a jungle of brambles and undergrowth. He went back to the tank and issued instructions, leaving Pierre by the roadside while he guided the vehicle some distance across a sun-baked field and well away from the bridge before they attempted the descent to the river bed: he was determined to leave no traces of their presence by smashing down undergrowth close to the bridge.

He checked the river depth again, returned to the tank, and ordered Reynolds to switch on the headlights, disliking the precaution but knowing that it was essential because it was almost dark now below the level of the banks. Then the tracks began to descend, smashing down undergrowth, dropping with a bump as the tank's centre of gravity pivoted on the brink and then plunged downwards, slithering and grinding over the brambles, hitting the water with a splash, the tank turning as Reynolds briefly halted the right track so that the revolutions of the left one swung the hull round through an angle of ninety degrees to face downstream. When Barnes shone his torch beam he saw that the river level was no more than a foot up the side of the tracks. As usual, Reynolds was handling the driving brilliantly even in this unusual environment. The tank advanced towards the bridge, a clearance from the banks on either side of several feet, moving forward over the firm river bed until they halted under the archway. Inside the hull Penn sat listening to the peaceful lapping of water round the tracks.

'Now,' said Barnes briskly, 'time for supper. Penn, you take up temporary guard duty on the bridge while Reynolds brews up – I'll come up and relieve you as soon as it's ready. I wonder what the devil has happened to Pierre?'

He climbed down to the footpath and started to climb the bank when he heard Pierre coming along the footpath from upstream; the lad was carrying something in his hands. When he switched on his torch he saw that Pierre was holding a large fish.

'I caught it in a pool higher up – we can have it for our supper. There are many more – easily enough for one each.'

Penn paused, halfway up the bank on his way to the bridge. 'What a marvellous idea – my mouth's watering already. Pity we haven't got some chips to go with them.'

'Give it to me!' Reynolds thrust an eager hand forward and Barnes remembered that the driver had been a fishmonger before he had signed on. 'I'll start cleaning it as soon as I get the brew-up going.'

'You really want raw fish for supper?' Barnes asked quietly.

'Raw?' Penn protested. 'We can cook the damned thing in no time.'

'There'll be no cooking here tonight. It's a warm evening, the air's absolutely still, and a cooking smell could linger round this bridge for hours. I'm not risking it. We'll have to make do with tea and bully beef. We've got the French bread Pierre brought, too,' he added.

'For Christ's sake!' exploded Penn.

'You're supposed to be up on that bridge keeping a lookout,' replied Barnes with deceptive calm.

'Sorry,' Penn spoke stiffly, turned away, and clambered up to the top of the slope.

Reynolds said nothing and went back to preparing a brew-up on his little stove. Barnes waited for the Belgian lad's reaction with interest. Putting his hands back behind his head, Pierre hurled the fish as far as he could downstream and sat down on the footpath, not looking at Barnes. Under the archway, Reynolds worked in silence, unpacking his spirit stove, inserting white metaldehyde tablets, applying a lighted match, and then replacing the metal cap over the flame. When he went off upstream to fill his kettle he was gone for several minutes and Barnes guessed that he had taken water from Pierre's pool so he could look at the fish.

The stove was not standard issue, but many of the items they carried, such as their sheath knives, had never appeared on any official list of equipment: Barnes had long ago decided that his tank must be able to operate as a self-contained unit without the normal supply facilities when necessary, although never in his wildest theorizing could he have visualized a situation like this where they would find themselves behind the enemy lines, cut off from all contact with their own army, let alone their own troop. I took the right decision, he told himself as he thought of Penn's irritability and watched Reynolds' abnormally slow movements in preparing the supper. Those two haven't enjoyed more than four hours' sleep a night since we landed at Fontaine and today was no picnic. Until we get some rest none of us is capable of taking part in action against the enemy, so the only thing to do is to keep our heads down until we've recovered. I hope to God we get a peaceful night. He went up to the bridge to relieve Penn.

Too tired to talk, they ate in silence by the light of the flickering spirit stove – Pierre, Penn and Reynolds sitting side by side along the pathway under the arch while the water gurgled past the tank's tracks. It was quite dark now and in the pale blue flame the tank looked enormous and strange, as though it stood in some war museum. Penn clapped a hand on the back of his neck and swore: it was after ten o'clock but the air was warm and muggy and the mosquitoes were active. He could hear one buzzing close to his ear and the blighter wouldn't go away. He hurried his meal because until he had finished, Barnes, who was standing guard on the bridge, would have to go hungry. Now that he had got used to the idea, Penn rather liked the feeling of security of being tucked away under the bridge: it was like camping out in a cave, something he'd always enjoyed as a boy. He must remember to change Barnes' dressing and he'd insist on taking first guard duty on the bridge. It would make up for some of his grumbling during the day.

Half an hour later he had changed the dressing and had gone up the bridge to mount guard. Barnes was sitting on the footpath as he put on his jacket again, thankful that the emergency dressing had been applied and feeling sufficiently better to appreciate his own state of incredible fatigue, but at least he felt more comfortable. As he dressed himself he looked sideways at Pierre. He had been conscious of the lad's fixed stare for several minutes.

'We may find somewhere to drop you off tomorrow,' he told him.

'That is for you to decide.'

'Yes, it is, isn't it? You'd better get some sleep now. We may have a long day ahead of us.'

'Can I take my share of guarding the bridge, Sergeant?'

'We'll see. Shut up chattering now and get down.'

Five minutes later Pierre was stretched out full length along the path, his feet to Barnes' head, his back against the wall of the bridge, an Army blanket loosely draped over his body. Reynolds had finished washing up in the stream and was settling down at the foot of the bank on the other side of Bert. Normally, he was a restless sleeper and he had wrapped himself in his blanket for fear of throwing it into the water during the night, but he had hardly put his head down before he was snoring loudly, deep in a sleep of sheer physical exhaustion.

Barnes, on the other hand, felt exhausted but not sleepy. It was eleven o'clock and in two hours' time he would take over guard duty from Penn and later hand over to Reynolds for the last turn. His mind raced round like an engine out of control: the great thing now was to find some really worthwhile objective, to give the Germans a tremendous blow on the nose. Without realizing it, he eventually fell into uneasy sleep, in spite of a tiny portion of his mind which desperately begged him to stay awake.

Chapter Three

Friday, 24 May

'Sergeant! Wake up! *Wake up!*'

Barnes opened his eyes instantly, blinking once, his hand automatically closing over the revolver he had hidden under the blanket.

'What is it, Penn?'

'Come up to the bridge – we've got company.'

Barnes had slept in his boots and now he sat up with the minimum of movement, glancing back at Pierre as he switched on the torch, shading it with his hand. Switching it off again immediately, he clambered to his feet and nearly fell into the river. Pierre lay in exactly the same position as when he had fallen asleep, one large hand resting limply outside the blanket. From the far side of the tank came a deep-throated snore. Reynolds was still putting his time to good use. Following Penn, Barnes climbed up the bank, digging in his toes and using his hand to follow the line of the wall. The illuminated hands of his watch, the watch he had borrowed from Penn, registered 1.30. Another two and a half hours to dawn. And Penn had let him oversleep by thirty minutes.

Coming up on the bridge he stopped as a chill ran

through him. The moon was up and through the palely illuminated night to the south a column of lights was advancing towards them. In the heavy stillness of the early morning he could faintly hear the purr of many engines. He made a quick estimate of the number of vehicles, stopped counting when he had reached twenty, which was only a fraction of the total number of tiny lights.

'Penn, go down and wake Reynolds – quietly. Tell him to get his damned boots on.'

'What about Pierre?'

'Don't wake him on any account.'

Barnes stood and waited, shivering a little from the cold. The nearest lights seemed closer now, the sound of the engines distinctly louder. This was no procession of refugees heading for the bridge: he could tell that from the orderly advance of the headlights, just sufficiently well spaced out to allow the whole endless column to move forward at a rate of about twenty miles an hour. Cocking his head to one side he listened carefully, but there was no sound of aircraft in the cloudless sky. Standing there on the bridge he could hear the gentle lapping of the river as it swirled round Bert in the cavern below, but the water sound was now being muffled by the steady revolutions of the motors of the approaching armada, which he was quite certain now was an Army column of enormous striking power. British, French, or German? Their very lives might hang on the answer to that question. A few minutes later he was listening even more intently as Penn stood by his side. No, he had not been mistaken. Above the engine rhythms he could detect a familiar sound – the steady rumble of tank trucks. They were standing in the path of an armoured column.

Scrambling down the side of the bank, finding his way by feel, he went in under the bridge and switched on his torch briefly. Reynolds was up and standing on the same side of the river as Pierre who had just laced up his shoes. The lad's hair was freshly combed and he was staring up at Reynolds who had a revolver in his hand.

'They'll be coming over the bridge in a few minutes,' Barnes snapped. 'It may be a Panzer column. Whatever happens you both stay here until I come back. Get it, Reynolds?'

He looked meaningfully at the driver and then scrambled back up the bank to where Penn still waited at the northern end of the bridge, just in time to see the corporal leave the road in a hurry as he plunged down the far side of the bridge. Instantly, Barnes moved sideways along the bank and hid himself behind a thick clump of wild shrubs. The next moment he heard the buoyant burst of a motor cycle. Lights flashed, crossed the bridge, swerved round the corner, and headed north, immediately followed by a second cycle. The lights of the second patrol briefly lit up the first and in the side-car he caught a glimpse of a seated soldier who wore a pudding-shaped helmet, a machine-pistol cradled across his chest. It was Jerry all right. Christ!

Instead of following the first patrol towards Fontaine, the second motor cycle reduced speed, swerved on to the grass, its headlights sweeping over the shrub where Barnes lay, then stopped, its engine still running. The soldier in the side-car stepped out and the cycle drove off, leaving the sentry who walked back to the bridge. Barnes lay very still as the German peered over the parapet on his side. A powerful torch beam flashed on and swept over the bank where they might have taken Bert down by the direct route to the river bed. Then it went out and he heard the sentry's feet march back to the end of the parapet. The torch flashed on again, pointing down the bank. It began to move forward and behind it feet slithered, recovered, and then started to feel their way down over the brambles. Barnes gritted his teeth. This was a thorough bastard. *He was going to check under the bridge.*

Without a sound, Barnes brought his right hand up to his hip, grasped the hilt of his knife and withdrew it from the sheath. The sound of the oncoming engines was much louder. He would have no time at all to work this trick. He lay still listening to the sentry moving down the bank, praying that Penn wouldn't open fire. The German was only a few feet from Barnes as he passed him and his feet were making a row as they trod through the undergrowth. Lifting himself carefully to his feet, Barnes moved across to the wall under cover of the sentry's shuffling feet, leaning out his hand to contact the stonework. Then he began to follow the German down, left hand on the right, right hand gripping the knife. He had to finish him with the first thrust. He could see the silhouette of the sentry clearly against the torch glow: any second now the torch would swivel left and shine on the stationary tank. What the German's reaction would be when he found that under the bridge was really something for the book. Stealthily, he went down the bank. There was one horrible moment when he nearly slipped, digging in his right heel desperately, his knife hand waving all over the place, but he regained his balance without the sentry hearing him. The German was about four feet ahead of him now, and beyond the bridge the purr of the motors grew steadily louder. He had to get a little closer. He stepped down farther and at that moment the German swung his torch sideways and the beam glared full on the menacing hull of the hidden tank, its two-pounder pointing downstream. Barnes sprang forward, knife held high, his body lunging forward and downward in one leap. The knife reached the sentry's back and stabbed clean through the greatcoat, penetrating the body deeply under the impetus of Barnes' violent thrust. They fell forward together on to the bank, the sentry groaning once as Barnes landed on top of him. The torch splashed in the river.

As he fell, Barnes smashed his forehead on the German's steel helmet, which stunned him for a second, but his brain forced him to his feet, still holding the knife hilt which he was pulling at savagely. It wouldn't come out. Penn appeared from under the arch.

'I was just going to shoot him.'

'That's what I was afraid of. Here, hold this.' He handed him his own torch which he had switched on. Then he was tugging the German over on his back, unhitching his steel helmet, which was a struggle because the head flopped back inside it. He got it loose and thrust the helmet at Penn. 'Get this on . . . someone's got to act as sentry – they'll expect to see him. I'm too short so you've just volunteered. Grab his machine-pistol, man.' He was unbuttoning the greatcoat, trying to push the body over on its stomach and only succeeding when Penn helped him. The throb of the advancing engines resounded in his ears. 'Reynolds, you stay there with Pierre.' They had the sentry over on his stomach now, both of them hauling a sleeve over limp arms.

'The knife,' said Penn, 'we can't . . .'

'Yes, we can. You stand with your back to the bridge wall so they can't see it.' The sleeves were free now. Taking a firm hold of the coat, Barnes ripped it clean up over the haft of the protruding knife and helped Penn inside the coat. 'Now, follow me, but keep out of sight till I tell you – we may be too late . . .'

Scrambling back up the bank like a terrier, ripping his hands and face on the brambles, he reached the top and peered over the parapet. The leading vehicle was alarmingly close but its headlight beams hadn't yet reached the bridge. He could hear that deep-throated mechanical rumble clearly. They had tanks, all right.

'Just in time, Penn. Here, your top button's undone. Get over that side, *your back to the wall*. Hold the machine-pistol across your chest. All you have to do is to stand there so they see you. Away you go!'

Penn dashed across the bridge and took up his position. With a last look at the headlights, Barnes felt his way rapidly back down the bank, hand scraping over the wall. At the bottom he trod straight into the river and retrieved the sentry's lighted torch. Switching it off, he flung it under the bridge and got back on to the bank. Now for the really difficult part. Feeling around in the dark, his hands touched the sentry's legs, grabbed his ankles. He took a deep breath and began to move backwards under the arch, hauling the German with him. He wondered if he was going to make it: the body weighed several stones more than Barnes and it was like trying to shift a buffalo, but inch by inch he pulled it back until it was well under the arch. Then he bent down and toppled it over the edge so that it fell into the water between the river bank and Bert's right hand track. As he stood up he found that his legs were trembling with the effort and sweat was streaming down his back and over his forehead. In standing up he bumped into someone. Pierre. His voice sounded strangled.

'I think I'm going to be ill – Reynolds attacked me.'

'Reynolds,' growled Reynolds, 'shoved a revolver into his belly – he was trying to play hero. Wanted to come up and help.'

'Don't be ill over us,' snapped Barnes. 'You asked for it.'

'I think I will be all right.'

'Sit down, Pierre, and stay down.' Barnes reached out a hand in the dark and pushed it against Pierre's chest until he felt him sitting down on the footpath. 'And if we have one cheep out of you Reynolds will empty his gun into you . . .'

He stopped speaking, holding the wall for support. A vehicle rolled over his head. Twin beams swept over the river bank and briefly passed over the small copse in the field. Then they were gone as the vehicle proceeded north. In no time at all more wheels moved over them, more beams swivelled, then vanished. To make sure that Pierre understood the situation Barnes touched his head lightly with the muzzle of his revolver, bending down to whisper.

'Just keep it quiet, laddie, and you've nothing to worry about.'

Nothing to worry about, that's a good one, thought Barnes. Four more vehicles rolled over and then he heard a different sound coming, the smooth grinding clatter of heavy caterpillar tracks. The arch seemed to shiver as it rumbled over, little more than twelve feet above them, a German tank moving at medium speed. Before the rumble had disappeared they could hear the next monster approaching the bridge, reducing speed slightly, the tracks clanking like the tread of a small leviathan. As he leant against the stone wall Barnes felt scared stiff and wondered how poor Penn was feeling.

Penn was petrified, gripped by such a paroxysm of fear that he had almost lost all sense of feeling any emotion. He had just taken up his position when the first vehicle arrived, headlights briefly glaring in his face, then sweeping over the bridge, round the corner, and up the road towards Fontaine. An armoured car. Penn had stationed himself at a point where the bridge wall curved away from the road, so that he presented a profile to the oncoming vehicles – a profile of a pudding-shaped helmet, a greatcoat, and a machine-pistol. He held the weapon at an angle, its muzzle pointed across the road to be sure that they would see it. Another armoured car swept past and Penn began counting: Barnes would want to record the make-up of the column afterwards, always assuming that there was going to be an afterwards. As he stood there Penn was horribly aware that it only needed one vehicle with an officer to stop and he would be done for. Four more armoured cars drove past and then Penn experienced an even sharper terror as he heard the approach of a familiar rumble. The tanks were coming – they would have commanders erect in their turrets, men who would have time to look him over as the huge vehicles turned the corner.

He froze rigidly, his hands locked so tightly over the machine-pistol that the muzzle began to quiver. Hastily, he loosened his grip and prayed as the first tank mounted the bridge, his eyes staring ahead at the opposite wall. When the vehicle drew level with his position his eyes were fixed at a point on the lower turret and he was conscious of the figure above. The tank moved past, went round the corner, picked up speed. He let out the breath he had been unaware he was holding and wondered how much more of this he could stand. The second one was coming over now . . .

In times of danger Penn had learnt to practise a little mental exercise which he called to himself 'putting the mind into cold storage'. It involved suppressing all feeling, all normal reactions, and was in fact a temporary suspension of the brain's activity by concentrating on one thing only: now he concentrated on his counting. He had counted the passage of twenty heavy tanks when he realized something – not one of the commanders had spared him a glance. As they came over the bridge they were far too concerned with getting their tank round the corner to bother about a sentry whose presence they accepted as part of the night landscape. Penn even reached the stage where he welcomed the arrival of a tank because he had discovered that the trucks of motorized infantry were far more dangerous. The first one to arrive gave him a frightful shock. As the headlights passed beyond him he was able to see it clearly – a replica of the one he had blown up with the two-pounder. The truck drove forward slowly and from under the rim of his helmet Penn saw the officer sitting beside the driver in his cab. The officer looked sideways at Penn, then the cab was past. Without warning the open back presented itself to Penn, a back crammed with helmeted German infantry nursing their weapons. A sea of blank faces stared out at him as the truck back-fired at the corner and almost stopped. For God's sake keep moving, keep moving! The truck went round the corner and vanished. His hands were so wet now that he had difficulty in holding the weapon straight. Count, keep on counting. Nothing else matters but counting. He wiped his hands quickly on his greatcoat. Another truck now. The same frowning glance from a peak-capped officer, then the sea of staring faces at the back of the truck. He could do without any more of those. Send me some more tanks, please. He almost giggled at the thought and his own reaction bothered him. Was the fearful strain driving him round the bend? Watch it, another damned truck. As the vehicle disappeared he heard Barnes' voice from behind the parapet at his back.

'Keep it up, Penn. You're a bloody marvel.'

Hearing Barnes' voice made him feel better: it counteracted the dreadful feeling of being mercilessly exposed to the enemy. And it can't be all that much fun down there, he thought. It's probably even worse not being able to see what's going on. He began counting again. Half an hour later, as though his nerves had not already been shredded, battered to a jelly, and then shredded again, fate decided to turn the screw tighter, to take him to breaking-point and then beyond to a region of terrified desperation he could never have dreamt existed, and the trial came without warning.

The truck approached the bridge like its predecessors, the headlights catching him briefly in the face. It rode up over the slope and passed him, first the cab with the officer and then the open back with its huddle of staring faces. As it started to turn the corner it backfired explosively again and again. The vehicle slowed down, its engine coughing and spluttering unpleasantly although it still took the truck forward. Penn could hear the driver fighting to keep the engine going and for a few seconds it throbbed perfectly. Then the awful coughing started again and the truck turned off the road, its headlights beamed directly on the copse. Driving forward a few yards farther into the field it stopped.

In a daze of horror Penn watched men jump down from the back and begin to walk about the field. An officer and a soldier, undoubtedly the driver, had the bonnet up and they were peering inside at the engine. The sentry Barnes killed, Penn thought grimly, must have some chums in this division and they could be outside that truck. How long would it be before a soldier came over to him? Even in the face of this new nightmare Penn realized what was happening as the next tank came over the bridge. Every vehicle must have the same instructions – in the event of a possible breakdown they had to get off the road at all cost. Whatever happened they mustn't impede the movement of the Panzers. And this lot could quite easily still be here by daylight.

'Penn!' Barnes hissed the name from behind the parapet. 'I know what's happened. Just keep still. They may get that truck moving in a minute . . .'

He broke off as another tank crossed the bridge, pressing himself flat against the wall so that it was impossible for the commander in the turret to spot him.

'Penn, I'm right behind you with one of their own machine-pistols if the balloon goes up. Don't move – just . . .'

The rest of his words were lost as another tank clattered by, but knowing that Barnes was waiting behind the wall gave Penn's morale a desperately needed boost. He gripped the machine-pistol tighter. If this was it, well this was it and there was nothing he could do except to keep up the masquerade to the bitter end. Several of the men from the truck were moving closer to the road and the officer and the driver were still bent double over the engine. If they didn't get it started pretty soon some of the waiting troops were going to cross the road to come and have a chat with him. He saw one soldier start to cross, then headlights flared and a truck swept over the bridge too quickly, pulling up at the corner with a squeal of brakes, gunning the engine as it navigated the corner. The soldier had stepped back on to the grass and stood there hesitantly. Something had to give soon.

Barnes had left the wall behind Penn and now he was scrambling up the southern bank, the bank nearest to the oncoming column. His hands were torn to pieces, covered in congealed blood from earlier struggles with the brambles, the congealed blood in its turn covered with a film of fresh blood so that both palms were sticky with gore and damp with sweat. He reached the top and fell flat as another vehicle arrived, waiting until it had passed before he parted the branches of a shrub, sucking in breath quickly at what he saw. They were almost too late. He scrambled down the bank again, picked up his machine-pistol from the path, plunged into the river, and climbed the other side. He waited until the next tank had crossed and then spoke rapidly.

'Penn, only four more vehicles to come – and the last two are probably motor cycles.'

'I think that truck in the field is leaving . . .'

'I know, I heard them starting the engine. Now listen. You let two more vehicles pass and then you get down here like a bat out of hell when I tell you.'

'But the truck in the field . . .'

'Shut up!'

It was going to be a damned close thing, Barnes knew that. He was peering round the end of the bridge where he could watch the truck. Soldiers were climbing into the back and the officer and the driver were inside the front cab. The last patrol at the rear of the column would be stopping on the bridge to collect Penn and they would have to deal with that patrol, but everything depended on the truckload of soldiers in the field driving away in time so that they had the bridge to themselves, and Barnes realized that the timing was going to be split-second. All the troops were aboard now, the tail-board had been pulled up. The truck started to turn in a half-circle. Another vehicle went over the bridge, an armoured car. One more to come. The truck was driving forward towards the road, bumping across the uneven field at a pain-fully slow pace. Would it slip on to the road before the next vehicle drove past, the last one before the patrols arrived? He gripped his machine-pistol firmly, his mind on edge for the lightning decision he would have to take within the next sixty seconds. The truck reached the edge of the road and paused to make sure that the way was clear. Barnes watched it grimly – that truck was the real enemy, the enemy which could mean the difference between life and death for his unit. It seemed reluctant to depart, almost as though the driver sensed that there was some unfinished business to attend to here. A thought flashed into his head and he hoped to heaven they were not about to die by mischance – the mischance that the officer in the cab would decide to collect the sentry himself. Then the truck turned on to the road and drove off as an armoured car came over the bridge, skidded round the corner, and followed the truck along the road to Fontaine. Barnes jumped up. 'Penn! Now!'

He grabbed Penn's arm as he came round the end of the bridge and hustled him along the bank.

'Down behind those bushes. Whatever happens, don't open fire unless you've got to. The first patrol will probably drive on, leaving the last one to pick you up. If the first one does stop we'll have to wipe them out and then deal with the second one.'

'They're bound to search for . . .'

'Not necessarily – they may think you were picked up by one of the last trucks when they can't find you. I'll be over on the other side.'

Barnes ran back flat-footed to avoid tripping. He crossed the road in a sprint, ran farther along the bank and dropped down behind some bushes twenty yards back from the road. From this position he commanded the northern side of the bridge and the road beyond. With Penn facing him they would have the patrols in a crossfire, although he hoped that it wouldn't come to that because the tail-end of the Panzer column wasn't far enough away yet. Let them be tired, he prayed, too tired to start poking around under the bridge. Then he saw lights and the first motor cycle and side-car arrived.

It came over the bridge at speed, braking with a snarl of exhaust, screaming round the corner explosively, then it was gone. It happened so quickly that it almost took Barnes' breath away. Now they were only faced with the last patrol, the one which was bound to stop to pick up the sentry. He pressed himself closer to the earth, the machine-pistol stretched out in front of him, also flat on the ground to avoid any danger of light reflecting off it. He could hear the machine coming now, coming flat out as though anxious to collect the sentry and catch up the column. An impatient type. That might just help – someone who didn't like to spend too much time hanging around lonely bridges in the middle of the night. Through the bushes he could see the light now, blurred by the tiny branches and leaves of the bushes, a light which rushed towards the bridge. His leg muscles tensed, his hands grasped the pistol. The roar of the motor cycle was almost on top of them, the light showing on the parapet. Then it arrived, crossed the bridge, swerved, skidded madly on the corner, recovered its balance, and raced off up the road after the column.

Barnes laughed silently, weakly, the spasm shaking his aching body. Of course! He'd got the system wrong! He must need a refresher course. The real sentry would have kept a close eye on the progress of the column and then waved down one of the last trucks to pick him up: motor cycles had no wireless communication, no way of being told that there was a sentry ahead to be collected, and that last patrol which had gone over the bridge already carried a soldier in the side-car. All that tension, all that nerve-racking anxiety – all for nothing. He went across the road and told Penn.

'Jolly good,' was all Penn could find to say. 'Anyway, now we can relax,' he added.

'I'm afraid not – there's one fatal question we need the answer to before morning.'

It was half an hour before dawn and beneath the bridge the world was pitch black. Barnes switched on his torch and shook Pierre awake. The lad stirred, blinked in the glow of the beam, sat up, and ran his hands through his hair.

'More trouble, Sergeant?'

'No, but you seem anxious to do your bit. We are all just about exhausted and I'd like you to relieve Reynolds from guard duty if you would. It means three hours on the bridge because we won't be moving off before seven.'

'Certainly!' Pierre began to lace up his shoes. 'I am most willing to take my turn with all guard duties. I said so.'

'We'll see how you make out. All you have to do is to stand on the bridge and listen. Don't assume that if a vehicle is coming it will have its lights on – and remember, it may not be coming from the south like the others. In fact, I'm more worried about them sending someone back from the north if they find out that they're one sentry missing.'

'I will watch very carefully.'

'At the first sight or sound of anything coming you run down here and wake me – is that clear?'

'Perfectly.' He reached out for the machine-pistol, but Barnes' hand closed over the weapon. 'I'll need something, won't I?' Pierre protested.

'Yes – your eyes and your ears. I'm not risking you letting loose at something in the dark which turns out to be a shrub instead of a crouching man. Up you go.'

Barnes waited until Pierre was climbing up to the bridge and then he ran back under the archway, crossed the river without making a sound, clambered up the opposite bank, and settled himself behind the shrub which had concealed him when he had watched the progress of the Panzer column. He was now hidden on all sides because the lower part of his body was submerged under a clump of brambles. From where he lay he could hear Pierre and Reynolds talking on the bridge, followed by the sound of the driver slithering down the bank as he returned to the archway. After that the only noise came from the bridge itself where Pierre had begun to patrol backwards and forwards, his footfalls a soft tread in the night. Gradually, Barnes found that he was able to see the patrolling figure as a vague silhouette beyond the parapet, a silhouette completely unaware that he was being checked. By the time the false dawn began to glow in the east Barnes had come to the conclusion that Pierre would make an excellent sentry: at frequent intervals the lad paused at either end of the bridge to listen for a whole minute before he resumed his march back and forth, and once or twice he glanced over the parapet wall and looked along the river as though he feared they might be subjected to a surprise attack either upstream or downstream. Dammit, thought Barnes, he might have been trained for the job.

The real dawn was beginning to show, pale shafts of cold light low down on the horizon, when Barnes found himself in difficulties. He had lain quite still ever since he had taken up his position, putting up with an ache in his right leg which steadily grew worse, when suddenly he was subjected to an attack of cramp. Forcing himself not to move, he felt the cramp take hold, compressing and kneading the leg muscles of his calf mercilessly, to such a fierce degree that he had to dig his fingers into the ground to bear it. He was determined not to move since Pierre had now stopped at his end of the bridge, his face turned towards where Barnes lay as he watched the dawn grow stronger, and any sound would alert Pierre and warn him that he was under observation. Sweat began to trickle over Barnes' face as he struggled with all his will-power to keep the leg flat until the pain receded, which gradually it did, and when the cramp had gone Pierre resumed his patrol, almost as though he had waited so as to cause Barnes the maximum agony.

Through the shrub Barnes could now see the field beyond which rose gently to a ridge. From his personal reconnaissance of the area shortly after they had first arrived he knew that beyond the ridge the ground fell away sharply to a lower level. It was, in fact, the one blind approach spot in the vicinity of the bridge, the one place where an enemy patrol could come close to the bridge without being observed at a distance. It was also the spot to which his eyes were now glued, and as he watched the line of the ridge grew clearer until it was sharply outlined against the dawn sky which was streaked with splashes of grey and gold, the genesis of another glorious day. Pierre had stopped again, this time on the far side of the bridge, and the absolute silence of early morning seemed uncanny, unreal, a silence that Barnes imagined he could almost *hear*. It was also chilly and several times he shivered as the cold penetrated his battledress and began to freeze his body, the low temperature accentuated by the presence of early morning dew which had settled on his uniform and coated his hands with a film of moisture. Beyond the ridge a spiral of white mist was rising from the ground, the curtain of vapour blurring the dawn light so that he could almost convince himself that there was movement behind the mist. A few minutes later he detected human movement beyond the ridge.

Gradually, the vague figure moved higher up the ridge and then stood stock still. Barnes tensed, fingers closing over the revolver in his right hand, his eyes staring at the silent figure half hidden in the mist so that it was impossible to identify the clothes it wore. The figure was two-dimensional, without depth, faintly outlined against the light behind it until the mist swirled away and he saw that it was the upper half of a soldier wearing a greatcoat and a pudding-shaped helmet. He could hear Pierre crossing the bridge again and then the footfalls ceased abruptly; when he glanced sideways Pierre had disappeared, crouched down behind the parapet wall. This will test his reflexes, Barnes told himself grimly.

The helmeted soldier remained motionless, staring in the general direction of the bridge as though he sensed danger. Now the silence was heavy and ominous, like the moment before the storm breaks. Barnes waited. Pierre waited. The German soldier waited. The soldier stood so still that he might have been a statue, and now Barnes' attention was concentrated on two points – the ridge in front of him and the parapet wall to his side. Then without warning the soldier marched up to the crest of the ridge and came down the other side, a slow deliberate approach as though he had not seen anything yet but he still didn't like the look of the bridge. He could easily be the advance guard of a patrol sent out to find out what had happened to the sentry, a patrol which had been clever enough to cross the river higher up so that they could approach the area unexpectedly from the south side in the hope of taking the enemy by surprise.

He came forward holding a machine-pistol across his body, a body which stooped forward, the face blurred by remnants of dissolving mist. Barnes heard a rustle from behind the parapet where Pierre crouched, and when the rustle stopped the only sound in the heavy stillness was the faint tread of the oncoming soldier's boots, a tread so light that Barnes knew he was trying to walk cat-footed as he crept forward. Halfway between the ridge and the bridge he stopped, head to one side, listening. Then he began to advance again and Barnes raised himself slightly. This was it. Any second now. He heard a scrabbling sound from the bridge and Pierre stood up, his hands in the air. He was calling out as he walked forward into the open, walking more rapidly when the soldier didn't open fire, calling out urgently. Barnes stood up, his battledress rumpled, hands by his sides, and also emerged into the open as Pierre reached a point midway between the bridge and the soldier who now swivelled his machine-pistol to train it on Barnes. Turning, Pierre saw Barnes and called out again, one hand pointing, jabbing in Barnes' direction. He began to run towards the soldier, shouting at the top of his voice, insistently, continuously. A short distance from the helmeted figure he stopped abruptly, his voice dying away as Barnes walked briskly across the field towards the two men. Pierre had been shouting non-stop in German until he saw the face under the helmet, the face of Penn wearing the German sentry's greatcoat and helmet.

'You were right about this rat, then.' Penn levelled his machine-pistol at Pierre's stomach.

'Strange behaviour for a Belgian patriot,' said Barnes. 'Very strange behaviour. He sees a German soldier come over the top and instead of calling me he runs up to him.'

Penn held the butt of the pistol under his arm, one hand still round the trigger guard while he used the other to undo the top button of his German greatcoat.

'This thing chokes me. As you were saying – I thought he'd never react. So we've trapped ourselves a dirty little spy.'

'He didn't react at once because he thought a whole infantry platoon would be coming over the ridge behind you. My appearance on the scene jolted him into action. You made several mistakes, Pierre.'

'What mistakes? I do not make mistakes.' Pierre drew himself up, a sneer on his young face, making no attempt to deny the charges. He even ran his fingers through his hair to straighten it.

'That, for one thing – you've an obsession with your personal appearance. After we'd shot up that truck yesterday you arrived on the scene with your hair neatly combed – and you'd just been sprawling in a ditch. No normal lad of seventeen would react like that. But a trained soldier who was fantastically conceited about his good looks might do that automatically – providing he was very tough and a bit of a bastard into the bargain. It was your lot we shot up, remember.'

Pierre's eyes blazed and he stood very erect. 'It was not possible to take any action at the time.'

'No, you were biding your time till you could hand over a Matilda tank intact for inspection by your own people. And another thing – your reaction to that cemetery round the wrecked truck wasn't right either, not for your supposed age.'

'The German soldier is not trained to hide under bridges from the enemy.'

Penn took a step forward but Barnes restrained him with a look, his voice still mild when he spoke again.

'Let him spit away – he's going to be shot in a minute unless he gives us some information.'

For the first time Barnes thought he detected a flicker of fear in the staring blue eyes, eyes which looked quickly over Penn's shoulder and then back at Barnes. He tried to speak indignantly but his voice couldn't quite manage it.

'That would be murder, Barnes.'

'You'll address me as Sergeant, and I would remind you that since you are not wearing uniform this puts you into the category of a spy who can be shot out of hand. What is your unit, Pierre?'

'I don't have to answer your questions.'

'No, that's right, you don't. You can be shot instead.'

'I might be prepared to answer certain questions.'

'That's better. How old are you?'

'Twenty.'

'And still with fluff on his cheeks.' Barnes looked at Penn. 'Maybe they wean them late in Germany.'

Pierre clenched his hands and stood rigidly, his feet close together, a pink spot on either cheek.

'What's your real name, Pierre?'

116

'Gerhard Seft. Sergeant Gerhard Seft.'

'And your unit?'

Silence. Seft's mouth was a tight line and he looked quickly over Penn's shoulder again.

'You haven't see any real war, then?' Barnes goaded him.

Seft's voice changed. He stiffened his shoulders and almost barked his reply as he glared at Barnes.

'I served with the Wehrmacht in the Polish campaign. I was at Warsaw. We cut the Poles to pieces, smashed them – and I was there!'

'Well, you really know the position of a soldier caught in civilian clothes, then.'

The German's eyes flickered and he changed the subject quickly. 'How did Corporal Penn get away from the bridge without me seeing him?'

'He slipped off up the river bed while Reynolds was handing over the guard to you.' Barnes waited for a reaction but the German said nothing, gazing back blankly as though waiting for something. 'Seft, why did they push you out on a limb – send you in civilian clothes behind enemy lines? I want to know. Why?'

'Because I speak perfect English and French. My mother was French.'

Had he put that last bit in to arouse sympathy, to remind his captors that he, too, was human? Barnes suspected as much; his hostility towards Seft grew. His voice was harsher now.

'Where does this road lead to?'

'Towards Arras – I told you.'

'You told me a lot of bloody lies, my lad. And while we're on the subject where have we come from?'

'From Fontaine, of course.'

Seft's manner was growing more confident again, a trace of the arrogance returning as he realized that he wasn't going to be shot out of hand.

'From Fontaine?' queried Barnes. 'Try that one again, too.'

'But he's right there,' protested Penn in surprise.

'Is he? Did anyone in the village except Seft tell you that it was Fontaine? I thought not. The road we were supposed to have taken from Fontaine runs south-west on the map, but this road ran due south for miles before it turned south-west. And we should have passed through at least a dozen villages – instead we came across four towns and not a single village anywhere. Seft's game was to lead us deeper into German-held territory until he got the chance to hand over Bert intact – and that would have been a feather in his cap. The German High Command would love to have one undamaged tank so they know exactly what they're up against. He must have been doing his nut when Reynolds held a revolver on him while a whole Panzer division rolled by overhead. And that, Seft, was a further mistake. You were just a little too anxious to come out from cover when your lot arrived. Now, what is the name of the village you called Fontaine?'

He stood looking up at the German, his eyes half-closed. This was his first encounter with a fanatical young Nazi and he found the attitude of sneering arrogance an interesting reaction under the circumstances. It neither startled nor impressed Barnes, he simply thought that it amounted to sheer bloody stupidity. Seft spoke loudly, his voice clipped.

'I am not permitted to reveal information which may be of assistance to the enemy. You are my enemy. Heil Hitler!'

Penn hit him across the side of the face, hit him hard with the back of his hand and the blow left a red weal across the German's pink flesh. He took a step back as Penn snapped at him.

'You've been told once, Seft, and you won't be told again. When you address Sergeant Barnes you address him as Sergeant. Next time you forget, you'll be minus a few teeth.'

Seft looked carefully at Penn as though memorizing his face. Then he deliberately rotated his cheeks and with an expression of supreme contempt spat on the ground. Again, Barnes' look restrained Penn.

'Don't waste your strength on the lad. He's hardly out of his nappies.'

Whether he understood the word or not, the insult galvanized Seft. He stood very erect, his chin thrust forward, his voice rasping like a drill sergeant's as he stepped forward.

'The German Army will be here very shortly. You are standing in German-occupied territory and you are now my prisoners-of-war. Sergeant Barnes, surrender your pistol.'

Taking two more steps forward, his face flushed with uncontrollable fury, he reached out to grab at Barnes' hand. The effrontery, the blind insanity of the manoeuvre, momentarily stunned Penn but Barnes reacted as though he had been expecting just such an attempt. Stepping backwards, he brought up the revolver from his side and swung it in a vicious arc. The barrel smashed against Seft's left temple and the blow was so powerful that the revolver almost leapt out of his hand. He took another step sideways as the German fell forward and slumped to the ground, his arms stretched out beyond his head, his fair hair all over the place. Barnes bent forward, felt the neck artery, and then looked up at Penn.

'The fool's dead. Just as well – we can't afford to be lumbered with prisoners at this stage.'

'He must have been stark raving bonkers.'

'He's a fanatic who thought he could get away with anything, but not completely bonkers. Take a look over your shoulder. I think Seft must have spotted them earlier than I did.'

A long way off to the south, where the road was now clearly visible in the early morning sunlight, Penn saw a thin trail of toy-like vehicles moving up the road towards them. The rear of the column was hidden behind a rise in the ground but more and more vehicles were appearing as the column advanced steadily forward. Barnes spoke grimly.

'I'll check with my glasses but that's another Panzer column on the way, bet your life on it. So that route's barred. And if we head back to so-called Fontaine we'll run into the other lot.'

'What the hell are we going to do? We'll never get away with it a second time.'

'Get out of here with Bert as fast as we can by the only route still open to us.'

Chapter Four

Friday, 24 May

At 4.30 a.m. they were fleeing for their lives. Moving at five miles an hour the tank emerged from under the bridge and drove along the river bed between the high bramble-covered banks like a monster metal barge sailing downstream. Standing up in the turret, Barnes was enormously relieved to find that he couldn't see over the tops of the banks which were two or three feet above his head, so that meant the enemy couldn't see them either. As they left the bridge behind he looked back to make sure that the tracks weren't leaving traces of their passage but apart from a muddying of the water there were no traces to give them away. Ahead, the river ran almost straight for about a hundred yards and then it disappeared round a bend. They had to reach that bend and get round it before the advance elements of the Panzer column reached the bridge. He rated the chances of success a good deal less than fifty-fifty, but it was their only hope of survival.

About halfway from the bridge to the bend a line of trees covered the banks on both sides, their branches spanning the river to form a tunnel of foliage which roofed in the water below, and it was so dark inside the tunnel that he couldn't see the river clearly. If it suddenly went deeper, they'd be finished anyway. Behind him the fording flap was closed down over the rear air outlets so now Bert was amphibious – amphibious, that was, in up to three foot six of water. He looked down at the grisly load roped on the back of the tank and hoped that they hadn't left their departure too late.

Their departure from the bridge had been held up by the necessity of disposing of the two bodies – the sentry's and Seft's – and since he was determined to leave nothing near the bridge which might arouse suspicion and provoke a search, he decided that the only safe thing to do was to bring the bodies with them. The bodies were now lying on the engine covers at the rear of the hull, attached to the turret by separate ropes.

The greatest danger was the motor-cycle patrols which he had seen through his glasses moving ahead of the column. They would follow the same procedure as the previous column, he felt sure of that. A patrol would arrive, halt to drop a sentry, and then drive on. The sentry would move on to the centre of the bridge and look straight down the river. Barnes looked down the river: yes, it was a good hundred yards to that bend. And there were other things to worry about. Driving a tank along the bed of a river, even a comparatively straight river, is not the easiest of manoeuvres, and he was constantly talking into the mike to guide Reynolds' progress between the banks. They might just make it, *so long as the river bed remained firm.* From his elevated position he strained his eyes desperately to see the ground ahead under the water, searching for any sign of a large area of mud or softness or, worse still, a threat of rapids. And then there was always the chance that the engine might stall, leaving them in full view of the approaching Germans. He put that thought out of his head quickly as Penn climbed up to join him.

'Think we'll make it?' Penn asked him quietly.

'If we can get round that bend in time.'

'Can't we get up a bit more speed – we're crawling.'

'Deliberately. This isn't the Great North Road, you know, and I'm bothered about the river bed – it's getting deeper.'

The water level was rising up the tracks quickly and he guessed the depth at over two feet. Three foot six was the maximum Bert could take. At the same time the river banks were closing in so that Reynolds barely had half a foot clearance on either side. The tracks ground forward, sloshing through the water, rattling over unseen rocks, grinding up mud discolouration, sinking deeper and deeper below the surface. Penn pulled a face as Barnes glanced back at the bridge.

'Must be three feet at least now.'

'All of that,' Barnes said tightly.

They were halfway between the bridge and the tunnel of trees when a new anxiety assailed them –

the sound of a plane. From the light-toned beat of the engine Barnes guessed that it was a small plane and it was flying very low. The Panzer column was using a spotter plane to check the ground ahead, which meant that the pilot would be searching every inch of countryside below him. If that plane flew over the river they were bound to be seen. Barnes could visualize it all clearly – the plane circling overhead while it wirelessed back to command HQ, the arrival of heavy tanks on both banks – in front, behind, above them. Then the remorseless shelling at point-blank range until Bert was reduced to a shattered hulk. It looked as though he'd taken them straight into a death-trap. He spoke into the mike.

'Driver, increase speed by five miles an hour. Follow my instructions exactly. You're too close to the left bank . . .'

The tunnel of trees still seemed a terribly long way off, and that tunnel could hide them from the plane if only they reached it in time. The sound of the plane's engine was very close and it was flying lower. It had probably spotted the bridge and was coming in to reconnoitre the whole river area intensively. At that moment the tank almost collided with the right bank and Barnes corrected Reynolds sharply, which wasn't fair because although the driver's head was poked up through the hatch and he had a clear view ahead, his vision was limited at the sides and he couldn't see the edges of the banks. The plane was losing even more height, Barnes could tell from the engine sound.

'This is going to be dicey,' Penn remarked.

'Keep an eye on the bridge, will you? I want to concentrate on the sky from now on.'

He wanted to concentrate on several things – checking the sky, observing the bridge, watching the clearance on either side of the tank, and keeping a sharp eye on the river course ahead, but it was impossible. As usual, Reynolds was doing a marvellous job – any other driver would have stalled the engines, driven hard into the bank, committed any number of understandable errors, but Reynolds ploughed stolidly on ... Barnes lurched sharply as the whole tank *dropped*, a really noticeable drop. Penn's face went white and he quickly glanced down and then resumed observation of the still-deserted bridge. They must have dropped at least another foot and now they were semi-submerged under the river. The hull would soon be awash. Barnes grunted, checked the clearance on both sides, and scanned the sky. They'd have to gamble now, gamble on the desperate hope that the river stayed the same depth. That plane was almost on top of them – his hand tightened on the rim as he waited for it to flash into view. The tank rocked over an obstacle and his moist hand slipped. He was recovering his balance, still looking up, when a roof of foliage blotted out the sky, a tangle of branches thickly covered with many layers of leaves. Above the green network the spotter plane sped across the river and continued on its course to the north.

'So far, so good, as the man said to the girl,' joked Penn.

'There's still the bridge.'

'Not a sausage yet, not even a German one.'

Barnes looked back. The stone arch was much smaller now and it looked amazingly peaceful from inside the tunnel of trees, the sunlight showing up its white stone with great clarity. It seemed incredible that at any second the engines of war would be streaming across it on their way to a battle zone. Barnes turned round to face the front, feeling the coolness of the foliage-wrapped tunnel on his face, and his heart leapt into his mouth. Their road was blocked.

The light was dimmer inside the tunnel, which was why he hadn't spotted the obstacle – in the very centre of the river, barely ten yards ahead, a giant boulder projected from the water. The rock was black and pointed at the summit, its nearside sheer and massive, forming an island round which the river divided into two separate channels. Bert was capable of mounting a vertical obstacle two feet high, but the height of the boulder was at least four feet. In the time it took the tank to move forward a couple of yards Barnes considered the alternatives: climbing it was out of the question; ramming it could be suicide – they'd stall the engine or damage the hull; bypassing the obstacle by driving Bert out of the river and along the bank slope would be near-suicide. But the third alternative was the only possible one so he immediately began issuing warning and instructions to poor Reynolds who was now being asked to overcome the insuperable. The operation called for no less than taking the tank from the river bed up on to the steep slope and then endeavouring to pass above the boulder with the vehicle tilted at a precipitous angle high above the river. Penn listened with a drawn face until Barnes had completed his preliminary instructions and when he spoke his voice was strained.

'Can we manage that? You could topple us over sideways.'

'It's the only way – we'll have to manage it. Keep a sharp lookout on that bridge.'

'Well,' said Penn lightly, 'it's a good job we've got plenty of time.'

'Do watch that damned bridge, Penn.'

Penn hadn't taken his eyes off the bridge except for the brief downward glance when the tank had dropped precipitately, but at the moment Barnes was in no mood for his corporal's pleasantries. They were very close to the boulder and the closer they came the more immovable it appeared. Yes, the only way was up the bank and along its side. Reynolds commenced the manoeuvre under Barnes' watchful eye, braking the left track so that the right one turned the tank towards the bank. As they left the water and mounted the left-hand slope a spasm of alarm ran through Barnes: the bank was much steeper than it had appeared. Instead of the undergrowth sinking several feet under the tank's weight it flattened down no more than a foot, enormously increasing the hazard because when Bert tried to move along the slope parallel to the river it would be like a cyclist riding up the wall of death. We could topple sideways, Penn had suggested. Well, Barnes knew what the likely result of that would be for the men in the turret: they would end up on the river bed and twenty-six tons of dead-weight tank on top of them. The tracks moved forward, the tank inched up the slope, and then began to turn which could prove quite fatal. Reynolds had braked the right-hand track and now the revolutions of the other track slowly swung the massive weight round on its axis, then he stopped briefly. The tank was parallel to the river below, the turret tilted out over the water, tilted so steeply that Barnes and Penn had difficulty in keeping their balance and their bodies were perched at an acute angle. Now for it.

They were all only too aware that even the slightest error of judgement would take the tank over sideways, and that even if they survived, which was unlikely, Bert would land on the bed of the river flat on his back like a helpless beetle, his tracks churning the air. And to Barnes it was quite clear that it all hinged on a few degrees of tilt; even a few extra pounds of weight on the right-hand side could be sufficient to start the fatal sideways topple. He gave the order. The tank began its forward movement. Foot by foot the tracks advanced, clutching at the earth below the undergrowth, and no one spoke, no one moved, every nerve end geared to the painfully slow revolutions of the steel tracks. They were beginning to creep past the huge boulder below when the crisis came. Barnes saw the left-hand track start to lift gently, increasing the tilt by several degrees. His hand gripped the turret rim as he took his decision. The bodies of Seft and the sentry were sliding over the engine covers to the right – he saw that when he glanced over his shoulder – and those bodies were adding well over twenty stone to their dead weight. Literally, dead weight, he thought grimly.

'Penn, cut those ropes – quickly!'

Reacting instantly, Penn pulled out his sheath knife and nervously leaned down over the back of the turret, being particularly careful not to lean sideways. The ropes were taut with the weight of the slithering bodies and he sawed rapidly, his nerves so keyed up that he observed each strand giving way until the rope, thinned to a few strands, suddenly snapped of its own accord. Seft's body rolled off the sloping hull and fell with a great splash into the channel of water alongside the boulder. Penn was so preoccupied in trying to watch the bridge while he cut through the second rope that he never even saw the first body land, but Barnes had a quick glimpse of the corpse sinking below the surface before he switched his gaze back to the front tracks. They were pressing down the undergrowth slowly, like an animal feeling its way across treacherous ground, and he knew that even the merest extra lift could unhinge Bert's precarious balance.

On his jacked-up seat in the nose of the tank, Trooper Reynolds was drawing on all his experience of the engines as he desperately tried to judge just how slowly he could keep moving without a fatal stalling of the motors, because if that happened he was sure that even the vibrations of restarting the engines might well tip them into the river, and this was an experience that no training had prepared him for. Only his intimate knowledge of the tank's structure and idiosyncrasies could pull the trick if anything could. For several minutes Barnes had not spoken a word, knowing that words were useless and that he must leave it entirely to Reynolds to perform this diabolical operation. They were three-quarters of the way past the boulder when Barnes saw the upper track move against a clump of brambles, but instead of pressing them down the track began to climb as it mounted some unseen obstacle beneath the undergrowth. Here we go, Barnes told himself. He prepared to shout to Penn to jump, knowing that he had to stay on board himself because Reynolds wouldn't have a dog's chance of scrambling up out of the hatchway in time. The track was still climbing, but Bert still clung limpet-like to the side of the bank, poised at an impossible angle. Then Barnes felt the *wobble* as the tank began to heel over. At that moment Penn sawed through the final strands of rope and the sentry's body broke free, toppling off the hull into the river. The wobble stopped, the upper track savagely trampled down undergrowth and dropped at least six inches to lower ground. They had recovered their balance. Penn's voice was breathless.

'Thought we were going, then. Two passengers couldn't stand the strain – they got off.'

'I think you were just in time, but we're not out of the wood yet. Any sign of the Panzers?'

'Bridge still like a picture postcard. Can't last like this much longer.'

'No, it can't. Keep watching.'

They weren't out of the wood yet because now Reynolds was faced with a fresh manoeuvre which promised to be at least as tricky as the one he had just completed. The upper track was still moving forward over the smooth slope so Barnes decided that they'd better get on with it before that track started to climb again. And they had passed the boulder now. He gave instructions and then waited, watching intently without saying another word to Reynolds. Again, it was strictly the driver's baby.

To move back down to river level Reynolds had to brake the right-hand track, keeping the upper track churning so that it revolved the tank on its own axis to face down the bank at an oblique angle. Here again there was ample opportunity for a fatal mistake: it was not only a topple that Reynolds feared, he was frightened that the revolutions of the upper track might cause a side-slip. He paused to wipe his clammy hands on his trousers and then firmly gripped the steering levers, knowing that Barnes was relying on him to pull it off. The upper track speeded up and they began to turn. Reynolds handled the manoeuvre largely by feel, handled it magnificently, although in his own estimation he lost a few marks when Bert slithered the last yard or two and flopped into the water with a thunderous splash. But he redeemed himself in his own eyes by missing the far bank as he completed the second turn. The tank now faced downstream again. Barnes spoke quickly.

'Well done. Now, drive like hell . . .'

Reynolds accelerated, the tracks churned up the water into a cauldron as the tank surged forward, pushing the river out of its way, heading non-stop for the bend which was now so close. South Pole or bust, he told himself, and increased speed more still. He could see part of the way round the bend now, could see that it turned gradually so there was no need to slow down. Instead, he speeded up! In the turret two pairs of eyes started back at the distant bridge which was still deserted, the stone intensely white in the sunlight. Barnes turned to see how close they were to the bend, shouted a warning to Penn, and two heads ducked down inside the turret. They heard the crack of the overhanging branch as it broke against the metal. When Barnes lifted his head Penn was already standing upright as he observed the bridge, his knuckles white with tension as he gripped the turret. They felt the tank veering under them as it entered the bend, saw the bank on their right gradually screening the bridge from view until it vanished together. Ahead, Barnes saw another long stretch of river still hidden under the tunnel of trees. They had made it.

Less than half an hour later, as though their shattered nerves had not alrady been tested almost beyond endurance, a new crisis burst upon them. German tanks were approaching from *downstream*.

They had halted Bert a hundred yards or so beyond the bend, had climbed the southern bank to catch their first sight of the advancing column they had so narrowly escaped, arriving at the top in time to see the first motor-cycle patrol reach the bridge. Because of the bend in the river they could see clearly across open fields to the bridge and Penn gulped as he peered through the trees: the cycle had stopped in the very centre of the bridge while a soldier dismounted from the side-car, and even at that distance Penn felt quite sure that the sentry was staring clear down the stretch of river they had just negotiated.

'God!' Penn gasped. 'That was closer than the shave I didn't get this morning.'

'Which reminds me,' Barnes replied, 'we'll have to clean up as soon as we get the chance.'

He focused his glasses and the bridge came up to him – the sentry walking to the northern side, gazing down over the parapet, making his way down through the brambles to check under the bridge before the column arrived. Yes, it had been damned close. He swivelled the glasses and the twin circles ran along the column – stubby armoured cars, squat self-propelled guns, heavy tanks with their deadly barrels pointed up the road. The lot, in fact. He began counting, recording the count cryptically in his note-book, a form of shorthand which only he could decipher, adding it to the notes he had already made under the bridge when he had recorded the composition of the previous column while he waited to wake up Pierre for his test watch.

Behind them Reynolds had stayed with the tank which was now resting in mid-stream like a strange steel island, the sunlight forming a patchwork of shadow across the hull where it penetrated the overhead foliage, foliage which was still dense enough to mask them from any spying plane which might fly over. The river was shallower at this point so the water flowed past no more than three feet up the sides of the vehicle, but it was also much wider and there was now a good three foot of clearance on either side. For Reynolds, who was seizing the opportunity for a little maintenance, it was more like scrambling about on the deck of a boat. Since he was over twelve feet down below the level of the banks he didn't hear the menacing rumble of the Panzers, a sound like the distant chunter of a concrete-mixer.

Under the trees Barnes made a further note while Penn stood with his arms folded as he asked his question.

'What happened to the bodies when they went in? I was too busy trying to observe the bridge at the time, you may remember.'

'They both sank – they've probably floated miles down-stream by now.'

He finished his note and frowned. The throb of powerful engines and the clattery grind of tank tracks drifted across the field as a muddled purr, but his acute hearing had detected a different sound. No, the same sound, but from a different direction. As he turned his head Penn noticed the movement.

'What's up?'

'Quiet.' He looked across the fields to his right. About half a mile away the ground sloped up gently to a low ridge so that the area beyond was hidden from view. Was there another road beyond that ridge? The sound of approaching engines was more distinct now, distinct enough for Penn to hear them.

'Not another lot?' He groaned in mock despair, but his feelings of despair were real enough, and he hadn't yet recovered from his ordeal on the bridge during the night, to say nothing of that mind-breaking experience when Barnes had taken the tank up the bank and past the boulder. It was not yet 6 a.m. and Penn's morale was at its lowest in the early hours, on top of which he was unshaven, unwashed, and unfed. There had been no time even to have a drink of water since they had left the bridge and now he was hungry and thirsty and his stomach was full of wind.

'I'd better take a look,' said Barnes eventually. 'You

stay here and keep on counting – start with that tank just coming up to the bridge now.'

'If it's Panzers coming up the river, they're bound to spot us.'

'Just wait here.'

Barnes was away for fifteen minutes, although to Penn it was more like an hour, and since he had loaned his watch to Barnes there was no way of checking the passage of time. Glumly, he went on with his counting, half his mind on making notes while the other half listened to the distant throb of engines downstream. We're caught in a pincer movement, he was thinking, trapped between two columns of the bastards. It was bound to happen, our luck's run out ... He turned as he heard a trampling of undergrowth and Barnes came up the bank behind him.

'It's Panzers, all right. About a hundred yards farther on there's another bend with a bridge just round the corner. It carries a road behind that ridge and there's another column going over the bridge – probably to protect the flank of this lot.'

'We're the meat in the sandwich.'

'Something like that. It's a good job we stopped here instead of pushing on downstream – we'd have run into them, or they'd have seen us after we'd passed the bridge. The river goes through open country just beyond there. And they've posted a sentry, of course. The chap was looking this way when I had a dekko through some trees.'

'So we just sit tight?' Penn made a note in the book Barnes had left him. 'I could do with a drop to drink before you start counting again.'

'I'll get your bottle from the tank.'

Barnes turned to make his way down the bank and froze.

Something had just floated downstream past the tank, a mis-shapen object which was now picking up speed in the current. Reynolds hadn't seen it because he had an engine cover up and was kneeling on the hull with his back to the near-side channel, but Penn had spotted it and he swore foully.

'That's the sentry's body – that German on the next bridge will see it.'

'You stay here!'

Barnes stumbled and slithered his way down the slope and then started to run along the overgrown bank side as though all the devils in hell were after him. He ran flat-footed, hammering his feet down and then lifting them straight up again to try and avoid tripping over the brambles which snared his path, and as he ran black despair threatened to smother his mind. Of all the bloody bad luck. It had all seemed so simple up to this moment: all they had to do was to keep their heads down and remain out of sight until the Panzers on both roads had disappeared to the north. And now this. It was like a drowning man within an ace of the shore suddenly feeling himself swept up by an ebb-tide. And the tide of the river was carrying their safety away from them in the form of the dead sentry's body. What the hell could have happened? It must have got caught on something and then later the current had freed it again. Barnes could have wept; instead, he kept on running, watching the ground but continually glancing up to see the progress of the corpse which was so clearly that of a German soldier.

The body was face down in the water but the shoulders and back and legs were well above the surface, exposing the jacket and trousers of a German infantryman, and it wouldn't take some bright officer too long to wonder why this had appeared now on a stretch of river between two bridges being crossed by the Wehrmacht. He increased speed, took several paces forward, and fell flat on his face. Scrambling up again he heardly noticed the tear and rip of the thorns as they reopened recent wounds, but he had fallen sideways on his right shoulder with a heavy thump and he did notice the sharp throb of his wound which immediately started up again. Swearing briefly, he ran on desperately. He had to reach that corpse before it swept round the bend and flowed on in full view of the sentry on the bridge, a sentry who had been looking this way. He fell flat again, his foot trapped by ropes of bramble, dragged himself to his feet, began running and then stopped. The floating body was approaching the bend, still drifting in the centre of the river. It was now or never. He threw off his battledress tunic, tore off his boots, and dived in.

The chill of the water took his breath away but he

ignored the shock and began swimming rapidly downstream, his arms flashing through the water, his body shooting forward under a momentum which was increased by the flow of the current. While stationed in India as a professional solider before the war Barnes had been champion swimmer in the division but he broke all records now, swimming as though his life were at stake, which it probably was – and the lives of two others. Under his shirt the wound was throbbing steadily, sucking away his energy when he needed it all for just the next few minutes. He swam with his teeth clenched, knowing that he was beginning to overtake the corpse. Foot by foot the gap closed, and foot by foot the bend came closer. He was only a few yards behind the floating body when his leg hit a rock under the surface, the blow sending an agonizing pain from his kneecap to his thigh. It stopped him for a second, then he was swimming on, his eyes fixed on the bend which was almost on top of him, the corpse still several yards ahead. The hump of German uniform picked up a little speed, bobbing slightly as it swept round the bend in full view of the bridge. He hadn't made it.

He had a quick glimpse – the curved bridge, the low parapet, the sentry on the far side, his back turned. Barnes took a deep breath and dived under, swimming now almost along the bed of the river, thrusting forward with powerful strokes until he saw a grey mass above him, barely one foot above him. He reached up with one arm, grabbed the body round the middle, hauled downwards with all his strength, feeling he was trying to drag down a ton-weight. It came down suddenly, rolling over sluggishly, and now his arms tried to swim two men. The bridge was very close to the bend but the distance seemed endless as he swam forward while the body tried to take on a life of its own, threatening at any moment to slip from his grasp. As he fought to retain control he was keeping a close eye upwards for the first sign of a change in the light which would warn him he was going under the bridge, and at the same time he was fighting his bursting lungs, his teeth a tight trap to hold back the carbon dioxide, to force his lungs to hold out just a few seconds longer as he felt the blood pumping like a steam hammer. No sign of a light change yet. He began to expel air, saw a shadow on the water surface, heaved upwards, broke surface under the bridge, blew out, took in oxygen as he threshed to the bank and grabbed at it with one hand.

A tank was crossing the bridge, he could hear the steel rumble, so no one would hear him threshing about. He clung on to the bank with his left hand while the right pinioned the sentry. Now for the rough part – getting out. The tank had gone, so he waited. When the next one approached he started to climb out and then he had the devil's own job hauling out the sodden body which seemed suddenly to have increased its weight ten-fold, at one point almost dragging Barnes himself back into the water as he lay face down in brambles while he struggled to heave the leaden burden up over the edge, both his arms wrapped round the waist and his hands locked together to make quite sure that it wouldn't slip back and float into view at the last moment. It was a grisly task and it became even more grisly when he succeeded in hoisting the corpse on to the bank because it rolled and he rolled with it, lying for a moment flat on his back with the sentry almost on top of him, sodden, dripping with water, its face close to his, the hair plastered flatly over the white skull.

He waited until another tank arrived and then he worked furiously to push the body deep inside a jungle of brambles, treating it like a sack of cement as he finally jerked the legs and bent them to thrust them after the rest of the corpse. The bridge he now lay under was much smaller than the one higher up, wide enough only to take single-line traffic, and the footpath had disappeared altogether long ago when the brambles flourished and took over the whole bank up to the stone wall. There, he'd done it. No one would find the sentry unless they searched for him and by now Barnes was becoming familiar with German bridge procedure: they checked underneath it before the column arrived but they certainly wouldn't come poking around down here a second time. Not unless he attracted attention.

Barnes was temporarily exhausted, the wound playing him up badly now, his kneecap aching steadily, his hands and face scratched to blazes with the ripping of the brambles. He lay quite still for several minutes, his revolver in his hand, although whether the weapon would work after its soaking was anybody's guess. He listened to the column rumbling past overhead and gradually he revived, his mind revolting at the thought that he was back to square one again. When he cautiously peered through the far side of the arch he saw the long shadow of the sentry above him spread over the upper bank, the top half of his body, the pudding-shaped helmet absurdly stretched out. The bastard was on the right side of the bridge – downstream – and Barnes had had a bellyful of being cooped up under bridges. He decided to risk it. And Penn would be doing his nut if he didn't get back soon. The real danger was that his swimming form might be spotted under the water before he reached the bend, but the river here was about four feet deep so he'd just have to swim with his face on the bed. Because a tank commander erect in his turret has an elevated view Barnes waited until one of the vehicles had moved across the bridge and then he took a deep breath, slipped back into the river noiselessly and began swimming upstream along the river bed.

This time he was going to swim the distance in two stages, pausing halfway along the stretch under the lee of the bank where long grasses trailed into the water. In fact, swimming as he was now against the current, he was going to have to take two bites at the cherry, a favourite Penn phrase for seeing the same girl twice. His face close to the flat-rocked bed, he was having to swim all-out to make headway, against the current which was stronger than he had expected; he began to veer in close to the bank, expelling air slowly, his eyes gazing ahead for underwater boulders as soft mushy weeds brushed against his face unpleasantly. When he reached the bank and surfaced behind the trailing grasses he found that he had covered half the distance. He stood crouched against the bank, his nose just above the water, watching the approach of yet another German tank, and it was rather like observing it through a green bead curtain, his first close-up look at the weapon which was sweeping across the plains of France in an annihilating wave.

As he waited hunched under the bank his mind raced over the problems ahead: taking Bert downstream when the coast was clear was something they might just manage in this depth, and beyond the bridge he could leave the river where the banks came lower, a fact he had observed from under the bridge. The tank was crossing now, the commander leaning out of the turret to check clearance. One we get away from this lot, Barnes thought, we'll head west-south-west: in spite of Seft's deception he was confident that he had a rough idea of where they were because he had found two places on the map which could correspond to the fictitious Fontaine. And west-south-west should lead in the general direction of Arras. The tank had crossed now. He slipped under the water.

He was immediately aware that his movements

were slower, that his strokes lacked thrust, so he redoubled his efforts, determined that this time he must get round that bend or else he was going to be spotted. He had pushed his luck to the limit and far beyond, so whatever happens, keep going, he told himself, for God's sake keep going. In his anxiety to succeed he took a short cut, veering to the left to take himself straight for the turn in the river, seeing a forest of trailing weeds ahead and projecting himself through the diabolical mess. He was almost through when he felt a tug above his right kneecap, the one he had injured, and when he endeavoured to swim forward he remained anchored to the spot where the weeds had twined themselves round him. Pausing for a split second, he lunged out savagely, felt the weed stranglehold tighten, and he didn't move forward an inch. He was running out of air: the only thing to do was to surface. He made to swim up and the grip tightened like the tentacles of an octopus. You can't drown in four feet of water, Barnes. But you can, you know – if your upper leg is locked down tight close to the bed. A tremble ran through his brain and transferred itself to his body as he felt panic rising. Grimly, he fought down the emotion and concentrated on freeing his damned leg. Think it out, quickly! Forward is no use – try sideways, out into mid-stream. His lungs were protesting again, building up a horrible balloon-like pressure, the water gyrating oddly, a singing in his ears growing. He thrust out sideways, felt the weed tighten. God, he really was done for this time. Keep moving, Barnes! He made one last effort, felt the weed tearing away as though reluctant to give up its victim, then he was free, stroking his way upstream, still under water until he came to the surface choking and spluttering as he gulped in water, his head turning automatically to check his position. He was round the bend.

And if it goes on like this much longer he thought as he headed for the bank, we'll all be round the bend. But his instinct told him that it would probably get worse.

Eight and a half hours later, at three o'clock in the afternoon and thirty miles away from the bridges, the tank was like a hunted animal, still alive but only because of the sharp eye and keen instinct for danger of its controller who had saved it on four separate occasions from detection by the hunters. At the same time the animal was still viciously armed with over seventy two-pounder shells and ten boxes of Besa ammunition secreted within its innards.

By 8.30 a.m. the Panzers had gone from the river area and by 9 a.m. the tank crew had shaved – at Barnes' insistence – and they had eaten bully beef and the last of the French bread Seft had brought, which reduced their rations to a meagre quantity of remaining bully beef and nothing else: the two tins of meat Seft had supplied were found to be blown, whether by accident or on purpose didn't matter any more, but it did mean that they were desperately short of food. They were also running low on water but this was due to an accident and an oversight which were the result of chance and fatigue. Before leaving the river they had attended to the radiator and filled a dixie with water for their own use: the accident had taken place an hour later when they mounted a steep bank into a wood to escape being spotted by a flight of Stuka bombers. The dixie had fallen over and spilt its precious contents on the turntable floor. The oversight was the fact that only Barnes had remembered to fill his water-bottle – he blamed himself for not checking to make sure that the others had filled their own. In a word, there was now one water-bottle to quench the growing thirst of three men. Although only briefly mentioned, the thirst was the reason for a bitter argument between Barnes and Penn soon after one o'clock.

'I think we ought to risk going in,' Penn had said emphatically, pointing towards the town on the skyline.

'We'll go round it, instead – across country,' Barnes had replied quietly.

Across the sun-baked fields, the town – another church spire and a line of buildings – had looked like a mirage as it trembled gently in the dazzling heat haze, an impression heightened by the absence of workers in the fields, although normally the farmers would have been busy at this time of the year. This absence of people troubled Barnes and strengthened his decision.

'It is possible to get a bit too cautious,' said Penn hotly.

'It's also possible to walk into something we won't get out of. There's no one about and I don't like the smell of it.'

'There's been no one about for miles – what makes this place so ruddy different?'

'The fact that there's a town over there. If it's under German occupation the locals may be lying low indoors – these are cultivated fields so there should be someone working them.' Barnes put a foot on the hull to climb back into the tank. 'Any more questions before we start?'

'We've seen no sign of Jerry on the ground since we left the river – what makes you think he's anywhere near here?'

'Penn, I've no idea where Jerry is. From what I've seen and from what you told me about those radio bulletins my guess is that the Germans have torn a huge gap in the Allied lines which may be up to twenty miles wide* – at the moment we're somewhere inside that gap but until I know more about it we'll avoid all towns and villages as long as we can. We're moving off now.'

---

* Barnes had badly underestimated the position: at this moment the gap torn in the Allied lines by the Wehrmacht was between fifty and sixty miles wide.

Two hours later they were moving along a deserted country road under the furnace blaze of the afternoon sun, and during those two long hours they had stopped three times to avoid detection by aircraft, halting twice in the lee of hedges and sheltering once inside an abandoned dairy farm where they had been surrounded by empty milk churns. As they had waited for the Stuka bombers to disappear a small herd of cows had gathered behind a fence, their udders horribly swollen, their strange cries a pathetic sound which had affected them more than the distant roar of the Stuka engines. But there was no one to milk the beasts so they had gone away, thankful when Bert's engines drowned the echoes of animal pain. It was not only people who were suffering in this war, Barnes had thought.

As they drove steadily along a hedge-lined road between a sea of empty fields which stretched away on all sides Barnes knew that he was feeling the strain, the strain of standing upright in the turret for long periods while the sun beat down fiercely on him, so fiercely that his shirt and trousers were almost as generously soaked with sweat as they had been with water when he had emerged from the river. His task of endless observation was arduous enough to test the strength of the fittest person since it involved keeping up a constant watch – on the road ahead and behind, on the landscape on both sides of the road, and above all on the sky, since they had good reason to know now that a moment's unguarded relaxation might be punished by the sudden swoop of a Messerschmitt. But Barnes was not feeling at his strongest and a further drain on his strength was the non-stop pounding of his shoulder wound which he was finding impossible to ignore, while at the same time he had to take his weight on the left leg because the right kneecap was badly bruised where it had struck the underwater rock. Mentally, Barnes was still functioning, but physically he was in a state.

Shading his eye against the sun's glare he stared along the road to where a small building stood by the verge, or rather to where the relics of a building stood. It must have received a direct hit from shell or bomb. But what caught his attention was a pole which spanned the road outside the wreckage, a red and white striped pole. He spoke into the mike.

'The frontier's dead ahead. We are just about to cross the border into France.'

He could see now that the Customs post beside the pole had camouflaged the existence of a gun position, a gun position which had been completely wiped out. The 75-mm barrel lay by itself and several French helmets were scattered across the ground, but there were still no German helmets to indicate that the enemy had also died. Bert rumbled forward, smashing aside the pole like matchwood. They were on French soil. When Penn asked permission to come up into the turret for a minute Barnes readily agreed. It must be like an inferno down inside the tank this afternoon.

'Back on home ground,' remarked Penn lightly.

'We're still a long way from home,' Barnes replied grimly.

'Any chance of a drop of mild-and-bitter?' He meant water.

'Not yet. We're down to half a bottle.'

'I do think we should have gone into that town,' Penn said hoarsely.

'And run into a Jerry ambush most likely. Tanks aren't for towns – not tanks on their own roaming about behind the enemy lines. It only needs a couple of anti-tank guns at either end of the street with us in the middle and we're finished. You should know that by now.'

'Well, we can't go on like this much longer. Reynolds must be near the end of his tether stuck out there in front driving on and on hour after hour.'

'Reynolds has not complained,' Barnes answered drily.

'But Reynolds is a good boy.'

'If this is going to be the quality of your conversation you'd better get back behind your gun.'

Penn clambered down into the fighting compartment without a word and Barnes immediately regretted his reply, but having said it he had to leave it. God, the strain must be telling for him to say a damned silly thing like that, but the tension was the product of strain. He reckoned it up. In twenty-four hours he had enjoyed barely two hours of uneasy sleep and Reynolds had made do with the same ration, but Penn hadn't slept at all, and prior to that both of them had made do with four hours' sleep a night for four nights while Barnes lay unconscious. Yes, they badly needed a safe bivouac for the night. And eight hours' sleep. He scanned the sky again

Inside the hull the temperature was ferocious, the air almost non-existent. Penn sat in his vest and trousers, hugging the shoulder-grip, his hand close to the trigger guard. Their experience with the lorryload of German infantry which had roared over the bridge in their faces had impressed on all of them the need for a constant state of alertness, although at this moment it was purely a reflex action with Penn to take up the position. His brain was becoming numbed, numbed with the heat, with the diesel-fuel odour, with the endess throb of the engines, with the hypnotic grind of the tracks. He had reached the stage where he was frightened he might faint and this was why he had gone up into the turret. The dizziness increased and he kept shaking his head to clear it. The thirst he was suffering from was so intense that his tongue clove to the top of his mouth and he could almost see foaming tankards of beer, wishing to God that his imagination wasn't so strong. The tank ground on.

In the nose of the tank Reynolds wore a stolid expression. He was hot and sticky and he was thirsty, too, but they would get a drink when Barnes gave permission. In the meantime he could wait. He was neither worried nor resigned – he was just doing his job, driving Bert in accordance with instructions. He had experienced a little trouble with the monotony of the road rolling towards him on and on like a slow-motion conveyor belt which never stopped, but he countered this by glancing sideways across the fields frequently. So they were inside France now, were they? It didn't seem to make much difference to Reynolds – one field was like another and if they hadn't put up that pole you'd never have noticed any change. Fuel was going down, of course, but Barnes would do something about that. The tank ground on.

Water, fuel, ammunition, food. These were the basic commodities, in that descending order of priority, vital to their existence as a fighting unit, and they always loomed in the front of Barnes' mind. They loomed large now while he was coping with his aching wound, his bruised kneecap, the heat and the thirst, maintaining all-round observation at the same time. He knew exactly what the position was – they had sixty gallons of diesel left, but the tanks at the rear of the hull had a capacity of ninety gallons; they had half a bottle of water; a meagre quantity of bully beef, sufficient for another meal, and some tea. They were stuffed to the gills with ammunition, of course. A pity they couldn't eat that. He began to think that perhaps they had better investigate the next place they came to and he shaded his eyes to make sure that he wasn't seeing things. No, there it was – a line of buildings on the horizon straight ahead of them. He spoke into the mike.

'We're approaching a town. I'll be taking us in to have a look at the place.'

From that moment the whole atmosphere changed for the better. Glancing down inside the turret Barnes saw Penn looking up at him. The corporal grinned and winked. Even Reynolds reacted, sitting up a little higher on his seat, straightening his shoulders, gripping the steering levers a little more tightly. It was like the approach to the promised land for them. Water, fuel, ammunition, food. If they were very lucky they might load up with everything they needed. And information, an item which Barnes was tempted to add high on his priority list. If they could only know exactly where they were what a weight off his shoulders that would be! He called to Penn to come up out of that hothouse again and the corporal almost sprinted up into the turret, his voice positively light-hearted.

'Maybe we'll be off the old bully beef tonight. I wonder what's on the menu at the Restaurant de la Gare.'

'We're behind the German lines,' Barnes reminded him.

'Even so, providing their lordships aren't in residence we may get a slap-up supper. Now, let me see, I wonder what I fancy.'

'A bottle of water to start with.'

'Boeuf à la Bourguignonne with haricots verts would be acceptable. Yes, that's it. Washed down with several bottles of vin ordinaire, of course. We can't really afford vintage wines on Army pay, can we?'

'Don't count your chickens.'

'Chickens? Well, poulet rôti might do at a pinch. It's rather plebeian, of course.'

They chattered on for several minutes and Penn's lively banter, plus the sight of the approaching town, revived Barnes, but soon he sent Penn down into the tank again as a precaution. It would be just their luck to meet another lorryload of German infantry leaving the town. He repeated his routine, scanning the hot blue empty sky, searching the surrounding country-side for signs of danger, and all the time the tank rumbled forward, taking them even closer to the unknown town, which he now had difficulty in seeing because the road was turning and the sun shone straight into his eyes.

As the town came closer he found himself shading his eyes more frequently, straining to catch the detail of the silhouette which looked oddly still in the blazing sunlight. Once again he checked his all-round obser-vation and then quickly looked ahead, his hand form-ing a peak over his eyes, his sense of unease growing. This town had been badly bombed. What he had taken for buildings from a distance on closer inspec-tion revealed themselves as stone façades of irregular shape, and now he was sure that at least half the town was in ruins. But in a place of this size there must be someone left, someone who could tell him the name. And they must find more diesel. A tank running low on fuel was a sitting duck, its second weapon – movement – immobilized. He'd better break the news to them. He spoke quietly.

'This place looks a bit of a wreck – I think Jerry has been here before us and he dropped a few carefully placed bombs.'

They were less than a quarter of a mile from the town now, a small town of possibly about thirty thousand inhabitants he estimated. He held his hand up again, screwing up his eyes, his mouth tight. It reminded him of pictures he had seen of Ypres taken during the First World War, although the one thing he did know was that they were many miles away from that ill-fated Belgian town. Grimly, he watched the advancing silhouette.

The outskirts had been gutted, no other word for it. The walls which were still standing were window-less, the upper frames like sightless eyes enclosing clear sky beyond. Halfway down the walls the scree slopes began, slopes of rubble and debris. These were relics of buildings and there was no sign of life anywhere – no women working in the fields nearby, no men clearing the mess out of the streets. Just nothing, nothing at all. And over the devastation there hung a curious atmosphere, a horrible silence which seemed even more unnatural in the bright sunny afternoon. Water, fuel, ammunition, food . . .

They crawled through the outskirts at minimum speed, hearing the tank tracks grinding their way over pieces of masonry, feeling the hull drop slightly as the stone was crushed to powder. Barnes ordered Reynolds to drive down the very centre of the rubble-littered highway as he anxiously watched the spectral walls of the bombed buildings they were passing, wondering whether they should turn back at once. It was by no means certain that the vibrations of the tank movement might not bring down one of those hanging walls. Some of them seemed to stay upright by a miracle of balance. Cautiously they edged their way round a corner and drove deeper into the town.

The devastation was getting worse, no doubt about that. Whereas before many buildings had at least one wall standing they were now entering an area of almost total annihilation. Any relationship between what Barnes saw and a town could only be visualized by stretching the imagination to its limits. He calculated that an area close to a quarter square mile was a sea of rubble. The rubble was arranged in cone shapes which rose up between huge craters, a scene more like a moon landscape than a town in northern France, and the going was getting worse.

'Driver, halt. Keep the engines running.'

He gave Penn permission to come up and climbed down to the street, resting one hand on the hull and then snatching it off as the heat seared his flesh. Changing his mind, he told Reynolds to switch off so that he could listen carefully to hear whether he could detect any sign of life; he still found it hard to believe that a town of this size had been abandoned.

'There's always someone who stays behind,' he

told Penn, 'someone who tried to make the best of it.'

'The Panzers may have been through as well,' objected Penn.

'But they're not here now, are they? If they have been this way they'll just have passed through without occupying the place – that's the sort of thing that's happening from what you told me about the news bulletins.'

'But no one would stay here – just look at the place.'

'I know, but it may not be so bad on the far side. We'll take a look.'

'I'd be quite happy to clear out altogether, thank you.'

Penn was voicing the feeling of all three men. There was something horribly oppressive about the deserted town, as though it had been sacked by barbarians who had taken all the inhabitants away into slavery. On the far side of the rubble sea a wall swayed gently, leaned and toppled out of sight. They heard a dull thud and saw a huge cloud of dust floating upwards. Barnes was still listening when suddenly he was galvanized into action, ordering Penn down inside the tank, warning Reynolds to close his hood, leaping up into the turret himself and ramming on his headset as he issued instructions.

The tank headed into the heart of the rubble sea, threading its way between the cones, slipping down the slope of a crater, crossing the floor and mounting the other side. They were near the centre of the area before the first planes appeared, a squadron of Stuka bombers flying low. Barnes issued the order to halt in the middle of a wide crater, went down inside the tank, slammed the lid closed and waited. The first stick of bombs fell some distance away, growing fainter as they fell farther off. Penn's voice was bewildered.

'Surely they couldn't have spotted us?'

'No, I think they were coming here anyway. I wanted us well clear of those walls.'

'But they've already smashed the place to bits . . .'

He stopped and they listened, staring at each other. The scream was starting again, the scream of a Stuka falling into a high-speed dive before it released its deadly load. Another stick was coming, but this one was different. The first explosion was a long way off, the next one closer, the third closer still, a frightful nerve-shattering crump. Penn began conducting an unspoken conversation with himself. It will be the next one that gets us, the next one . . . The bomb exploded in their ears and the shock wave was like a hammer-blow. The hull of the tank shook, wobbled, settled again. Then a fifth crump farther off. A sixth, fainter still.

'They must be stark raving bonkers.' Penn sounded indignant, a highly strung form of indignation. 'They did the job last time – are they running out of space to store their perishing bombs?'

'There's an encouraging side to this,' said Barnes,

going on quickly as he saw Penn's expression. 'They must have come back to make the place absolutely impassable – which looks as though they're frightened Allied reinforcements will be moving up here soon.'

'Glad to hear it. I feel so much better, Sergeant, now you've told me that.'

The scream of another plane starting its dive commenced, a plane which sounded to be directly overhead, the scream rising in a crescendo as it came down as though the machine were out of control, a scream which sent cold water down Barnes' spine. Then the explosions came, heart-shaking crumps landing all round them, pinpointing Bert's position. Between explosions he head another distant sound, a heavy thump. One of the remaining walls had gone. At least he had taken them clear of those insidious hanging walls. Barnes was well aware that the majority of casualties during an air raid on a built-up area are caused by the inhabitants being buried under collapsing masonry. He glanced at Penn to see how the corporal was standing up to the bombardment and Penn looked back, deliberately quivering the ends of his moustache in mock terror.

Mock terror? Penn's nerves were shuddering like plucked violin strings. Another bomb exploded almost on top of them and the tank rattled like a toy under the impact, fitments coming loose and falling on to the turntable. Bombing is a grim experience wherever the recipients may be hiding, but it is particularly grim for those inside a tank. Penn had an awful sensation of being exposed: the brick wall of a building may give as little protection as the 70-mm steel which protects the lower sides of a tank, but inside a building there *feels* to be more protection, and locked inside the Matilda the assault on the eardrums was tremendous. As Penn sat tensely the sound of the explosions seemed, to slice clean through the metal skin, but once inside the hull the cannonade reverberated from wall to wall as though a ten-ton hammer were beating on the plates, setting up vibrations which shook him to the guts. While the raid proceeded he struggled to put his mind into cold storage, as he had on the bridge when the Panzers were moving past, but now the method didn't work. He had decided to count up to a hundred explosions, telling himself that long before he reached that figure the raid would be over, but already he had lost count and he gave it up, living now from one explosion to the next.

In the nose of the tank, locked away from the other two men, Reynolds sat huddled forward, his hands still gripping the steering levers, his brain dazed with fear. It wasn't so much the thought of a direct hit which frightened him, because if that happened there would be nothing to worry about. Instead, Reynolds was desperately trying to forget a technical factor in the construction of Bert – the four six-volt batteries which were housed in the nose of the tank. And above all else Reynolds had a gibbering horror of being blinded. He was well aware that even a near-miss could deal the hull such a shattering blow that those batteries might burst – spilling sulphuric acid all over his face and hands. He sat there silently, waiting for the next one, cursing the man who had designed the Matilda for exposing him to this terrible hazard. Miss us or kill us, he prayed, gripping his hands even tighter as they slipped wetly on the levers. Here it comes, right in front of me. Oh God, no! The explosion battered the nose and he heard debris spatter the armoured glass beyond the slit window, then he realized he was all right this time. He still sat with his head down, facing his lap, his eyes tightly closed.

'So far, so good,' said Barnes, repeating Penn's joke.

'Yes.'

Penn spat out the word, wondering how much longer it was going to last, his imagination working at a feverish pitch as he saw so clearly what was coming – the bomb which was a direct hit. The hull would rip open, letting inside the monstrous gases which are the product of high-explosion, tearing their flesh apart, disintegrating the three men and scattering their pulped relics across the rubble. No one would ever know what had happened to them: they would simply disappear. 'Reported missing in action . . .' My God, he thought, my poor people. I was just going to write to them the day we moved across the frontier. That was how many days ago? He couldn't work it out and he didn't even try to any longer as the next stick came down, straddling the tank so that for a few agonizing seconds three men were convinced that they were on the verge of death.

The raid lasted fifteen minutes and during that time they were bombed almost non-stop. After a short pause they endured a series of near-misses which terrorized poor Reynolds very close to breaking-point: it was probably only the unseen presence of Barnes just beyond the plate behind him that saved the driver from opening the hatch and climbing out to escape those dreaded batteries. He had reached the stage where he was quite prepared to take his chance out in the open. Then the second pause came, a pause which went on and on while they waited for the bombardment to start again. It was Barnes who recovered first, climbing up into the turret and cautiously raising the lid, starting to cough as soon as he had poked his head up into the dust-laden air, feeling the heat of the sun on the back of his neck. The turret rim was hot to the touch.

Many of the hanging walls were no longer there and over the whole area was suspended a pall of dust, a pall so dense that the sun was a blurred disc. He looked down and saw that the hull was coated with a film of dust as though Bert had been camouflaged to operate across a grey desert, and when he stepped down on the hull his foot slipped and he almost banged his knee again. He told both of them to get out of the tank and join him where they could breathe in the dust for themselves, but at least they were out in the open, outside the claustrophobic confines of what had so nearly become a metal coffin.

The tank stood inside an old square in the western, less-ruined sector of the town while its crew waited for the unknown intruder to make his appearance, the first sound of life they had met since entering the devastated town. The square was enclosed by hanging walls and the weird tomb-like atmosphere seemed to grow as they waited, Reynolds still in his driver's seat, Penn standing in the turret grasping a machine-pistol, while Barnes stood next to a corner of the square with his back to a wall. Instinctively, he did not lean against it and he held the revolver across his chest so that the muzzle was aimed at the corner.

Little more than ten minutes after they had stopped inside the square for Reynolds to check the tank, Barnes' acute hearing had detected the sounds, odd rustling sounds as though the approaching feet were scuffling furtively through rubble. The footsteps were very close now, moving more quickly. Barnes elevated his gun and at the same moment Penn aimed his machine-pistol. A man came round the corner and stopped abruptly.

Over his shoulder he carried a limp sack and for an instant his bony face expressed extreme fear, but he recovered quickly, removing a cap from his head and smiling unctuously. Small and lean, he was dressed strangely, his suit old and shabby, but round his neck he wore an expensive silk tie and Barnes caught a glimpse of a gold wristwatch before he wriggled his sleeve. His feet were encased in a pair of brand new crocodile shoes. Barnes spoke quietly.

'Sorry we frightened you, but can you tell us the name of this place?'

'British soldiers, yes?'

He was still smiling in a forced way and he had begun to step away from Barnes, shooting a quick glance at the tank as though he expected it to advance on him at any moment. Barnes tried again.

'We're British soldiers. There's nothing to worry about – we won't hurt you. But I would like to know the name of this place.'

He began jabbering away in French, speaking at a tremendous rate, so quickly that neither Barnes nor Penn could understand what he was saying, and as he went on talking he retreated step by step. He was close to the next corner when he lifted a hand and gestured furiously in the direction the tank had come from, waving his cap and then replacing it on his head. Barnes was walking slowly towards the tank when the man with the sack scuttled round the corner out of sight. Penn looked puzzled and sounded irritable when Barnes reached the tank.

'Why didn't you grab him? He could have told us . . .'

'Quick, Penn – give me that machine-pistol.'

'What . . .'

'Hurry it up, man.'

'Here . . . what's the big idea?'

'Both of you wait. If you hear me using this thing get a move on – but come with Bert.'

He ran to the corner, peering round just in time to see the man leave the road as he scrambled over a heap of rubble in the distance. He followed him, running lightly on the balls of his feet and holding the machine-pistol across his chest. The man had vanished behind the wall of a building and when he reached the point where he had scrambled over the rubble he was vanishing again behind the stunted relic of a house, still without a backward glance. Barnes slowed down as he approached the house, and now he held the machine-pistol under his arm ready for instant use as he peered round the end wall, quite unprepared for what he saw.

Beyond the house was a road comparatively free of debris and standing in the road was a single-decker bus, its sides covered with dust. Four people stood outside the bus and they appered to be arguing. The bus was empty of passengers but its interior was crammed with a motley collection of goods, and beyond the open door he saw a seat piled high with miscellaneous articles. Bottles of wine, their necks protruding from a wicker basket, some red material which might be curtains or a bedspread, an up-ended silver tray, the upper half of a small chair with a brocaded back, and an old hunting rifle with a silver-plated stock. The quartet which stood arguing were almost as strange a collection as the contents of their bus.

The bony-faced man stood on one side, putting in a word every now and again, while the other three men formed a circle, facing each other as they talked. The leader of the group appeared to be a short squat man with a swarthy complexion and a large black moustache. He wore a crumpled business suit, a dark slouch hat pushed well back over his head, and round his neck was tied a coloured handkerchief. Barnes was reminded of a Corsican he had once met in a bar at Port Said when his troopship stopped there on the way home from India. The other two men were very thin and tall and they seemed to defer to the swarthy individual when the argument became too heated; they were dressed in blue denim jackets and trousers and wore black berets pulled tightly over their heads. Barnes walked out from behind the wall, his machine-pistol aimed at the group, his voice harsh.

'What the devil's going on here?'

Three bodies spun round to face him, then froze. The Corsican was the first to recover and he came forward a few paces, smiling as he said something in French.

'Talk in English,' snapped Barnes.

The Corsican made a show of not understanding. Jabbing forward his pistol, Barnes rasped out the words.

'Get your hands up or I'll cut you to pieces.'

The Corsican shot up his hands, saying something

quickly over his shoulder, and three more pairs of hands jumped above shoulder level.

'I'm glad you speak English,' Barnes commented. 'Who are you? Come on – be quick about it.'

'Joseph Lebrun, sir. Fur salesman from Le Cateau.'

'What's the name of this place?'

'Beaucaire, sir. You are the British Army?'

'The advance guard. That road which comes into the town from the west – where does it lead to?'

'To Cambrai. Arras is beyond.'

God, Barnes was thinking, we're miles farther south than I'd thought. He stepped back several paces because Lebrun was showing a tendency to edge closer. He kept his voice crisp and hard.

'Stay where you are. Lebrun, how close are the Germans?'

'They have gone.' Lebrun looked astonished. 'They passed through here several days ago soon after the first bombing . . .'

'Soldiers in trucks, you mean?'

'No nothing like that. It was a long column of huge tanks, enormous guns.'

'But no soldiers in trucks?' Barnes repeated.

'No, nothing like that.' He stared at the machine-pistol, frowning. 'That is a German gun?'

He's quick, this one, Barnes warned himself, and probably treacherous. He kept the pistol aimed at Lebrun's stomach as he pressed home his cross-examination.

'How long ago was this? You said several days ago – exactly how many days?'

'Six or seven days since. We did not see them ourselves – we were told. We do not live here.'

He stopped quickly and his face went blank as though he had said the wrong thing. Barnes went on talking quickly, determined to extract the maximum information from this gangster while he was still off-balance.

'Lebrun, where are the Germans now?'

'In Abbeville.'

Barnes felt as though he had been rabbit-punched. If this were true the BEF and the French armies in the north would be severed from the main French armies to the south, a catastrophe without precedent during the whole of the First World War. Then he recovered. The so-and-so was lying, of course.

'Abbeville's on the coast, Lebrun. Now try again and this time be a bit more careful.'

'I tell you.' He became excited, waving his hands above his head. 'I tell you, they are in Abbeville – we met refugees who were from the town. The German tanks are everywhere. They have thousands of tanks and they are all over France.'

'But not near here?'

The squat man's eyes became cunning and he stared hard at Barnes before replying.

'Only the big tank outside Beaucaire – on the road towards Cambrai.'

'A German tank, you mean? How far along the road outside Beaucaire?'

'Seven or eight kilometres – we passed it on our way back here. It is there by accident, I am sure. It has broken down in a field and four soldiers are trying to make the repairs. They are working stripped to the waist like peasants. This was two hours ago.'

'On which side of the road as you drive towards Cambrai?'

'To the right, about half a kilometre from the road.'

Barnes nodded and gave them instructions, forming them into a line spread out across the full width of the road with plenty of space between each man. Then he marched them back towards the square, halting at a side turning which led down to the road from the square, at the corner he made them lie down in the dust, flat on their stomachs with their arms stretched out full length, firing one burst from his machine-pistol into the air. The prone bodies jumped and he knew that for a brief second they had believed they were about to die. In the distance he heard the throb of Bert's engines and he fired a second short burst, bringing the tank round the corner. Only Lebrun plucked up the courage to look over his shoulder as the tank pulled up.

'Who are these birds?' inquired Penn from the turret.

'Looters.' Barnes spat out the word. 'While their own chaps are trying to hold off Jerry this lot goes round scavenging. There's a bus-load of the stuff up the road.'

'How did you catch on?'

'Bony-Face was wearing some of it. He's wearing a filthy old suit but the tie and the shoes don't go with it – to say nothing of the gold watch.'

He ordered Penn to stay in the turret while Reynolds searched the four men. From Lebrun and one of the thin men the driver extracted two pistols, German 9-mm Luger pistols, and when Barnes asked where they had obtained these Lebrun explained that they had taken them off two dead German soldiers they had found lying beside a crashed motor cycle and side-car. Barnes made no comment on the fact that only German officers were armed with Luger pistols and he left Penn to guard the four men while he walked back to the bus with Reynolds.

The seats of the bus were littered with a variety of loot which included a glass case containing old gold coins and Barnes was burrowing deeper into the strange cargo when he heard Reynolds give a whoop. The driver had thrown out of the door the hunting rifle, the silk curtains, the little chair and silver tray when he called out. Barnes looked up.

'Found some champagne?'

'Yes, for Bert!'

He was holding a heavy rectangular can and had taken off the cap while he examined the contents. Replacing the cap, he carried it off the bus and put it down on the roadside as though it were a fragile glass vase. Then they began searching the bus ruthlessly, finding more cans of the precious diesel fuel which they carried to the roadside. Within five minutes Reynolds had arranged twenty cans in a neat row and still Barnes found it hard to believe their good luck. Bert ran on diesel fuel and possibly the only vehicle in northern France which used this was a bus. Reynolds stood guard over the cans as though he were afraid they might walk away, his voice almost purring.

'They must have pinched the bus from a depot, so they pinched plenty of spare fuel to go with it.'

'You can load up Bert now, but get a move on.'

While Reynolds was carrying the cans back to the tank Barnes made a further search of the bus and when his fingers pressed through a coverlet he felt bottles underneath. At least not only Bert would have plenty to drink. Ripping away the coverlet he found a dozen bottles of mineral water: clearly, Mr Lebrun liked to dilute his wine. And underneath the last two mineral waters he found the jackpot – a half-bottle of Five Star Bisquit cognac.

He carried his own treasures back to the tank and the four men were still lying sprawled in the blazing sun while Penn mounted guard over them from the turret. Reynolds was humming to himself as he fussed about the tank, lifting back the engine cover, removing the cap and inserting the large tin funnel which he used to fill up with diesel. As he poured in the precious liquid he was taking as much pleasure over the operation as if he were enjoying a five-course dinner himself. They had almost completed the loading operation when Lebrun couldn't stand it any longer. Lifting his head cautiously, his face streaming with greasy sweat, he spoke over his shoulder, his tone of voice petulant.

'Please, sir . . .'

'What is it, Lebrun?'

'Please leave us two or three of the containers for the bus.'

'Too late – we've poured it all in the tank.'

Lebrun glared savagely and Barnes was startled by the look of bitter hatred in the squat man's eyes. He had his mouth open and between the thick lips several mis-shapen gold teeth showed. Barnes told him to get his head down, took a heavy wrench from the tool kit and went back to wreck the bus's engine. He smashed the motor systematically, putting it completely out of action. Lebrun wouldn't be using this bus again to plunder his own people and now there was no risk of the looters driving out of Beaucaire ahead of them to warn that German tank of Bert's existence. When he returned to the tank Lebrun was settling his face back on the ground as Penn swore at him.

'He's a sensitive soul,' Penn explained. 'The noise you were making was getting on his nerves.'

'I wish you'd told me that – I'd have wrapped a

cloth round the wrench.' Barnes' voice hardened. 'Lebrun, get on your feet. The others can get up, too.'

Lebrun said something quickly in French and rose slowly to his feet, facing Barnes alongside his companions, an expression of the utmost venom on his face. He's an ugly customer, this one, thought Barnes, but he can't do much without his Lugers. He spoke abruptly.

'You can all push off now – that way, to the east. If we see any of you again we'll shoot.'

'The Germans come from the east ...' began Lebrun.

'That's right. I doubt if they'll like you any better than we do. Get moving.'

They followed the four men down the road in the tank and then halted after they had turned on to the highway which led westward. Amid the sunlit ruins they ate a quick meal and quenched their thirst with mineral water while Barnes pointed out their position on the map and outlined what the Corsican had told him. The news almost spoilt Penn's appetite.

'The Germans in Abbeville!' The corporal looked stunned. 'You don't believe that, do you?'

'With these Panzers roaming all over the place I'm not sure what to believe. I just hope he's wrong, that's all.'

'We're heading for Cambrai first, then?'

'It's in the right direction, if there is such a thing.'

They talked about the problem – a single tank

roaming behind the enemy lines, unaware of its position, because they couldn't be absolutely sure that this was Beaucaire, the Germans unaware of its presence – and then Barnes said it was time to move, but at the last moment he jumped down to the ground again. 'What's up?' inquired Penn, leaning out of the turret.

'I'm going back to the bus – I forget to look in the tool box at the back and there may be something useful in it.'

He left Penn standing in the turret, hurried back up the road, and turned the corner out of sight of the tank, the machine-pistol under his arm. As he reached the bus he glanced down at the pile of loot which Reynolds had thrown out and wondered why it looked different. Dismissing the thought as imagination, he boarded the bus and made his way to the back. All the windows were closed and it was appallingly hot and airless and there was a smell of wine. His foot kicked an empty bottle which rolled under a seat and he stiffened: the bottle hadn't been there when he left the bus. Inside the tool box he found a large wrench which he put in his pocket, still trying to work out how the bottle had appeared. He was leaving the bus when his glance fell again on the pile of loot strewn across the ground and a warning signal flashed in his brain. *The rifle had gone.*

A sense of foreboding gripped him as he ran back towards the corner. Why take an old hunting rifle? Lebrun must have doubled back round the ruins while they were eating, must have found a bottle of wine, drunk it and made off with the weapon. He was midway to the corner when he heard the sound of a single report, one sharp crack, then an awful silence. He reached the corner and at first sight nothing appeared to be wrong: the tank was where he had left it and Penn was still in the turret, but as he ran closer Reynolds scrambled clear of the hatch and stood on the hull close to Penn who was no longer standing erect. When he reached them he saw that the driver was holding Penn up, his right hand sticky with blood. Penn spoke hoarsely, his face ashen.

'Blighter got me in the shoulder ... Lebrun ... watch it – he's behind that building ...'

'Take it easy ...'

Reynolds spoke quickly. 'It's all right, I can see to him.'

Barnes ran across the rubble towards the stunted house from where he had first seen Lebrun and his gang, ran crouched low, his eyes everywhere, the machine-pistol held forward in front of his stomach, his mind calculating and murderous. The house came closer and he watched both corners, watched a window which faced his approach, the only three points from which Lebrun could take him by surprise. As he ran he cursed himself for overlooking that rifle, but who would dream of checking an ancient weapon like that? Some idiot must have kept the damned thing loaded in his house and Lebrun had pinched it because of the silver-plated stock. He reached the house, crept round the outer walls, looked inside through a half-wrecked doorway, and saw the entire ground floor at one glance because the internal walls had collapsed, leaving only a stone staircase which led upwards past the still intact ceiling. On an impulse he stepped inside and carefully mounted the staircase which trembled under his footsteps. He merged on to a flat roof, the floor of the upper storey which had vanished, and it gave him an all-round view over the rubble-strewn desolation behind the house, a region of large bomb craters. Inside one huge hole something flashed in the sunlight.

Lebrun knew instantly that Barnes had spotted him and now he began to scramble to his feet, kicking up dust from the crater floor, shouting hysterically at the top of his voice as he lifted the rifle and waved it harmlessly. The silver on the stock flashed again and again in the sun. Was he saying that the rifle wasn't loaded, was he begging for mercy? Barnes neither knew nor cared. Without pity, without any real emotion, he lowered the muzzle of the machine-pistol, braced his legs and fired, sweeping the fusillade of bullets over the crater floor where they coughed up spurts of dust. Lebrun was on his feet and suddenly he jerked, then he fell over backwards and lay still. The bombed zone was terribly silent.

Barnes pulled a face. His tank crew was now down to two men.

Chapter Five

Friday, 24 May

Penn was in a bad way. Barnes only had to look at his face to tell that; a face which was normally pink and fresh was now the colour of grey mud and his eyes lacked life. He sat up on his seat inside the tank, a folded blanket behind his back, and Reynolds had just finished cleaning the wound which was in the right shoulder, a similar wound to Barnes', but in Penn's case the bullet had entered from the back instead of from above. Reynolds was just about to apply a field dressing but he waited while Barnes examined it. The driver constantly had to swab up fresh blood and Barnes wasted no time.

'What's the verdict?' Penn asked weakly.

'I've seen worse, much worse, and they survived.'

'I'm afraid I'm not much use at the moment . . .'

'You will be, soon enough. Put the dressing on.'

As Reynolds applied the dressing Penn stiffened his back against the blanket and took the bottle of cognac which Barnes had opened for him.

'Just a few sips now – don't get greedy.'

'Rationing me?' Penn managed the pale imitation of a smile.

'You can have a stiffer tot, in a minute. Do you think you can stay in that seat when Bert's on the move?'

'Course I can – anything to get away from this bloody hole. This place gives me the creeps. Did you get Lebrun? I heard . . .' He stopped and winced as Reynolds tightened the dressing.

'Yes, he's dead. He took half a magazine in the guts.'

'I should have seen him . . . my fault . . .'

'No, it isn't. There was no reason for you to think that he might be armed, or even come back at all for that matter.'

'Anything in the tool box?'

'A big monkey wrench – it will replace the one we lost at Etreux. We'll get you out of this beauty spot . . .'

'Join the Army and see the world. Thanks, Reynolds, that's better. What was I saying? Oh, yes. The people you meet in this man's Army. When this is all over I'll publish my memoirs. You didn't know I was keeping a diary, did you, Sergeant?'

'No,' lied Barnes.

'Strictly against regulations. You'll have to put me on a charge. Three days' CB – confined to Bert. Looks as though I'll be confined to him anyway.'

He laughed feebly and then stopped abruptly, his face cramping in a spasm of pain. Barnes handed him the cognac bottle again and told him to take several mouthfuls, watching him closely. The vital thing was for Penn to stay conscious until they got clear of Beaucaire. At least a little colour was flowing back into his face as the alcohol penetrated his bloodstream. Reynolds gathered up a number of blood-soaked swabs and climbed out of the turret. Barnes didn't like the look of those swabs – Penn must have lost a lot of blood and among the swabs there had been two sodden field dressings, which meant that Reynolds had twice failed to stem the flow.

'We'll be moving off now, Penn. I'll try and avoid the rough patches, but it won't be like driving along Brighton Prom.'

'Let's get on with it. We're heading for Cambrai?'

'In that general direction, yes.'

'Don't forget the Jerry tank Lebrun warned us about – the swine could have been telling the truth about that. Sorry I can't handle the gun,' he repeated.

'Don't worry about it. I'll act as my own gunner till we get you fixed up.'

'Bet you could do with a bit of a sit-down yourself.'

'More fresh air up there, my lad. We'll get under way now.'

Yes, I could do with a bit of a sit-down, Barnes thought as he gave the order to advance from the turret. It was five o'clock in the afternoon and the sun scorched down as the tank headed westward, the tracks grinding up fresh clouds of dust from the powdered rubble, dust which obscured his vision so that he was constantly waving his hand in an attempt to see clear ahead. To ease the strain on Penn he had told Reynolds to move at low speed, but it was not entirely a feeling for his corporal's comfort which prompted his instruction. He wanted Penn to be as strong as possible when the time came – the time to take out the bullet.

Heaven knew when they would find a doctor and Barnes was not prepared to leave the leaden obstruction festering in Penn's shoulder. He wished that he knew whether a missile fired from an old hunting rifle was more or less dangerous than a .303 bullet lodged in the same place. He simply had no idea, but there was one small mercy – the bullet appeared to be close to the surface, wedged in down the side of the bone. Extracting the bullet successfully was not likely to be an easy matter, but at least he had had to perform a similar operation once before in India when they had come under fire from hostile tribesmen in a remote spot. He hoped that he could remember how he had managed it then. One basic thing it did involve and that was laying Penn face down on his stomach, and there were less cruel surfaces than dust and rubble for such an operation. He shaded his eyes and gazed ahead, eager for his first sight of open country and fresh green.

They reached the end of the town without warning. One minute they were driving through a street of badly bombed houses and then they turned a corner and France spread away in front of them, a vast landscape of green fields as far as the eye could see, a haze of shimmering heat close to the horizon. Barnes heaved an audible sigh of relief.

Half an hour later there was still no sign of the German tank which Lebrun had mentioned but they were approaching a spot which seemed ideal for Barnes' purpose. They had just come over a small rise and close to the road stood a large empty farm building: he could see that it was empty because the large double doors had been left wide open. There was no sign of a farmhouse nearby and he could scan the road in both directions for over a mile. Nothing in sight anywhere. The building provided perfect cover for Bert in case enemy aircraft flew over while he was at work, and bombing was the last activity he wished to attract while he was treating Penn. He gave Reynolds the order to turn off the road and they moved along a short track which led inside the building. As the engines were switched off he went down inside the tank and saw that Penn was looking better in spite of the ride.

'Penn,' he said, 'you'd better treat yourself to another tot of cognac. I'm taking out that bullet.'

The floor of the farm building showed traces of animals, which would increase the danger of infection enormously, so reluctantly Barnes decided that they would have to do it outside. At least the light was better there. They spread blankets over clean grass and laid a groundsheet over the blankets. Then Penn lay stomach down on the groundsheet while Reynolds boiled water. He was stripped to the waist now. Barnes had removed his jacket and rolled up his shirt-sleeves. When the water was ready he took one last look along the road in both directions, scanned the sky, and started.

'Reynolds is going to sit on your shoulders,' he explained. 'We've got to be sure you're kept perfectly still.'

'I can dig my fingers into the ground.'

'You'll be doing that, anyway, my lad. And Reynolds will be holding down your elbows.'

'Good old Reynolds. With his weight he'll probably flatten me to a pancake.'

'And don't be in such a hurry to kiss mother earth, Penn. Here, drink this.'

He poured a generous quantity of cognac into a mug and made Penn drink it quickly. If only he could get him drunk that would help, but he knew from previous experience that Penn's ability to absorb alcohol was phenomenal.

'There'll be the same for you afterwards,' he told him.

'Almost worth it – to get rations like this.'

'Ready?'

'Get it over with.'

Reynolds sat his whole weight on Penn's shoulders, twisting himself sideways so that he could press his huge hands over Penn's elbows. The field dressing came off with a quick rip and Barnes used antiseptic cottonwool to sponge off a mess of ooze. Then he reached for the knife in the boiling water: he was using Reynolds' sheath knife, a knife the driver kept honed sharp as a razor, the point like a needle. Barnes took a deep breath, he wanted to get this over with quickly.

It took him five long minutes, and whether this time was longer for Barnes or Penn no one would ever know. Only Penn experienced the searing, agonizing, hellish pain which went on and on, stabbing and gouging into the ultra-sensitive wound like a red-hot poker, then turning and grinding and driving deeper and deeper until he thought that he must have reached the ultimate of all pain, only to feel through the burning hot scalpel another wave of torture twisting and disembowelling flesh which had become a million times more sensitive to even the lightest of touches, let alone to this fiendish probe which was thrusting and tearing right through his body until his brain pleaded and screamed for relief, for death, for anything but a continuation of this incredible agony . . .

Barnes drew the knife firmly between bullet and bone, and the scrape of knife on bone brought on the ultimate agony for Penn. He really felt that his entire shoulder was being amputated with a blunt butcher's knife. Moaning horribly, as he had been doing for several minutes, he buried his fingers deep in the ground, biting his teeth together like a steel vice. In some superhuman way he was still managing to keep his tongue at the back of his mouth, knowing in a strangely disembodied corner of his brain that he was in grave danger of biting clean through his tongue. And at that moment Barnes remembered and his hand almost slipped. He'd forgotten. He should have rammed a handkerchief into Penn's mouth. *He'd bite his tongue in half*. He couldn't stop now. He pressed the knife in deeper between bone and bullet, not realizing that it may have been this omission which kept Penn sane and conscious – the knowledge that he must protect his tongue, keeping it well back, well back. And in his stupefied state Penn had no idea that Barnes was in trouble: the bullet wouldn't shift. He had cut all round, he had loosened it from the bone, he had prised underneath, but the bullet simply wouldn't shift. Then he heard the planes coming.

Glancing up he saw the flight of Messerschmitts. They were flying in formation about a thousand feet above the ground, their course roughly parallel with the road. Without hesitation Barnes put his head down and went on with his task, refusing to allow the oncoming roar of the engines to divert him. Penn had his fingers dug deep in the groundsheet now, turning his head from side to side as he moaned quietly like an animal in its death throes. Reynolds was leaning his whole weight on the elbows, and he hadn't looked up once when he heard the planes coming. If it was all right with Barnes it was all right with him. They were almost overhead now, and then they sped past, unaware of the drama below. Barnes took a deep breath, said *Sorry, laddie* under his breath, and scooped

much deeper, turning the knife with great delibera-
tion, then he hoisted. The bullet flicked up from his
knife and landed on the groundsheet. Done it!

As he disinfected, sponged and dressed the wound
he tried to tell Penn that it was all over, that it was all
right now, but Penn was too far gone to understand.
Barnes applied the dressing quickly but carefully,
feeling an enormous wave of relief, and then a wave
of fatigue swept over him and he nodded to Reynolds
to get up as he gripped Penn's left arm.

'It's done, Penn. The bullet's out and I've put a
fresh dressing on. It's all right, Penn.'

Penn turned his head, his eyes dazed, his face wet
and drawn, looking at Barnes without seeing him.

'It's all right now, Penn. You can have your cognac.'

Penn opened his mouth to say something and
fainted.

'Damn him,' said Barnes. 'Why couldn't he have
done that five minutes ago?'

It was close to dusk and the tank was rumbling
steadily forward when they first saw the farm, an
isolated spot in the middle of nowhere. Would the
inhabitants be friendly? Barnes wondered, and he
prayed that they would be because the tank crew was
near the end of its tether.

It had been eight o'clock in the evening before he
had felt that Penn was fit enough to travel, as far as
any man could be said to be fit to travel inside a tank

two hours after a bullet had been removed from his shoulder. While Penn rested, Barnes and Reynolds had worked non-stop under the heat of the sun attending to the tank's maintenance. Their work completed, they had turned to the nightmare task of lowering and settling Penn inside the tank and as they wedged him in with several blankets he had protested.

'You don't have to make all this fuss. For your information I'm already feeling a lot better with that bullet outside me.'

'Shut up and try to get some rest,' Barnes had told him. 'You ought to be blind drunk now with the cognac you've consumed.'

'When I was in London, Sergeant, the deb girls used to have some trouble getting me drunk.'

'I thought it was supposed to be the other way round.'

'Then clearly you weren't in demand like I was.'

Even this short exchange of banter seemed to exhaust Penn and he relapsed into silence as Barnes checked the firing mechanism and then climbed back into the turret. Giving the order to advance, he forced himself to stand erect as the tank left the building, proceeded down the track and turned on to the road to the west – the road to Cambrai, with Arras beyond.

An hour later Barnes was still in the turret and the tank was still rolling forward. To make sure Reynolds kept alert he spoke to him frequently over the intercom because by now even the driver was showing signs of strain and Barnes was hoping to God that they wouldn't meet the enemy before nightfall. The unit was in no shape to fight a cat at the moment. They were approaching the top of a hill and he couldn't yet see over the other side. Standing up on his toes, he waited for the moment when he could see what lay ahead. When they moved over the top he saw the farm.

It was standing by the roadside half a mile ahead. Focusing his glasses he saw a farmhouse, several outbuildings, a haystack close to the verge, and a man working in the fields. As they came closer he saw a woman leave the man to walk back to the farmhouse while nearby another man was driving across the fields on an orange tractor. From the farmhouse chimney a coil of smoke rose, climbing vertically into the evening sky as the sun neared the horizon, a blood-red disc which promised yet another glorious tomorrow. Would they be friendly? Was it possible that they could tell him of a place where the tank and its crew could spent the night out of sight? And, above all else, would they sell them some food? He doubted it. They were under partial German occupation and probably already they were learning to watch their step. 'German occupation.' The phrase ran through his mind and he thought of what Lebrun had said. 'The Germans are in Abbeville . . .' Lebrun must have lied about that: if it were true it could mean that the war was lost. Perhaps at least this farmer would be able to tell him about Abbeville. As they drew close to the farm the man left the field and stood waiting by the roadside, and as he watched him Barnes heard a familiar sound a long way off, no more than a distant mutter but he immediately identified the sound of heavy artillery firing. The guns of Arras? They were approaching the battle area. It was the evening of Friday, 24 May.

Four days earlier, at 7 p.m. on Monday, 20 May, the Panzers entered Abbeville. Before dusk General Storch had set up his new headquarters inside a school building on the northern outskirts of the town.

He always made a point of establishing new field headquarters as close as possible to the point where his next advance would begin, and the new direction for the Panzer onrush would be north, north towards the Channel ports. But as he completed inspecting his temporary new home Storch was in a state of almost uncontrollable fury, a fury which as usual he vented on Meyer.

'They must be mad,' he thundered, 'completely insane. Out of their minds, Meyer!'

'The High Command, General?'

Meyer straightened some papers on the desk, making a neat pile by squaring them up with the palms of his hands. He was standing up because Storch had just risen from his chair, sending it over backwards with the abruptness of his movement, but in spite of the fact that he was the victim of Storch's tirade Meyer was in an excellent humour.

'The people who drafted this order, Meyer.' Storch waved the wireless message savagely. 'All Panzer divisions are to halt temporarily on their present positions pending further instructions. Why stop when you are winning? Always go on to the end, Meyer, always go on as long as your tanks have a litre of diesel left. That is the way to win wars.'

'I suppose General Guderian has his reasons.'

Their normal roles were almost reversed, because now it was Meyer who spoke silkily, careful to keep his voice sympathetic, but underneath he was experiencing a sense of triumph. At last the High Command was seeing the folly of this reckless onrush into the unknown. But here Meyer had overplayed his hand because Storch had a sensitive ear for voice tones and now regarded his GSO1 thoughtfully, his manner suddenly calm.

'You mean General Guderian is worried about the Panzers?'

It was a subtle manoeuvre and Meyer instantly felt that he was losing ground. Everyone was aware that Guderian, the Corps Commander, was almost as great a firebrand as Storch himself, and Meyer had little doubt that Guderian was at this moment raging and fuming about the order he had been compelled to pass on to the divisional commanders. So if Storch took it into his head to dismiss Meyer from his post

Guderian would completely agree with the decision – once it came out that Meyer had said Guderian wished to halt the Panzers.

'I was referring to Army Headquarters,* of course,' he said hastily.

But now Storch was re-reading the message and the cynical expression under the peaked cap bothered Meyer. Surely he couldn't twist this order to his advantage? Storch threw the message down on his desk and asked Meyer to read it again, then went on speaking.

'They probably don't realize that we are still as fresh as when we came over the bridges at Sedan. It's understandable, is it not, Meyer, when you think of the remoteness of Army Headquarters? I think a little reassurance would help. Send this message. Road to Boulogne open. Division ready to advance.'

'Ready to advance?' Meyer stared in amazement at Storch. 'Fifty per cent of our vehicles are in desperate need of maintenance and the men have had very little sleep for over ten days.'

'You mean half our tanks have broken down?'

Meyer swallowed. Storch knew perfectly well that he hadn't meant that. 'No, sir, but there may soon be breakdowns . . .'

---

* Meyer was actually referring to the Army Group Commander, General von Rundstedt, who personally sent this halt order. The conflict between the two schools of thought – those for advancing non-stop and those who preached caution – raged ferociously through the entire campaign.

'The tanks require urgent maintenance?' Storch's own voice was silky now, almost a purr. 'That's what you mean, isn't it, Meyer?'

'Yes, sir.'

'I agree. You are right, of course. It therefore becomes a matter of top priority to work on the tanks through the night.'

'We have arranged for a night shift . . .'

'*All* the fitters, Meyer. They must all work non-stop through the night if they are capable of standing on their feet. Any fitter on the sick list who is capable of walking must immediately be put to work.'

'But the men themselves . . .'

'I expect you to supervise the operation personally. Through the night,' he added maliciously.

Meyer screwed in his monocle, his face blank. Storch was well aware that he had been up most of last night and Meyer was a man who needed eight hours' sleep. He's punishing me, Meyer thought, punishing me because I dared to look pleased at the order to halt the Panzers. He waited, seeing that Storch hadn't finished with him yet. The general picked up the order again.

'I think we have misunderstood what lies behind this message, Meyer. It ends with the words "pending further instructions". I think I can predict that those will be for us to resume our advance, so it becomes vitally important to be ready, Meyer. Do you not agree?'

'Yes, sir.'

'We are now close to the jugular vein of the British Expeditionary Force – the Channel ports. Once we start moving north we shall capture Boulogne, Calais and Dunkirk within two days, maybe even only one day. Then the British are finished.'

'Two days?' Meyer was stunned.

'At the most. Now, you must hurry.' Storch walked to the door and then turned before leaving the room. 'And don't forget that message, Meyer. Road to Boulogne open. Division ready to advance.'

The farmer's name was Mandel, and without hesitation he invited them into the farmhouse, but first he asked them to hide the tank in a distant outhouse which lay about half a kilometre from the Cambrai road. Before parking Bert, Barnes and Reynolds helped Penn to walk from the tank into the farmhouse where they lowered him into an armchair in the kitchen. Barnes was almost too exhausted to worry about other people but he did warn Mandel that it could be very dangerous for him if the Germans arrived and found them helping the British.

'You do not worry about that,' Mandel assured him. 'Once the tank is hidden in that distant outhouse the Germans will never find it. As for yourselves, Etienne, my nephew, will keep watch. We can see the road for a long way in both directions, so if anything happens there will be time for you to hide in a ditch well away from here.'

This was another stroke of good luck – the fact that Mandel spoke good English. Barnes asked him where he had learned the language.

'In your country, of course! For several years I worked as an onion-seller. I come from Brest, you see, where I was employed by the Syndicate. I used to take my bicycle on the boat over to Southampton, collect my onions from the depot and then cycle all round Hampshire and Surrey. You soon learn English that way!'

'We'd better park the tank.'

'Etienne will show you. You go up the track and . . . I will leave it to Etienne.'

As far as Barnes could see there was no sign of a telephone, so it wouldn't be possible for Mandel to phone the Germans to tell them that they were here. Not that he thought there was any likelihood of that happening for when he looked at Mandel he felt pretty sure that he could trust him. The farmer was in his fifties, a short, heavily-built man with a strong red face and a large grey moustache which matched his great bush of hair. Even his wife, Marianne, showed no signs of alarm at the arrival of these dangerous visitors. A woman of about the same age as her husband, she wore her hair tied back in a bun and her features were shrewd and decisive. She said she would prepare a meal for them and went away before Barnes could protest. They made a formidable pair.

Leaving Penn with the Mandels, he followed Etienne to where Reynolds had returned to the tank.

The track was stony, barely visible under the grass, and Etienne had to guide them along it to the distant outhouse. He could hardly speak a word of English but frequently he banged his fist on the side of the turret and said 'Good, good!' He was probably just under military age, Barnes decided, very close to his seventeenth birthday, the age which Seft had claimed. But Etienne was very different from the German fifth columnist. This lad was thin and wiry, his freckled face fresh and alert, and there was a look of wicked humour in his eye. He'll be a devil with the girls, thought Barnes as they reached the isolated building. Etienne jumped down off the hull to open the huge doors.

While Reynolds was driving the tank inside Barnes walked all round the building which stood in the middle of nowhere. Green fields stretched away to the skyline and the only approach was by the track they had driven along. He was on the horns of a dilemma because his small unit was now reduced to two effectives – himself and Reynolds. Leaving Bert here meant either leaving the driver to guard it or not guarding the vehicle at all. Reluctantly, he took a decision which would have horrified his troop commander – he decided to leave Bert on his own for the night. They had to keep some sort of watch through the hours of darkness – for the sake of the Mandels as well as their own – and he knew that in their present state of exhaustion keeping awake and alert all night was impossible. He would have to split the guard duty between himself and Reynolds, so both of them would take turns in watching the road, because it was along the road where any danger would come from. As they walked back with Etienne through the gathering dusk he still wasn't happy about putting the Mandels at risk by staying with them, but the fact was they couldn't move another kilometre without rest. On one point he was quite determined: they wouldn't sleep in the house.

Well after dark they sat down to the hot cooked meal which Marianne had prepared. Roast chicken, potatoes and some green vegetables they didn't recognize. They ate together at a scrubbed wood table in the huge kitchen at the back of the house, the stone walls hung with burnished copper pans, and the family ate with them. Barnes was famished and joined Reynolds in attacking the meal with vigour, but Penn held his knife and fork and then put them down. Marianne said something and Mandel, sitting at the head of the table, smiled sadly.

'Your friend can't eat – it will be his wound.'

'I'm terribly sorry . . .' began Penn.

Marianne spoke rapidly in French, taking up his glass of wine and making insistent gestures that he should at least drink. Then she took away his plate and when she came back Penn was drinking. Nodding to herself with satisfaction, she said something to Mandel, who nodded in his turn.

'I can manage a gallon of this,' said Penn.

Mandel spoke to his wife in French and laughed at her reply.

'She says that as long as he drinks a gallon he will be all right. And, Sergeant Barnes, do stop listening so carefully while you are eating – Etienne is outside watching the road and will warn us if there is anything coming.'

'It's just that it's well after dark. Would he see them?'

'Of course! These Germans drive through the night with their lamps blazing away as though they owned France. Les salles Boches!' He made a gesture of cutting a throat with his knife and Marianne frowned, which caused Mandel to laugh again as he reassured Barnes. 'Do not worry. She is a good woman. Because I want to help you that is enough for her – she wants to help you also. Certainly we are more happy to see your tank than we were to see the others.'

'The others?'

'Yes, a tremendous column of Germans which went on and on past our front door – huge tanks, big guns, armoured cars. I think it was a whole division.'

'When was this?'

'Six days ago – last Saturday. There have been other since, but they are mainly supply columns. The first one was the big one. Of course, you know that the Germans are in Abbeville?'

'We had heard a rumour,' said Barnes slowly.

'It is true, I fear. We may have a visitor from

Abbeville later tonight – my other nephew, Jacques. He comes from Lemont near Dunkirk, where he lives with his father, but at the moment he is living with his married sister in Abbeville. He may have interesting news for you.'

'How will he get here – you're behind the German lines.'

'I know, but this is not like the last war. The Germans are in Abbeville but only with tanks and guns – so if you can get the petrol, and if you are crazy like Jacques, you can drive about as you wish as long as you avoid their road-blocks. He has already made the journey once and he said he might come to see us again tonight. It has become a game with him but do not ask me how he gets the petrol – he will not even tell me. I am sure that he has stolen it from a German store.'

'He'll get shot.'

'Do not look so surprised – it may not be as difficult as you think. The Germans seem very short of troops to guard even important places like petrol and ammunition stores. The foot-sloggers – is not that the right word – the foot-sloggers have not caught up with the tanks yet. I was a foot-slogger myself once.'

Mandel nodded towards the fireplace where a frame hung above the mantelpiece. Inside the frame hung Mandel's Croix de Guerre, the medal polished, the ribbon faded. Barnes was frowning as he spoke.

'I find that hard to believe, Mandel – that they don't guard their ammunition dumps.'

'I did not say exactly that – I said that they have not enough troops to guard them properly, as with the petrol. You can ask Jacques yourself when he arrives, he learnt to speak English when he lived with a British family. You see, his father has ideas that one day the boy will be a great international advocate.'

'What happens when the Germans pass here, Mandel?'

'They make us stand by the roadside so that we can see how powerful they are.'

'Very good of them. Where are the nearest Allied troops now? Do you have any idea?'

'In Arras, I believe. You are going to Arras?'

'Possibly.'

'It would be suicide.' Mandel waved his knife. 'The German Army is between here and Arras and the closer you get to the front line the more of them there are, naturally. You would do far better to go west beyond Cambrai and then turn north towards the Channel ports. That way you might just meet the Allies before you met the Boche.'

They went on talking and eating but still half Barnes' mind strained to hear any unusual sound outside the farmhouse. After spending days in the open with the tank he felt nervous indoors and he couldn't get out of his mind the thought of Bert lying unprotected in that outhouse. He was picking up his last piece of chicken when he saw Penn staring at his fork. Without a word, Marianne went to the oven at the far end of the kitchen and came back with a plate which she put in front of Penn. Mandel grinned.

'She kept his meal warm because she thought that would happen. When he sees other people eating his appetite returns.' He raised his glass to Penn. *'Bon appétit!'*

While Penn wolfed down his chicken the others tackled their second course, an almost unlimited supply of cheese. Again Mandel returned to the question of which way Barnes should take in the morning and while he spoke Barnes listened without committing himself. Half an hour later they were all drinking strong bitter coffee when Etienne came into the room and spoke quickly, a hint of urgency in his voice. Mandel stood up.

'A car is coming along the road from the west at high speed. It may be Jacques, but I think you should hide.'

Mandel led the way out of the farmhouse and across a field with his torch, stopping as they reached a large haystack close to the road.

'Wait behind here until I call you. It is rather too early for Jacques but one never can tell – he drives like the devil. If it is him, I will come out and shout.'

'Should he know we are here?' queried Barnes.

'The last time he was here he spent the night with my brother who lives at Fontenoy, a village close to Beaucaire. But he did not sleep much – he was up half the night with some friends. They tied a piece of telephone wire across the road just high enough to catch a motor-cycle rider. The Germans always send such patrols ahead and they caught a fish. At seventeen and a half he has killed his first German, the young devil.'

'Pretty risky, isn't it? You might get reprisals.'

'Like the last one, this war will last four years and we shall get many reprisals, and Jacques will join the Army soon and will kill many more Germans. But it is spirit like his which will save France. Now, I must go. And don't mention any of this in front of Marianne – she doesn't know and sometimes she understands a little English!'

They could hear the car's engine as Mandel hurried away, the engine of a car being driven at recklessly high speed, and now the headlights were coming closer. Penn's voice whispered in the dark.

'These people seem all right.'

'Yes, you want to forget about Lebrun and his gang. It's people like the Mandels we're fighting for. Keep well in – I hope to God this is Jacques.'

Jacques was more mature than Etienne, more heavily built, and he had the face of a monkey, a monkey with jet-black hair. His eyes were intelligent and quick-moving and Barnes took to him at once as he shook hands all round with a firm grasp.

'Uncle has told me about you, Sergeant Barnes. The Germans are in Abbeville with their Panzers. I have just come from that town.'

'How did you manage to get here past the Germans?' Barnes asked quietly.

'By knowing the side roads very well, by keeping my eyes well open, by asking friends on the way what the situation was.'

By keeping his eyes well open. They were large eyes and they had the same look of the devil in them which Barnes had detected in Etienne, but they were bolder, more challenging, and now they seemed humorously to challenge Barnes to call him a liar.

'So you came most of the way by side roads?'

'No, Sergeant.' Was there a hint of mockery in this young man's expression? Barnes thought so as the lad went on. 'I came most of the distance along the same main roads the Panzers have used, but I turned on to side roads to avoid road-blocks.'

'There are a lot of road-blocks?'

'There are three – all outside Abbeville. But you should not go through Cambrai. They have set up some kind of headquarters in the town hall and there is a curfew at sunset. But no one takes any notice of it because they have so few troops to see that their orders are carried out.' He grinned. 'Even so, your tank will not be welcome in Cambrai.'

Damn! thought Barnes. I wish Mandel hadn't mentioned Bert to him. I'm sure he trusts too many people. He hesitated. It didn't seem quite the thing to cross-examine Mandel's nephew in front of them all. Marianne was washing up and Reynolds was helping her while Penn sagged in the armchair. Mandel finished lighting his pipe and laughed.

'Go on, Sergeant Barnes, ask him questions. He expects it!'

'So apart from Cambrai and the three road-blocks the road to Abbeville is open?'

'It was for me this evening. I took side roads to miss the road-blocks and Cambrai but otherwise I came straight here. It was easy.'

'Are there many Germans in Abbeville?'

'The town is full of their tanks and guns.' He frowned, his black eyebrows close together, moving swiftly like a comedian's. 'That is not quite correct. Most of the tanks and guns were on the north side two days ago and I haven't been to that district since. There is a curfew, too.'

'When does the curfew start?'

'Half an hour before sunset and it goes on until half an hour after dawn. They have said they will shoot anyone they find outside during the curfew but that has not happened yet. I could take you towards Abbeville,' he added hopefully, 'and then you could turn north to Boulogne. The Allies are in Boulogne.'

'I should damned well hope so. What about German aircraft – are there a lot about during the daytime?'

'Yes, there are, but they fly very high. If there were many of you I think they might see you, but not just one tank if you are careful. There are many miles where you do not see any Germans except for the occasional supply column. And they will not be expecting you in this area,' he pointed out shrewdly.

'Thanks, Jacques. There may be some more questions I'll think of to ask you – you'll be staying here for the night, I suppose?'

'No,' interjected Mandel quickly, 'he will be staying with my brother at Fontenoy, but there is plenty of time to ask him as many questions as you wish.'

It wasn't a matter of more questions to be asked, but now he knew that Jacques wasn't going to spend the night at the farm, Barnes' mind was filled with foreboding, driving away in a flash the soothing effect of the food and the wine, forcing his tired brain to weigh and calculate just when he had hoped that for a few brief hours at least he would be able to relax, to recuperate from the terrible strain of the events of the past two days. The lad was probably loyal: Mandel seemed confident enough and the Frenchman was no fool. But was it only a question of loyalty? Supposing he went out again tonight with his friends on one of those wild escapades, that he was captured and interrogated, possibly even by the SS? Since there was nothing he could do about it he smiled amiably.

'That's all right. I've asked all the questions I can think of for the moment.'

Mandel offered them two bedrooms but Barnes firmly refused, saying they would sleep outside by the haystack in case the Germans arrived unexpectedly, and he suspected that Mandel was secretly relieved at his refusal. Before they left the house the farmer said that they must listen to the news bulletin and Barnes was interested to see that he automatically tuned in to London as though he regarded that source as being the most reliable at the moment. They listened in silence as the calm detached voice of Stuart Hibberd began speaking.

'. . . fighting in Boulogne.'

It was after eleven o'clock when they opened their bed-rolls which they had carried back from the tank after parking it, and they laid them out behind the haystack. As they arranged the blankets the moon was coming up and Barnes welcomed this pale illumination since it would make their watch on the road easier; he was by no means convinced that the Germans would announce their arrival with warning headlights. Firmly, he gave Penn his instructions.

'You get to bed and stay there – you'll have little enough sleep as it is.'

'When do I go on duty?'

'You don't – I'm sharing it with Reynolds.'

'And may I ask at what hour reveille will be blowing?'

'At dawn – four o'clock on the dot.'

'That's five hours away, which means you'd get two and a half hours' sleep each. It's not good enough. I'm afraid you're in for a touch of insubordination – I'm doing my whack.'

'And you're due for a whack on the head if you don't shut up. Get down and stay down – that's an order, Penn. If I need you, I'll wake you.'

He only had to wait a few minutes before Penn was fast asleep, dead to the world, lying on his left side to take the weight off his wound. He gave Reynolds his orders.

'You go down as well. I'll do two and a half hours and then wake you at one-thirty. After I've gone down you're to wake me at four – we must be away very early tomorrow. While you're on guard it's just a matter of keeping a sharp eye along the road in both directions. Down you go.'

A few minutes later and with some trepidation he watched Jacques drive away towards Beaucaire in his four-seater green Renault, still unable to rid himself of the feeling that this was the fly in the ointment. Physically, he was having an awful time keeping on his feet and he walked up and down the moonlit road to take his mind off his gently throbbing wound, realizing now that it would have probably been wiser to change the dressing, but his brain went on racing round. They'd have to head north for the Boulogne–Calais area, not so far from where Jacques came from. It would mean the devil of a right-hand sweep, west and then north, and he doubted whether they'd ever make it, but at least on the way they might meet some really worthwhile objective. The search for some massive objective against which they could deal the Germans a hammer-blow was now looming larger in

Barnes' mind than finding a way back to the Allied lines. The position was becoming terribly serious, the news bulletin proved that. It was a warm muggy night and this didn't help to keep him on the alert. He'd be glad when morning came, and then they could get on with it. As he paced up and down Barnes had a strong feeling that this was the last haven of peace they would find, that from tomorrow they would be in the thick of it all the way.

Shortly after midnight the lights in the farmhouse went out and he heard a window open and then close. It was probably Mandel listening to him pacing up and down. In the distance he could still hear the mutter of those guns, but just before it was time to wake Reynolds the guns stopped, and this disturbed Barnes greatly as though it were an omen of disaster. He woke up Reynolds and settled down to sleep under the stars, which seemed far bigger than usual. An hour later he was still awake, his mind twitching with anxiety, then without knowing it he fell asleep. The emergency he had feared came just after dawn.

Chapter Six

Saturday, 25 May

The tank emerged from the outhouse into the eerie light of the false dawn. It seemed to kick up the devil of a row as it moved slowly down the stony track, following the beams of the headlights which made the pale grey gloom even weirder. Across the fields coils of mist floated above the ground and a curtain of vapour fogged the beams.

They had risen at four like ghosts in a half-world, bleary-eyed, thick-tongued, thirsty, hardly able to carry their bed-rolls along the stony track, but they had the world to themselves, a world which was dark and chilly. They had brewed up, drunk their tea and, at Barnes' insistence, had a shave. After the tea and the shave they had begun to revive sufficiently to eat some of the remaining bully beef and a packet of biscuits which Reynolds had quietly kept for an emergency. There was general agreement that the morning qualified. The horizon was a faint line against a bleak glow when they drove out of the building and along the track. Barnes already realized that Penn had not benefited from his night's rest to anything like the extent he had hoped and the corporal's peevishness had confirmed this.

'What about the Mandels?' he had asked. 'Are you running off and leaving them without a word of thanks?'

'Of course not. We'll park Bert by the road and then I'll pop back to see them.'

As they moved down the track he saw that lights had appeared in the upper windows of the farmhouse. Mandel must have heard them coming. It seemed ungrateful not to warn him the night before of their plans for a very early start but Jacques had been there until they had left the farmhouse. Rubbing his arm to get the chill out of his bones Barnes looked both ways along the road and saw nothing. It would be an enormous relief when they had left the Mandels in peace. Within ten minutes they would be on their way towards Abbeville. He had chosen that route because it was the only one they had heard to be clear of traffic. They were very close to the farmhouse when he stiffened, swore, and gave the order.

'Halt! Lights off!'

From the direction of Beaucaire tiny headlights glowed in the distance, just one pair. They'd have to let the vehicle go past without seeing them. He issued more orders and the tank moved across the field until it was completely hidden by the dim bulk of the haystack, when he ordered a halt. Standing in the turret behind the stack he saw that the top was at least six feet above his head and when he leant far out

from the rim his fingers touched the edges of projecting hay. Jumping down, he checked the front and
rear: there was at least four feet of stack which
concealed the tank from the road at either end. It was
just a question of letting this early bird drive past
before he went to see Mandel. He might even be able
to buy some food off the farmer.

Going down on one knee behind the rear track he
waited, feeling the early morning dew soak through
his trousers, gripping the revolver in his right hand.
His brain was becoming very alert now as he watched
the headlights growing larger, a sense of alarm beginning to sting his nerves: this could be trouble, but at
least there was only one car. Pull yourself together,
Barnes – one car could contain four Germans armed
with machine-pistols. Climbing up on the hull he told
Penn to hand him up a machine-pistol, then he
assumed his position behind the track. The car was
very close now, moving at a tremendous speed,
probably well over sixty. Tension built up inside him
like the crackle of electricity. Thank God he had got
them up early. With a scream of brakes the car turned
off the road, headlights sweeping over the rear of the
tank, then it stopped.

Had they seen the tank? The headlights had continued in their ninety-degree turn without a quiver,
but a strong-willed driver might manage that. The
slam of the car door. Footsteps. A solitary figure
reached the front door and hammered on it like a
German drill-sergeant demanding entry. Barnes lifted

the gun as the front door opened, shedding a pool of light into the yard and then closing again. Could it be Jacques? The parked car looked like a Renault although in this weird light it was difficult to tell. He wasn't at all sure that there weren't other people inside the darkened car. He'd better check this.

He ran, racing forward until he reached the side of the house out of sight of the car, creeping along the wall to a window which showed light behind curtains. He couldn't see through the material but faintly he heard voices, one of them excited. This voice was doing most of the talking. Cautiously he crept towards the front of the house and as he reached the corner he heard the front door open. Footsteps came into the yard. He froze.

'Sergeant Barnes, it's only Jacques. He's brought some news, some alarming news. Barnes!'

'Here, Mandel.'

He stepped out into the courtyard, lowering his machine-pistol, and when Mandel saw it he must have recognized the gun since he looked at it in surprise but without comment. Beside him stood Jacques, his chin unshaven and his collar open, while Etienne waited in the floodlit doorway. Mandel hurried forward, his shirt only half-tucked inside his trousers, speaking quickly.

'There is great trouble. From his bedroom in Fontenoy Jacques can see across the fields to Beaucaire – or rather to the road here from Beaucaire – and he heard something early this morning. Then he saw a lot of lights so he walked across the fields and hid behind a hedge close to these lights. A large German column has reached Beaucaire, has come round it to the south, you understand, and camped on this side of the town . . .'

'Camped?'

'No, that is the wrong word. Apparently it has halted for a short time. When they move again they must come this way – past here.'

'What makes him say it has only halted for a short time?'

Jacques stepped forward, his manner so different from the night before that he seemed a different person. He spoke urgently.

'May I explain? It is part of a Panzer divison – the usual big tanks and guns. It has to come this way and may move at any time. They are using this route as their highway to the west – but can you keep ahead of them?'

'We'll have to. We'd better start at once. Mandel, can I buy some food off you or are you short yourselves?'

'Etienne.' Mandel turned and took a parcel from his nephew and handed it to Barnes. 'Take this – my wife packed it before we went to bed last night. No, any suggestion of payment will be taken as an insult. Now you must go!'

Thanking him, Barnes tucked the parcel under his arm and ran back to the tank. The three Mandels followed him and waited while he climbed into the turret, put on his headset and gave Reynolds the order to start the engines. While he waited he looked down and saw grey stubble on Mandel's chin. Looking back in the growing light he could see no sign of traffic on the road from Beaucaire. The engines coughed, sputtered, and died. Barnes said nothing and waited. Reynolds tried again. The engines repeated their surly reaction. Mandel put his hands on his hips and waited. They all waited while Reynolds fought desperately to start the motors. Five minutes later the dawn light was spreading gradually over the fields and now there was a glint of gold in the east. Soon it would be broad daylight. Reynolds tried again and again but not once did the engines give any sign of activating. Patiently, Mandel stood waiting without showing any traces of alarm but the two lads were now staring fixedly along the road to the east.

'No good?' Barnes called down from the turret to Reynolds.

The driver's head inside the hatch turned to look up. 'I think it's the starter system.'

'Do your best – that Panzer column may be here soon.'

'I'll still have to look at the starter wiring.'

'How long do you think it will take?'

Immediately he regretted the question. How on earth could Reynolds be expected to predict that? It was the only sign of anxiety Barnes had allowed himself to show.

'Could be two minutes, could be two hours. I

noticed it was coughing nastily when we came down that track.'

'Have another go before you start checking.' Barnes leaned over the turret to speak to Jacques. 'What exactly made you think the column would be on the move soon?'

'The men in the tanks hadn't left them – they were eating a meal and they had stayed in the towers to eat.'

Barnes looked down at Mandel. 'That sounds as though it's just a short stop and then they'll be coming this way.'

'I think so, too.'

'We'll have a few more shots at starting.'

Reynolds was persisting non-stop now and while he struggled to coax life out of Bert it became daylight. Again no one spoke. Barnes stared backwards at the distant hill crest which was now clearly to be seen, the crest over which the Panzers would appear. Jacques and Etienne stood stock still, hands in their pockets to keep warm. Only Mandel was moving during the agonizing wait when nerves were stretched and a fresh chill, the chill of fear, seeped into the waiting men. Walking round the haystack, Mandel disappeared from view and then reappered at the other side in front of the tank. His face was thoughtful, his thick brow scowling, and he looked at the tank closely and then spoke quickly to Etienne. The lad ran away across the field to an outhouse just behind the farm.

'Sergeant, it's no good,' said Reynolds firmly. 'I've

got to have a look at the engines. It may take quite a while.'

'Just do the best you can as quickly as possible.'

He had just finished speaking when he heard the purr of a motor. Turning round, he saw Etienne emerging from the building as he drove a large orange-coloured machine towards them. In front of the machine a huge power-grab shovel was hoisted at an angle, wobbling as it moved closer. Mandel came forward and stood directly under the turret.

'The tank will not move. Is that not so?'

'Not yet, anyway.'

'And the German tank column will soon be on the move and will pass there?'

'That seems pretty evident,' Barnes replied irritably.

'So the only solution is to hide the tank. Is that not so?'

'You can't shift it with that power-grab machine. This tank weights twenty-six and a half tons and you won't budge it an inch with that thing. You're pretty well-equipped out here, aren't you?' he added.

'I borrow it from a wealthy neighbour to clear my ditches. Now, I agree that this machine won't move your tank, Sergeant Barnes. So we must proceed logically – we must leave the tank where it is and yet still hide it. That is the only possible solution.'

'I don't follow you.'

'We shall have to turn it into something else – a haystack.'

'How the devil are you going to manage that?'

'This haystack is constructed of square bales of hay which have been placed on top of each other – this method makes it easier for us to take away only a small portion of the stack when we require it. The bales were lifted up by the power-grab, as you call it. All we have to do is to take the haystack to pieces and then rebuild it round the tank which will, of course, sit in the hollow inside it. But we must start at once – all of us helping.'

'Even if it would work there may not be time.'

'It will be much quicker than you think. Etienne!'

He poured forth a stream of French as Barnes told Reynolds to help Penn out of the tank. Between them they got him sat down on the grass and by now Etienne was working the grab to Mandel's instructions. To start with he tackled the corner of the stack nearest the road, driving the machine forward, inserting the huge metal hand and emerging with a bale of hay which he dumped on the ground. Immediately he began repeating the process as Mandel developed his idea.

'We leave the wall of hay next to the tank because we can use that where it is. To surround the tank will take a lot of hay but there will be plenty left over by the hollow inside. We shall use that hay to build the roof over the tank.'

While he was talking Etienne was moving more bales, dropping them at random as he attacked the haystack ferociously along the side nearest the road.

Barnes looked again towards the east. In the light of day the deserted highway bore a sinister aspect and he could just picture the scene. One moment it would be still like this, a peaceful scene devoid of traffic: then the first tank would crawl over the crest and head towards them, followed by a whole armada of Panzers. And if they found the tank here all the Mandels might well be shot. He made up his mind.

'We'll try it. Penn, your job is to watch that hill crest. At the first sign of movement bellow like the bull of Bashan. Reynolds, stop tinkering with that engine, there's work to do.'

Between them, Barnes and Mandel organized a work system: while Etienne dismantled the stack on one side, Reynolds and Jacques began lifting bales of hay and moving them to form a wall parallel to the rear of the tank. At the same time Barnes and Mandel formed a second team, carrying their own bales to build a wall across the front of the tank. Even here, Mandel was showing foresight.

'If the Panzers arrive too soon,' he explained, 'we may at least have two walls up. If we were very lucky they might not see the open back.'

'Let's hope we don't have to be that lucky.'

Half an hour later it all seemed to be taking too long to Barnes. The Germans would arrive and catch them in the middle of it. He urged everyone to move faster. It was still chilly but they were all working feverishly, their jackets lying on the ground as they heaved the huge bales up, balancing the load between them, staggering across to the walls to lay their new 'bricks', and then going straight back for another load. The two side walls were still only half-built when Marianne appeared with a tray of coffee. Laying it on the ground she watched them working for a minute and then went indoors without a word. Mandel grinned across a bale at Barnes.

'You have misunderstood her – she knows that when men are working women must keep out of the way. She is the same when she brings us wine in the fields.'

'She must be worried, though.'

'We are all worried. So let us finish building our new haystack and then we can stop worrying.'

He's wrong there, Barnes thought. If we do get the job done in time the big worry will then start – will the Germans find the tank? He glanced towards where Penn stood leaning against a fence as he stared towards the ominous hill crest. They're going to catch us in the middle of this, Barnes felt sure of it.

'Mandel, whether we get the tank hidden or not in time I think you should clear out until the Germans have gone – take your family into the fields.'

'We could hide, certainly – and if they come too early we shall. But if we have finished, then we must stay. It would look strange if the place was deserted at this hour of the day.'

'No, it won't. People are fleeing all over France.'

'Yes, my friend, but they take things with them. Anyone who goes inside our house will see that we have taken nothing and will know we are hiding. They might well burn down the house. And do not forget Jacques' car – that will show someone is about.'

'Hide that in the outhouse where we hid Bert.'

They had laid the fresh bale on top of the wall in front of the tank, a wall which was now about the same height as the rear wall, Reynolds and Jacques were building, and so far both walls only concealed half the hull. It was all taking far too long.

'Your idea about the car is good,' said Mandel. 'If they ask to see Jacques' papers they will see that he comes from Lemont and may wonder why he is here – so take him with you when you hide and I will get him to move the car at once.'

An hour later they were making tremendous progress, encouraged by the sight of the tank sinking lower and lower behind the walls of hay. The work had been considerably speeded up by Etienne who had now completed dismantling three quarters of the haystack and was using his power-grab to transport the loose bales right up to the walls, so that all the others had to do was to manoeuvre the 'bricks' into position. Soon the end walls were finished and within another half-hour the rear wall was over five feet high: even at the back only the turret still protruded, looking rather like the conning tower of an invisible submarine submerged in a sea of hay. They were all working in a frenzy now, standing on the rear wall, on the hull of the tank as they wrestled the bales into position, never stopping for a moment. The unspoken thought that they might just fail for the sake of a few bales gave added impetus to their efforts and now Mandel and Reynolds worked stripped to the waist, their bodies running with sweat in the warm sunshine. It was going to be another lovely day – for the Germans.

There had been no traffic along the main road since they had started, not even a farm cart, and this puzzled Barnes until he mentioned it to Mandel who laughed grimly.

'No one comes this way at the moment because they know that the Panzers use the highway, so what happens? My neighbours go miles out of their way along side roads when they could use this road easily, but they will not risk the Panzers.'

'What happens when the Panzers meet something?'

'If they meet a vehicle or catch it up they tip it into the ditch. Nothing must stop the progress of the Panzers. That is why people are keeping away from here. You see, Sergeant Barnes, soon we shall be finished.'

With the four walls completed they turned to the final task – the roofing-in of the new structure. Putting the icing on the cake, as Mandel called it. For this stage Barnes and Reynolds stood on top of the walls while Etienne handed up bales with the power-grab. It proved to be a more difficult stage than they had anticipated, because first they had to fill in the area round the turret, dropping bales down on to the hull and tracks and fitting these in round the gun. The gun was a nuisance because they had to wedge in bales round the long barrel and it slowed them down, but they persisted and then suddenly they had done the job. The drawback was that they ended up with an irregular roof which looked strange; once again Mandel came up with the solution, telling Etienne to use the power-grab in a certain way. Standing back on the road Barnes watched as the machine moved forward, the grab hoisted to its highest elevation. When it stopped Etienne brought the shovel down full force again and again, hammering the roof of hay flat. When he had completed the job even Barnes had to agree that from the road the haystack looked perfectly normal and he could hardly believe that Bert nestled inside the new structure. Then his eyes dropped to the ground in front of the stack and his mouth tightened. The earth was littered with hay relics and flattened dead grass which described a neat-rectangle clearly locating the original site of the stack.

'Mandel – the Germans will see that. It's a dead giveaway.'

'All has been prepared. Do not worry. You will see!'

Reynolds and Etienne were now walking slowly back from the farm and between them they carried an enormous tarpaulin which they proceeded to spread over the marked area under Mandel's guidance. When it was in place the farmer began pulling hay from underneath the sheet and throwing it at random over the top.

'Now it means nothing. Perfect camouflage! This cover could have slipped off the haystack or been pulled off to let the sun dry the stack out. So now we can go inside and wait for them.'

'I still think you ought to hide in the fields with us.'

'No, we shall stay here to welcome them. More camouflage! So long as we line up on the roadside acknowledging their achievements they are quite happy. You will come in for some wine?'

'No, I'll wait here and relieve Penn. Why is Etienne dumping those spare bales in your yard?'

'To create a diversion. If something exciting is happening when they arrive it will take their minds off other things – including that haystack. Leave this to me and do not worry if you see signs of fire when the Boche comes. Marianne will bring a glass of wine to you and inside we shall drink a toast. To the tank!'

Barnes went into the middle of the road and waited alone as he watched the deserted hill crest. Supposing that after all their troubles the Panzers didn't come? But they were halted on this side of Beaucaire and he remembered that apart from one or two country lanes there had been no major road leading off this one. Could they possibly get away with it? He looked at the stack again, amazed by its appearance of normality. Just so long as they didn't start pushing bayonets into it, although it would need a pretty long bayonet to reach Bert through those walls. And this, he thought, is a method of camouflage you won't find in the textbooks.

Frequently he looked behind him along the road towards Cambrai and then he looked up into the brilliantly blue morning sky. Not a cloud anywhere, but more important still, not a plane either. Again it was hard to believe there was a war on. A few minutes later, at 7.15 a.m., he was running at top speed towards the house when he met Marianne on her way out with a glass of wine, a glass he knew that he would never drink. He had just seen the first German tank coming over the hill crest.

They lay full length in a ditch some distance from the house but at a point where Barnes could still see it. The ditch was dry and disused and thick with tall weeds. A German would have to be on top of them before there was the remotest chance of their being spotted, and the ditch was a long way from the outhouse where the Renault was now hidden. Penn, Jacques and Reynolds were sprawled out along the ditch behind him and the machine-pistol rested in front of his chest. Barnes had deliberately placed Jacques between the two men because he was fairly sure that they would have to lie there for two or three hours and he had no knowledge of the lad's endurance. When he had taken Reynolds aside his instructions had been quite precise.

'If he gets panicky and there's no other way out – knock him on the head with your revolver butt.'

Through a clump of weeds Barnes could see the farmhouse and a section of the road. The view looked incredibly peaceful, a pastoral scene with not a soul in sight. His eye fell on the haystack, an innocent piece of furniture one might expect to find anywhere out in the country. For the second time in twelve hours Bert was all on his own. He stiffened. From the road beyond the house he heard the high-pitched engine sound of a motor cycle: a patrol must have overtaken the leading tank and roared on ahead. A cycle with a side-car came into view, turned, and drove out of sight into the farmyard. Penn kept his own voice down as he spoke, although it wasn't necessary.

'Have they arrived?'

'Just a motor bike and side-car. They've gone into the yard.'

'Let's hope Mandel can handle them.'

'He'll handle them all right just so long as they don't start investigating that haystack.'

'Something's smoking – look, just beyond the roof.' Penn rested his chin on the edge of the ditch. 'They can't have set the place on fire already.'

'Got it! The artful old devil set fire to those spare

bales Etienne dumped in the yard. That's his diversion to keep them occupied.'

For the first time Barnes wondered what rank Mandel had attained during the First World War.

'Any sign of the two Jerries?' inquired Penn.

'No, they must still be at the house ... keep your head down! Tell the others.'

Along the road from behind the house the first German heavy tank appeared, its commander erect in the turret. The machine seemed to glide along the highway and across the field they could hear the low grumble of its revolving tracks. He estimated the vehicle's speed at fifteen miles an hour and the gun barrel was elevated at an angle of about ten degrees. Another tank moved into view, then another and another. They were certainly in a hurry to get somewhere and he was suprised that they were not spaced farther apart. The column's commander was either foolhardy or else he had very good reason to know that they risked no danger of air attack. Grimly he watched the enemy tanks and then thought of the Mandels again.

What on earth was happening at the farm? There had been no sign of the Mandels and the motor-cycle patrol was still on the premises. Gradually, the smoke from the fire died down until only a thin wisp rose above the rooftop. By the side of the machine-pistol lay Barnes' field-glasses but he was reluctant to use them except in an emergency – the sun could so easily reflect off the lenses and if one of those commanders in the turrets spotted it the fat would be in the fire. He settled himself down to a long wait. Providing all went well at the farm there wasn't a great deal of risk to fear: it was largely a matter of patience, of waiting for the enemy to go away. This comfortable thought had just passed through his mind when he heard the plane.

Instantly he was reminded of the machine which had spied out the ground for the Panzers crossing the country south of Fontaine. He would always remember that place as Fontaine. His body tensed, his nerves twanged as he realized the implications, and he could have kicked himself for his complacency. The element of comparative safety had now been turned into one of maximum danger. He could tell that the plane was flying very low, and from the way its engine sound faded, and then grew louder he guessed that it was travelling in a circle. It was the one hazard which he should have foreseen, the one which had completely escaped him. Turning on his side he spoke rapidly over his shoulder.

'It's a spotter plane, probably flying very low. From now on no one moves a whisker. Pass it on.'

'I'm the only one with a whisker to move,' said Penn.

From observation on land they were completely concealed but aerial observation was quite a different matter. There were four of them stretched out close together and the machine sounded to be only a few hundred feet up. They should still escape detection so long as they remained motionless, but in that still empty countryside only a small movement at the wrong moment could easily locate them. Pressing his body into the ditch, Barnes slowly turned his head to one side until he could see a narrow oblong of pure blue sky. The plane was very close now, almost on top of them from the sound, then it flashed into view. It was barely two hundred feet up, so low that he could see the outline of the pilot's helmet, a helmet which was tilted downwards. Then it vanished. Barnes wet his lips and then stiffened again. The plane was turning to come back again. Surely they couldn't have been spotted so quickly? Unless someone had moved. Jacques flashed into his mind and he stifled a groan. If he had moved Reynolds could hardly have warned the lad in time, the damage would have been done. Yes, it was definitely turning back, coming closer. What on earth could have attracted the pilot's attention? Suddenly he went ice-cold as the reason for the pilot's return flashed through his brain. *He was coming back to examine the haystack.*

With an awful clarity Barnes saw their fatal mistake. He had personally checked the appearance of the stack from the road which had seemed the obvious danger point. But he had forgotten the air! In his mind he re-lived the final stages of the camouflage operation. The roof of the stack had looked bumpy so Etienne had used the power-grab shovel to flatten the top. Supposing some of the bales had sunk into the hollow, perhaps falling down into a space between the tank and the hay walls? It could easily have happened and this meant that from the air Bert was now exposed to view. Penn's finger tapped him on the shoulder.

'Anything wrong? I saw your hand grip the pistol.'

'No,' said Barnes firmly, 'but keep absolutely still. That plane's coming back.'

Even though he couldn't see it yet he could hear it quite clearly now. The machine was describing another circle, but this time it was a smaller circle, a circle whose centre could well be the farmhouse – or the haystack. Very slowly, inch by inch, he raised his head above ditch level, taking care not to disturb the weeds. The Mandels, all three of them, were out standing by the roadside as a self-propelled gun rolled past. There was no sign of the motor-cycle patrol which must have driven off while his head was buried in the ditch. He studied the Mandels, trying to tell something from the way they stood. Then between the weeds the plane darted into view, flying straight towards him across the road. He kept perfectly still, resisting the temptation to duck. As it went over, the Mandels looked up and then dutifully turned their gaze back to the road as another heavy tank rolled past. The commander's head was turned towards them. Had he made some remark? The spotter plane swooped even lower and roared over their heads. What had caught his attention?

He tried to put himself in the position of the pilot.

What would he do? At his first sight of the tank inside its huge box of hay he would hardly believe his eyes, so he would circle in again for a closer look, which could well be the operation he had just completed. Then he would circle again and come in for a third and final look before he wirelessed the commander of the column. At least that's the way I'd handle it, Barnes told himself grimly. Had the plane gone away? He strained his ears for the sound of its engine. His wound was throbbing badly this morning and lying in that fixed position he could feel his right knee stiffening, the knee which had struck the underwater rock. No, the bloody plane hadn't gone away – it was coming back now for the third time round. It flew directly over the haystack and headed straight for him, waggling its wings from side to side. Why the waggle? Was it a signal? He felt stiff, clammy and sweat-soaked. They were trapped and all they could do was to wait inside the trap, hoping that these alarming manoeuvres of the plane had some other explanation. It passed directly over them and turned back to follow its familiar course. Still counting, he watched the endless column of vehicles move past to the west.

It was only ten minutes later when he was still waiting for a plane that never reappeared that he grasped the fact that Bert had not been spotted. For over an hour he refused to accept the idea completely, expecting that at any moment the haystack would be surrounded, but still the column rolled past and still the Mandels patiently witnessed its progress. Just how many Panzers did the Germans possess? He made a rough-and-ready estimate of what they had seen since leaving Etreux and then doubled it, arriving at the conclusion that the German High Command must be deploying three or four fully-equipped Panzer divisions in northern France.* The BEF complement was one tank brigade and one tank regiment. A tap on his back told him that Penn wanted to speak.

'I thought you might like to know, Sergeant, that I've got ants crawling all over me and cramp in my leg. It's nothing to worry about, mind you, but I knew you'd want to know.'

'Good of you to keep me informed, Penn.'

'I'll be issuing regular bulletins from now on.'

The ants were crawling over Barnes, too, crawling inside his uniform. He had first felt the tickle of their tiny bodies when the plane was flying over, at the very moment when they had to lie as still as death. Since then he had been constantly aware of this minute enemy. Lying full length in the ditch there was no way of ejecting them and by now the tickling sensation had invaded the lower part of his body, crawling over his stomach and his groin until he thought that he would go mad if this went on much longer. Penn tapped him on the shoulder again.

---

* Barnes underestimated. General von Rundstedt's Army Group A deployed seven Panzer divisions – over two thousand armoured vehicles.

'I haven't heard anything recently ... what's that?'

'The end of the column's gone, I think. A staff car's just stopped ...'

'It's probably the general – they always ride at the rear of the column!'

'The officer's just gone into the house with the Mandels. It shouldn't be long now – the driver's stayed with the car.'

Fortunately, Barnes was too far away to hear the conversation which had preceded the Mandels' return to their home, otherwise his mind might have been racked with anxiety.

Outwardly Mandel showed no traces of alarm as the staff car slowed down and then stopped. His expression was sleepy, the hands by his sides limp, but he sensed that just at the moment when he had thought all would be well fate had dealt him a bad hand. The major who sat by his driver's side was immaculately dressed, his uniform newly pressed, the peaked cap resting squarely on his head. He stared down the road after the tail of the Panzer column when he first spoke, presenting them a profile which might have been carved out of stone. His French was highly guttural.

'I trust that you are now convinced of the invincibility of the German Army after what you have seen?'

'We could hardly fail to be,' Mandel replied quietly.

'Good, good.' The major stood up, got out of his

car, closed the door, and stared down at Mandel from his great height. 'You still have plenty to eat?'

'We have sufficient for the moment, but as to later . . .' He spread his hands and dropped them.

'And to drink?'

'For the moment, just enough.'

'Good, good. Aren't you going to ask me inside? I may even furnish you with a certificate saying you are reliable citizens. That would come in useful when the next column arrives. There have been cases of French civilians firing on German troops and some commanders are a trifle hasty in their judgement.'

Without a word Mandel turned and led the way into the farmyard, his face still expressionless. When he reached the front door he stopped to let his wife and Etienne enter first and then waited for the German officer. The major had stopped in the middle of the yard to take a cigarette from a gold case. While he lit it he looked towards the remnants of burnt hay.

'I see that you have had a fire here very recently.'

'It started just before your column arrived – two of your men very kindly helped us to put it out.'

'That does not surprise me – in spite of what the lying British propagandists say the German soldier is always chivalrous. Now you will be able to tell your friends the truth in future.'

Mandel made no reply and the officer stood for a minute looking round him while he smoked. Gazing at the haystack he pointed with the cigarette.

'It is a good thing something like that didn't catch fire – that would be a tragedy for you, I'm sure.'

'We take care not to smoke near it,' said Mandel, feeling it wiser to make some reply.

'Ah well, we must not keep your good lady waiting. And I'm sure she dislikes smoking inside her house.'

He threw down his smoking cigarette among some pieces of straw which began to burn almost at once. Seeing that there was no danger of the fire spreading Mandel walked after the German and found him standing in the kitchen looking at the framed decoration above the mantelpiece.

'The Croix de Guerre! I am in the presence of an old soldier then. I imagine you earned this fighting in the last war?'

'Probably at the same time as you obtained the Iron Cross on your tunic,' Mandel replied politely.

The officer glanced at him quickly, fingering the cross. Marianne stood by the table, her arms folded over her chest as she stared out of the window across the fields. Mandel wished that she had gone upstairs but he was aware that she was staying in the hope of keeping down the temperature. By her side Etienne gazed into the fireplace. The major spoke abruptly, his voice harsh.

'You said you had plenty to drink. Since my men so kindly helped you to put out the fire I think they should be suitably rewarded. Would you not agree?

Two or three bottles of cognac would be acceptable, I'm sure.'

So that's it, Mandel thought, he's after loot. And they make a man like this an officer. Since he's a heavy cognac drinker his temper is probably uncertain. I'll have to watch this carefully.

'I have no cognac, Major, but possibly a bottle of wine or two? Would your men prefer red or white, do you think?'

'They would prefer cognac.' His voice was a whiplash now. He stood very erect, his nostrils flared, his eyes glowing. 'Since you say you are running short we will give them three bottles only, which is a meagre enough reward. Had the fire spread this house might have been burnt down. And understand this, my men are here to fight a war – not to help profiteering French farmers save their capital!'

'I'm sorry – you can search the place. We have wine but no cognac. Not a single bottle.'

The German eyed him grimly. 'You hid it when the first column came through here. I have little doubt of that.'

Casually, he unbuttoned the flap of his leather hip holster and withdrew the pistol, holding it sideways in one hand, the muzzle pointing towards Marianne. Mandel moved quickly in front of her, while behind him his wife slipped a hand towards her throat. He saw Etienne's eyes on the heavy poker in the fireplace and almost imperceptibly he frowned, giving a little shake of his head. Knowing that at any moment there might be a tragedy he took the initiative quickly.

'Major, the cupboard in that corner is full of wine – may I show you and then you can make your choice?'

Slowly he moved towards the cupboard and the pistol turned away from Marianne to point at the wall. Without further hesitation Mandel threw open both doors and started lifting out bottles on to the table. The German waited until a dozen stood in a row and then he put away his gun.

'That will have to do if you persist in being obstinate. You and the boy – bring all the bottles on the table out to my car.'

They hurried out across the yard, three bottles under each arm, while the officer followed slowly. The driver snapped something at them, indicating that they should store the bottles on the back seat. When they had emptied their arms he leaned over and pulled a greatcoat across the bottles to conceal them. The major had left the yard now and strolled along the road to stand close to the haystack. He looked at it with interest while he extracted a fresh cigarette and lit it in a leisurely fashion. Mandel sent Etienne away to the farmhouse and waited tensely, feeling quite sure that their ordeal was not ended yet. From the direction of Beaucaire a motor-cycle patrol drove up, slowing down and then speeding away as the officer waved them on. The driver had started the engine of the staff car but the major seemed in no hurry to depart: in fact, the haystack appeared to fascinate him and he began to walk round it as he took short puffs at his cigarette.

Nothing shows, Mandel told himself, nothing shows at all. He cannot possibly suspect anything so why is he taking such a great interst in it? With a tremendous effort he compelled himself to assume an attitude of complete indifference, even going so far as to clasp his hands over his stomach while he looked up at the sky as though checking the weather situation. The major had walked right round the haystack now and he made a small gesture with his free hand. Driving forward, the car pulled up close to the officer who now stood wih his back to the road facing the haystack. Again he spoke without looking at Mandel.

'I do fear that the cognac you so stubbornly concealed is going to prove a most expensive proposition.'

Raising his right hand he aimed with great care, tossing the burning cigarette high in the air so that when it fell it landed out of sight on top of the stack. Then he stood and waited, one hand close to his holster flap, studying Mandel's face closely. Appalled, the Frenchman showed only the reaction expected. Hanging his shoulders, he gazed at the stack in glum despair, then very slowly he turned away and walked back to the farmhouse, forcing himself not to hurry, hoping that by removing himself from the scene of the conflagration the German would lose interest and go away.

The officer stood watching the top of the stack which was now crackling and sputtering, suddenly flaring up until the entire roof was a crown of flames. Satisfied, he got back into his seat and the car drove off at a high speed.

Only by exerting his will-power far beyond its normal limits was Barnes able to keep himself pressed down inside the ditch. He had seen the German officer studying the stack, he had even seen that he was smoking because now he risked using his field-glasses. But as if some telepathic intuition had been transmitted between them he had understood Man-del's action when he slowly trailed back to the house. Seen from this great distance the burning stack pre-sented an even more alarming spectacle as grey-black smoke billowed in a huge cloud above the road, and from where he lay Barnes could see red tongues of flame licking their way along the full length of the roof of hay. He felt Penn stirring as Mandel walked away.

'We'd better get moving – we've got to try and put that lot out. We can shoot those two while we're about it.'

'Keep yourself down,' Barnes rasped. 'We're not moving till that staff car is well on its way.'

'You've got the machine-pistol,' Penn protested. 'And we've got our revolvers.'

'And they've got their car, you idiot. As soon as

they see us coming they'll drive off and then be back with half that column.'

It wasn't only the unit he was thinking of. More important still he had no intention of putting the Mandels into further danger, no matter what the cost. And the cost could be very high.

'You're just going to let Bert burn?' Penn protested again.

'The car's off now. No one gets up till I give the word.'

Lifting himself cautiously only a few feet, his body still well concealed behind the weeds, he watched the car racing away. When it reached the next hill crest and vanished he started running, running as he had never run before, keeping easily ahead of the others in spite of his smallness. The stack was roofed with flames, flames which drove the smoke several feet above the top of the stack. He was drawing close to the conflagration when he heard the power-grab coming across the field, moving forward so fast that the elevated arm was swaying wildly. They were all arriving at once – Etienne with the power-grab, Barnes, Mandel hauling and heaving desperately at a huge coil of hosepipe.

'Give Reynolds the grab,' Barnes shouted. 'I'll take that hose. Leave this to us – the tank is full of diesel and it may blow at any minute. Get back inside the house.'

'No!' Mandel shouted back. 'Etienne knows how to

use the grab. Help me with this hose. It will take all of us to save it. The tank, I mean – the stack is gone.'

Marianne came running forward with several pitch-forks and Mandel told her to drop them and go straight back to the house. It was developing into a horrible muddle until Barnes took charge. Pitch-forks for Reynolds and Jacques. Etienne was left to work the grab. Barnes began to unloop the hose while Mandel fixed the other end to an outlet pipe from a small pump-house. While he worked Barnes was shouting instructions for Mandel to pass on to Etienne.

'Get Etienne to scoop the burning bales off the top – he's to drop them well clear of the stack so the men with forks can carry them to the road. But the grab must be used to clear off the burning hay. I'll hose down the lower walls – we'll never save the top.'

They worked like demons. As Barnes directed the powerful jet of water on the lower walls he tried to keep an eye on the spread of the fire, scared stiff that at any moment the fuel tanks would go up, wondering whether there had been a blow-back of fire from the top down into the hollow interior, a disaster which might not be seen until the whole stack suddenly burst into flames. And there was high-explosive inside that inferno – seventy rounds of two-pounder shells and ten boxes of Besa ammunition. He was close to the front wall now, spraying his jet in a steady arc, while nearby the grab was scooping up burning masses of hay above his head and throwing them clear. As the scorching bales hit the ground they crackled and spat angrily like live things. The heat was almost unbearable and Barnes was shielding his face with one hand while he held the bucking hose in the other, hardly able to see what was happening as acrid smoke filled his lungs and blinded his eyes. Behind him the men with pitch-forks were skewering the burning bales and carrying them over to the road where they dumped them and then ran back for more. Each bale was so heavy and unmanageable that it took two men to spear one bale and then lift it betwen them, and unknown to Barnes his corporal had seized a fork and formed a team with Mandel, holding the fork low down because he found it impossible to lift his right arm.

The turret of the tank was visible now, again protruding strangely like the conning tower of a submarine, but this time like a submarine trapped in a sea of burning oil. It gave Barnes a pang to see it standing there and for a moment he moved back out of the smoke to assess the position. It looked quite hopeless. They had removed the greater part of the upper walls and the roof but the haystack still seethed with smoke and from inside it he could hear that horrid flame crackle working farther down. He saw Penn helping Mandel to carry away another bale and he opened his mouth to stop him, then closed it again without saying anything as he directed the water jet on to the hull of the tank. The temperature inside there must be ferocious and never for a second could

he forget that Bert was bloated – bloated with fuel,
with shells, with ammunition – a state of affairs which
only a few hours ago he had congratulated himself on
but which might now bring about the death of the
tank and several of its would-be rescuers. They were
working at such a frenzied pitch that they hardly
realized the injuries they were suffering from the
scorching heat, but Barnes had already noticed that
Reynolds' right forearm was an ugly mass of blisters.
As he began hosing down the outer walls again Barnes
himself narrowly escaped the most appalling injuries.
He was directing the jet low down when he heard a
shout from Etienne above him. Instinctively he
jumped sideways. A mass of burning hay which had
been balancing precariously in the power-grab shovel
smothered the spot where he had stood a moment
before. He swivelled the jet and drenched the hay, but
it took several minutes to put the fire out and afterwards he couldn't understand why it hadn't set light
to the main wall low down.

Some time later he again stepped well back from
the stack to see how much progress they were making,
almost bumping into Reynolds who was carrying a
blazing mass of hay towards the road when suddenly
it disintegrated, almost collapsing in the driver's face.
He just had time to jump clear but a shower of red-
hot sparks sprayed over his already badly-blistered
arm. Wiping his hand over his sweating forehead,
Reynolds headed back to the stack while Jacques, who
had been leaning on his own fork, joined him.

'We've nearly done it,' said Mandel.

'Have we?'

Barnes was astonished. Once he had emerged from the clouds of smoke the stack looked far quieter than he could ever have dared to hope. Bert was now exposed to halfway down his hull at the front, and although the turret was only occasionally visible behind the pall of smoke the vicious redness of the flames had died away. He paused to wipe his eyes with his handkerchief and then ran forward, switching on the hose: a line of flame had appeared along the top of the front wall and was growing with alarming speed. They'd never get the thing out. And close to the tank the temperature was still incredible, so fiercely concentrated that it seemed to come towards him in an invisible glow from the metal plates. It could happen so suddenly that they would probably have no warning – fuel first, one blasting outward thump, then the series of sharp explosions as the ammunition started to burn, but they would probably never hear that second sound being as close to the tank as they were. It's like being on top of a ruddy great bomb, he thought. Through the smoke he could see figures moving without knowing who they were. Then, some time later, he thought they at last had the inferno finally under control. It should only be a matter of dousing with water until even the smoke faded away. At that moment he heard a frenzied shout from Reynolds.

'A burning bale's just dropped down Bert's side – it's flaring up close to the fuel tank.'

Barnes tried to run forward through the smoke and was jerked backwards. The hose was trapped round the wheel of the power-grab. He lost precious seconds releasing it and then jumped up on to the front wall. The flaring bale had fallen down over the far side but someone had got there first. Reynolds. He lifted his pitch-fork behind him to the fullest extent and then rammed it down like a bayonet, plunging the fork deep into the huge bale which was trapped betwen the hull and the rear wall of hay. Twisting it to tighten the fork's grip, he began to lift. From behind him Barnes could see the veins standing out on his left arm under the frightful strain. Two men had been handling these intact bales and now Reynolds was trying to hoist one by himself, to hoist it upwards from a position below him. Incredibly the bale began to come loose, edging upwards as flames danced round the buried fork. Reynolds went on lifting, his legs splayed wide on the hull, his broad back arching. The bale came up suddenly with a rush, but Reynolds was ready for that and he regained his balance by leaning back against the turret. He must have seen Barnes waiting with the hose because as he turned he shouted, 'Get out of my way!'

Without the least idea of what the driver was going to do Barnes leapt back to the ground. Reynolds began to swing the bale in a slow arc through a hundred and eighty degrees, holding the massive weight at arm's length as the fire spread towards him along the fork. Stepping down off the wall he nearly lost his balance, but again he recovered as flames burst out all over the bale. Then he calmly walked across the grass to the road, still holding the flaming mass at arm's length. He had almost reached the road when it ignited into a small inferno, burning back and enveloping Reynolds. Barnes saw him hurl the bale forward, pitchfork and all. It landed in the road and burst as Reynolds turned round to face the stack, both arms badly burned now, his hair singed, his face a brick-red colour. Ten minutes later Barnes was moving the hose over hay which barely smoked and the fire was out, but he still played the hose over the remaining walls and across the hull. He had sent the others back to the house and now only Mandel wandered round the relic of the stack, holding a pitch-fork and finding nothing to do with it. Leaning over the wall Barnes touched the hull and quickly snatched his hand away.

'You think it's safe now?' asked Mandel. 'The diesel, I mean.'

'If it was going up it should have gone up by now. Can you get Etienne to use his grab to shift the hay in front of the tank? When it cools down I'll have another go at the engine, but that won't be for a while yet. You'll be damned glad to see the back of us, Mandel.'

'This is our war effort. Who knows – your tank may strike a decisive blow at the enemy.'

A decisive blow? It seemed a little unlikely to

Barnes at that moment and even less likely when later he followed them into the house to assess the damage to his crew. The kitchen had all the appearances of a casualty clearing station. Jacques, who was now out-side watching the road, and Etienne, had escaped with only minor burns, but Penn and Reynolds had borne the brunt of the injuries. Reynolds seemed to be in the worst state: he was sitting in a chair with his arms stretched out across the table and both arms had been bandaged by Marianne from wrist to just below the shoulder. As Barnes came in the driver stood up swaying slightly, and Mandel began to help him on with his shirt while Marianne attended to Penn who was flopped in the armchair. She had just finished applying a bandage which covered the whole of his left forearm and he winced as she tied the knot. But when he saw Barnes he managed a grin.

'Now it really looks as though your crew has been in the wars.'

'How are you feeling, Penn?'

'Like a fortnight by the sea. Would Abbeville be a good idea do you think?'

'What about you, Reynolds?'

Barnes turned to his driver with a special anxiety because without Reynolds the status of the unit was definitely noncombatant. Barnes could drive the tank but he couldn't from the driving compartment and at the same time keep close all-round observation and oper-ate the guns when necessary. Clinically he watched the process of Reynolds finding his way back inside the shirt Mandel was holding, noticing that Reynolds was able to bend his elbows and seemed to have full use of his hands. It was his face which worried Barnes most at the moment. Normally, Reynolds looked the picture of physical well-being, his complexion ruddy like that of a man who spent most of his life outdoors, but now the driver's face was chalk-white, drained of all colour.

It's hitting him, thought Barnes. He's in a state of shock. It just depends on how he comes out of it. Reynolds still hadn't replied to the question and he remained silent while he fumbled with the shirt buttons. Then he reached for his battledress jacket but Mandel lifted it off the table, holding it open for his arms. Carefully, Reynolds slipped inside it, doing up the cuffs and then the buttons down the front. When he had finished he sat down heavily on the chair and picked up a glass of wine, draining the contents in one long swallow. Putting the glass down he looked up at Barnes, his voice a growl.

'Give me half an hour and I'll drive you to the coast.'

He's indestructible, Barnes told himself. He's been driving almost non-stop most of yesterday; he had two and a half hours' sleep last night, less the night before; both his arms have been badly burned, and even now his voice sounds vigorous. He decided he still had a driver and went over to Penn, another face as white as death but here there was an awful weariness, and whereas Reynolds sat stiffly upright at the table Penn sank back limply as though he might never move again. He grinned up at Barnes.

'I'm not as bad as I look. Fortunately.'

'Of course you're not. I didn't see your arm – what's it like?'

'A bit of a mess – but you should see Reynolds! I suppose you know the back of your own hand could do with a little attention?'

He had just made the remark when Marianne took charge of Barnes, guiding him over to the sink where she held his hand under the cold water tap. The sudden icy douche made him jump and he saw that raw skin was peeled back and hanging loose. While she applied ointment and then a bandage he looked round the kitchen. At least the Mandels had avoided severe burning: Mandel himself had a few blisters on his right arm and he had lost half his eyebrows, but apart from a singed hair-line Etienne was untouched, probably because he had fought the fire from the seat of the power-grab. When he tried to thank them Mandel wouldn't listen, repeating that it was part of their war effort and that in any case the British were fighting for France as well as for themselves. Because there seemed to be no more to say Barnes went back outside to struggle with the engine.

The hull was still very hot but he found that he could cope and he spent half an hour checking for the fault, feeling an enormous sense of relief that the tank had survived and enjoying himself once more with mechanical work, work which gradually drained away the tensions from his body. When he climbed down inside the driver's compartment the engine started first time. They were on their way.

Chapter Seven

Saturday, 25 May

West and then north – that would be the route they would follow. The tank climbed up to the summit of the hill crest at top speed in the mid-morning sunshine. The rim of the turret was hot to the touch, but this heat came from the steady blaze of the sun rather than from the incandescence of fire. Looking back for the last time Barnes saw the tiny figures of the Mandel family standing outside their farm, then they vanished as Bert moved down the other side of the hill. The road ahead to Cambrai was deserted and the only sign of movement came from people working in the fields several kilometres from the roadside.

In spite of his throbbing shoulder, his aching knee, his hand which burned as though a fire smouldered under Marianne's bandage, Barnes experienced a sense of quiet exhilaration: they were on the move again once more and now he knew exactly where he was heading for. His fateful decision to change direction – to head west and then north for Calais instead of north-west to Arras* – was based on a process of

---

* The Allied forces had withdrawn from Arras at 10 p.m. on Thursday, 23 May. During their brief counter-attack, 1 Army Tank

thought which had been going on inside Barnes' head for nearly two days, and he was compelled to rely on only two sources of information – the sketchy news bulletins and the evidence of his own eyes. It was what he had seen which more than anything else had convinced him that this was a revolutionary development in warfare based on the fantastic mobility of the tank.

The Germans had disrupted all previous ideas of a static front line by driving their Panzer divisions nonstop across France, driving forward without any attempt to consolidate what they had conquered, relying almost entirely on the elements of surprise and terror to disorganize their enemy. The conclusion to be drawn seemed clear enough – providing one threw out of the window nearly all one's previous ideas of tank warfare. If the Panzers could move across such huge distances without waiting for the infantry to occupy them, then it should be possible for a lone British tank to come up behind them providing that it escaped detection. And then there was the question of the dumps. Barnes thought back over the conversation he had had with Jacques as he wrestled with the engine.

'If you can drive all the way here from Abbeville, Jacques, you must have plenty of petrol.'

Brigade halted the 7th Panzer Division commanded by Major-General Erwin Rommel and caused a panic in the German High Command.

'The Germans have plenty of petrol.'

'What does that mean?'

'You won't tell my uncle – he worries about these things?'

'I asked you because we're out here on our own.' Barnes stopped working for a moment. 'Look Jacques, I've got to get an idea of the position as accurately as I can. You've been haring all over the countryside and you're the only one who can tell me.'

'I took it from a German petrol dump near Abbeville. All I had to do was to creep under a wire fence well away from the guards and take what I wanted. They've threatened to shoot anyone found on what they call German property – but that's to scare people off because they can't guard the petrol.'

'Something was said about ammunition dumps, too.'

'The same with them. I got inside one place with a friend and there were shells and boxes of ammunition all over the place.'

'I find that hard to believe, Jacques.'

He flushed and then grinned. 'That is because you do not know what is happening. The German tanks and guns have broken through with their supply columns but the infantry have not yet reached them – so they can't guard their dumps properly.'

'I'm beginning to get the idea,' Barnes encouraged him.

'It is like the curfew in Cambrai. They say they will shoot anyone found on the streets at night but that is to scare people. I have heard that you can walk all through the town after dark without seeing one German soldier except near the town hall. I think,' he said shrewdly, 'the main reason for the curfew is so that people will not know how few Germans there are in Cambrai at the moment.'

'And you say the road to Abbeville is clear all the way?'

'Except for Cambrai and the three road-blocks outside Abbeville. I could mark their position on this,' he offered, pointing to the map spread out over the hull.

'Do that, would you?'

He went on checking the engine while Jacques marked the road-blocks and then asked a fresh question.

'What about the roads south towards the Somme?'

'I don't know the position there – I have not been that way, you see.'

'And which route do you take when you bypass Cambrai?'

'This way, to the south. I will mark it for you.' When he had finished he looked up, his expression blank. 'If you turned north beyond Cambrai you might get through to Boulogne. I know a way which goes close to St Pol and Fruges, but it is not the main road – it ends up at Lemont where I live, near Gravelines. I have often used the route when driving from Lemont to Abbeville. I will mark that, too, just in case.'

'Might as well.' Barnes was peering at the engine.

'I feel perhaps I should have driven there instead of here,' went on Jacques as he marked in the route.

'You'd have run into the Panzers.'

'Possibly. I wonder? I think they went up the coast road here and my route is much farther inland. From what I have heard I believe there is a gap between the Panzers along the coast and the Allied lines near the frontier.'

'Really?' Barnes kept his face blank, wondering whether he was fooling the sharp-witted youth. It hadn't escaped him that Jacques had carefully refrained from asking him which route they would be taking.

'I'm going back to Abbeville later this morning. I want to tell my sister that Uncle is all right. Then I may drive on to Lemont. Plenty of petrol!'

The trouble with this lad, Barnes was thinking, is that he's so excited by the war that he can't keep still, so he pinches Jerry petrol and then goes flying about all over the countryside to see what's going on. If he's not careful he's going to run into something.

But it was from this conversation that Barnes had gleaned the final scraps of information which led to his ultimate decision, and as the tank rumbled down the hill away from the Mandels he was pretty confident that the French lad had no idea which route he was taking – something he had been particularly careful about in case the lad were picked up by the Germans and made to talk. He scanned the sky and it was empty, further proof that they were still moving through a vast gap in the Allied lines, since had there been any Allied forces in the area the Luftwaffe would have been bombing them. An hour later they had turned off the main road to Cambrai and had almost bypassed the southern approaches to the town. He called a temporary halt to go down and see Penn.

'How's it going?' he asked him.

'Not too bad, although I do feel a bit woozy. I'm getting double vision every now and again.'

Penn was propped up with a wedge of blankets and he was trying to hold himself upright, but earlier when he had looked down into the fighting compartment Barnes had seen him sagging limply, his head flopped forward as though he couldn't hold it up any more. What the devil are we going to do with him, Barnes thought, but he spoke cheerfully.

'Can you stand a bit more of this? I know the movement of the tank must be giving you hell.'

'It's not so much that as the lack of fresh air down here. It's like sitting inside a furnace.'

The description was apt enough. Even standing on the turntable for only a few minutes was enough to bring Barnes out in a prickly sweat and he was surprised that Penn was still conscious.

'I'll be all right,' said Penn.

'Do you want to try and stick your head out of the turret for a while?'

'I doubt if I could get up there.'

Barnes kept his face blank but a chill of fear gripped

him. He had to keep moving, had to keep the tank heading west and then north, but he had to find a doctor for Penn, too. It seemed as though fate had deliberately kept Penn in a state where he was wounded but not desperately ill until they had left the Mandel farm, and now Penn was becoming desperately ill, Barnes had little doubt of that. His skin was a strangely pallid colour and his eyes appeared to have sunk.

'The next place we come to we'll see if we can find a doctor,' he said.

'Not necessary. I'm not doing anything except sitting and I'll probably feel better by evening. It's just this heat.' He tried to speak lightly. 'Calais next stop?'

'We've a long way to go before we get there, Penn.'

'How far is it?'

'About a hundred miles.'

'Seven hours' drive if Bert goes flat out.'

'You're assuming there'll be nothing in the way, Penn. We can count on there being plenty in the way.'

It seemed an odd way for Barnes to be talking to a seriously wounded man but already he was foreseeing the moment when they would have to leave Penn behind if they could find a sanctuary for him. The realization of what they were driving into might make that moment when they left him a little less hard to bear. He hoped so. He also hoped that they found that sanctuary soon. Considering his physical state, Penn's mind was remarkably alert.

'A hundred miles, you said. Have we got the diesel for that?'

'Yes, with what we took off Lebrun, that is, providing we keep to the road all the way, which we probably won't. You know what happens when we move across country – fuel consumption is doubled.'

'You know what,' Penn began brightly, 'I think we're going to make it. I've had a bit of time to think down here and it strikes me there may not be all that much in our way if we keep a sharp lookout.' He paused and Barnes realized that Penn was wondering whether anyone was observing.

'It's all right, Penn. I told Reynolds to get out and stand on the hull while I was down here. Now, what were you thinking?'

'Well, Jerry is pushing on fast with his tanks and his popguns but the old foot-sloggers haven't put in much of an appearance down here yet. I reckon that with a lot of luck we could sneak up behind those Panzers before we run into much. Then it's up to us.'

'We might do just that, Penn.'

'And by that time I'll have pulled myself together. You'll see me hugging the old two-pounder again before we reach Calais. You can bet on it.'

'I never bet on certainties, Penn.'

With a heavy heart Barnes climbed back into the turret, told Reynolds in a loud voice that Penn was coming along nicely, and then gave the order to advance. Half an hour later he looked back along the road, frowned, and grabbed his binoculars. The twin circles of glass brought forward a four-seater Renault with a single occupant, the driver. Jacques was racing towards them on his way to Abbeville.

The twin circles of glass focused and brought forward a toy line of white cliffs glistening in the sunlight. The white cliffs of Dover. General Storch lowered his binoculars and frowned.

'There we are, Meyer, the citadel of the enemy – the main enemy. Let us hope the 14th Panzer Division will be the first to be put ashore on the British beaches.'

'We have to beat them over here first,' Meyer pointed out.

'That will be dealt with in the next forty-eight hours. Here we stand on the coast west of Calais with our forward troops on the Gravelines waterline and Calais is under siege. Now we only have to take Dunkirk and the whole British Army is surrounded.'

Meyer screwed his monocle into his eye and found that he was looking through a film of perspiration. In the hour of victory he felt exhausted, overwhelmed by the dazzling series of triumphs Storch had produced since that day so long ago when they crossed the Meuse at Sedan. So long ago? It was the afternoon of Saturday, 25 May, and they had made their way over the pontoons at Sedan on 14 May. Meyer felt stunned. Perhaps, after all, this was a war for the younger men, for the Storches. The general stood gazing out to sea, talking rapidly.

'I want an immediate investigation made of this French Fascist's story – that informant from Lemont. He says there is a second road direct to Dunkirk – a road the enemy may not know about now that the sluice gates have been opened.'

'The French were very quick about that – the floods will make it very difficult for the Panzers to move on Dunkirk . . .'

Storch broke in impatiently. 'This is why this second road may be decisive. I want you to interrogate this man personally.'

'I can't find such a road on any map . . .'

'But that is the whole point, Meyer. Our Fascist friend has explained that for some reason it is not included on most French maps. So if the British are holding the sector at the other end they may not know it exists now it is under water. Even if there are French units in that sector they will probably come from another part of France. That road could be the key to final victory – the road along which the Panzers will advance to Dunkirk.'

'I don't think we should count on it.'

They paused as they heard the humming sound of a host of engines above them. Craning their necks they stared into the sky where an armada of small grey dots was approaching from the east, the humming growing steadily louder as the planes came forward like a swarm of angry bees. Storch nodded his head in satisfaction.

'General Goering is on time again and I see he has the sky to himself. When Mr Churchill opened the cupboard this morning he must have found his shelves bare.'

'We mustn't count on air immunity any longer,' said Meyer sharply. 'After all, we can actually see England from here.'

Storch tightened his lips at this sign of caution. 'I want a very detailed report about your conversation with this Fascist. He says this road will be covered by only a few inches of water – sufficient to conceal its existence but not enough to prevent the passage of the Panzers. Since he is a local he may well know what he is talking about.'

'I'd better go now.'

But Meyer did not go immediately because his sharp ears had heard a fresh sound in the sky, an engine sound different from that of Goering's huge aerial fleet. Whipping up his glasses he focused them towards the west while beside him Storch also stood with his binoculars aimed upwards. High above the Channel, at an altitude much greater than the Luftwaffe bombers, several squadrons of RAF fighters flew steadily on course, heading for an invisible point which would take them over the heart of the oncoming bombers, although from the ground it seemed that the two air fleets were advancing on a collision course.

Less than a minute later the RAF formations dived to the attack, roaring down like avenging hornets on the massed planes below, weaving in and out of the pattern of bombers which was now becoming disorganized as the pilots forgot their objectives and desperately began to take evading action. In less than two minutes the huge German air armada was flying in all directions, its attack formation completely shattered. One bomber spiralled to the ground and crashed into the fields a mile away, to be followed by a second, but this one was heading for the coast close to where Storch and Meyer stood. As one man they dropped flat behind the hull of a nearby tank only seconds before the bomber hit the earth three hundred yards away, its bomb load exploding a few seconds after the moment of impact. The vibrations of the shock wave rattled the tank behind which they sheltered and a shower of soil rained down on Storch's neck and shoulders. Meyer spoke quietly.

'Mr Churchill must have found something at the bottom of his cupboard.'

'Driver, halt! There's a parachute coming down,' Barnes warned.

The air battle had raged over their heads, out of sight, for several minutes – out of sight even though the sky was cloudless because the planes were high and against the glare of the early afternoon sun. From the noise it sounded as though several machines were

wheeling and diving as they fought each other to
death in the sunlight. The engine sounds had come
closer and faintly he had heard the stutter of machine-
guns but they went on manoeuvring in front of the
sun so that he had found it impossible to locate them
until he had heard the ominous sound of a plane
plunging into a tremendous power dive. Then he had
located a small dark shape spinning earthwards a long
way to the west, much too far off to identify its
nationality quite apart from the fantastic speed at
which it approached the ground. It vanished and he
heard a distant cough. Petrol tank gone. A thread of
black smoke crept up from the horizon. Overhead the
sky was full of warm silence. He gave the order to
advance, reversing that order almost at once as he
saw the tiny inverted cone of the single parachute
floating down. He waited.

While he waited he thought about Penn. Since noon
they had passed through three abandoned villages,
and when he had halted the tank and walked through
their deserted streets he had in each place found a
house with the tantalising word *Médecin* on a door-
plate, but there had been no one behind the doors.
Inside the third village they had stopped briefly for a
quick meal from the Mandels' food parcel but Penn
hadn't shared the meal because he appeared to have
fallen into a state of unconsciousness. Alarmed,
Barnes had checked his pulse but the beat was steady.
When he felt his forehead it was hot and damp, and
now everything in Barnes' mind was dominated by

his new priority – finding a doctor. They were within four miles of the next village before the air battle going on overhead had attracted his attention as he halted the tank to attend to a call of nature. Reynolds twisted his head above the hatch to follow the course of the cone as it grew larger and larger drifting straight for them across the deserted fields. He called up from the hatch.

'Ours or theirs?'

'No idea.'

It was a good question, a vital question, in fact. The last thing they could cope with at the present was a Luftwaffe pilot as a prisoner. But if he had seen them and they let him go free it might be less than an hour before German headquarters in Cambrai knew of the presence of a British tank prowling behind their lines. As he watched the parachutist drift lower Barnes swore to himself. He had already shot one German for mercy reasons beside the wrecked infantry truck, but the idea of shooting one down in cold blood for their own protection was rather a different business. Maybe he'll open fire on me, Barnes told himself. If he does I'll let him have half the magazine. There was, of course, just the chance that the pilot wouldn't see them. The parachute was drifting lower and lower – and closer – the tiny figure underneath pulling at cords to guide himself, bobbing about so erratically that Barnes found it impossible to focus the glasses on him. Reynolds called up from the hatch.

'What if it is a Jerry?'

'Then we'll have a problem on our hands.'

'I'd shoot the bastard. He's probably just back from machine-gunning one of those refugee columns.'

Barnes was surprised. It was the first time that Reynolds had ever expressed an opinion without being asked for one. His burnt arms must be playing him up badly. Reaching down, he picked up the machine-pistol and tucked it under his arm. There was no hope now that the parachutist might not see them – as he drifted close to the earth he was floating nearer and nearer to the tank. From that height and distance he couldn't possibly miss seeing them. Climbing down from the turret he stood on the hull so that he could see the exact landing point. The parachutist was now tugging frantically at the cords so that the cone which had been almost overhead was floating away from them along the country road. He jumped down off the hull.

'I can follow him in the tank,' offered Reynolds.

'No, I'll investigate this blighter myself – get another machine-pistol out of the turret and wait here.'

'Watch yourself, Sergeant. Don't forget Seft.'

That was the trouble at the moment, Barnes thought. We're in a general state of jitters. Apart from the Mandel farm, which had been a brief oasis of peace in a nightmare world, ever since they had arrived at Fontaine they had met either the enemy in the form of Panzers or treachery in the form of Lebrun; in the case of Seft the enemy and treachery had combined into one menace. So what was he going to encounter now? Let him give me just one reason, just one small reason, and I'll press the trigger.

He was running along the dusty road when the pilot landed in the field close to the verge, the parachute billowing as it dragged its owner across the grass. The cloth cone collapsed slowly. Barnes ran faster. He wanted to get there before the pilot disentangled himself from the cords, but as he came closer the man released himself from the parachute and climbed to his knees, facing Barnes who ran up with the machine-pistol thrust forward. Were pilots armed? He didn't think so but he wasn't taking any chances. The kneeling figure saw the gun and stayed on his knees, throwing his arms wide to show that he was unarmed. The next second will tell, Barnes thought grimly, and then the man spoke.

'And what is a Limey doing in this part of France, I'd like to know? Don't shoot the pilot – he's done his best!'

'You're an RAF pilot?'

Barnes asked the question sharply, his pistol still aimed at the pilot's chest as his eyes roamed over every inch of the man's flying suit. From underneath goggles pushed up over the leather helmet a rugged face stared upwards at Barnes, the face of a man who might be any age between twenty-five and thirty-five. His skin was tanned brown, the texture almost as leathery as the suit he wore; his huge nose, strongly boned, overhung a broad, firm-lipped mouth, and his jaw-line suggested great strength of character. This, thought Barnes, is a tough egg, a very tough egg. But the overall impression of toughness was tempered by the humorous expression in his blue eyes, a humour which came to the surface with his reply.

'If I'm not RAF the Luftwaffe is employing some pretty dubious characters.'

His accent was heavily American and this alone was disconcerting, plus the fact that the pilot himself appeared more amused than disconcerted, an unusual reaction when a man found himself at the wrong end of a gun. But Barnes couldn't forget that Penn had thought Seft a genuine Belgian, and it was just possible that the Luftwaffe employed a few renegade Americans.

'Get on your feet,' Barnes said tightly.

'Coming down I think I broke both me legs, Sergeant.'

God, another lame duck to take aboard Bert. As if it wasn't enough having to cope with Penn he was now going to have another patient on his hands. The tank was rapidly turning into a casualty clearing station: the only trouble was that there was nowhere to clear them to. He went back several paces as the pilot clambered carefully to his feet. The stranger grinned.

'Correction, Sergeant. I just *feel* as though I've broken both me legs. Ever landed in one of those things? The ground looks to be coming up so peacefully and then at the last minute it flies up and hits you like a steam-hammer.'

'I didn't know the RAF were recruiting Americans,' Barnes said grimly.

'Canadians, please!' He lifted one gloved hand in mock horror. 'Although your error of geography is understandable, Sergeant. My mother is Canadian and my father was American, but I was born in Canada. Ever heard of Wainwright, Alberta? No, I didn't think you would have. It's about the size of a pinhead but the CNR expresses do stop there to unload drums of ice-cream for the locals.' He gestured behind Barnes. 'Is that your tin can back there?'

'The tin can is a Matilda tank. Have you any way of proving your identity?'

'Sure. If I unbutton my jacket and slip my hand inside real slow you'll promise not to pull the trigger?'

Barnes didn't reply and he watched the pilot's hand carefully as it ferreted inside the jacket, but when the fingers came out again they only held an RAF identity card. The pilot held it between his fingers for a moment.

'Now if I try and hand it to you there's a danger you'll think I'm going to jump you. On the other hand, if I drop it on the ground for you to pick it up, I could just possibly land a boot in your eye. So which is it to be?'

'Drop it on the ground – then take six paces back.'

The pilot was still pacing backwards when Barnes stooped quickly to grab the identity card. Using only his left hand he fingered open the card, wondering whether he was carrying on with his check through caution or sheer cussedness at Colburn's attitude. Because that was the name in the card. Flying Officer James Q. Colburn.

'The Q. is for Quinn,' Colburn explained helpfully, 'which comes from my mother's side of the family. The Quinns are an old British Columbia family – old, that is, by Canadian standards – although . . .'

'All right, Colburn.' Barnes skimmed the card through the air and the pilot caught it with his left hand. 'What happened up there near the sun?'

'You're satisfied with my identity, then, Sergeant?'

'I think so.'

'Well how about letting me see your pay-book – or am I supposed to take you at face value alone?'

Barnes looked at the six-foot pilot. He had a seriously ill loader-operator on his hands, he was in a great hurry to push on to the next village in search of medical help, and he had expected to find a Luftwaffe pilot struggling to free himself from the cords. He was certainly in no mood for wisecracks with freelance Canadians.

'I'm Sergeant Barnes and if you think I'm going to show you my pay-book you're out of your tiny mind. What do you think that thing standing behind me is – a Jerry tank? And even you must have seen a British Army uniform.'

'All right! All right!' Colburn waved a placatory hand. 'And don't think I don't appreciate you've probably had a hell of a fortnight, whereas I'm just over here for the afternoon. At least I thought I was,' he added. 'But may I point out that I'm wearing RAF flying kit and that what you saw come down in flames wasn't a vacuum cleaner. It was, at the time of take-off from Manston, a perfectly good Hurricane.'

'It came down so quickly I hardly saw it till the crash. A Messerschmitt got you, I suppose?'

'Three of them – although that's no excuse. They chased me down here from the coast, which was a bad reaction on my part since I hadn't the petrol to make home base even if I could have clobbered the lot. Let's face it – they out-manoeuvred me. And, Sergeant, do I have to sing *Auld Lang Syne* before you'll put away the carbine?'

Barnes lowered the machine-pistol and nodded. 'Sorry, but we had a little trouble with a German fifth columnist who said he was Belgian so I'm taking nothing for granted. You could have been one yourself, Colburn.'

'Out of the sky?' queried the Canadian ironically, then his expression changed. 'I'm sorry – you're right to check everything. Those characters really exist, then? We've heard plenty of rumours – so many you'd think France was swarming with them.'

'The only thing this part of France swarms with is Panzers.' Barnes stared hard at Colburn before he went on. Was Colburn really as tough as he looked?

'You've come down in the middle of a gigantic no man's land which could be at least twenty miles wide, but the only troops we've seen are parts of armoured divisions. We're completely on our own – just one Matilda tank.'

Barnes had relaxed a little now and he was prepared to wait for a few more precious minutes while he made up his mind. He was studying Colburn quite dispassionately, without the least trace of sentiment, weighing him up ruthlessly. And Barnes had some experience of weighing up men. In this instance he was applying only one criterion – would Colburn be an asset or a liability? If he was going to be the latter then he wasn't coming with them. Colburn stared at him steadily.

'You mean the rest of your outfit got wiped out?'

'I mean we got separated from them at the very beginning and it's been that way ever since. If you come with us you'd better understand we have one two-pounder gun, one light machine-gun, several machine-pistols and three revolvers. That's the extent of our armament and so far we've escaped detection by three separate Panzer columns by the skin of our teeth.'

'Sounds a little one-sided. I'd have thought you could do with a little reinforcement.'

'We could, but tanks don't fly and you're a pilot.'

'You may have a point there. What's the alternative?'

'The alternative, Colburn, is to make your own way

home.' He paused. 'Unless you'd sooner take the easier way out and walk down that road into Cambrai where the Germans are. Then you could spend the rest of your war in a nice quiet POW camp.'

He waited for the Canadian's reaction, but still nothing had changed in the steady expression. Even the voice was mild when he retaliated.

'I suppose if I were to hit you in the mouth for that, Sergeant, your pal in the tank would gun me down?'

'I'm sure he would. Don't let me get under your skin, Colburn. It's just that I have to be sure.'

'Sure of what? I thought you'd have realized by now that I was taking off from Manston half an hour ago.'

'I have to be sure you won't get in the way. You're a Canadian, you say, yet you're in the RAF.'

'I volunteered. It was very hot weather at the time and the heat can make you do silly things . . .'

'What were you in civvy street, Colburn?'

'I took my medical degree and then . . .'

'You're a doctor?' Barnes didn't attempt to keep the eagerness out of his voice.

'No, I'm not. I never practised. I found I didn't like it so I became a chemist.'

'A chemist?' Barnes found it difficult to visualize Colburn behind a counter handing out aspirin.

'An industrial chemist. I developed an interest in high-explosives and had my own outfit after a few years. We supplied stuff for quarry-blasting operations all over Canada. So now you'll know how crazy I was to volunteer.'

'You had your own business and you gave it up?' Barnes stared even more closely at Colburn's sun-tanned features, wondering what made a man throw up everything to travel three thousand miles to fight someone else's war. His decision was crystallizing rapidly now.

'No, it wasn't as bad as that. I handed over to my brother and he's running things till I get back.' Colburn smiled faintly. 'Ed doesn't see any reason why the British shouldn't be left to fight their own wars. He could be right at that. Sergeant, what made you jump half a mile when I said I'd taken my medical degree?'

'My corporal's seriously wounded and I've been praying to run into a doctor for hours. Would you take a look at him for me?'

'Be glad to – but remember, I'm the most qualified non-practising doctor in the western hemisphere. Where is he?'

Barnes stayed behind to gather up the collapsed parachute while Colburn walked back to where Reynolds waited on the hull of the tank. It took him several minutes to bundle up the cloth and cords into a package which resembled an overblown eiderdown and then he hid it inside a drainage ditch. There was no point in alerting any German patrol which might arrive later to the fact that there was a British airman in the district. When he returned to the tank Reynolds was out of sight inside the hull but Colburn's head emerged from the turret. He looked down at Barnes, his voice quiet.

'The guy down there is a close friend of yours?'

'He's my corporal,' replied Barnes flatly.

'Sorry, that was badly put. The news isn't good, I'm afraid.'

'He may not make it?'

'He didn't make it – he's dead.'

It took them well over an hour to dig the grave out of the sun-baked French soil. They worked with the same shovels which had been used to dig them out of the tunnel at Etreux, and they took it in turns when Colburn insisted on helping. During his rest period Barnes watched Colburn closely: on the basis of sheer physical strength there was very little to choose between the Canadian and Reynolds, but the main thing he liked about Colburn was his quick acceptance of an entirely new situation. By now the poor devil might well have expected to be landing at Manston prior to a trip to the nearest local: instead of which he was marooned in the middle of the battle zone helping to bury the body of a man he had never known alive. As he watched them dig out the final shovelfuls his mind was stunned. Penn had spent three years with him and in that time they had established a working relationship which functioned so smoothly they might have known each other all their lives. Penn, who had never really believed in anything, who found his sergeant's intense preoccupation with his profession rather amusing, Penn was a man who could always be relied upon. And, by God, they'd relied on him during that endless night when he'd stood sentry-go on the bridge while the Panzers rolled past. Penn had found his sanctuary now, although not the sanctuary Barnes had planned for him.

What had seemed to be the simplest part of their mournful task proved to be the hardest – the lowering of the body. The grave was ready and Colburn stood aside, leaving it to Barnes and Reynolds to lift the body which they had swathed in a blanket and then further protected by folding a groundsheet round it. To enable them to lower their burden slowly they had looped two ropes round the groundsheet – one over the chest and the other over the legs. All went well until the body was halfway down inside the grave, then it stuck, wedged in at the shoulders at a point where the hole narrowed. They raised it and then lowered it a second time, but again it stuck. Barnes looked at Colburn.

'Would you take over this rope for me?'

He waited until the Canadian was in position and then he knelt down, placing the flat of his hand on the groundsheet. As he pressed he could feel the thickness of the bandage over Penn's left arm. Colburn had said that it was probably the shock of severe burning on top of his shoulder wound which had finally dictated that he couldn't survive. The heavily wrapped body still wouldn't go down. He pressed harder, feeling that Penn didn't want to be buried here and was resisting him. What was it he had said? 'You'll see me hugging the old two-pounder again before we reach Calais.' Well, they were a long way from Calais and now Penn would never know whether they made it or not. He pressed harder still, knowing that they hadn't time to embark on fresh digging because out here they were horribly exposed to view. The body gave up the struggle suddenly, sinking down so unexpectedly that Barnes almost overbalanced. When he stood up his face and hands were running with sweat and all he wanted to do was to get away from this place.

'Shouldn't we say something over him?' mumbled Reynolds.

'No,' said Barnes abruptly, 'nothing. Didn't you know – he was an agnostic.'

When they had filled in the grave they erected a crude marker, and they used a shovel because it was the only instrument they could find for their purpose. The shovel was dug deep into the ground and on the handle Barnes had inscribed simple wording which he cut into the wood with his knife. '18972451 Corporal M. Penn. Killed in Action. May 25th, 1940.'

Before they moved off he asked Colburn to check his shoulder wound. While he had been leaning over into the grave, at the moment when the body had

suddenly slipped down into its resting place, he had
jerked his shoulder, feeling something give: he had
ripped open the wound again. He sat on the warm
hull while the Canadian removed the bandage and
Colburn's voice spoke volumes of disapproval.

'I can see this dressing hasn't been changed
recently.'

'You mean it's turned septic?' Barnes inquired
quietly.

'No, you were lucky there. I'm talking about the
state of the outside of the dressing. You've reopened
it again, all right, but it looks clean and that's the
main thing. Now, keep still. This may hurt.'

Cleaning the freshly opened wound thoroughly, he
applied a new dressing and then helped Barnes on
with his shirt and jacket. The shoulder was starting to
throb steadily, a nagging ache which absorbed far too
much energy. When he was dressed he took out a
pencil from the pocket containing Penn's pay-book
and diary, spread out his map over the hull and
roughly marked the spot where the corporal was
buried. One day Penn's parents might wish to make a
pilgrimage to this spot, but by then anything could
have happened to the shovel. Really, he told himself,
it's a waste of time. All he could hope for was that the
whole ruddy war wasn't a waste of time. He began
discussing the battlefield situation with Colburn but
soon found out that the Canadian could tell him little
more than he already knew.

'As far as I can make out,' Barnes went on, 'the BEF

is roughly north of this line with the Belgian Army on its left. We're standing in the middle of a huge no man's land . . .'

'The gap,' said Colburn.

'You mean they're actually calling it that?'

'Yes, it's referred to as that on our briefing maps. As you say, you're slap in the middle of it but there's a lot of argument as to how wide it is. My squadron came over to mix it with Hun fighters but as a sideline we were told to shoot up any Panzers we found. They think reinforcements may come through here soon.'

'They were right – they came through early this morning.'

'Late again.' He smiled faintly. 'Going back to those Panzers, I raised a query about the risk of shooting up our own guys and you're not going to like the answer they gave. They said that if we found a whole lot of heavy tanks strung out along a road they were bound to be German – the British only have a handful and the French have cleverly scattered theirs in penny packets over the whole front.'

'You don't seem to know a great deal more than I do, Colburn.'

'Sergeant, you're over here in the thick of it, and it's my opinion that you're far too close to be able to take in the general picture.'

'That, Colburn,' said Barnes irritably, 'is what I'm trying to extract from you. You get detailed briefings before you take to the air, you fly over the battlefield – if anyone has a general picture it should be you.'

'Oh, I've got it, all right, but from your questions I get the idea you're looking for some sort of clear pattern I should draw you, some nice neat little map which will show the Germans here, your lot there, and the French some other place. Well, I can't do that, and again it's only my opinion, but I'm pretty sure that when this war is only a memory and the historians get busy with their tidy little analyses they still won't be able to say exactly which unit was where and on what day. This, for what it's worth, is the biggest muddle of a battle that ever was.'

'What are you trying to say?'

'That there isn't any information worth a damn – these boys, the generals, are just making it up as they go along. Just like Wellington in the Peninsular War when he said it was like knotting a rope – you tie one knot, then you tie another and hope for the best. But don't try to kid me that any of them are working to a tidy little plan in a war room any more.'

'Not even the Germans?' Barnes asked quietly.

'Not even those bastards – not any more. Ask me how I know and I'll tell you it's the well-known Colburn intuition – that and the fact that I'm a minor student of the history of warfare. But there's one thing, Barnes, I'd bet money on – I'd bet that at this moment the German generals are so intoxicated with their success that they don't know what to do with it. Generals are always divided into pushers and pullers – one lot will be saying press on, push 'em into the sea, and the other lot will be yelling blue murder that they've over-reached themselves and had better dig in quick before they get their heads chopped off.'

'It doesn't help me much,' remarked Barnes.

'Well, maybe this will help you. When I flew in today I came down south-east over Calais and I'm pretty sure there's another gap between the coast road and the main battle area to the east. That could just be the way for us to go.'

'It is the way we're going.'

'So I get a free ride to Calais, but on one condition – that you don't ever ask me again for the general picture. There isn't one. This is such a bloody mixed-up mess they'll never be able to describe it – not in a hundred years' time. Not unless they call on the aid of Shakespeare who did have a word for a complete one hundred per cent shambles. The general picture, Sergeant Barnes, is hugger-mugger.'

'Which simply means we could run into Jerry at any time now.'

Chapter Eight

Saturday, 25 May

The Stuka bomber, one hundred feet up, smoke pouring from its tail, was heading straight for them as though aimed at the mouth of the quarry. Barnes stood perfectly still, his gaze fixed on the approaching projectile as he prayed that it would maintain its height for at least a few hundred yards more. It screamed in closer, its nose dipping like a suicide bomber guided to penetrate the quarry mouth and explode against the rear wall where Bert was parked. Beside him Colburn froze as he automatically assessed the Stuka's line of flight. Then it roared over them, still losing height, and ten seconds later they heard it hit France a mile away as its bomb load blew up.

'This place reminds me of high-explosives,' said Colburn.

The tank was parked inside a chalk quarry cut out of the hillside and the giant alcove was filled with shadow. It was half past six in the evening and they had been standing at the narrow entrance while Reynolds mounted guard on the rim of the quarry high above them. The driver shouted down to tell them that the plane had crashed a long distance off and then resumed his all-round observation.

'I'm none too fond of high-explosive myself at the moment,' Barnes replied drily as he swirled tea in his mug.

'That's because you've been on the receiving end – I'm talking about quarry-blasting operations. There's something very satisfying about laying the charges just right, going back to the plunger, pressing it, and seeing exactly the right area of rock slice away.'

'I thought you just supplied the stuff.'

'Oh, they were always asking me for advice and I ended up by doing the job for them. I have a talent for destruction, Barnes. What's more to the point, I enjoyed my work.'

They walked away from the tank and through the narrow defile which formed the entrance to the quarry. Stopping in the entrance, they looked out across the fields of France. They had done very well, Barnes was thinking, and he estimated they were now less than thirty miles from Calais. All through the late afternoon and early evening Bert had moved at top speed along the road and only twice had they stopped and prayed. Once when a flight of German planes had flown across the eastern sky, and once when a cloud of dust had warned them of the approach of a German supply column. For over half an hour they had waited concealed inside a nearby wood, only emerging when the last escorting tank had driven out of sight in the opposite direction. And then Bert had ground forward non-stop heading north, always north towards Calais.

They had finished their meal and once again bully beef hadn't been featured on the menu. When they reopened the parcel which Mandel had provided they had found several sticks of French bread, an earthenware pot of butter, a whole cold chicken, and four bottles of wine. They had dined well but Barnes had not enjoyed it because at the beginning of the meal he had remembered Penn who had never tasted any of the food. As a crew they were probably in better condition than at any time since they had left Fontaine, except that now the fighting crew comprised only two men – unless Colburn could absorb enough of a rudimentary training to make him useful. Beyond the quarry, several miles across the sunlit plain, Barnes saw a long thin trail of dust moving at an oblique angle to where they stood. It looked as though the column were heading for the coast. He focused his glasses.

'Panzers?' inquired Colburn.

'Probably. Too far away to see properly and that dust is fogging the view. They're not coming this way, which is something to be thankful for. Now, Colburn, let's see how much you can learn about a tank in no time at all.'

At the most, Barnes had hoped he might show Colburn how to use the Besa, but the Canadian was no sooner down on the turntable when he wanted to know how to traverse the turret. Within five minutes he was showing that he possessed real mechanical aptitude and an ability to grasp the traverse system which surprised Barnes, a surprise which grew as he experienced the Canadian's endless persistence. Once he found he was able to traverse he asked Barnes to go up to the turret and give him instructions over the intercom. Settling down to indoctrinate his quick-witted pupil Barnes showed him no mercy, correcting his faults with the ruthlessness of a drill-sergeant.

'Right, Colburn! I said traverse right! You now have the distinction of presenting our bloody rear to the enemy. That's better. Left! Traverse left!'

It quickly dawned on Barnes that he had a tiger by the tail. Colburn wouldn't give up until he could operate the traverse on instruction without mistake. He simply went on and on and on, tirelessly as though his life might depend on getting this right. And, Barnes thought, it could just work out that way. In all his experience he had never trained a pupil who learned so quickly, even though it was only the rudiments he was grasping. When he went back into the fighting compartment Colburn demanded to know something about the two-pounder, but here Barnes felt that any attempt to show him how the weapon worked would be a waste of time. He suggested, instead, that Colburn should tackle the Besa.

'Five minutes will do that,' said Colburn briskly.

Barnes stared. So the Canadian was a braggart, which meant he would be totally unreliable in an emergency. Colburn read something of the thought in his expression and grinned.

'You may have forgotten, Barnes, that we do carry a certain armament in the Hurricane. Like the Besa it's called a machine-gun.'

'Sorry.' Barnes closed his mouth rightly. The throb-throb of the shoulder wound had started up again and was pounding his mind to a jelly. 'I'd overlooked that. As you say, five minutes should do the Besa.'

Two hours later Barnes called a halt to the training exercise. It would be dark in half an hour and he wanted to move farther north to a more open position which still provided some cover: being trapped inside the quarry for the night didn't appeal to him when he remembered their experience under the bridge. By now Colburn had grasped some of the basic lore of how to fight a tank, including the use of the periscope for observation by the gunner. It was quite impossible to cram months of basic training into two hours even for Colburn, but Barnes was amazed at how much the Canadian had picked up. Calling Reynolds down from the top of the quarry he prepared to depart.

'That was fun,' said Colburn with enthusiasm. 'I'm not quite the spare wheel I was two hours back.'

'You'll do – in an emergency.' Barnes smiled drily.

'At least I can cope with the traverse and the Besa, so try and find me some running Germans within range, but if you're counting on the two-pounder,' he grinned, 'you'll be lucky.'

It struck Barnes that perhaps he shouldn't be too surprised at the Canadian's achievements; after all, it needed plenty of mechanical ability to handle a plane and the one quality no fighter pilot could do without was quick-wittedness. He was more surprised still when Reynolds spoke, pausing as he climbed down into the hatch.

'It just goes to show, Sergeant, that training course is far too long like I've always said – strictly for village idiots. A right old load of bullshit.' He disappeared inside his own compartment.

For the first time it flashed through Barnes' mind that maybe Reynolds had always been so silent because Penn had always been so talkative. The relationships inside the unit were changing rapidly and he was pleased to see that Reynolds obviously liked Colburn.

Three minutes later the tank left the quarry, moved on to the road and headed north. Up in the turret Barnes' expression was grim: he was conscious that they were approaching a crisis and that within the next twenty-four hours at the outside they might well all be dead or taken prisoner. There was, of course, the third alternative – that they might get the chance of striking a great blow against the Germans. If only they could locate a really vital objective. Over seventy two-pounder shells under me, he thought. They could make a mess of something.

He was still turning over an idea which he had not yet mentioned to the others – the idea of keeping going through the night, headlights ablaze like the Panzers. The Germans won't be expecting anything coming up behind them. He felt sure that their eyes would be glued to the battlefield ahead, and a vehicle moving through the night with its headlights full on looked very innocent from a distance, until they had the enemy within two-pounder range, anyway.

They were moving into a more populated area and now he saw people working in the fields some distance from the road. To the north several orange-coloured tractors moved slowly across the landscape which was so flat that it reminded him of Holland, although there was a small ridge over to the right. They were in the heart of the Pas de Calais now, roughly midway between Béthune and Etaples. It was incredible, thought Barnes, to have come all this way from Etreux in a vast semicircle round the southern flank of the battle zone – but no more incredible than the lightning dash of the Panzer spearhead from the German border to the gates of Boulogne. I'll go on through the night, he decided, by God, I will. The people in the fields had stopped work to watch the tank, standing as motionless as scarecrows on a windless day. Then he caught sight of movement to his left, lifted his glasses, and his heart jumped. Another of those sinister dust clouds, only just visible in the fading light, but under the cloud he could see small square shapes moving towards him across country. Panzers!

He issued orders instantly and the tank turned off

the road to the right, moving over the field towards the low ridge, the only defence feature in sight. When they reached it he manoeuvred Bert until he faced the oncoming enemy in a hull-down position, the greater part of the tank concealed behind the ridge so that only the turret projected in the open. A quarter of a mile away a farmer on his orange tractor changed direction, heading across the field to take a closer look at the intruder. Flip off, Barnes told him mentally, or you'll cop a Jerry shell.

'Two-pounder. Traverse right. Right! Steady!'

The turret swung him round and steadied. Perfect. Davis could have done no better, and Davis had been good.

'Range six hundred. Six hundred.'

Barnes had the glasses pressed into his eyes as he watched the dust cloud's progress. It appeared to be moving *across* their line of fire now. Was it possible that in the uncertain light of dusk that they hadn't been spotted after all? In less than five minutes he knew that the Panzers had another objective altogether, somewhere far to the north. He didn't know whether to feel relieved or disappointed. It was almost dark as he gave them the news over the intercom, following it up with the order to advance.

To save time and to avoid the farmer on the tractor who was close behind him now, Barnes guided the tank towards the road along a different course from the one which had brought them to the ridge, moving at an oblique angle which would take them back on to the road some distance north of the point where they had left it. The tank completed its quarter-turn and rumbled forward over the grass, leaving a faint trail of chalk as the substance disengaged itself from the tracks. It may have been the treacherous light of dusk, or it may have been the throbbing of his wound which grew worse towards night: it may have been a combination of these two factors which momentarily robbed him of his normal lynx-eyed observation, but whatever the cause Barnes failed to see the change in the texture of the land they were crossing, failed to see that whereas a moment ago they were passing over green grass and baked earth, now the grass was sparser, growing in isolated tufts, and even where it grew its colour was a strange, almost sinister acid green colour.

His first warning of the danger was the moment when the tank stopped moving forward, although its huge tracks continued to churn round, moving uselessly as the whole tank slowly began to tilt. The tilting motion was in a backward direction, so slight that at first Barnes wondered whether he was suffering from an attack of dizziness, but as the motion continued and he looked quickly over the side the awful truth dawned. They were sinking, sinking more rapidly as the quagmire sucked at the tracks, dragging over twenty-six tons of tank downward into its drowning grip.

Chapter Nine

Saturday, 25 May

His instinct was to give the order to reverse, to take the tank backwards on to the firm ground they had left. Opening his mouth, he closed it again without speaking. Work this out, Barnes, and quickly. The front seems stable, so it may be on solid ground; only the back is going down. If you reverse you may never reach firm ground. Switching on his pocket torch, he swept the beam behind the tank. They appeared to have broken up a very thick crust of earth baked hard by weeks of sunshine, exposing a horrible sticky ooze lower down which gleamed in the torchlight. Go forward then? Climbing out of the turret he walked forward over the left-hand track, sat down and gingerly lowered one leg. Firm enough. But in the beams of the headlights he had told Reynolds to switch on he could see the same type of pallid baked earth, the surface cracked with tiny fissures. Was that firm ground or were they perched on an island of solidity with more quagmire ahead? At least the tank had stopped tilting backwards now, as though it had found a precarious equilibrium. Colburn came out of the turret and climbed down on to the hull.

'What are you playing at, Sergeant?'

'We've run into a bog. It's as soft as butter behind us now and I'm not too sure of this lot. Get ready to grab me – I'm going to test it for firmness.'

He lowered his full weight on his right leg and the ground held, but it was rather like treading on a sponge. He slipped the other leg down and stood up, felt a crumbling sensation under his left leg and the ground caved in. He started to go down, suddenly up to his knees in filthy ooze. Hands grabbed him from behind, hauled him bodily backwards and lifted, sitting him back on the track, legs astraddle it. Carefully, he turned round and scrambled back on to the hull.

'Thanks, Colburn. You just about saved my bacon there. No way ahead and no way back. Get me a rope from that box near the compass. I've got to find out how far away we are from the shore.'

He waited until Colburn had emerged from the turret again and then tied a loop under his shoulders, handing the free end to the Canadian. The tractor had arrived now and it stood on the bank of the quagmire with its headlights beamed direct on to the tank, blinding Barnes as he made his way along the rear track while Colburn stayed on the hull. The farmer was shouting non-stop across the quagmire in French and with his limited knowledge of the language Barnes couldn't understand a word. If only they'd speak slower. He shouted back slowly in English that he was crossing to the bank and received an outburst in reply. Looking back to make sure that Colburn was in position, he pulled a face.

'Pity you don't speak French as well as handling machine guns.'

'I know German. Do you think he might savvy that?'

'Don't try it, for God's sake. He's probably only friendly because we're British.'

'How can he know that?'

'Because of the uniform – he must have seen enough of them before we decided to trot off into Belgium. Here goes. Don't haul me back unless I'm in real trouble. I've got to find out how far it is to the bank.'

'You can see that by the tractor.'

'He'll be yards farther back than he need be. It must be his quagmire.'

Reaching out sideways well beyond the track his right foot touched firmness. But for how long? He put his full weight on it and the ground held. He put his other leg down and there was no feeling of sponginess. He was away from the tank now. Get on with it. A bold step forward with the right leg: it landed on more firmness, a tuft of grass. Were they really as close as this to safety? He lifted the other foot and when it reached the earth it went on going down at an alarming rate, straight through the crust into liquid mud which sent up a dank nauseating smell. Jerking his other foot off the tuft he thrust it forward as far as he could and it hit solid earth, his legs splayed wide apart in front and behind him. He tried to heave the rear foot loose but found he was in serious trouble: it had sunk in up to the knee and the quagmire was wrapped round his leg like some monstrous sea creature determined to suck him down into its lair. Fighting down a rising sense of panic, he heaved again with all his strength, feeling the leg coming up reluctantly, mud oozing and sucking as he pulled. Then it came free with a jerk and he fell flat on his face, aware that the ground under his body was hard and still. Strong hands locked under his shoulders and helped him to his feet. By the light of the tractor's beams he looked into the farmer's face, the long lean face of a man in his forties, still babbling away in French.

'Thanks,' said Barnes. 'Can you speak more slowly?'

Unlooping the rope from his shoulders, he looked behind the Frenchman to where the tractor stood and then walked up to it. Tied to the side were half a dozen iron stakes with ring heads: the stakes were at least six feet long and the farmer had obviously been erecting a fence. With sign language he indicated that he needed the stakes and the farmer nodded his head vigorously in agreement. Cutting the rope with his knife he carried three of the stakes to the bank and called out:

'Get Reynolds up on to the hull. He's to get the two steel tow-lines and attach them to the rear of Bert. I need a hammer over here, too. This chap's got some iron stakes – if we can fix the tow-lines to them it may stop Bert sinking any deeper while we think up something.'

'OK.'

While he was waiting the farmer began to make a great effort to tell him something in a few words of English, spacing out the words one by one in his anxiety to convey the message.

'Stop ... stop ... there!' He pointed at the tank. 'I bring big big wood.' He was gesturing madly, scooping his hand as he pointed at the tank again. 'Big wood. Back soon. You wait.'

What the hell else can we do, Barnes wondered. Colburn had reacted quickly and he threw the hammer into the pool of light from the tractor just before the machine was driven off. To start with, Barnes had to hammer the stakes down in the dark, but once he had them firmly embedded he held the torch in his left hand and hammered with his right. Reynolds had attached the two lines to the rear of the hull long before Barnes had driven in the stakes so deep that he thought they should hold up Bert for at least a while, at least until the farmer came back, if he came back.

The quagmire was an eerie place at night and even though it was now completely dark he could see the tank's silhouette outlined against its own lights. The shadows of Reynolds and Colburn waited on the hull and somewhere far above them a squadron of planes flew through the night at a great height. It was still very warm and muggy and the mosquitoes were active now, biting the back of his neck. He was only satisfied when the stakes were several feet into the ground and then he flashed his torch to show the edge of the quagmire.

'Before you throw me the tow-lines, is Bert still sinking?'

'I don't think so.' Colburn's voice. 'I think the tank's balanced on the island for the moment but it's still badly tilted at the back.'

'As far as I could make out that farmer is coming back with a load of heavy wood. That's all I could get but I imagine he's got some idea of bridging this gap. Now, I'll stand well back, Reynolds, so throw me the first line.'

The loop landed within inches of the stakes where Barnes had left his lighted torch on the ground. He wrapped the line tightly round the stakes close to the ground and then passed the end through an iron ring. When the second tow-line arrived he repeated the process. Now all they could do was to wait, hoping that the farmer would come back and that he would bring something they could use. Occasionally he called out to the men on the tank, but carrying on a conversation across the quagmire seemed pretty unsatisfactory so soon they said nothing and the minutes dragged by with agonizing slowness. Leaving the headlights on bothered Barnes because this drew attention to them from the road, but he decided that they must risk keeping them on to make sure that

the farmer could find them. They waited a whole hour
before lights appeared across the field behind them,
and then the tractor chugged across the grass and
pulled up close to the bank. Barnes ran forward to see
what the farmer had brought, and for a moment he
couldn't see anything until the man pointed to behind
the vehicle. He had dragged across the field two
immense beams of wood which were attached to the
back of the tractor by chains. While the farmer undid
the chains Barnes measured their length by pacing.
About ten feet long. He would have put the distance
between the shore and the front of the tank at twelve
feet, but that was only a rough guess. They'd just
have to try it, anyway – as a fighting vehicle Bert
might just as well be at the bottom of the swamp as
immobilized on that island when daylight came. He
stood on the bank and explained the plan carefully to
Colburn and Reynolds, but that was the easy part. He
now had to explain it to the farmer, and this was only
achieved by careful gesturing. It became clearer when
Reynolds had thrown two coils of rope on to the bank,
and then they started.

The first stage involved careful cooperation
between Barnes and the farmer because the wooden
beams were enormously heavy and extremely
unwieldy. They tied one rope tightly round the end of
the longest beam and then began to invert it so that
the roped end was lifted over their heads. As the huge
beam rose higher and higher Barnes kept a firm grip
on the loose end of the rope. The beam was slowly

moving up to the vertical but the really tricky part was coming when they tried to control its falling movement as it passed beyond the vertical, lowering it under control so that the far end could be dropped just below the right-hand track and form a bridge to dry land – if the beam would reach that far. The beam reached its apex and began to topple. They just managed to prevent it crashing down as they both held on to the rope, and the farmer was sensible enough to let Barnes guide its controlled fall. It dropped lower and lower, scraped the front end of the right-hand track and settled. Would it begin sinking or had they managed to prop it on the tip of the island? The lights of the tractor were again beamed directly on the tank and as far as he could tell the beam was stable.

'Nice work,' shouted Colburn. 'Looks OK to me.'

'Right. Now for the next one.'

The second beam was successfully manoeuvred in direct line with the left-hand track, but it fell short. Not more than a foot, Colburn informed him, but it had fallen short of the island and was sinking slowly. Slowly? Barnes wondered – did that mean it had settled on a patch of fairly firm ground? The quagmire must be unusually solid at this particular point if a beam of such enormous weight was sinking slowly – whereas Barnes had felt his leg knifing through the mud. They'd just have to risk it, and at least they had the two beams placed so that they formed a bridge from the present position of the tank to the shore. He

295

reached up and felt his shoulder gingerly. He'd ripped that wound open again. When he was lowering the second beam he had been aware of a slow tearing sensation and now he could feel stickiness round the edge of the dressing. He set about enlisting the farmer's aid for the final, possibly fatal, stage, and this time he was able to explain quickly what he wanted by sign language. They undid the tow-lines from the iron stakes after the farmer had reversed his tractor, then re-attached them to the rear of the tractor. Barnes tried to explain that he must synchronize his movements with those of the tank – that they must both move at the same moment, and he hoped to God that the farmer understood that the signal would be when Barnes shouted 'Maintenant'. Now. Since the farmer went on repeating the word about two dozen times Barnes felt that he had probably grasped it. Now to get back to the tank.

He was careful to choose the right-hand timber and when he walked along it he lit his way with his torch beam which splayed over the edge, showing a gleam of insidious ooze waiting for him where the crust had broken. Reaching the tank, he checked the position of the timbers. The right-hand one was fine, perfect, in fact, but the left-hand one wasn't at all good. The breadth of the gap between timber and island looked more like eighteen inches. He explained it carefully to Reynolds.

'You'll have to reverse back along exactly the course we came over – then the tracks will move along the beams. This isn't going to be a picnic and you might as well know what could go wrong. The beams could crack under Bert's weight, and they probably will at some stage. One of them could slip off this island after we've started. Or your tracks could slip off the beams – take your choice.'

'Not much of a choice, is it, Sergeant? But we can't stay here.'

'That's the whole point – we've got to risk it. You'll have to follow my orders very precisely. I've fixed up with that farmer chap to shout "Maintenant" when we're coming, and I'll do that as soon as you start moving. He'll drive his tractor like hell to help pull us out – every extra bit of power might just turn the trick. That's why he's revving up now.'

'You'll give me the usual order when you want me to go?'

'No, in this case I'll say "Now". I want you to rev up first so that when we do go we'll go back at a hell of a lick. If we can shoot back fast enough before those beams give way there's a chance the rear tracks will reach the bank. If they do we might just make it – with the added pull the tractor will give us. And I can't guarantee it will work.'

'You're telling me you can't,' said Colburn. 'Once this weight moves on to the beams my bet is they'll sink like a stone.'

'You're probably right – but by then our impetus may take us on to the bank. There's no other way, Colburn. We're damned lucky that farmer turned up.'

'You're right there – I wonder if he has any idea what he's risking if a German patrol turns up? Don't tell me he can push off in the dark because he can't – not with all those tons of tank tied to his tail.'

'He must know that,' replied Barnes quietly. 'If the generals had fought this war the way some of these people fight when they get the chance we'd be over the Rhine by now.' He paused. 'I want you to stay on the rear of the hull, Colburn. Then if anything goes wrong you jump. We're bound to move back at least a bit and with your legs you should be able to hit the bank.'

'What about you?'

'I'll be jumping off myself as soon as Reynolds is clear of the hatch.'

'Let's just see what happens, shall we?' Colburn suggested. 'And for your information you can stop treating me as a privileged person. There won't be any passengers on this trip.'

Reynolds moved on to the front of the turret to lower himself inside the driving compartment but Barnes stopped him.

'There's one point, Reynolds, and I'm sure you'll agree it's a good one – and no reflection on your driving abilities.' He grinned drily. 'When we do start to move be sure that you are in *reverse* gear!'

'I'll do my best, Sergeant,' Reynolds replied stolidly. He climbed down through the hatch and began revving up.

At the last moment Barnes scrambled down inside

the hull, collected a second torch, and handed this to Colburn when he emerged from the turret, telling him to shine it along the right-hand beam. He used his own torch to illuminate the other beam: at least they could now see where they were going and it was vital that he had as much warning as possible if they were on the edge of disaster. Any moment now. He waited a little longer to give Reynolds more time to warm up – the ulitmate disaster would be an engine failure when they were halfway back along those beams. And as he contemplated the weird scene behind the tank he felt that their attempt was doomed to failure. The torchlight showed up clearly the improvised bridge they hoped to move over and above it the tow-lines were taut and strained, vanishing in the darkness where they continued across to the rear of the tractor. In the brief intervals between the deep-throated revving up of the tank's engines he could hear the snarl and spit of the tractor's motor. Would there be enough horsepower to get them clear in time before the beams sank so deep that mud engulfed and choked the tracks – because of one thing Barnes was perfectly sure: those beams were going to sink rapidly under the tank's weight and they would probably split in half long before Bert reached the bank. Standing on the engine covers at the rear of the tank, Colburn should make it so long as he jumped quickly, but if their first rush didn't carry them to the bank Barnes didn't think that he would make it – he would have to stay behind to help Reynolds, and the driver had to climb upwards out of his hatch before he was even standing on the front hull. There was every chance that the twenty-six-ton weight of the tank would sink like a stone long before Reynolds had come out, in which case they would both die without the aid of enemy action just as poor Penn had died. In fact, just as Davis had died. Barnes had an awful vision of what would happen as the tank went down, the mud and ooze rising hungrily up over the tracks, enveloping the hull, welling up over his chest and neck, his head going down as the quagmire swept over him and shut out the world for ever. His hand gripped the mike and he spoke.

'Now!'

Then he immediately bawled out 'Maintenant!' three times at the top of his voice and the tank was moving backwards. The tow-lines drooped, went slack. The farmer hadn't heard him! He opened his mouth again and saw the lines whip up, tighten, twanging as the tractor lurched forward. The tracks were on the beams now and instantly he was aware of a sinking sensation. Both beams had slipped off the island and Reynolds' end was going down. He was revving up non-stop and the tracks were churning through mud, sending up great gouts of ooze which sprayed through the torchlight rays as their bridge sank deeper and deeper. They weren't going to make it. The front end of the bridge was still firmly anchored to the bank so the rear end submerged more and more and now the tank was climbing at a steep angle. He looked back and saw liquid brown ooze lap over the end of the rear tracks, bubbling and slithering over the top. Soon the hull would be under. It was going to be too late, too late ever to reach firm ground and the tank was dropping like a slow-moving lift. Colburn still stood on the hull, leaning back now against the turret but still aiming his torch along the right-hand beam. Hand over the mike Barnes shouted to him to jump, removed the hand and sucked in his breath to order Reynolds up. Looking back he saw that the quagmire had reached the top of the hull – Reynolds must be frightened out of his life.

Inside the nose of the tank Reynolds was more terrified than he had ever been while under German bombardment, and he had been terrified from the moment he lowered himself through the hatch. His seat was jacked up so that when he sat down his head was well clear of the hatch rim and he could see exactly what was happening. It was the change of angle which finally confirmed that he was going to die horribly. Before Barnes had given the order to move the tank was tilted so that the nose was higher than the tail and this had been of some comfort to Reynolds while they waited for him to rev up. If the tank did start to go down at the rear he might have time to get out and jump back on to the island. It was at least a chance. In the earphones he heard Barnes' order. *Now!* The tank began to move backwards, dropping to an even keel as the nose left the island and proceeded over the beams. Seconds later the angle began to change, so that now the nose was sinking, leaving the rear higher, and Reynolds knew that he was finished. The floor seemed to go down at an alarming pace and he could see mud flying past the headlights as the tracks churned deeper and his compartment went on sinking. The downward angle let him see the mud rising up over the tracks and he knew that in the next few seconds it would come over the line of the hull and creep towards his chin. Then, suddenly, it would be pouring into the hatchway, flooding his compartment as the quagmire swamped him. But Barnes hadn't yet given the order to bale out, so he stayed.

Colburn still hadn't jumped and Barnes had taken in breath to order Reynolds up when a tuft of grass flew past his torch ray. A second later the rear of the tank dropped and there was a slight bump as the tracks hit something solid. Colburn was shouting sentences Barnes couldn't hear but he understood what had happened. Climbing up over the steeply-angled beams the tracks had moved on upwards into the air until the centre of gravity had passed the end of the beams and they dropped. *They had reached firm ground.* The tracks went on up the shallow slope of the bank as he spoke quickly into the mike.

'Keep it up! We've done it!'

At that moment the engine coughed, sputtered, stalled, but they were ashore. The tow-lines were still taut as the tractor heaved at its immense load so Barnes jumped to the ground and ran forward to tell the farmer to stop. When the engine was switched off he thumped the Frenchman on the back and kept on thanking him regardless of the fact that the man couldn't understand half what he was saying. He stopped suddenly as he heard Colburn calling out urgently and when he turned round to face the quagmire his body went completely rigid and he froze.

The giant vehicle must have driven along the road while they were preoccupied with saving the tank. They wouldn't have heard its motor because of their own engines and that of the tractor, and Reynolds, the only one facing the road, must have been too concerned with what was happening to notice the road. Worse still, the new arrivals could easily locate their position because Bert's headlights were still on, to say nothing of the tractor's lamp. The moon had now risen and this enabled Barnes to make instant recognition of the huge vehicle and the silhouette of its load – a tank transporter with a tank aboard. As if to complete the process of recognition a soldier walked past the headlights of the transporter, a soldier carrying something which could only be a machine-pistol and wearing a pudding-shaped helmet. The Germans had arrived.

It took a very short time for Barnes to recover from his stunned state, and this was replaced by an upsurge of cold, murderous fury. They had come all this way;

they had lost Davis and Penn; they had almost lost their tank and their own lives a few minutes ago, and now this lot was poking its nose in to snatch it all away from them. Running back to the tank, he leapt on to the hull, grabbed a machine-pistol off the ledge inside the turret, and jumped down behind the tank. He spoke briefly to Reynolds and Colburn.

'Wait here – behind Bert. Don't switch the lights off – that will alert them.'

Then he was running back into the field, following as closely as he could the course the tank had taken when it first turned off the road. To avoid any risk of going into the quagmire he ran a little farther round than he thought was necessary, circling back so that he would come out on the road a good hundred yards behind where the transporter was parked. And as he ran his mind worked with icy detachment. How many Germans would there be? One transporter carrying one heavy tank to the repair shop: four men at the most, he guessed. Possibly only three – the Germans were short of ground troops. He dropped flat suddenly. The first soldier he had seen was standing in the field just beyond the grass verge, and now a second one had walked in front of the headlights and he was looking in Barnes' direction. He didn't think he had been spotted. He had kept his body crouched low and the moonlight wasn't very strong yet, its illumination blurred by a faint white mist rising off the field. The second soldier joined his companion and they both stood staring across the field. They couldn't be too worried yet because otherwise they wouldn't have walked in front of those headlights, and they could have no reason to suspect the presence of hostile troops in this area. Had they done that in the first place they would never have stopped the transporter. A third soldier appeared and stood right in front of the headlights, his machine-pistol clearly visible. He walked forward to join the others.

Barnes was very close to the road now and when he stood up the road was only a dozen yards away. A curtain of mist floated between himself and the Germans and he ran forward, crossing the road and continuing several yards into the field beyond. When he turned, the bulk of the transporter shielded him from where the soldiers waited. Why didn't they either investigate or go away? He found the answer when he looked back across the road and saw that the scene on the edge of the quagmire from that distance looked like anything but what it was. The lights of the tank were tilted downwards and he remembered the shallow slope at the edge of the quagmire. The odd angle of Bert's headlights gave the strange impression that there had just been a car crash. The turret of the tank was invisible and the light of the tractor was too far away to show up the tank's silhouette. The Germans might well be imagining that there was another road just across the fields, and from the passive way they were standing by the roadside he felt certain that Bert's engine had stalled just in time, otherwise they must have recognized the grind of the tracks. It was a tableau made to order, if only he could take advantage of it in time. He moved across the field towards the transporter, his boots making no sound on the grass.

He was close to the rear of the vehicle when he heard someone call out in German. Peering round the end he saw two soldiers still standing on the verge just beyond the front of the transporter while a third one made his way across the field, flashing a torch in front of him. The mist was blurring Bert's lights now and hung over the quagmire like a noxious gas rising from the swamp. Was there a fourth man in the cab? The two Germans by the roadside presented a tempting target but Barnes waited. He had to try and get them all at once to avoid them scattering.

The soldier walking across the field had stopped, the machine-pistol tucked under one arm while he waved the torch with the other hand. The curtain of mist had drifted lower now and soon he would have to walk into it. He shouted across the field in German, waited, and then shouted again, several sentences. It was deathly quiet when he stopped shouting. The transporter's engine had been switched off and the mist seemed to cover the field like a leather glove which smothered even the slightest sound. Barnes waited. The Germans waited. He was fairly sure that the soldier in the field was going to give up his search and return to the others, which meant that for a brief moment all three men might be close together. He hoped so because as he stood by the elevated ramp at the rear of the transporter an entirely new idea was developing at the back of his mind, an idea which made it imperative that he would wipe out the whole German escort. Then he heard one of the men who stood by the roadside call out; the soldier with the torch answered and began to move deeper into the field, sweeping his torch towards the mist wall which was now less than a dozen yards ahead of him.

It happened without warning. The German walked up to the remnants of a wire fence, paused at a point where two posts tilted at a drunken angle, the wire between them sagging, and stepped over the wires, walking forward again. Then he fell forward, losing his torch which skidded sideways over baked mud, and shouted. His shout rose to a shriek of alarm. Jesus, thought Barnes, he's in the quagmire. One of the soldiers by the roadside ran forward, flashing on a torch beam, while the other stayed to guard the transporter. It was at this moment that Barnes climbed silently up on to the side of the huge vehicle, creeping forward and taking up a fresh position behind the German tank. The soldier was running across the field now, waving his torch in front of him as his comrade in the swamp screamed his head off, a scream of pure terror. As the running soldier stopped abruptly his torch beam focused on a horrifying sight: the first German was already up to his waist as the quagmire sucked him steadily downwards; his arms were waving frantically as he kept padding them down on the mud to arrest his sinking movement and he was still shrieking frenziedly. The third German by the roadside ran up to the transporter, feeling under the tank only feet away from where Barnes was crouched, pulled out a coil of rope and started running across the field. The soldier in the quagmire had sunk in up to the chest now, waving his arms high above his head, and only a few feet from where he struggled the lighted torch he had dropped lay on the top of unbroken crust. The man with the rope was close now and while he ran he held the rope coil ready to throw. As he reached the spot where the German holding the torch stood the struggling man sank lower, only his head and upstretched arms visible now, his voice an agonized moan. The rope was thrown, falling several feet short. The head in the swamp sank out of sight, the voice dying in a strangled gurgle, the vertical arms sliding under the surface, vanishing. Barnes wiped sweat off his forehead, slipped his finger back inside the trigger guard, stood up behind the tank and waited.

The two Germans came back slowly, machine-pistols hoisted over their shoulders, talking in low tones. They were less than a dozen yards away when Barnes lifted the machine-pistol. He fired one contin-uous burst, shifting the muzzle slightly from side to side to cover them both. They were still collapsing to the ground when he ceased fire, half a magazine still unused. At that moment the engine of the transporter kicked into life. There had been a fourth man – the driver, with instructions never to leave his cab. Barnes leapt down on to the grass verge and the door on his side was still open as he ran forward, pulling up short just before he reached the opening. Keeping back out of sight he shoved the muzzle of his pistol round the corner, aiming it upwards, firing one short burst. As he ran back to the rear of the vehicle, round the end and along the other side, the engine was still ticking over but the transporter hadn't started moving. He was still cautious when he reached the closed cab door. Grabbing the handle, he hauled the door open and jumped back, his pistol levelled, but the precaution wasn't necessary. As the door opened the driver's body toppled sideways, landing in the road with a soft thud. The German was dead, his right side riddled with bullets. Switching off the motor, Barnes went across to have a look at the other two soldiers. They were also dead. Sergeant Barnes was in sole possession of one German tank transporter.

Chapter Ten

Saturday, 25 May

They were roaring through the night like a thunder-bolt, twin headlights ablaze, the long beams stretching far into the darkness, the giant transporter swaying gently from side to side as Reynolds stepped up the speed. Fifty-five, sixty, sixty-five miles an hour. On the other side of the cab Barnes gazed along the beams which still showed only endless open road, while between them Colburn turned round to peer through the tiny window at the back of the cab.

'Don't worry,' Barnes assured him. 'Bert's still there – his weight alone will keep him on board even moving at this pace.'

His mind travelled back to what had taken place at the edge of the quagmire before they started their headlong dash to the north, and he smiled grimly as he thought that whatever happened now they had been responsible for eliminating at least one German heavy tank, even if the method used had been, to put it mildly, unorthodox. When he had examined the vehicle he found that it was in perfect working order except for the machine-gun and the wireless set. To Barnes' mind it should have been possible to repair the firing mechanism in a few hours but instead the Germans had loaded the tank on to a transporter. This action alone pointed up the Germans' prodigal use of equipment. He had just finished his examination when he heard a heart-warming sound – the sound of Bert's engines tuning up faultlessly. By the time that Reynolds and Colburn arrived inside the tank he had decided exactly what he was going to do.

He was going to head all-out for Calais, the last port before Dunkirk, possibly the twin keys to the whole campaign. If they could come up behind the Germans, causing the maximum possible damage to their rear, then they might be able to strike a heavy blow at a decisive moment. Above all else, he prayed that they would find a really major objective. Bert, going all-out, had a maximum speed of fifteen miles an hour, whereas the German transporter, if driven to its utmost limits, could multiply that rate by four. But as a preliminary they had to get rid of one Wehrmacht heavy tank. This operation took less than thirty minutes.

First, they made a cautious reconnaissance to find out where the quagmire began. The wire fence proved to be the boundary and a short way from the gap through which the German soldier had walked to his death they found a faded notice board which carried a warning. The next stage was an even more cautious reversal of the transporter to a position close to the edge of the swamp. Barnes drove the vehicle while Colburn guided him with a torch. The third stage was the lowering of the ramp at the rear of the vehicle, followed by the infinitely satisfying moment when Barnes climbed into the driving compartment of the tank, fiddled with the controls, drove it backwards and forwards a few feet along the deck, and then reversed it for its final journey. He climbed out of the hatch and jumped clear as the machine was clattering down the ramp.

Wobbling erratically in the moonlight it proceeded across the field. It travelled backwards a dozen yards on an even keel, like a robot moving through the night, then suddenly it lost its stability, the front tilting downwards as the tracks churned up a rain of wet mud. It continued at that angle for a short distance, advancing without pause, hurling back great goutfuls of ooze which made them jump sideways. A few seconds later the engine sound changed, coughing and spluttering as the huge tracks sank so deep that only the hull and turret were visible. The hull went under. The engine sound cut out altogether while the turret submerged and Barnes saw with amazement the turret disappear in a matter of seconds, leaving behind only a disturbed whirlpool of mud and water. They had been lucky – they had driven Bert into the harder end of the swamp.

'What happened to that farmer?' he asked Colburn.

'As soon as he heard the rattle of your machine-pistol he cleared off across the fields. I don't think he liked the idea of being mixed up with dead Germans.'

'And yet he had the guts to fetch those beams.'

'I guess he thought he'd done his bit – you can't blame him, he probably had a wife and family.'

'I don't blame him but I'd like to have thanked him with a bottle of Mandel's wine.'

It took them another ten minutes to put Bert aboard the transporter and to cover his silhouette with the tarpaulin they always carried. Under Barnes' instructions, Reynolds had reversed Bert back up the ramp and along the deck until his rear rested behind the cab wall so that in an emergency he could be driven off in the minimum possible time. Then they had carried the dead Germans well away from the roadside into the field opposite the quagmire, collected all the spare machine-pistol magazines they could lay their hands on, and climbed aboard.

It was surprising, Barnes thought as he sat in the cab of the transporter which was now thundering north like an express train, it was surprising what you could do in thirty minutes. The question now was what they could do behind the German lines near Calais. He looked at his watch, Penn's watch. Thirty minutes to midnight. At this rate they would reach the Calais area soon after midnight, that was assuming they drove all the way without interception, which of course wouldn't happen. It was the surprise element which they had on their side, surprise plus audacity. He had a vivid picture of that Panzer column which had driven through the night with its lights full on. Well, they had their lights full on and this was a German vehicle they were driving. Finally, there would be an element of near-chaos close to the battle zone.

'I still say these might come in very useful,' remarked Colburn. He produced three German helmets piled on top of each other from under the seat.

'Under what circumstances?' demanded Barnes. 'Put one of those on and you can get shot as a spy.'

'Just a thought.' He put them away again and produced a machine-pistol. 'This baby is very good. While you were killing Germans back at the quagmire I found out from Reynolds how to use it – just in case. Look.'

Extracting the magazine, he hunched the weapon under his shoulder and gave a demonstration. Then he replaced the magazine and slipped the pistol under the seat. The energy of the Canadians, thought Barnes. This laddie never stops going. A distinct asset.

'I still can't understand why you liked handling explosives as a peacetime occupation,' he told Colburn.

'The satisfaction of doing a good job.' He paused. 'Hell, let's face it – I'm a bastard who likes a good blow-up.'

'You've come to the right place.' He pointed to the right.

Beyond Barnes' side window the night was lit up with distant flashes, flashes which succeeded each other almost instantaneously like an electric storm. They were racing north through Colburn's 'gap' with the southern flank of the main battle area on their right, although as yet they couldn't hear the sound of the guns. For the third time in a minute Reynolds glanced in his rear-view mirror.

'I thought so, Sergeant. We've got company. There's a truck coming up behind us and I think it's like the one Penn put a shell through.'

'How far back?'

'Coming up on our tail. I think he'll be passing us in a minute. He's coming at a helluva lick.'

'Keep your present speed.'

Barnes tightened his grip on the machine-pistol which lay across his lap and Colburn produced the German helmets again with a flourish.

'Sergeant Barnes, how many men do you think there could be aboard this truck?'

'At least twenty,' said Barnes shortly.

'And we would like to get to Calais rather than fight Custer's Last Stand here?'

'That is the general idea.'

'Then may I offer these – going very cheap? I've noticed that in wartime you don't look at a soldier's face – you look at his uniform, and the most distinctive part of a German soldier's uniform is this elegant helmet.'

They said no more, they put the helmets on, and it struck Barnes that he had never seen anyone look more like a German soldier than Reynolds in his helmet which was perhaps just as well since he would be closest to the truck. They could hear the horn blaring behind them now, warning the transporter they were about to be overtaken, and now a chill silence descended on the cab as the tension rose rapidly. Barnes remembered the open-backed trucks which Penn had described and how the sea of faces had stared at him as they went past. If this lot suspects anything, Barnes thought grimly, all they have to do is to play innocent, pass us, and the next thing we'll know is when a spray of bullets comes through this windscreen. One burst should do for all three of us. He crouched lower in his seat, peering from under the rim of the helmet which was too large for him, changing his grip on the pistol so he could raise and fire in one movement. The only comforting thing was that Reynolds would keep on driving without his nerve cracking as long as he was physically capable of the action. Ah, here they come.

He could see the headlights of the truck now. It seemed to drive part way along the side of the transporter and then hold its speed. Had the tarpaulin come undone? Could they see that it wasn't a German tank under the sheet? He peered back through the little window and the bulk of the tank blocked his view, but he could see that the tarpaulin was still firmly in place over the rear. The trouble was it was the side which counted. The headlights were moving forward now and out of the corner of his eye he saw the cab of the other vehicle draw level and then move ahead. Any minute now. The cloth-covered side of the truck slid past and the truck was ahead of them. A huddle of helmeted German soldiers stared back into the fierce glare of the headlights, their faces white under the pudding-shaped helmets. Barnes stared back, knowing that they couldn't see him because of the headlights. They looked dazed, bored, tired. As the truck sped away from them he wondered how many of the soldiers would be alive when the war was over. They took off their helmets and handed them to Colburn.

'Well, that worked,' he said, 'but I can't say I fancied the experience all that much. Have you had a lot of this sort of thing since you left Etreux?'

'Not more than six times a day,' Barnes replied humorously.

'Oh, well, that's fine. I thought maybe it happened frequently.'

You could sense the drop in temperature inside the cab, the relief at still being alive, the sheer enjoyment of still being in one piece. Colburn found he had an almost uncontrollable impulse to chatter and it was with difficulty that he restrained himself from over-doing it. These boys really had something to put up with; this long-drawn-out business wasn't his forte. Give him the air every time. It was short but sharp up there, over with quickly. Ten minutes later the tension crept back into the cab when Reynolds informed them that there were headlights behind again.

'Another truck?' queried Barnes.

'No, I think this is a car. He's in a hurry, too. I

thought I was driving this bus over the speed limits but some of these drivers need certifying. The car behind came up from nowhere like a dirt-track rider.'

'Let him pass.'

'Helmets on?' queried Colburn.

'Not this time. Whoever it is won't be able to see clearly into the cab from a car.'

'He'll see Reynolds if he looks,' Colburn objected.

'I don't like wearing Jerry helmets,' said Reynolds flatly.

Headlights had appeared beyond Reynolds' window and the car began to move up fast. Reynolds glanced down, looked ahead quickly, and then glanced down again. The car moved forward and then stayed alongside the transporter's bonnet, the driver's arm projecting and waving madly as he flagged them down. Barnes' eyes narrowed and he lifted the pistol, a movement which caught Reynolds' eye.

'Don't, Sergeant.'

'What's the matter?'

'It looked like Jacques. I think he wants us to stop.'

'Jacques! It can't be. He passed us this morning on his way to Abbeville.'

'It's a green Renault and I'm sure it's Jacques. In fact,' Reynolds concluded heavily as though not enjoying contradicting Barnes, 'I saw him twice. It's definitely Jacques.'

'All right. Slow down and then pull in, but keep your engine running. Was he alone?'

'As far as I could see, yes.'

The darkest suspicion flooded into Barnes' mind and he put one hand on the door handle ready to jump out as soon as the vehicle stopped. If this really was Jacques no possible stretch of the imagination could explain his presence up here in the Pas de Calais, yet what was he doing so far from the Mandel farm and Abbeville? Still not at all sure that Reynolds hadn't made some ghastly mistake, he jumped down as soon as the transporter pulled up. When he reached the ground the Renault was stopping a dozen yards ahead. The engine was switched off and a man got out. He ran towards them, shielding his eyes against the powerful beams. It was Jacques.

'I've been driving up and down this road for three hours hoping to see you, Sergeant Barnes. But I didn't really expect I ever would – I thought you'd follow that route I marked on your map, though.'

'I didn't expect to see you either,' Barnes replied grimly.

'You amazed me when I saw Reynolds in that cab – it is a German transporter, isn't it?'

His face looked chalk-white, although it might have been the light of the beams, and his voice was harsh and strained.

'Yes, it's a transporter. What are you doing here, Jacques? You said you were on your way to Abbeville.'

'A terrible thing has happened. The Germans have shot my sister.'

Had his voice trembled? Barnes thought so, but the

fleeting expression of pain was succeeded by an expression of bitterness and hate.

'How did it happen?' Barnes asked quietly.

'The Germans are trying to say it was an accident – their interpreter told me that – but they killed her. She was standing in a square in Abbeville and some German tanks arrived. Someone leaned out from a window and shot one of their men in the tower of a tank. They fired their machine-guns all round the square and my sister was killed. Boches!' He spat out the word.

'I'm very sorry to hear that, Jacques.' Barnes spoke gently. 'But what are you doing in this part of the world?'

'After what happened I decided I must come home to tell my father. I live in Lemont – that is near Gravelines. I told you that,' he ended accusingly. 'Then I shall kill some Germans.'

'I'd think about that, if I were you. Killing Germans takes training and skill.'

'Not with a knife in the back in a dark street.'

He spoke without hysteria, his mouth tight. He means just what he says, Barnes thought, and he'll do it coldly and clinically. This was the lad who led a gang to put wire across a road, wire which killed a German cyclist.

'On the other hand,' Jacques said suddenly, 'I could come with you.'

'Thanks, but nothing doing.'

Jacques was peering up at Colburn who leant out

of the cab window to listen to the conversation. He frowned and turned to Barnes.

'Who is that?'

'A soldier – someone we picked up on the way.'

'And where is Mr Penn?'

'He died.'

'I am so sorry. I liked Mr Penn. He was so jolly, is that the word?'

'Jolly would do.'

'And you will not let me come with you?'

'Sorry. No. You get home to your people at Lemont.'

'This is the road to Calais as well as to Gravelines. You are going to one of those places – to Calais, perhaps?'

'Perhaps.'

'I could drive ahead at least some of the way and warn you of danger.'

'It's no good, Jacques. That would put you in a crossfire between us and the Germans.'

'I don't mind. No, that won't make you change your mind.' He paused. 'You are travelling on the main road at the moment, the most dangerous road. If you are going to Calais I know another road which turns off this one and it would be much safer, I'm sure. The Germans are less likely to expect someone coming that way. If I take you along it I can leave you before you reach Calais and drive back to Lemont. In fact,' he added slyly, 'if I insist on driving ahead of you, you can't really stop me, can you?'

In the end, reluctantly, Barnes agreed. Before the night was out the lad was going to do something silly, anyway, and he was within a few months of being called up when he would have no choice. If they were very lucky they might get him behind the Allied lines where he would be safer while he got over his sister's death. The only alternative, in view of his obstinacy, was to throw away the ignition key and leave him stranded, and he wasn't prepared to do that. He gave Jacques careful instructions – he was always to drive at least one hundred yards ahead of them and if they ran into trouble he was to leave his car at once and run. Climbing back up into the cab, Barnes watched him walk back to the Renault.

'I still don't like it,' he told Colburn, 'but if he keeps that distance ahead of us it won't look as though he's leading the way.'

'There's a war on and he looked pretty mature to me. If you'd made him leave us he'd have been up to his back-stabbing tricks and sooner or later they'd get him.'

'Let's go, Reynolds,' said Barnes.

As the transporter moved on through the night the air of tension returned to the cab and it never went away again. There was no longer much conversation and Barnes found himself holding the machine-pistol in a vice-like grip as his eyes followed Jacques' tail-light. He had already made up his mind that as soon as Jacques put them on the side road the lad would have to leave them and go home to Lemont. Telling

Colburn to keep a close eye on the tail-light, he took out his map folded to the Pas de Calais area and found Lemont, a dot little more than a large village close to Gravelines, the town east-north-east of Calais. Both places were on the waterline, a system of canals with sluice gates to control the flow. Closing the map, he lowered his window and looked to the east where the flashes now rivalled the moonlight as they illuminated the sky, but it was no longer the flashes alone which told him they were moving very close to the battle area, for now he could hear in the distance the thump of big guns. He wiped more sweat off his forehead and dried his hands on his trousers. The rising sense of tension had almost become a physical presence inside the cab, something they could all *feel*. Was it simply the growing sound of the guns or was it also the realization that with every second which passed, with every yard they moved forward, they drew closer to the inevitable encounter with the Germans? Five more minutes passed, five minutes of loaded silence, and then the crisis broke with alarming suddenness.

They had followed Jacques round a sharp corner and immediately Reynolds was jamming on the brakes, the huge vehicle still trying to move forward against the restraining pressure. The Renault was stationary perhaps seventy yards ahead, and no farther than fifty yards beyond the stopped car, lights were strung across the road. One of the lights, a red lamp, moved from side to side.

'Road-block,' said Barnes tersely.

Colburn stirred beside him. 'Hadn't we better move up closer to Jacques?'

'No, we stay here. Reynolds, switch off the head-lights but leave the side ones on – we may have a visitor in a minute. And turn off the motor – I want to hear what's going on – but get ready to start it again as soon as I tell you.'

Leaning out of the window, he turned his head and listened. The big guns had obligingly paused with their cannonade and he heard a voice, a staccato voice probably speaking in German. Then Jacques began to turn the car round in the road. He had only commenced the operation when a burst of machine-pistol fire shattered the night. The car stopped in mid-turn and ran back into the ditch, its front wheels still on the road. Barnes had his head poked out of the window when he heard another burst. As it broke off he detected a faint noise and looked up the road but it was difficult to see anything between the transporter and the Renault, whose lights were now beamed across the road. Colburn grasped Barnes by the arm.

'For God's sake . . .'

'Quiet! I think he's almost here.'

The running footsteps were very close and as Barnes jumped down into the road Jacques appeared, his breathing laboured, his expression bleak. He spoke rapidly.

'I'm all right. They opened fire when I wouldn't drive up to them. As far as I could see there's only three or four of them but they've got a pole across the road . . .'

'Any sign of a field gun? A gun with a shield and a big barrel?'

'No, but there was one man crouched by the roadside behind a sort of rifle on legs.'

'Anti-tank rifle. Which side is he on?'

'The left as you approach them. I saw a motorcycle and side-car behind the rifle . . .'

'Anyone in it?'

'No, but there are three more men behind the barrier – it was one of them that fired at me. I managed to get out of the car on this side.'

'Get up here quick.' Barnes was unfastening one corner of the tarpaulin and he held it while Jacques scrambled up on to the transporter deck. 'Get on to the tank behind the cab and lie flat on the engine covers – the turret should shield you from any bullets that may be flying about.'

'We're going through it?' asked Jacques.

'Yes, so keep your head down.'

Re-fastening the tarpaulin, he climbed back into the cab and gave the order to move. He held the muzzle of his machine-pistol well below windscreen level and Colburn extracted his own pistol from under the seat. The transporter began to move forward, headlights blazing again, while inside the cab three men gazed fixedly ahead.

'No shooting unless we can't avoid it,' Barnes warned. 'We stopped and they'll think there's something funny about that but they'll recognize their own vehicle. We're not stopping whatever happens and they may lift the pole. Reynolds, get up some speed and keep going – I'd like at least forty miles an hour when we reach that barrier, more if you can manage it.'

The transporter began picking up speed fast as Reynolds put his foot down. He had reached a speed well in excess of forty as they flew past the abandoned Renault and ahead the lights of the road-block rushed towards them. Barnes was leaning well forward now, straining his eyes to see as much as possible before they reached the obstacle, which was clearly visible in their headlights – a narrow pole mounted several feet above the road. And something else, too. On the left a soldier lay behind the anti-tank rifle, while beyond rose the silhouette of the motor-cycle and side-car, a soldier already astride the cycle. The pole remained obstinately down. Barnes shouted.

'Reynolds, if you can, drive over that rifle and the cycle – as long as you can get us back off the verge to the road. Leave it to you . . .'

Reynolds made no reply, his broad shoulders hunched forward over the wheel, his head quite still as he stared through the windscreen. They hadn't opened fire yet. The fact that it was a German vehicle was confusing them. Barnes braced himself for the impact, grabbing the edge of the window and spreading his left arm across Colburn's chest to hold him back. Cleverly, Reynolds left his manoeuvre until the last possible moment, driving straight down the centre of the road, heading for the middle of the barrier, increasing speed. Twenty yards. Fifteen. Ten. He turned the wheel. The anti-tank rifle, the soldier, the man on the cycle, rushed towards them and then the huge transporter loaded with twenty-six tons of tank smashed past the impediments. The wheels ground over something, the cycle and side-car were hurled sideways, the soldiers catapulted through the air, and then they were through the barrier as Reynolds swung the transporter back on to the centre of the road. Not a shot had been fired. In his concentration on the anti-tank rifle Barnes had never even seen the pole go: and the beams from the Renault were fading into the distance. He gave one simple order.

'Accelerate.'

Chapter Eleven

Sunday, 26 May

General Storch stormed into the Lemont farmhouse which was his temporary headquarters, his voice preceding him down the narrow passage.

'Meyer! Where are you?' He reached the entrance to the room serving as his office, closed the door quickly and took off his cap. 'Ah, there you are! What has gone wrong?' He was talking rapidly as he strode to a table clothed with a large-scale map of the area. 'I have just heard that you have sent an instruction countermanding my order.'

'Only provisionally, sir.' Colonel Meyer stood up behind the table and screwed the monocle into his eyes, his expression worried. This was going to be another bad night.

'But it was only an hour ago that we went over the order together – the order to attack at dawn, at 04.00 hours. That road to Dunkirk is only three inches under the waterline in spite of the fact that the French opened the sluice gates at Gravelines – so what has happened since?'

Meyer picked up the message form from the table and held it out for the general to read, but

Storch ignored it, stripping off his gloves, his voice urgent.

'You've read it, so tell me.'

'It's a message from GHQ, which came in after you'd left, sir. It was because of this that I issued my order – to be confirmed later subject to your approval.'

'What are the armchair lot up to now?'

'The message is not complete – it was garbled in transmission. We're still having trouble with the wireless but I'm sure the meaning is clear.'

'We haven't much time,' the general reminded him, examining the map as he spoke.

'It orders us to halt on the waterline, to stay where we are now. General von Bock will attack the BEF from Belgium. I gather that General von Rundstedt is worried about the condition of the tanks, and that's why he's halting us.'

'May I see it?' Storch took the message and read it through several times, then looked up cynically. 'It doesn't really say all that – and it's certainly garbled.'

Meyer took a deep breath. 'When I was talking to Rundstedt on the field telephone several days ago in your absence he explained his views – he wishes to preserve the armoured forces for the coming battle against the French south of the Somme.'

'Yes, I remember.' Storch hardly seemed to be listening. 'I have just heard from Keller that this submerged road is not covered by the enemy – our patrol advanced halfway along it before dark without meeting any opposition. I've had the patrol pulled back to Lemont for the night.'

'On the surface it does look promising,' Meyer reluctantly agreed.

'Actually, the road is under the surface.' Storch flashed a confident smile and it made Meyer feel even more exhausted to see the general looking as though he had just risen from an excellent night's sleep. 'So the road to Dunkirk really is open, Meyer. Even allowing for a cautious passage by our tanks the advance forces will be inside Dunkirk two hours after dawn. And once we have Dunkirk the whole BEF is in our hands – over a quarter of a million men.'

'But the message from GHQ . . .' Meyer began.

'I think we can deal with this. It's badly garbled and the most recent order we received was quite clear – advance up the coast and seize the ports. That is what we shall do – we shall seize the last port. Dunkirk.'

'I have asked the wireless operator to try and get through to obtain clarification.'

'Then we shall have another confused reply which will make matters worse. Cancel the request for clarification.'

He waited while Meyer picked up the phone and gave the order, replacing the receiver reluctantly.

'What is really worrying you, Meyer?'

'I'm bothered about the huge concentration of ammunition at the dump. In this confined area inside the waterline . . .'

'You have sufficient for the operation?'

'Too much really . . .'

'We can never have too much.' He pulled his cap on firmly. 'So we can record the receipt of this latest message as being so garbled that it is meaningless. And now you can send off the confirmatory copy of my order to attack to Advanced Headquarters. We should be able to spare one staff car from our entry into Dunkirk. Send off the car within the hour.'

The colonel swallowed. Storch had now covered himself completely. By the time the staff car reached Advanced Headquarters the Panzers would be on the move along the partially submerged road.

'Our rear, sir,' Meyer persisted. 'It is hardly protected at all, everything is facing north and east.'

'Precisely! The British are in front of us, Meyer, not behind us. We advance at dawn as planned.'

The clock on Meyer's desk registered 12.10 a.m.

Racing through the night, the transporter weaved steadily from one side of the road to the other and then back again as Reynolds struggled desperately to prevent the German truck from passing them. Again, the crisis had arisen with hardly any warning. Barnes checked his watch. 12.15 a.m.

Reynolds had warned them that headlights were coming up behind them very fast and that he thought it was another truckload of German soldiers. A sixth sense had told Barnes that it was highly unlikely that they would be able to repeat their previous deception and then he heard the horn blowing. The horn had gone on blowing ever since, and for a while the truck had been content to stay on their tail.

'Sounds as though he'd like a word with us,' said Colburn.

'I'm sure he would,' replied Barnes grimly.

'I don't see how they could have cottoned on to us.'

'The road-block we smashed up. Someone must have sounded the alarm and sent this lot after us.'

Reynolds glanced in his rear-view mirror. 'He's going to try and pass us.'

'Don't let him.'

So Reynolds had started waving the giant vehicle, backwards and forwards across the road, blocking the truck's path each time it attempted to move up. Colburn had been surprised that they hadn't opened fire, but Barnes had pointed out that behind the cab stood a tank with a 70-mm armour-plating and that the Germans must realize there was a tank aboard from the shape of the tarpaulin. They must also have realized that machine-pistol fire would scarcely scratch the plating, let alone penetrate the full length of the tank to reach the cab. And that, Barnes supposed, was why they were so anxious to pass – so that they could send a blast of bullets into the cab from the front. It couldn't go on like this much longer, he was quite sure. They had to do something about that truck. He explained his plan briefly to them and then he opened the door and threw it back flat against the side of the transporter. The horn behind them was still blowing like a banshee. He went out backwards, holding on to the upper door frame while his right foot stepped inside the metal climbing rung. Looped over his shoulder, the machine-pistol didn't help his balance and at the speed they were travelling the wind velocity buffeted his body like a minor hurricane and tried to tear him away from his precarious grip. He stayed there for a second and wondered whether he was in full view of the truck, but the tarpaulin-shrouded tank was acting as a screen. Very carefully he sent his left foot out into space, feeling for the deck behind the cab. The foot felt nothing as the transporter lurched sideways and he nearly came off. There were too many things to cope with at once – keeping his grip, anticipating the violent swerves of the trans-porter, feeling around for the deck – and all the time the wind rush tore savagely at his body. This was worse, far worse, than he had expected. It was taking him all his time to hang on. Then his shoulder wound began to throb viciously and suddenly he felt dizzy and his head started to swim. That decided him. All or nothing. Gritting his teeth he made a supreme effort, lifting his left leg high, bringing it down where the deck should be. His foot hammered down on hard flat wood. He let go with his left hand and grabbed for the tarpaulin rope, praying that it was firmly attached to the rear of the cab. He pulled at the rope and when it held firm he let go with his right hand, his whole weight suspended from the rope now. At that moment the transporter swerved again and the violence of the momentum hurled him outwards.

His body described a complete arc of a hundred and eighty degrees, his left foot pivoting under him, his hand sliding down the rope, then his body slammed back against the tank with fearful impact and he ended up facing outwards, still clutching the rope with only his left hand as his right foot scrabbled for a hold on the deck. For several seconds he hung there helplessly, dazed with pain because when the swing of the arc had brought him round to crash backwards against the covered hull the first point of impact which took the shock was his wounded shoulder. Waves of dizziness trembled through his brain, a feeling of sickness welled up, and beyond it all the guns boomed, the horn shrieked, and the transporter swayed crazily from side to side. He was done for, he couldn't summon up enough will-power to do anything but hang on. He fought down the sickness, tasted salty blood in his mouth where he had bitten through his lip, and then he felt Jacques grasp him, one hand round each upper arm. The grip steadied him while he grasped the rope with both hands, hauling himself in between the cab and the rear of the tank. Then he flopped forward on the canvas over the engine covers and lay quite still, gulping in great breaths of air, desperately fighting for self-control as his wound screamed at him. He was vaguely aware that Jacques was lying beside him next to the turret. And all the time the vehicle swayed insidiously from side to side under him as he tried to push away the feeling that he was blacking out.

It was a terrible struggle to recover quickly, to get his choking breath back to normal, to push under the blinding waves of pain, but two things stimulated his recovery – the rush of fresh air and the insistent shrieking of the horn which continually alerted him of the imminent danger. Telling Jacques to keep flat he forced himself up on his knees, scooping up a ridge of tarpaulin to conceal his position. Then he extracted two spare magazines from his pockets, rested them behind the ridge and lowered himself flat, the machine-pistol next to his shoulder. Clubbing his fist he gave the agreed signal, banging three times on the rear of the cab.

The transporter stopped weaving and pulled over to the right side of the road, still moving at high speed, allowing free access for the truck to pass. I've got to get this just right, Barnes told himself. Head down until the exact moment when the covered part of the truck is alongside us – the part which sheltered the troops inside. No need to fire at the driver at once – I want to get the lot – and they won't shoot at Reynolds from their own cab for fear he swerves into them. He kept his head down and heard the truck coming up as Reynolds drove well into his own lane. The truck was coming up with a roar. He felt the transporter lift slightly as they started going uphill. Now! He flattened the canvas ridge with the gun muzzle and his heart sank – the truck was much farther past than he had expected, the cab already beyond Reynolds, the covered side spread out in front of him. Pressing the trigger he swivelled the gun methodically low down along the canvas wall, just above the wooden side, sweeping the muzzle in slow arcs. Empty! He was ramming in a fresh magazine when Jacques called out: a German soldier peered round the end of the truck, machine-pistol aimed. Barnes fired, the man fell into the road as Barnes swivelled the muzzle back again, his finger pressing steadily on the trigger, a stream of bullets ripping and tearing through the canvas along one continuous strip. At that moment Reynolds took a hand.

The road was climbing an embankment up to a bridge and the driver gave the pre-arranged signal, two long blasts on his own horn. Barnes shouted to Jacques to hold on tight and braced himself for the impact as the transporter began to speed up and edge across the road, moving ahead of the truck as it shifted its course to hit the truck broadside on. They were close to the summit when the German driver lost his nerve, swerving away when the colossus was only inches from him. Lifting his head Barnes saw the truck spin over sideways, falling from view. As they went over the bridge he heard a muffled thump, a boom, and then flames flared in the night behind them. The petrol tank had gone. The next thing he heard was a terrifying shriek of brakes, the transporter's brakes.

The view from the cab was frightening. Reynolds had heard the stutter of Barnes' gun, had concentrated half his attention on that final manoeuvre which had destroyed the truck, then he was sweeping over the bridge at high speed. The road was going down now and he saw what faced him in a flash. Headlights blazed on a stone wall dead ahead, a right-hand turn at the bottom. Then the headlights were swinging wildly as he desperately tried to negotiate the unexpected hazard, braking, turning, going straight through the wall with a tremendous smash, the immense weight of the vehicle piercing the wall like butter. The whole transporter shuddered, knocking aside a small tree, skidded across the garden, then it stopped.

Barnes lay still for a moment, collecting himself, still clutching the machine-pistol. He had been warned by the shriek of brakes and he had been saved by the pillow of spare canvas between himself and the rear of the cab, and his own body had saved Jacques when the lad was thrown against him. They got up cautiously, like men expecting a limb to fall off, and Colburn was waiting for them at the foot of the open cab door, his pistol under his arm, blood oozing from a cut on his forehead and gash on the back of his left hand. He said they were little more than scratches.

'Is Reynolds all right?' asked Barnes.

'Reynolds is all right,' said Reynolds from the cab. 'I don't know why, but he's all right. Probably only because he was inside this brute – we went through that wall like going through paper. I'm sorry, Sergeant,' he added, 'but I was concentrating on the truck and when we got over the bridge the wall was on top of me. And by the way, this job,' he banged the wheel, 'is a write-off. So it's back to Bert now.'

'You did damned well. No one could have survived in that truck – I riddled it before you bounced it over the edge and then the petrol went up – but I'll go back and make sure in a minute. It's a good job you braked when you did – we wouldn't have gone through that like paper.'

He pointed to the house. Barely six feet beyond where the transporter had pulled up stood an ancient three-storey mansion. All the windows were broken, a wall creeper almost covered the front door, and the garden in which the transporter rested was knee-deep in weeds. No one had lived there for a long time, which was probably just as well: opening the front door to find a tank transporter in the garden could be a disconcerting experience. Reynolds tried the engine several times but it refused to function, and while Barnes went back over the bridge Colburn and Jacques helped the driver to pull the tarpaulin off Bert.

Barnes approached the bridge with caution. Reaching the top he crouched behind the wall and peered over the edge to where the wrecked truck was still on fire. There was no sign of life but there was every sign of death. The vehicle had landed with its wheels in the air and by the light of the flames he saw huddled shapes lying in the grass, but the only thing which moved was the flames. Few of the men in the back could have survived the murderous fire of his machine-pistol, and any who did would have perished when the truck tumbled down the steep embankment. He doubted whether anyone was alive when the petrol tank blew. When he turned round to walk back he froze, his taut nerves trying to cope with the fact that a new crisis was at hand.

Headlights were coming down the road from the opposite direction. They were still some distance away but he gained the impression that they were approaching at speed. Running down the slope he heard the welcome sound of Bert's engines starting up, but they still had to lower the ramp and bring Bert down it, and he knew there wouldn't be time to do that before the oncoming vehicle arrived. Colburn must have seen something in his face because he asked the question immediately.

'More trouble?'

'I'm not sure. There's something coming down the road from the north – on its own.'

'We'd better set up an ambush. I'll take the other side of the road . . .'

'No, stick with me – otherwise we may end up shooting each other. Jacques, tell Reynolds to switch off his engine and sit tight. You get behind the end wall of the house and stay there. Come on, Colburn . . .'

The vehicle was quite close now and it sounded like a car, but it was still hidden by the bend in the road, and it was still travelling at high speed. They ran a short distance into the garden, stopping at a point where an undamaged section of the wall was shoulder-high. Peering over the wall-top beyond the bend Barnes saw that the headlights were quite close. He ducked out of sight and heard the car begin to lose speed as the headlights reached the bend. Well, they wouldn't get far once they turned the corner and found half the wall strewn in their path. He looked back and wasn't too happy to see that the glow of fire beyond the bridge clearly silhouetted the transporter with a British tank nestling on its deck.

'I think it's stopping,' Colburn whispered.

'It's bloody well going to have to.'

'It may be a civilian.'

'Only people like Jacques are mad enough to drive about in battle zones.'

He timed it carefully, keeping low as the car crawled round the bend and then pulled up, its engine still ticking over. As he lifted his head he heard a clash of gears and the car began to reverse back round the bend. He had a quick impression – a black Mercedes staff car, the hood back, a German soldier driving and beside him an officer in a peaked cap clutching something to his chest. It was almost beyond the bend now, reversing rapidly. He lifted the machine-pistol, cradled it into his shoulder, and rested the barrel on the wall-top. Aiming about two feet above the headlights he fired. One long burst. He hard a brief shatter of breaking glass and the car went crazy, still reversing but snaking from side to side. He fired again, arcing the gun. The car swung wildly sideways, crashed its rear into the wall and halted, its headlights shining on the opposite wall. The engine had stopped.

The driver was hunched over the wheel, head and shoulders drenched in blood. The passenger-seat door was open and the officer lay in the roadway on his back, capless, arms outstretched, staring up at the stars. A few feet from his right hand lay a half-open briefcase, the case he had clutched so firmly to his chest when the emergency had arisen. Barnes checked the officer, whose chest was torn with the bullets where the arc had moved across him and lifted one shoulder. He was a major, a dead major. Picking up the briefcase, Barnes took out a paper while Colburn examined the rear seat; holding the paper in front of the headlights he grunted.

'This is your pigeon. You said you could speak German, Colburn, can you read it as well? This looks as though it could be interesting.'

'Let me have a look.'

He scanned the lines briefly and then looked up, his face very serious.

'This *is* interesting. It's a battle order and this copy is for some Advanced Headquarters. Let me check it again to make sure I've got it right.'

'This staff car can tell us something,' said Barnes thoughtfully. 'They can't possibly be expecting anyone coming up from this direction or else it wouldn't be travelling without escort. We may surprise the bastards yet.'

'This document* is going to surprise you, Barnes. The German 14th Panzer Division is going to attack Dunkirk at dawn. They've found some secret road to the port just under the water – the whole area must be flooded along that part of the front as far as I can gather. Apparently this road is built up from the surrounding countryside so it's only a few inches under the floods.'

'Does it give the start-line for the attack?'

'Yes, the funny thing is it's Jacques' home town – the attack is being launched from Lemont at 04.00 hours.'

Barnes knew that at the eleventh hour he had found his worthwhile objective. He checked his watch. 12.25 a.m.

'We'll forget about Calais,' he said. 'Jacques is going to take us home.'

'It gives the name of the general who's leading the attack.'

'Really?' Barnes wasn't too interested as they hurried back to the transporter.

'Yes. A General Heinrich Storch.'

---

* Not only sergeants are lucky with documents. Twenty-four hours earlier, Lieutenant-General Sir Alan Brooke, commander 11 Corps BEF, was handed a battle order captured from a German staff car which warned of an imminent offensive by General von Bock's Army Group B – just in time for him to move more troops into the threatened area.

Chapter Twelve

Sunday, 26 May

Storch jumped out of the staff car, checked his watch, briefly acknowledged the salute of the waiting officer, walked down the hedge-lined lane on the outskirts of Lemont. 12.45 a.m. Less than four hours to dawn. The lights of an armoured car at the end of the lane showed him the way while beyond the hedge on his left, to the north, the light of the moon shone down over the flooded areas, a vast lake which might have been the sea. When he reached the car he stopped and turned to the officer who had followed him.

'So here it is, Keller – the start-line of the final advance. It doesn't look much from here, does it?'

The lights of the armoured car beamed north across a flooded field below the level of the lane. Water stretched as far as the eye could see towards Dunkirk, but standing up above the surface of the lake ran a double line of six-foot poles like slim telegraph poles immersed by the inundation.

'Keller, how far do the marker posts stretch?'

'Ten kilometres, sir. We felt it inadvisable to mark the passage any further at the moment.'

'Quite right, Keller, quite right.'

Storch paused, slapping his gloves slowly against the side of his leg. He was in an excellent humour and when this mood took him he liked to show his subordinates that their general was capable of a certain light-hearted touch.

'So, Keller, you are telling me that between those posts lies the road to Dunkirk – that we do not have to possess supernatural powers like Christ to walk upon the waters?'

Keller, a religious man, as Storch knew well, blinked and stirred uneasily. What could be in Storch's mind now? He kept his face expressionless and answered with admirable brevity.

'Yes, sir.'

Keller waited anxiously. He was never quite sure how to deal with the situation when Storch talked like this for it was closely akin to another mood which could be the precursor to an almighty row. He said nothing further and waited while the general walked to the front of the armoured car, standing to gaze for a moment through the gap in the hedge. Then, without warning, Storch marched forward between the posts, his boots splashing up water but never sinking more than six inches below the waterline. He walked on and on, almost out of sight, and then came back again, deliberately kicking up great spurts of water like a small child on its first day by the sea. Reaching the armoured car, he paused and lifted his night glasses to look the other way, focusing his gaze to the south where a line of heavy tanks was drawn up along the extension of the road on higher ground. Beyond the tanks he could see the small airfield which was serving as the main tank laager and beyond the groups of small dark shapes loomed the hangar, the main ammunition dump. Meyer had once again complained that everything was crammed into too confined an area but the floods had dictated that. At that moment Keller had the misfortune to say the wrong thing.

'I hear, sir, that the main dump is very close the laager.'

'You'd like to move it, Keller?' Storch inquired.

'No, sir. I just thought ... that is ... Colonel Meyer ...'

'Meyer has been here recently?'

'Only a few minutes – to check the water level ...'

'Really, Keller, it is most fortunate for you that I have only wet my boots. Had the water risen to my thighs we might well have had to look for your replacement. Till 04.00 hours, Keller!'

Barnes rubbed his eyes and checked his watch. 12.45 a.m. The tank rumbled along the side road, its lights full on, the tracks churning round at top speed. In the turret beside him Jacques warned that they were approaching the southern outskirts of Lemont. The French lad knew exactly where he was and now he felt strangely excited as the road he had known since boyhood rolled past under them. He had chosen a roundabout route to enter the village and Barnes had asked him to find a place where they could park Bert safely for a short time. He thought he knew just the place.

Inside the tank Colburn sat behind the two-pounder in Davis' old seat. A loaded machine-pistol lay across his lap and already he was becoming accustomed to the small metal room, the gentle sway of the hull, the endless grumble of the tracks. He missed the fresh air of five thousand feet up but at least here he had solid ground under his body. Oddly enough, now that they were so close to the battle zone the thunder of the guns had died, as though preserving their energies – and their ammunition – for one final effort when day came. And daylight was close now. But he was on edge because he had nothing definite to do, and in this respect he envied Reynolds. The driver in the nose of the tank had his head projecting above the hatch and gazed stolidly forward. His hands held the steering levers stiffly because his arms felt as though they were on fire and even the slightest movement increased the pain. They were almost there, Barnes had said, and Reynolds was anxious to get it over with. Now that they were so close to the Allied lines and that Dover was just across the water he found himself thinking of England and home. With a bit of luck they'd soon be there. He'd be able to get some leave and go back to Peckham. A pint of bitter at The Grey Horse. It made him feel thirsty and then he

forgot about it as Barnes' voice came down the intercom with a fresh instruction.

'You turn left,' Jacques had just told Barnes, 'just
beyond that white building.'

Barnes gave the order. 'And that farm you mentioned, Jacques, those isolated outhouses . . .'

He broke off as the tank turned down a narrow
track. At the edge of the headlights he could see a
strangely familiar shape, and when the track curved
the beams played full on the bulky silhouette. Barnes
stiffened and as Jacques pointed to the farm buildings
beyond an open gateway he gave the order to halt.
The stationary vehicle which had startled him was
tilted over at an acute angle, lying just inside the field
with one track caught in a deep ditch. It was Bert's
twin brother – a Matilda tank. Jumping to the ground
he walked towards it, hearing Colburn's footsteps
behind him. When he played his torch over the tank
he saw that it was derelict, half the turret blown away,
its right-hand track torn loose, the rear of the hull
burnt black.

'Looks like one of yours,' Colburn suggested
quietly.

'It's one of ours all right. There's been a helluva
scrap here. Look.'

In the field behind the tank uniformed bodies lay
scattered across the grass, on their stomachs, on their
backs, on their sides, and sometimes the uniforms
were German but many were British and all dead.

Barnes picked up several rifles and found them empty. There was only one tank, the single Matilda, and in its solitude it seemed to emphasize the terrible shortage of armoured forces with the BEF.

'The Panzers came through,' he remarked to Colburn, who made no reply.

They walked farther down the track and by the gateway they found more empty rifles, British .303s, their dead owners lying close by. Barnes followed his torch beam cautiously into a yard surrounded by outbuildings and when they searched them they found that the place was deserted – deserted of human life but there were several British fifteen-hundredweight trucks parked round the edges of the yard which had obviously been some minor transport depot. Inside the buildings were more trucks and further evidence that a unit had been in residence recently – a pile of unwashed billy cans, a dixie full of scummy water, several respirators and a Lewis gun without a magazine.

'I'd like to have another look at that truck in there,' said Colburn, flashing his torch on a truck with an RE flash at the rear.

'I'll be back in a minute. I want to get Bert parked.'

Barnes left the Canadian and explored the area immediately round the buildings, finding only empty fields which were strangely still and silent in the pale warm moonlight, the air heavy and muggy as the earth released the heat of yesterday, the buzz of unseen insects in his ears. Across the fields he could see a roof-line which looked as though it had been cut from cardboard – the roofs of Lemont – and behind them a solitary searchlight wearily probed the sky. When he returned to where he had left the Canadian he found him inside the truck which carried the RE flash. He was shining his torch over layers of wooden boxes.

'I want to do a recce into Lemont on foot from here,' Barnes told him. 'Jacques has agreed to take me in so I'm leaving you and Reynolds with the tank. This is a better pláce than I thought we'd get to park Bert – the Germans are hardly likely to come poking around a place where there's already been a dust-up and this stuff's no use to them. It's only a handful of bits and pieces, anyway.'

'There's more than a handful of these, Barnes. You know what they are, of course – detonators. There's enough stuff here to blow up half Ottawa – including gun-cotton, a plunger, and God knows what else. This truck belonged to a demolition unit.'

'For God's sake mind what you're doing, then ... Sorry, I'd forgotten. Detonators are your business.'

Barnes sat down on an old wooden crate pushed against the wall and tried to think straight. His shoulder wound had been playing him foully ever since he had crashed back into the trank transporter when he was trying to reach the deck from the cab. It was pounding like an iron hammer now and he wondered whether he had the energy to walk one step farther. Well, he'd have to walk quite a few steps farther if they were going to try and find out what the position was inside Lemont, and Jacques had blithely told him the best thing would be to try and reach his father. The fact that his father lived in a house in the main part of the village on top of a small hill overlooking some private airfield, and that this meant a long walk from where they were now, hadn't seemed to worry Jacques, but it worried Barnes when he thought of them making their way through enemy-held streets. He made the effort and was walking out to give instructions to Reynolds when he stopped in the doorway in surprise. Colburn was whistling under his breath, a tuneless melody. Colburn was in his element as he explored more boxes.

'Barnes, there's wire here – there's even some phosphorus. This goodamned truck is one huge potential bomb . . .'

'Well, we shan't be needing any bombs,' Barnes replied, his voice edged with irritation.

'Can't understand the bastards leaving this lot unguarded.'

'They haven't got enough men to guard their own stuff according to Jacques.'

'This I could really do something with, Barnes. I haven't had my hands on such a hoard since I joined the RAF. If I'd bumped into this outfit instead of your own mob I could really have earned my daily bread. And say, look you here . . .'

Barnes wasn't too interested in Colburn's enthusiasms and the Canadian's burst of energy seemed to underline his own state of desperate fatigue to an extent which made him feel more irritable than ever. He spoke quickly.

'I'm off with Jacques now. Reynolds is staying with Bert next door so you'll have someone to chat to.'

'I'm quite happy here. You're going to Jacques's father's place?'

'I doubt if we'll get that far.'

'The old boy might know what's what. And watch yourself – we don't want any nasty accidents now we're at the end of the line.'

'That's right. So for Pete's sake, Colburn, don't drop one of those detonators.'

Barnes checked his watch, Penn's watch. 2.25 a.m. Ninety minutes to dawn. The recce was completed and they were almost home, if you could call 'home' three outbuildings they had never known before, one of them stuffed with high-explosive. He looked back along the silent street and saw Jacques a long way behind him – Jacques who was still a problem because the village of Lemont was abandoned, all the inhabitants either evacuated or driven away by the Germans when the tide of war had rolled this way. The lad waved a hand and pointed ahead, an unnecessary precaution because Barnes was already trying to locate the German sentry they had skirted on their way in. He had been standing on guard outside a small single-storey house where light had shown round the edges of drawn blinds. On the outskirts of Lemont all the houses were single storey and this was the only house which had shown any sign of life in the deserted tree-lined street. Who was hidden behind those drawn blinds? And where was that damned sentry now? The empty motor cycle and side-car was still parked in front of the house.

He took several cautious steps forward again and halted. He could still see the light round the blinds but the sentry had vanished. It worried Barnes and he glanced back again to make sure that the lad was still behind him. Jacques opened his hands to express puzzlement and Barnes knew that he also had spotted the sentry's absence. The only thing to do was to go round the back way as they had before, but cautiously. He held up a warning hand to indicate to Jacques that he should stay well back and then he crept forward, turning down a path which led between the houses.

His nerves were keyed up tautly, his mind oscillating between two impulses – the need for caution on the last lap and the need to move quickly because they were running out of time just when he had found his supreme objective. The path was bordered with shoulder-high stone walls and he knew that when the path turned at the bottom the walls continued along the backs of the houses. Keeping his head down, his revolver in his hand, he crept past a closed gate let into the wall. He was concentrating on placing his feet carefully because he remembered that there was a deep ditch on the left. Perhaps he heard something at the last moment. He might even have started to turn his head, but he could never remember the details afterwards. A rifle butt struck his head with such vicious force that he lost consciousness immediately . . .

When he woke up he knew that he was going to be sick, but he forced it down into the churning pit of his stomach. His wound ached abominably but now the pounding hammer was at work inside his head, and because it felt hollow he seemed to receive each blow twice as the blows echoed. Get a grip on yourself, man. With an immense effort he forced open eyelids which felt to be made of lead. A blinding light hit him, so he closed them quickly. A voice spoke, gutturally. In English.

'So pleased you are recovering, Sergeant Barnes.'

Barnes jerked his eyes open a fraction and peered through slitted lids. From behind the lamp a uniformed arm appeared and lowered the light cone so that it shone on to the desk. The arm belonged to a thin-faced man of about thirty who wore the uniform of a German officer. Glancing round the darkened room Barnes could see no sign of Jacques; the French lad must have escaped into the village during the ambush.

'Tell me when you are ready to speak,' the German suggested.

Barnes swore inwardly. He was seated in a high-backed wooden chair and his wrists were bound with wire to the arms. When he tried to shift his body surreptitiously he felt a broad band strapped round his waist; only his legs were still free. They had sewed him up nicely. Another uniformed officer appeared from behind his chair and like his colleague behind the desk he was wearing his peaked cap. He spread pine needles along the desk under the cone of light, arranging them carefully in varying lengths, apparently taking no notice of Barnes while he completed his little display. Barnes gritted his teeth, wondering whether the prelude to torture was a bluff to sap his nerves. The officer behind the desk.

'I am Major Berg. You, of course, are Sergeant Barnes.' He lifted a British Army pay-book off the desk and waved it. 'And if you are wondering why I speak such good English it is since I was military attaché in London before the war.' His voice changed and he spoke rapidly, his manner bleak. 'Barnes, where is your unit and from where will the British be attacking us in the rear?'

Barnes said it. Name, rank, serial number. Then he shut his mouth. He opened it a moment later when the officer who had been bending over the desk swung the stiffened side of his hand savagely across Barnes' lips. He felt something give inside his mouth, felt around with his tongue, tasted blood, and spat out a broken tooth. Through half-closed eyes he saw Berg shake his head as though cautioning his fellow officer.

'I should have introduced you,' Berg went on. 'This is Captain Dahlheim. Normally our method is to ask questions politely first and then exert pressure later, but we are short of hours. I should warn you that Captain Dahlheim becomes annoyed when people do not answer my questions properly.'

Barnes said it again. Name, rank, serial number, adding that under the Geneva Convention this was all the information he was obliged to give. Dahlheim was fiddling with the pine needles now and while his body temporarily masked him from Berg, Barnes lifted his wrists hard against the wire. It was quite impossible to get his hands loose.

'But you are a spy,' went on the unseen Berg. 'Show him the clothes he was wearing when we found him.'

Dahlheim picked up a bundle from a chair and showed the clothes. For a horrible moment Barnes wondered whether they belonged to Jacques but he saw that they were a jacket and a pair of trousers of blue denim, common apparel for French workers in the fields. Jacques had worn a lounge suit. He must have escaped.

'I've never worn those in my life and you know it.'

'Captain Dahlheim can confirm that we took those clothes off you while you were still unconscious. We can say you wore them to hide your uniform. And you had no means of identification. No pay-book.' He dropped the pay-book into a drawer and closed it. 'So you are a spy and can be treated in any way we like.'

Was Berg bluffing? Barnes could see his white face now and as he became accustomed to the single desk light he thought the German was older than he had thought at first. He felt sick with fury. He had been on the last lap, had completed the most difficult reconnaissance he had ever undertaken, had been within a five-minute walk of Bert's refuge, and because of a momentary lack of alertness he had been captured. And as the realization dawned on him, the realization of how unlikely it was that he would ever escape, he found one thought torturing his mind. He had come to Lemont because the battle plan they had taken from the German staff car showed beyond doubt that here was the point of maximum peril for the BEF. And now he believed that he had found a way of striking a blow against the 14th Panzer Division, the spearhead of the attack on Dunkirk, only to find himself a prisoner. What was it Berg was saying?'

'We have not a great deal of time, Sergeant Barnes.'

'None of us have that here.'

'For various reasons it is a matter of urgency that you answer my questions quickly. What is your unit? What is the British plan?' He paused. 'Dahlheim! Barnes is not going to reply again.'

Dahlheim straightened up and turned round. The needles were arranged in a neat row, their sharp points turned towards Barnes under the cone of light. Beneath the peaked cap Dahlheim's face was round, his eyes seeming half asleep, and for the first time Barnes saw that he wore a black and silver collar-patch bearing a curious runic sign. Captain Dahlheim was a member of the SS.

By now Barnes found that his eyes were growing

accustomed to the semi-darkness beyond the cone of light and behind the seated Berg he could see a window. The curtain was drawn across it but at one side there was a gap, and because of the deep shadow beyond the desk light he could see a wedge of moonlit night. Dahlheim was reaching his hand to his side and Barnes expected him to draw the pistol from his leather hip holster, but instead he took a length of cord from his pocket and wrapped it round both hands. He took his time over this little exercise, watching Barnes carefully, then without speaking he went past the chair and disappeared behind it. Guessing what was coming, Barnes tensed himself.

Reynolds could see the sentry standing outside the small house and he also saw the stationary motor cycle and side-car close by. It was the first sign of life he had seen since entering the village. He took several quiet paces away from the road down a pathway between stone walls. Now he was well under cover, two houses away from where the sentry mounted guard. For a minute he stood there, undecided what to do. It was probably the first time in his Army career that he had performed these two actions and both of them worried him – he had disobeyed an order and he had taken an initiative without reference to any superior. He kept wondering whether he ought not to go back.

Barnes had specifically told him to stay with the

tank and now Bert was a good five minutes' walk away. Only an overwhelming feeling that something had happened to Barnes had prompted his action and he had firmly refused Colburn's offer to come instead. A pilot's place was in the air – they weren't much good on the ground, Reynolds had reasoned to himself. Now his great dread was that he had missed Barnes and Jacques coming back and that already his sergeant was asking Colburn where the devil Reynolds was. He'd better go back, he decided, but not along the road – that was far too dangerous. There must be another way back along the rear of these houses. Yes, he'd go back immediately. Barnes was able to look after himself.

He reached the end of the wall and lifted his head cautiously. Light from a window two houses away spilled out into the night. It must be some sort of German HQ, a good place to keep away from. He started retreating along the footpath which ran behind the back garden wall and then looked over his shoulder. The light puzzled him. Perhaps he'd better check: Barnes might want to know who was there. In for a penny, in for a pound, as his father was fond of saying. Keeping his head well down, he crept along the back wall, counting gates. This must be the right one. The gate wasn't quite closed and when he pushed it gently it swung back inwards without making a sound. The vague outline of the lighted window was broken up by the branches of fruit trees which stood in the garden. He listened carefully and peered round the end wall to look along another pathway which led back to the road. If the sentry decided to walk up there while he was inside the garden he would be nicely trapped. In for a penny . . .

Creeping down a garden path he reached the back of the house close to the window and saw that there was a gap in the curtain. Ten-to-one the people inside would be staring straight at the window when he looked in, but he felt he must see what was going on, so he pressed one hand against the wall, eased himself forward, caught a quick glimpse and stepped back. He had glanced inside at the moment when Dahlheim had walked behind Barnes' chair. He had seen his sergeant helpless, the only time he had ever seen Barnes in this state, and for a few seconds he was stunned, but his mood swiftly changed to one of fury.

He went back up the garden, out of the gateway, down the pathway between the houses, his hand extracting the knife from its sheath, a knife which he had carefully honed to a razor's edge, the point like a needle, the condition in which an ex-fishmonger was prone to keep his knives. At the end of the path he waited behind the wall and listened to the sentry's footsteps. The German must have become bored with standing and now he paced a steady sentry-go – ten paces away, ten paces back again. While he listened Reynolds remembered a certain guard duty he had mounted late one night at a remote camp outside Hull. Alone in the dark, he had particularly disliked the moment when he had stopped to turn, still keeping step as he revolved through one hundred and eighty degrees, and this was the moment he was waiting for now.

The sentry was coming his way again. Eight, nine, ten . . . Leaving the safety of the wall Reynolds moved with a terrible determination, seeing the back of the German only six feet away. His hand rose above shoulder level and with the same movement he crept forward three quiet paces, driving the knife savagely down into the uniformed back. He felt it shearing through cloth, driving down deeper, jerking briefly as it grazed bone and then sank deeper still. The back fell away from him and the sentry let out one howling shriek. Reynolds was sure half the street had heard the sound as he bent over to grab the rifle and fixed bayonet, tearing the strap loose from the limp arm.

His reactions now were an echo of his early basic training – taking up the rifle, one hand gripping the stock, the other stretched well along the barrel as he grasped it close to the bayonet. He was running full pelt for the front door when it opened in his face, revealing a uniformed figure. Dahlheim held a Luger pistol in his hand but before he could press the trigger Reynolds was on him, his headlong rush carrying the bayonet deep into Dahlheim's stomach. He groaned and went over backwards, carried to the floor by the still-moving impetus of Reynolds' violent charge. Automatically, the driver stood a foot on the sprawled body and used it as leverage to withdraw the bayonet with one quick hard pull, his eyes searching the room beyond.

When they heard the sentry's awful cry Dahlheim had just gripped Barnes round the neck. At Berg's instant command he had taken out his Luger and rushed to the front door, opening it as Berg came round the side of the desk, his own gun already in his hand. Barnes heard Dahlheim's horrible groan while Berg was passing him. Shooting out his left leg, he caught the German between his own legs and tripped him. Berg was on the floor when Barnes flung his whole weight sideways, carrying himself and the chair over on top of Berg, the fall smashing the left chair arm so that his wrist was immediately released still encircled with wire. He was half on top of Berg, still tied inside the chair as he raised his left fist and clubbed him viciously in the face. Then the chair slipped and took him over farther sideways so that now he was lying on the floor trapped by the chair behind him. He saw Berg blink, spit blood from his mouth where the fist had broken teeth, and then he raised the revolver which he still held and aimed it point-blank in Barnes' face. Anchored to the floor by the heavy chair, just too far away to get at Berg, even in that moment of terror Barnes was aware of movement above him and then the rifle butt in Reynold's grip smashed down on Berg's head with a terrible impact. The hand fell back with a thud to the floor and the Luger slipped from the hand as it went slack.

'Good work, Reynolds.' Barnes gasped out the trite phrase automatically and just as automatically thought of Dahlheim. 'Make sure of that other bastard.'

'He's finished. Keep still while I get your hand free.'

'Smash the support off under the chair arm with your rifle butt and then I can slip my wrist off. Go on, man, we're hellishly short of time.'

They could hear Dahlheim groaning continually behind them as Reynolds aimed the rifle butt carefully, destroying the wooden support under the chair arm so that Barnes could slip his wrist off the end. Then he pressed the wire bracelets down over his hands while Reynolds unfastened the leather belt which bound him to the chair. Barnes had his back to Dahlheim but he could still hear the agonized moans of the SS officer, the clumping of his shoes on the floor. The moment he was released he swung round and instantly shouted a warning. Dahlheim was turned over on one side clutching his left hand to his stomach, a hand covered with blood, his face twisted almost out of recognition with the pain, but his right hand had found the pistol. At the moment when Barnes shouted the gun went off.

Dahlheim had fired at random, Barnes felt sure of it because the barrel had been wobbling all over the place. Two more shots entered the ceiling and then the gun fell harmlessly on the floor. Jerking his head round as the pistol skidded against the wall, Barnes looked up and saw Reynolds topple, an expression of amazed disbelief on his large face as he fell and hit the floor with a tremendous crash. Groggily, Barnes climbed to his feet and his legs nearly gave way under him as he picked up the rifle, wobbled forward, and took up a position behind Dahlheim who was now rolling on the floor. He managed to lift the weapon several feet and bring it down again. Even in his weakened state the force of the blow was so great that the rifle jumped out of his hands and fell beside the now motionless German. Kicking the rifle away against the wall he picked up the pistol which still held five cartridges and pushed it down inside his own empty holster, wondering what the devil they had done with his own gun.

'Reynolds!'

He had a terrible job turning the driver over and then Reynolds began stirring and cursing foully. There was plenty of blood on his left thigh but on making a quick examination Barnes found that the bullet had passed through without lodging in the flesh. He applied a field dressing he always carried and managed to seat the driver in Berg's chair, an operation which took away nearly all his remaining strength. Inwardly he was swearing. Of all the bloody bad luck. Davis killed by the accident of falling rock. Penn shot down by an envenomed looter. And now Reynolds wounded by a wobbling hand that had hardly been able to hold the gun, let alone aim the bloody thing.

Then his eyes fell on his watch. When the chair had gone over sideways the face had been smashed in the fall and the hands had stopped at 2.40 a.m.

He stood by the desk for a moment, looking down at Reynolds' haggard face, his thoughts torn and muddled between his wounded driver and the knowledge that within eighty minutes the Panzers he had seen with Jacques from the ridge above the airfield would be on the move, creeping along the underwater road which the French lad had pointed towards. He pulled himself together, refusing to give way to the fatigue clogging his limbs. Think, Barnes, there are things to do.

He opened Berg's drawer to collect his pay-book, found his own revolver inside, still loaded, and substituted it for the German's gun.

Reynolds suddenly became talkative and told his sergeant to leave him there since he couldn't possibly walk or drive. But Barnes just nodded, went to the front door and looked carefully along the silent street. He wasted several precious minutes dragging the dead sentry's body inside the house, but if a patrol came along he didn't want the alarm raised if it could be avoided. Dropping the body next to Dahlheim's he took a deep breath and began the intricate manoeuvre of hoisting the driver on to his back. Bent double under the great weight, hearing Reynold's feet trailing on the floor, he staggered out of the house and wrestled him inside the side-car while his burden protested that the noise of the engine would give them away. Without replying, Barnes went back into the house, switched off the desk light and came out again, closing the door behind him.

The starting of the motor cycle seemed a louder noise than any he had ever heard, but he had made up his mind – he must find a safer place to park Reynolds. The street was still deserted as he drove away from Lemont and reached the outbuildings, cutting the engine quickly and calling out to warn Colburn who emerged from behind a wall with a machine-pistol at the ready. They made Reynolds as comfortable as possible by sitting him on some straw inside one of the buildings – Barnes was determined that this time he would take no wounded crew member on what might be Bert's final journey. And, he thought grimly, for this journey his crew was now reduced to two – himself and Colburn.

At 3.20 a.m. they were ready to move, but only because they had worked like Trojans. Barnes looked up at Colburn who now occupied his own position inside the turret – the tank commander himself was going to have to drive Bert on his last trip.

'You really think it will work, Colburn?'

'It's more likely to than your idea of firing shells into the dump. That way there's no guarantee at all that you'll get a major explosion, but you can bet your sweet life that when this lot goes it'll lift the whole dump sky-high – just supposing we ever get close enough and just suppose we don't go up before we get there. If we do, they won't have any burial problems with us. Just look down there – this tank is one ruddy great bomb.'

The floor of the turntable at the base of the turret had been tightly packed with gun-cotton slabs and to this lethal foundation Colburn had added a quantity of instantaneous detonating fuses, several cans of petrol, a quantity of phosphorus and some grenades he had found in a satchel. The remaining grenades were still in the satchel hanging from the top of the turret where he could reach them easily. Even closer to hand was the plunger mechanism and a large spool of wire. Colburn pointed to the plunger.

'And just supposing, Barnes, that we do get a chance to get clear of the tank before this lot goes up . . .'

'Don't bet on that, Colburn.'

'Hell, I'm not betting on a damned thing. But just supposing you're on your own then, don't forget to take the coil of wire as well as the plunger with you. The wire's paid out through the gun slit so you can ram the lid shut – ramming the lid shut is important because it locks everything inside and increases the power of the explosion quite a bit . . .'

'We've got to get moving, Colburn.'

'For Christ's sake, I know I'm telling you twice but it may save your life. Before you press the plunger you must turn this switch. This device is as harmless as a kitten until you do turn the switch. Come to think of it, Barnes, I reckon we've got rather too many "supposings" in this equation.'

'We've also got seventy two-pounder shells and ten boxes of Besa ammunition to pep up the explosion.'

'I know. I just hope I'm around when that lot goes up – it will be the crowning blow-up of my career to date. When I say "around" I do mean at the very end of that paid-out wire,' he added.

'We'd better get moving, Colburn. I've a nasty idea we're too late already with fiddling around with your little toy. You'll have to handle all the observation and talk to me over the intercom. Think you can manage?'

'Damn sight better than I'd manage driving Bert. OK. As the bomber crew guys say, this is the final run-in.'

'Which is pretty appropriate since it's a mobile bomb we've got for delivery to General Storch.'

Three minutes later the tank was moving through the village at full speed, its headlights ablaze, rumbling down the deserted street like an avenging phantom. It was their only chance, Barnes felt sure of that – to press forward as though they owned the place in the same way that Mandel had described the advance of the Panzers across France. And it was their one advantage – the element of total surprise, an element which must be rammed home ruthlessly right up to the moment when they reached the airfield, if they ever did reach it. The appearance of a tank in the early hours with its lights full on must cause a reaction of doubt, of indecision, for at least a few vital seconds, and in that time Bert should pass any patrol they might encounter. It was all a question of how soon they ran up against the big stuff.

They were moving past the house where Reynolds had saved him, he felt sure of it, although his vision was limited and he was relying heavily on Colburn's guidance over the intercom. The driver's seat was closed to its lowest level and the hood over his head was shut, sealing him off from the outside world so that his only view was through the slit window in front. Four inches of bullet-proof glass protected that slit while 70 millimetres of armour-plate shielded him from shell-fire – the thickest plate covered the front hull – so theoretically he was fairly safe. Unless the tank caught fire and when he rolled back the hood he found the two-pounder barrel pointed straight ahead and depressed to its lowest elevation, in which case the barrel would form a steel bar preventing him from climbing out at all while the tank burned. Cynical drivers said that was why the driver was issued with a revolver – to give him an easier way out than frying alive. Why the hell am I thinking like this, Barnes wondered? Perhaps only now he was really appreciating what poor Reynolds had gone through.

He hoped that if it really came to it, Colburn did know how to use a Mills hand grenade. The Canadian had told him that a British staff sergeant had demonstrated their use on a bombing range and Barnes could imagine Colburn taking a great interest in how the mechanism worked. Still . . .

'Barnes,' Colburn's voice came clearly over the one-way intercom. 'We're approaching a square and from that sketchmap you drew me we go straight over, but there may be a problem – I can see light. Keep moving. I'll keep you in touch.'

Up in the turret Colburn stared anxiously ahead. The lights shone through some trees in an open square surrounded with two-storey houses and the beams were stationary. He couldn't see any sign of troops, any hint of danger, just those lights coming through the trees. Barnes had told him that as far as he had been able to make out when he reconnoitred the village with Jacques the place had been evacuated of civilians, which would be logical since the Germans were using it as a forward base. They had penetrated as far as the house of Jacques's father and he had not been at home. So any sign of life was likely to be hostile life. The square, apparently deserted, came closer and Colburn moved from side to side as he tried to see behind the trees. There was something there, then he saw them.

'Barnes. A couple of motor cycles and side-cars at the edge of this square. They've got lights on but there doesn't seem to be anyone about . . .'

Barnes coaxed a little more speed from the engine, staring along his headlight beams which now stretched across the small square to the street beyond.

He sat wedged in between the boxes of detonators which were stacked on either side and the proximity of so much explosive wasn't a comfortable feeling, but he had insisted on loading these spare boxes to increase the power of the bomb. Now he wondered whether he had overdone it. Highly unstable, British detonators, Colburn had said. The Germans used Trotyl, which was far less temperamental. And Colburn was a man who should know. They were half-way across the square now and subconsciously he was listening for the first sound of Colburn's voice, because if he spoke now that would mean trouble. The avenue of darkness ahead moved towards him and then they left the square and the beams stabbed along a straight street. Colburn's voice was tense.

'They came out just as we left the square – a couple of Germans. They stopped and stared for a few seconds and then ran for one of the bikes.'

Barnes gazed ahead. It was starting already. There was a turning down to the left he had to negotiate soon and that would mean reducing speed a lot, and this was the last moment they should be slowing down if one of those motorcycles was after them. He wished to God that the intercom was two-way, that he could warn Colburn to watch the man in the side-car, the one who would be carrying a machine-pistol. Colburn's voice again.

'The cycle is following us down this street. I know there's a left turn soon but keep up your speed. Don't worry, I'll handle it.'

Colburn was really worried. He looked back to where the lights of the oncoming cycle were closing the gap rapidly. He realized the danger to himself perched up in the turret – if the cycle was allowed to come close enough the man in the side-car would blast his head off with the machine-pistol he had seen him running with. He took one grenade out of the satchel and then he took another, laying the second one behind the plunger box where it couldn't roll: it wasn't an action that many would have taken but to Colburn the box was dead until the switch was turned. He also glanced down inside the turret towards the bed of gun-cotton. Don't drop this little feller down there, he told himself. He had his finger inside the ring-head of the pin now. Get it right, Colburn: allow for the tank's speed and the onrush of the cycle. And get it good. You're pitching the ball at Toronto. Removing bomb from pin, he counted. One, two three, four. He threw. Without waiting, his hand whipped over the second grenade, inserting his finger. Withdraw. Count. He had his head down as the first grenade blew only feet in front of the Germans. A hard lethal crack split the street. The flash lit the walls and the cycle climbed, taking the side-car with it, wheels spinning futilely, the side-car ripping away from the cycle. He threw the second one from inside the turret, just to get rid of it now that it was no longer needed, and by the flash of the second bomb he saw a shadowed wreck in the street behind it. Even the lights had gone. He let out his breath and the sound travelled down the intercom to Barnes.

'Got them.'

Colburn leant back against the turret and wiped sweat off his hands on his flying suit. He had shot men out of the air but this was different. He had caught a brief glimpse of the man in the side-car pitching out head first towards the ground and he was amazed it was all over so quickly. He had been very frightened for those few minutes, so frightened that he had made a bad mistake in not wiping his hand earlier – that second grenade had nearly slipped, had nearly gone down inside the turret. The very thought of it made him sweat again but now it was all over he felt enormously relieved, relieved that he was still alive. And this was a mere bagatelle, a single motor cycle and side-car. What faced them somewhere just ahead would be on a far bigger scale. The headlights played on a distant wall with wording painted on the plaster. Restaurant de la Gare. He spoke quickly into the mike.

'That building's coming up – the restaurant place. Prepare to turn left. I'll guide you.'

Barnes was already reducing speed and he began turning very slowly, his hands an extension of Colburn's instructions as they eased Bert round. The turning was sharp and almost at once they moved on to a downward slope of cobbles. He had to crawl round, edging his way as Colburn leaned out of the turret to check wall clearance, talking down the intercom all the time. They nearly scraped the right-hand wall, then they were round the corner, the tank straightening up and proceeding down the cobbled street, its metal tracks grinding and clattering over the stones. That was close, Colburn was thinking, but we managed it nicely between us. He peered along the beams, still savouring the sensation of relief, wondering how Barnes was feeling.

Inside the nose of the tank Barnes was experiencing a rather different sensation – Barnes was in serious trouble and he wondered whether they had a dog's chance of making it as a chill of fear seeped through him. *One of the detonator boxes had broken loose.* It had happened on that last bend while he was struggling grimly to negotiate the corner and allow for the drop in street level. They were almost round the turning when he felt a heavy blow strike his right shoulder. Still in the process of taking Bert round the corner he only had time for a quick glance sideways and this showed him the heavy box projecting well beyond the one it rested on, kept stable now only by the obstacle of his own body. As he moved down the hill, the tank wobbling slightly as it rumbled over the cobbles, he tried to ease the box back into position with his shoulder. The action nearly made him jump out of his seat as pain from the maltreated wound screamed through his body, stabbing at his brain. For one terrible second he thought he was going to faint. He bit down on his lips to drive away the dizziness and reopened the cut in his mouth, tasting his own blood for the second time that night. The heavy box was pressing against his shoulder all the time and there wasn't a thing he could do about it, except to pray that at the next right-hand turn the box would regain its balance. Was he still driving straight? The forced himself to concentrate on the view through the slit window.

'Barnes, I can see the canal embankment beyond the bottom of this street, so we're on the right road. And we turn right in a minute.'

Barnes had been waiting for that right-hand turn but he knew that with both hands occupied with the steering levers his shoulder was still going to have to bear the brunt of shoving that box back against the wall. Would he be able to stand the pain; Colburn's voice again, a voice edged with tension, the sure sign of further trouble.

'Something coming up . . . a soldier in a doorway, a sentry, I think. Keep moving at this speed – we'll have to turn in less than a hundred yards . . .'

Colburn ducked his head inside the turret and waited, waited for the challenge, the pause, then the first burst of fire from the machine-pistol the sentry held across his chest. His own machine-pistol was gripped in his hands and he looked upward beyond the open rim of the turret. The tank clattered down over the cobbles, the dark silhouette of irregular rooftops slid past beyond the turret rim, cold specks of starlight glittered distantly in the late night sky. The moon was low now and an early morning chill prickled the back of his neck. Still no sound from the sentry. He couldn't stand it any longer: he peered over the rim. Nothing moving but he thought that he could still see the shadowed figure by the doorway, a motionless figure. It was incredible. Some of his astonishment travelled down the intercom.

'Barnes, he never moved – he never moved. And we're in a British tank.'

It worked, Barnes thought, the element of surprise worked there. Perhaps the sentry hadn't done his homework on tank silhouettes. He might have been posted there from other duties and he was tired out, so when a vehicle came down the streets of German-occupied Lemont with its headlights blazing he assumed that it must be all right. He could even have been asleep on his feet. But the main thing was it had worked once and it could work again. Colburn's voice spoke urgently.

'I can see the embankment clearly now – we're close to the turn. You'll have to watch this one, it's narrow. I'll guide you round . . .'

Barnes reduced his speed close to zero. He remembered this bend and it was the worst one they would have to negotiate. The route they were following had been so simple that he had known exactly where they were ever since leaving the farm building. Once they had entered the village the way had led straight forward down the first street, across the square, continuing along the street beyond up to the first left-handed turn down the hill. At the bottom of the hill they turned right and then it was straight on again by the side road at the foot of the canal embankment. If they could only manage this corner ... They were almost round the sharp turn when it happened. They were moving slowly forward and then there was a terrific jolt and the tank stopped, its engines still ticking over. Barnes had jammed on the brake, warned by the impact and the scraping sound he had heard just before the jarring crash which rammed the detonator box savagely against his shoulder. He struggled against an overwhelming desire to be sick, too shaken to try and thrust the box back while his hands were free. Then he heard Colburn.

'Track's jammed against the left wall. Sorry – my fault. We'll have to get out of here quickly – that sentry has started to walk down the hill. Reverse slowly. We can't go forward.'

Inside the hull Barnes heard the harsh grind of metal plate along immovable wall as he reversed carefully. Then the tank stuck. He grimaced and thought for a few seconds. If they weren't very lucky he could immobilize them. He remembered once seeing a track split and come apart, so that the tank hull moved for a few yards while it splayed out track like unrolling a metal carpet. If that happened they were done for, and there was that little matter of the sentry coming down the hill to investigate. They couldn't go forward so they'd have to go back. Gritting his teeth, he reversed, hearing, feeling, the agonized grind of metal over stone. Then they were free again. And still intact. Colburn guided him round without haste and then they were moving along the next street, the headlights probing its emptiness and desolation. Barnes glanced at his watch, the one he had borrowed from Colburn. 3.30 a.m.

Up in the turret Colburn put the revolver back on the ledge next to the plunger box and wiped both his hands dry. The revolver had seemed a more appropriate weapon for one sentry. Taking a last look back at the dangerous corner he concentrated on observing the view ahead, issuing occasional instructions to keep Barnes in the dead centre of the street, his mind chilled. On his right a row of two-storey houses ran down the side of the street as a continuous wall, the upper-floor windows just above the level of his turret. To his left ran the high embankment of the unseen canal, a steep-sloped embankment at least twenty feet high which closed off the view across open fields. Ahead lay the street, a canyon of shadow, apparently deserted, the forward movement of the beams exposing only empty road. It seemed quite uncanny and as the tank ground forward Colburn found his nerves screwing up to an almost unbearable pitch of tension. Within the next few minutes they were bound to run into something very big.

Barnes was experiencing the same emotion, as far as he could experience anything beyond the mounting pain which gripped his whole body. The tenderness of the shoulder wound was almost unendurable now as the side of the detonator box sagged against him, a relentless pain which should have obscured all others, but he could still feel the aching bruise on top of his head where the German sentry had knocked him out and the back of his burnt left hand felt strangely disembodied, as though it might float off the end of his arm. And over it all flooded a tidal wave of fatigue which threatened to drown his mind, a wave held back more by pain than by any effort of will.

Another part of his mind mechanically operated the steering levers and the two control pedals – the gear-box clutch pedal on the left and the accelerator on the right. There was a hill in front of them, a hill which rose almost level with the embankment then a steady drop with a side turning off to the right, then another hill beyond that . . .

Colburn's voice was taut. 'We're running alongside the canal embankment now – there's a line of houses on the right. Still no sign of trouble.'

Which was exactly how Barnes was visualizing it. Had they got away with it? Already they were driving along this road at the very edge of Lemont – the village ended abruptly at the embankment and beyond there was open country. Jacques had told him that it was very much of a side road, which was why they had reconnoitred along this route. And now they had left behind what Barnes had anticipated might well be the grimmest part of their journey – the dash through the village. What lay ahead didn't bear thinking about but it almost looked as though they might reach the airfield. In his mind's eye he saw the lie of the land ahead. They had come in one way, along this road to the empty house of Jacques's father, and then for safety's sake they had come back across the fields on the far side of the embankment ... He heard the shot, one single report. Then another.

Colburn had been striving to watch all ways at once – the road ahead, the road behind, the line of two-storey houses to his right and the silhouette of the high embankment which showed more clearly now against a faint glow. Dawn was on the way. He looked for his watch and remembered that he had loaned it to Barnes. The line of the embankment was dropping now as they began to move uphill. He knew that soon he would be able to see across it and he kept reminding himself to keep a sharp eye on those houses. There was no reason to suspect any danger from their darkened windows but they worried him because they were so close and the upper windows looked down on the tank. He picked up the revolver and the weapon gave him a sense of security.

The emergency happened so unexpectedly that it almost took his breath away. A window on an upper floor was flung open and the curtain must have been attached to it: a pool of light flooded out and illuminated the tank below. Colburn looked up and saw a German soldier, his pudding-shaped helmet clearly visible, staring down. He heard him shout, saw him reach back into the room and then lift a machine-pistol. Colburn reacted instantly, raising his revolver, he fired twice. As the tank moved on the German toppled into the garden below.

'Barnes, a Jerry opened a window and spotted us. He was going to shoot but I got in first.' Colburn wished that the damned intercom wasn't simply one-way. It was like talking to a ghost. 'If they've got a phone in the house they'll be all over us soon now. Unless he was alone with a girl. He had his helmet on,' he added with unconscious humour.

Barnes thought of the joke and smiled grimly. He hoped that the German had been with a girl: if that were the case she'd probably try and get a neighbour to dump the body into the convenient canal. Not that it was likely if the village had been evacuated, so they'd better assume a warning was going out. They must be close to the top of this hill now, and close to where he had crossed the canal with Jacques over that huge barge. Was there something wrong? He could have sworn he had heard Colburn suck in his breath. Colburn had sucked in his breath and now he was no longer looking at the houses or at the embankment. He was gazing straight ahead and as they moved over the hill-top his mouth was dry with fear such as he had not known since they started their fateful journey through Lemont.

From his vantage point at the hill crest he could see over the summit of the hill beyond where a chain of headlights moved towards him, an endless chain which threw up a great glow of light behind the next hill summit. He had no doubt at all that he was looking at a column of armoured vehicles advancing down the road they were moving along, probably a column sent for the express purpose of intercepting them. My God, he thought, and I was kidding myself that we might have got away with it. We're finished now, finished.

'Barnes! There's a whole stream of traffic on the road ahead. It's still some distance off but it's coming towards us and we'll meet it in the next few minutes. They're on to us – it must be Panzers, a helluva lot of them.'

Barnes' reaction staggered him. He felt the tank pick up speed as it moved down the hill, the tracks grinding round faster and faster as they rumbled forward at ever-increasing pace as though Barnes couldn't wait to meet the oncoming column in head-on collision. For a moment he thought he had gone mad and then they reached the bottom of the hill and stopped. The headlights went out and Barnes rolled back the hood. He paused for a second while he heaved the detonator box back into position, using both hands to push the case firmly against the side of the hull. Then he jacked up the seat so that when he sat down his head would be above the hatch. He called up to the anxious Colburn.

'How far away are those vehicles?'

'Half a mile, I'd guess. I can't be certain.'

'Maybe only a quarter?'

'No, at least half a mile. Barnes, our lights have gone.'

'I put them out. I don't want to risk them seeing us go up the embankment.'

'Up there?'

Colburn stared in horror up the steep slope which rose twenty feet above them. Had Barnes lost his judgement? He must have decided to make a last stand from the top of the embankment, if they ever got up there. He couldn't have realized the strength of the column which was moving against them. He called down from the turret.

'There must be at least twenty or thirty vehicles heading towards us.'

'Listen, Colburn.' Barnes' voice was urgent. 'We're not going to fight them – we're trying to dodge them. I came back over this canal with Jacques dead opposite this road behind us which leads back into Lemont. We came over a huge barge with a deck like an aircraft carrier – it almost fills the canal. We're going to reverse into this side street until Bert's nose is pointed up that embankment – then up there is where we go.'

'Will the tank make it?'

'I don't know till we try it but it's our only chance. It's close to dawn, so if we don't make it now we never will. When we reach the top there'll be a split second for you to see whether we're driving on to the centre of the barge. I'll be ready to brake, but I can't

382

do that till we're off the slope. You'll have to react damned quickly. Got it?'

'If it's OK to go on, I'll say OK. If it isn't I'll say stop.'

The side road which led off at right-angles to the embankment was wide enough to give ample room for Barnes to reverse into quickly. Then he paused briefly to flex his fingers. Without thinking about the chances against success he went forward, guessing that Colburn thought it was a maniac's last throw, and up in the turret confidence was the last of the emotions which inspired Colburn. He would have liked to look two ways at once – up to the hill crest behind which the armoured column was advancing and straight ahead where the slope loomed like the side of a mountain. Beneath him the tracks began to claw and grind up the gradient as though finding it difficult to hold on to the lower slope and Colburn found himself tilted backwards against the rear of the turret. Barnes seemed to be going up at a fantastic pace. Supposing the barge wasn't in the right position to act as a bridge? Supposing the enemy column poured over the hill crest when they were halfway up the embankment? Grimly he recalled his remark to Barnes just before they had started out. Were there, after all, too many 'supposings' in this equation? I don't think we'll make this one, Colburn told himself.

Barnes had decided, and now he never asked

himself whether or not they could make it. His pain-battered mind was concentrated on one idea only – get Bert over the top. Because the tilt of the tank was longitudinal rather than sideways the detonator boxes were holding their position well, but could they stand up to this sort of treatment? The tank rocked badly as the forward tracks moved into a depression and then climbed out of it, the engines revving madly as Barnes fought to take the tank higher. Very unstable, Colburn had called British detonators, the Germans use Trotyl. The left-hand track sank alarmingly into another depression and the box slipped again, slamming hard against his shoulder, grating its weight into the sensitive wound. He stiffened abruptly, swearing that he would throw out that box if they ever reached the other side, and, knowing that he was approaching the summit, he accelerated.

Colburn was standing upright in the turret now, holding himself erect by grasping the front rim with both hands, because it was vital to see instantly whether they were correctly placed to move across that barge, a barge he couldn't even see yet. But he felt the acceleration and knew that Barnes was going to rush it. Anxiously he leaned farther forward. They reached the top.

'OK, Barnes! OK! OK!'

There it was – the barge. They were going to hit it dead centre. The tank paused, its forward tracks in the air briefly, then dropped level to the tow-path. It moved forward again across a few inches of water and landed in the middle of the flat deck. The barge suddered under the impact of its immense visitor and the tank moved on until it was halfway across the deck. Then the engines stalled.

Colburn forced himself to say nothing. They were now trapped on top of the embankment in full view of the approaching column once it breasted the summit of the hill. He heard Barnes trying again and again to start the engine. Instinctively his eyes swept over the summit of the hill behind which the column was advancing. Nothing yet, but the front of the column must be very close now. He could imagine the scene so clearly – the first heavy tank cresting the hill, spotting them clearly silhouetted against the pale light, wirelessing back to the column, continuing down the hill as more vehicles followed, the barrage of shells aimed point-blank ... He found he was holding his revolver tightly and forced himself to relax his grip. His eyes rested on the plunger below him and then he looked again at the glow of light behind the hill, a glow which seemed to grow stronger every second as Barnes repeated his efforts to start the engines without success. Colburn glanced back the way they had come and the street was still deserted. Who had summoned the armoured column? Probably the owners of the second motor cycle and side-car in the square they had crossed. Then the engines fired, the tank jerked forward, left the barge and plunged down the far slope at speed. At the bottom Barnes turned in a wide curve and halted the tank facing along the canal. He switched off the engines, rolled back the hood and climbed out quickly.

'I thought we'd stall at the top,' he remarked. 'No sign of that column? Good. Colburn, could you come down and give me a hand to dump this bloody box?'

He checked his watch. 3.40 a.m. Twenty minutes to zero hour.

The field below the embankment was firm hard earth and there were no hidden quagmires to hold up their advance, although not so far off to the left was a vague glimmer of flooded areas. The tank rumbled forward as Barnes gazed through the slit window from his lowered seat, following the same course he had taken when he had returned from the reconnaissance with Jacques. The next twenty minutes would decide the whole issue, would decide whether the 14th Panzer Division would advance across the waterline to spring on an unsuspecting Dunkirk, or whether they could muddle things so drastically that the Panzers would be delayed, perhaps fatally. Colburn was talking now.

'I think I can see the archway under the embankment.'

That archway was the end of the line, a phrase Colburn had spoken just before Barnes had set off on the reconnaissance which had deprived them of Reynolds, but without that reconnaissance they would never have reached this point. Through the archway

lay an open field with the aerodrome beyond – the
site of a huge ammunition dump and the laager of the
waiting Panzers. Tight-lipped, Barnes peered through
the slit window as the tank rolled forward in the early
morning light.

He found that he had increased speed without
realizing it and he wondered about that archway.
Would it be wide enough? He had paced out its
width, immediately thinking of Bert when he had
crept under it with Jacques, and he had estimated that
in an emergency they should just be able to manage
it. They *had* to manage it – the archway was the only
means of approaching the target from this side of the
canal. The growing light was apparent even through
his narrow window and he prayed that the defences
had not been reinforced since they had left the place,
but there was always the chance that the Germans
would confidently rely on the heavy column they had
sent along the road to investigate the intruders. He
wondered how Colburn was feeling, knowing that
these might be his last few minutes of life.

In the turret Colburn kept looking to the east where
the pale glow of dawn was spreading across the
horizon. If they had been half an hour later they
would never have passed through the village successfully – and even if they had got through the 14th
Panzer Division would already have been on the
move. Would they really manage it? He glanced down
at the plunger again with a feeling of wonderment,
suddenly conscious of the fact that he might be dead

within the hour, or sooner. It was an odd sensation and involuntarily he shivered. There was a sharp chill in the air now and white mist was rising off the fields. He had seen the same mist rising off the early morning fields near Manston. Then he saw the archway clearly and Manston faded.

The archway looked far too narrow to allow the passage of the tank, its stone walls so close together that Colburn thought they could let through nothing larger than a farm wagon. A feeling of bitter disappointment swept through him – they were going to be stopped at the last moment because of a single archway. There was no question of driving the tank up the embankment a second time – the slope here was even more steeply-angled, to say nothing of the fact that if they reached the top their advanced would be stopped by the canal itself. A sense of overwhelming frustration was in his voice when he spoke.

'Barnes, this archway's too narrow to get through – I'm sure of it.'

The tank ground forward, moving away from the embankment in a wide semicircle until Barnes had brought it into a position where it directly faced the arch, and now he could see that the field beyond was shrouded in mist, masking their approach from the Germans. Colburn gave up protesting and leaned far out as he guided Barnes forward every inch of the way, his gaze switching backwards and forwards between the incredibly narrow arch and the forward tracks. The ground was very uneven at this point and

Barnes found it difficult to follow the Canadian's instructions precisely. He was close to the archway when Colburn called out urgently for him to halt: he was too far over to the right. He reversed some distance and changed his angle of direction a fraction, moving forward at a crawl, his eyes straining to see more clearly, forcing himself not to look at the wristwatch which was ticking away vital minutes. They must get through this time. The dark archway crept towards him and now the light beyond was stronger, illuminating the semicircle clearly. It was almost daylight now. The front hull moved inside. Suddenly there was a jarring sound, the screech of steel grating along stonework. The tank shuddered violently through the length of its hull and then stopped abruptly as Barnes braked. Perhaps it was useless. This could be one obstacle they might never overcome, not even in broad daylight. He rolled back the hood and from above him a torch beam flashed along the wall.

The vicious clash of steel against stone had frightened Colburn and now he tried to estimate the position by the light of his beam. They had driven into the left-hand wall, of course. In their anxiety not to repeat their earlier mistake they had erred too far in the opposite direction, but was the manoeuvre even possible? He flashed the torch on the other side and the light penetrated a gap between tank and wall, a gap no more than six inches wide, if that. So theoretically it was possible, but with such a narrow clearance they would be extraordinarily lucky to pass clear through the archway in this light. He called down direct to Barnes.

'Six inches clearance on the other side. Six inches maximum, maybe less.'

'Then we can do it, providing nothing gives when I reverse.'

'It'll take a miracle.'

'Maybe we're entitled to one.'

For the second time Barnes went into reverse, handling the controls with a concentration he had probably never equalled before, hearing the metal scraping harshly against the wall every inch of the way. But they were moving. The tearing sound petered out following the painful withdrawal, his heart in his mouth until he saw that they were clear of the imprisoning arch once more. They had to manage it this time. Colburn guided Barnes back a short distance and then gave no further instructions. The change of direction required was so fine that unless Barnes could *feel* what was needed they would end up smashing into the other wall.

Gripping the rim he saw the arch coming towards him again, his torch shining on the right-hand side now to make sure that Barnes hadn't overdone it again. He ignored the other wall completely, knowing that if they could move through with the right-hand track barely scraping the wall they should be able to make it. So great was his concentration on the wall that Colburn nearly died at that moment. Just in time he remembered the solid stone arch coming towards his head: he dived down inside the turret and something brushed the crown of his head, and as he went down a fresh fear darted into his mind – would the turret go under the arch? He reached up a hand and felt his fingers graze stonework as the tank rumbled forward. They were almost through when their nerve ends were seared again as the familiar grinding noise started. The tank increased speed and they were out in the open, driving across the field in a weird early morning half-glow mingled with white mist.

Barnes halted the tank briefly, switched off the engines, and stood up to listen. The vaporous fog bank was dispersing and beyond it he detected a staccato mutter which sounded like the power-drills of a tank repair shop, and beyond that he was damned sure he could hear the mechanical grumble of Panzers on the move. With a bit of luck these two background noises might help to conceal Bert's approach until the very last moment. And now he looked at his watch. 3.48 a.m. Twelve minutes to the Panzer attack.

'The mist's clearing,' said Colburn quietly. 'I can just see the ammunition hangar. I'll stick it out up here until we get close and then I'll pop downstairs and observe through the periscope.'

'If you don't, you'll be dead mutton.'

'And I'll use the Besa when the time comes – machine-guns are my forte. The mist's clearly rapidly. That hangar is dead ahead. Good luck, Barnes. Advance!'

'Thanks for coming, Colburn. Thanks a lot.' It sounded trite, horribly trite, but he felt he must say something at this moment. Sitting down again, he closed the hood.

The tank moved forward rapidly over the level ground, brushing mist trails aside, picking up more speed every second. Colburn felt chilled to the bone, scared stiff of what was coming, but he looked curiously at the high bank which rose immediately behind the rear of the hangar. The houses behind the ridge were a faint silhouette of rooftops in the early morning light. It was from this ridge that Barnes and Jacques had looked down on the airfield, from here they had seen the sinister huddles of tanks which comprised the armoured striking force of the Panzer division which General Storch was about to hurl against Dunkirk. Ahead he could see the outer defences of the tank laager, a screen of barbed wire hastily thrown up to cordon off the airfield, and as the pale glow of the coming day increased he saw beyond the hangar a score or more of low dark shapes. His heart thumped when he saw them. Heavy tanks of the 14th Panzer Division. The laager was in view.

Quickly he gave Barnes an instruction to veer on to a fresh course which would head him straight for the entrance to the hangar which they were approaching broadside on. As to going below and watching through the periscope, that would be useless: he'd have to stay in the turret to keep the perfect observation they needed. He lifted his machine-pistol. As they approached the line of barbed wire Colburn almost forgot the holocaust which must await them; there was so much to see, to note. An armoured car parked close to the hangar, the outline of another vehicle which seemed familiar, signs of movement over to the left behind the mist. He recognized the vehicle now – a giant transporter with a tank on its deck. It was then that he saw the first Germans – small figures on the deck working by the light of shaded lamps. His hands tightened on the machine-pistol as the tank rumbled closer and closer. Surely those men must have seen them, must have heard them coming? But as he watched he saw a violet glow and sparks flashed strangely in the mist. They were using welding equipment and the sound of their tools had smothered the sound of Bert's engines. Still there was no indication that they had been spotted and the line of wire was very close now, coils of mist like gun-smoke floating behind the tangled network.

It was pure luck that he turned his head in the right direction and saw movement low down on the ground just beyond the wire, fifty yards away to the right. In the deceptive light he made out a square shield, the profile of a long barrel, a barrel which was swivelling. The barrel of the field piece was traversing as though it had not yet locked on to its target. Scrambling down inside the fighting compartment he jammed himself into the gunner's seat, hugging the shoulder-grip, his hand grasping the traverse lever. The compartment rotated too fast and too far, so he had to bring it round again, his eye glued to the telescopic sight. The range was point-blank, for field piece as well as for two-pounder. He had to get his shot in first. The cross-wires locked on to the shield smudge as he depressed the barrel a few degrees. He squeezed the trigger and the tank bucked under the impact of the recoil. God! The explosives! He waited for the tank to disintegrate but it was still grinding forward. He traversed to find the target and saw a cloud of white smoke replacing the white mist swirls. Dead on target. Climbing back up into the turret he looked round quickly. The tank had reached the wire and then the scratching noises began as it threshed over the coils. The field piece had vanished inside the smoke and from now on it all became a kaleidoscope, for Colburn as he went on speaking to Barnes automatically, guiding him towards the hangar entrance.

Men had appeared from nowhere, running towards the stationary armoured car. Colburn realized the danger at once and he raised his machine-pistol and took careful aim. As his finger pulled firmly on the trigger he swivelled the gun. He swivelled from a point close to the armoured car outwards, so that his hail of bullets cut them down before they could reach the vehicle, bringing down three men while a fourth man ran straight into the fusillade, stopping suddenly in mid-stride as he flung up his arms and fell to the ground. As Colburn inserted a fresh magazine he gave a direction change. The tank was still moving forward, passing within inches of the steel-plated sides of the armoured car, its nose pointed towards a machine-gun which had just been manned by a soldier who had darted out from the shadow of the hangar. Colburn ducked, hearing bullets spatter the sides of the turret, and the tank accelerated, its steel bulk thrust forward and driving over man and gun, crushing flesh and metal under its pulverizing tracks.

Their course was now taking them close to the tank transporter and Colburn remembered the men who had worked on it. Pressing the trigger, he swept the deck with a semicircle of fire, seeing men falling over the side. He heard a brief burst of answering fire before another German fell forward after his machine-pistol had dropped under the tank's tracks. Colburn knew that he had been hit in the left shoulder, which had suddenly gone numb. He also realized that he had emptied his magazine as a capless figure in overall came out from behind the tank and jumped from the deck on to Bert's hull. Dropping his machine-pistol on to the ledge he grabbed his revolver as the overalled figure lifted something he held in his hand – a spanner? Colburn never knew as he raised his revolver and shot the German once in the face, saw him topple backwards and fall under the tracks which ground forward over him. He spoke breathlessly into the mike.

'We're almost there. Keep straight on . . .'

It was the tanks which worried Barnes. His own kind. He knew what they were capable of. They had to reach the hangar entrance before the Germans brought up heavy tanks. Without a loader-operator to re-load the two-pounder Colburn would never stand a chance against them, even supposing he could hit one of them if he tried. Down in the tank nose Barnes never knew about the smashed field piece. He was concentrating on keeping going. The element of surprise. Ram it down their bloody throats till the end. He thought they *must* be pretty close now, close to General Heinrich Storch. Colburn was coping well. He could hear machine-gun bullets ricocheting off the hull now, angry metal bees glancing harmlessly off the armour-plate. Sweat streamed off his face and hands but the pain had receded as his nerves strung up to fever pitch took over for one last effort. They'd almost made it. If they were hit with a shell which penetrated, this lot round him would blow and it ought to take the dump with it, but he'd like to be certain, absolutely certain. He wanted Bert in the mouth of that hangar. Through the slit window he saw men coming round the end of the building, but had Colburn seen them? Colburn had seen them. With great difficulty he had inserted a fresh magazine and now he was slumped forward over the turret, the machine-pistol crooked under his right armpit, his right hand curled round the trigger as he lifted the muzzle high. It was like lifting a cannon and the tank seemed to be rocking strangely like a ship in a choppy sea. His left shoulder was beginning to ache now, a thudding ache which affected his whole body as though it were being plucked like an immense violin string.

He managed it, he lifted the gun higher and squeezed hard, vibrating the muzzle madly from side to side as he sprayed it wildly over the running group of men. They collapsed in a heap, too closely bunched together to spread out in time, only one man firing a few random shots, so random that they missed even the tank which was bearing down on them non-stop. Colburn's finger relaxed on the trigger and he slumped forward over the turret rim, still holding on to the pistol, the weapon now held between his chest and the rim.

Colburn was still hanging on desperately to consciousness when Barnes reached the end of the hangar, braked his right-hand track, carrying the tank round on the left-hand track, advancing several yards again and then stopping in the mouth of the open hangar. Colburn was vaguely aware that they had arrived and he lifted his head, catching a brief glimpse of the shell dump, of great stacks of wooden boxes. Then his eyes switched to the next hangar corner which he instinctively felt to be the danger point. A group of helmeted figures ran recklessly round the corner and he operated the gun with one arm and one hand, swivelling the muzzle as he poured out a hail of bullets at point-blank range into the compact mass of running bodies. It became a muddle and a massacre, the front men falling, the ones behind tripping over their bodies and dying in the subsequent rain of fire. Then his magazine was empty and he knew that he could never reload. Beyond the inert bodies he could see a squat dark shape moving from the laager towards him. He whispered down the mike.

'Tank coming . . . don't forget . . . close lid.'

Looking sideways, he stared dazedly beyond the open doors of the hangar into the vast stockpile of shells and ammunition, his last sight before a German soldier hidden behind a pile of crates aimed his rifle and fired once, killing Colburn instantly. The machine-pistol fell and narrowly missed Barnes who was beginning to emerge from the hatch, his revolver in his hand. He looked quickly towards the corner where the huddle of Germans lay and then switched his gaze to the inside of the hangar. His revolver jerked up and he fired twice. The German with the half-aimed rifle collapsed behind the crates. Jumping to the ground, Barnes ran round the back of the tank, climbed on to the hull, took a quick glance at Colburn and went down inside the turret. The Canadian who had just come over for the afternoon had been shot through the temple.

Settling himself into the gunner's seat, he remembered that the two-pounder wasn't loaded. Cursing, he stood up, flopping in a fresh round with sufficient force to make the breech-block close, settled himself again and traversed the turret. Using the shoulder-grip, he elevated the barrel several degrees. The German tank came up behind the cross-wires, crawling forward like a huge dark beetle, a silhouette he had seen so many times in the past battle-scared fortnight.

He squeezed the trigger and Bert shuddered under the spasm. The shot reached the target, the German tank stopped, flames flaring over the superstructure. Bert had just killed his first German tank. Barnes climbed back into the turret and looked at the plunger. It was extraordinarily quiet all of a sudden. Without thinking about it he gripped the handle firmly, paused, then pressed down.

Nothing happened. He had forgotten the switch. He lifted his head above the rim and looked round the airfield. The burning tank was well ablaze now but he couldn't see any sign of Germans. Again without thinking about it he picked up the plunger-box and the spool of wire. Climbing down on to the hull, he closed the lid and dropped to the ground, paying out the wire which led back inside the gun slit. Peering round the corner of the hangar along the side they had come he saw no sign of life. He began to walk rapidly back under the hangar wall, paying out wire from the spool, going past the Germans Colburn had killed, past the tank transporter where an arc welding torch lay on the deck, still spitting out a spray of sparks. Feeding out the wire behind him close to the wall, he kept on walking like a robot, wondering whether the wire would last out.

To his exhausted, pain-racked mind the act of forgetting to turn the switch had seemed a sign, a sign that he might just survive if he refused to give up. He reached the end of the hangar and found that the area between the rear wall and the high bank was deserted. Still paying out wire, he crossed the concrete strip and began to climb the slope, the same slope from which he had looked down on the airfield with Jacques before they had made a detour round the airfield to the point where Barnes had seen inside the open hangar mouth with his field-glasses. He had almost reached the top of the slope when he heard trucks arriving on the concrete strip below him. He flopped on the slope, still holding the box, and lay perfectly still, his head turned sideways. Soldiers were spilling out the trucks and forming up into two sections, then one section made its way down one side of the hangar while the second section followed the officer along the other side. Barnes climbed over the top of the ridge and staggered down inside a huge bomb crater close to the houses. Sitting down on the floor he looked at his watch, Colburn's watch, stared up at the pale sky he might never see again, turned the switch and pressed the plunger. At 3.58 a.m. the world blew apart.

The initial explosion came in two shock waves which blew away from Lemont straight across the laager – the detonation of the tank-bomb followed almost at once by the subsequent blowing of the immense dump, which was then succeeded by fire which created a chain reaction of exploding ammunition. The first two shock waves swept over the laager like a tidal wave of destruction, caving in the tank walls like paper. Beyond the laager the shock waves smashed in the walls of the farm which housed German headquarters, and when Meyer, blood streaming from his forehead, staggered into his general's office he found Storch lying across the floor, his skull crushed under a rafter which had fallen from the ceiling, one clawed hand stretched out towards the telephone which lay in a heap of plaster. Reaching down for the phone, Meyer sank to his knees, picking up the receiver and found that the field telephone had survived. He asked for Keller. He knew exactly what he must do – he must retrieve the situation from the disaster he had always feared since that day so long ago when they had crossed the Sedan pontoons. He had already heard the report that British tanks were moving up through Lemont to attack their rear and a column had been dispatched to intercept them without success. What Meyer had dreaded had now happened – the enemy had counter-attacked. The tremendous explosion which had just killed Storch was the final confirmation: there were no enemy planes reported so the British must have heavy artillery which had blown up the dump. He heard a voice speaking and broke in.

'Keller, this is Meyer. General Storch is dead. The British are attacking from the south – yes, the south.

Cancel the order for the advance on Dunkirk immediately. Do you understand? You have the waterline at
your backs so now you must . . .'

Halfway through the conversation the line went
dead, but Meyer was satisfied that Keller had grasped
his order. From the tank laager there was now a series
of explosions of increasing violence and for the first
time Meyer had the terrible thought that he might be
wrong. He *could* hear planes now, planes flying low
overhead, and the ack-ack guns had opened up. With
a curse he left the wrecked office and ran out into the
garden. He heard the whistle of the bomb coming
down and turned to run, just in time to receive the
relics of the farmhouse full in his face as the bomb
scored a direct hit.

At exactly 3.55 a.m. Squadron Leader Paddy Browne
was approaching the coast of France, leading his
Blenheims on a dawn raid. His instructions gave him
unusual latitude, but then the situation was, to say
the least of it, unusual. Evacuation·of the BEF imminent, the German Panzers lording it over the battlefield, the position changing almost from minute to
minute. 'Fluid,' as the war communiqués would say.
His primary objective was the key rail junction at
Arras, but if he saw enemy ground forces and could
positively identify them, the choice of target was left
to his discretion. 'But for Pete's sake, don't paste our
own chaps,' the briefing officer had added.

Browne wasn't particularly concerned with the Gravelines–Lemont area, but as he led his squadron over the coast his attention was drawn to it by a huge mushroom of smoke rising into the early morning sky, a mushroom which rose higher every second as though the whole of that corner of France were detonating. We'd better have a quick look, thought Browne, so he signalled to the squadron and took his Blenheim down. Two factors quickly convinced him that this lot was the other lot – he met flak at once and his keen eye saw beetles scuttling around on the ground as though they had gone mad. He could hardly believe it for a moment but he believed it the next moment. Hun tanks – a whole laager of them. Browne exercised his discretion: he gave the order to bomb. An avalanche of high-explosive rained down and when the squadron turned away there was no sign of movement anywhere between the breaks in the smoke pall. Browne's only comment on the way back was typical.

'Good of them to send up a smoke signal.'

Lieutenant Jean Durand of the 14th French Chasseurs found it difficult to believe his eyes as he focused his glasses across the flooded zone. His unit was charged with the defence of this forward sector of the Dunkirk perimeter and so far it had been a quiet morning, but then this is what he had expected because how could Panzers advance across water? And, Durand asked himself, how can this idiot advance across water? Speaking into the field telephone, he asked the British liaison officer to come at once. This was a sight which must be shared.

The lone figure on the bicycle was crouched low over his machine as though he could hardly stay on it, but still he cycled steadily across the sheet of water, never once looking up, as though he knew the way by heart. Barnes had to ride in that fashion because it was the only way he could see the road surface under six inches of water. His pedalling motion had long since become mechanical, a movement which had no relation to thought. In fact, he had now reached the stage where he hadn't looked up for some time and he had no idea he was so close to the Allied lines.

The British liaison officer, Lieutenant Miller, had now joined his colleague and his eyes narrowed behind the field-glasses as he recognized the uniform. Apart from the fact that the cyclist could cross water, this sudden arrival of another apparition was not a complete surprise to Miller because in the present state of the battlefield men kept stumbling into the perimeter with increasing frequency. A dog's breakfast, that's what it is, Miller told himself. All over the bloody shop.

The cyclist was within a hundred yards of where they stood when there was almost a disaster. Unknown to either Durand or Miller, because they had been unaware of the road's existence, and unknown to Barnes because he hadn't been this way before, the road suddenly dipped and before he knew what was happening he was cylcling up to his chest in water, and then he fell off. They dragged him out spluttering and choking, holding him up between them until they reached dry land where they laid him out on the grass. Barnes was desperately trying to say something and in spite of Miller's attempt to restrain him he burst out with it.

'Road goes all the way ... all the way to Lemont ... Jerry Panzers.'

'Got it,' said Miller. 'Not to worry. Hospital for you, my lad.'

Barnes spent two days at the Dunkirk field station for the seriously wounded although he kept trying to tell them that he was only seriously exhausted. In spite of his efforts to leave they refused to listen to him, so he waited his opportunity until the ward was empty of staff and then he crept out behind the hospital still in his pyjamas, his bundle of clothes under his arm. It took him half an hour to dress himself behind the hanging wall of a bombed house, and when he reached the beaches he made a tremendous effort to walk upright as though there was nothing wrong with him. He was still only vaguely aware that a total evacuation was taking place and he was frightened that they might not take him if he didn't look fit.

Afterwards he could only recall the journey as a blur, like a film run too quickly through the projector. The endless wait on the beaches, the sand coughing up as bombs fell, the crowded boat which threatened to sink under the great weight of men who sat shoulder to shoulder, the incredible calm of the Channel as they crossed to England under bombardment and in a blaze of sunshine. Then Dover. Dover was the same thing all over again. A tremendous muddle, hundreds of men moving off in trains with hardly any supervision so far as he could see.

He waited alone for long hours, searching the sea of faces so intently that eventually he feared he was incapable of seeing what he was looking for. Twice he had persuaded a military policeman to let him wait a little longer and he was on the point of giving up when his heart jumped. Three soldiers were helping a fourth along the platform to a waiting train and he recognized the stoop of the broad shoulders, the tilt of the head of the limping man who was being helped. Reynolds! He could hardly believe it as he ran forward and when the three men saw his stripes they left the driver in his care and wearily climbed aboard the train. Reynolds managed a faint grin, leaning on his stick.

'Those three Jocks found me outside Lemont – we helped ourselves to one of the fifteen-hundredweight trucks. I woke up as they drove inside the Dunkirk perimeter.'

They were boarding the densely packed train when the military policeman questioned Barnes for the third time, inquiring his destination.

'Colchester,' Barnes replied.

Colchester was his base depot. Barnes now had one fixed idea in mind. He had to get a new tank.